Shadows Unveiled

Elves of Vacari

T.A. McEvoy

T. McEvoy

Dedication

Tom Vick

To my wonderful boyfriend, Tom—thank you for reading every draft of this book. Since we met, my life has improved in more ways than I can express. Your constant encouragement, always having my back, and reminding me that I can achieve anything means the world to me. A special thanks for handling all the marketers and promoters—though they seem too scared to contact you after they're told to! Guess you've got them figured out, huh?

Forward

"Welcome back to the enchanting realm of Vacari in this the second installment of the Elves of Vacari series. If you've embarked on this journey with us from the beginning, you might recall our first book, 'The Wicked Phoenix,' which provided vital background information. However, fear not, for 'Shadows Unveiled' can also be enjoyed as a standalone adventure. For those who journeyed with us in 'Shadows Unveiled,' the second installment, you will find familiar threads that continue to weave the tapestry of this intricate world.

As we delve deeper into the lore of Vacari, you will re-encounter the High Elves, known as 'Eladrin,' and the enigmatic Dark Elves, referred to as 'Druchii.' These names have become synonymous with our elven kin's rich heritage and complex hierarchy.

In our previous tale, the High Elves were known as the 'Eladrin,' while the Dark Elves were called the 'Druchii.' These distinctive names carry forward in this book, especially when referring to specific elves.

We extend our heartfelt gratitude for your continued support, and it is our sincere hope that you'll find immense enjoyment in this latest installment of the 'Elves of Vacari' saga.

Content Warning

This book may contain themes of violence, dark fantasy elements, and mature situations. Reader discretion is advised.

(There are no graphic or explicit scenes herein.)

Thank you for reading Shadows Unveiled

If you enjoyed the book, we would be immensely grateful if you could take a moment to leave a review at the location where you purchased the book.

Your feedback is invaluable to us and helps other readers discover our work. Thank you for your support!

Also, by T.A. McEvoy

<u>The Elves of Vacari Series:</u>

The Wicked Published 11-01-2023

Shadows Unveiled- Published 12-05-2023.

Vacari's Resurgence: Healing Bonds 04-12-2024

<u>Dragons of Vacari Series:</u>

Rise of the Ancients

Coming Soon

<u>Shadows of the Sylvan Series</u>

Coming Soon

<u>Depth of Destiny: A Merfolk Saga</u>

Coming Soon

<u>Passion's Quest</u>

Coming Soon

Explore more about each book and series at: https://www.tamcevoy.com/

World Map

VACARI
CORALUNA
FLAMEFORD
EMBERWOODS
FEL THALOR
PURPLEFIRE WOODS
GOLDMOOR
E'VANHONA
BRIDGE OF CONNECTIVITY
CRYSTAL VALE
ABYSSAL SOVEREIGN
HIDDEN ISLES
EMERALD WOODS
IVORY MOONBEAM
CERULEAN EXPANSE
LUMINAQUA
TWILIGHT GLADE
AFOR
SHADOWHAVEN
ARDINIA
LYRA'EL

Various Locations

Main Realm

Vacari

Vacari is an enchanting realm where nature's vibrant tapestry weaves together diverse landscapes, fostering a peaceful coexistence among elves, humans, dragons, and merfolk. Majestic cities like Goldmoor and Crystal Vale thrive in prosperity, their gleaming spires and flourishing trade routes nestled amidst lush forests, shimmering lakes, and serene oceans. Ancient magic flows through the very soil, influencing both the land and its people, while the skies above remain guarded by the vigilant wings of dragons. Vacari's rich cultural heritage reflects the harmonious balance between its peoples, sustained by an intricate connection to the natural and mystical forces that shape the land.

Main City inside Vacari

Goldmoor

Goldmoor, the shining jewel of Vacari, radiates a harmonious fusion of elven grace and human ingenuity. Majestic spires, adorned with intricate gold and silver filigree, reach toward the heavens, their gleaming surfaces catching and reflecting the sunlight like beacons of prosperity. The bustling streets form a living tapestry of elven elegance and human vitality, where vibrant marketplaces brim with goods from every corner of the realm. Artisan stalls display exquisitely crafted wares—delicate elven jewelry, sturdy human armor, and magical artifacts—while the aromas of exotic foods fill the air. At the heart of the city stands the grand castle, its walls a testament to the unity between elves and humans, built with precision and artistry that mirrors the strengths of both races. The city hums with life, laughter, and camaraderie, celebrating the enduring bond that has forged not only a shared kingdom but a shared destiny.

Notable City inside Vacari

Crystal Vale

Crystal Vale, a mesmerizing gem nestled in the heart of Vacari, stands as a testament to the perfect fusion of elven grace and human ingenuity. Its crystalline structures shimmer like diamonds, refracting sunlight into breathtaking cascades of light that dance across the city. Elven and human artisans work in harmony, crafting architectural wonders—delicate bridges that span glistening waterfalls and elegant towers that soar toward the heavens, their surfaces glinting with ethereal brilliance. The city's pulse resonates with the unity of its people, and nowhere is this more poignantly symbolized than in the union of Ong Swifthammer and Keisha. Their marriage, a celebration of love and alliance, echoes eternally through the crystal spires, binding the city's legacy to their story.

Celestial Realm

Lyra'el

Lyra'el, the celestial realm, is a magnificent and ethereal domain where dragons and celestial beings converge in harmony. Floating high above the mortal world, this radiant realm is bathed in the soft glow of starlight and cosmic energies. The skies shimmer with hues of gold and silver, and vast, crystalline mountains rise from the celestial plains, their peaks touching the heavens. Here, dragons of divine origin soar alongside majestic celestial beings, their forms radiant with the essence of the stars.

In Lyra'el, the boundaries between time and space seem to blur, creating a timeless sanctuary where both beings of incredible power come together in unity. The realm pulses with an ancient magic, one that governs both the heavens and the mortal world below, and its inhabitants are entrusted with the balance of cosmic forces. It is a place of unparalleled beauty and serenity, where the celestial and draconic realms intertwine, their destinies forever linked by the will of the stars.

Dark Cities inside Vacari

Fel Thalor

Fel Thalor, once the forsaken city of the Druchii, now stirs with life once more, yet remains a haunting monument to its dark past. Its once-majestic spires, though still scarred by time, rise defiantly against a brooding sky, casting long shadows over the streets where whispers of ancient power still linger. The air is thick with the weight of forgotten rituals, as if the city itself remembers the blood sacrifices and dark magic that once permeated its core. At the heart of Fel Thalor, the sacrificial altar—a grim relic of the Druchii's ruthless practices—has stirred from its long dormancy, as though waiting for its masters to reclaim their sinister legacy. Though no longer abandoned, the city remains shrouded in an unsettling stillness, a place where the line between past and present blurs, and the presence of its dark history can be felt in every stone.

Old Flameford

Old Flameford, once the formidable stronghold of the warlock Phoenix Shadowwalker, was a city cloaked in darkness. Its ominous atmosphere, enhanced by the oppressive hues of black and red that covered every building, created an ever-present sense of dread. At its heart stood the Dark Tower, a foreboding structure that pierced the very heavens, once the source of Phoenix's malevolent power. This was the seat of his dark rule, where nefarious plans were forged and dark magic flowed freely—until the alliance rose against him, driving him into exile.

However, Old Flameford has since undergone a dramatic transformation. While the tower still looms over the city like a grim reminder of its past, the landscape has become even more treacherous. Evil dragon lairs now scatter the land, their dark inhabitants adding to the already sinister aura of the city. These draconic overlords have made their homes among the crumbling ruins, solidifying Old Flameford as a place of darkness where evil continues to fester, waiting for the moment to rise once again.

Shadowhaven

Shadowhaven lies on the edge of Twilight Glade, adjacent to the foreboding Cerulean Expanse. This dark and shadowy city is a place where the light barely penetrates, and an air of mystery and danger lingers over every corner. Once a thriving figure in Goldmoor, Maldrak now rules over Shadowhaven, having been exiled by King Alex for his treacherous actions. Under his iron grip, the city has become a haven for those who seek to escape the law, as well as those drawn to its darker energies.

The architecture of Shadowhaven is as oppressive as its atmosphere—blackened stone towers and gloomy streets blend into the ever-present twilight, illuminated only by the faint, eerie glow from hidden sources. Maldrak's influence casts a long shadow over the city, where whispers of rebellion and secrets seem to thrive in the gloom. Its residents, a mix of outcasts and dark-hearted souls, have adapted to this realm of constant dusk, living under the ever-watchful gaze of their exiled ruler.

Though menacing and dangerous, Shadowhaven also holds a certain allure for those seeking power or refuge from the light. It is a place where alliances are forged in the shadows, and where Maldrak's dark ambitions may one day extend far beyond the city's borders.

Forests inside Vacari

Purplefire Woods

Purplefire Woods, awash in a mesmerizing kaleidoscope of purples, stands as an enchanting testament to nature's vibrant palette. Every shade, from deep amethyst to soft lavender, blends harmoniously with the gentle rustle of leaves, creating a forest alive with color and serenity. This breathtaking realm, beloved by Keisha for its beauty and tranquility, became the perfect setting for her union with Ong in a magical wedding ceremony that will forever be etched in the hearts of those who attended. The regal shades of purple that drape the trees and blanket the ground serve as both a backdrop and witness to this sacred event. Beyond its beauty, Purplefire Woods is a vital passage, guiding travelers through its enchanted paths toward the majestic city of Goldmoor, making it a place of both natural wonder and symbolic importance.

Emeraldwoods

Emeraldwoods, a lush, verdant realm bathed in the soothing embrace of emerald green, serves as a breathtaking passage to Crystal Vale. The vibrant hues of the forest, coupled with its serene ambiance, create an enchanting landscape where nature feels alive and welcoming. This sacred forest witnessed the engagement ceremony of Ong and Keisha, marking the union of their souls in a celebration of love and harmony. Beneath the emerald canopy, they pledged their bond, setting the stage for the joyous festivities that awaited them in Crystal Vale. The forest stands as a symbol of new beginnings, a tranquil sanctuary where love and life intertwine before travelers continue their journey to the majestic city.

Emberwooods

Emberwoods, a captivating forest bathed in fiery hues of red and orange, stands near the volatile volcanic region, lending it an otherworldly glow. Despite the inherent dangers lurking within, the forest retains a haunting, untamed beauty that entices both awe and caution. Traveling through Emberwoods is a perilous journey, as it leads to the formidable Druchii stronghold of Fel Thalor. Now, a new layer of mystery and challenge awaits all who venture there. Copper dragons and pixies have woven their magic to create an intricate, twisting maze at the very gates of Fel Thalor, a cunning trap meant to confuse and thwart the evil Druchii. This enchanted maze, alive with illusions and deceptions, tests the wit and endurance of any who dare to enter, making the path to Fel Thalor even more treacherous than before.

Ivory Moonbeams

Ivory Moonbeam, the mystical home of the Sylvan Elves, is a realm bathed in hues of white and ivory, its landscape reflecting the pure, radiant beauty of its name. The trees, with bark that gleams like polished pearl, rise tall and graceful, their leaves and flowers shimmering with a soft, ethereal glow beneath the moon's gentle light. The entire forest comes alive at night, as the moonlight casts an otherworldly brilliance upon the landscape, enhancing its serene and enchanting atmosphere.

The Sylvan Elves, known for their deep connection to nature, dwell harmoniously within these enchanted depths, their lives intertwined with the magic of the forest. The pristine color palette, dominated by shades of ivory and white, reflects the purity and tranquility that permeates Ivory Moonbeam, making it a sanctuary of peace and wonder. Those who wander through its glistening paths feel the quiet magic of the place, as though they've stepped into a world untouched by time, where nature and mysticism reign supreme.

Twilight Glade

Twilight Glade lies in the delicate balance between the ethereal beauty of Ivory Moonbeam and the mysterious darkness of Shadowhaven. The color palette of this enchanted forest reflects its name, with soft hues of purple, blue, and gray blending seamlessly into the landscape. The interplay of light and shadow creates an ever-changing tapestry of colors, as the sunlight filters gently through the thick canopy by day, casting dappled shades across the forest floor. By night, moonbeams weave through the trees, their silvery glow dancing upon the ground, adding an air of quiet magic to the glade.

The forest itself seems alive with the subtle transitions of light, as if caught between two realms—one of purity and one of shadow. Twilight Glade serves as a mystical bridge, embodying both serenity and mystery, a place where travelers can experience the magic of both worlds. The shifting hues create a dreamlike atmosphere, inviting those who wander through to lose themselves in the tranquil beauty and the soft whispers of the wind

Sub-Areas inside of Vacari

Shimmering Coast

The Shimmering Coast stretches along the borders of the Cerulean Expanse, where the ocean's azure waves gently meet the land. This radiant coastline serves as a peaceful convergence point, where merfolk from Coraluna emerge from the depths to bask in the sun's warmth and converse with visitors from the surface world. The coast is named for the way the waters shimmer and sparkle as sunlight dances across them, creating a breathtaking spectacle of light and color.

More than just a place of beauty, the Shimmering Coast acts as a vital meeting point between the realms of land and sea, fostering friendships and alliances among different civilizations. Here, merfolk and surface dwellers exchange knowledge, form bonds, and strengthen ties between their worlds. The coast has become a symbol of harmony, a place where the boundaries between ocean and land blur, and the people of both realms come together in peace.

Hidden Sub-Realm inside Vacari

E'vahona

E'vahona, the hidden jewel of the Eladrin, was a sacred gift from Kadona, the benevolent goddess of light. Shielded by divine magic, it remains untouched and unseen by the evil Dominion, a sanctuary of peace and purity. Crystal pathways wind gracefully through the city, leading to homes seamlessly crafted from a delicate fusion of crystal and wood, blending the natural with the ethereal. Within the enchanting boundaries of E'vahona, the Eladrin share their lives with magnificent companions—majestic wolves and mythical creatures like Pumpkin the panther—who roam freely, adding to the city's mystical charm. The air carries the gentle, harmonious melody of nature, resonating with an otherworldly beauty that reflects the close bond between the Eladrin and their divine patron. E'vahona is not just a city; it is a living testament to the light and protection of Kadona, and a place where magic and nature dance in perfect harmony.

The Sacred Grove

Nestled within the heart of E'vahona, a breathtaking garden flourishes under the divine caress of Kadona, the goddess of light. Crystal-clear waterfalls cascade gently from moss-covered cliffs, their soothing symphony echoing throughout the lush, vibrant landscape. The air is perfumed with the delicate fragrance of exotic blossoms, their brilliant hues creating a mesmerizing tapestry of color and life. Elaborate pathways, adorned with luminescent flora, weave gracefully through the garden, guiding visitors on a journey through this enchanted paradise where ethereal creatures roam freely. Butterflies, shimmering in the soft glow of the flora, dance in a harmonious choreography, while the gentle hum of mystical energies pulses in perfect resonance with the natural world. In this sacred space, the beauty of nature and the divine touch of Kadona converge, creating a serene haven of peace and wonder.

Sub-Realm inside Vacari

The Hidden Isles

Tucked behind a mystical barrier, The Hidden Isles emerge as a sanctuary of breathtaking beauty. This ethereal realm, a collection of isles adorned with vibrant flora and encircled by cascading waterfalls, welcomes only those who can pass through its enchanted protections. At the heart of these mystical isles stands a majestic golden castle, a symbol of the noble dragons' grandeur and the sacred meeting place for allies from various races. The crystal-clear waters below reflect the brilliance of the azure sky, while the air hums with the harmonious melodies of unseen creatures that dwell among the isles. This hidden paradise, untouched by time or conflict, is a place where nature, magic, and dragonkind exist in perfect harmony, offering refuge and counsel to those deemed worthy.

Ardinia

Ardinia, a haven of enchantment shielded by a magical barrier, unfolds as a breathtaking realm where nature's beauty reigns supreme. Towering trees, their branches adorned with blossoms in every imaginable hue, stretch toward the heavens, creating a lush canopy that murmurs the ancient secrets of the forest. Crystal-clear streams weave gracefully through the verdant landscape, reflecting the vibrant colors of the surrounding flora and adding to the tranquility of the realm. In this mystical sanctuary, nymphs, fairies, and the elusive white unicorns roam freely, their presence adding an ethereal grace to the serene atmosphere. Occasionally, the skies above Ardinia are graced by the majestic flight of Pegasus, a rare and awe-inspiring sight reserved for those fortunate enough to glimpse the magic that thrives in this protected paradise.

Cerulean Expanse

Beyond the shores of Vacari lies the Cerulean Expanse, a vast and seemingly endless ocean teeming with life and untold mysteries. The azure depths of this boundless sea conceal countless wonders, from vibrant coral reefs brimming with marine life to the forgotten shipwrecks of ancient vessels long lost to time. The ocean's surface glistens under the sun's rays, reflecting a shimmering, almost magical light that stretches to the horizon.

Beneath the waves, the merfolk dwell in majestic underwater kingdoms, their cities crafted from coral and pearl—a breathtaking testament to the beauty and grandeur of the ocean realm. These hidden cities are sanctuaries of peace and wonder, where the ocean's currents carry stories of the deep and where nature and magic intertwine. The Cerulean Expanse holds many secrets, its waters whispering of adventures yet to be uncovered, making it a place where both beauty and danger coexist in the vastness of the sea.,

Underwater Kingdom inside Vacari

Coraluna:

Coraluna, a mesmerizing underwater kingdom, unfolds as a realm of vibrant beauty beneath the azure waves. Vast coral reefs, adorned with a kaleidoscope of colorful corals and teeming with exotic fish, create a breathtaking tapestry that stretches across the ocean floor. Lush underwater plants sway gracefully with the gentle currents, their movements in perfect harmony with the ebb and flow of the sea. The merfolk, diligent and wise, tend to the well-being of their aquatic home, ensuring that Coraluna remains a thriving and serene sanctuary. King Oceanous, a majestic and benevolent ruler, watches over the kingdom with compassionate eyes, guiding his people and maintaining the delicate balance of the underwater world. In Coraluna, the harmony between nature and its inhabitants creates a tranquil and magical realm, hidden beneath the waves yet brimming with life.

Luminaqua

Nestled in the heart of the ocean's embrace, Luminaqua stands as a stunning testament to the ingenuity and harmony of the Aquanar Elves. This underwater haven is a marvel of elven and aquatic architecture, where the boundaries between nature and artifice blur, creating a breathtaking spectacle. The city's structures are masterfully crafted from luminescent coral, casting a gentle, ethereal glow that bathes Luminaqua in perpetual light. Towers and buildings, adorned with pearlescent shells, shimmer like jewels beneath the caress of the ocean's currents, their surfaces reflecting the serene beauty of the underwater world. The city's layout flows seamlessly, mirroring the graceful movement of the tides, with elegant bridges and pathways connecting its various districts in fluid harmony.

Luminaqua is not merely a city; it is a living, breathing masterpiece, pulsing with the ocean's rhythm and the spirit of its elven inhabitants. The Aquanar Elves live in perfect balance with the sea, their culture deeply intertwined with the ebb and flow of the tides. Life in Luminaqua is a dance of elegance and resilience, as this sanctuary, hidden in the ocean's depths, has withstood the test of time. A glittering jewel in the vast underwater world, Luminaqua remains a beacon of beauty, unity, and strength, a place where magic and nature are forever intertwined.

Underwater Realm inside Coraluna

Abyssal Sovereign:

Nestled within the ocean's depths, Abyssal Sovereign is a magnificent underwater realm governed by the divine watch of Lysander, the God of the Sea. This ethereal kingdom is a breathtaking display of aquatic wonders, where vibrant corals sway gently with the currents and schools of iridescent fish dance in perfect harmony. The tranquil kingdom is adorned with stunning structures, masterfully crafted from seashells and precious gems, their surfaces reflecting the divine touch of Lysander. His protective aura envelops Abyssal Sovereign, ensuring that no darkness or malevolence can breach its serene depths.

The merfolk inhabitants, guided by their benevolent ruler, maintain the flourishing marine life, tending to the ocean's vibrant ecosystem with care and devotion. Under Lysander's divine leadership, Abyssal Sovereign has become a haven of peace and beauty, where the sea's mysteries and magic coexist in perfect balance. It is a realm untouched by conflict, its calm waters a reflection of the god's power and wisdom, a sanctuary beneath the waves where tranquility reigns supreme.

Neighbor Realms

Afor

The Neighboring Realm of Afor has undergone a dramatic transformation over time. Once a vast, treacherous swampland where Phoenix and the Druchii were exiled, Afor's landscape was forever altered when Vuarus, the god of the abyss, was released from his imprisonment. His chaotic power scorched the land, transforming the swamp into an unforgiving desert, a barren region of shifting sands and desolation.

Since the defeat of both Phoenix and Vuarus, Afor has begun to rebuild. Amidst the harsh desert, new cities have emerged, built by resilient inhabitants who have adapted to the unforgiving climate. Yet, due to the realm's dark history, the Noble dragons (Bronze) maintain a vigilant watch over the region, patrolling the skies and ensuring that no lingering threats arise from its troubled past. Though Afor still bears the scars of its dark legacy, life continues to flourish as its people and their noble dragon protectors carve out a new future in this once-forsaken land.

Etharyon

A secluded realm of ethereal beauty, Etharyon is home to the Moon Elves. Known for its harmony with nature, the realm features Silvaraen, a serene valley city glowing with bioluminescent lights, and Aerindral, the Sapphire City, a cultural and diplomatic hub with canals and sapphire-inspired architecture. Etharyon embodies clarity, wisdom, and resilience.

List of Characters

Shadows Unveiled Character List

Main Characters:

Keisha - A courageous Eladrin adventurer with elemental magic that ties into the forest of Vacari, excellent archery skills, and a powerful sense of justice.

Ong Swifthammer - A loyal and skilled warrior, Keisha's trusted husband.

Pumpkin - An adorable and mischievous young panther with a mysterious connection to Keisha.

Qellaun Deadcrusher - A powerful and fearsome Druchii of the Abyssal Dominion, serving Phoenix and Vuarus.

Lyra Deadcrusher - A cunning and skilled Druchii sorceress with a mysterious past working for Phoenix and Vuarus.

Good/Neutral Dragons (Council Members):

Kimras, Gold Dragon - Regal and authoritative, Kimras embodies the quintessence of leadership with his golden scales symbolizing wisdom and benevolence.

Silvara, Silver Dragon - Gentle and nurturing, Silvara radiates serenity and calm, her silver scales reflecting her soothing and peaceful nature.

Talleoss, Silver Dragon - Majestic and wise, Talleoss is marked by his battle-scarred silver scales, symbolizing his resilience and the freedom he fiercely upholds.

Dirona, Bronze Dragon - Ancient and dignified, Dirona's bronze scales are a testament to her profound wisdom and the respect she commands.

Aurelia, Crystal Dragon - Mysterious and ethereal, Aurelia's crystalline form exudes an otherworldly beauty, hinting at her vast, ancient knowledge.

Verdantia, Emerald Dragon - Deeply connected to nature, Verdantia's emerald scales mirror the vitality of the natural world, reflecting her nurturing spirit.

Amara, Amethyst Dragon - Strong and spiritually insightful, Amara's amethyst scales gleam with an aura of power, and her playful teasing often lightens her presence.

Caelum, Copper Dragon - Mischievous and cunning, Raelithar's copper scales shine with a playful light, reflecting his witty and clever nature.

Sylvana, Sapphire Dragon - Wise and graceful and possessing an aura of calm and deep insight.

Hespherus, Brass Dragon - Powerful and charismatic whose eloquence could sway hearts and minds.

Eladrin High Council Members:

Lady Seraphina - A wise and graceful figure.

Lord Karrenen - Revered throughout Vacari for his extraordinary mastery of magic, with unmatched command over the arcane arts.

Lord Thaldir - A wise and respected elder known for deep knowledge of ancient lore.

Lady Elowen - A skilled diplomat with a keen eye for politics and negotiation.

Lady Lythia - A talented healer and empathetic counselor supporting the Eladrin community.

Lord Alaric - An expert strategist and tactician, advising the council on matters of defense and strategy.

Lord Eldrion - A stern and ancient scholar.

Lady Isadora - A young and graceful figure.

Lord Galadon - A fierce warrior and defender of the Eladrin, renowned for his bravery.

Lady Mirabelle - An enchanting sorceress gifted in the mystical arts and arcane knowledge.

Evil Dragons:

Zylron, Red Dragon - Once a loyal servant, Zylron's fiery scales now mirror his tainted allegiance. His presence is as intimidating as a raging inferno, reflecting a fierce and unpredictable nature born from his betrayal.

Glaciera, White Dragon - Glaciera's icy scales are a chilling testament to her cold and ruthless demeanor. Her aura is as frigid as the deepest winter, capable of instilling fear into the hearts of even the most courageous.

Drakthor, Black Dragon - Cunning and ruthless whose scales were as dark as the depths of the abyss.

Venfyr, Green Dragon - Cunning and manipulative who delights in sowing discord and mistrust among the evil force.

Thundria, Topaz Dragon - Power now bolstered after joining the dark dragons leaving no doubt that the evil dragons' council held sway over those who succumbed to darkness.

Divine and Significant Beings:

Kadona - Goddess of Light and protector of the Eladrin Elves.

Lysander - God of the Sea.

Aeliana - Guardian of the Mystic Realm of Ardinia.

Talleoss - Once a Silver Dragon, loyal to Kadona and imprisoned in a crystal.

Nerissa - Protector of the Heart of Twilight.

Merfolk:

King Oceanous - Ruler of Coraluna.

Adrianna - Daughter of King Oceanous.

Aqilus - Right hand of King Oceanous and Adrianna's mate.

Kaelen - Merman of Coraluna.

Thalorin - Merman of Coraluna.

Others:

King Manard - King of Crystal Vale.

Malrik - Chief Priest of Vuarus.

King Alex - King of Goldmoor.

Queen Jeanne - Queen of Goldmoor.

Contents

Prologue

Phoenix's brow furrowed as he peered through the window, his gaze capturing the bleak expanse that was once the vibrant city of New Flameford. The cityscape now stood as a somber tableau. Adorned with serpents like ominous ornaments, Lifeless trees painted a macabre scene against desolation. The gnarled branches of these once proud trees now hung low, their twisted forms reaching out like skeletal hands, as if yearning for a lifelong past. A dull gray haze crept into the tower, shrouding it in a gloomy pallor and triggering an involuntary cough from Phoenix.

'Exile to this forsaken place by those Eladrin!' he muttered, the bitterness in his voice evident. His words echoed through the chamber, swallowed by the oppressive silence that clung to the air. The decaying state of the buildings below stoked the fires of his anger. Crumbling facades and shattered windows whispered tales of forgotten glory, now reduced to rubble and despair. 'This decay, a testament to her meddling! That persistent elf should have refrained from rallying the masses against me. Soon, she'll bear the weight of her interference,' Phoenix growled, his fists clenching in anger. It was as if the very stones bore witness to his fury, trembling beneath the weight of his resentment.

Emerging from the shadows, a figure cloaked in a dark metallic robe adorned with delicate gold trims materialized. Beneath the hood, only crimson eyes gleamed, like embers in the night. Stepping forward, the newcomer exuded an undeniable aura of authority. Shadows seemed to bend and sway in deference to his presence.

'Who stands before me, and by what means did you infiltrate my sanctuary?' Phoenix questioned, his gaze wary and persistent, like a sentinel guarding a fortress.

A subtle, almost mischievous smile played upon Vuarus's lips, concealed in shadow. 'Vuarus, the God of Shadows, answers your unspoken query. I bring an offer of assistance, Phoenix,' the figure revealed, his voice holding an irresistible air of intrigue, like the siren's call of forbidden knowledge.

Phoenix's thoughts brushed against the whispers of ancient tales, stories often casting Vuarus in a dubious light. Skepticism etched his features as he narrowed his eyes, blending caution with resentment. 'I am no stranger to the cost of your aid. So, what price do you expect for your services?' Phoenix inquired, his words cautious yet curious, like a gambler at the edge of uncertainty.

A nod passed between them, acknowledging the undeniable truth in Phoenix's words. 'Indeed, my assistance demands its due. I seek the destruction of Kadona, the Guardian of Light, who oversees the Eladrin,' Vuarus divulged, his gaze unyielding and relentless, like a predator locking onto its prey.

A wry smirk touched Phoenix's lips. 'The Eladrin's shield. Very well, Kadona's fall aligns with my intent. However, time is fleeting – a mere four years,' he conceded, vengeance churning within his thoughts, like a storm gathering on the horizon.

With resolve solidified, Phoenix affirmed his accord with Vuarus. A fresh staff materialized in response – a symbol of his heightened might. Crowned with a sapphire crystal entwined with golden threads, the staff cradled an intricately carved emerald dragon. 'Talleoss, from this moment, you are mine to command,' Phoenix declared, his grip unwavering. The staff seemed to pulsate with a life of its own, resonating with his newfound power.

Agony seared Phoenix's hand as he asserted his dominance over Talleoss, the newly summoned dragon. The chamber was shrouded in mist, the air crackling with their struggle's intensity. The dragon materialized, its iridescent eyes locking onto Phoenix with feral intensity. A battle of wills raged, Phoenix weathering Talleoss' fierce assault and emerging victorious. The dragon, now subservient, inclined its head in reluctant submission, a testament to the indomitable spirit of both master and servant.

With Talleoss under his sway, Phoenix's determination crystallized. 'Raise a temple in New Flameford, another within Flameford itself. The Druchii shall be drafted as devotees in the temple,' Phoenix relayed to Vuarus, a vicious grin spreading across his face like a sinister omen. His words echoed through the chamber, sealing the dark pact with a promise of conquest and domination.

Vuarus chuckled, a melody of dark amusement threading through his voice. 'Druchii, both enchanting and obedient. Your proposition is accepted. But remember Phoenix, and failure is not an option,' he cautioned before vanishing into the abyss, like a shadow fading into the night.

As Vuarus dissolved into shadows, leaving only his lingering essence behind, Phoenix's mind became a cauldron of contemplation. Memories of battles waged against the Eladrin and their valiant dragon allies surged forward. 'Accepting this pact would crown me the unmatched warlock of Vacari. Even the Eladrin will cower before my power. Vengeance will finally be mine,' he whispered, a glint of malice igniting his eyes like a blade forged in the fires of hatred.

But there was more to Vuarus's offer than met the eye. A secret he kept well hidden, a revelation that would shake the foundations of their dominion. As Phoenix clung to his resolve, unaware of the darkness lurking in the shadows, he had no clue of the impending revelation that would test the very limits of his ambition, like a hidden trap waiting to be sprung.

Phoenix turned his attention to a collapsed tunnel hidden beneath the tower of New Flameford. Commanding Talleoss, he directed the dragon to restore and expand the passage, linking New Flameford's ruins to the ancient Flameford in Vacari. A wicked smile curved his lips as he envisioned this tunnel as a vault for his most prized captives, a gateway to his darkest desires. Once more, Phoenix's gaze sought the horizon, envisioning the indomitable archer Keisha ensnared within his web. The mental tableau depicted her futile struggle against the tide of Druchii, and a twisted satisfaction coursed through him. 'Your intervention will not pass unpunished. Keisha, the time approaches when you'll beg for mercy,' he whispered, power surging through his veins as he relished the impending dominion, like a puppeteer savoring the anticipation of his grand performance."

Chapter 1

Shadows Unveiled: Normalcy in Vacari

In the heart of E'vahona, a majestic Eladrin forest city, the morning sun painted the treetops in shades of gold and amber. Towering buildings, fashioned from a harmonious fusion of crystals and nature's bounty, stood above the forest floor as crystalline sanctuaries. These homes were interconnected by intricate walkways and graceful staircases that spiraled skyward. Equally breathtaking in their design, the residences reflected the hues of the forest canopy on their crystalline facades, their windows framing views that were nothing short of divine.

Keisha, a rare red-haired elf with emerald green eyes, moved gracefully through this enchanted city, commanding attention wherever she went. Her every step seemed like a dance, a harmonious rhythm with the forest and the crystalline homes surrounding her. Beside her, Ong, a tall and sturdy human with dark hair and piercing blue eyes, walked with quiet confidence, a steady presence that complemented Keisha's more exuberant nature. Their love for each other and the city they called home was evident in their every glance and touch.

Their bond was a testament to the enduring beauty of E'vahona. As Ong glanced at Keisha, his eyes caught the glimmer of the necklace he had lovingly given her four years ago, symbolizing their enduring love and commitment. A warm smile tugged at his lips, memories of that special gift flooding his mind, a small but cherished moment amid their journeys.

As they moved, Ong couldn't help but admire Keisha's fiery spirit, always eager to embrace life's challenges head-on. Her presence in the city was like a vibrant splash of color against the crystalline backdrop, a reminder of the beauty and vitality of their world. Keisha, in turn, found herself drawn to Ong's steadfast loyalty and the quiet strength he brought to their partnership. He was not just her partner in adventure but her beloved husband, the anchor of her heart.

Pumpkin, their loyal companion and a sleek black panther, moved with feline grace in their wake. Her green eyes were alert and curious, reflecting an intelligence beyond the ordinary. She was not just a pet but a protector and an integral part of their adventurous trio. Years ago, during a dangerous quest, Keisha had rescued Pumpkin from a helpless baby panther. From that moment, an unbreakable bond formed between them. Pumpkin had grown alongside Keisha, evolving into a fierce and devoted companion, her lithe form a testament to the wild spirit that ran through their group."

"In the heart of E'vahona, where crystalline homes and nature's bounty coexisted perfectly, Keisha, Ong, and Pumpkin embodied the essence of their cherished realm. Their presence was a testament to the beauty of their world, where love and bonds forged through adversity were as unyielding as the ancient trees and crystalline structures surrounding them.

When Ong entered their lives four years ago, Pumpkin's loyalty expanded to encompass him. In battles, she fearlessly stood by his side, a formidable guardian. Her sleek black form moved like a shadow of protection, her green eyes gleaming with a fierce determination. Pumpkin's bravery shone during the climactic confrontations against Phoenix and his dark forces, a beacon of unwavering devotion. On one occasion, she had leaped into action, positioning herself between Ong and an assailant, thwarting a potentially fatal blow with a grace that belied her wild nature.

Since then, Pumpkin remained an unwavering presence, a guardian and friend. Her loyalty and bravery made her an indispensable member of their trio, their adventures woven together with shared courage and love.

As Keisha and Ong approached the shimmering lake known as Shimmering Coast, a sense of calm and serenity enveloped them. The lake's crystal-clear waters mirrored the beauty of the surrounding forest, inviting them to immerse themselves in its tranquil embrace. Leaves rustled softly, and woodland creatures added their melodies to the symphony of peace that enfolded the cove.

This hidden sanctuary held a magical allure, frequented by elusive merfolk – graceful mermaids and mermen who emerged from the depths, basking on shimmering rocks and sands. Keisha, Ong, and Pumpkin had forged a unique connection with these mystical beings, their encounters marked by curiosity and mutual respect.

Pumpkin raced alongside them, her lithe form embodying feline grace. Her green eyes sparkled with excitement, mirroring the anticipation of her human companions. With each step, she conveyed her eagerness for the wonders of Shimmering Cove. As they drew nearer to the water's edge, they could almost hear the merfolk's laughter echoing through the waves, blending with the gentle lap of the lake.

Keisha turned to Ong with carefree abandon, mischief dancing in her eyes. "Race you to the water!" she declared with a playful grin, her adventurous spirit ignited by the beauty around them.

Ong chuckled, his laughter a testament to his competitive nature. "You're on!" he called back, the sparkle in his blue eyes revealing his readiness for the challenge.

Ever eager for adventure, Pumpkin joined the race, her lithe form keeping pace with her human companions. The trio dashed through the vibrant foliage, their laughter and joy merging with the harmonious symphony of nature.

As they neared the water's edge, the shimmering lake welcomed them, its crystal-clear surface inviting them to revel in its tranquility. They could almost sense the merfolk playfully gliding through the glistening waves, their laughter harmonizing with the gentle lapping of the lake, creating an enchanting melody of nature and friendship."

But just as they were about to embrace the serene cove in all its splendor, the distant sound of horns resonated through the forest. The melody of peace was replaced by an urgent tone, causing Keisha, Ong, and Pumpkin to exchange puzzled glances. The horns' foreboding call highlighted significant importance, shattering the moment's serenity, like a sudden thunderclap interrupting a tranquil reverie.

Before they could ponder further, a group of Eladrin warriors, led by Lord Karrenen Adan, emerged from the trees. As the most skilled mage of the Eladrin Council, his presence demanded respect. His silver hair cascaded over his shoulders, a crown of wisdom earned through years of experience. The sight of him alone indicated that his visit held gravitas, like a living embodiment of the ancient wisdom that guided the Eladrin.

Lord Karrenen's mastery over magic had turned the tide in the decisive battle against Phoenix and the Druchii, leading to their exile in Afor. As he approached

Keisha and Ong, his voice carried an air of authority from a lifetime of wielding arcane power. "Keisha, Ong," he greeted with a nod, acknowledging their presence. "I come with urgent news from King Manard of Crystal Vale."

Curiosity mingled with concern as Keisha and Ong focused on the venerable mage. They had heard tales of his exploits and knew the magnitude of his magical prowess. When Lord Karrenen spoke, his words carried the weight of truth, and they understood that his news would be of utmost importance, like the pronouncement of fate itself.

"It seems darkness is spreading in our lands," Lord Karrenen continued, his silver eyes reflecting the gravity of the situation. "Strange occurrences, sightings of dark creatures, and disturbances in the magical ley lines have been reported. King Manard has requested aid from allies he trusts, and you both are among them."

Ong's brow furrowed as he considered the implications. "Could Phoenix have found a way to extend his reach beyond Afor?" he asked, his voice edged with concern, like a sentinel guarding against an unseen threat.

Lord Karrenen's gaze turned grave. "We cannot dismiss the notion entirely," he replied. "Though exiled, Phoenix is a cunning adversary. His thirst for revenge may have driven him to seek ways to sow chaos and darkness in our lands, like a shadowy puppeteer orchestrating a sinister performance."

"The weight of responsibility settled upon Keisha and Ong's shoulders. They grasped the importance of the mission and the potential consequences if they failed to act. The safety of Crystal Vale and Vacari depended on their courage and determination, like a fragile thread holding back the encroaching darkness.

Keisha's grip on Ong's hand tightened, memories of their past battles resurfacing. "If he's responsible, we must be prepared for a formidable challenge," she asserted firmly, her determination unwavering, like the unyielding roots of an ancient tree.

"We'll need to be vigilant," Ong added, his warrior instincts awakening. "Even a possibility of Phoenix's involvement requires us to stay on guard, like sentinels protecting our homeland."

Lord Karrenen nodded in agreement. "Your caution is wise. I trust that both of you, along with your loyal companion," he glanced at Pumpkin, "will bring courage and skill to aid King Manard in securing Crystal Vale from this looming darkness."

With renewed determination, Keisha and Ong exchanged resolute glances. They knew the journey ahead would be perilous but were ready to meet it head-on, like heroes of old marching toward their destiny. As the sun dipped below the horizon, casting a warm glow over Vacari, Keisha, Ong, and Pumpkin bid farewell to their serene haven, the promise of their purpose guiding them toward Crystal Vale and thoughts of Phoenix lingering like shadows in their minds, a reminder of the darkness they must confront."

"Meanwhile, in the ominous city of New Flameford, Phoenix's dark influence had taken root like a poisonous vine, choking the life out of what was once a vibrant community. Lyra and Quellaun, swayed by his manipulative grasp, now aided him in his evil schemes, their once-bright spirits dimmed by the shadow of his power. Once a thriving city, New Flameford had transformed into a sinister place, cloaked in an eerie atmosphere that seemed to seep from the cobblestones.

Black and red banners bearing the mark of Phoenix's twisted emblem draped the streets, their tattered edges fluttering in the tainted wind. The tunnel leading to the underworld bore markings that seemed to writhe like serpents, evoking an unsettling feeling that sent shivers down the spine of any who dared to pass through. Sinister dragon statues, wrought from the darkest obsidian, cast their malevolent gazes upon all who walked the twisted streets, symbols of Phoenix's dominance and the terror he instilled.

The city's once-vibrant and diverse population now lived in fear, oppressed under Phoenix's rule like prisoners in their homes. His insatiable desire for power and vengeance had tainted the city's soul, casting an oppressive shadow over every corner, as if a dark cloud hung perpetually over New Flameford."

"As Keisha, Ong, and Pumpkin prepared to depart for Crystal Vale, they gathered a group of elves, selecting one among them for a critical task. "We must alert the benevolent dragons of the growing threat," Keisha asserted, her green eyes unwavering and filled with determination. "Phoenix may be exiled, but his reach extends beyond Afor. We need the dragons' aid to safeguard our lands."

Ong nodded in agreement, his blue eyes reflecting his unwavering commitment to the mission. "Indeed. The dragons have stood by us in the past and should be aware of the looming darkness."

The elves listened attentively, understanding the gravity of the situation. They chose a skilled messenger, adept at communicating with the dragons and delivering the urgent message. Armed with a scroll bearing the details of Phoenix's resurgence and the potential threat to their world, the elf embarked on a swift journey to the Hidden Isles.

The Hidden Isles, a realm of serenity hidden beyond conventional maps, served as the dwelling place of the benevolent dragons. The messenger navigated dense forests and treacherous mountains, overcoming the obstacles with unwavering determination to reach the entrance of this secret realm. A shimmering portal, concealed beneath the bark of an ancient oak tree, marked the path to the isles.

As the elf approached, the portal's magic recognized their pure intent, responding with a swirl of light that revealed the awe-inspiring beauty of the Hidden Isles. Verdant valleys stretched in all directions, adorned with exotic flowers that painted the landscape in a vivid tapestry of color. Towering trees with shimmering gold and silver leaves seemed to touch the sky in reverence. Birds of stunning hues danced through the air, their melodic songs harmonizing with the gentle rustling of leaves.

Yet, the true wonder of the Hidden Isles lay in its majestic waterfalls. They cascaded from sheer cliffs with an ethereal grace, each waterfall a unique masterpiece of nature's design. Some flowed like delicate veils, trailing in the breeze like silken ribbons. Others roared with thunderous might, casting mists that shimmered with rainbows in the sunlight as if the very tears of the heavens fell upon the land."

Amidst meandering rivers and pools formed by the waterfalls' descent, crystal-clear lakes sparkled like gems. The water held pristine clarity, reflecting the essence of purity and tranquility. Silverfish darted gracefully through the water, adding to the enchanting spectacle, their movements like a ballet in the aquatic realm.

Throughout the Hidden Isles, nature's symphony played on, a melody of life and magic resonating in the hearts of those who set foot upon this sacred land. Benevolent dragons soared gracefully above, their wings casting fleeting shadows that danced upon the earth below, like guardian spirits watching over their cherished realm.

The Hidden Isles' beauty ran deeper than aesthetics; it was a living testament to the delicate balance between light and shadow, something the benevolent dragons held dear as the messenger ventured toward the heart of the isles. A sense of reverence and wonder filled them. They stood in a realm untouched by the darkness that threatened to engulf Vacari, a realm unaffected by the chaos that Phoenix's return could bring. It was a sanctuary of purity and tranquility, a beacon of hope in a world teetering on the edge of darkness.

In the heart of the Hidden Isles, surrounded by nature's splendor, stood a grand stone castle—the council chamber of the dragons. Here, the dragons convened to discuss matters of utmost importance, their collective wisdom a guiding light in times of peril. The castle's architecture was a testament to craftsmanship, adorned with carvings that told ancient wisdom and history stories, like the pages of a living tome.

Approaching the grand council chamber, awe swept over the messenger. The castle's colossal doors, etched with ancient runes that whispered of ancient secrets, welcomed those who sought the counsel of Kimras, the wise and venerable gold dragon. Inside the hallowed halls, shelves lined with scrolls held the accumulated knowledge of the dragons, containing wisdom spanning centuries, like a repository of the world's history and the dragons' unwavering commitment to its preservation.

With a humble heart, the messenger presented the scroll to Kimras, whose eyes shimmered with the wisdom of ages, like pools of liquid gold reflecting the world's wisdom. Kimras, leader of the grand council, emanated regal grace, their presence commanding respect from all who were fortunate enough to stand in their presence. Beside them sat Dirona, the ancient bronze dragon known for her unmatched wisdom, her scales gleaming with the patina of age and experience. And next to her was Hespherus, the powerful brass dragon whose eloquence could sway hearts and minds, his words like a mesmerizing melody.

Further down the table, Silvara, the nurturing silver dragon, exuded serenity that soothed troubled souls, her presence a balm to those in need. Caelum, the clever copper dragon, observed with keen intelligence, his eyes gleaming with a mischievous glint that hinted at the depth of his knowledge and wit.

Surrounded by the grandeur of the Hidden Isles, the council of dragons deliberated. Kimras's voice resonated like a harmonious symphony, their words imbued with ancient wisdom and a deep sense of purpose, "Rahgot krosis, vanuul elf. Foduniid niin viingah. Dovahzul, dii duniir. Klo dovah, daar lein fahdon dovah." ("We shall answer your call, young elf. Phoenix's return must not be taken lightly. Together, we shall safeguard our lands from this darkness.")

With the dragons' support assurance, the messenger returned to Keisha and Ong, bearing hope and strength. Though challenges loomed, the knowledge that allies worldwide were standing vigilant against Phoenix's schemes provided comfort and resolve. The path ahead was treacherous, yet they were not alone in their struggle. They carried with them the wisdom and strength of the dragons, a force that would bolster their determination and guide them through the darkest times.

As the sun dipped below the horizon, casting a warm glow over Vacari, Keisha, Ong, and Pumpkin took a final moment to bid farewell to their tranquil haven. Thoughts of Phoenix's malevolent plans weighed heavily on their minds as they set out toward Crystal Vale, the city of Ong's birth. The journey ahead was a test of their mettle, a confrontation with an adversary who threatened to plunge Vacari into eternal darkness. But with the dragons by their side, they faced the future with unwavering courage and the hope of a brighter tomorrow.

Chapter 2

Shadows Unveiled: Tidings of Darkness

The foreboding city of New Flameford stood as an ominous testament to the hostility of Phoenix Shadowwalker, where his dark influence had taken root and tainted everything it touched. Within the obsidian walls, a cauldron of sinister machinations simmered, and the once vibrant thoroughfares now sagged under the weight of encroaching darkness, like a festering wound upon the land.

Banners, a sinister dance of black and red, twisted in the wind above, their tattered edges fluttering like the torn fabric of hope. The evil eyes of dragon statues, once symbols of protection, now surveyed all who traversed the shadowed streets with a cold, unfeeling gaze—a chilling display of Phoenix's supremacy over the city.

Hidden deep within treacherous mountains, shrouded from prying gazes, lay the Dread Spire—a clandestine haven for malevolent dragons. This desolate expanse, perpetually surrounded in inky darkness, was circumscribed by erupting volcanoes, casting fiery tumult and enigmatic shadows across its desolate canvas. The towering peaks, their serrated edges reaching skyward like jagged teeth, channeled icy gales that whispered through the craggy crevices, rendering the land inhospitable to all but the darkest hearts. It was a place where the very earth rejected the presence of light.

In the heart of the Dread Spire, a sinister conclave gathered—a pantheon of destruction and despair. Zylron, once devoted, now marred by allegiance to Phoenix, presided at the helm—a crimson dragon now tainted, his scales like smoldering embers. By his side, Drakthor, a black-scaled paragon of cruelty and cunning, brooded with an aura of abyssal depths, his eyes gleaming with malice. The alabaster presence of Glaciera exuded an aura of frigid elegance, concealing a perilous sagacity beneath her icy exterior, her breath forming frosty tendrils in the air. Completing this council of hostility, the emerald-green Venfyr reveled in sowing seeds of discord, his manipulations a delight amongst wicked forces, his laughter echoing through the chamber like a venomous serpent's hiss.

A recent addition, Thundria, the Topaz dragon, marked a shift—once neutral, now shackled by Phoenix's beguiling charm. Her powers lent fresh vigor to their ranks, underscoring the sinister sway of the evil dragon council. This dominion held all who had succumbed to darkness, like a web of malice ensnaring their souls."

Meanwhile, concealed beneath the facade of New Flameford, an arcane passageway slithered through the city's embrace, connecting the city to its ancient twin, Old Flameford, nestled within the Realm of Vacari. This subterranean conduit wove a tapestry of obscurity, ferrying malevolent forces unnoticed between realms—each step a whispered progression toward their clandestine objectives. A web of darkness spanned the realms, a sinister thread connecting the heart of hostility.

As the Abyssal Dominion readied itself to unleash chaos upon an unsuspecting Vacari, rumors of their nefarious stratagems crept like serpentine shadows through New Flameford's corridors. Whispers of the evil dragon council's sinister designs ignited like wildfire, weaving a lattice of fear and uncertainty amongst the innocent denizens—a populace cowed by the looming specter of Phoenix's wrath. Once a vibrant hub of life and culture, the city had become a breeding ground for fear and despair.

Within the recesses of the Dread Spire, the malevolent council convened, each breath drawing power from the malevolence permeating the very land. Unfettered by restraint, their ambitions soared, aimed at seizing the Abyssal Dominion over Vacari and Afor—an enigmatic realm of exile concealed in the tapestry of worlds. It was a gathering of hostility that threatened to tip the balance of power in the realms, a dark symphony of conspiracies and treachery.

In the depths of the ominous city of New Flameford, a sinister aura clung heavily to the air, an unmistakable sign of the evil force that had firmly taken root. Within the towering citadel's shadowed heart, Phoenix Shadowwalker, a human warlock with hair-like silver threads and eyes as deep as the night, stood surrounded by a gathering of nefarious figures. Among them stood Lyra and Qellaun Deadcrusher, siblings and Druchii with a lineage tainted by darkness, bound by an oath to serve Phoenix Shadowwalker in his evil pursuits.

Lyra, her hair cascading like a river of shadows, eyes burning like crimson embers, and adorned in a gown that melded silver and crimson, emanated an aura of cunning and treachery that infected the air around her. In stark contrast, Qellaun Deadcrusher, his hair a blend of midnight and silver, eyes fierce like the ocean in a storm, clad in armor that mirrored the dance of shadows, stood resolute, ready to execute Phoenix's every whispered wish. United by unwavering loyalty to their sinister patron, they were prepared to unleash chaos and devastation upon the Realm of Vacari, their allegiance an unholy pact that bound them to a path of hostility. From the shadowy recesses of New Flameford, dark creatures began to stir, summoned forth by the evil might of Phoenix and his devoted followers. The once-vibrant streets had metamorphosed into a fortress of obscurity, its inhabitants shackled by the weight of oppressive darkness that now governed their lives. Menacing dragon statues, embodying Phoenix's supremacy, loomed over the thoroughfares, casting a frigid shroud over the hearts of all who walked beneath. The city had become a twisted reflection of its former glory, a realm where fear thrived, and hope dwindled.

As Phoenix and his loyal confidants plotted the course of their impending actions, the Realm of Vacari remained enshrouded in blissful ignorance of the burgeoning malevolence that loomed, threatening to engulf their world. Yet, unbeknownst to them, destiny prepared to weave their fates into an epic tapestry of light clashing against shadow. In the face of impossible darkness, the courage of a chosen few would be thrust to the forefront, their destinies entwined with the very survival of Vacari.

With an unsettling grin, Lyra watched the creatures writhe and slither into their new reality, their presence heralding an impending cataclysm. Her shrewd intellect delighted in the havoc she foresaw, soon to be unleashed upon unsuspecting lands. Her eyes glittered with an evil gleam, and her heart beat in time with the impending chaos, relishing in the power she would wield as darkness spread.

"Welcome, my minions," the resonance of Phoenix's voice carried a potent power as he addressed the shadow-born creatures. "Your task is simple—spread fear, chaos, and despair wherever your steps fall. Let lands quake with trepidation at the mere whisper of your arrival. Show them the tranquility they once cherished is a fleeting mirage in the face of true malice."

The dark beings hissed and growled in macabre harmony, comprehending their master's edict without needing spoken words. As they dispersed, their malevolence infused the heart of New Flameford, transmuting the once-vibrant city into a realm of eerie shadows and haunting whispers. The air seemed to thicken with malice, and the streets echoed with the eerie laughter of the shadow-born.

Lyra's eyes gleamed with gratification as she beheld the malevolent entities commence their ominous errands. Each stride they took further fueled her insatiable thirst for chaos and dominion. She was a conductor of calamity, reveling in the discord she sowed, and her loyalty to Phoenix was unwavering. Together, they would reshape the world in their image, and New Flameford was the first step in their grand design.

New Flameford shall serve as the nexus of our operations," Phoenix declared, his expression suffused with smug satisfaction. "From here, we shall unfurl our dominion, reducing the world of Vacari to its knees, powerless before our might." His words hung like a dark omen, a foreboding promise of the calamity yet to come.

Meanwhile, in the lands of Vacari, the sun's descent painted the sky with hues of orange and gold as Keisha and Ong ventured into Crystal Vale. The city sprawled before them, a tapestry of vibrant colors woven into the fabric of nature's grandeur. Surrounded by the embrace of a sprawling lake, Crystal Vale exuded breathtaking beauty, its tranquility further amplified by the majestic waterfalls that cascaded down towering cliffs. The architecture, an exquisite blend of craftsmanship and creativity, stood as a testament to the city's elegance, while the warm glow of street lanterns welcomed them with a comforting embrace.

Yet, beneath this picturesque serenity, an undercurrent of unease tugged at the edges of Keisha and Ong's perceptions. The citizens of Crystal Vale, accustomed to sharing warm smiles and cheerful greetings, now exchanged cautious glances and hushed whispers. Like leaves rustling before a gathering storm, the residents hinted at unsettling events that had recently shaken their peaceful abode.

In the heart of this city stood King Manard, a figure of wisdom and age, who greeted Keisha and Ong with a mixture of gratitude and concern etched onto his features. His voice carried a solemn weight as he addressed them, "Thank you for coming, my friends. The dark creatures now treading upon our lands are not the ordinary foes we have encountered. An air of malevolence clings to their presence, and I fear forces beyond guide them."

Keisha and Ong exchanged knowing glances, their thoughts coalescing around a single name: Phoenix, the evil sorcerer banished to the forsaken Realm of Afor. Though his physical distance was great, his power and influence stretched far beyond the line of sight, like the shadow of a looming storm cast upon a distant horizon. The tendrils of his malevolence seemed to reach out, whispering dark commands to creatures that acted as extensions of his will.

"The dragons have been made aware of the unfolding threat," Keisha reassured the king, her voice a steady pillar of confidence. "They stand ready to lend their might should the need arise."

King Manard nodded, his expression a blend of gratitude and worry. His gaze drifted to the lake, where the water's surface shimmered like a mirror to the city's inner turmoil. "I pray that it shall not come to that," he confessed, his voice carrying the weight of a ruler burdened by the safety of his city. "For Crystal Vale has long been a sanctuary of peace and prosperity, and I fear what shadows these ominous times may cast upon it."

Gently, Keisha placed a reassuring hand upon the king's shoulder, her touch an anchor of resolve. "Rest assured, King Manard. We shall wield every ounce of our strength to shield Crystal Vale and safeguard the lands of Vacari," she vowed.

Ong, the stoic guardian, echoed her words with unyielding conviction. "You have our steadfast loyalty, King Manard. We shall stand as an unbreakable shield against the trials that lie ahead."

As the trio gazed out upon the serene vista of Crystal Vale, they understood that appearances were often deceiving. Beneath the façade of tranquility, a storm brewed. The evil forces that Phoenix had set in motion threatened to shroud the entire realm in an all-encompassing darkness. The path ahead would test their courage, unity, and commitment to safeguarding the fragile balance between light and shadow in the world of Vacari.

Unbeknownst to the inhabitants of Vacari, within the shadows of New Flameford, the evil dominion continued to weave their webs of deception and wicked scheming. Like insidious darkness, their plans unfurled, casting a looming threat that sought to engulf the world in an unending abyss of night. The epic clash between the forces of light and the depths of darkness had commenced, and the destiny of Vacari precariously teetered on the precipice.

While the fate of Vacari hung in the balance, in the desolate expanse of Afor—a realm forsaken and shrouded in malevolence—Phoenix's influence churned. The barren landscape stirred with newfound agitation, as if the land was responding to an invisible orchestrator of chaos.

Within the heart of Afor, concealed by darkness and despair, lay Phoenix's lair—a somber reflection of his malevolent dominion. Here, he convened with sinister forces, seeking to extend his malefic grip beyond the confines of New Flameford, eager to lay his cruel hand upon the unsuspecting lands of Vacari.

Emerging from the shadows, Qellaun Deadcrusher, Lyra's loyal brother, approached with a demeanor of unwavering allegiance. His dark eyes mirrored his loyalty to Phoenix as he conveyed the successful deployment of evil creatures to sow discord within New Flameford.

Phoenix's silver hair shimmered in the dim light as he intently absorbed Qellaun's report. "Exceptional work, Qellaun," he commended, his voice reflecting his pride. "With New Flameford firmly under our control, the rest of Vacari shall inevitably follow suit."

In the concealed depths of New Flameford and the desolate Realm of Afor, the evil dominion persisted in their dark stratagems, their nefarious intentions veiled within the tendrils of shadow. Lyra's heart seethed with a potent blend of ambition and envy. Though equally devoted to Phoenix as her brother, Qellaun, Lyra's aspirations stretched beyond mere loyalty. She yearned for more—a more profound connection that transcended servitude, kindling both romantic longing and the desperate desire to ascend to the role of Phoenix's closest confidante and companion.

With pride and envy intertwined, Lyra observed her brother's interactions with Phoenix, her eyes lingering on the graceful articulation of his report. She thirsted for such praise and acknowledgment from Phoenix, to be recognized as his most cherished and indispensable servant. The notion of an elevated status, not just in their malevolent endeavors but also in a profoundly intimate manner, consumed her every thought.

As the vicious creatures proliferated chaos and terror within New Flameford, Lyra seized each opportunity to showcase her cunning and treacherous nature. She wove a tapestry of sinister plots, sowing manipulative seeds among the ranks of followers, all aimed at securing her ascendance in Phoenix's regard.

In her heart, Lyra nurtured the belief that by proving herself invaluable to Phoenix, she could transcend the bounds of servitude and be regarded as an irreplaceable companion. She envisioned standing by his side, ruling with him from a throne bathed in malevolence, sharing in power and passion within a shadow-drenched embrace.

Yet, she concealed these fervent desires beneath a veneer of composure, acutely aware that revealing such vulnerability to Phoenix would be risky. He was a master manipulator skilled at exploiting weaknesses for his gain.

Despite her growing envy towards Qellaun, Lyra remained a shrewd ally to her sibling. Their bond as Druchii siblings was steeped in shared darkness. However, Lyra's aspirations propelled her beyond familial connections, compelling her to seek a unique distinction that would set her apart and render her indispensable in Phoenix's malevolent realm.

As the vicious dominion continued their shadowed machinations, Lyra's ambitions smoldered, a simmering ember awaiting the opportunity to ignite into an inferno of darkness and longing. Unbeknownst to all, her twisted yearning for Phoenix's favor would soon propel her toward choices that could reshape the trajectory of their malevolent quest and alter the destiny of Vacari itself.

In the depths of the evil temple devoted to the sinister deity Vuarus, the imprisoned creatures of darkness brooded, their malefic presence a dire threat to the Realm of Vacari. The unholy alliance between Phoenix and the cult of Vuarus had unleashed a sinister connection that bridged the gap between New Flameford and the malevolent temple in Afor, allowing for the malefic forces to flow freely between realms.

The evil cells held captive creatures of unparalleled darkness within the confines of the temple's stygian heart. Each of these beings was a harbinger of chaos and devastation, their powers carefully contained but ready to be unleashed upon the unsuspecting world.

The first cell housed the Shadow Wraith, a vile entity that thrived on fear and despair. Its mere presence could drive individuals to madness, and its woeful shrieks reverberated through the void, chilling the hearts of all who heard them.

In another chamber, the Maelstrom Serpent lay imprisoned, wielding dominion over the elements and conjuring tempests and storms with catastrophic fervor. The sinister hisses and flashes of lightning from its enclosure cast a foreboding pall over any who dared to approach.

The third cell contained the Wraithbound, an ethereal entity capable of feasting upon its prey's life force. Its spectral form drifted through the darkness, and the mere glimpse of its glowing eyes could reduce even the bravest souls to trembling fear.

These malevolent captives embodied darkness, each with the potential to unleash unimaginable horrors upon the Realm of Vacari. The cells were enchanted to drain the prisoners of their strength, rendering them enervated and docile. However, the ever-present concern was that these enchantments might weaken, leading to the unleashing of the maleficence contained within.

The evil forces within New Flameford and the temple in Afor saw these captives as weapons of cataclysmic destruction, ready to be unshackled upon any who dared to oppose their nefarious aspirations. The path ahead for Vacari was fraught with peril, as the venom plotted its ascent to dominance, threatening to plunge the realm into an abyss of darkness and despair. The destiny of Vacari hung in the balance, and the forces of light would have to muster their strength and courage to confront the impending cataclysm.

The shadow-clad cells within the malevolent temple held prisoners whose powers were as dangerous as they were insidious. With the ability to exploit the deepest fears and darkest desires of anyone who crossed their path, these captives posed a grave threat to the very essence of those who encountered them. The convergence of light and darkness was poised to escalate, testing the core beliefs and convictions of those who stood in their way and reshaping the understanding of courage and heroism in the face of such hostility.

In the heart of New Flameford, concealed within the realm's shadow-draped core, an underground chamber remained shrouded in potent enchantments, safeguarding Phoenix's most prized captives. This hidden labyrinth of hostility bore eerie runes and sinuous shadows that seemed to observe with malefic intent. At its center lay individual cells, each meticulously designed to imprison those whose powers threatened Phoenix's dominion of dread.

One cell's walls were etched with runes that leeched elemental might from its inmate, rendering them feeble and powerless. Enchanted crystals drained all sorcery from their prisoners in another chamber, leaving them bereft of their arcane mastery.

Within a particularly ominous cell, shadows undulated and whispered, a sinister incarnation of psychic energy capable of infiltrating minds and afflicting inmates with haunting phantasms.

Yet, the most ominous of all was a cell steeped in eternal darkness, impervious to any attempt at escape. No ray of light could pierce its inky abyss, and any endeavor to break free summoned an implacable force, compelling prisoners into an abyssal descent from which there seemed to be no return.

These malevolent captives represented a dire threat to Vacari, their powers harnessed to further Phoenix's malefic designs. As the forces of light and darkness clashed on the precipice of destiny, the path forward remained treacherous and uncertain, with the realm's fate hanging in the balance. Courage and heroism would be tested like never before, as Vacari braced itself for an epic confrontation that would determine its survival.

As Keisha's fiery red tresses and noble elven lineage marked her as a significant threat to Phoenix's nefarious designs, he spared no effort in ensuring her captivity within one of the evil cells. This cell was meticulously tailored to quash her intrinsic magical might, designed to neutralize her formidable abilities.

As the evil dominion readied itself to sow chaos upon the unsuspecting Realm of Vacari, the vacant cells concealed within New Flameford's covert chamber harbored a plot far more intricate than the city's superficial malevolence suggested. Unbeknownst to the masses, a clandestine network of passageways wound through the very core of Afor, entwining New Flameford with its counterpart in Vacari – Old Flameford.

Among these hidden routes, one passage remained shrouded in darkness, immune to prying eyes. It descended underground, delving into the fathomless depths of an unnamed ocean expanse that separated the two realms. This enigmatic body of water teemed with creatures of mystery, its currents murmuring secrets only the courageous or the reckless dared to pursue.

The underground tunnel, hewed from bedrock by malevolent hands in ages past, offered an unholy conduit for New Flameford's dark forces to traverse the dangerous waters. Enchanted magic bound into the very essence of the tunnel shielded it from the crushing weight of the abyssal ocean, granting passage to the wicked while sparing them the ocean's wrath.

Meandering toward Old Flameford, the tunnel gradually ascended, weaving a path through concealed caverns. These underground chambers, adorned with age-old phosphorescent mosses and luminescent crystals, cast an eerie radiance that illuminated the way for those brave enough to tread its course.

Embedded within the walls of these ancient passages, whispers of bygone tales lingered, as if the stones retained memories of the hostility that once trod this very path. Legends spoke of grim rituals performed in the deepest recesses, where malevolent entities offered homage to their nefarious deity.

The malefic connection between New Flameford and Old Flameford remained hidden from the eyes of the world, a sinister thread that bound these two cities across realms, facilitating the flow of darkness and treacherous plans that would soon be unleashed upon the unsuspecting lands of Vacari.

His covert passage remained among Vacari's most closely guarded secrets, a gateway for the malevolence festering in Afor to infiltrate the once harmonious lands. As the dominion poised to set its sinister stratagems into motion, the tunnel remained enshrouded by the cloak of night, biding its time until the forces of darkness would ascend from the abyssal depths, plunging the world into disarray.

Amidst the serenity of Crystal Vale, a growing unease gnawed at King Manard's heart. Unseen to his eyes, the nefarious schemes weaving through New Flameford and the malevolent temple of Afor were poised to intersect with his city. This calamitous convergence would examine the bravery and unity of those who dared to defy the encroaching obscurity.

Within the protective embrace of Crystal Vale's walls, Keisha, Ong, and their steadfast companions had arrived with an unyielding resolve to safeguard their cherished world. Yet, their understanding of the hostility ahead remained incomplete. As they steeled themselves for the impending trials, their course would propel them to confront the evil forces that had unfurled from the depths of New Flameford and the age-old sanctum of Afor's temple.

Chapter 3

Shadows Unveiled: Abyssal Dominion

Amidst the sinister assembly, Zylron presided as the council's leader with his scales now smoldering like embers. His eyes, once ablaze with fervor for a different cause, now harbored the cold, calculated cruelty of one who had succumbed to Phoenix's insidious influence.

He was the crimson beacon of Phoenix's malevolent might, symbolizing the darkness that had consumed his once-noble soul.

Drakthor, a dragon born of abyssal depths, exuded an aura of sinister intellect. His ebony scales seemed to absorb the very light around him, and his eyes gleamed with malice. His cunning and ruthlessness were unmatched, making him a key strategist in the council's dark designs.

Glaciera, the alabaster presence among the council, possessed an elegance that concealed her perilous sagacity. Her icy exterior belied the lethal power she held, capable of freezing the very hearts of those who dared to oppose her. Her breath formed frosty tendrils in the air, a chilling reminder of the frigid depths of her cruelty.

Venfyr, the emerald-green dragon, reveled in sowing discord and chaos. His manipulative talents were a source of delight among the evil forces, and his laughter echoed through the chamber like a venomous serpent's hiss. He was the mastermind behind many of the council's treacherous plots.

Thundria, adorned in topaz splendor, marked a shift within the council. Once a neutral entity, she succumbed to Phoenix's beguiling charm, adding considerable power to the council's ranks. Her presence lent fresh vigor to their dark aspirations, highlighting the sway of the evil dragon council over those who had embraced the darkness.

This sinister conclave gathered in the heart of the Dread Spire, their very breath drawing power from the malevolence that permeated the land. Unrestrained by morality or compassion, their ambitions soared, aimed at securing the Abyssal Dominion over Vacari and Afor—a gathering of hostility that threatened to tip the balance of power in the realms, a dark symphony of conspiracies and treachery.

Within the ominous confines of the Dread Spire, the malevolent council convened, their discussions steeped in treachery and dark machinations. At the heart of their assembly lay a subtle undercurrent of wariness, particularly within the mind of Zylron, the red dragon who harbored a shared history with Talleoss. Despite their united front in malevolent unity, the presence of the ancient staff cast a shadow of ambiguity upon their gathering, a reminder of the enigma dwelling within their midst.

Talleoss, now bound within the staff wielded by Phoenix, emanated an enigmatic aura that both intrigued and unnerved the assembled dragons. While they acknowledged the staff's formidable might, they could not fully trust the ancient consciousness residing within it. Talleoss had traversed ages, amassing knowledge beyond even the most erudite dragon's grasp, and his presence within the staff added an unpredictable element to their plans.

As Zylron's gaze locked onto Talleoss, an inexplicable chill coursed down his scaled spine. It was as if the staff's ancient gaze penetrated his soul, probing for hidden vulnerabilities. He resisted the instinctual urge to break eye contact, maintaining his unwavering focus on the staff, determined not to show weakness in front of the council.

The council members noticed Zylron's discomfort and exchanged knowing looks that betrayed their awareness of his unease. Drakthor, always keenly perceptive, sought to reassure him, emphasizing Talleoss's captivity and tethering to Phoenix's will.

Glaciera, her icy demeanor unwavering, echoed the sentiment, emphasizing the importance of keeping Talleoss dormant within the staff.

Venfyr, the master of manipulation, played with sly amusement, reminding them that even the most discerning dragons had their vulnerabilities.

Despite the council's reassurances, Zylron remained circumspect, recognizing Talleoss as both a potential asset and a precarious wildcard in their evil pursuits. He couldn't shake the feeling that the ancient entity held secrets that could alter the course of their evil plans, and that their control over him might not be as absolute as they believed. As twilight descended, Vacari's fate hung in the balance, poised on the precipice of darkness's unshackling, ready to plunge the realm into chaos.

As shadows lengthened and malevolent tides surged closer, the sinister forces of the Abyssal Dominion gathered their might, poised to unleash pandemonium upon the unsuspecting Realm of Vacari. Whispers of the evil council's nefarious machinations spread like wildfire, sowing dread and uncertainty among the innocent residents trapped by the specter of Phoenix's vengeful ire.

Within the staff's heart, the essence of Talleoss seethed with an unrelenting fusion of anger and frustration. Entrapped within the confines of the enchanted artifact, his spirit yearned for liberation, a return to the majestic form he once embodied. It was an eternal clash of resolve, a ceaseless contest between the imprisoned dragon's essence and the arcane shackles that trapped him.

Once, in the annals of time, Talleoss had soared as a magnificent silver dragon, revered by Vacari's denizens. His scales mirrored the moon's luminescence, casting a radiance that filled the skies with wonder. He had traversed the heavens, spewing fire to safeguard the realm, a beacon of hope and brilliance amidst darkness's shadow.

But epochs shifted when malevolence unfurled its wings over the land, a precursor of treacherous designs by the sorcerer Phoenix Shadowwalker. Kadona, the Goddess of Light, witnessed the realm's veering corruption and shielded Talleoss from Phoenix's clutches.

In an ethereal confrontation, Kadona's luminous visage illuminated their realm. "Talleoss, noble guardian," she had begun, sorrow lacing her words, "I perceive the looming abyss. To thwart this menace, I shall bind your spirit to this staff until freedom's path emerges."

Torn between his understanding of Kadona's motive and the urge to resist his captivity, Talleoss implored, "My lady, I am a beacon of light, protector of these lands. Please spare me my liberty, and I shall stand as your ally against the encroaching darkness."

Kadona's radiant gaze had softened, her touch delicate upon Talleoss's snout. "Your heart radiates purity, gallant one," she had intoned, "and your devotion is unwavering. Yet, malevolence's seduction runs deep. We must veil you within this staff to preserve your valor, safeguarding your noble spirit."

With resolve interlaced with reluctance, Talleoss had yielded to Kadona's wisdom. Radiance had flowed from her, magic woven, and his argent scales transformed into deep, earthy verdancy—a testament to his newfound role as guardian from within, an emblem of protection shrouded in mystical containment.

Initially, Talleoss had waged an inner war against this fate, resenting the encased confinement. Frustration surged like a smoldering ember, reverberating through the enchantments that fettered him. Yet, as temporal currents coursed, understanding dawned, unveiling Kadona's profound design.

Despite his captivity, Talleoss evolved into an enduring font of strength and counsel, a reservoir of sagacity for those wielding the staff. His erudition and age-old lore fortified the battlefront against darkness's tide. He murmured words of courage and sowed hope from within his crystalline prison, buttressing the champions who rose to shield Vacari from the looming malevolence.

Nevertheless, the shackles bore heavily upon the once-unfettered dragon. He yearned for the caress of wind under his wings, the exhilaration of flight, and the guardianship of his cherished realm. Yet, Kadona's sorcery held unyielding, so Talleoss endured, embracing the faith that the Goddess's grander purpose would one day unfurl him from his arcane cocoon.

Within the dimly illuminated sanctum of the temple, shadows waltzed upon the walls as Malrik, chief priest of Vuarus, genuflected before the towering effigy of Vuarus, the God of Shadows. "My Lord Vuarus," Malrik chanted with reverence, his words a melody of devotion, "my years of faithful service stir questions within me. Why not simply remove Kadona, the Goddess of Light? With your might, a realm bereft of her influence could fuel your ascendancy."

Vuarus, eyes aglow with an otherworldly luminescence, cast his gaze upon his fervent disciple. "Ah, Malrik, my unwavering servant," he began, his voice akin to a gentle breeze laden with age-old sagacity, "you venture into places that elude mortal comprehension. The cosmic laws that tether us forbid direct harm among us, the divine entities. Veridius, the Chief God of Balance and Harmony, decreed such laws—indeed, even I, Vuarus, am bound by their tenets."

In concord, Malrik acknowledged the intricate equilibrium governing the divine plane. "Yet, my Lord Vuarus, could an alternative route not lead us to our aspirations?" he inquired, his words tentative. "If direct intercession is taboo, maybe we can manipulate the tides of fate to our favor?" A sidelong smirk curled upon Vuarus' lips, a precursor of veiled machinations. "Indubitably,

my loyal acolyte," he responded, a subtle glint in his gaze, "the mortal realms sprawl with complexities, a tapestry of souls seeking purpose and direction. Though we cannot directly intervene, our might can provoke and shape the destiny of mortals."

"But who among mortals could best serve as your vessel of intent, my Lord?" Malrik ventured, intrigue sparking within his eyes.

Vuarus' gaze traversed the ethereal horizon, contemplating the myriad threads of human existence. "One harbors potential," he disclosed, his tone tinged with fascination. "Phoenix Shadowwalker, an exile aflame with torment and resentment, his spirit corroded by pain. He hungers for revenge against a realm that spurned him—unbeknownst to him, he stands poised as a pawn in our intricate symphony."

Comprehension lit up Malrik's eyes as he grasped the profound nature of his god's design. "You aim to harness Phoenix's vengeance and wrath to sculpt our ambitions," he voiced, awe and trepidation melding within his words.

Vuarus nodded, the grin deepening. "Indeed. By whispering subtle guidance and stoking the fires of his malice, we can mold his actions to our ends. The weft of destiny threads through all creatures, and the ripples of Phoenix's conduct may well shepherd Kadona's demise."

Malrik was enthralled and disquieted by the intricacy of his deity's stratagem. "And if Phoenix unearths our hand within his path?" he inquired, a note of caution clinging to his words.

Vuarus' gaze retained its enigmatic quality. "Fear not, stalwart servant. Phoenix's heart brims with darkness, shrouding him from the divine's subtler orchestrations. He shall remain ignorant as long as our presence remains unseen, dancing to a melody he does not recognize."

With renewed resolve, Malrik exited the chamber, aware that he had been enlisted as a pivotal figure in the grand tapestry of destiny. Vuarus surveyed his devotee's departure with contentment, a conviction unwavering that the skeins of fate were converging to usher in the metamorphosis that would convulse the bedrock of Vacari.

Qellaun Deadcrusher, a formidable Druchii warrior born and raised in the shadowed city of Fel Thalor, held an unyielding loyalty that ran deep. From his earliest days, his sacred duty was safeguarding and standing sentinel over the young Phoenix Shadowwalker. This pledge wasn't taken lightly; it forged an unbreakable bond between him and the boy who would eventually rise to become the feared malevolent sorcerer.

As a Druchii, Qellaun's training in martial arts commenced at a tender age, honing his mastery over the blade and bow. His movements melded swiftness with grace, his combat finesse as lethal as the keen edge of his weapon. Infused with the eldritch shadows of Fel Thalor, his character bore the marks of cunning and ruthlessness. But it was his unwavering allegiance to Phoenix that truly defined him.

As Phoenix's powers burgeoned during their formative years, Qellaun remained an ever-present figure at his side. He bore witness to the boy's struggles and victories, the ghosts of his past, and the emergence of his ominous talents. Their connection transcended verbal articulation—a profound understanding woven through the fabric of shared chronicles.

Qellaun Deadcrusher beheld the evolution of Phoenix from fragile youth to force to be reckoned with. The warrior admired Phoenix's indomitable spirit and resilience, remaining unwavering throughout every ordeal. To Qellaun, no more tremendous honor existed than serving the one he had vowed to safeguard—even if it meant traversing a path veiled in shadows.

While many quaked before Phoenix's malevolence, Qellaun perceived the soul beneath the veneer of wickedness. He envisioned a dominion that could construct a realm where acceptance and respect trumped their disparate origins. Yet, this journey wasn't devoid of trials. Qellaun apprehended the perils of their partnership with Vuarus, the God of Shadows and Vengeance—a pact that could upend Vacari's bedrock. The ferocity of their adversaries wasn't lost on him. Nonetheless, his allegiance to Phoenix fortified him, allowing him to surmount any hurdle, even if it demanded the ultimate sacrifice.

Amidst the heart of darkness, Qellaun Deadcrusher emerged as an unyielding guardian—an embodiment of loyalty's potency and the impervious connections that could bind even the most improbable companions. His destiny intertwined with Phoenix's, their fates irrevocably intertwined. Embarking on this treacherous odyssey, Qellaun embraced the unknown, understanding that he would stand unflinching at Phoenix's side until the journey's terminus, regardless of the daunting path ahead.

In the evil confines of New Flameford, Lyra Deadcrusher—a beguiling Druchii sorceress—dwelled as an ambitious and artful enigma. Enthralled by the allure of the black arts from a tender age, her yearning for power knew no bounds. Her teaching in the sinister realms of magic molded her into a deadly maestro, her skills a precise manipulation instrument.

Lyra's inaugural encounter with Phoenix Shadowwalker transpired three years prior during his bid to subdue Goldmoor. Drawn to his malevolent charisma and the tantalizing prospect of ultimate dominion, she perceived a gateway to satiate her craving for supremacy. Hence, she affixed her loyalty to him, pledging allegiance to aid him in realizing his nefarious aspirations.

While her elder sibling, Qellaun Deadcrusher, harbored unwavering devotion for Phoenix, Lyra had a hidden agenda. Her allegiance to the evil sorcerer was a stepping stone—a means to seize the ultimate boon of power. She conceived that reigning at Phoenix's side would bestow the authority she hungered for, sating her thirst for dominion over others.

However, Lyra's ambitions extended beyond mere servitude to Phoenix. The dominion with Vuarus, the God of Shadows and Revenge, grated against her thirst for supremacy. Yet, she was no fool to challenge her evil master's will openly. For the time being, she begrudgingly embraced the dominion while clandestinely plotting to turn Phoenix to her cause and eliminate the god she deemed a hindrance to her ascent.

Beneath her veneer of beauty and allure, Lyra concealed a treacherous nature. She wielded her charms as adeptly as her magic, mastering the art of manipulating those around her. Her enchantments ensnared hearts and minds, converting potential pawns into pliable instruments in her pursuit of power.

As the Abyssal Dominion's potency burgeoned, Lyra practiced patience, awaiting the precise moment to execute her maneuver. She recognized the dominion's fragile power equilibrium and aimed to tilt it in her favor.

While the entwining with Vuarus unsettled her, Lyra's ambitions adhered to a solitary path — grasping power's reins and ascending to unparalleled authority. She acknowledged no obstruction, not even the evil god who shadowed Phoenix. With her brother by her side and her treacherous sorcery as her arsenal, Lyra emerged as a formidable presence. The sinister forces of New Flameford would soon taste the full measure of her craftiness and ambition.

Phoenix stood as a multi-faceted and imposing figure, driven by ambitions that flamed within him and sustained by his resentment for certain factions within the realm. His past experiences and upbringing in Fel Thalor fanned a sincere distaste for the Eladrin, and this hatred kindled his hunger for dominion and dominance. A firm believer in his peerless strength and talents, Phoenix was resolute in his conviction that he could surpass all in Vacari and Afor. To advance his objectives, he harnessed the power of Vuarus, manipulating it to his ends. His ultimate aspiration was to claim supremacy over both realms, which he pursued with unwavering resolve.

Raised in a city where trust was scarce, Phoenix's heart had grown impervious to caring for anyone save a select few. Qellaun was an exception, their bond a testament to their intertwined guardianship. Phoenix's soul was cloaked in shadows, an entity that rejected emotions and compassion as weaknesses fit only for abandonment.

Yet, his loathing for Keisha transcended all other enmities. Attributing his thwarted plans in Goldmoor to her interference, his disdain for the brave dragon rider ran deep. Keisha embodied a formidable adversary and a symbol of everything he loathed. She represented the light and hope that imperiled his malevolent machinations—a barricade he was determined to dismantle at any cost.

As Phoenix advanced with his sinister dominion, propelled by vengeance and insatiable power lust, the virtuous forces of Vacari and Afor prepared for the impending clash that would determine their world's destiny. Unbeknownst to them, the puppeteer Vuarus deftly manipulated the strings, orchestrating a grand scheme capable of unsettling their very foundations. The impending battle between light and darkness drew near, casting its shadow over both realms' fates.

Chapter 4

Shadows Unveiled: Brush with Dark Forces

The once-thriving Emeraldwoods had indeed succumbed to an evil influence, its vibrant life giving way to the encroaching darkness. Keisha, Ong, and Pumpkin continued their cautious journey through the transformed forest, their steps punctuated by the eerie silence that enveloped them. The absence of the forest's usual vitality weighed heavily on their hearts.

As they ventured deeper, they noticed signs of corruption within the flora and fauna. Twisted trees with gnarled branches reached out like skeletal hands, and the once-colorful flowers had wilted, their petals now ashen and lifeless. Even the ground beneath their feet seemed tainted, the soil dark and barren.

Pumpkin's unease communicated itself to her companions, and they remained vigilant, knowing that they were walking through a realm touched by malevolence. The forest's resistance to their presence was palpable, as if the land recoiled from the Abyssal Dominion's influence.

With each step, Keisha's determination burned brighter, a resolve to push back against the encroaching darkness that threatened Vacari. Ong's connection to the elements surged, and he sought to restore balance to this once-pristine place. Together with Pumpkin, they forged ahead, their hearts set on reclaiming the Emeraldwoods and dispelling the shadows that had taken root in their beloved realm.

Keisha, Ong, and Pumpkin continued their trek through the corrupted heart of the Emeraldwoods, their determination unwavering. The trio's bond, forged through years of training and shared experiences, was a source of strength in the face of the encroaching darkness. Keisha's command over the elements, Ong's mastery of archery and connection to nature, and Pumpkin's loyalty all converged to form a formidable team.

As they moved forward, the forest's resistance grew stronger, but so did their resolve. Keisha's water orb shimmered with potential, ready to unleash its power when needed. Ong's bow remained steady, a symbol of his unwavering skill and connection to the natural world. And Pumpkin, torn between her protective instincts and the turmoil within, remained a steadfast companion.

Their journey was not just a physical one but a spiritual and emotional quest to restore the purity and serenity that had once defined Vacari. The darkness that had taken hold of the Emeraldwoods was but a microcosm of the larger clash between light and dark that threatened their realm.

In their unity and shared commitment, Keisha, Ong, and Pumpkin found the strength to confront malevolence and work toward reestablishing the delicate equilibrium of their world. As they pressed forward, their bond served as a beacon of hope, a reminder that even in the darkest of times, the power of unity and determination could prevail.

Their unity and determination were their greatest assets. They knew that they faced physical challenges and tests of their inner strength and the newfound powers that had developed within them.

Each step they took was a testament to their growth and transformation from the beginning of their journey. They had become stronger, both individually and as a team, and they drew strength from the extraordinary forces that now resided within them. The hostility that surrounded them was palpable, but their resolve remained unshaken.

The forest itself seemed to conspire against them, with dark symbols etched upon the trees and evil energy emanating from the earth. Illusions and twisted creatures lurked in the shadows, seeking to confound and terrify. Yet, Keisha, Ong, and Pumpkin met these challenges head-on, drawing upon their newfound abilities.

Keisha's bow had become a conduit for her archery skills and elemental magic, allowing her to strike with precision and power. Ong's arrows found their marks with deadly accuracy, cutting through illusions and shadows. With her graceful agility and unwavering loyalty, Pumpkin acted as a protective shield against the evil entities.

The trio was a force to be reckoned with in their unity and determination, a beacon of hope against the encroaching darkness. They knew that their journey was far from over, and that even greater challenges awaited them. But with their bond and their newfound abilities, they were ready to face whatever lay ahead and protect their land from the shadows that threatened it.

As Keisha, Ong, and Pumpkin pressed on through the tainted woods, their journey became a true test of courage, resolve, and unity. With every step, they could feel the evil presence of the venom growing stronger, a constant reminder that the darkness was just one aspect of the evil force threatening Vacari. Yet, they remained steadfast, committed to facing the shadows and ensuring that darkness would not forever consume their realm.

Meanwhile, unbeknownst to them, the evil council of the Abyssal Dominion was gathering within the ominous Dread Spire. Phoenix Shadowwalker, driven by his insatiable thirst for power, saw this as the perfect moment to unleash a terrifying entity upon Vacari. With a sinister grin that sent shivers down the spines of his loyal followers, he commanded one of his devoted servants to release the Maelstrom Serpent from its ancient prison.

The Maelstrom Serpent was a colossal and awe-inspiring entity that had slumbered for eons in the depths of Afor. It had been sealed away by ancient custodians who understood its power to manipulate the elements, causing storms, cyclones, and chaos on a grand scale. Under Phoenix's dark directive, the creature was set free, its massive form directed toward the forest outside Crystal Vale. Its purpose was clear: to unleash its elemental might, summon fierce storms, and disrupt the very balance of nature. Phoenix planned to spread confusion and fear, further destabilizing a land already tainted by darkness.

As the Maelstrom Serpent stirred, its arrival threatened to escalate the already dire situation in Vacari. Unaware of this new threat, Keisha, Ong, and Pumpkin pressed on in their quest to confront the shadows and restore their realm. Little did they know that an even greater challenge lay ahead, one that would test their abilities and determination to the fullest.

As the elemental turmoil escalated, Keisha, Ong, and Pumpkin couldn't ignore the growing danger. The once-vibrant forest had transformed into a swirling vortex of darkness, and the skies above gradually darkened. The air was charged with hostility, as if the forces of darkness were toying with the very fabric of reality.

Pumpkin's instincts were on high alert as they ventured closer to the epicenter of this unnatural disturbance. Her sleek form tensed, emitting low growls to warn them to stop. Her green eyes conveyed a deep sense of concern and urgency, marking her as the sentinel of the group, attuned to the imminent danger.

Keisha and Ong exchanged knowing glances, realizing Pumpkin's instincts were not to be taken lightly. Reluctantly, they heeded her unspoken command to go no further into the disturbed forest.

With her bold and protective stance, Pumpkin positioned herself firmly in front of them, like a sentinel guarding their safety. Her posture left no room for doubt – proceeding deeper into the darkened woods would be unwise. The trio paused, fully acknowledging the significance of Pumpkin's warning. They were on the verge of a dangerous path filled with unknown dangers.

A shiver ran down their collective spines as they looked upon the colossal Maelstrom Serpent, coiling through the skies with an aura of chaos. This sighting only reinforced the wisdom in Pumpkin's caution, and her green eyes reflected an even deeper sense of concern. They knew they were facing a formidable and unpredictable adversary that would test their abilities and unity to the fullest.

The evil creature fulfilled its grim task, and with tremendous force, it retreated to Afor's Realm. Ong gently pulled Keisha backward, his innate protector instincts surging forth. They understood that confronting such a formidable adversary would be futile. Their battles must be chosen strategically.

As the skies cleared, the trio regrouped. Though the Maelstrom Serpent remained beyond their confrontation, their determination intensified. They had glimpsed the malevolence the Abyssal Dominion could unleash, a dire forewarning. Their resolve to safeguard Vacari was redoubled, fortified by their guardian panther's instincts and the magical arsenal they possessed.

Pumpkin's allegiance, Keisha's elemental empowerment, and Ong's archery expertise and communion with nature stood poised against the shadows. Together, they pledged to shield their homeland, one another, even as dark machinations unfurled, threatening to submerge Vacari in an eternal abyss.

As the echoes of the Maelstrom Serpent's roars faded into the distance, the trio stood amidst the forest's aftermath—a testament to chaos. The once-vibrant trees lay toppled, their branches twisted and broken. The forest floor was littered with debris, leaves, and shattered fragments of what was once a serene sanctuary. Keisha turned to Ong, a furrow in her brow, contemplation etched in her expression. "Something isn't right," she murmured, her voice laden with concern.

Ong's agreement was solemn. "You're correct. Phoenix's power has never been this formidable before. It's as though something or someone has amplified his malice."

Unease prickled Keisha's skin. She knew Phoenix's might, but this escalation was disconcerting. "But who could it be?" she pondered aloud, a whirl of thoughts racing through her mind.

Pumpkin, her green eyes troubled, observed the exchange. Though she couldn't vocalize insights, her attunement to the forest's malevolence amplified the tension.

Ong's gaze turned inward, his thoughts filled with contemplation. "There are ancient entities, beings of darkness that seek to tilt the balance toward malevolence," he ventured. "Perhaps one of them has seen promise in Phoenix and forged a dominion."

Keisha's mind raced with urgency as she absorbed Ong's words. "We must unveil the puppeteer behind this Abyssal Dominion," she declared firmly. "If they can manipulate Phoenix, others may also be pawns."

A shared, unwavering glance between them conveyed their commitment to this newfound mission. As they continued, the encroaching shadows tightened their grip, ensnaring trees with sinister symbols. They followed a path where Phoenix's newfound power demanded scrutiny, knowing that uncovering the secrets hidden within the shadows was crucial.

Their unity propelled them into the unknown, where they would unmask the sinister puppeteer behind the Abyssal Dominion. As they strode forth, they understood that their journey had just begun. Their threat loomed more extensive than ever, but their bond and determination remained steadfast. In a world gripped by darkness, they clung to their mission—to rekindle the brilliance of light and restore the heart of Vacari to its resplendent glory. Returning to King Manard in the serenity of Crystal Vale, Keisha, and Ong shared the grim news of the eerie changes in Emeraldwoods. The king's face grew graver as he listened, understanding the gravity of the situation. His voice carried concern and resolve as he spoke, "We must act swiftly to counter this malevolence, for every day it thrives, our world suffers."

Together, they decided to embark on a new phase of their quest. "We need to uncover who is aiding Phoenix in his malevolent schemes," King Manard declared. "To do that, we must seek information from Fel Thalor and Old Flameford. These cities have long histories, and it's possible that someone there knows more about the hidden supporters of the Abyssal Dominion."

Keisha and Ong nodded in agreement. Their path was clear, their purpose unwavering. With Crystal Vale behind them and Fel Thalor and Old Flameford ahead, they set forth, driven by the knowledge that their journey would reveal not only the depth of the hostility threatening Vacari but also the strength of their bond and the resilience of their world.

Chapter 5

Shadows Unveiled: Journey Through Emberwood Forest

Ong, Keisha, and Pumpkin stood at the edge of Emberwood Forest, a once-thriving woodland now transformed into a desolate wasteland by evil forces. The once-lush trees now stood as charred skeletons, their vibrant foliage replaced by an aura of darkness that clung to the air like a suffocating shroud.

Keisha's heart ached as she gazed upon the once beautiful Emberwoods, now marred by the devastation. Memories of their earlier journey through the forest's enchanting beauty flooded her thoughts. She couldn't help but compare it to the grim reality before her.

As she turned to Ong, her voice trembled with sorrow. "Ong, do you remember our earlier journey through these woods?" Her words carried the weight of melancholy as her eyes swept across the desolation. "Now, as we pass through it again, look at what has happened."

Ong's gaze mirrored her somberness as he surveyed the scene. Memories of a conversation from four years ago resurfaced in his mind. He had inquired about Keisha's connection to the forests, her unique bond with these mystical places. At that time, they had never imagined that the forests would fall victim to evil and destruction; it had been beyond their comprehension.

Turning to Keisha, Ong's eyes held a deep understanding. "I remember, Keisha," he said softly, his voice touched by regret. "Four years ago, I asked about your connection to these forests. You spoke of a deep bond that ran within your veins. We never thought that these sacred places would be targeted by malevolence and brought to ruin. I didn't fully grasp it then, but now, I see it. The forests are a part of you; as they suffer, so do you."

Keisha nodded, her eyes mirroring the pain of that truth. "Yes, Ong. My connection to these lands is both a gift and a burden. When they thrive, I feel their vitality coursing through me. But when they suffer, it's as if a part of me withers away."

Ong's heart ached as he looked at Keisha, knowing her suffering was his too. He longed to protect her from the pain but wasn't sure how to go about it. "Keisha," he began, his voice filled with a deep desire to shield her from harm, "I can't bear to see you suffer like this. I want to protect you, to shield you from the pain that engulfs you when the forests are harmed. But I don't know how to do that, how to ease your burden."

Keisha gently placed her hand over Ong's, her eyes radiating gratitude and affection. "Ong, just being by my side, facing these challenges together, that's all the protection I need. Your presence gives me strength, and together, we'll find a way to heal the forests and protect Vacari. We'll confront the darkness and bring back the light."

Ong pulled her close, his embrace filled with determination. "We will do everything we can to heal these lands, Keisha. To restore them to their former glory. Your connection to the forests is a potent force, and together, we'll wield it to defeat the Abyssal Dominion and restore light to Vacari."

Continuing their journey through the devastated Emberwoods, their determination to confront the hostility and shield the realms burned with an intensity that outshone the surrounding darkness. They were fueled by the stark realization that even the most sacred places could succumb to the depths of shadow.

Ong's gaze remained somber as he surveyed the scene. "The Abyssal Dominion's taint has marred even this once-thriving forest. Malevolence has found its roots here, leaving only desolation in its wake."

Venturing deeper into the forest, an eerie silence enveloped them, interrupted only by the sinister hiss of serpents, now the sole inhabitants of this land. The ground was strewn with the remains of creatures drained by the pervasive darkness that saturated the area.

Pumpkin moved with heightened caution, her instincts on high alert. The distorted landscape unsettled her, and her sleek form remained taut with readiness. Her senses detected a hostile presence lurking in the shadows.

The few creatures they encountered were no longer the gentle woodland inhabitants of yore. Their eyes glowed with an unnatural light, their once-melodic voices replaced by dissonant sounds that sent shivers down Keisha's spine.

Continuing their journey, they caught glimpses of shadowy figures flitting among the trees, elusive and cunning. Keisha and Ong wisely refrained from pursuit, aware of the deceptive nature of the evil forces.

The hostility seemed to intensify with every step, its weight pressing heavily on their spirits. Yet, their unwavering determination to uncover the truth and confront the encroaching darkness propelled them forward.

Within the desolation of Emberwood, they bore witness to the aftermath of evil influence. What other horrors lay concealed in the forest's unfathomable depths were left to the imagination.

The faint glimmers of dawn brought hope, a poignant reminder of the urgency of their mission. The Abyssal Dominion must not succeed; Vacari and Afor depended on their unyielding resolve. Keisha, Ong, and Pumpkin pressed ahead, their unity unwavering, their strength in their bond.

As they journeyed, the forest seemed to conspire to divide them, its hostility testing the strength of their companionship. However, their solidarity remained steadfast, a resilient bulwark against the insidious intentions of malice.

With the approach of dawn, a distant tumult reached their ears, drawing them ever closer. Pumpkin surged forward, guided by instinct. Keisha and Ong followed, their hearts and minds focused on the source of the disturbance that awaited them.

Before them lay an Amethyst dragon, ensnared by the evil forces—her majestic limbs trapped, her once-mighty wings cruelly restrained. The dragon's scales shimmered with iridescent violet hues—a breathtaking testament to her elemental power.

Ong's arrows found their mark, striking down serpents that slithered menacingly toward her. Meanwhile, Pumpkin growled fiercely, her teeth bared in readiness to defend. Keisha summoned the forces of water and wind, creating a protective barrier that sent the serpents recoiling, at least for the moment.

Their harmonious efforts combined to dispel the assailants, and the Amethyst dragon's gratitude was unmistakable in the shimmer of her eyes.

"Heroes, I am Amara," the dragon spoke, her voice resonating with the elements' might. "Your timely arrival spared me from a fate worse than you can imagine. The forces of darkness have grown bold, and it seems someone is aiding Phoenix in his evil schemes."

They exchanged names and expressions of gratitude. "I must make my way to the council," Amara declared. "The roots of this darkness run deep, and unity is our greatest shield against it."

Amara soared into the heavens with graceful wings unfurled, leaving a trail of violet brilliance that faded into the night. Keisha and Ong watched in awe, a sense of determination burning in their hearts.

"We continue our journey to Fel Thalor and Flameford," Ong asserted. "Answers await us there, and we must uncover the identity of Phoenix's ally."

Keisha nodded, her resolve unwavering. "The forest's darkness may have tested us, but our unity will guide us through whatever trials lie ahead."

And so, their journey recommenced, leaving the desolation of Emberwood behind. As the stars adorned the night sky, they knew that more trials awaited them, but their unbreakable bond fortified their spirits for the challenges ahead.

Glaciera watched from her vantage point above as they pressed onward, her curiosity thoroughly piqued. She tracked Amara's movements and later followed the trail of Keisha and Ong, a notion forming in her crystalline mind: to test their resilience in nature's unforgiving face. Glaciera manipulated the breeze into icy gusts with a graceful sweep of her wings. Delicate snowflakes danced around Keisha and Ong, their breaths forming fleeting clouds in the frigid air.

Glaciera's intent was clear—to challenge their adaptability and test the strength of their spirits.

The snow-covered forest offered respite from the frosty onslaught, but the cave's interior held an eerie aura. Whispers and elusive shadows filled the space, conjuring visions that probed the depths of their spirits.

Throughout the long night, Keisha's elemental magic responded to the mystical energy that permeated the cave, while Ong's instincts remained sharp. They confronted their innermost fears and doubts, facing the enigma of Emberwood head-on.

As dawn's first light marked Glaciera's departure, her observations bound for the dragon council, Ong and Keisha emerged from the cave, their spirits shaken but resilient.

The night's trials had strained them, but their bond remained unbroken. Keisha's thoughts mirrored Ong's—these challenges had only served to prepare them for the trials that lay ahead.

With their eyes fixed on the edge of Emberwood, Keisha and Ong anticipated the journey ahead. Each step brought them closer to Fel Thalor and Flameford, where secrets and further trials awaited them.

They embraced the rising sun's warmth, drawing strength from each other, ready to unveil the evil puppeteer lurking in the shadows. The forest's haunting had kindled their resolve, and the flames of courage within them burned unwaveringly.

In the shadowy recesses of Emberwood, Vuarus and Phoenix plotted, their partnership a tangled web of secrets and enigma that mirrored the forest's malevolence. Phoenix's restless energy was palpable, his frustration bubbling to the surface. "Vuarus, this darkness here... I had no idea you possessed such power."

Vuarus, as enigmatic as ever, calmly explained his role in the venom. "My power sowed discord, testing the strength of their bond. Doubt weakens unity."

Phoenix's fiery glare met Vuarus's calm gaze. "You meddled without consulting me? We are allies, after all!"

Vuarus's grin held a touch of malice. "A subtle nudge sets the stage. The forest's darkness tests their unity, making them vulnerable."

Torn between anger and reluctant acceptance, Phoenix finally relented. "Very well, but from now on, no more secrets between us."

Vuarus's response carried a veneer of mocking deference, but he harbored a hidden truth beneath his shadowed thoughts. He had noticed something unique and potent—an unspoken connection that Keisha held with the very essence of nature itself. It was a secret he chose to keep to himself for the time being, a card to play when the opportune moment arose. "Transparency shall be the cornerstone of our partnership," he declared, concealing his agenda.

Even as they conversed, the malice of Emberwood lingered, its shadows probing hearts and minds. Their dominion continued to twist events, unexpectedly shaping Keisha and Ong's journey. The shadows aimed to fracture their bond, creating challenges that tested the very core of their unity.

Despite their trials and tribulations in Emberwood, Keisha, Ong, and Pumpkin stood unwavering. Their shared purpose eclipsed any looming darkness. With unity and hope as their guiding lights, they approached the imposing gates of Fel Thalor, determined to unearth the secrets concealed within the ancient city's walls. The battle against malevolence and the quest for truth had just begun, but their indomitable spirit burned brightly even in the darkest hours.

In the aftermath of Emberwood's haunting, Keisha and Ong remained steadfast, their bond unbreakable. As the first rays of dawn broke, they moved into the heart of the ancient city, fortified by their connection and the promise of uncovering hidden truths. The trials that awaited them would test their resolve, but their courage remained unshaken.

The heart of darkness lay ahead within the city's confines, yet Keisha and Ong ventured forth with unyielding determination. Through unity, love, and unwavering resolve, they embarked on the path that would save Vacari from the abyss that threatened to consume it.

Chapter 6

Shadows Unveiled: Investigating Fel Thalor

As Keisha and Ong ventured deeper into the heart of Fel Thalor, an eerie stillness enveloped them, seeming to permeate every breath they took. The once-grand city, now in ruins, stood desolate and forsaken, its streets devoid of living residents. It exuded a palpable aura of foreboding that hung heavily in the air. Shadows writhed like restless spirits along the cracked walls of narrow alleys, and an oppressive silence seemed to weigh down every footstep. It was as though the city itself had absorbed the hostility that had led to its downfall, retaining an unsettling essence long after its inhabitants had been exiled alongside Phoenix.

As they ventured further, the ancient spirits of the Druchii stirred from their slumber, and their presence felt deep within Keisha's and Ong's souls. Ethereal wisps of spectral figures flitted at the periphery of their vision, carrying haunting whispers upon the wind that swept through the deserted streets. Keisha and Ong couldn't help but sense the lingering hostility in the air, the spirits seemingly trapped in perpetual unrest, as if they were prisoners of their history.

Amid the crumbling ruins, a grand circular stage emerged, encircling a trench bubbling with molten lava. The fiery heat cast an ominous and flickering glow upon the surrounding darkness, accentuating the stark contrast between the ancient stones and the churning depths below. This stage had once been a site of sinister rituals and dark machinations, where prisoners had been suspended high above the lava-filled chasm to extract confessions through the sheer terror of their impending fate.

The spirits of the Druchii appeared to linger around the stage, their ethereal forms resembling tendrils of swirling dark mist. As Keisha and Ong approached cautiously, they felt the weight of the city's tormented history pressing down upon them. The evil aura was almost suffocating, yet they steeled themselves, resolute in their determination to continue despite the overwhelming darkness.

Stepping onto the stage, the presence of the spirits surged, their spectral forms converging into shadowy figures that encircled Keisha and Ong. The intensity of their collective consciousness, brimming with despair and malice, sought to engulf the two intruders in the city of ghosts.

Keisha refused to succumb to the overpowering darkness and called upon her latent elemental powers. She enveloped herself and Ong in a protective shield of wind and water. The spirits recoiled, their grip weakened by the essence of the elements. It was as if these ancient specters recognized the potency within Keisha, acknowledging her lineage as a descendant of the Guardians of Vacari, and hesitated in their evil intentions.

Unfazed by the evil spirits and the haunting cries that echoed through the desolate streets of Fel Thalor, Keisha and Ong pressed on with an unshaken determination. The source of the darkness that gripped the city had to be confronted, and they were willing to brave all obstacles, even the restless souls of this forsaken place.

With every deliberate step they took, the hostility seemed to intensify, becoming a formidable trial that tested not only their physical prowess but also the strength of their bond. Yet, they were far from alone in this harrowing journey. Their connection deepened with each challenge they faced, becoming a beacon of light amidst the encroaching shadows.

United and resolute, Keisha and Ong stood firmly against the hostility that sought to devour Vacari. Their courage remained unwavering as they embarked on their mission to unveil the sinister secrets concealed within the ancient city's heart. The spirits that haunted Fel Thalor may have cast an ominous pall over their path, but Keisha and Ong remained steadfast in their unwavering commitment to restore hope to their world, even in the bleakest circumstances.

Within the dimly lit chamber of the Abyssal Dominion, Phoenix and Vuarus stood facing each other, shrouded in an aura of malice and secrecy. The flickering candles cast eerie, dancing shadows on the walls, creating an atmosphere thick with foreboding. Phoenix's crimson eyes gleamed with sinister anticipation as he addressed Vuarus.

"Vuarus," Phoenix began, his voice carrying a chilling undertone that seemed to echo in the chamber, "I require your unique abilities. I want you to conjure a vision from the past – a memory that holds the key to our adversaries' vulnerabilities."

Vuarus, with his enigmatic aura and an expression that danced between amusement and intrigue, regarded Phoenix with a knowing smile. "Ah, dear Phoenix, your desires never cease to amuse and intrigue me. Pray tell, which memory do you seek to unravel?"

As he spoke his dark intent, Phoenix's crimson eyes narrowed with unwavering determination. "I yearn to witness the downfall of Keisha's ancestors, the Guardians of Vacari. Within their defeat lies the secrets we need to exploit their weaknesses."

Vuarus nodded, fully comprehending the gravity of Phoenix's request. "Indeed, a formidable endeavor," he replied, his voice tinged with a hint of fascination. "To evoke such a potent memory, we must delve deep into the currents of time."

Advancing toward the chamber's center, a circle of ancient runes adorned the floor. Vuarus traced intricate patterns in the air with a flourish of his hand, and each movement carried an essence of dark magic. The runes etched on the floor responded, emitting an ominous glow that resonated with the arcane energy flowing through Vuarus's fingertips.

"Time flows as a river, and memories are naught but ripples within its current," Vuarus murmured, his words carrying the weight of eons. "To beckon forth the past, we must precisely navigate its currents."

His eyes radiated a dark intensity as he delved deeper into the temporal river. The chamber seemed to quiver with an uncontainable surge of power, as if the fabric of time was bending to Vuarus's unyielding will.

However, Vuarus was acutely aware of the intricate complexity of this task. The past was not merely a tapestry to be casually unraveled; it was a labyrinth of intertwined events and emotions. To summon a specific memory demanded finesse and skill, lest he become trapped in the turbulent torrents of history.

Drawing upon his mastery of the arcane arts, Vuarus honed his focus on the image of the Guardians of Vacari, meticulously seeking the thread that held the memory Phoenix desired. An ethereal mist began to coalesce within the chamber, giving form to ghostly apparitions that seemed to materialize from the very fabric of time.

Yet, the desired image remained elusive, requiring Vuarus's unwavering patience and expertise. He trod cautiously, keenly aware of the danger of becoming trapped by the tumultuous currents of the past. "Almost there," Vuarus whispered, his voice but a breath amidst the swirling mist.

At last, the vision materialized in a burst of dark energy, unfurling before them. Phoenix observed with unwavering focus as the memory of the Guardians' downfall played out like a grim tapestry. He witnessed their battles, strategies, and the vulnerabilities exposed amidst the heat of combat.

However, Vuarus understood that this vision was merely a fleeting glimpse, a carefully selected fragment from the tapestry of time. Withdrawing his magical influence, he allowed the vision to dissipate, turning to Phoenix with an enigmatic expression.

"Behold, a glimpse of the past," Vuarus declared cryptically. "Yet remember, the true secrets do not solely reside in the past but in the hearts of our adversaries here and now."

Phoenix's eyes blazed with a newfound resolve, intensifying their crimson hue. "Indeed, Vuarus. Armed with this knowledge, we shall unearth the weaknesses of the Guardians and plunge Vacari into darkness once and for all."

As the haunting vision waned, leaving only the spectral remnants of the past within their minds, Phoenix and Vuarus were acutely aware of the formidable challenges and malevolent schemes ahead. The darkness within the Abyssal Dominion had discovered a potent ally in Vuarus's abilities, and together, they aimed to reshape Vacari's fate according to their twisted ambitions.

Yet, amidst the lingering malevolence that clung to the chamber, Keisha couldn't help but be deeply affected by the scene she had witnessed. Her heart ached as the vision unfolded, and her emotions ran tumultuously as she grappled with the horrors of her father's torment.

As the memory replayed in her mind, Keisha felt an inexorable pull toward the lava stage in Fel Thalor, as if an unseen force guided her every step. Ong watched with growing concern as Keisha appeared entranced, unresponsive to his inquiries and appeals.

"Keisha, what's happening? Where are you going?" Ong's voice trembled with worry, yet she remained unyielding to his pleas, her gaze fixed on the haunting scene before her.

Approaching the lava stage, Keisha shattered the eerie stillness of the forsaken city with the haunting echoes of her father's anguished cries. He materialized before her, a red-haired mage in the throes of suffering, suspended above the churning sea of molten lava. His visage contorted with agony and torment, though a glimmer of hope persisted as the head sorceress of the Druchii extended a lifeline to him.

The sorceress's tone was icy as she declared, "Disclose E'vahona's whereabouts, and you shall be liberated to rejoin your wife and infant daughter."

Caught between the excruciating pain of his predicament and the instinct to safeguard his kin, her father's countenance wavered. Understanding the torment he must have endured in that pivotal moment, Keisha's heart plunged into a maelstrom of conflicting emotions, torn between self-preservation and the well-being of his beloved family.

"No..." Keisha's voice escaped in a hushed breath, scarcely audible, as the heart-wrenching tableau played out before her.

Yet, in the face of his oppressors, her father remained resolute, steadfastly refusing to betray his people. The Druchii sorceress's patience frayed, worn thin by his stubbornness. She commanded her minions to cast him into the seething lava with a mere gesture. The anguished screams of her father pierced the very fabric of the air, and Keisha's vision blurred through the haze of tears.

"No! Cease this!" Keisha's cry echoed through the empty streets, unable to bear the gut-wrenching scene that unfolded before her. The anguish etched upon her father's features, the pervading sense of desolation and helplessness seemed tangibly real, a harrowing reminder of the darkness that had plagued their world for so long.

Ong watched in horrified helplessness as Keisha's torment played out in vivid detail. He could taste the bitterness of her anguish, the weight of her sorrow, and her unrelenting grief. "Keisha, break free from this! It's a fabrication!" he shouted, his fervent words brushing against the walls of her distress, an anchor of reality amidst the nightmarish illusion.

As the vision neared its unbearable zenith, Keisha crumbled to her knees, her sobs intermingling with anguished cries. Ong surged forward, enshrouding her in his arms, his gaze ablaze with anger and unwavering determination.

"Phoenix, I shall eliminate you for the torment you inflict upon her," Ong's voice resounded with zeal, a tempestuous declaration cast toward the shadows that cloaked the city. His protective embrace was a bulwark against the hostility that sought to break her spirit.

He held Keisha close, a bastion of strength amidst the storm of her nightmare. The weight of her past and the inky darkness of Phoenix's plotting bore heavily on Keisha's spirit, and she clung to Ong, her lifeline in the turbulent sea of despair.

Slowly, the vision faded, and Keisha's sobs subsided. She blinked, returning to reality, enveloped in Ong's comforting embrace. The memory of the vision lingered vividly in her mind, haunting her, but she drew strength from Ong's unwavering presence and the realization that it had been nothing more than a twisted illusion.

"Ong... I saw my father," Keisha murmured, her voice trembling with the weight of the emotions that had surged through her.

"I know, Keisha. But he's not here. It was just a vision, a dark trick orchestrated by Phoenix," Ong reassured her, gently brushing a strand of hair away from her tear-streaked face.

Keisha gazed up at him, her eyes shimmering with gratitude for his steadfast support. "Thank you, Ong. You're right. We can't allow Phoenix's malevolent games to shatter us. We must remain resolute and united."

With Ong by her side, Keisha regained her composure, the strength of their bond buoying her amidst the shadows and foreboding of Fel Thalor. As they confronted the hostility of the Abyssal Dominion and navigated the treacherous landscape surrounding them, their connection grew even more potent, fueled by their shared determination to safeguard their world and each other.

The vision had tested the limits of Keisha's spirit, yet she understood that yielding to despair was not an option. With unwavering love and unbreakable unity, they would confront Phoenix and his sinister designs head-on. The looming shadows of Fel Thalor only served to fortify their resolve as Keisha and Ong steeled themselves to face the next phase of their heroic journey. They knew their unbreakable bond would be their most potent weapon as they ventured into the battles that awaited them.

Meanwhile, deep within the inner sanctum of the Abyssal Dominion, Phoenix turned to Vuarus, his anticipation evident in his gaze. The enigmatic sorcerer met Phoenix's gaze with a slow, deliberate nod, his dark eyes gleaming with satisfaction and intrigue.

"Did the vision achieve the desired effect?" Phoenix inquired, his dark eyes fixated on Vuarus.

Vuarus's lips curled into a sinister smirk, his amusement was evident. "Oh, it worked as planned, Phoenix. Her pain was palpable, and the memory of her father's suffering now lingers in her mind, tormenting her just as we intended."

Phoenix's satisfaction manifested as a wicked smile. "Excellent. Her resolve will weaken, leaving her susceptible to our manipulation."

"And it will drive a wedge between her and Ong," Vuarus said, relishing the prospect of exploiting their deep bond. "Love can be a potent weapon, yet it can transform into a liability when infused with doubt and despair."

Phoenix's gaze turned icy, a ruthless determination gleaming within. "Keisha will succumb to the weight of her emotions, and Ong will bear the consequences. Their spirits will shatter, rendering them defenseless and easily molded."

A dark chuckle escaped Vuarus, satisfaction radiating from him at the success of their cunning plan. "My friend, with Keisha in her vulnerable state and Ong consumed by his anger, they will prove no match for the overwhelming power at our disposal."

As they reveled in the evil depths of their scheme, an oppressive aura settled around them, heavy with their shared malevolence. The dominion forged between Phoenix and Vuarus stood as an overpowering force, and they reveled in the impending chaos they were about to unleash upon Vacari.

"Now, Phoenix, let us push Keisha and Ong even further," Vuarus suggested, a wicked gleam lighting up his eyes. "We shall drive them to the brink of despair, where the shadows of their past and the weight of their emotions will relentlessly torment them."

Phoenix nodded, eager to see their design come to fruition. "Indeed, Vuarus. Let the darkness enshroud them until they are nothing more than pawns in our grand design."

With that, the evil partnership sprang their twisted machinations into motion, poised to exploit every chink in the armor of Keisha and Ong. The destiny of Vacari hung precariously in the balance, and the unwavering love and resilience of the heroes would be subjected to the ultimate crucible. As they confronted the hostility of the Abyssal Dominion, their mettle would be tested like never before.

As the events unfolded, Vuarus observed with a calculating eye. While Ong's vulnerabilities were apparent, it was Keisha who intrigued him the most. There was a unique and potent essence within her, a connection to the very heart of Vacari itself. He recognized it as a potential tool, but as always, Vuarus kept his thoughts and intentions shrouded in secrecy, revealing nothing of his true motives.

Unbeknownst to them, a glimmer of hope still burned within Keisha and Ong, an unbreakable resolve that would navigate them through the shadows and illuminate the path to their true strength. Little did Phoenix and Vuarus comprehend that Vacari's destiny rested not solely in their malice but in the power of unity, love, and the unwavering spirit of its heroes.

In the ethereal realm, distant from the dark machinations of the mortal world, Kadona, the Goddess of Light, observed with sorrowful eyes as the unfolding events played out below. The vision that had tormented Keisha was laid bare before her, and her heart ached for the young heroine and her steadfast companion, Ong.

With a gentle sigh, Kadona whispered words of solace across the realm, hoping that Keisha and Ong might hear her voice resonating in their hearts. "Hold on, dear ones, to the love that intertwines you. Embrace the light that resides within, for it shall guide you through the most somber of hours."

Kadona's divine presence infused a glimmer of hope amidst the malevolence that sought to engulf the world. She understood that the potency of Keisha and Ong's love, their resolute connection, was an energy that not even the darkest shadows could extinguish.

"Search for the truths concealed within the shadows," Kadona continued, her voice carrying the warmth of a thousand suns. "Unveil the riddle of the enigmatic force assisting Phoenix, for within that revelation lies the pivotal key to unraveling his malicious designs."

As a deity of light, Kadona was forbidden from directly intervening in the affairs of mortals. Yet, she endeavored to instill bravery and purpose within the hearts of

Keisha and Ong, recognizing that their quest was pivotal in preserving the world's equilibrium.

With a final whisper of encouragement, Kadona receded from view, her divine presence leaving behind a sense of tranquility and hope. Keisha and Ong, still reeling from the vision and the hostility they confronted, could sense the echo of the Goddess's words reverberating within them—a soothing antidote against the encroaching darkness.

United by love and guided by Kadona's divine wisdom, the heroic pair pledged to persist with renewed determination. Their journey was far from its conclusion, and the path ahead was dangerous. However, they would face it united, with their bond and resolve serving as their most potent weapons against the evil forces in motion.

Amidst the abyss of darkness, the radiance of their love and the guidance of the Goddess would lead them forward, drawing them ever closer to the truths they sought. Thus, with fortified hearts and resolute spirits, Keisha and Ong embarked on their mission, poised to confront the hostility that engulfed their world. They clung to the love they held dear and hoped it would suffice to triumph in the bleakest moments.

As Keisha and Ong ventured deeper into Fel Thalor, the dark city gradually unveiled more of its secrets. They chanced upon a concealed entrance amid the foreboding alleys and enigmatic structures. This expansive library had defied the ravages of time, and within its walls resided forgotten knowledge, a repository of ancient wisdom.

The library's towering bookshelves were laden with age-old tomes, scrolls, and manuscripts, each harboring fragments of history and long-forgotten truths. As they meticulously studied the texts, deciphering the cryptic symbols and puzzling passages, they unearthed clues illuminating the evil forces that manipulated their world.

"These writings speak of a potent relic, the Heart of Twilight," Keisha murmured, her gaze sweeping across the pages of a weathered tome. "Legend holds that it possesses the capacity to tip the delicate balance between light and darkness, conferring unimaginable might upon its possessor."

Ong's visage took on a somber cast as he absorbed Keisha's revelations. "That must be Phoenix's objective. He could plunge our realm into an eternal abyss of shadow with such an artifact."

Keisha and Ong's determination remained unshaken as they departed from the ancient and evil city of Fel Thalor. The revelations they had uncovered in the library only deepened their resolve to confront the Abyssal Dominion and thwart Phoenix's sinister plans.

As they ventured toward Old Flameford, they were acutely aware of the arduous journey that lay ahead. The hostility that clung to Fel Thalor was but a glimpse of the darkness they would encounter in their quest. However, their unwavering bond and their newfound knowledge were their greatest assets.

"We shall proceed with caution and unwavering determination," Keisha affirmed, her voice filled with resolve. "The Abyssal Dominion will stop at nothing to achieve their goals, but we have the power of love and unity on our side."

Ong nodded in agreement, his eyes reflecting the same determination. "Old Flameford may hold the answers we seek, and we must be prepared for whatever challenges await us there. Together, we are strong."

Hand in hand, they continued their journey, their hearts filled with hope and their minds focused on their mission. The fate of Vacari rested upon their shoulders, and they were determined to face whatever trials lay ahead with courage and unwavering resolve.

Chapter 7

Shadows Unveiled: Investigating Old Flameford

With the unsettling mysteries of Fel Thalor behind them, Keisha and Ong prepared to embark on the next leg of their journey. The morning sun cast a golden glow upon the land as they stood just beyond Fel Thalor's gates, ready to set their course for Old Flameford.

Before them, the city of Old Flameford beckoned, its gates mirroring those of New Flameford but with a sinister twist. Dragon statues, much like those they had encountered before, adorned the city's entrance, but the colors were now tainted with darkness. The once noble and awe-inspiring figures had been corrupted, their eyes gleaming with malice. Zylron, the red dragon, symbolized the fire of destruction that Phoenix wielded to impose his will upon others. Glaciera, the white dragon, represented the chilling frost that threatened to freeze the hearts of those who dared oppose the Abyssal Dominion. Drakthor, the black dragon, epitomized the shadows and deceit that masked the true intentions of the evil forces. Venfyr, the green dragon, embodied the poison of manipulation, corrupting the minds of the unsuspecting. Thundria, the topaz dragon, symbolized the electrical storms of chaos and turmoil that plagued Vacari. Lastly, Talleoss, the greenish dragon, stood tall, representing the ancient and arcane magic that fueled the Abyssal Dominion's schemes.

Keisha and Ong shared a knowing look, their determination unwavering despite the foreboding sight before them. They knew that the hostility they sought to challenge lay within Old Flameford's dark heart, and they could not turn away from the truth that awaited within its walls.

As they stepped forward, the city's gates loomed large, and the dragon statues watched them with a chilling intensity. The shadows of the past whispered in the wind, but Keisha and Ong clung to the love and resilience that had brought them this far.

Hand in hand, they passed through the gates, ready to face the hostility that lurked within Old Flameford. The journey ahead would test their bond like never before, but they remained united, their hearts alight, hoping to uncover the secrets that would shatter the darkness and bring light back to their world.

Beyond the gates of Old Flameford, a treacherous path lay ahead, fraught with challenges and dangers. However, Keisha and Ong stepped forward, driven by determination and love, as they ventured deeper into the heart of darkness. With each stride, they drew strength from their unity and the unwavering spirit of Vacari's heroes. Their mission to save their land from eternal shadow was far from over, and the shadows they would confront in Old Flameford would test their resolve like never before. Yet, their determination remained steadfast, fueled by the knowledge that hope and love would be their guiding light even in the darkest times.

Hand in hand, Keisha and Ong pressed forward, poised to confront whatever trials awaited them on their quest to unveil the secrets hidden within the ancient city and confront the darkness that threatened to engulf their land.

As they entered the ominous city of Old Flameford, they couldn't escape the weight of its dark atmosphere. The dragon statues loomed over them, each representing a different element, yet all infused with an eerie aura. Keisha noticed Pumpkin's apprehensive gaze as she scanned the dragon statues, her instincts on high alert.

Attempting to lighten the mood, Ong leaned down and whispered to Pumpkin, "What do you think, girl? Quite the collection of dragons, huh?"

Pumpkin's ears perked up as if comprehending his words, and a playful glint sparkled in her eyes. Swiftly, she darted from one dragon statue to another, sniffing and growling at each of them, as though sizing up the competition.

Keisha and Ong burst into laughter while watching their loyal companion's antics. Pumpkin's brave display lifted the oppressive atmosphere, momentarily pushing the impending darkness aside.

"She's guarding us from those dragon statues!" Keisha chuckled, wiping a tear of laughter from her eye.

Ong nodded, his infectious smile spreading. "Indeed. Good girl, Pumpkin," he praised, gently patting her head.

With Pumpkin faithfully by their side, they felt renewed courage and camaraderie. The darkness might have enveloped Old Flameford, but they knew they weren't alone on their journey.

Hand in hand, Keisha and Ong ventured further into the city, ready to face whatever challenges awaited them. With Pumpkin leading the way, they felt a glimmer of hope in the face of the hostility that loomed large in Old Flameford. Their bond, fortified by moments of fun and laughter, would be their guiding light in the dark days to come.

As Keisha and Ong walked through the ancient streets of Old Flameford, they couldn't help but be struck by the eerie contrast before them. The city stood grand and majestic, untouched by the passage of time or the hostility that had engulfed Old Flameford. It was as if Old Flameford had been preserved in a timeless bubble, frozen in a moment that defied the reality they knew.

"This is strange," Ong mused, furrowing his brows. "Phoenix was exiled over four years ago, yet Old Flameford shows no signs of decay or ruin."

Keisha nodded, her eyes scanning the immaculate buildings and pristine streets. "You're right. It's as if the city has been waiting for us to arrive. But how can that be? Could Phoenix have returned here and somehow concealed his presence?"

"Unlikely," Ong replied thoughtfully. "The elven sentries would have detected any unauthorized entry into Old Flameford. They have to ensure the city remains secure."

Keisha sighed, feeling a growing sense of unease. "Then what could explain this phenomenon? Something feels off, Ong, and it worries me."

Pumpkin, who had been playfully darting around the dragon statues, suddenly came to their side as if sensing their concern. She let out a low growl, her stance protective as if to assure them she was there to watch over them.

"I agree with Pumpkin," Ong said, glancing around cautiously. "We need to be on our guard.

There's more to this than meets the eye, and I don't like the feeling of being watched."

As they continued their exploration of Old Flameford, the mystery deepened. The streets remained deserted, and an eerie silence hung in the air. No signs of life or habitation were evident, and it was as if the city held its breath, awaiting the arrival of its unexpected visitors.

As the sun cast its warm glow upon the city, they couldn't help but feel a sense of trepidation. The answers they sought lay within the heart of Old Flameford, but so did the enigma of its pristine state. They couldn't shake the feeling of being drawn into a carefully woven web of deception.

"Let's be cautious," Keisha whispered, her hand instinctively finding Ong's. "There's more to this city than we can comprehend now. We must tread carefully and trust in our instincts."

Ong nodded, his grip tightening on Keisha's hand. "Agreed. We'll uncover the truth, but we won't do it unthinkingly. We'll find a way to expose whatever is hiding within these seemingly perfect streets."

Pumpkin let out a low whine as if empathizing with their concerns. Keisha bent down to pat her, finding comfort in their bond.

Keisha, Ong, and Pumpkin pressed on with determination, knowing that whatever awaited them in Old Flameford would test their resilience and unity like never before. The city's mysteries and the Abyssal Dominion that threatened their world were intricately linked, and they were determined to unveil the secrets concealed within its ancient walls. Their resolve grew stronger with each step, and they steeled themselves for the challenges ahead.

As Keisha and Ong walked through the empty streets of Old Flameford, they were suddenly interrupted by the sound of powerful wings beating the air above them. They looked up to see Zylron, the red dragon, hovering overhead, his fiery eyes fixed on them.

"What is he doing here?" Ong whispered, his hand instinctively reaching for his bow.

Before they could react, a voice resonated in their minds—a dark and familiar voice that sent shivers down their spines. It was Phoenix, communicating through their connection with Zylron. "Ah, Keisha and Ong, how delightful to see you in Old Flameford," Phoenix's voice taunted.

"It seems you're quite the tenacious ones, always poking your noses where they don't belong." "What do you want, Phoenix?" Keisha's voice betrayed a mix of defiance and unease.

"Oh, I simply want to invite you to a little gathering in the heart of Old Flameford," Phoenix replied, his tone dripping with malice. "Zylron here will ensure you don't wander off before the party starts."

Zylron let out a low growl, circling above them, effectively herding them toward the imposing tower in the middle of the city.

"We don't have time for this," Ong said, his eyes locked on the tower. "But we can't ignore it either. It might hold the answers we seek."

Keisha nodded, but her uneasiness was evident. "I can't shake the feeling that this is a trap, Ong. We need to be cautious."

As they approached the tower's base, its dark and foreboding presence loomed over them. The stairs to the entrance seemed to stretch on forever, and an overwhelming feeling of dread washed over them.

"I've faced many challenges in my life, but this tower gives me pause," Keisha admitted, her grip on her staff tightening.

Ong agreed, his usual confidence tinged with uncertainty. "I share your apprehension, Keisha. But we can't turn back now. We need to confront Phoenix and uncover the truth."

Standing before the daunting entrance, they hesitated, exchanging glances that conveyed fear and determination. The tower radiated hostility, and they couldn't shake the feeling of walking into the heart of darkness.

"Let's go together," Keisha said, mustering her courage. "Whatever we find inside, we'll face it together."

Ong nodded, a sense of resolve returning to his features. "Together, always."

With that unspoken promise, Keisha and Ong took their first step up the stairs, the weight of their quest pressing upon them. What lay ahead was unknown and filled with peril, but they knew their unity and the love that bound them together would be their guiding light in the darkest times.

As they ascended the tower's stairs, the air grew heavier, and the darkness enveloped them. But they pressed on, their steps echoing in the silence, each taking them closer to the answers they sought. What awaited them at the top of the tower remained a mystery, but Keisha and Ong were determined to face whatever darkness lurked within and bring hope back to their world. The clash of light and shadow was inevitable, and the fate of Vacari hung in the balance. It was a battle that would test their physical prowess and their inner strength and resilience against the darkness that threatened to consume them all.

In the dimly lit chamber of the Abyssal Dominion, Phoenix and Vuarus engaged in a heated discussion about the fate that awaited Keisha and Ong when they opened the door of the imposing tower in Old Flameford.

"We should send the Shadow Wraith after them," Phoenix insisted, his eyes ablaze with malevolence. "It's the perfect time to crush their spirits and bend them to our will."

Vuarus shook his head, his dark eyes gleaming with cunning. "No, not yet. Keisha and Ong still possess the strength to resist the Shadow Wraith's influence. We should savor the anticipation of their eventual downfall."

"They are more resilient than you give them credit for," Phoenix retorted, eager to see the heroes succumb to darkness. "I grow tired of your cautious approach, Vuarus. It's time to strike fear into their hearts."

"Patience, my friend," Vuarus replied with a twisted smile. "There will be a time for the Shadow Wraith, but for now, I believe it's time to reveal my presence to them."

Phoenix raised an eyebrow, intrigued. "You want them to know you're behind this malevolence?"

"Yes, it's time they see the puppeteer pulling the strings," Vuarus explained. "They have been chasing shadows but need to know who truly holds the power in this game."

"You risk revealing too much," Phoenix warned, though a hint of excitement danced in his eyes.

"I assure you, it will be worth it," Vuarus said, his confidence unwavering.

After a moment of deliberation, they finally reached a compromise. They decided to send shadows into the tower to sow fear and chaos while keeping the Shadow

Wraith as a trump card for later. With their plan in place, they focused their dark energies, and the shadows slithered away from them, disappearing into the tower.

As Keisha and Ong reached the top of the tower, they found themselves surrounded by an onslaught of shadows that poured out of the opened door. The door slammed shut behind them, leaving them trapped inside, unable to open it. Faced with the encroaching darkness, Keisha drew upon her elemental magic, creating a protective light shield around them. The shadows hissed and writhed, unable to breach the barrier of light.

As they stood beneath the shield, Keisha and Ong caught their breath, their hearts pounding from the sudden onslaught. The shadows seemed relentless, but Keisha's light provided them a momentary rest. Though shaken, they knew they couldn't stay trapped forever. With their renewed determination, they steeled themselves for the challenges ahead. The tower may have concealed dark secrets, but Keisha and Ong were determined to uncover the truth and emerge victorious against the hostility that sought to consume them.

In the heart of Old Flameford's foreboding tower, the heroes prepared to face the shadows and confront the darkness that awaited them, united in their bond and unwavering resolve to bring hope back to Vacari.

As the relentless shadows continued assaulting Keisha's protective barrier of light, Ong notched an arrow on his bow and aimed. He hoped his arrows would at least slow down some dark entities, giving Keisha a brief rest. With each arrow that hit a shadow, it dissipated momentarily before reforming and renewing its assault.

But the shadows were cunning. Sensing the pair's growing weariness, they began to weave illusions, trying to exploit their deepest fears and insecurities. Keisha saw visions of her father, tortured and screaming in the clutches of darkness. On the other hand, Ong saw haunting images of his lost comrades, blaming him for their demise.

"Keisha," Ong called out, his voice strained, "I'm not sure how long you can hold this barrier!" Keisha's brow furrowed with concern as she fought to maintain the shield. Her elemental magic was powerful but was being pushed to its limits. She knew they couldn't endure this assault much longer.

Amidst the chaos, Phoenix's wicked laughter echoed through the tower. He reveled in their torment, believing that victory was within his grasp. Just as he was about to issue an ultimatum, a sudden commotion diverted his attention. Loyal and resourceful, Pumpkin had clawed through the stone door, allowing a stream of light to pierce the darkness within. Spurred on by Pumpkin's efforts, Ong pushed against the weakened door with all his might. Cracks began to form, and finally, the door gave way, allowing them to escape the clutches of the evil tower.

As Keisha and Ong descended the tower steps, their breaths heavy, they were immediately greeted by their steadfast companion, Pumpkin. Overwhelmed with gratitude for the feline's timely intervention, they knelt down and embraced her, thanking her for saving them from the relentless shadows. At that moment, they realized the strength they drew from their love for one another and the loyalty of their companions. Together, they were an unyielding force against the encroaching darkness. They had survived the tower's trial, but the true challenge was yet to come. United and determined, they set their sights on the next step of their journey, ready to face whatever malevolence awaited them in their pursuit of truth and justice.

Phoenix's furious screams filled the air in the dimly lit chambers of the Abyssal Dominion. "I hate that panther! How dare it interfere and foil my plans!" His eyes blazed with anger and frustration.

Vuarus, standing nearby, nodded in response to Phoenix's outburst. However, as the commotion settled, a calculating look crossed Vuarus' face. A slight smirk tugged at the corner of his lips as he couldn't help but see even more potential in Keisha, especially after witnessing the unbreakable bond with Pumpkin, though he kept this observation to himself. "You failed to mention the panther before," he said coolly, fixing his gaze on Phoenix. "Its bond with Keisha and Ong could significantly hinder our endeavors."

Phoenix's anger waned slightly, replaced by curiosity at Vuarus' words. "What do you mean, its bond?" he inquired, the flames of his rage smoldering beneath the surface.

Vuarus folded his arms, his expression grave. "The panther shares a deep and unbreakable bond with Keisha and Ong," he explained. "It is not merely a companion but a guardian and protector, intrinsically linked to their well-being. Its presence gives them strength and resilience, something you underestimated."

Phoenix's brow furrowed as he considered the implications of the panther's bond. "So, it won't be as easy to dispose of them as I thought," he grumbled, his frustration evident.

Vuarus nodded, his smirk hidden behind his composed demeanor. "No, it won't. The panther's connection to them makes them formidable adversaries. We must devise a different strategy if we are to defeat them."

Phoenix's eyes gleamed with renewed determination. "Very well. If the panther is their strength, we will find a way to turn it into their weakness. I want you to explore any possible means to exploit this bond and bring them to their knees."

Vuarus nodded, accepting the task. "Consider it done. I will leave no stone unturned in my search for weakness."

As they delved deeper into their sinister plotting, neither of them realized that the bond between Keisha, Ong, and their loyal feline companion was not just a source of strength but also a beacon of hope in their darkest hours. The trials ahead would test their unity, but the power of their bond would prove to be a potent force against the hostility that sought to consume them.

With their hearts still pounding from their encounter in the tower, Keisha and Ong decided to return to Old Flameford to investigate further. The imposing tower's dark secrets had only intensified their determination to uncover the truth behind Phoenix's rise to power. Their loyal companion, Pumpkin, followed closely behind, her senses ever vigilant.

As they explored the city again, Keisha and Ong searched for clues that might shed light on the mystery of Phoenix's newfound strength. They knew he was unlikely to have grown so powerful in such a brief time since his exile. Someone had to be aiding him, pulling the strings from the shadows.

Their search led them to a hidden chamber within one of the ancient buildings. In the chamber, they discovered a collection of ancient texts written in a language neither could decipher. The texts were vital to understanding the hostility overtaking Vacari but remained out of reach.

"I feel these texts are vital to our mission," Ong said, crossing his fingers over the enigmatic symbols. "But without the ability to read them, we are at a loss."

Keisha nodded in agreement, her mind racing about who could help them unlock the knowledge in the texts. "We should seek counsel from Lord Karrenen, the Eladrin high council member and mage. He is renowned for his wisdom and knowledge of ancient languages," she suggested.

"An excellent idea," Ong replied, his eyes brightening with hope. "Lord Karrenen has always been a trusted advisor and may hold the key to unraveling this mystery."

With a shared sense of purpose, the trio left Old Flameford and began their journey back home, where they would seek the guidance of Lord Karrenen. The weight of the knowledge they sought weighed heavily on them, and they could feel the shadows of uncertainty and danger lurking in the corners of their minds.

As they journeyed, Ong and Keisha discussed their findings and pondered the possibility of someone aiding Phoenix. "Who could be powerful enough to rival the ancient dragons and aid him in his malevolent plans?" Keisha wondered aloud.

Ong's brow furrowed in thought. "It must be someone with immense magical prowess and a deep understanding of the dark arts," he mused. "But why would they choose to align themselves with Phoenix?"

Keisha shook her head. "Perhaps they share a common goal or desire for power," she speculated. "Or maybe Phoenix has something to offer them in return."

The possibilities swirled in their minds as they continued on their journey. The road back home was long and filled with uncertainty, but they were determined to find the answers they sought. Lord Karrenen's wisdom could be the missing piece of the puzzle they needed to confront the darkness that threatened to engulf their world.

As the sun set on the horizon, painting the sky in hues of orange and purple, Keisha and Ong knew that their quest was far from over. The journey ahead would be filled with challenges, but they were prepared to face them with every ounce of courage they possessed.

In the heart of Vacari, a dangerous dominion had been forged, and darkness loomed on the horizon. But Keisha, Ong, and Pumpkin would persist. With their bond unyielding and their determination unwavering, they would continue their pursuit of the truth and stand united against the hostility that sought to devour their world. The stage was set for a battle of epic proportions, and they were ready to face whatever trials awaited them with the strength of their unbreakable bond and the hope that light would prevail over darkness.

Chapter 8

Shadows Unveiled: Uncovering Vuarus

As the sun dipped below the horizon, casting long shadows across the ancient city of Old Flameford, Keisha and Ong retreated from the imposing tower. They clutched the mysterious ancient texts they had discovered in their arms, filled with both excitement and trepidation about the knowledge they might contain. Pumpkin, their loyal panther companion, padded silently beside them, her eyes glinting with intelligence as she sensed their urgency.

Finding a secluded spot within the city, they sat down and carefully spread out the texts before them. The writings were inscribed in an archaic language, unfamiliar to Keisha and Ong. They exchanged worried glances, realizing that deciphering these texts might require more help than they initially thought.

"We need to find someone who can read this," Keisha murmured, gently tracing the enigmatic symbols. "Perhaps Lord Karrenen will be able to shed some light on these ancient writings."

Ong nodded in agreement. "He's been a great ally to us, and if there's anyone who can help, it's him. But it's strange. How could Phoenix have amassed such power so quickly after his exile?" "That's what worries me," Keisha replied, her brow furrowing. "It's as if he has an ally, someone aiding him in his quest for revenge. But who could it be?"

Their minds raced with possibilities, but they couldn't jump to conclusions without more concrete evidence. After carefully securing the texts in their bags, they decided to head back to their home in Vacari to consult with Lord Karrenen.

Upon their return, they were greeted by the comforting sight of their quaint cottage nestled amidst the serene landscape of E'vahona. The scent of pine and the gentle rustle of leaves greeted them as they entered. Keisha and Ong sank into the familiar warmth of their home, feeling the weight of their journey settle on their shoulders.

"We'll have to set out for Lord Karrenen's in the morning," Ong said, stoking the fireplace to ward off the evening chill. "We can't waste any time."

Keisha nodded, her thoughts still consumed by the mysteries they had encountered. "I just hope he can decipher the texts and give us some answers. We need to know who or what is behind Phoenix's sudden rise in power."

As they settled down for the night, the weight of unrevealed secrets hung heavily in the air. Keisha and Ong knew their journey was far from over, and the truth they sought remained elusive. Little did they suspect that the shadows concealed the secrets of the past and the lurking presence of Vuarus, the enigmatic and formidable sorcerer hidden in the darkness.

With the morning sun painting the sky in soft hues, Keisha and Ong stood amidst the tranquility of E'vahona. Remarkably, they couldn't sense any trace of the darkness that had plagued their previous journeys. Relief was evident in their expressions as they came to the shared decision that the time had come to seek counsel from Lord Karrenen, the Eladrin high council member and mage, regarding the cryptic texts they had acquired.

In Lord Karrenen's serene study, they recounted their trials and tribulations in Fel Thalor and Old Flameford. Their words conveyed the eerie emptiness of Fel Thalor, the hostility that shrouded the Druchii city, and the perplexing preservation of Old Flameford despite Phoenix's exile. They detailed their encounters with the ethereal spirits in Fel Thalor and the ominous shadows that pursued them in Old Flameford.

Lord Karrenen listened with rapt attention, his wise gaze absorbing every detail. Once they had finished, he reclined in his chair, thoughtfully considering their experiences. "The absence of darkness within E'vahona is not coincidental," he softly imparted. "Kadona, the Goddess of Light, shields and protects this city. Her divine influence repels the grasp of darkness, ensuring its safety."

This revelation struck Keisha and Ong with astonishment. "Kadona, the Goddess of Light?" Keisha uttered in awe.

Lord Karrenen nodded in affirmation. "Indeed, a potent and benevolent deity. E'vahona has long been a sacred refuge under her vigilant gaze, hidden from Phoenix's malevolence and sinister forces. Find comfort in knowing you are under her vigilant care while you reside here."

Keisha and Ong felt renewed hope and gratitude for this newfound understanding. With Kadona's protective shield enveloping them, they could confidently plan their next steps. Yet, much remained to be unraveled, particularly concerning Vuarus and his enigmatic connection to Phoenix. With this insight in mind, they expressed their gratitude to Lord Karrenen. They returned to their dwelling, eager to meticulously examine the ancient texts they had obtained, laying the groundwork for their forthcoming actions.

In the depths of the Abyssal Dominion's lair, Phoenix and Vuarus seethed with frustration. Their attempts to locate Keisha and Ong proved fruitless, leaving the two adventurers vanishing. Phoenix's agitation was palpable as he paced back and forth, his icy demeanor thinly veiling his boiling anger.

"Where have they disappeared to?" Phoenix growled, his eyes blazing with vexation. "It's as though they've slipped through our fingers entirely!"

Even Vuarus, typically composed and calculating, shared in the vexation. "It's infuriating, Phoenix," he muttered, his usually calm voice tinged with exasperation. "They must have discovered a way to evade our pursuit."

But Phoenix's anger soon became a steely determination as a sudden insight dawned upon him. "Of course!" he exclaimed, a twisted smile forming. "They've undoubtedly sought refuge in E'vahona. It's the only place they could remain so effectively hidden from our reach."

Phoenix's theory caught Vuarus off guard, and skepticism crept into his expression. "E'vahona? But that city is shielded by Kadona, the Goddess of Light. She wouldn't permit their return so easily."

Phoenix's grin widened, revealing a sinister delight. "Ah, but Vuarus, my friend, every shield has its vulnerabilities. If they have taken refuge in E'vahona, we shall exploit those vulnerabilities and return them to our grasp. The Goddess of Light cannot protect them forever."

Phoenix's eyes gleamed with malicious intent. "Kadona, the alleged protector," he scoffed. "Her meddling presence has always hindered our grand ambitions.

But her shield won't safeguard them indefinitely. And by the way, I might have neglected to mention that Keisha is, in fact, an Eladrin."

Vuarus' shock mingled with his anger. "An Eladrin?" he spat, the intensity of his frustration evident. "And you deemed this revelation unimportant to share with me?"

Phoenix waved off Vuarus' agitation dismissively. "I saw no reason to burden you with insignificant details. Besides, it hardly matters. While Kadona may have reasons for granting them sanctuary, her protection won't shield them forever."

Vuarus' frustration lingered, and he felt compelled to caution Phoenix. "You underestimate Eladrin at your peril. Their powers are far-reaching, even beyond our understanding. If Kadona is indeed involved, tread with caution."

Phoenix's patience waned, and his tone grew curt. "Spare me your warnings. I'm aware of the capabilities of Eladrin. Divine intervention won't dissuade me."

Vuarus, though simmering with anger, recognized the futility of arguing further. He took a deep breath, endeavoring to regain his composure. "Very well, but do not dismiss Kadona's significance. She may play a larger role than we anticipate."

Phoenix's impatience flashed in his eyes. "Enough of this. Our focus should be on breaching her protection and reclaiming our 'assets.'"

Vuarus nodded outwardly but couldn't hide the subtle smile that played across his lips. He knew Keisha's Eladrin heritage could be an unexpected advantage in his plans. As they turned their attention back to their sinister plotting, the complex web of dominions and rivalries continued to evolve in the shadows, each move taking them closer to a reckoning that would shape the destiny of Vacari.

Unbeknownst to them, Keisha and Ong, ensconced within E'vahona, were under Kadona's watchful gaze. The clash of darkness and light remained far from its resolution, and the revelation of Keisha's heritage added more intricacy to the unfolding events.

In the sacred city of E'vahona, where ethereal light intertwined with ever-present shadows, Kadona, the Goddess of Light, stood before a shimmering crystal. Within its crystalline depths resided Talleoss, the ancient and wise dragon spirit trapped by the machinations of the Abyssal Dominion.

Kadona's gaze was fixed upon the crystal, a gentle radiance illuminating her serene visage. With a delicate motion, she extended her hand, her touch sending ripples of light across the crystal's surface. In response, the spirit of Talleoss stirred within its confines.

"Talleoss," Kadona's voice echoed with the weight of ages, resonating like a timeless melody. "I sense your presence, dear friend. What brings your unease to this realm of shadows?"

The spirit's voice resonated within her consciousness, its tones carrying wisdom and apprehension. "Kadona, Goddess of Light, I bear somber tidings," Talleoss conveyed, his words heavy with concern. "The forces of darkness are in motion, their gaze fixed upon E'vahona."

Kadona's brow furrowed with worry. "The Abyssal Dominion," she sighed, a faint sadness in her eyes. "Their malevolence has long been sensed, but what knowledge do you bring of their current designs?"

"They seek passage through E'vahona's sacred boundaries," Talleoss warned, his presence within the crystal flickering like a distant star. "Phoenix and Vuarus have unearthed a way to breach your protective shield. Their intentions extend beyond capturing Keisha and Ong; they harbor plans that threaten the very essence of this city."

A surge of determination ignited within Kadona's gaze. "We cannot permit their success," she proclaimed, her voice unwavering. "E'vahona shall remain a haven of light and sanctuary."

"I knew your strength would not waver," Talleoss reassured, his voice echoing with the resonance of ages past. "However, exercise caution, for the darkness they wield holds knowledge that could challenge even the most formidable defenses."

With solemn resolve, Kadona nodded. "The guardians of E'vahona shall be placed on heightened vigilance," she pledged. "While darkness may wield its strength, the light that safeguards this realm shall prove an unassailable bulwark."

Within the crystal, Talleoss' spirit stirred, embodying his unwavering loyalty to Kadona and the realm they both cherished. "In my crystalline prison, I shall watch and guide as best I can," he vowed, his spirit swirling within like a fierce wind.

Renewed and fortified by their pact, Kadona turned her gaze toward the distant horizon, where the shadows of the Abyssal Dominion lurked. "Together, we shall face this looming threat," she murmured, her words a solemn promise. "The balance of light and darkness shall endure unbroken."

Thus, the Goddess of Light and the spirit of the ancient dragon forged an unbreakable bond, united in their determination to safeguard E'vahona from the malevolence that sought to consume it. As the struggle for the city's fate escalated, the alliance between Kadona and Talleoss stood as an indomitable force against the encroaching darkness.

Within the grand halls of Lord Karrenen's ancient library, Keisha and Ong stood in the presence of the Eldarin high council member and esteemed mage. The texts they had retrieved from their perilous journeys through Fel Thalor and Old Flameford were carefully arranged on an ornate table, their faded pages adorned with enigmatic symbols and ancient script.

As the soft glow of candlelight danced upon the pages, Lord Karrenen's wise eyes perused the intricate writings with reverence and intrigue. "These texts are nothing short of extraordinary," he mused, his voice a melodic cadence resonating through the hall. "They hold the essence of an era long past, containing knowledge that time has sought to bury."

Keisha's curiosity gleamed in her eyes as she leaned forward. "Can you decipher their meanings?" she inquired, her anticipation palpable. The cryptic contents promised to unravel the enigma surrounding their unfolding adventure.

Lord Karrenen's lips curved into a knowing smile. "Deciphering these texts will require both time and collaboration," he responded, his voice carrying the weight of his vast experience. "I shall convene a special council meeting at once. Our collective wisdom shall be pooled to unlock the secrets woven within these ancient words."

Ong nodded in appreciation, acknowledging Lord Karrenen's dedication to the task. "We stumbled upon a mention of the Heart of Twilight," he said, selecting and presenting a specific text. "Do you possess any knowledge of this artifact?"

A contemplative expression crossed Lord Karrenen's countenance as he regarded the text before him. "The Heart of Twilight," he murmured, the words seeming to hold a whisper of mystery. "A relic of profound significance, veiled in myth and legend. It is rumored to possess the ability to transcend the boundaries between realms, forging connections between our world and others."

Keisha's gaze widened as the implications settled upon her. "Could Phoenix be seeking the Heart of Twilight?" she pondered aloud, her thoughts racing ahead.

"In the realm of possibility," Lord Karrenen conceded, his voice measured. "The machinations of the Abyssal Dominion are intricate, and the Heart of Twilight could undoubtedly play a pivotal role in their nefarious designs. Yet, the true essence of this artifact eludes even our understanding."

Determination ignited in Ong's eyes as he exchanged a resolute glance with Keisha. "We cannot allow Phoenix to harness such power," he asserted, his voice unwavering.

Lord Karrenen nodded in agreement. "Agreed. However, I advise both of you to return home and rest. Deciphering these texts will require time and meticulous effort. When the council requires your presence, I shall send word."

Grateful for the reprieve, Keisha and Ong shared a meaningful look, fully aware of the gravity of the situation. They bid their farewells to Lord Karrenen, stepping out of the hallowed library and embarking on their journey back to their dwelling. The air hummed with the intrigue of the mysteries they had uncovered, each step bringing them closer to unveiling the truth that lay shrouded within the ancient texts.

Amidst the serenity of their homely refuge, Keisha and Ong walked side by side, their hearts burdened with the weight of uncertainty. The shadows had proven more pervasive than they could have fathomed, and their path was shrouded in ambiguity. Yet, within the walls of their sanctuary, they found solace, strength, and the assurance of companionship, all of which encouraged them to face the daunting trials ahead.

With the knowledge that the council of E'vahona had taken up the mantle of deciphering the texts, Keisha and Ong took solace that their quest for truth was not embarked upon in isolation. The presence of their comrades-in-arms lent credence to their cause, fostering a sense of unity that would serve them well in the impending confrontation that would shape the destiny of their world.

In the grandeur of E'vahona's majestic halls, Keisha and Ong found themselves in the company of esteemed figures, standing before Lord Karrenen and the assembly of distinguished Eladrin council members. The chamber exuded an air of reverence, adorned with intricate carvings that told tales of ages past, while the soft luminescence of enchanted crystals bathed the space in an ethereal glow.

The council consisted of three venerable Eladrin, each possessing a unique presence. Lady Seraphina exuded wisdom and grace, her gentle countenance reflecting her profound insights. Lord Eldrion, a figure of seasoned scholarship, bore the weight of history upon his shoulders, his demeanor stern yet sagacious. Lady Isadora, youthful and vibrant, radiated intellectual enthusiasm that belied her age.

The texts were presented before the council, and a peaceful anticipation settled over the assembly. Lord Karrenen's voice, imbued with authority and sagacity, resonated within the chamber as he addressed the council. "These texts," he began, his tone measured, "are relics of a bygone era, their origins obscured by the veils of time. Caution and meticulousness must guide our every step to unravel their concealed truths."

Lady Seraphina leaned in, her gentle eyes tracing the contours of the ancient symbols. "These texts possess an aura of significance," she remarked, her voice soft and contemplative. "Yet, the question remains: what tale do they seek to tell? And who is this enigmatic 'Vuarus' whose name graces some of these passages?"

Lord Eldrion adjusted his spectacles, his scholarly demeanor commanding attention. "Vuarus," he mused, his tone a mixture of thoughtfulness and recollection. "The name is not unfamiliar. It harkens back to a time of ancient legends, a time when darkness and potency were synonymous with his name. He was said to have been defeated by a united front of luminous forces."

Lady Isadora interjected, her eyes alight with curiosity. "If the texts speak true, then the resurgence of Vuarus heralds the return of the malevolent forces we once thought banished."

Lord Karrenen's gaze turned solemn as he nodded. "A somber possibility, indeed. But let us exercise prudence and refrain from prematurely divulging our suspicions to the broader council. Before we conclude, we must secure further evidence."

The council chambers were filled with a sense of purpose and shared determination. Keisha and Ong watched as the council members exchanged knowing glances, aware of the gravity of the situation. They had embarked on a journey that now intertwined with the fate of E'vahona itself, and the path ahead promised challenges and revelations that would shape the destiny of their world.

As the council delved into deliberation, Keisha and Ong stood as witnesses to the discourse that held the fate of their world in balance. Amidst the exchange of insights and interpretations, Lord Karrenen's attention turned toward the determined adventurers. His voice resonated with a blend of approval and insight.

"Your efforts in recovering these texts have not gone unnoticed," he acknowl-edged. "And I sense that your journey is far from its conclusion."

Keisha met Ong's gaze with a resolute nod, her voice unwavering. "We shall stand ready to assist in any way necessary to uncover the truth."

Lord Karrenen's expression softened into a benevolent smile. "Then, I beseech you to take these texts to Hidden Isles and consult the council of good dragons," he instructed. "Their wisdom and perspective may be key to unlocking the enig-mas buried within these ancient pages."

Ong's affirmation was steadfast as he pledged, "We shall heed your counsel and seek the guidance of the good dragons at Hidden Isles."

Leaving the council chamber, Keisha and Ong embraced the unfolding journey with unyielding hearts. With every step they took, the mysteries they had un-raveled beckoned them closer to revelations that would shed light on Vuarus, Keisha's lineage, and the imminent trials awaiting them. The path to Hidden Isles was a bridge to the answers they sought, and they were resolute in their determination to confront the enigmatic truths that lay in wait.

The ancient texts lay before the council of wise and regal dragons in the Grand Hall of the Good Dragons Council on the Hidden Isles. Their presence evoked a profound sense of importance, and the dragons' collective wisdom focused on the scrolls' intricate symbols and hidden meanings.

Kimras, the venerable leader of the council, peered into the texts with eyes that held the weight of eons. Beside him, Dirona, the majestic bronze dragon, nodded with the gravity of understanding. Hespherus, the charismatic brass dragon, leaned forward, his gaze reflecting the seriousness of the situation.

Silvara, the serene silver dragon, approached the scrolls gracefully, her wisdom radiating like moonlight. Caelum, the clever copper dragon, examined the texts with a keen intellect, his curiosity burning bright.

As the dragons delved into the texts, a profound connection unfolded. Their minds merged, forming a shared comprehension of the writings' importance. Their eyes met in silent understanding, and Kimras broke the silence with a voice that held ancient authority.

"These texts weave a tale of ancient darkness," Kimras began, his voice a resonant echo of ages past. "Vuarus, a name thought to be buried in history, awakens in the shadows once more."

Dirona's voice joined the chorus, her tone laden with wisdom. "His darkness is potent, and his resurgence threatens to tip the balance of our realm."

Hespherus, with his charismatic aura, continued, "The signs unmistakably point to Vuarus' hand in the recent turmoil. His malevolence seeks to reclaim dominion."

Silvara's gentle voice added to the discourse. "We cannot afford hesitation. The Eladrin Council must be informed, and our united efforts must stave off Vuarus' impending menace."

As he contributed, Caelum's keen eyes gleamed. "Keisha and Ong, you bear the key to unlocking the truths concealed within these texts. Seek the Eladrin Council's guidance and share our revelations."

With the unanimous resolve of the dragon council, Keisha and Ong embraced their newfound duty: to relay the warnings of the good dragons to the Eladrin Council. They bid farewell to the dragons with gratitude and purpose and returned to E'vahona.

In the heart of E'vahona's halls, Keisha and Ong stood before Lord Karrenen and the gathered Eladrin council members, conveying the insights and gravitas of the dragon council's revelations. Lord Karrenen listened intently, his features a blend of concern and determination.

"Time is of the essence," Lord Karrenen declared resolutely. "Vuarus' resurgence jeopardizes our world's very essence. We must pool our knowledge and resources to counteract this ancient malevolence."

The council of Eladrin nodded in unison, united in their purpose. Together, they commenced the arduous task of crafting a strategy to face the looming threat. Keisha and Ong's journey had brought them to the epicenter of a battle that spanned the spectrum between light and darkness. They recognized that their destinies had become entwined with E'vahona's fate and the broader world beyond.

While the path ahead was fraught with peril, the wisdom of dragons and the unity of the Eladrin fortified them. Standing on the cusp of a looming confrontation, Keisha and Ong shouldered the weight of responsibility. They understood that their choices could irrevocably mold their world's destiny and determine the ultimate supremacy of light over darkness.

Chapter 9

Shadows Unveiled: The Revelation of Vuarus

In the grand chambers of the Eladrin Council in Goldmoor, Keisha and Ong stood as still as statues, their every movement echoing the moment's gravity. The air was thick with solemnity, and the council's assembly held its breath, waiting for the truth to be revealed. Lord Karrenen, a figure of earnest concern and unyielding determination, stood at the forefront, flanked by the council members like sentinels of an ancient order.

"Now is the hour to unveil the truth about Vuarus," Lord Karrenen's voice pierced through the silence, resonating with unwavering authority. It was a voice that carried the weight of centuries and demanded attention and respect. "In ages past, he stood as a formidable sorcerer, a master of the arcane arts who dared to delve into the forbidden, driven by an insatiable hunger for supremacy. He journeyed into the abyss of illicit magic, coveting the most obscure and evil forces."

As Lord Karrenen spoke, the very air seemed to shimmer with an eerie intensity. Keisha and Ong exchanged a meaningful glance, their eyes reflecting the profound weight of this revelation. The name Vuarus had long been a spectral whisper, a shadowy enigma, but now, the true identity of this mysterious figure was laid bare before them.

"He aspired to capture the very essence of shadows," Lord Karrenen's narrative flowed like an unyielding river, "to bend darkness to his will and ascend as a deity. Yet, such audacious ambitions took a harrowing toll, and Vuarus paid the ultimate price. In his reckless pursuit of dominion, he relinquished his humanity, consumed by the shadows he sought to command."

The council members nodded solemnly in agreement, their expressions mirroring the gravity of the history unveiled. Lady Thessara, a living embodiment of wisdom and antiquity, stepped forward. Her presence was like a beacon of ancient knowledge in the chamber, and her voice, a gentle river of profound sagacity, seemed to carry the weight of countless years.

"Vuarus' insatiable craving for dominion knew no bounds," Lady Thessara elucidated, her words carrying the weight of ancient knowledge. Her tone was a quiet river of wisdom flowing through the chamber and into the hearts of those who listened. "His lust for power birthed unspeakable horrors, a cataclysm of suffering unleashed upon the world. His wake left behind annihilation that scarred the lands for eternity."

As the harrowing truth of Vuarus' narrative unfolded, Keisha and Ong found themselves caught in a whirlwind of emotions—sadness and anger intertwined. The exposure of his transgressions painted a chilling portrait of an evil power that had sown boundless agony.

"It was universally believed that he had been imprisoned, his darkness forever contained," Lord Karrenen continued his unwavering discourse, his voice a steady beacon of guidance. "Yet, it seems he has resurfaced from the abyss of oblivion, intent on reclaiming the omnipotence he once coveted."

Keisha's fists clenched, her determination unwavering. "Success is not an option for him," she declared steadfastly. "No matter the cost, we shall thwart his ambitions and stand as guardians for E'vahona and Vacari."

Ong's nod conveyed both agreement and a flame of unyielding determination. "Side by side, we shall brave this encroaching darkness and stand firm against Vuarus, regardless of the challenges ahead."

Lord Karrenen's countenance softened into a smile, a flicker of hope illuminating his underlying concern. "Your valor and steadfastness are virtues to be admired," he remarked. "However, let us not discard caution. Vuarus is a cunning master, prepared to employ any means to achieve his sinister aspirations. We must scour every nook for advantage."

Keisha and Ong exchanged resolute glances, poised to embrace the trials that awaited them. The revelation of Vuarus' true nature had stoked their fierce determination. They understood that the journey to conquer this darkness would be arduous. But armed with the sagacity of the Eladrin Council and the wisdom of the benevolent dragon council, they possessed the means to safeguard E'vahona from the malevolence that coveted it.

Their quest to thwart Vuarus was a nascent flame, and Keisha and Ong were keenly aware that the destiny of their realm rested upon their shoulders. Empowered by an intimate understanding of their adversary, they were ready to confront the enigma with unwavering courage, guided by the brilliance of their determination and the unity of their allies. The chamber held its breath, anticipating the birth of a new legend in Vacari's storied history.

Amid the backdrop of the Dread Spire, where darkness thrived, Drakthor, the colossal black dragon, made his dramatic entrance. His immense form sinuously slithered into the chamber, and his wings twitched with restless energy. His sharp gaze locked onto Phoenix, the master of this evil domain. Like distant thunder, his voice resonated through the chamber, filling it with an ominous presence. "Master, I have fulfilled your command, returning from Fel Thalor and Old Flameford. Yet, the ancient tomes we sought have vanished, as if they were naught but whispers in the wind."

A storm of anger momentarily twisted Phoenix's features as he absorbed this unwelcome news. His attention swung toward Vuarus, his trusted confidant, his tone demanding and laced with frustration, "Vuarus, did you falter in securing the texts? This setback is infuriating."

Vuarus clenched his teeth, and his frustration was palpable. "Phoenix, my actions were executed with utmost precision," he replied, a sharp edge to his voice. "The tomes were untouched upon my departure. It is plausible that another hand has reached them before us, or perhaps the guardianship of the Eladrin Council has been invoked."

Phoenix's eyes narrowed, suspicion taking root in his mind. "The Eladrin Council," he mused aloud, his voice like smoldering embers. "Their meddling in our affairs has persisted for far too long. I would not be surprised if their influence is at play here."

Drakthor, ever attuned to his Master's volatile temperament, added his insights, "It is within the realm of possibility that the Eladrin Council has unearthed the truth about Vuarus and seeks to disrupt our designs."

Vuarus shook his head, a veneer of frustration overlaying his anger. "Implausible," he growled. "I have taken pains to conceal my true self. None outside the Abyssal Dominion should know me."

Though his frustration lingered, Phoenix recognized that dwelling on it was fruitless. "Very well," he conceded, his voice a taut rein on his emotions. "We shall retrieve the texts, whatever the cost. Any who dare oppose us will know the depths of suffering."

Vuarus nodded, his determination a mirror of Phoenix's resolve. "Indeed, Master. This setback shall not dismantle our plans. We will unveil the mystery surrounding the absent texts and extinguish any opposition."

A shared glance between the sinister pair conveyed a profound understanding, their resolve steeling against the challenges ahead. The path to secure the ancient texts had taken an unforeseen twist, yet their unquenchable thirst for power and retribution burned fiercer than ever before. In the shadowy depths of the Dread Spire, their dark ambitions forged an unbreakable bond.

Within the grand chamber of the Eladrin Council in Goldmoor, Keisha and Ong stood, their presence imbued with anticipation, as they faced the venerable assembly. The chamber held its breath in expectation as a symphony of knowing glances traversed the council members before Lord Eldrion, their sage leader, spoke. His voice carried the weight of epochs, echoing through the chamber with a resonance that commanded attention.

"Keisha and Ong, your unyielding dedication to unraveling the enigma of Vuarus and safeguarding our realm from encroaching darkness are commendable," Lord Eldrion said with measured solemnity. "As you are well aware, the lifespans of dragons span centuries, affording them a unique perspective across time. Among the dragons residing in the Hidden Isles, there might be those who hold invaluable knowledge about Vuarus."

A nod of agreement came from Lady Seraphina, a figure of gentleness and nurture. "Undoubtedly," she affirmed. "The Hidden Isles have long provided sanctuary for an array of beings, some of whom have witnessed epochs when another name knew Vuarus."

Lady Isadora, an embodiment of youth and vibrancy, enthusiastically chimed in. "Dragons possess a penchant for storytelling, a means to weave the tapestry of history. It is conceivable that within their narratives, clues slumber that could illuminate your quest."

Lord Karrenen, observing with his discerning gaze, interjected with his wisdom. "Keisha and Ong, it would be judicious to seek the guidance of the dragon council members dwelling in the Hidden Isles. Their counsel could unveil Vuarus' history, potentially unearthing the motives steering his actions."

Locked in determined eye contact, Keisha and Ong voiced their shared conviction. "To the Hidden Isles, we shall journey to seek the ear of these ancient beings," Keisha proclaimed resolutely. "Until we have peeled back the layers obscuring Vuarus' tale and thwarted his nefarious designs, our pursuit shall not waver."

A raised brow of approval arched from Lord Eldrion. "Your valor is laudable," he acknowledged. "Remember, these beings are not easily swayed. Approach them with deference and humility, and they might be more inclined to share their lore."

Adding a note of gratitude and determination, Ong appended, "Understood. We shall exhaust every effort to garner their trust, to glean insights into Vuarus' shadowed past."

A warm smile danced upon Lord Eldrion's lips. "The blessings of the Eladrin Council rest upon you," he bestowed his blessing. "May the luminance of guidance illuminate your path, leading you to the revelations you seek within the Hidden Isles." The chamber seemed to resonate with a sense of hope as Keisha and Ong prepared to embark on their quest to uncover the secrets of Vuarus and protect their realm from the encroaching darkness.

Keisha and Ong lowered their heads in respectful acknowledgment, their determination and hope further strengthened by the support of the Eladrin Council. As they departed from the grand chamber, they carried the harmonious blend of hope and resolve that would guide them through the challenges of their quest for truth.

Deep within the heart of the Hidden Isles, surrounded by the majestic presence of the Gold Dragon, Kimras, the trio sought an audience with the esteemed dragon council. With hearts filled with humility, Keisha addressed the towering creature, her words carrying the weight of their purpose. "Kimras, we beseech your permission to approach the council and discuss a matter of paramount significance. It pertains to Vuarus, the dark warlock whose sinister designs imperil our realm."

Kimras inclined his regal head solemnly, his ancient eyes reflecting the wisdom of countless epochs. "Your earnest concern does not elude me, young ones," he replied, his voice resonating like a deep and harmonious melody. "I shall carry forth your request to the council, but their final decision shall govern."

With a graceful unfurling of his majestic wings, Kimras ascended, soaring towards the grand chamber where the dragon council convened. Within, the council members greeted him with profound respect, their luminous scales aglow in the gentle illumination that permeated the chamber.

Addressing the council with authority, Kimras intoned, "Honorable members, Keisha and Ong seek an audience with you, driven by a shared apprehension regarding Vuarus and the looming shadow that imperils our domain. They entreat your wisdom and the repository of knowledge you wield, for dragons have borne witness to myriad epochs and may possess invaluable insights into this evil force."

A tacit exchange of glances ensued among the council members, each countenance reflecting a moment of contemplation. Following a measured pause, Sylvana, the Sapphire Dragon, known for her wisdom, opined, "This matter concerns us all. We ought not to deny entry to those who seek illumination."

Aurelia, the Crystal Dragon affirmed, "Truly so, especially considering Keisha's valor and mettle demonstrated when she fought valiantly alongside us during the clash against Phoenix."

Verdantia, the Emerald Dragon contributed, "The equilibrium hangs in the balance. It is incumbent upon us to ensure the tide of darkness is stemmed."

Amara, the Amethyst Dragon, heralded as the most formidable of the neutral dragons, added her voice last, "Permit their passage. The answers they quest for may be enshrined within the annals of our memories."

With the council's decision, a path to knowledge and illumination was paved for Keisha, Ong, and Pumpkin. They would now have the opportunity to delve into the ancient wisdom of the dragon council, seeking the insights and revelations necessary to confront the evil force of Vuarus and protect their realm from its shadowed grasp.

At the chamber entrance, Kimras returned to Keisha, Ong, and Pumpkin, bearing news of the council's decision. "The council accedes to your request," he declared, a trace of approval underlying his words. "They recognize your dedication and grasp the gravity of the circumstances. Keisha, your actions have already garnered merit; your presence in the Goldmoor battle against Phoenix, riding on my back, testifies to your courage. Such courage has granted you their consideration."

Grateful glances passed between Keisha and Ong, uplifted by the council's decision. "We extend our gratitude, Kimras," Keisha articulated genuinely. "Your benevolence and guidance shall remain etched within our hearts."

Kimras responded with a nod, his gaze a repository of profound sagacity. "May the wealth of council knowledge illuminate your quest. I shall stand as your companion as we enter the chamber. We shall present your case before the council, uniting in this pursuit of truth."

Guided by the regal presence of Kimras, Keisha, Ong, and Pumpkin ventured deeper into the heart of Hidden Isles, their spirits fortified for the imminent encounter with the venerable council of ancient dragons. They aspired to glean the wisdom within these sacred halls to unlock the veiled secrets shrouding Vuarus' enigmatic past.

In the sanctified expanse of the dragon council's chamber, wise and time-honored dragons met Keisha, Ong, and Pumpkin. Each figure bore a unique repository of wisdom and experience, each willing to impart their insights about the enigmatic Vuarus.

Kimras, the Gold Dragon of regal bearing, initiated the discourse. "Vuarus, in the days of old, bore the name Azeron. He was a figure steeped in shadow, once a trusted council member, until an insatiable lust for dominion and an unquenchable desire to manipulate the shadows consumed him. He turned to the abyssal arts, intent on bending the very essence of darkness to his will. Gradually, his fall into corruption escalated, and evil forces recognized his potential, ultimately reshaping him into the deity we now know as the God of Shadows."

Dirona, the Bronze Dragon, ancient and distinguished, supplemented, "He plumbed the depths of forbidden knowledge, mastering chants and rituals that marred the purity of his soul. His descent isolated him, severing bonds with those who once cherished him."

Hespherus, the charismatic Brass Dragon, spoke with a trace of melancholy. "Our attempts to salvage him, to draw him back from the precipice, were met with resistance. He surrendered to his ambition, a choice that severed our bonds of fellowship."

Caelum, the playful Copper Dragon, interjected wryly, "Vuarus reveled in cunning and manipulation. His newfound shadowy prowess fomented strife among factions, sowing discord to advance his designs."

Amidst the tapestry of revelations, Keisha and Ong absorbed the disclosures with rapt attention. The realization of Vuarus' grievous acts and his posed peril gradually crystallized. Beyond an individual driven by ambition, he embodied malevolence, a force that had deliberately veered down a path of darkness, imperiling all that was cherished. The council's disclosures fortified their resolution, reinforcing their determination to thwart Vuarus and shield their world from his nefarious intents. The weight of their quest hung heavy in the air, but they were now armed with knowledge and purpose, ready to confront the shadowed enigma that threatened their realm.

Amidst the revelations and the weighty history of Vuarus, Silvara, the Silver Dragon of gentle and nurturing disposition, remained subdued and withdrawn. Her eyes bore a poignant glimmer, her voice carrying a heavy burden of sorrow as she finally broke her silence. "I fear Vuarus may have wrought grievous harm upon Talleoss," her words barely rising above a whisper.

During this emotional admission, Keisha and Ong exchanged a glance wrought with concern, comprehending the profound depths of Silvara's anguish. "Talleoss, a silver dragon renowned for his kindness and devotion," she continued, her voice trembling with sorrow. "We were more than mates, our bond transcending all. For untold years, our connection was a beacon of strength."

Silvara's voice carried a bittersweet resonance, a testament to the intricate tapestry of emotions woven into the narrative of Vuarus' darkness.

Silvara's emotions seemed to swell within her, and the council members regarded her with profound empathy, a shared understanding of the weight she bore. "When Vuarus plunged into the abyss of darkness, Talleoss endeavored to reason with him, to guide him from the treacherous path he treads," she confessed, her voice a delicate tremor. "But Vuarus was engulfed by his unquenchable thirst for power, heedless of reason. To witness his once-friend transmute into such a vile entity shattered Talleoss's heart."

Tears shimmered in Silvara's eyes as her tale continued, "Talleoss's presence has eluded me for an enduring span. Dread whispers that misfortune might have befallen him. A glimmer of hope remains that Kadona's radiant embrace has shielded him. Yet, the specter of uncertainty gnaws at my soul."

The weight of Silvara's revelations enveloped the chamber in a somber hush, the pall of sorrow casting its shadow upon all assembled. Keisha and Ong, their hearts now infused with an augmented urgency, resolved to confront Vuarus and terminate his dark machinations—for the well-being of their world and to bring closure to those trapped in his hostility. The memory of Talleoss and the pain in Silvara's eyes were potent reminders of the cost of Vuarus' descent into darkness.

Kimras, the sagacious Gold Dragon, conveyed compassion in his words, "Your grief resonates within us, Silvara. Vuarus's malevolence has sown pain aplenty, but our mettle must not falter as we persist in quelling his designs."

Keisha, encouraged by the council's support, advanced with resolute determination etched on her features. "Talleoss's fate and Vuarus's tyranny shall not evade our grasp," she declared with unwavering conviction.

Ong nodded in agreement, his voice unwavering, "Our dedication to curbing Vuarus's havoc shall remain unyielding. Our world and its inhabitants deserve naught but our relentless pursuit of justice."

The dragon council members nodded in unanimous approval, their ancient eyes bearing the weight of understanding. They acknowledged that the destiny of their world lay squarely in the capable hands of these brave champions. They embraced the belief that, guided by courage and determination, Keisha and Ong could defeat the darkness that sought to engulf their realm.

As the council session neared its conclusion, and the resonance of their disclosures lingered in the air, Kimras, the sagacious Gold Dragon, voiced counsel anew. "Before your journey commences, seek counsel from another, a being of great importance," he suggested, his gaze resting upon Keisha and Ong with a knowing intensity. "Visit Kadona, the Goddess of Light. In the annals of Vuarus's history, she played a pivotal role. Her insights might offer guidance on how to face him once more."

Silvara, the silver dragon, added her assent. "Talleoss served Kadona with devotion, and her depths harbor the most intimate knowledge of Vuarus and the darkness he wields," she affirmed. "Her guidance might illuminate your path, a beacon that the council's wisdom cannot replicate." Keisha and Ong exchanged steadfast glances, the import of this suggestion dawning upon them. To stand against Vuarus, seeking the counsel of the Goddess of Light emerged as an inescapable necessity. "To Kadona, we shall journey, beseeching her guidance," Keisha articulated, her tone unwavering, resonating with their resolution. "In our pursuit of justice and safeguarding our world, no avenue shall remain unexplored."

"May her luminance illuminate your passage, furnishing you with the strength to combat the encroaching shadows," Silvara whispered, her melancholy lingering but her hope kindling anew.

Empowered by the blessings of the dragon council and armed with the legacy of Talleoss, their fellow dragons, Keisha, Ong, and Pumpkin, embarked on their journey anew. Their course was illuminated by a singular purpose: to seek Kadona, the embodiment of light's grace, and to decipher the concealed chronicles that would sculpt a brighter destiny. The trials ahead were formidable, yet their hearts brimmed with determination, for the very existence of their realm was poised on a precarious precipice.

Within the tranquil enclave of Lord Karrenen's tower, Keisha and Ong stood before the venerable Eladrin mage, their visages radiant with resolve and anticipation. In hushed tones, they delineated their strategy, detailing their intent to approach Kadona and unravel the veiled enigma of Vuarus. The chamber, adorned with relics and scrolls of ages past, whispered of the arcane wisdom that resonated within its walls.

Lord Karrenen, a sage figure clad in silver hair and adorned with the wisdom of epochs, listened with unwavering attention. His ageless eyes, steeped in profundity and compassion, met the steadfast gaze of the adventurers. As their plea reached its conclusion, a thoughtful nod acknowledged the magnitude of their mission.

"This is a pursuit of great magnitude," Lord Karrenen pronounced, his voice a bastion of sagacity. "To approach a deity of Kadona's stature demands reverence and humility. Her dominion spans cosmic realms, and her designs are as intricate as the constellations. Are you prepared to traverse the potential perils?"

Locked in a shared understanding, Keisha and Ong exchanged a significant glance, recognizing the challenges ahead. "We are fully cognizant of the perils that await," Keisha asserted unwaveringly. "However, the insights we seek from Kadona could hold the blueprint for comprehending and thwarting Vuarus. We are willing to embrace the risks."

Lord Karrenen, acknowledging their resolve, nodded anew. "Very well," he intoned, a glimmer of pride underscoring his words. "I shall present your petition before the council. Their esteem for Kadona's sagacity is profound, and their verdict shall serve as a lodestar in this weighty affair."

With this pronouncement, the die was cast on Keisha and Ong. Their trajectory was now in motion, their fate swaying in the balance as they awaited the council's

decree. As the sands of time sifted through the hourglass, they steeled themselves for the odyssey that loomed, an expedition fraught with trials. Yet,
unwavering, they trod onward, cognizant that their world's destiny and the
realms beyond danced on the edge of a blade. Their commitment to unearth
the truth and guard against encroaching darkness would remain unyielding,
echoing their proclamation that they would not waver in their pursuit.

In the grand hall of E'vahona, Keisha and Ong stood in the presence of the
esteemed Eladrin Council members, their hearts a blend of anticipation and
resolve. Lord Karrenen, the sagacious mage and trusted advisor to the council,
excused himself, saying his purpose was to convey Keisha and Ong's petition
to the remaining members for consideration.

In the interim, Lady Seraphina, embodying gentleness and nurturing
warmth, assumed the speech mantle. "The approach to Kadona necessitates
utmost care," she began, her voice a soothing melody. "A goddess of immense
power, we must tread lightly to win her favor."

Lord Thaldir, the venerable figure of wisdom and respect, augmented the
discourse. "Kadona's entwinement with Vuarus transcends mere happen-
stance. She was instrumental in his binding, and her motives may elude our
understanding."

In her characteristic youth and vibrancy, Lady Isadora contributed her perspective. "Kadona's ties to the equilibrium of light and darkness are profound.
It is conceivable that her insights could serve our mission to thwart Vuarus."

Yet, with a tempered tone, Lord Galadon interjected caution. "Stepping into
the presence of a goddess is no trivial endeavor. We must be prepared for any
response she deems fit."

Lady Lythia, the embodiment of healing and counsel, interposed a glimmer
of optimism. "Kadona's benevolence is renowned. Approached with sincerity
and humility, she might extend her assistance."

Lastly, Lord Alaric, the architect of strategic insight, contributed a calculated
approach. "Our petition must be both lucid and respectful. Intentions must
align with the greater good, unwavering in their earnestness."

With the discourse complete, Lord Karrenen rejoined Keisha and Ong, ushering
them into the council chamber where their fates would be sealed. Stepping into
the chamber, a deep breath was drawn in tandem, mindful of the momentous

nature of the proceedings. The council members' gaze bore the weight of anticipation, an audience prepared to receive their plea.

With resolute voices, Keisha and Ong unveiled their intentions. They intended to beseech Kadona for her guidance and insights into the enigma of Vuarus. Their commitment to safeguarding the realm from the grasp of darkness and their unwavering aspiration to lay bare Vuarus' shadowed past were conveyed with steadfast fervor.

The council absorbed their words with palpable intensity. The room enveloped itself in contemplative silence, the gravity of their appeal rippling through the air. Knowing glances exchanged amongst the council members, a tacit understanding of the moment's significance. Lord Karrenen's voice broke the silence, laden with purpose, "Your request bears weight. It shall be subjected to meticulous deliberation, and our petition shall reach Kadona."

As Keisha and Ong exited the grand chamber of the Eladrin Council, a profound sense of anticipation and uncertainty hung in the air. With its towering arches and ancient tapestries, the hallowed chamber held the weight of their realm's destiny in its very stones. They left behind the council members, their faces etched with hope and trepidation, as the council prepared to reach out to Kadona, the Goddess of Light.

In the days that followed, Keisha and Ong found themselves enveloped in an atmosphere of eager anticipation. Time seemed to stretch, each passing moment a heartbeat echoing the resounding echoes of their request within the hushed chamber. Their hearts pounded in rhythm with time, their thoughts consumed by the outcome that awaited them.

Unwavering in their dedication, the council dispatched emissaries and supplications to Kadona. Their messages carried the weight of their realm's destiny, beseeching the goddess for her guidance and consent regarding Keisha and Ong's entreaty. The threads of fate, delicate and intricate, now lay ensnared in Kadona's ethereal grasp, awaiting her divine response.

On an evening bathed in serene, golden light, the sun's descent into the horizon was a spectacle of breathtaking beauty. As the last rays of daylight kissed the world, a radiant presence began to materialize within Keisha's dreamscape. Ethereal and resplendent, Kadona stood before her, a vision of divine luminance that emanated a soothing, benevolent light. Her form glowed with otherworldly grace, and when they came, her words resonated like a celestial symphony, filling the very air with profound insight.

"Child of the mortal realm," Kadona's voice flowed forth, cadence a harmonious blend of divinity, "your quest is not to be embarked upon lightly. Yet, your intentions shine with the purity of your heart. I extend to you the privilege to seek me within the veiled sanctuary of E'vahona."

Keisha was overwhelmed by an influx of awe and gratitude, her dream self instinctively bowing in respectful homage to the goddess. "Goddess Kadona, I am humbled and grateful," she murmured gently in the ethereal realm.

But Kadona's guidance was far from over. "Before you tread the path to me," she continued, her iridescent gaze seeming to penetrate the essence of Keisha's being, "seek the Sacred Grove concealed within E'vahona. It is a bastion of ancient potency and shelter, hidden from the world's prying eyes. There, you shall unearth the passageway to my presence."

Keisha clung to Kadona's words with unwavering focus, her curiosity driving her to seek clarity. "How shall I recognize the Sacred Grove?" she inquired, her voice a thread of curiosity woven into the dreamscape.

A gentle smile graced Kadona's visage, akin to the soft radiance of dawn's first light. "Chase," she began, her words flowing like a gentle breeze, "the whispers of zephyrs as they embrace the mellifluous ballad of the river's course. Immerse yourself in the cadence of ancient arboreal heartbeats, for they shall be your compass. Repose trust in the symphony of nature enveloping you, for it is the key to unlocking the path unto the Sacred Grove."

With these profound directives, Kadona's ephemeral presence began to dissipate, like morning mist slowly yielding to the embrace of the rising sun. "Go forth, dear child," her voice lingered in the air, a whisper of ethereal wisdom, "and may the light illuminate your path."

As the tendrils of slumber reluctantly relinquished their hold upon Keisha's senses, she awoke to a newfound sense of purpose. She relayed Kadona's celestial message to Ong and Pumpkin with unwavering determination. In harmonious unity, they embarked on their expedition, their hearts ablaze with anticipation. Their objective was clear—unveiling the enigmatic Sacred Grove in the heart of E'vahona. This veiled sanctuary, concealed within the city's very embrace, held the potential to unearth secrets that could mold the contours of their odyssey, forging a trajectory that inched them ever closer to comprehending the enigma of Vuarus and his shrouded machinations.

Chapter 10

Shadows Unveiled: E'vahona, the Eladrin's Hidden City

In the mystical embrace of E'vahona, a city woven with enchantment and wonder, two brave souls, Keisha and Ong, embarked on an odyssey as wondrous as the shifting hues of twilight. Their purpose: to unveil the veiled mysteries of the Sacred Grove, an ethereal haven cradled in the heart of the land. The hallowed Eladrin council, in a rare benediction, had extended its blessing, granting passage into the presence of Kadona, the resplendent Goddess of Light. But as with otherworldly significance, this sacred meeting ground was not readily laid bare; it was nestled behind the weft of potent sorceries, a concealed and elusive realm.

As they traversed the cobbled thoroughfares of E'vahona, alive with the symphony of Eladrin lives intertwining, Keisha and Ong strode with resolute purpose, their determination a beacon that outshone the bustling city's myriad lights. The scents of mystical spices wafted through the air, a fragrant offering to the senses, yet the duo remained steadfast, their focus rigidly fixed upon the clandestine quest.

The city's enchantment extended beyond mere architecture; it was a living, breathing entity, resonating with the ancient magic that coursed through its veins. Eladrin, adorned in splendid robes that mirrored the colors of the setting sun, moved with a grace that defied mortal understanding. The buildings, decorated with intricate carvings that told stories of epochs long past, seemed to whisper secrets to those who cared to listen.

As Keisha and Ong ventured deeper into E'vahona, they could feel the presence of the Sacred Grove drawing nearer. It was a subtle pull, like a distant melody growing more transparent with every step. Their anticipation grew, fueled by the tantalizing promise of the unknown that lay ahead.

Ancient tomes, their pages heavy with the secrets of bygone ages, beckoned to them like long-lost friends. In the hallowed halls of knowledge, the city's venerable sages lent their wisdom, transmuting enigmatic verses into whispers of guidance. Each acquired morsel of lore was a shard of a greater whole, a luminescent tile in the grand mosaic of their destined voyage. The air seemed to hum with an undercurrent of arcane knowledge, and every step they took was a pilgrimage through the annals of time itself.

In the heart of this dance of destiny, Lady Mirabelle, a sorceress whose aura resonated with the mysteries of eons, extended her hand. Her eyes, twin pools of pale luminescence, fixated on the veil between worlds as incantations flowed from her lips like liquid moonlight. Yet, the Sacred Grove's secrets proved immune even to her arcane prowess as the elusive realm shimmered beyond her conjured visions. It was as if the Grove existed in the interstitial spaces of reality, where even the most skilled sorcery faltered.

Amidst the labyrinthine corridors of knowledge, Lord Alaric emerged, his intellect a beacon that pierced the haze of uncertainty. With the grace of a master strategist, he and Mirabelle sought the tomes that whispered of hidden sanctuaries, their fingers trailing across the spines of ancient volumes. Yet, like a gemstone cloaked in shadows, the name of the Sacred Grove eluded their grasp, its resonance a distant echo veiled by time-honored incantations.

As the celestial clock marked the passage of days and then weeks, Keisha and Ong remained unyielding in their pursuit, shadows cast by their unwavering purpose. Lady Isadora emerged among the council's constellation of supporters, a comet of youthful brilliance streaking through the sky. Her keen intellect guided the duo to the concealed seams of the city's fabric—forgotten niches where whispered echoes of forgotten lore seemed to harmonize with their quest. In these dim-lit alleys and age-worn corners, they found that profound truths often slumbered beneath layers of neglect, awaiting the touch of seekers with the correct key.

Guided by this revelation, Keisha and Ong ventured into E'vahona's oldest districts, where time had sculpted memories into stone and history was etched upon every archaic edifice. Drenched in the patina of countless sunsets, towering spires cast elongated shadows that danced with tales of a bygone era. With each step upon cobblestone streets, the pulse of time seemed to resonate through their very bones, connecting them with the tapestry of generations long past.

In the tapestry of fate, a fated encounter with Thaldir, an Eladrin historian marked by the ebb and flow of years, breathed life into the flickering ember of hope. From the corners of time, Thaldir wove sagas of enigmatic passages that slumbered beneath the very heartbeat of E'vahona, whispered secrets known only to the chosen of the council. A labyrinthine web of concealed tunnels, they whispered, held the promise of an audience with Kadona, the luminous Goddess herself.

Following Thaldir's whispered guidance, Keisha, Ong, and their steadfast companion Pumpkin ventured towards the city's core, where an unassuming stone sentinel stood sentinel. Awash in a cascade of emotions, the trio discovered that this statue, aged by the hands of eons, was the lynchpin to unfurling the enigma that bound them. With the enchantment passed through generations, the statue stirred, yielding to the pull of ancient sorcery, and thus, a portal into the arcane underbelly of E'vahona was unveiled. It was as if the city had acknowledged their purpose, opening hidden doors to the determined souls who sought the light in the heart of its mysteries.

Into the heart of shadow, they stepped, a trinity of seekers guided by the starlight of destiny. The passage, a whispering corridor of hidden truths, led them through the labyrinthine catacombs and sinuous chambers that nestled beneath the city's bosom. With each step, the air seemed to thicken with the weight of time, anticipation, and the secrets woven into the very stone. The walls bore ancient carvings, tales etched in the language of forgotten epochs, their meanings veiled by the passage of ages.

Emerging from the labyrinthine embrace of the tunnels, they found themselves in a sanctum suffused with a transcendent glow. A pool, the vessel of Kadona's ethereal essence, shimmered with the luminescence of a thousand stars, mirroring the boundless firmament itself. The presence of the Goddess of Light was an enveloping embrace of tender and otherworldly energy as they ventured closer. The pool's surface was a canvas of iridescent ripples reflecting cosmic mysteries.

Keisha and Ong, their hearts an offering of reverence, knelt by the side of the radiant pool. In the hushed language between souls and divine beings, Keisha's voice emerged, laden with humility, "Kadona, we pray for your wisdom and guidance. The tides of darkness rise, and we stand at the crossroads, yearning to unveil the enigma of Vuarus and his veiled designs."

The waters of the pool responded with ripples that mirrored the starlight dance on an endless sea, Kadona's mellifluous voice a symphony within their minds, "Bold are your steps to seek me, children of this realm. Vuarus, once a paragon of my council, now strays along the precipice of power's allure. The storm of his ambitions seeks to unweave the harmony of night and day."

With Kadona's words, the pool's luminance surged, casting its brilliance upon a concealed path. An ethereal yet potent gesture urged them to continue their journey, to tread the threads woven in light and shadow. "Embark upon the path unveiled before you, but tread with the caution born of wisdom," her voice echoed, imbued with the weight of ages. "For within these veiled tunnels, the dark has entwined false whispers amidst the true."

Firm in their resolve, Keisha and Ong shared a nod, each heartbeat echoing their determination. With Kadona's celestial counsel as their North Star, they ventured forth into the labyrinthine heart of the tunnels. All-encompassing darkness enveloped them as the passages spiraled into infinity, each bending a new mystery, a shroud of obscurity drawing tighter. The path ahead was uncertain, but their purpose burned as brightly as the stars, lighting the way through the shadowed labyrinth of revelations.

Time flowed like a river whose course they could not gauge, and eventually, they arrived at a crossroads, a decision poised on the cusp of their fate. Keisha's gaze met Ong's, a silent conversation of trust and uncertainty. Pumpkin, attuned to the arcane currents, growled, her hackles raised as she perceived the malevolent resonance cloaked around one path. Trusting the wisdom woven into their instincts, Keisha led the way along the other passage. The abandoned path, once tempting, unveiled itself as a labyrinth of deception, its corners pregnant with sinister forms.

Unfazed, they retraced their steps, their spirits unbroken by the web of shadows. The next fork beckoned, like a riddle demanding their wits. This time, the path whispered promises of promise, but its true nature revealed itself in time, where grotesque guardians lay in wait, their hunger for light clawing at their core. Keisha and Ong, warriors of resilience, stood poised, the bond between them an unbreakable shield. Yet, Pumpkin's ferocity growl resonated beyond, a crescendo of defiance that stilled the creatures' advance. Their malevolence wavered before an enigma too potent to grasp, and they slinked back into the ink-black veil from whence they came. Empowered by this newfound unity, Keisha, Ong, and Pumpkin advanced, unyielding in their quest. Their determination was a fire that lit their path, each step carving a furrow in the tapestry of destiny. And so, they reached yet another fork, the air trembling with the resonance of choice. Here, Kadona's unseen hand was felt, a warmth that guided them toward a passage aglow with an otherworldly luminescence.

The illuminated corridor beckoned, a haven of resplendence amidst the darkness. With each stride, the weight of the obscurity lifted, giving way to an enchanting radiance that repainted the world. The tunnel's embrace unfurled into a grand chamber, where their eyes, like moths to a celestial flame, fixed upon a towering tree aglow with leaves of gilded light.

Exhaustion hung upon them like a mantle, yet as they stood in the presence of the majestic tree, tranquility swept over them like a soothing breeze. The tree's energy flowed like a healing river, a balm that caressed their weary souls. It was an acknowledgment, a whisper in their hearts, that they had found Kadona's hidden sanctuary. In unity, they decided to rest beneath the watchful gaze of the Goddess of Light, their bodies and spirits cradled in the tender embrace of her divine protection.

Beneath the golden canopy of the ancient tree, Keisha and Ong found rest and wonderment, their senses entwined with the enchantment surrounding them. Although their destination was not yet within grasp, the ethereal encounter with Kadona and the sanctuary of the luminous tree had given them a precious gift: hope. Wrapped in the warmth of the Goddess's benediction, they fortified their spirits, unwavering in their readiness to confront whatever shadows may dance ahead and to unveil the enigmatic tapestry of Vuarus' nefarious designs.

Enthralled by the whisper of destiny courting through their veins, Keisha, Ong, and Pumpkin remained the fellowship of seekers, emboldened by Kadona's spectral touch. The path, shrouded in the embrace of night, unfurled before them. Darkness stretched its velvety fingers, an inky abyss where sight was a luxury. Here, amidst the obsidian expanse, the realm of senses transformed. Instinct became a compass, a map carved on the heart's walls, their unspoken connection, a guiding constellation.

Entwined, Keisha and Ong ventured through the stygian expanse, their movements measured and cautious. Hand in hand, they trudged the precipice of uncertainty, their steps reverberating with a symphony of trust and reliance. Pumpkin, a sentinel of vigilant awareness, lingered sentinel—keen ears tuned to the cadence of the void.

A tightening corridor beckoned, the way narrowing as if echoing the heartbeat of a challenge. Here, Keisha sensed the precipice yawning at her feet, a chasm unseen but palpable. Fear, a coiling serpent, threatened to seize her heart, but Ong's presence was her sanctuary. Hand clasping hand, they navigated the tightrope of shadows, their united resolve a lifeline against the abyss. In the timeless expanse, they persevered, minutes stretched like a canvas awaiting destiny's brushstroke. A murmur, a whisper, a serenade of droplets—water's tender call reached their ears. The sound danced like an invitation in this dark cocoon, drawing them toward its source. Keisha's hopes, fragile as gossamer, hitched onto the melody, praying it heralded a haven of rest.

Then, as if fate's hand had rewoven the tapestry of their journey, the path unveiled its newfound breadth. Before them, an expanse of pure wonder lay. A fountain, a crystalline marvel, adorned the chamber, radiant in its otherworldly glow. Waters pirouetted gracefully, weaving a murmured melody that danced through the air. The chamber's atmosphere vibrated with ethereal luminescence, a resplendence that echoed the heartbeats of the realms beyond.

In the presence of this marvel, Kcisha, Ong, and Pumpkin basked in an oasis of tranquility within the labyrinthine embrace of night. Their weary forms, cradled by the warmth of divine design, found solace in the gentle cascade of light-infused waters, their spirits echoing the soft symphony that wove through the heart of the enchanted chamber.

A tranquil exhalation escaped Keisha, Ong, and Pumpkin as they approached the radiant fountain, their souls resonating with the calm cadence of the waters. The gentle symphony of liquid notes played a soothing lullaby, weaving threads of serenity around their frayed nerves. The fountain's luminous aura whispered to their senses, an elixir of rest that flowed not only into their weary bodies but also through the labyrinthine corridors of their spirits. Keisha's hands dipped into the cool embrace of the waters and trembled with the touch of rejuvenation, an energy that coursed through her like the tendrils of starlight.

"We've come through," Ong's voice emerged from his weary breath, a blend of exhaustion and the fierce flames of triumph that danced in his eyes.

A gentle nod from Keisha, her lips curling into a smile that bore witness to their shared triumph. "Indeed, we have," she responded, the words laden with echoes of their shared trials and victories. "Our journey wasn't walked alone, but side by side."

A merry chuff from Pumpkin seemed to echo her sentiment. Settling by the fountain's edge, they embraced a moment of rest, a reprieve nestled in the heart of this celestial oasis. The arduous trek through shadows had tested the seams of their companionship, stretching the bonds that held them. Yet, like the crafting of a tempered blade, the fire of challenge had only refined their connection. It was here, by the fountain's tranquil pool, that their trust was tempered, their love rekindled.

As their breaths synchronized with the melody of the waters, Keisha found her heart swelling with gratitude for the benevolent hand of Kadona that had guided them to this juncture. She couldn't help but feel that their path was ordained by a more remarkable design. The fountain, an emblem of purity, was a sanctuary nestled within the shroud of darkness—a living testament to the presence of hope even when despair's veil was thickest.

Resolute as the blaze of dawn, Keisha, Ong, and Pumpkin cast themselves once more into the abyssal tapestry of the tunnels. Like the snares of destiny, entwined vines wound around their path, testing their resolve as they wove through the twisted gauntlet. Each step was an assertion of their will against the grip of adversity, a declaration that their strength was inexhaustible.

Emerging from the coils of darkness, they were met with the towering figure of the guardian, an enigma in form and purpose. Telepathic whispers brushed against their minds, questions cloaked in riddles. Pumpkin, the sentinel of their unity, responded with a growl of vigilance, an oath to protect the ones she cherished.

"Only one shall tread the Sacred Grove," the guardian's ethereal voice resonated within their consciousness, a weighty choice suspended in the air. "The other must find an end. Decide."

Keisha's eyes met Ong's, a symphony of unspoken words echoing in the depths of their gaze. Love and sacrifice entwined their hearts in a constellation of devotion. The air grew heavy with the weight of the choice, an echo of eternity's embrace.

"I choose to fade so Ong may embrace the Sacred Grove's secrets," Keisha's tender yet resolute words etched a testament to her love.

Ong's breath caught, and his resolve kindled into a blaze. "No, I cannot allow that. I shall relinquish that Keisha may find the heart of the Sacred Grove."

The guardian's sentinel gaze recognized the purity of their intent, a nod as solemn as the pages of time turning. Their passage was granted, the gatekeeper of destiny stepped aside, and the final challenge was overcome. Their love, their sacrifice, an illumination that banished the shrouds of darkness, a testament that even within the crucible of trials, the flame of devotion burned brighter.

Stepping into the sacred embrace of the Grove, a new guardian awaited—an ethereal warden of serenity and guidance. The guardian's voice, a melody spinning from the dream strands, welcomed Keisha and Ong. "Rest here, within this hallowed sanctuary," Their words flowed like a gentle stream, carrying promises of reprieve. With a sigh like a breeze, the guardian vanished, leaving only the ethereal beauty of the Grove to envelop them.

Amidst the cradle of ancient trees, Keisha and Ong found rest, their bodies and minds bearing the weight of their odyssey. In the twilight lull of anticipation, they retraced the tapestry of their journey—the shadowed paths, the choices like stars guiding their way. The stillness of the Grove seemed to echo with the rhythms of their hearts, a testament to their worthiness of Kadona's grace and the truths she held.

Within the sacred heart, Keisha and Ong's beings converged with the sanctuary, their essence in harmony. Rest became an offering, a preparation for the impending communion with the Goddess of Light. Their repose was a prelude to the wisdom that danced on the precipice of their thoughts, a solace woven from the threads of determination.

And so, within the sanctum of the Grove, Keisha and Ong rested, poised to be touched by Kadona's luminous counsel. They stood ready, guardians of their world's fate, the emissaries of light poised against the encroaching shadows that sought to dim their realm's brilliance.

In the heart of the Grove, where the susurrus of ancient trees wove whispered conversations with the gentle harmony of nature, Keisha and Ong's slumber yielded to the soft touch of awakening. The morning sun, a painter of worlds, brushed the sky with hues of gold, casting a tender glow upon the figure that graced their presence.

Kadona, the embodiment of splendor beyond mortal imagination, stood before them. Hair cascading like liquid gold, her presence flowed with the grace of waterfalls. Eyes, deep pools of azure, shimmered with the wisdom that had bloomed over countless ages. Her raiment mirrored the forest's palette, an ethereal fusion with the world she presided over—an attire woven from the threads of nature itself. Such was the ethereal vision that greeted Keisha and Ong, a presence that stirred their souls like a timeless melody.

As Kadona's steps carried her nearer, her lips curved in a serene smile that echoed the tranquil pulse of the Grove. In her wake, Pumpkin, guided by an ancient rhythm, bounded forth with gleeful meows—a dance of joy meeting the embrace of divine aura. The Goddess's hand, an embodiment of gentleness, reached out to meet Pumpkin's eager spirit, bridging the gap between realms with a single gesture—a bridge between the immense and the small, the cosmic and the earthly.

With a gentle turn of her gaze, Kadona directed her attention back to Keisha and Ong, her voice carrying the embrace of sunbeams and the whisper of a tranquil breeze. "Welcome, children of E'vahona, to this hallowed haven," her words flowed like a melodic river, their resonance brushing tenderly against the very fibers of their souls. "Your journey through trials has not been in vain, for in your valor, you have shown yourselves worthy of my counsel."

Grove responded with an awakening symphony. Trees of majestic splendor swayed in rhythmic unity, leaves humming a melody known only to the whispers of the wind. Blossoms, every hue imaginable, erupted in a vibrant spectacle, saturating the atmosphere with the heady aroma of nature's canvas.

The ground underfoot, imbued with life's pulse, embraced them with an affectionate resonance—a union between earth and soul. As clear as the truths it harbored, a brook meandered with a gentle murmur, capturing the radiant light in its fluid choreography.

"Here," Kadona's voice reverberated like an echo from the heart of time, her gaze a wellspring of understanding that reached beyond the bounds of mere existence, "lies the font of wisdom you seek. The ancient and the unborn intertwine within this sanctuary, secrets awaiting their hour to unfurl."

Once more, her hand extended—a gesture of beckoning, of invitation—and Keisha and Ong followed. Through the tapestry of enchantment, they walked, their footsteps composing verses of lore in the air. As they moved, the ambiance seemed to sing with echoes of eons past—a symphony of truths resounding with a celestial vibration while a hush of serenity enfolded them. Cradled within the Sacred Grove's embrace and guided by Kadona's benevolent presence, Keisha and Ong felt purpose stirring within their souls. The answers they sought, the enlightenment they craved, stood tantalizingly close, waiting to unfurl their revelations in this realm of mystique.

Kadona, with a turn of her gaze, directed her attention to Ong, her eyes shimmering with a depth that bridged the chasm between realms. "Ong," her voice, a cadence of celestial harmony, carried within it the appreciation of the ages, "your devotion to Keisha and the Eladrin is an accolade of unwavering loyalty. Your chosen path is paved with the stones of sacrifice, a guardian of E'vahona's hidden heart, the custodian of its veiled brilliance."

Ong's response was a nod, a beacon of his unwavering convictions. His gaze met Kadona's with uncompromising sincerity, a reflection of his commitment to his chosen course. "I have not once looked back to the world of Crystal Vale," his words unfurled a testament to his allegiance, "for E'vahona's secrets are treasures beyond measure. Its enigma is a symphony of wonders, and the Elven union's rituals are woven with enchantment threads. My heart has found its sanctuary among the Eladrin, and I shall remain a sentinel of their cause, shielding E'vahona from those who would exploit its potent grace."

Kadona's smile, a radiant blossom of approval, graced her lips, her eyes aglow with a kindling pride. "Within our hidden city, your presence has woven threads of enrichment," her voice, a cascade of starlight, carried the weight of admiration within it. "The bond that you and Keisha share is a tapestry of strength, breathing unity into the very fabric of our community. The courage you've wielded in embracing this new world and its enigmatic customs—valor deserving of my utmost esteem."

As they meandered through the Grove's enchantment, Ong was drawn into an intricate dance of connection, an ethereal waltz with the Goddess of Light. Her words, a symphony of affirmation, rekindled the torch of his purpose, a beacon to protect E'vahona's sanctuary and stand unyielding by Keisha's side. Amidst the refuge of this mystical expanse, Ong unearthed the wellspring of fortitude, an assurance that his path was veined with shared determination.

In the tranquil cradle of the Grove, Kadona's gaze, a repository of sagacity and compassion, turned to Keisha, deep blue eyes holding a trove of stories untold. "Keisha, do you know the story of your mother and father?" her question, as gentle as a whisper, shimmered like starlight.

Keisha nodded, her voice a ripple of remembrance. "I have heard fragments of their tale. My mother, Serena, a wielder of the elven bow, and my father, Eldric, a conjurer of flame with hair aflame, embarked on a love that transcended the boundaries of their worlds. Their union was consecrated in elven rites, yet their love was tested, as my father confronted a choice—much like the one Ong and I stood before—concerning E'vahona."

Kadona's nod, a gesture of understanding, painted the scene with empathy. "Indeed, Serena and Eldric journeyed the same labyrinth you have, pledging to shield our hidden city. The price of their allegiance was steep, a sacrifice paid willingly. But let me ask you, Keisha, do you deem their choice amiss?"

Keisha's gaze, a tapestry woven with gratitude and understanding, found its way to Ong—a silent acknowledgment of his significance. "No," she responded, her voice a tapestry of certainties. "My father's decision was far from wrong. Though I yearn to understand him better, his choice was a sentinel of E'vahona's sanctuary. Its preservation was a treasure transcending the confines of individual stories."

Kadona's smile bloomed like a sunbeam, embodying Keisha's wisdom and perspective. And so, beneath the arching canopy of ancient trees, they walked—a trio of souls entwined in shared purpose, their footfalls a soft cadence against the Grove's mosaic of existence. In time, Kadona's gaze circled back, the compass of her attention returning to the ones who stood at the precipice of destiny.

"Do you, perchance, have familiarity with the Guardians of E'vahona?" Kadona's inquiry danced like a silver thread through the air, a question that unfurled the scrolls of curiosity.

Keisha's nod, a gentle ripple of acknowledgment, found its response. "I've heard fragments of their legends," she admitted.

Kadona's voice, a tapestry woven with ethereal threads, unveiled the tapestry of truth. "Guardians are ordained with the sacred mantle—their charge, the cradling of our enshrouded city. They stand sentinel against those who would pluck its veiled mysteries, champions of its sanctum. And it is you both who have been chosen, embossed with E'vahona's sigil."

A weighty hush drifted upon them, an echo of destiny. Keisha and Ong exchanged glances, their gaze weaving together the threads of realization. The significance of their roles, their responsibility to keep E'vahona's heart beating in clandestine rhythm, settled upon them—an orchestration that the Grove itself seemed to hold within its verdant palm, a secret whispered on the breath of the wind.

Amidst the tranquil symphony of their surroundings, they strolled further, each footfall a note in the song of their purpose. Pumpkin, their jubilant companion, wove between them, her playful spirit a reminder that life, even in its weightiest moments, had room for joy.

Approaching Kadona, Pumpkin's spirit seemed to query, "What of me?" Laughter cascaded, a chorus shared between the three as Kadona extended her benevolent touch. Fingers met fur, an exchange of affection as words wove an explanation. "Little one," Kadona's voice, a lullaby brushed with sunlight, resonated like a whisper of secrets between realms, "your part is of utmost consequence—you stand guardian, sentry of their souls, a sentinel against the shadows."

With reverence, Kadona donned Pumpkin's neck with a golden collar, its intricate design a testament to elven artistry. Like a sprite infused with newfound magic, Pumpkin danced back to Keisha and Ong—a gesture of shared celebration. Their fingers brushed against golden strands, a tactile connection to the greater purpose they embraced.

Kadona's smile reflected their unity, echoing their vows to shield one another. And so, with their four hearts beating in shared cadence, they continued within the Grove's embrace, each step invoking the enchantment it held.

In the woven tapestry of their journey, they found themselves basking in the wellspring of knowledge and the magic that surrounded them. With each stride, the enchanting beauty of the Grove whispered a symphony of destiny, and the understanding of their role as E'vahona's defenders breathed life into their souls.

With Pumpkin's joyful spirit as their guide, they traversed the realm, carrying the mantle of Guardianship—an embodiment of their promise to the city they cherished. Bound by their shared purpose, Keisha, Ong, and Pumpkin felt the pulse of E'vahona resonate within them, a symphony of loyalty, and they stood ready to defend their secrets from the encroaching tide of darkness.

Ong's curiosity, a seeking flame, could no longer be contained. His voice, a vessel of longing, finally breached the silence. "Kadona," he began, his words dancing like wind-kissed leaves, "can you, with your boundless wisdom, unveil more of Vuarus' shadowed tale? What revelations do you possess about his evil desires?"

Kadona's visage, a portrait of tranquil wisdom, waded into somber waters as she unraveled the tapestry of history. "Vuarus, once cloaked in the name Azeron, was a star among the celestial council of dragons. His luminous potential could have heralded untold greatness, but alas, darkness coiled around his heart, a serpent's whisper that dulled his radiance. A zealous hunger for dominion eclipsed his once-gentle brilliance."

"In the beginning," Kadona's voice, a chorus of memories, carried the tale forward, "he treaded the fringes of forbidden knowledge, entwining his fate with the esoteric arts. Dark spells and incantations, like tendrils of corruption, wound around his spirit, irrevocably altering his course. He wandered into the labyrinthine alleys of isolation, severing ties with those who once cherished his presence. Friends turned to whispers, and the abyss beckoned him."

Sorrow and regret, as tangible as the caress of twilight, tinged Kadona's voice as she painted the portrait of Azeron's descent. "Despite our endeavors to rescue him from his storm, his ambition was a disruption that swallowed his whole soul. Embracing the shadows, he exiled the bonds that once knit us as kin. Friendship's tapestry, once vibrant, was torn asunder."

Kadona's voice, a vessel of memory, carried the weight of ages as she continued her chronicle. "His newfound sorcery, a reflection of his dark odyssey, became a weapon of dissonance. He sowed discord among the factions of our world, fanning flames of chaos to fuel his ascension. The scales that once balanced light and shadow now trembled under his weight as he sought to harness the very core of darkness itself."

"As history weaves onward," she narrated, her voice both bard and sage, "Vuarus was shackled, his malevolence imprisoned. Yet, the ember of his ambition smoldered, and now he has resurfaced, entwined with Phoenix, a turbulent dominion. Their designs unfurl in shadows, a symphony of impending turmoil."

Kadona's narrative ceased with those words, a curtain drawn over the chronicle. An aura of gravitas lingered, the air heavy with the weight of her revelation. Keisha and Ong exchanged glances, a silent exchange heavy with comprehending what lay ahead. Vuarus was not a mere antagonist; he manifested noble aspirations twisted by the maw of power's allure. Now, as the Guardians of E'vahona, the mantle fell upon their shoulders to counter this evil tide and safeguard the city from its impending darkness.

Keisha's inquiry, a symphony of astonishment and concern, cast a shimmer of uncertainty into the air. Her gaze, vast as the moon's reflection on a tranquil lake, sought Kadona's wisdom—an oracle in the realm of revelations. "Wait," her voice, a chorus of wonder, wove through the moment, "Are you telling us that Vuarus, once a dragon, has now become a God?" The disclosure unfurled before her like a map charting unexplored territories.

Kadona's expression, a portrait of serene empathy, softened like twilight's touch upon a sacred grove. Her response, a gentle breeze carrying secrets, embraced Keisha's inquiry with understanding. "Indeed, Keisha," her words, like a thread stitching the narrative, bound the truth, "Vuarus was once enshrouded in the form of a dragon—a being steeped in both wisdom and power, revered as a custodian of ages past. His very essence wove into the tapestry of our realm."

The tendrils of Kadona's narrative, like ivy on ancient stones, wound around their understanding. Ong, his eyes twin pools of reflection, ventured a question. "What is the extent of his powers as the God of Shadows? How formidable a foe do we face?"

Kadona's response, a ripple in the pool of knowledge, washed over them. "Vuarus, in his divine form, wields a mastery over shadows that transcends mortal understanding. His control over darkness is akin to an artist wielding a canvas—a domain where he can manipulate and shape the very fabric of shadows, concealing truth, and revealing deception. His powers extend beyond the physical realm, allowing him to traverse the boundaries between worlds and dimensions, rendering him a formidable and elusive adversary."

Ong's thoughts, like an intricate tapestry, weaved with newfound information. "And his connection to Phoenix?" His voice, a curious whisper, sought to unravel the entwined strands of their enemy's alliance.

Kadona's reply, a beacon of illumination, offered insight. "Phoenix, a realm of chaotic energies, stands as a turbulent dominion. Its inherent instability and volatility complement Vuarus' mastery over shadows. Their alliance serves to amplify his powers, providing him with the means to harness the fierce forces of Phoenix to further his evil designs. Together, they pose a threat that extends beyond the boundaries of E'vahona, endangering the very balance of the realms."

Keisha's brows furrowed as she considered the implications of this alliance. "So, they aim to disrupt not only E'vahona but also the balance of all realms connected to Phoenix?"

Kadona's solemn affirmation nod painted the canvas of their understanding. "Indeed, Keisha. Their ambitions are far-reaching, with the potential to unleash chaos that could ripple through the tapestry of existence itself. The threads of fate are intertwined, and the destinies of many worlds hang in the balance."

Ong, his determination a burning ember, spoke with resolve. "Then, as Guardians of E'vahona, it falls upon us to thwart their malevolent designs, to protect not only our hidden city but also the harmony of all realms connected to Phoenix."

Kadona's smile, a blessing etched in moonlight, graced their commitment. "Your resolve is a beacon of hope, and your purpose, is noble and true. The path ahead is fraught with trials, but your unity, guided by the light of E'vahona, will illuminate the shadows and preserve the sanctity of our realm."

As the weight of their newfound knowledge settled upon them, Keisha, Ong, and Pumpkin stood as Guardians of E'vahona, their spirits entwined with destiny's thread. The sacred Grove bore witness to their pledge, and the whispers of ancient trees echoed with the promise of their quest—their journey to safeguard their world from the encroaching darkness.

"As Kadona's words settled into the air like an ancient melody, Keisha and Ong felt the call to action reverberate within their core. Vuarus, the embodiment of darkness, was no mere adversary, but a former dragon of prodigious might, now veiled in godly garments. The burden was monumental, but their resolve, a steadfast beacon, illuminated their path. They would rise against this colossal threat, safeguarding their world from the clutches of his evil machinations.

Ong, with the demeanor of an interested and steadfast warrior, shifted his attention to Kadona. His gaze, a steady beacon amidst uncertainty, carried the weight of his query. "You spoke of Vuarus as a dragon. Yet, has he forsaken his draconic origins in his pursuit of power? Is he still bound by the form he once bore?" His voice, firm as the roots of an ancient oak, held the undertone of curiosity woven with concern.

Kadona's gaze, a wellspring of insight, softened as she met Ong's inquiry. "It is a question that lingers in the hearts of many, woven into the tapestry of his transformation," she replied, her words a delicate dance. "Vuarus's path, steeped in shadow, led him to become the harbinger of the God of Shadows."

Kadona's voice, like a whisper from ancient chronicles, wove through the air, drawing them deeper into the tale. "The purity of his dragon nature, once noble and revered, became marred by the inky tendrils of darkness. Imagine, if you will, a once-glorious tapestry with vibrant threads slowly consumed by creeping shadows. Remnants of his former form may still linger in the depths of his being, like fragments of a forgotten melody, but his essence has undergone a profound metamorphosis. It's now an intricate amalgam, a bewildering synthesis of his dragon heritage and the malevolent hostility he willingly embraced."

Keisha, her eyes now holding the weight of an epic saga, found herself amidst the labyrinthine revelation. "So," she spoke with the voice of comprehension, her words the weaver's thread stitching together the puzzle's elusive pieces, "Vuarus no longer resides within the majestic form of the dragon he once was. Instead, he embodies the evil essence of a dark God—a deity draped in shadows?" The conflicting duality of Vuarus's existence unfolded before her like a riddle in a forgotten language, waiting to be deciphered.

Kadona's nod, a ripple on the surface of an ancient river, conveyed a sense of age and wisdom etched into her ethereal shoulders. "Indeed," her response held the gravitas of eons, "your insight is keen, like a gemstone gleaming in the depths of a hidden cave. Vuarus now stands at the convergence of these disparate aspects—an enigmatic blend, fueled by an insatiable hunger for dominion. This force threatens to eclipse even his once-majestic dragon heritage."

Ong, his visage a canvas painted with worry and determination, spoke with the unwavering voice of a hero poised for the most significant quest. "Should the chance for redemption, for the rekindling of the dragon he once was, present itself, we must grasp it," his words rang out like the clarion call of a brave knight, ready to face the unknown.

Kadona, a wellspring of empathy, laid her soothing hand upon Ong's shoulder, and her touch radiated solace like the gentle caress of a comforting breeze. "Your compassion, Ong, is both a well of strength and a beacon of virtue," her voice flowed softly, like the murmurs of a serene stream. "Yet, you must fathom the depths of darkness that entwine Vuarus. The path you contemplate is fraught with thorns and shadows, and the journey ahead is daunting. Prepare yourselves for the possibility that his salvation may dwell beyond the reach of even your noblest intentions."

Keisha's steadfast and unyielding voice cut through the solemn moment, her unwavering conviction palpable as the determined roots of ancient trees. "We comprehend the gravity of this quest," she declared, her gaze unflinching, "and with resolute determination, we shall thwart his malevolence and shield our realm from its insidious taint."

Kadona's countenance, radiant as the morning sun breaking through the leaves of the ancient forest, shone with admiration for their courage. Like the warm embrace of the sunlight, a smile graced her lips. "My faith in your abilities is unwavering," she confessed, her words carrying the warmth of a hearth's fire. "Your unwavering devotion to E'vahona radiates like a beacon in the night. Assume your mantle as Guardians with grace and grit, for within your hearts. You bear the potent light to confront this impending storm."

The Sacred Grove enveloped them as they walked its ethereal pathways, a living tapestry of nature's beauty. The air was thick with purpose, and an unbreakable connection to their roles as Guardians took root in their souls, fortifying their spirits to confront the encroaching darkness that threatened their world. The journey ahead would undoubtedly be arduous, but with Kadona's guidance and unwavering resolve, they were poised to face Vuarus and unravel the veiled shadows gripping their realm.

Keisha's gaze turned to Kadona, curiosity sparking in her eyes. "May I pose one more question, Kadona?" she ventured, her voice tinged with a hint of hesitation. "Are you acquainted with a silver dragon named Talleoss? He once served under your tutelage, and his companion, Silvara, has been troubled by his prolonged absence."

Kadona regarded Keisha's inquiry with a mix of understanding and nostalgia, her expression softening as if a cherished memory had resurfaced. "Ah, Talleoss," she echoed, her voice like the delicate threads of a long-forgotten tale. "In the early days of E'vahona, he stood as a devoted silver dragon, a Guardian sworn to protect our realm. However, in keeping with the nature of all dragons, his path was not dictated by decree but guided by the rhythm of his destiny."

Keisha found solace in Kadona's words, though a lingering concern remained. "Is Talleoss's spirit still alive?" she inquired, yearning for confirmation that her worries might be alleviated.

A gentle smile graced Kadona's lips, a reassuring beacon in uncertainty. "Indeed, he lives on," she affirmed with a nod, her voice carrying the weight of assurance. "The winds of time have carried Talleoss to distant horizons beyond the embrace of E'vahona. Yet, the connection he shares with Silvara endures, a steadfast bond that transcends the boundaries of mere distance."

While not entirely dispelled, Keisha's apprehension found some relief in Kadona's words. Still, a shadow of concern lingered in her eyes as she posed another question. "But has his path been fraught with danger? Has peril befallen him?"

Kadona enveloped the Grove in a moment of contemplative silence as she chose her words carefully, her gaze resting upon Keisha with the depth of age. "In the pursuit of safeguarding and nurturing, peril often dances along the trails tread by noble hearts," she responded enigmatically. "Talleoss's journey has woven through places where shadows gather, as is the destiny of all who bear the mantle of protector. Place your trust in his resilience and understanding; he can navigate the challenges that unfurl before him."

Kadona's serene smile graced her countenance once more, a testament to her faith in their determination. "I harbor no doubt that your spirits will shine as beacons against the encroaching shadows," she responded with a soft assurance. "But remember, Guardians, that unity is your greatest strength in the face of adversity. The bond between you two, and with Pumpkin, shall be your steadfast foundation."

Keisha and Ong exchanged a knowing glance, their connection deeper than mere words could express. It was a connection forged in the crucible of their journey, a bond that transcended the mundane and embraced the extraordinary.

As they stood within the embrace of the Sacred Grove, their roles as Guardians solidified, and the weight of their destiny settled upon them like a sacred mantle. They were ready to face the challenges that lay ahead, to confront Vuarus and protect E'vahona from the looming darkness. The Grove seemed to pulse with anticipation, as if the heart of their world beat in rhythm with their resolve.

Under the solemn canopy of the Sacred Grove, Keisha and Ong absorbed Kadona's words like sacred verses, etching them into the tapestry of their souls. The wisdom of the ancient woodland and the profound connection between themselves and E'vahona's hidden heart resonated within them, strengthening their purpose.

Kadona's presence, like a guardian of time itself, stood as a testament to their role as Guardians. She radiated an aura of grace and wisdom, and they found guidance and solace in her gaze. They remained poised in the tranquil sanctuary, ready to embrace further the knowledge and blessings that the Grove and its ethereal residents had to offer.

"As Guardians, you have earned the trust and blessing of the spirits that protect this realm," Kadona's voice resounded, a gentle melody that seemed to harmonize with the very essence of the Sacred Grove. "May your journey be illuminated by the radiant beams of light and the profound depths of wisdom and may the bond between your hearts and the Grove grow ever stronger."

Kadona's words lingered in the air, their resonance igniting a fresh blaze of determination within Keisha and Ong. The road ahead stretched steep and arduous, yet they stood poised to tread it with a courageous spirit, bolstered by resolve that knew no bounds. As the sun descended, casting its golden embers across the Grove, Keisha and Ong felt an unbreakable connection unfurl between their souls and the enigmatic city of E'vahona. This relationship affirmed the sacred oath they had sworn to uphold.

A furrow etched its mark upon Ong's brow, concern manifesting in his gaze. His query emerged laden with a shadow of unease, disrupting the serene tapestry that Kadona had woven. "Kadona, do you know how Vuarus reclaimed his freedom?"

Kadona's countenance dipped into somber hues, the light in her eyes waning as she delivered her response. "His adherents, through their unwavering belief in his malevolent dominion, unearthed a means," she said, painting a chilling tableau. "As the roots of his dark influence deepened, the collective strength of their faith and rituals gnawed at the constraints that had entrapped him. Regrettably, the power of their belief became a blade that severed his chains."

A shiver coursed down the spines of Keisha and Ong as the realization took form—an unholy congregation fueled by a twisted creed, yearning to plunge the world into abyssal chaos once more.

Kadona's voice took on a gravity that matched the weight of her message, a note of caution that echoed with solemn resonance. "Bear in mind, Vuarus walks not alone. In the confinement of his captivity, he wove a web that ensnared companions, and the threads of darkness extend beyond his solitary malevolence. To stand against him, you shall require allies of your own."

A silent exchange of glances passed between Keisha and Ong, each comprehending the depth of Kadona's warning. The magnitude of their duty to safeguard E'vahona and confront Vuarus unfurled its immense wings, casting a shadow even grander than before. Nonetheless, their determination held steadfast.

"We shall rally allies to our cause and marshal every ounce of our strength to shield E'vahona," Keisha declared, the fire in her eyes ablaze with resolute purpose.

Ong's nod resounded with his unshakeable resolve. "Darkness shall not eclipse the brilliance of E'vahona's light," he affirmed.

As the night deepened, the Sacred Grove enveloped them in its protective embrace, enfolding Keisha, Ong, and Pumpkin within its tranquil heart. Amidst its embrace, they discovered solace—the serene beauty of their concealed city, their steadfast companion. The Guardians' task loomed, weighty and demanding, yet with the wisdom of the Grove as their compass and the promise of allies yet undiscovered, they stood primed to unveil the truth concealed in the enigma of Vuarus's resurgence.

Thus, within the heart of the Sacred Grove, where the silent sentinels of ancient trees stood vigil, the destiny of E'vahona and the realm beyond found their bastion—a trio of intrepid souls united by bonds of love, friendship, and an unwavering will to shield their cherished haven from the encroaching shadows.

As Ong and Keisha returned home, Ong received a message from Kadona, a whisper from the depths of their shared history. "My newest guardian, remember your pledge when you entered E'vahona before your marriage to Keisha." The message carried the weight of tradition and duty, a reminder of the sacred oath they had undertaken, and the profound destiny that now lay before them.

Chapter 11

Shadows Unveiled - The Abyssal Dominion's' Schemes

Deep within the concealed fortress of the enigmatic Abyssal Dominion, the air hung heavy with the scent of smoldering embers, mirroring Phoenix's unrestrained intensity. The dimly lit chamber flickered with eerie shadows as the fire-wielder paced restlessly. His aura, a swirling vortex of crimson and gold, mirrored the frustration within him.

Phoenix's voice thundered through the chamber, reverberating off the obsidian walls. The shadows trembled at his fury. 'Ong and Keisha should be entangled in our snares by now! Their resistance exceeds my initial estimations!'

Vuarus, an imposing figure seated upon a sinister throne carved from the essence of darkness, observed Phoenix with calculated calmness. His presence extended beyond the fortress as if he embodied the surrounding shadows. His voice, a resonant cadence that held dominion even over the storm within Phoenix's spirit, cut through the turmoil.

'Patience, Phoenix,' Vuarus uttered, his words a hypnotic melody that sought to soothe the fiery storm. 'We must not permit anger to eclipse our judgment. While Ong and Keisha possess resourcefulness, so do we. Their actions are but a thread in the larger tapestry.'"

With a deep breath, Phoenix consciously quelled the smoldering ember of fury that still burned within him. His eyes, like twin infernos, smoldered with remnants of rage. "Your words hold wisdom, Vuarus," he reluctantly conceded. Our focus should be on our ultimate objective. The shroud of darkness expands, and the domains of Afor and Vacari will inevitably bend to our dominion."

Vuarus inclined his head, satisfaction ghosting across his features. Indeed, the time has come to unveil our complete design," he said with a chilling smile. "The seeds of malevolence have been meticulously sown, and it's time for their wicked harvest."

The obsidian canopy above thickened as they conversed, darkness absorbing their sinister intentions. Their discussions wove a haunting symphony, resonating with impending doom, each word echoing in the shadowy chamber like a foreboding prophecy. The weight of their menace pressed upon the fortress's foundations, a palpable harbinger of a veiled darkness storm.

With each passing moment, Ong and Keisha's absence intensified the tension that loomed over the Abyssal Dominion's stronghold."

As the dialogue between Phoenix and Vuarus delved deeper into the intricacies of their nefarious designs, a realization took shape. With her Eladrin heritage, Keisha held the potential to unlock a strategic advantage for their sinister goals.

Vuarus, a mastermind of manipulation, voiced his insight with a sly smile that twisted the corners of his lips upward. "Perhaps it's time to refocus our efforts," he purred, his voice dripping with honeyed malevolence. "Keisha's Eladrin lineage might be a critical asset to us. If we trap her, her existence could become leverage to bend her kin to our will."

His dark eyes gleamed with wicked anticipation as his plans began to unfurl before him. The sinister atmosphere thickened as Phoenix and Vuarus discussed their dark plans for Keisha. The fortress seemed to absorb their absorbed walls echoing with the foreboding of what was to come. The shadows in the room deepened, and the air grew heavy with malice as they laid out the intricate details of their nefarious scheme.

Tainted by wicked anticipation, Phoenix's grin danced across his face like a shadowy specter. His eyes gleamed with the promise of evil triumph, and his words were laced with sadistic glee as he envisioned breaking the spirit of the Eladrin through Keisha's capture.

Vuarus, the mastermind orchestrating this sinister plot, exuded chilling confidence that seemed to stretch beyond the confines of the fortress. His nod of agreement was like a pact sealed in darkness, and his words carried the weight of authority as he outlined the strategic importance of Keisha's capture.

As they described the subterranean abyss they had prepared for Keisha, the mere thought of it sent shivers down the spine. The chamber they had fashioned was a nightmarish creation, a place where light dared not tread, and where the embrace of nature itself was severed—a true manifestation of despair and isolation."

The laughter that punctuated their discourse was a macabre symphony, a cruel counterpoint to the benevolent harmony of the Grove. It symbolized the perversion of their objectives, the depths of their malice, and the impending darkness that threatened to engulf Keisha and their world.

With each word, the malefic plan became more precise, and the impending doom loomed ever larger, setting the stage for the clash between light and shadow that would define the fate of E'vahona and its Guardians.

The members of the Abyssal Dominion, their intentions cloaked in shadows, found common ground in their sinister schemes. Keisha's capture became the linchpin of their evil plans, a pivotal step in their grand design to plunge Afor and Vacari into chaos.

Amid this diabolical assembly, a figure emerged from the shadows, stepping forward with a respectful bow. Malrik, Vuarus's chief priest, sought an audience with his dark lord. He broached a disquieting possibility with carefully chosen words—Ong and Keisha may have already obtained the texts and delivered them to the Eladrin council for interpretation.

"Suspicion took root in Phoenix's mind, his paranoia growing as he contemplated the implications. Could these mortal adversaries have outsmarted their agents and secured the texts before them?"

"Malrik, however, remained resolute in his suggestion, his tone respectful but unwavering. He acknowledged the resourcefulness of Ong and Keisha and the faltering progress of their pursuit. The notion that the texts were now in the hands of the Eladrin council lingered like a shadow."

"Vuarus's fury simmered, his countenance darkening. The possibility that the Eladrin council might decipher the texts and gain an advantage over them was unacceptable. Failure was not an option, Phoenix affirmed with renewed determination."

With steely resolve, Vuarus commanded Malrik to lead a cadre tasked with hunting down Ong and Keisha. Their escape could not be tolerated, and if the texts were indeed in their possession, they must be reclaimed at all costs.

Malrik nods solemnly, accepting the weight of his mission. 'As you command, my lord,' he pledges, 'We shall pursue them relentlessly until those texts are back in our possession.' The die is cast, and the hunt for Ong and Keisha intensifies, setting the stage for a dangerous game of cat and mouse in the shadows.

The members of the Abyssal Dominion disband once more, their minds consumed by the urgency of their newfound task. The knowledge that Ong and Keisha might have gained a lead on them stirs the air with tension, setting the stage for a race against the relentless march of time, where the fate of Afor and Vacari trembles precariously on the precipice.

Meanwhile, Thundria's encounter with the fledgling crystal dragon proves to be a fruitful source of information for the Abyssal Dominion. She wastes no time and swiftly travels to New Flameford, where Vuarus and Phoenix await her with brooding anticipation. As she enters the dimly lit chamber, her eyes shimmer with the thrill of triumph.

"'I have succeeded,' she announces with a victorious tone. 'Keisha and Ong are rumored to have sought refuge in the enigmatic city of E'vahona. However, they've also visited the sanctuary of the benevolent dragons twice since their return.'"

Phoenix's glare deepens into a fiery glint, his hands clenching in barely contained fury as he absorbs the implications. 'E'vahona, that elusive fortress,' he hisses, his irritation palpable.

Vuarus, though equally vexed, directs his concern toward a different matter. 'The fact that the Eladrin has glimpsed my secrets troubles me deeply,' he muses in a voice tinged with the promise of impending danger. 'Their presence within E'vahona may have already compromised the delicate balance of our plan.'"

Thundria nods gravely, fully aware of the severity of the situation. 'They must be dealt with swiftly to prevent any further revelations to the Eladrin council,' she suggests, her words urgent."

Phoenix's fury ignites like a wildfire, his eyes ablaze with vindictive determination. 'Indeed. We can no longer allow them free rein. Once they are within our grasp, they will regret the day they dared to cross paths with the Abyssal Dominion.'"

The evil dominion, united in their resolve, sets their sights on Ong and Keisha with renewed purpose, ready to enact their sinister designs.

Vuarus reclined on his ominous throne, a predatory smile curving his lips with sinister satisfaction. 'Very well, let the spotlight of our designs shine on E'vahona. The time has come to tighten our grip on Keisha and Ong, to weave them into the intricate tapestry of our ambitions.'"

Amidst the labyrinthine scheming of the Abyssal Dominion, the realms of Afor and Vacari remained oblivious to the brooding tempest that brewed on the horizon. Unbeknownst to the residents of these worlds, an explosive clash between light and shadow was poised to erupt, with Keisha and Ong thrust into the heart of the impending maelstrom. A tapestry of fate was weaving itself, threads of destiny entwining to unveil the enigma of veiled shadows in all their ominous magnificence.

In the concealed alcoves of the Abyssal Dominion's sinister abode, Qellaun and Lyra found a brief sanctuary, the heavy air pregnant with unspoken tensions. Their glances exchanged in secrecy spoke volumes, silently acknowledging the widening chasm that severed them from Phoenix's once unwavering allegiance. Unease festered within the members of the Dragon Council, their devotion to Phoenix faltering like a dying ember.

Lyra's words were punctuated with an undercurrent of exasperation as she hissed, her voice an evil whisper, 'I am weary of being naught but a pawn. Our prowess merits a loftier station than mere messengers for Phoenix's desires. His reliance on Vuarus has eclipsed our significance.'"

Qellaun's somber nod mirrored her sentiments. His brow furrowed, burdened by the strain of their predicament. 'Your observation holds truth,' he confessed, his voice tinged with worry. 'Phoenix's preference for Vuarus over our council's fealty has grown conspicuous. We are sent on trivial quests that hardly warrant our abilities.'"

Lyra's bitterness dripped like venom from her words, her frustration palpable. 'Deserving of more, we are. Potent and cunning, we deserve acknowledgment that extends beyond mundane errands.'"

Qellaun's sigh carried the weight of his internal struggle, torn between loyalty to the Abyssal Dominion and a burgeoning discontent. 'I comprehend your sentiments, Lyra. Yet, to sway Phoenix is no simple task, and extricating Vuarus from his confidence is a labyrinthine endeavor. The roots of trust run deep.'"

A gleam of resolve ignited Lyra's gaze, her determination alight like smoldering embers. 'Then alter the scales of power we must,' she declared fervently. 'If Vuarus's removal eludes us, securing our standing in this dominion becomes paramount. Our potent secrets are weapons to wrest control from Phoenix's grip. We shall exploit them to cement our dominance within these shadows.'"

Qellaun mulled over her proposal, aware of its risks and the consequences that could follow. Yet, the days of servitude were no longer tenable, and the hour had come to cast their influence upon the dominion's destiny.

'A perilous gambit,' he admitted reluctantly, 'but one we must undertake. We shall tread this precarious path cautiously, leveraging our knowledge to reshape our status within these darkened halls. Through careful maneuvering, we might sway the scales in our favor.'"

Thus, as they wove their stratagem, a charged atmosphere of intrigue and duplicity permeated the heart of the Abyssal Dominion. The equilibrium of supremacy teetered precariously, and in the obscure undercurrents of their manipulations, a dance of associations began, where loyalties wavered, trust was weighed, and the insatiable thirst for power guided each step down the treacherous corridors of fate.

In the majestic expanse of E'vahona's grand chamber, Lord Karrenen and the esteemed members of the Eladrin High Council convened, their presence lending an aura of wisdom and authority to the space. The chamber was a masterpiece of artistry, adorned with intricately carved motifs and glistening crystals that mirrored the depths of knowledge and might harbor within its walls.

Lord Eldrion, a venerable scholar bearing the weight of age and wisdom, broke the hush with his voice, resonating with gravitas. 'The Heart of Twilight,' an artifact of untold potency, is said to cradle both the essence of light and the shadow. Its origin, veiled in the tapestry of myth, remains a riddle that eludes our grasp.'

A solemn nod from Lady Seraphina, a paragon of grace and sagacity, affirmed his words. 'The Heart is a relic of paramount importance to our kind. Its handling necessitates prudence, for within its core lies the potential for both symphony and ruin.'"

The poised figure of Lady Isadora, youthful and keen of mind, interjected with a tinge of concern, 'But should the Heart stray into the clutches of malevolence, its very essence might disrupt Afor and Vacari's delicate equilibrium, tilting the scales towards the shadow.'"

Lord Thaldir, a venerable sage immersed in ancient lore, provided his insight, his voice a wellspring of wisdom. 'Our charge is the guardianship of the Heart, to keep it shrouded within the embrace of Coraluna's sanctuary. It is a might not to be taken lightly, veiled in its enigma, to be safeguarded from inquiring eyes.'"

The contemplative pause that followed spoke volumes, Lord Karrenen's stature as a master of arcane arts demanding thoughtfulness. 'A blade that cleaves both ways,' he mused, the gravity of his words mirrored in his tone. 'A harbinger of fortune, yet with an abyss of shadow lurking beneath. Such is the nature of the Heart.'"

Lady Elowen, adept in the diplomatic craft, her gaze shrewd, put forth the imperative. 'Our judgment must be a shared symphony, woven with prudence. In ripples shall our resolution traverse through Afor and Vacari, touching the Eladrin and every resident that graces these realms.'"

Lord Galadon, a warrior without equal whose valor was renowned, contributed his conviction. 'Unity shall be our anthem, strength our chorus. In the counsel of our forebears and the spirits of our land, may we unearth the path that lies luminous before us.'"

The sage advice found an echo in Lady Lythia's empathetic voice, a healer's touch evident. 'E'vahona's serenity is our charge to uphold. If the Heart's peril outweighs its promise, alternate roads must be ventured.'"

Lord Alaric, a strategist of unparalleled insight, issued his counsel with a tactical edge. 'Whatever our resolve, it must forge through the crucible of unity. The Heart is a testament to our vigilance, a sentinel against the backdrop of our world's fragility.'"

Lady Mirabelle, a sorceress whose eyes arcane secrets danced, concluded the council's discourse with an enigmatic murmur. 'Unveiling endless secrets, the Heart's siren call is undeniable. Let wisdom and compassion be our North Star as we navigate its seductive embrace.'" "As deliberations rippled, the fate of the Heart of Twilight poised on a precipice, a juncture where worlds teetered on the cusp of transformation. The ancient relic's weight bore the potential to weave nations' fates and inscribe history's tomes. Each member of the Eladrin High Council accepted the mantle of choice, the solemnity of their decisions entwined with the destinies of Afor, Vacari, and all that nestled beneath their guardianship. Kept ensconced within Coralune's enigmatic depths for centuries, its sovereignty protected by the merfolk's solemn pact, the Heart's destiny remained cloaked, awaiting the symphony of choices to resound."

Amid the shadowed realm where Phoenix and Vuarus conspire over the enigmatic Heart of Twilight, an unexpected interjection breaks through the scheming air. Lyra and Qellaun, with a fusion of resolve and confidence, venture forth with their proposal. 'Perhaps our skills might unveil the Heart of Twilight,' Lyra suggests, her voice poised and confident."

Vuarus's derisive chuckle reverberates, laden with skepticism. 'What could you accomplish that we have not already attempted? You lack the tomes of old that might guide you through the labyrinth.'"

Lyra's gaze sharpens with unyielding determination, and her response is, 'True, the texts elude us, yet other resources and talents lay within our grasp. The texts have thus far led you astray from the Heart's embrace, have they not?'"

Qellaun adds his voice, a counterpoint to Lyra's. 'An attempt is still valid. Our expertise in stealth and intelligence-gathering is unmatched. Into places shunned by others, we dare to tread.'" "Phoenix's intrigue surfaces as he leans back, curiosity written across his features. 'And how do you intend to embark on this endeavor?'"

Lyra and Qellaun's eyes meet in mutual understanding before they unfold their strategic draft. A plan conceived within, they propose, commencing from the heart of Coralune, whispered to be the cradle of the Heart of Twilight among the merfolk. Their journey unfolds further, aiming to unravel the ancient sea's depths for creatures bearing whispered knowledge of the coveted artifact."

Vuarus's skepticism persists, though an evil grin paints his countenance. 'Very well. Proceed on this venture but under one caveat. Should you fail to unveil the Heart of Twilight, your standing in the Abyssal Dominion shall crumble, rendering you our lowly vassals, bending at our will.'"

Lyra and Qellaun exchange a measured look, undeterred by the dire pact. 'Agreed,' their voices intertwine with unyielding conviction.

Meanwhile, as Phoenix and Vuarus muse over the idea of the Heart concealed within Coralune's depths, skepticism brims in their gazes. 'Coralune?' Phoenix's scoff carries a trace of amusement. 'Do you genuinely believe the artifact would rest where air-breathing beings can scarcely survive? Merfolk and their fables are but tales spun by imagination.'"

Vuarus's dark laughter fills the air, an echo of concurrence. 'Truly, entertaining the notion that the Heart of Twilight is ensconced beneath waves is ludicrous.

Merfolk, ensnared by whimsical legends of treasures adrift and ancient powers forgotten.'"

Yet, undeterred by their comrades' cynicism, Lyra and Qellaun hold firm, unyielding in their stance. 'Judging by appearances alone is a fallible path,' Lyra asserts, a flash of certainty igniting her eyes. 'Legends are often fragments of truth, and the merfolk have guarded their history in shadows.'"

Qellaun joins, his assertion unwavering. 'Our ways are nuanced, our strategies adaptable. If the Heart resides in Coralune's realm, we shall find a path to its embrace.'"

Phoenix rolls his eyes, dismissing their conviction as naive. 'As you wish. Chase your mirage yet heed my words – you shall return with naught.'"

Vuarus's smirk deepens. 'I await your venture into this 'mythical' pursuit with intrigue.'" "Yet, undaunted by their allies' doubt, Lyra and Qellaun set forth on their quest, unswayed by skepticism. Driven by a belief in Coralune's whispered legends, they venture into the realm of the merfolk, determined to illuminate the enigma of the Heart of Twilight. As their odyssey unfurls, they tread a precipice where conviction battles skepticism, knowing their journey could either culminate in glorious triumph or condemn them to obscurity within the folds of the Abyssal Dominion's grip."

Amidst the shadow's embrace, Phoenix and Vuarus delve into the labyrinthine discourse surrounding the elusive Heart of Twilight, contemplating its whereabouts with a tinge of intrigue. Vuarus's lips curl in a knowing smirk, his voice oozing with calculated confidence. 'Why bother sifting through the annals of a relic's past when we can wield its potency in the present? The Eladrin Council, true to their ponderous nature, shall indulge in scholarly debates and historical meanderings before even fathom the idea of pursuit.'"

Phoenix, perpetually one for rash decisions, inclines his head in accord. 'Your insight is astute. We shall surge ahead while they wade through their deliberations, laying claim to the artifact's might before their senses can even grasp its absence. The Eladrin, blindsided and enfeebled, will find themselves trailing far behind.'"

In the wake of their leaders' deliberations, Lyra and Qellaun, entrusted with a high-stakes mission, absorb each word attentively. A subtle exchange of glances between them hints at the gravity of their task, the looming potential for failure palpable. A silent pact is formed – their resolve solidified, their allegiance undivided – as they grasp the daunting challenge within the Abyssal Dominion.

Vuarus leans closer, his voice now a velvety undercurrent, tinged with malice. 'Remember, should you falter, your status in the annals of the Abyssal Dominion will crumble. Reduced to mere pawns, your worth shall dwindle into insignificance, lost and forsaken.'"

"Lyra's gaze narrows, reflecting her unyielding determination, as she replies, 'We comprehend the stakes, Vuarus. You can trust that we shall not falter. Our commitment is steadfast.'"

Thus, with their destinies irrevocably interwoven with the pursuit of the Heart of Twilight, the residents of the Abyssal Dominion set forth on their treacherous journey. The allure of supremacy drives their purpose, while the promise of unprecedented power fuels their steps.

In parallel, within the grand chamber of E'vahona, Lord Karrenen, a venerable figure of distinction, assembles his council. Their discourse revolves around the Heart's elusive location and the dire repercussions that hang in the balance should its potency fall into evil hands.

Within the hallowed halls of the Eladrin Council's chambers, a haven of serenity amidst the tumultuous currents of fate, Lord Karrenen's voice reverberates with measured wisdom. 'Our approach demands the utmost circumspection. The Heart of Twilight, a vessel brimming with unparalleled potential, is a dichotomy of blessings and curses. We cannot plunge into this odyssey blindly; understanding its lineage and capacities must precede our foray.'"

Lady Isadora, a sentinel of sagacity, inclines her head in accord. 'Indeed, to recklessly court the enigmatic unknown would court disaster. Each step must be measured against a scale of risks and benefits.'"

A harmonious nod from Lady Seraphina accompanies her words. 'The merfolk of Coralune, guardians through epochs of the Heart's enigmatic existence, embody a living testament to its lore. Their counsel, a beacon of enlightenment, should guide our course.'"

Lord Thaldir's age-etched presence brings forth mellifluous murmurs, his voice a gentle lull of contemplation. 'As our actions reverberate not solely within E'vahona's sanctum but echo throughout the very sinews of Vacari, we bear the mantle of destiny itself. We must not falter, for the relentless grasp of darkness spans horizons beyond our vision. The very essence of our realm hangs in equipoise.'"

While the Eladrin Council navigates the currents of discourse, deliberating the facets of their path, the tendrils of an unfolding epic reach across realms. Within the enclaves of the Abyssal Dominion, their members surge forward on a treacherous odyssey driven by fervent ambition. The Heart of Twilight, a luminary beacon of invincible power, ignites their pursuit, each step further entwining them within the embrace of a war that transcends the boundaries of light and shadow."

Chapter 12

Shadows Unveiled: The Heart of Twilight's Secrets

Beneath the enchanting embrace of the sea's glistening waves lay Coraluna, a realm of unfathomable wonder. Its ethereal beauty was a symphony of colors that seemed to have been woven by the hands of celestial artists. The ocean's depths held secrets painted in purples that whispered of twilight's mysteries, blues that mirrored the vast expanse above, and fiery reds that blazed like the heart of an underwater star. Every coral reef was a luminescent masterpiece, casting a spellbinding radiance that unveiled the enigmatic underwater world.

Amidst the undulating currents, a mesmerizing ballet of sea creatures unfolded. Iridescent fish, bedecked in scales that rivaled precious gems, choreographed aquatic ballets in the crystal waters. Majestic sea turtles, bearing the wisdom of eons in their ancient eyes, glided with regal grace, beholding the marvels of their liquid realm. Delicate sea anemones, like living rainbows, swayed in a tranquil dance, their tendrils reaching out in a peaceful embrace, painting the water with vibrant hues.

Glorious sea flowers blossomed within the coral gardens in an explosion of hues. The inhabitants of Coraluna, an assembly of otherworldly beings, had fashioned this hidden sanctuary into their abode. From elusive seahorses, their tails like filigree artistry, to the sublime manta rays that soared through aquatic heavens, a symphony of life orchestrated a breathtaking ballet. Among them moved the merfolk, enigmatic sentinels of the Heart of Twilight, seamlessly intertwined with the sea's splendor, their iridescent scales shimmering like reflections of the coral's luminosity.

In this veiled sanctuary, the ocean exhaled its ancient tales, carried on currents that whispered long-forgotten secrets. Coraluna was a realm woven from dreams and veiled in enigma, its essence guarded by the merfolk, sworn protectors of the Heart of Twilight, a fount of unimaginable power forever shielded from those who sought dominion.

In the profound abyss of Coraluna, where the coral tapestries glowed with the mysteries of twilight, a sovereign figure reigned with dominion over the boundless ocean expanse. Lysander, God of the Sea, held sway as a being of unparalleled majesty and enigma. His presence commanded a reverence born of deep-seated awe. To all the residents of the depths, he was both guardian and patron, his splendor rivaling the sea itself.

Towering and formidable, Lysander bore a visage touched by the shimmering iridescence of the sea's ever-shifting palette. Cascading tresses, akin to the tendrils of seaweed, were adorned with pearls and seashells, a testament to his affinity with the ocean's treasures. His eyes, profound as the ocean's abyss, captured the tranquil balance between serenity and the raw might that surged within. Within his grasp, he wielded a trident fashioned from the very coral that adorned Coraluna's expanse, each rare sea stone embedded within emanating an otherworldly luminescence, a whisper of the ocean's arcane power.

Within the mystical embrace of the undersea dominion, Lysander had chosen a mermaid whose beauty and grace outshone the pearls that adorned the ocean's depths, entrusting her with the mantle of the Heart of Twilight's guardian. Known as Nerissa, she bore a cascade of hair that seemed woven from the tapestry of the sea's most enchanting hues - purples that whispered of dusk's secrets, blues that echoed the heavens above, and teals that shimmered like the hidden mysteries of the coral enclaves. Like deep azure pools, her eyes held the ageless wisdom of an ocean that had witnessed the passage of epochs.

The ornate patterns of seashells and pearls that graced Nerissa's tail marked her as the anointed sentinel of Lysander's choosing. Draped around her neck, an amulet of delicate craftsmanship held a sea crystal that pulsed with the very essence of the Heart of Twilight's power. As she glided through the aqueous realm, her presence exuded an ethereal luminescence that turned the waters into liquid starlight, revealing the wonders concealed beneath the sea's surface. Beloved by both the denizens of the depths and her fellow merfolk, Nerissa's reputation for compassion and kindness resonated as harmoniously as the songs of the ocean. Yet, beneath her gentle demeanor, an unyielding determination was forged in the crucible of her responsibility to safeguard the Heart of Twilight. She comprehended the dual nature of its potency – a force capable of heralding salvation or cataclysmic downfall to the ocean's realm and all those who inhabited its liquid embrace. Guided by Lysander's divine wisdom, she had bound herself by an oath to keep the Heart of Twilight shrouded from prying eyes, shielding it from those who sought dominion over its unparalleled might.

In the tranquil expanse of Coraluna, the ancient relic found its sanctuary, placed under Nerissa's unwavering vigilance and the watchful gaze of the Sea God himself. Their guardianship was a pact that ensured the artifact's enigmatic secrets remained veiled, nestled far beneath the undulating waves. It remained beyond the reach of covetous hands, forever shielded from those who would exploit its boundless power.

As Nerissa's radiant form glided with ethereal grace through the shimmering tapestry of Coraluna's waters, the world around her shining in her presence, her path was intersected by a curious young merman named Kaelen. His inquisitive nature had led him to ponder the significance of the ancient artifact Nerissa so fervently safeguarded. Today, his curiosity swelled beyond containment, compelling him to approach her, his voice carrying a gentle timidity, "Nerissa, the Heart of Twilight holds an importance that kindles your unswerving dedication. Might you share its secrets with me?"

Nerissa pivoted toward Kaelen, her azure gaze reflecting the solemnity that came with ageless guardianship and the wisdom she bore, an understanding woven from the ocean's myriad stories. "Indeed, Kaelen. The Heart of Twilight is no ordinary relic. Legend whispers that it was forged by the hands of gods, an artifact that cradles the essence of twilight within its core."

Amidst the ebb and flow of their aquatic sanctuary, Nerissa took a momentary pause, her thoughts weaving the delicate threads of significance into words that could begin to encapsulate the essence of the Heart of Twilight. "The Heart of Twilight," she began, her tone holding the weight of ancient sagas, "possesses the power to sway the equilibrium between light and shadow. Within its essence lies the ability to weave the radiant tapestry of day and the enigmatic veil of night. The sun's brilliance and the moon's mysteries are but threads within its grasp. Yet, such power bears the burden of profound responsibility."

A shadow of solemnity darkened Nerissa's features as she pressed on, her words etching a more profound gravity upon her listener's heart. "Imagine, Kaelen, if the Heart were to slip into hands tainted by ambition or malevolence. The result would be a storm of catastrophe, a torrent that could engulf our realm and cascade into realms beyond. The delicate symphony of nature and its harmony could be unraveled, birthing chaos and devastation. It is a charge the gods have entrusted me with to thwart such a disastrous future from descending upon our beloved ocean and the myriad souls it cradles."

Kaelen's gaze remained riveted, his youthful countenance etched with awe and a newfound respect for the venerable artifact that had for so long rested beneath Nerissa's vigilant care. "So, it's more than a vessel of might. It's a guardian of equilibrium," he reflected, his voice laced with contemplation.

Nerissa's affirmation came with a graceful nod, a ripple of understanding passing between them. "Exactly, Kaelen. This is why it must remain veiled and shielded. Lysander, the God of the Sea, has proclaimed Coraluna the most secure haven for the Heart of Twilight, and I am humbled and honored to stand as its sentinel."

A shared comprehension dawned in Kaelen's eyes, a newfound reverence unfurling like a hidden treasure long concealed. "Thank you for unveiling its mysteries to me, Nerissa. I now grasp the weight of its guardianship."

Nerissa's smile was like the caress of a sunbeam on the ocean's surface, a warmth transcending their world's depths. She held Kaelen's gaze, gratitude etching her features. "This duty I bear, Kaelen, shall be etched upon my heart, unwavering as the tides themselves." Her words echoed with a vow, the sacred undertone of her commitment resonating through the underwater realm they called home.

In the sanctified halls of E'vahona, the resplendent Eladrin High Council gathered, drawn together to unravel the veiled enigma of the Heart of Twilight. Lord Karrenen, a figure of profound eminence, presided over the assembly, his argent tresses cascading like liquid moonlight down his regal attire.

"In the pursuit of enlightenment, I bestow upon two of our most accomplished minds the mantle of unearthing the secrets veiled by the Heart of Twilight," Lord Karrenen proclaimed, his voice a command that drew every gaze. "Lord Thaldir, your mastery of the ancient chronicles has long been the beacon of our people's knowledge. In your eternal wisdom lies the key to unlocking the esoteric passages of time."

Lord Thaldir, venerable and adorned with the map of ages etched upon his visage, inclined his head in a respectful nod. "I embrace this solemn duty, Lord Karrenen. I shall comb through the tomes of history, peering into the past to illuminate the mysteries hidden within the Heart of Twilight."

Turning his gaze to the other chosen scholar, Lord Karrenen pressed onward, "And to you, Lady Mirabelle, whose mastery of the arcane rivals the very weft of the cosmos. Your spells have woven safeguards around our realm for generations untold. It is your unique craft that shall lay bare the arcane facets of this artifact."

Lady Mirabelle, an enchantress whose eyes held the luminescence of stars and the secrets of forgotten incantations, offered a graceful nod. "Your trust, Lord Karrenen, humbles me. My sorcery shall be a torch that illuminates the arcane truths of the Heart of Twilight, revealing its hidden facets."

Throughout the assembly, the council members nodded, acknowledging the sagacity of Lord Karrenen's choices. Like veins of unwavering purpose, the determination coursing through Thaldir and Mirabelle mirrored the gravity of the task.

As the council's directive unfurled, E'vahona set forth on a voyage of enlightenment, their collective curiosity aimed at comprehending the Heart of Twilight's aura and the threads it might weave through the fates of Afor, Vacari, and their very kin. The chambers reverberated with an atmosphere of anticipation and gravity as the destiny of their realm teetered on the cusp of revelation, the pursuit of knowledge igniting in full enthusiasm.

Within the tranquil recesses of E'vahona, Lord Karrenen embarked on a quest of his own, seeking out the envoys of destiny itself - Keisha and Ong, recognizing the symphony of fate that had woven them into this tale. By the tranquil expanse of the Moonlit Fountain, where waters danced with the moon's whispers, the trio converged, their presence a harmonious echo in the sacred stillness.

"Keisha, Ong," Lord Karrenen's voice resonated like a kindled ember, warming the night air. "I have faith that you are attuned to the ripples of significance unfurling around us—the ceaseless tide of our research into the Heart of Twilight. A relic that cradles the weight of power beyond measure, a force that demands our reverence and prudence."

Keisha's affirmation was hushed yet resolute, a promise in her gaze. "Indeed, Lord Karrenen. The import of this artifact is etched upon us. We stand poised to lend our aid in the preservation of balance."

"Yet," Lord Karrenen continued, "it is not merely power enshrined within its form. The Heart of Twilight is a narrative woven through the scrolls of ages, a symphony of enigmas. As we navigate this trove of hidden knowledge, I encourage you both to extend your thoughts toward those whose presence could illuminate the path. Our alliances, the bridges we've built to other realms, could serve as the compass that guides us."

Ong's manner was pensive as he weighed the counsel, his response reflecting contemplative wisdom. "In the tapestry of our journeys, we've woven connections with diverse races. Among them, the merfolk stand united in their guardianship of the Heart of Twilight, a bond steeped in solemnity. Their insights, if shared, might light our way."

Keisha's accord danced in the rhythm of her nod, a melody of agreement. "Indeed, Ong speaks true. The merfolk's lore, an ancient echo of the sea's whisper, might hold keys to the Heart's mysteries."

A smile as ethereal as moonbeams curved Lord Karrenen's lips. "Your choices mirror understanding, for the merfolk's embrace of the Heart's legacy is as old as the tides themselves. Their counsel could be a lantern guiding us through shadowed passages."

In this moonlit rendezvous, the realms of possibility and unity converged, veiled beneath the starlit tapestry of destiny. The journey ahead held the promise of revelations and challenges yet unknown, a tale that unfolded beyond the horizon of imagination.

"Yet, shall we not entertain the prospect of uncharted alliances?" Ong's inquiry cut through the air like a blade of curiosity, his thoughts reaching beyond the familiar boundaries of their realm. "Beyond the horizons we've touched, realms unexplored hold races with unique gifts and perspectives. Should we not venture to seek their counsel and camaraderie?"

Lord Karrenen's affirmation was a spark in his eyes, a glint of approval that acknowledged the depth of Ong's insight. "Your instincts guide you wisely, Ong. The tapestry of alliances we weave could stand as our fortress against the looming tides of the Abyssal Dominion. To tread the path uncharted, forging connections with those whose hearts resonate with our cause, is a course worthy of pursuit. Together, united in purpose, we can stand resilient against the shadow that threatens to engulf Afor and Vacari."

Keisha and Ong exchanged resolute gazes, understanding the mantle of duty that now cloaked them. The weight of E'vahona's hopes and the promise of newfound bonds lay upon their shoulders. With unity as their strength and the legacy of the Heart of Twilight as their guide, they embarked on a journey that would test their determination and lead them to confront the evil specters that hungered for chaos and ruin.

As they prepared to gather the threads of destiny, the very fate of Afor and Vacari swayed on a precipice of uncertainty. The Eladrin and their burgeoning allies stood poised, ready to unveil the enigma that was the Heart of Twilight. Their resolve was a beacon of hope, a testament to the delicate equilibrium they vowed to protect against the encroaching tide of darkness.

Within the sacred chambers of E'vahona, Lord Thaldir and Lady Mirabelle were ensconced in a symphony of discourse, surrounded by tomes whose pages whispered the echoes of ancient epochs. Arcane lights bathed the repository in a mellifluous glow, a dance of enchantment that heightened the aura of their scholarly endeavor.

"This passage," Lord Thaldir's voice was as melodic as the ancient hymns, his fingers tracing the illuminated scripts with the reverence of a minstrel's touch. "It unveils the Heart of Twilight as a vessel of cosmic resonance, a confluence of celestial energies. Its essence draws from the eternal waltz between light and shadow, balancing the cosmic forces that ripple through existence."

Lady Mirabelle's nod was a constellation in motion, her eyes starlit with rapt enchantment. "And here, within these lines, a connection to the heavens is laid bare. The Heart is believed to be aligned with the stellar patterns, resonating in symphony with their cadence during celestial crescendos."

"But the heart of its purpose?" Lord Thaldir's brow furrowed, his voice a melody of contemplation. "In allegory and metaphor, the texts often cloak its intention."

Lady Mirabelle's finger, akin to the wand of an enchantress, illuminated a passage, her voice weaving the revelation. "This verse implies its role as a tether bridging worlds. A conduit through the veils that shroud our realm from others. A key to unsealing hidden portals or tapping into wellsprings of magic hitherto unknown."

"Within the contours of these chronicles, we must heed a solemn dictum," Lord Thaldir intoned, his gaze as ancient as the texts they deciphered, "that an artifact bearing such celestial might be not only a vessel of power but a ward of careful stewardship. A sentinel of wisdom that guards against its misuse, a guardian against the disruption of unwary hands."

Lady Mirabelle's agreement was a spark that kindled the chamber's air. "Indeed, Thaldir, there lies more than potential within these pages. The Heart of Twilight whispers a cautionary note. Its magic, a cascade of cosmic energy, must be approached with reverence. For the power contained within is as inconsistent as it is commanding."

As the texts yielded their secrets, revealing verses of ages long past, the enigma of the Heart of Twilight burgeoned, each revelation threading the fabric of awe and wariness that cloaked the relic.

In the tranquil embrace of Coralune's depths, Nerissa's graceful movements wove an ethereal dance through the radiant coral gardens. Each sway of her tail was a musical note in the symphony of the underwater world, a harmonious response to the pulsing energy emanating from the Heart of Twilight. The currents themselves seemed to acknowledge her presence, their gentle undulations resonating with the cosmic heartbeat of the artifact.

Nerissa's connection to the relic deepened as she glided through the coral gardens. She and the Heart of Twilight were entwined in a timeless duet, their energies harmonizing in a cosmic ballet. This sacred pact had endured through epochs, an unbroken bond between the merfolk and the artifact, bestowing upon them the precious gift of equilibrium in their submerged dominion. Nerissa's countenance exuded serenity as she fulfilled her solemn role. Like windows to the ocean's wisdom, her eyes held the weight of countless ages, a repository of knowledge passed down through generations. She was more than a guardian; she embodied the ocean's secrets, a living testament to the merfolk's dedication to preserving the balance of the Heart of Twilight.

In the quiet depths of Coralune, Nerissa's presence remained a vigilant sentinel, an ever-watchful guardian ensuring that the Heart of Twilight remained concealed from covetous hands, its cosmic power shielded from those who might seek to manipulate it for their ends. The relic's secrets were safe in her care, and the ocean's embrace cradled their shared destiny.

In the sacred halls of E'vahona, the Eladrin of the High Council delved deeper into the enigma of the Heart of Twilight, guided by the whispers of starlit prophecy and the weight of their responsibility. Unbeknownst to them, their relentless pursuit of knowledge was mirrored by the vigilant guardianship of the merfolk in Coralune. These two realms, distinct yet intricately connected by the enigmatic relic, embarked on a journey that would shape the destiny of Afor and Vacari in ways they could not yet fathom.

With their exhaustive scholarship nearing its culmination, Lord Thaldir and Lady Mirabelle recognized the urgency of convening the Eladrin High Council. This gathering of enlightened minds would become the crucible in which the new-found revelations would be shared and analyzed. The word of summons, issued by Lord Karrenen, resonated like a clarion call to stand against the encroaching shadows, a testament to the gravity of the impending revelations etched into every line.

As the council members took their designated positions within the grand chamber, they embodied the legacy of wisdom that had guided their realm through countless ages. At the forefront of this assembly stood Lord Thaldir and Lady Mirabelle, their roles as custodians of arcane and historical knowledge positioning them as the precursors of the truths they had uncovered. The atmosphere within the chamber crackled with anticipation, a palpable sense that the veils concealing understanding were about to be drawn aside, revealing the path ahead for Afor, Vacari, and the Heart of Twilight.

Within the hallowed chamber of E'vahona, the words of Lord Thaldir, Lady Mirabelle, and Lord Karrenen resonated like an intricately woven tapestry, each phrase carrying the weight of their revelations and the echoes of ages past. Their collective understanding of the Heart of Twilight had unveiled its essence as a celestial masterpiece. This vessel harnessed the essence of cosmic forces to maintain their realm's delicate balance.

As Lord Thaldir's voice unfurled, it was as if the chamber itself had become a living tapestry, its threads intertwined with the knowledge they had uncovered. The relic, they understood, was a conduit for star-kissed energies, a guardian of equilibrium in a realm defined by the interplay of light and shadow.

Lady Mirabelle's eyes mirrored their uncovered revelations, shining with the brilliance of arcane enlightenment. The Heart of Twilight was more than a mere artifact; it was a beacon in the cosmic void, anointed by the grace of constellations. It could unseal realms beyond their comprehension and tap into wellsprings of magic that transcended their realm's understanding.

Lord Karrenen, the embodiment of wisdom, contemplated the knowledge before them. He acknowledged the duality of the relic—the promise of its power and the peril it posed. The mantle of guardianship weighed heavily upon them, and the question that hung in the air was profound: How would they wield this cosmic power, and what shadows might their ambitions cast if they dared to reach for its potential?

The council members, gathered in this sanctified conclave of wisdom, felt the gravity of their responsibility pressing upon them. The Heart of Twilight held the destiny of their realm within its cosmic embrace, and the path they would choose to tread was fraught with both promise and peril.

Lord Karrenen's attention shifted like a raptor's gaze, honing in on Keisha and Ong as the council's musings continued to unfurl. The air in the chamber seemed to thicken, charged with anticipation, as their presence, a convergence of diverse narratives, stood poised to breathe life into the tapestry of secrets.

"Keisha, Ong," Lord Karrenen's voice carried the weight of anticipation, "your voices are not just welcomed; they are the very breath of life in this chamber. What vibrant colors have your journeys painted upon this ever-unfolding canvas? Share your revelations about the Heart of Twilight."

With each word, Keisha and Ong embarked on a vivid narrative journey. Their words danced with the grace of firelight on water, weaving a tale resonating through the core of the council's souls. They recounted the story of Kadona, the guardian of knowledge, and the revelation of the relic's existence. Their voices painted pictures of the ocean's depths, where Lysander and his merfolk cradled the Heart within their protective embrace.

"Kadona," Keisha intoned, "believed that the merfolk's haven would be an unyielding bulwark against any heedless claims upon the Heart. Its protection stands fortified within the ocean's depths, a citadel of elemental guardianship."

The exchange of glances among the council members was like a living tableau of gravitas. The Heart of Twilight, they knew, was no ordinary artifact; it was the fulcrum upon which destinies balanced. The weight of deliberation lay heavy upon the Eladrin High Council, for within their hands rested the power to shape or shatter realms.

As the cadence of the council meeting continued, their discourse echoed through the hallowed bounds of the chamber. The wisdom shared by Lord Thaldir, Lady Mirabelle, Keisha, and Ong now nestled within their minds as seeds of contemplation, poised to sprout into solutions, visions, and purpose. The heart of the enigma held them all enraptured, each soul ensnared by its irresistible allure and profound mystery. Allies and guardians, united by the threads of fate, gazed upon it with a shared understanding—a token of power and the deep responsibilities that came with it.

Within the chamber's intimate hush, the council members found themselves standing at the crossroads of a decision that had the potential to echo through the annals of history. Lord Karrenen's voice, like the striking of a sacred chime, heralded the beginning of the momentous journey that lay ahead.

"Esteemed colleagues," Lord Thaldir's voice resonated like an invocation, "within our grasp, we hold the luminous secret of the Heart of Twilight—a revelation that stirs the very stars in their celestial dance. Let us not underestimate the treacherous precipice upon which we now stand. The artifact's potential for upheaval is as boundless as the cosmos itself. Therefore, I propose a course of action—let us scrutinize our Alliances, reforge bonds, and embrace the unknown."

The wise words of Lady Elowen wove seamlessly into the tapestry of intent. "Indeed, Lord Thaldir. We must expand our unity web beyond the familiar threads. To quell the gathering storm, let word reach Goldmoor and Crystal Vale, ensuring their shields are ready for the impending disruption wrought by the Abyssal Dominion."

Lord Galadon, his resolve unwavering, contributed to the symphony of wisdom. "And further still, the heart of the ancient Ardinian woods beckons. The forest's arcane lineage, held by the Nymphs, could be the shield we need to safeguard the Heart of Twilight."

As the council's discussion unfolded, the air became heavy with contemplation. Amidst the discourse, Ong's curiosity surged like a swift current, prompting him to inquire, "Pray, who are these forest dwellers of Ardinia, and what enchantments do they bring to our cause?"

"With the wisdom of roots and branches intertwined, Lord Galadon replied, 'Ardinia is home to Nymphs, ethereal guardians born from the very essence of the forest. They are intricately woven into the ancient enchantments of these woods, their luminous beings pulsating in harmony with the heart of the woodlands. As protectors, they hold the ancient forest's deepest secrets, and their magic sings in harmony with the melodies of nature.'

Keisha's gaze sparkled with moonlit fascination as the word 'Nymphs' danced upon her ears. It was as if she had stumbled upon the secret notes of an age-old symphony hidden within the forest's embrace. What enigmatic wonders might the Nymphs reveal, and what ancient harmonies could she learn from their existence?

Council members nodded in unison, their expressions akin to seasoned explorers, mapping the uncharted territory that lay before them. An Alliance with the Nymphs—the guardians of nature's sanctum—was not merely a proposal but a destiny intertwined with their own. Keisha and Ong felt the tides of fate shift, beckoning them towards Ardinia to seek the Nymphs' counsel and forge a pact that could harness the very forces of nature against the shadows that loomed.

With the weight of destiny heavy upon their shoulders, the council members reached a consensus. The first course of action would be to rekindle their Alliance with Crystal Vale and Goldmoor, reinforcing their defenses against the Abyssal Dominion's impending threat. Once this foundation was secure, they would embark on their journey to Ardinia, seeking the wisdom and partnership of the Nymphs to wield the primal forces of nature against the encroaching shadows. The council's decision reverberated through the chamber, a beacon of hope in the face of uncertainty, as they prepared to face the challenges ahead to safeguard the Heart of Twilight and the delicate equilibrium of their realm."

Chapter 13

Shadows Unveiled: Glistening Goldmoor

Lord Karrenen's visage was a mosaic of contemplation, each line, and furrow etched by the weight of decisions balanced upon destiny's scale. Like ancient sapphires, his silver deep-set eyes harbored secrets and glimpses of the realms they were about to traverse. His brow, furrowed with purpose, seemed to channel the essence of Vacari itself, a realm in which every choice carried profound consequences.

"The hour cometh to chart your course," he mused, his voice resonant, like the ancient songs of Goldmoor's bards. His words carried the gravity of a realm's compass, guiding them through uncharted waters. "Goldmoor or Crystal Vale beckons—cities that hold both familiarity and allegiance, binding threads we may weave anew."

Ong, an oracle of introspection, stood beside him, his sapphire eyes as deep and reflective as the emerald depths of Emeraldwoods. He nodded in accord with the unspoken wisdom that flowed between them. "Verily, the tendrils of history embrace us in Goldsmoor's embrace. King Alex awaits our tidings, and our footprints are etched through his city's corridors."

With her lips dancing with the fleeting grace of a fae, Keisha added a touch of whimsy to the solemn moment. Her voice descended upon the air like a gentle breeze rustling through Purplefire Woods. "A trip to Goldsmoor not only mends ties but lets us tread the verdant aisle of the Purple Forest." The words spun from her lips like whispers of forgotten spells, conjuring visions of lush greenery and mystical enchantments.

Ong's smile, radiant as the noonday sun, mirrored Keisha's delight. "Aye, a sanctuary you've cherished—a cradle of memories." Their shared glances held histories, worlds birthed from chance encounters, and bonds forged in the crucible of adventure.

Lord Karrenen's approving nod sewed the tapestry of decision, his gaze like a guiding star in the night sky. "Goldsmoor it shall be. But heed, as you venture beyond E'vahona's embrace, the guardian's mantle that Kadona's wisdom grants shall wane." His words were a reminder of the delicate balance between the known and the unknown, the familiar and the uncharted.

Their nods were solemn affirmations, bearing the yoke of responsibility, the key to their kinship. "Place trust in each other," Lord Karrenen advised, his eyes alighting upon Pumpkin, guardian and steadfast friend. And thus, a trinity bound by purpose, they embarked—footfalls echoing with a sense of purpose, hearts pulsing with the rhythm of destiny. Their path unfurled before them like a road to dreams, illuminated by the radiance of their shared resolve.

The journey to Goldsmoor unfurled like an enchantment scroll, each step etching landscapes painted in magic and memory. The Purple Forest, a realm veiled in hues of amethyst and dreams, welcomed them with open arms. Keisha's heart beat in cadence with the forest's breath, each rustle of leaves and cascading waterfall a symphony to her spirit, a reminder of the ancient connection between Vacari and its inhabitants.

As the verdant tapestry enveloped them, Keisha's steps felt like a dance of destiny, a rhythm guided by the whispers of the forest's secrets. In the heart of the Purple Forest, where petals danced on the breeze and the air shimmered with enchantment, Keisha and Ong's steps spoke of a journey beyond the mundane—a journey of friendship, courage, and the pursuit of harmony. In this forest of amethyst beauty, their footfalls echoed like the heartbeats of heroes, heralding a future yet unwritten.

Yet, as their footsteps embraced the forest's heart, an unexpected revelation was unveiled—a stark divergence from its once-celestial countenance. Once iridescent and alive with an otherworldly glow, petals now bore a trace of shadow, a veiled foreboding seeping into their vivid hues. The once-merry symphony of cascading waterfalls was silenced, replaced by a haunting stillness that draped the woods like a shroud.

Keisha's movement faltered, her heartstrings tethered to the lament of the transformed woods. Here, where her memories had been a symphony of light and laughter, an elegy of somber notes now resided. Ong's touch, a gentle reassurance, weighed upon her shoulder, and their eyes converged in shared melancholy. At that glance, the gravity of their world's shift was palpable.

"It's as if time has wept upon this land," Keisha murmured, her voice a tremor of sorrow and frustration. "A lament that whispers of a world altered."

Ong's grip, sturdy and steadfast, conveyed both empathy and resolve. "We stand at the crossroads of restoration, Keisha. A testament to our Alliance, to the essence that birthed our camaraderie. We are the harbingers of the dawn, the guardians of hope."

Keisha nodded, tears lingering upon her lashes, yet within her gaze kindled an ember of unyielding determination. As Ong's arms encircled her, a shelter against the encroaching darkness, she found solace in the haven of his presence, in the sanctuary they had built together.

"Phoenix and Vuarus may seek to shroud the realm in the twilight," Ong proclaimed, his voice resolute as forged steel. "But our unity, our resilience, shall form an impenetrable shield. This forest, your sanctuary, shall flourish anew."

In those words, Keisha felt her spirit lift. She knew that once the realm was free from the darkness, Purplefire would once again become a beautiful sanctuary. Amidst the sad shadows, her memories of the Purple Forest stood as beacons of courage, whispered promises that could not be extinguished. They stood in unity, unearthing the sword of resolve, daring the darkness to encroach no further, for in their hearts, the light of Vacari still burned brightly.

Venfyr, the emerald guardian of the skies, watched keenly as Keisha, Ong, and Pumpkin ventured deeper into the mystical embrace of the Purple Forest. His thoughts flowed like the wind, bridging the chasm of space and time in swift communion. With every movement of the trio, Venfyr conveyed their every step to Vuarus, a sinister smirk curling upon his lips, foretelling the malevolent symphony that would soon unfold. The twisted alliance between the enigmatic Eladrin and the dark forces of Phoenix and Vuarus was revealed in this clandestine exchange—an intricate dance of malevolence and cunning plotting, all fueled by the unwitting steps of Keisha and her companions into the labyrinthine heart of danger.

In a realm far removed from the unfolding drama, Lyra and Qellaun wrestled with the arduous quest of unveiling the elusive sanctuary hidden within Coraluna. Their tireless pursuit was met with vexing adversity, as the ancient manuscripts holding the realm's secret were tucked away within cryptic ink. Shared glances of exasperation communicated their deepening quandary; this endeavor required more than their traditional techniques. A sense of revelation dawned upon them: a diversion from their norm was essential to conquering the mysteries woven into the fabric of Coraluna.

In the enchanting embrace of the Purple Forest, Keisha and Ong retraced the tapestry of their past encounters, each step a brushstroke in the tableau of their memories. But as their journey delved deeper, the ambiance transformed, a palpable weight encircling them. Unbeknownst to them, Lyra's dark sorcery had merged, giving birth to a sinister entity—an amalgamation of shadows and dread. This grotesque embodiment slithered through the verdant undergrowth, malevolent eyes aglow, its purpose clear: to sow terror in the hearts of the unsuspecting travelers. The vigilant companion, Pumpkin, emitted a low growl, a sentinel poised for defense.

Keisha's intuition resonated with unease, a latent warning of impending danger. Swiftly, her arcane prowess sculpted a shimmering shield, a temporary bulwark against the encroaching abyss.

Ong's practiced precision took form, an arrow drawn and released with a resounding thrum. Impact met the creature's core, an electrifying convergence of energies that ignited the air. The creature's shriek was a sonic rending as it dissolved into obsidian tendrils, its nefarious intent scattered to the winds.

Yet, concealed in the unseen depths, Phoenix observed this dramatic scene, tethered by his malevolent link with Lyra. A fierce storm brewed in his consciousness, anger and thwarted scheming to merge into a tumultuous torrent that engulfed her mind. The evil forces continued to weave their web of darkness, and the fate of Keisha and her companions hung in the balance, entangled in the threads of a sinister conspiracy.

"How dare thee to disrupt my plots, Lyra?" Phoenix's words bore the serrated edge of venom, lacing her thoughts with a maelstrom of rage. His anger simmered like a smoldering volcano, threatening to erupt violently.

Vuarus, a voice of reason and calculated foresight, interceded, his measured tone a balm to soothe the storm. "Phoenix, though our approach stumbled, let us not forget our ultimate aim. This misstep, properly finessed, could serve our ends."

Vuarus's words were a lifeline thrown into the storm, a reminder of the dark purpose that bound them together.

Phoenix's rage ebbed, quelled by Vuarus's rationality. However, as the cyclone receded, his gaze remained fixed on Lyra, an unnerving leer curving his lips, and within that expression lingered a portentous promise, the unspoken prophecy of repercussions looming, like a shadow waiting to consume the unwary.

Lyra, her disquiet concealed beneath a façade of unwavering poise, returned Phoenix's gaze with a measure of defiance. While her intent may have strayed, her spirit burned with an indomitable fire, resolute to stride the treacherous path to power, undaunted by the abyss she walked. Her eyes held the glint of a forbidden ambition, a desire to seize control of the darkness that had trapped them all, even if it meant dancing on the precipice of chaos.

Emerging from the enshrouded embrace of the Purple Forest, Keisha, Ong, and Pumpkin stepped into the pale light, their footsteps the only sound that broke the forest's silence. Like ancient sentinels, the trees silently witnessed their passage, their gnarled branches reaching out as if to offer a wordless farewell. Keisha's gaze lingered on the once-thriving foliage with a profound ache, for the verdant haven that had once provided solace now bore the stains of darkness – a mirror to the world's turmoil.

Ong's gentle yet steadfast touch drew her near, his embrace a protective barrier against the weight of their arduous journey. His presence was a soothing balm, a reminder that they were not alone in their struggle to restore Vacari to its former glory.

Pumpkin, ever the empathetic companion, sensed Keisha's emotional upheaval. With affectionate loyalty, she strode over, a warm nuzzle against her hand. The brush of her devoted tongue was a gentle reassurance, a wordless reminder that they navigated this problematic path together, a trio bound by a profound connection.

Summoning resolve from the depths of her being, Keisha exhaled a determined breath. She pivoted away from the forest that had been both sanctuary and sorrow, her gaze shifting to the horizon where Goldmoor's radiant spires beckoned like beacons of hope. The name bestowed upon the city was more than luck – the structures composing its skyline emanated a soft, luminous glow that seemed to repel the surrounding shadows.

As they neared the city, its intricate features began to crystallize. Goldmoor was an architectural marvel where aesthetics and practicality coalesced in harmonious union. Towers of grandeur pierced the sky, their facades adorned with intricate motifs that ensnared the sunlight, radiating a welcome warmth. Graceful bridges spanned the glistening rivers, connecting the city with an ethereal elegance. Bazaars teemed with life, each stall a microcosm of vibrancy, a testament to the unyielding spirit of its inhabitants.

Gazing upon the grandeur of Goldmoor, Keisha and Ong were bathed in reverential wonder. It was an awe-stark contrast to the ruins they had witnessed four years prior, evidence that the seeds of resurgence could be sown even amidst desolation. As they approached the city's gates, they carried with them the hope that their journey would not only mend the ties of allegiance but also rekindle the spirit of Vacari itself, one step at a time.

With each step toward Goldmoor, anticipation and trepidation coursed through their veins like a powerful undercurrent. The city represented a potential ally and a bastion against the encroaching Abyssal Dominion. It was where Alliances might be forged, strategies woven, and a refuge for the weary. Yet, each footfall was a stark reminder of the arduous task, the battles already fought, and the sacrifices etched into their souls.

In cadence with their determined footfalls, the journey gained an air of profundity, a tangible testament to the unwavering bond shared between Keisha, Ong, and Pumpkin. With every step, the imposing gates of Goldmoor loomed ever nearer, their radiant splendor an invitation and a challenge. These steadfast companions steeled themselves for the trials yet concealed, poised to confront the enigmas and uncertainties with an unyielding unity of purpose.

Meanwhile, within the shadow-draped depths of the Abyssal Dominion's lair, Qellaun's voice carried a sinister cadence, dripping with the honeyed satisfaction of impending malice as he unveiled his proposal to Phoenix. "My lord, I bring before you a scheme. Goldmoor's recovery unfurls an opportunity for us to wound them deeply. To target none other than Queen Jeanne herself."

Phoenix's eyes, akin to burning rubies, gleamed with curiosity, a silent invitation for Qellaun to expound further. "Continue."

With an evil smirk that danced upon his lips, Qellaun elaborated, "Allow the Shadow Wraith to ensnare Goldmoor in its tendrils of fear. A calculated act of terror meant to send a message to Queen Jeanne – a reminder of the price she extracted from us."

Vuarus, seated on his somber throne, leaned back contemplatively, his hands entwined as he weighed the suggestion's ramifications. "Revenge wielded with precision possesses a potent influence. However, we must not reveal our intentions prematurely. Subtlety and timing are crucial."

Phoenix's contemplative gaze met Vuarus's, and in that silent exchange, profound understanding passed between them. When at last he spoke, Phoenix's words were measured, laden with calculation. "Quellan, your counsel bears merit. Yet, let us temper our eagerness with strategic wisdom. The day for such measures approaches, but it must coincide with the apex of our designs."

Quellan's gaze gleamed with anticipatory hunger, yet he yielded to Phoenix's discernment. "As you command, my lord."

Vuarus, however, bore a thoughtful countenance, his eyes locked on Qellaun. The proposal had piqued his interest, yet his ambitions transcended these immediate machinations. He harbored visions that would shatter the very foundations of Afor and Vacari, and these tendrils of revenge were but one strand woven into his intricate tapestry.

With the proposition lingering in the chamber like an unspoken decree, the members of the Abyssal Dominion dispersed, each cloaked in their ambitions and secretive plots, a network of shadows veiling their impending malevolence. The stage was set for a complex dance of power and revenge, with the fate of Vacari hanging in the balance.

As Ong, Keisha, and Pumpkin strolled through the vibrant thoroughfares of Goldmoor, they found themselves enveloped in a living tapestry of life. The city's residents, adorned in colorful attire and brimming with steadfast determination, cast warm smiles and curious glances upon the trio. Amid the bustling ambiance, hope thrived as a defiant flame, pushing back against the encroaching shadows that sought dominion over the realm. Vendors lined the streets like artisans of delight, and each stall was a treasure trove of wares that whispered tales of resilience and unity.

One such vendor, an elderly sage with eyes that held the twinkle of ages past, emerged from his stall with a gracious gesture. His voice carried an air of genuine merriment as he extended a savory confection toward Pumpkin, the faithful companion. "A noble companion, indeed!" his words flourished lightheartedly. He presented a small, golden-crusted pastry with a delicate flourish, its allure heightened by the sun's tender caress. "For your loyal friend, a token of our gratitude for gracing our city."

Keisha's lips curved into a gracious smile, her eyes reflecting gratitude as she accepted the offering. "Thank you, kind sir. Pumpkin will surely relish this treat."

Pumpkin's wagging tail was a symphony of joy as she received the delectable gift, her mannerisms exuding a delicate appreciation with each dainty nibble. The vendor's eyes sparkled like ancient stars, contentment radiating as he beheld the communion of kindness, a simple gesture that spoke volumes about the resilience and generosity of Goldmoor's people.

Progressing through the bustling streets, the trio became enveloped in the city's collective spirit of camaraderie. It was a haven of solace, a sanctuary from their arduous journey and the shadows that sought dominion. Goldmoor resonated with unity, a symphony of heartbeats that resonated with their own, forging an unbreakable connection. Every step carried the weight of their mission, a determination to strengthen this bond, and to offer their aid in the city's time of need.

Each stride fostered anticipation as the palace's grandeur drew near, its towering edifice standing as a crossroads where their destinies could shift profoundly. Donned in regal armor, the palace guards bestowed a dignified nod of acknowledgment as the visitors approached, a silent affirmation of their significance. As they waited for an audience with King Alex and Queen Jeanne, their thoughts danced upon the precipice of possibilities, contemplating how their presence could intertwine with the future of Goldmoor and its cherished inhabitants. The journey had brought them to this pivotal moment, where their resolve would meet a city's resilience, and the fate of Vacari hung in the balance.

Unbeknownst to them, an ominous gift had already infiltrated the palace's sanctum – an eerie creation known as the Whispering Shadows, birthed by the nefarious hands of the Abyssal Dominion. These enigmatic phantoms wielded the power of covert espionage, able to seize fragments of conversations and transmit them to their evil architects. The trio of Ong, Keisha, and Pumpkin remained oblivious to the spectral spies lurking in the shadows, clandestinely chronicling their every utterance and gesture, the strands of their fate woven into the sinister designs of those who sought dominion.

As the trio crossed the threshold into Goldmoor's grand palace, they stepped into a transformed city—a sanctuary of tranquility that stood in stark contrast to the bustling streets they had left behind. The luxury that adorned the palace was a testament to the realm's resurgence, its intricate motifs and lavish decor speaking volumes of a land that had rekindled its magnificence after enduring years of tribulation. The air carried a refined hush in this regal domain, as if the walls held stories of past trials and future hopes.

Goldmoor's reception embraced them with the same warmth they had experienced in the streets, but the gestures took on an air of ceremonial hospitality within the palace's exquisite chambers. The sumptuous grandeur of the surroundings amplified the grace and courtesy with which they were treated. Every encounter and smile affirmed the city's resilience and triumphant restoration.

The city's vitality, rekindled through their journey, reassured the trio that Goldmoor's glow remained undimmed by the encroaching darkness. Yet, the conversations with its citizens were a stark reminder that borders or boundaries did not limit the peril posed by the Abyssal Dominion —it was a shadow that could eclipse even the brightest of realms.

After a sequence of corridors adorned with history and luxury, the trio stood before King Alex and Queen Jeanne, embodying authority and benevolence. At this moment, their expressions bridged a delicate balance between deference and determination. The significance of their mission hung in the air, an unspoken understanding that their words held the power to shape destinies. The fate of Vacari rested in this pivotal audience, a meeting of minds that would chart the course of their realm's future.

Keisha and Ong stepped forward, their voices a harmonious blend of earnestness and urgency, as they recounted their recent encounters with the sinister Phoenix and his ally, Vuarus. Their narrative was a tapestry of danger, woven with threads of caution and concern.

King Alex, however, raised his hand in a gesture of interjection, his eyes a blend of skepticism and conviction. "I value your concerns," he responded, a voice of experience and grit, "but you might overestimated Phoenix. Ambitious, though he may be, he also recognizes the limits of his endeavors. Goldmoor stands as an unwavering bastion. Our defenses are unyielding."

"Your Majesty," Keisha's words carried weight, "while we respect your stance, we must convey the gravity of the situation. Vuarus wields an arsenal of darkness—a power that directly threatens your city's safety."

Ong's voice joined the chorus, a resonance of alarm, "His command over malevolent entities is absolute. These creatures of shadows heed his every bidding, and we fear that Goldmoor's tranquility could be shattered if they are summoned."

Keisha and Ong exchanged glances, the fervor of their convictions unswayed. In tandem, they addressed the king, their words a blend of both gentleness and resolve. "Your Majesty," Keisha's tone held both steadfastness and tenderness, "permit us to divulge more. The Abyssal Dominion seeks an ancient relic—the Heart of Twilight. This artifact is rumored to possess unparalleled power. Were Phoenix and Vuarus to seize it, the repercussions would be catastrophic."

Queen Jeanne's gaze held concern as she regarded the two visitors. "And what do you propose we do?"

Keisha looked at Ong, a shared understanding passing between them. "We suggest allying, pooling our strengths to confront this threat head-on. Your city's safety is our concern; we can face any challenge together."

King Alex's gaze softened, the skepticism giving way to contemplation. He glanced at Queen Jeanne, who nodded in agreement. "We will consider your words," he finally replied.

As the trio turned to leave the palace, Keisha and Ong exchanged a quiet conversation with their eyes. They knew that their task still needed to be finished. Phoenix's influence and the looming darkness were not to be taken lightly, and they were determined to ensure Goldmoor's safety. The Alliance they sought was a lifeline for both realms, a bond that could hold back the encroaching shadows and preserve the light of hope.

In New Flameford, anger simmered within Phoenix as he brooded over how King Alex had dismissed his concerns.

Vuarus, attuned to Phoenix's emotions, shared his sentiments. "It seems King Alex needs a reminder of the power we wield," Vuarus mused, his voice dripping with a sinister tone.

Phoenix's eyes gleamed with malicious satisfaction, a dangerous fire burning within. "Indeed, a lesson in humility." The decision was swift.

The Abyssal Dominion resolved to send not one but two of their most fearsome minions to Goldmoor. The Maelstrom Serpent is a creature born of chaos and darkness, and the Shadow Wraith embodies terror. Their mission was to create a sense of urgency, without causing irreversible damage.

The two creatures were unleashed upon Goldmoor with specific instructions. The Maelstrom Serpent's power lay in its ability to manipulate the elements, causing temporary natural disruptions that would signal the Alliance's capabilities.

The Shadow Wraith, on the other hand, was a master of fear, its very presence striking terror into the hearts of those who beheld it. Its primary target was Queen Jeanne, to make her realize the gravity of the situation.

The Abyssal Dominion aimed to instill a sense of vulnerability and urgency in Goldmoor's leadership, hoping that this display would lead to reconsidering their position without causing lasting harm to the city.

As the citizens of Goldmoor went about their lives, the sudden onslaught of darkness was swift and relentless. Panic swept through the streets as the Maelstrom Serpent's tempestuous power wreaked havoc, and the Shadow Wraith cast its eerie silhouette upon the city, sowing dread and despair.

Keisha and Ong, who had stood before the king and queen just moments ago, now thrust themselves into a nightmarish scene. Their faces tightened with resolve as they watched the citizens scatter, their expressions contorted by terror and confusion. Pumpkin barked and growled, her protective instincts kicking in as she sensed the impending danger.

Keisha and Ong fought valiantly to shield the citizens from the onslaught, their movements a symphony of agility and determination. Arrows met darkness in mid-air, and magic crackled through the chaos.

Yet, the Maelstrom Serpent's sheer force and the Shadow Wraith's suffocating aura proved formidable adversaries. The very fabric of reality seemed to shiver under their evil presence. The chaos and terror escalated to a crescendo as minutes stretched into what felt like an eternity. But then, unexpectedly, the oppressive aura began to wane.

The creatures that had instilled terror in the hearts of the citizens vanished as abruptly as they had appeared, leaving behind a scene of destruction and disbelief. Amidst the swirling smoke and debris, Keisha and Ong exchanged a surprised and relieved glance. They had shielded the city from immediate devastation, but the lingering questions hung heavily. Why had the creatures retreated? What had been the true intention behind their attack?

The citizens of Goldmoor emerged cautiously from their hiding places, their faces painted with relief and trepidation. Keisha, Ong, and Pumpkin remained vigilant, their watchful eyes scanning for any lingering signs of danger. The atmosphere was thick with unease and uncertainty, the aftermath of fear still tangible.

King Alex's heart raced as he found Queen Jeanne sprawled on the floor, her face etched with indescribable terror. He rushed to her side, his voice trembling as he called her name in desperate concern. His trembling fingers brushed against her cold cheek, his emotions blending with overwhelming worry and growing fear that she might be lost in the darkness.

With a heavy heart, he beckoned Keisha and Ong back to the palace. Their footsteps reverberated through the corridor as they returned, their expressions mirroring the gravity of the situation.

Keisha's eyes widened with sympathy and urgency as she saw King Alex cradling his wife, her heart aching at the queen's vacant stare. Ong's gaze turned equally solemn, understanding their now dire straits.

Keisha knelt beside them, her hand gently touching Queen Jeanne's forehead. Ong met King Alex's gaze and offered a solemn nod, a silent understanding passing between them regarding the queen's condition.

"She's not lost," King Alex managed, his voice strained. "But she's... changed. Her visage, a mask of frozen fear."

Ong and Keisha exchanged a knowing glance. Their shared awareness was palpable. "The work of the Shadow Wraith," Ong declared, his tone tinged with simmering anger. "Its malevolent aura is a force few can withstand."

King Alex's shoulders sagged under the weight of realization. "I should have heeded your words," he confessed, his voice heavy with regret. "Taken your warning seriously."

Keisha's touch on his shoulder was a gentle reassurance amidst the turmoil. "We understand, King Alex. The power of the Abyssal Dominion is not to be trifled with."

The king exhaled a mixture of guilt and resolve, his eyes reflecting his inner turmoil. "You have Goldmoor's support. Do whatever is necessary."

Ong and Keisha shared a nod of gratitude. "We are committed to safeguarding Goldmoor," Keisha vowed.

As they turned away from the palace, the weight of their mission pressed heavily upon them. Keisha's gaze flickered back briefly, the image of King Alex carrying his afflicted wife etched into her mind. The haunting sight remained with her as they stepped out into the city, the devastation around them a stark testament to the darkness they fought. The streets sprawled before them, a canvas of chaos and despair. The once-golden city had lost its luster, tarnished by the recent onslaught. Keisha and Ong exchanged a stubborn look, a silent agreement forming about their next course of action.

As Keisha and Ong embarked on their journey toward Crystal Vale, their steps were propelled by determination and a sense of urgency. The shadows of darkness that had touched Goldmoor had only strengthened their resolve to gather allies and confront the looming menace of the Abyssal Dominion.

Crystal Vale, a city bathed in the ethereal light of crystalline formations, awaited their arrival. It was a realm known for its mystic wonders and residents' affinity for harnessing the power of crystals in their magic. In these trying times, they sought to bond with the Eladrin of Crystal Vale, hoping the realm's unique abilities and knowledge would aid them in the impending battle.

Meanwhile, in their shadow-clad sanctum, Vuarus and Phoenix reveled in the success of their calculated manipulation of the Shadow Wraith and the Maelstrom Serpent. The havoc unleashed upon Goldmoor had achieved its intended effect—sowing fear and chaos among its people. The news of King Alex's decision to ally with the Eladrin did not deter their malevolent satisfaction but fueled their determination to bring about their dark designs.

Phoenix's wicked delight was evident as he mused about the king's shaken foundation and the city's turmoil. His crimson eyes gleamed with an evil spark, mirroring the sinister contentment of his very being.

Vuarus, equally amused by the turn of events, emphasized the futility of evading the Abyssal Dominion's grasp, regardless of a realm's prosperity. Their power and influence seemed unassailable, their dominion absolute.

A messenger's arrival interrupted their gloating, bringing news of King Alex's decision to ally with the Eladrin. Phoenix's gaze bore into the messenger, and he demanded a report. The messenger conveyed the king's acknowledgment of the imminent danger and the necessity of unity.

Vuarus's laughter echoed through the chamber, a chilling sound that underscored his disdain for King Alex's belief that Alliances could shield him from their wrath.

Phoenix's dark smile and sinister satisfaction were palpable as he stated that assembling allies would not alter the inevitable course that awaited their enemies. Vuarus, with an eerie finality, declared that no matter how many allies they gathered, they could not escape the destiny woven meticulously by the Abyssal Dominion.

With these ominous words, the two evil figures solidified their intent, and their shadowy influence continued to cast a long and menacing shadow over the realms of Vacari and Afor.

Chapter 14

Shadows Unveiled: Revisiting Crystal Vale

Ong, Keisha, and their loyal companion Pumpkin pressed forward on their journey to Crystal Vale, their minds trapped by the recent upheaval that had unfolded in Goldmoor.

The weight of concern etched deeper lines onto Ong's weathered face, furrowing his brow like the rugged contours of the surrounding mountain ranges. His words flowed with a profound introspection, adding gravitas to the moment. "Could you not sense it as well? The striking intimacy of that attack, as if the tendrils of the Shadow Wraith were woven with a personal vendetta against Queen Jeanne herself."

Keisha responded with a nod, her expressive eyes becoming a mosaic of emotions that danced in the dappled sunlight filtering through the trees. "Indeed, the hostility unleashed upon Queen Jeanne felt far from arbitrary. It was as if Phoenix intended to sow terror into the very depths of her heart."

In a measured tone that mirrored the gravity of their thoughts, Ong's gaze locked onto Keisha's, and his voice carried a somber timbre. "But this raises a vexing question – how did Phoenix come to possess knowledge of our conversations with the King?"

As if a long-held secret had suddenly been unveiled, realization crashed upon Keisha's consciousness, widening her eyes in astonishment. "Unless... there was a listener within the palace's confines, a puppeteer with access to the symphony of conversations, orchestrating the dark overture for Phoenix."

Their pace slowed as if the revelation itself had weighed down their steps. Pumpkin, ever attuned to their emotional currents, raised her gaze toward them, the innocence in her eyes accentuating the moment's gravity. Ong's fingers clenched, and his words hung heavy in the air, "Lyra..."

Keisha's once-clear features now bore the shadow of concern, and her voice carried the weight of her thoughts. "Lyra, whose cunning has always been a well-known trait, yet to fathom her capable of treachery of this magnitude..."

Ong's jaw set with unyielding determination, his resolve taking on the form of the imposing mountains that bordered their path. "Caution must guide us. If she schemes against us, her machinations shall not bear fruit."

Keisha's gaze mirrored his determination, and her voice resonated with enthusiasm. "Indeed. But our vigilance must extend to all corners. We must lead in this intricate dance of allies and traitors woven by Phoenix and Vuarus."

As their journey continued, doubts and suspicions wove an intricate tapestry of shadows along their path. The certainty of their quest became crystallized: to dismantle the evil embrace of the Abyssal Dominion and unveil the treachery concealed within unexpected allies.

Meanwhile, Vuarus turned to Phoenix, a twisted smile of approval curling upon his lips like a serpent's coil. "The elegance of the Whispering Shadows, Lyra, proves to be a masterstroke. Its tendrils of terror have woven chaos with exquisite precision—a potent weapon deserving further strategic exploration."

Phoenix's eyes shimmered with malevolent satisfaction, akin to a dagger's glint in the moonlight. "Indeed, these enigmatic messengers possess untapped potential. Delve into their arcane intricacies, Lyra. Unleash their latent might."

Lyra nodded in subservient accord, her steps carrying her away from the infamous duo. Her thoughts spiraled through a labyrinth of possibilities as she retreated, a mere pawn in the orchestration of sinister symphonies. Meanwhile, Vuarus leaned in closer to Phoenix, his words a hissed counsel, "Stay vigilant, Phoenix. Ambition is a double-edged sword; it can entwine loyalty and twist it to darker paths."

Phoenix's lips unfurled into a smile born of shadows, a delight that whispered of concealed malice. "Rest assured, Vuarus. My gaze never falters from those who aspire to ascend."

With a shared understanding carved from treacherous realms, the two figures, draped in the attire of darkness, delved deeper into their unholy parley. Like architects of impending doom, they wove the threads of their malevolent tapestry while casting vigilant eyes upon the seeds of deceit and ambition lurking within their ranks. A cadence of malefic intention echoed beneath their words, casting a specter of portentous shadow over the designs of the Abyssal Dominion.

Meanwhile, as the shadows deepened and the whispers of intrigue carried through the air, Ong and Keisha walked side by side, their murmured conversation a dance of cautious words beneath the overarching canopy of Crystal Vale. Ong's voice bore the weight of his concerns, and a resonance mirrored the rustling of leaves caught in an anticipatory breeze. "Caution must weave through every thread of our discourse," he mused, the tapestry of his thoughts intertwined with apprehension. "The sanctity of Coraluna's secret and the guardianship the merfolk hold over the Heart of Twilight must be veiled from the prying gaze of the Abyssal Dominion."

Keisha's nod held a gravity that matched the looming mountains in the distance, her countenance marked with the seriousness of their task. "You speak true. To expose the depth of Coraluna's significance is to hang the realm over a chasm of peril. Our companions, too, must be made aware of the stakes."

Ong's brow furrowed, and his gaze descended with a fire that kindled resolve. "Indeed. Until our strength is honed to a blade's edge and our allies marshaled to stand beside us, the fewer souls entrusted with the secret of Coraluna, the safer our world remains. It is a fragile ember, shielded from the gusts that might unravel our labyrinthine stratagems."

Keisha's eyes met his in an unspoken bond, a covenant forged amidst the rustling leaves and murmuring streams. "Our steps must tread as lightly as moonbeams on water, ensuring that our words and confidences remain far from the hungry ears of darkness. The truth of Coraluna must slumber, awaiting the auspicious hour."

With a resolute gesture, Ong's hand clasped Keisha's briefly, a gesture of unity amidst the enigmatic landscape. "In unity, our shield is steadfast against the disruptions to come. Afor and Vacari shall find safeguard in our unwavering dedication."

Closer to the threshold of the revered Emeraldwood forest, Ong and Keisha found their discourse adopting a reflective cadence. This lyrical exchange resonated with the whispers of ancient trees and the rustle of unseen spirits. Ong's voice dipped in a nostalgic hue wove the initial thread, each word a tapestry of memory and longing, "The Emeraldwood, once an enchantment to the eyes, a spectacle that transcended the forest of mere mortals. Trees, verdant and towering, embraced the heavens, meadows sprawled like the painter's palette, adorned in a profusion of untamed wildflowers. And the streams, oh, how they wove their liquid melodies through this living tapestry."

Keisha's response, a respectful nod accompanied by a faraway gaze, mirrored Ong's sentiment. "How vividly I recollect our last expedition there, driven by the disturbances that ruptured its serenity. The forest's tranquility splintered, some of its venerable residents already beset by the touch of decay."

Ong's gaze, a vista unto the horizon of memories, unfocused as if to grasp those recollections anew, intoned, "Indeed, to witness the affliction gnawing at those ancients – once imbued with vitality – was akin to witnessing stars fade from the night sky. In those moments, the warnings of a sinister presence took root."

In an unspoken but palpable gesture, Pumpkin, their loyal confidant, eased closer, an embodiment of solidarity within their journey's labyrinthine passages. Keisha's voice unfurled like a whispered promise, "And now, we return, not only to Crystal Vale's embrace but to the heart of the Emeraldwood, where shadows have taken root."

Thus, beneath the watchful eyes of the sky and the spirits that whispered through the trees, their pact was etched into the very fabric of the land, a vow to guard Coraluna's mysteries and the Heart of Twilight from the clutches of malevolence that yearned for dominion.

Ong's voice, now a steady flame of conviction, lit the path ahead, "That beauty shall be rekindled, its resonance echoing through time. Just as the schemes of the Abyssal Dominion shall find their twilight."

Their unspoken accord, a symphony of vows and resolutions, propelled them through the verdant gateway. The Emeraldwood forest unfurled its visage before them – an intricate tableau rendered in reverence and lament. Its vibrant expanse, once a mosaic of emerald hues, bore the insidious smudges of shadow and patches of withered green. With each footfall, the whispers of yesteryear resonated with a call to arms against the looming darkness.

Serenity met tumult within the heart of the Emeraldwood as if two opposing tides clashed. From the obsidian depths emerged minions, embodiments of malevolence swathed in sinister auras, their emergence casting an ethereal pall over the once-hushed domain. But their presence paled beside the harbinger of havoc, the Maelstrom Serpent – a colossus of coils and fury, its curved form carving paths of devastation through the underbrush. In a ghastly symphony, minions and serpent conspired, their shared intent etched in chaos and ruin, a clarion call for the realm to brace against the oncoming storm.

As the intrepid trio of Ong, Keisha, and Pumpkin tread deeper into the forest's heart, their footfalls merged with the eerie symphony of rustling leaves. This susurrus spoke of unseen shadows and ominous secrets. The enchantment that once painted the woods in picturesque hues now bore an uncanny distortion, where the once-proud trees appeared like misshapen sentinels, twisted by an evil hand. The air, once kissed by tranquility, now hung heavy with the acrid tang of sinister energies.

Amid this disquiet, the presence of the Maelstrom Serpent loomed like a spectral colossus, its sinewy form a serpentine tapestry of maleficence that wound through the very essence of the forest. Each coil of its vast body spoke to an ancient power, and its eyes – twin orbs of smoldering malevolence – fixed upon its prey with an unholy gleam. Its approach was heralded by a sinister hiss, a promise of impending doom as it undulated, its immense presence a living embodiment of dread.

The trio interconnected through an unspoken understanding, exchanged fleeting glances – a code that conveyed volumes in silence. The truth was undeniable: confronting these nefarious entities in the open would be folly. With the air thickening with urgency, Ong assumed the role of a guide, leading his companions to the shelter of a nearby cave. Its entrance yawned like the maw of a sentinel, offering rest from the encroaching darkness.

The trio's footsteps echoed into the cavern's depths, swallowed by the earthy embrace as they ventured deeper. Within the sanctum of stone, Keisha's arcane prowess blossomed, a manifestation of her innate magic. With a flourish of her hands, a protective barrier, ethereal and iridescent, materialized around them, a beacon of safety amidst the gathering storm.

As the dark minions slithered nearer, propelled by the serpent's evil will, the barrier shimmered – a resolute sentinel against the encroaching tide. It withstood the dark forces' assaults, the malevolence crashing upon it like waves upon a steadfast shore.

Ong's stance, that of a seasoned archer poised for destiny's dance, was unwavering. His fingers caressed the bowstring, and he drew back and released with uncanny precision. The arrow sliced the air, seeking its mark with uncanny accuracy, and found its fateful destination – the serpent's scaled visage. A roar, a discordant symphony of pain, echoed as the serpent recoiled, momentarily undone by the sting of Ong's arrow.

Pumpkin's primal instincts flared at the forefront, her feline form a testament to her indomitable spirit. Teeth bared, eyes ablaze, she stood as a sentinel of loyalty, ready to unleash her fury upon the forces of darkness.

A spellbinding ballet of magic and resolve ensued within the cave's depths. Keisha's shield held firm against the malevolent surge, repelling the minions' advances, while Ong's arrows wove an intricate dance of death through the air. Pumpkin's unyielding presence – a ferocious guardian – repelled any who dared approach.

Just as the crescendo of conflict seemed nigh, a distant call, a brief siren's song, reached the ears of the dark forces. In a cascade of hissing, retreating scales, the Maelstrom Serpent slithered away, a phantom amidst the woods. Like shadows relinquishing their human form, its minions followed in a re-treating march. Once fraught with tension and magic, the cave reverberated with a newfound silence.

In the wake of their departure, the trio – Ong, Keisha, and Pumpkin – stood within the hallowed chamber, their breath a harmonious echo. Their shared ordeal, a convergence of wills against malevolent might, left a lingering sense of triumph in the air, resting within the hollow heart of the forest.

Though the immediacy of peril had dissipated like a storm, the encounter with the evil forces that constituted the backbone of the Abyssal Dominion had left an indelible scar. In the cavern's embrace, the trio's glances spoke volumes, a silent language of shared understanding and a consensus that their journey had yet to unfurl its concluding chapter. Resilient and steadfast, they ensconced themselves within the cave's sheltering confines, every nerve attuned to the shifting tides of darkness.

Within the heart of the Abyssal Dominion's lair, where shadows converged and malevolence festered, Vuarus and Phoenix conspired like sorcerers, or-chestrating a symphony of deceit and betrayal. Their eyes met an unspoken communion that bespoke the macabre ballet of their designs. In the wake of the Maelstrom Serpent's echoing retreat, they focused on a discourse that held the delicate weight of fate.

Observe her magic," Phoenix's voice was a languid caress of contemplation, his gaze an anchor in the abyss of his thoughts. "It has evolved, burgeoned into something unfamiliar. That shield she wove, manifesting her latent might, bore a potency hitherto unseen."

Vuarus, a maestro of manipulation, nodded with a smile that tugged at the corners of his lips, a gesture suggestive of concealed amusement. "Indeed, the chrysalis of her arcane capabilities has broken open since our last engagement."

A furrow of contemplation creased Phoenix's brow, a cavern where thoughts dwelled. "Curious, she never wove such magic during our encounter in Goldmoor."

Vuarus, in a reclining pose that hinted at a feline grace, offered a honeyed retort, "Perhaps she harbored this potency all along, a dormant wildfire awaiting the spark of knowledge and experience to enkindle it."

The realization struck Phoenix, an epiphany that etched frustration upon his visage. His clenched fist spoke of unresolved vexation. "She's progressing rapidly."

Vuarus's laughter danced like candle flames flickering, soft, and sinister. "Aye, her ascent in the arcane arts is swift indeed. A testament to her inherent strength."

A sinister glint kindled within Phoenix's gaze, a spark that signaled an emerging scheme. "When she's in our grasp, we shall ensure her mastery bends to our will. Her power shall be harnessed solely for our ends."

Vuarus, the mastermind orchestrating dark symphonies, acknowledged with a nod a pact between them woven in shadows. "Keisha's magic will no longer serve her once she is our captive. We will take her magic from her."

The pact between Phoenix and Vuarus deepened in this chilling communion, their sinister aspirations solidifying with a steel resolve. As they plied their nefarious arts, the tendrils of their evil intentions intertwined, casting elongated shadows over the future. The echoes of their foreboding dominion lingered like a lament, a harbinger of dark tides awaiting release.

"Escape this place, we must," Ong's voice bore a cadence of urgency, resonating like a call to arms amidst the tumultuous encounter with the disgusting denizens of the Emeraldwood Forest. His gaze swept over the aftermath, a canvas of chaos painted with dark hues. "To Crystal Vale, before these unholy creatures reclaim the field."

Keisha's nod was a semaphore of determination, a silent accord amidst the lingering tremors of unease—step by step. They advanced, each footfall a tribute to their unwavering spirit. The distance unfurled, like a tapestry of fate threading its design toward the horizon where the beacon of Crystal Vale once shone. Yet, what they encountered deviated from the sincere hope that had taken root.

The aftermath of desolation stood before them, a tableau of destruction etched across what was once the vibrant heart of Crystal Vale. Towers that once kissed the heavens now lay prostrate, gardens of opulent flora mangled tapestries of ruin. Smoke still swirled in tendrils from the remnants of homes that had been reduced to ash. Ong's soul echoed the fallen city's lament.

"How... how could this darkness descend with such velocity?" The murmur danced on Ong's lips, a sonnet of disbelief and sorrow in equal measure, a symphony of heartache.

In the shared space between turmoil and fortitude, Keisha's hand found solace in his, a touch that conveyed both reassurance and unity. "The Abyssal Dominion's insidious touch spreads as ravenous flames, consuming all in its path. But we shall not stand as spectators, Ong. This shadow will recede."

Their gazes entwined, a dialogue inscribed upon the silent canvas of understanding. Their journey had borne trials aplenty, but the stakes were unprecedented, the threads of their choices interweaving with the very fabric of their realm.

Keisha's embrace, a sanctuary amidst the chaos, pulled Ong from the precipice of his contemplations. "Phoenix and Vuarus shall not triumph," her voice was a whispered vow, unwavering as a lighthouse against the storm. "Their dominion shall be thwarted. Crystal Vale shall know light again."

In the dance of affirmation, Ong's nod was a solemn oath, shoulders bearing the mantle of destiny. With Pumpkin, their faithful companion, as their sentinel, they pressed on toward Crystal Vale, where adversity and uncertainty converged like rivers destined to meet. They stood at the vanguard, fortified by an unbreakable bond, a resolute bastion against the encroaching tide of darkness.

In their unity, the trio moved forward, resolute and indomitable. The whispers of the wind carried their silent resolve, a promise woven into the tapestry of their hearts. In the face of adversity, their unity burgeoned, a beacon illuminating the path ahead, igniting the flames of their resolve to safeguard their home, loved ones, and the fragile tapestry of existence.

Through the time-worn gates of Crystal Vale, they strode Ong and Keisha, their footsteps laden with the weight of witnessing the unbridled devastation that had cast its somber veil upon the once-thriving city. Where vibrant buildings once kissed the sky now lay ruins as haunting remnants. The streets, once lively thoroughfares, bore the scars of upheaval. The air held the echoes of loss, an unspoken elegy for the city's former glory. Their eyes met in a shared glance, a mutual exchange of grief and resolute purpose, a silent affirmation of the immense task ahead. Even amidst the wreckage, their resolve stood unyielding – they would restore Crystal Vale to its former splendor.

Like a solitary beacon amidst turbulent seas, the palace's imposing façade symbolized unwavering hope amid the engulfing chaos. As they approached, a guardian of the realm emerged, his countenance a canvas painted with urgency. His voice, a timbre laced with respect, cut through the air, "King Manard awaits your presence," his words held a note of gravitas as if the winds of fate whispered secrets to him. "He has been expecting you."

Their nods of assent were the only reply needed, a tacit agreement to heed the summons of a realm in dire straits. The warrior led them through corridors steeped in history, a journey that seemed both ethereal and ephemeral until they arrived at a chamber – a sanctuary veiled in solemnity. The juxtaposition of grandeur and grief was palpable within its confines, as if the walls absorbed the sorrow that lingered in the air.

Seated at a table, King Manard's gaze, wearied by the burdens of rulership and sorrow, lifted to meet theirs. The warmth of familiarity mingled with the gravity of circumstance as he spoke, his words carrying a symphony of emotions, "To see you both alive is a rest amidst the tempest," a sigh of relief intermingled with the tendrils of sorrow wrapped around his voice.

As the trio gathered in this sanctuary, insulated from the world's gaze, King Manard's gaze spoke of a city in mourning. His eyes, like twin pools of reflection, held the collective anguish of his people. Every furrow etched into his brow was a testament to his weight. In a calm voice, as if confiding in kindred spirits, he articulated the anguish that lay heavy upon his heart, "Our losses are insurmountable – homes, lives, and the very tapestry of hope that once wove this land."

Ong and Keisha listened, their hearts echoing the cadence of sorrow that threaded through his words. When King Manard's voice eventually fell into the embrace of silence, Ong's voice ventured forth, a conduit of empathy and resolve. "Your

Majesty, Goldmoor bears the scars of the Dominion's wrath. Their intent is clear – to fray the strands of our realms before the final blow."

The monarch's gaze met theirs, and within that gaze ignited a glimmer of hope, a beacon in the darkness. "What course of action do you propose?" he inquired, urgently threading his tone.

A shared glance passed between Ong and Keisha, an unspoken understanding of their intention. Keisha, her breath a measured sigh, initiated the revelation, choosing her words as carefully as one might tend to a fragile flame. "In our pursuit to counter the Dominion's forces, we have come across knowledge of a relic – the Heart of Twilight. It wields ancient and immense power, and it is this artifact they seek. We believe it to be a pivotal piece in their designs."

In this quiet chamber, veiled by history's embrace, the cogs of destiny continued to turn. A new chapter unfurled, heralded by whispers of power and the echo of choices that resonated across realms.

King Manard's regal brow furrowed as he delved into contemplation. "The Heart of Twilight... a name whispered in the tapestries of lore, its essence shrouded in enigma, a symphony of secrets that eludes our grasp."

Ong, a sentinel of wisdom, nodded in solemn agreement. "The whispers have reached far and wide. They speak of its profound power, the capacity to mold the threads of fate, to wield the very currents of balance."

The king's gaze turned introspective, like a seer peering into veiled destinies. "Yet, where does this relic rest, concealed from prying eyes?"

Keisha's gaze, relentless and unyielding, held the weight of knowledge. "Its sanctuary remains known to the chosen few, a secret safeguarded by silence. Its whereabouts must remain veiled, lest the shadows sniff the trail."

The monarch's visage, a tableau of steadfast resolve, chiseled his thoughts into form. "To safeguard our realms, I pledge my support to this endeavor."

The resonance of unity was palpable, an undercurrent of shared purpose that surged through the chamber. No longer were Keisha and Ong alone in this formidable conflict – the mantle of Crystal Vale's strength bolstered their cause. The Alliance they wove was a cornerstone for the trials that lay ahead.

Amidst strategies and Alliances forged in the crucible of discussion, unbeknownst to them, the twisted tendrils of shadows wove a parallel narrative.

Shrouded in the umbral recesses of unknown intentions, an observer watched their every utterance, a puppeteer's strings poised for manipulation.

"Keisha, Ong," King Manard's voice resurfaced, laden with concern as he ventured into darker territories. "Whispers carry unsettling tales of the unholy pact between Phoenix and Vuarus. A partnership where prices are steep, bargains sealed in darkness. Do you, perchance, know the weight of that price?"

Ong, his expression a mirror of the gravity within the room, shared a silent communication with Keisha. His voice emerged as a timbre of solemnity, his words echoing like a lament of revelation. "Your Majesty, it is with gravest concern that we inform you that Vuarus demanded the annihilation of Kadona, the guardian of E'vahona, as his toll for marching alongside Phoenix."

The king's countenance, a storm of emotions, shifted from contemplation to stormy realization. His jaw was set in stone, and his eyes darkened like clouds veiling the moon's radiance. "The downfall of Kadona a price weighty enough to tip the scales of fate. But what desires of Vuarus could this price satisfy?"

Keisha's eyes narrowed, her thoughts forming a tapestry of calculation. "We surmise that Vuarus sees Kadona as a pillar of strength, a beacon of influence that dominates the Eladrin. By dismantling her, Vuarus would sow the seeds of turmoil, leaving our defenses fractured and feeble – a fertile ground for the harvest of the Dark Dominion's ambitions."

The monarch's gaze gleamed with the kindling of resolve, his voice a steel-edged blade. "This dominion, this bond is woven in shadow and deceit, cannot be allowed to thrive. With Kadona's fall, E'vahona's stability trembles, and the specter of darkness looms over Vacari's realm."

A collective understanding was forged in the chamber's sanctuary as destiny's threads intertwined. The echoes of their conversation lingered like the strains of a haunting melody, a prelude to the symphony of conflict awaited.

We are not blind to the peril, Your Majesty," Ong's voice resonated like the steady beat of a war drum. "Our determination is unshakable – we stand united to thwart their nefarious designs. With the strength of our allies, the Dark Dominions shall crumble, and their reign of terror shall be defeated."

Unbeknownst to them, their words were like ethereal notes carried by the wind, wafting beyond the boundaries of their dialogue into the enigmatic tapestry of forces that wove destinies beyond their ken.

Vuarus and Phoenix shared a furtive glance in the shadows of their machinations – an exchange that painted surprise upon their visages, an intricate dance of pretense. Phoenix's lips curved an embodiment of sly amusement, his eyes narrowing as he parsed the implications of the revelation that Ong and Keisha possessed.

"Well, well," Phoenix's voice, akin to liquid silver, dripped with calculated intrigue. "Our foes harbor more insight than we accorded them. There's a touch of intelligence behind those resolute eyes."

Vuarus, the orchestrator of shadows, leaned back, his fingers forming an intricate lattice. "Indeed. Yet, they tread upon the surface, unaware of the depths that my motivations plummet."

The incandescence of Phoenix's gaze danced with curiosity. "And what sentiments lie beneath your motivations, Vuarus?"

Leaning in, Vuarus's voice dropped to an intimate hush, a whisper woven with secrets. "The removal of Kadona is a solitary thread in the grand tapestry I unfurl. The fall of the Eladrin guardian would fray the edges of their unity, but the currents run deeper still."

Phoenix's intrigue unfurled like a raven's wing, ink-black and elegant. "Share your thoughts, Vuarus. What fragments of the puzzle elude our view?"

A smile, beguiling and malevolent, curled upon Vuarus's lips. "Know this, Phoenix – the Eladrin realm, E'vahona, is a fragile lattice spun of magic, power, and age-old pacts. By tearing those threads asunder, their realm shall falter, and the echo of their submission will resound throughout the realm."

Phoenix's eyes gleamed with a sinister gleefulness, like fire licking at the edges of parchment. "A masterful gambit, Vuarus. A symphony of manipulation and strategy. I tried to find the location of E'vahona once before, but this time, we will succeed. I want E'vahona!"

Amid shadow and secrecy, their discourse carved ripples through the fabric of destiny. Unseen forces, like specters of intrigue, conspired to advance pieces on the cosmic chessboard. A tale of heroes and malevolence unfolded – one where even knowledge and insight danced upon the strings of fate, their purpose a chord in the grand symphony of the unknown.

Vuarus's laughter was a subtle melody, weaving through the air like an echo from the depths of darkness. "A symphony of genius indeed, my dear Phoenix. But for now, let us allow them to waltz within the realm of illusions, believing their strategies to be a masterstroke. When the moment aligns with the stars, their realm shall crumble, leaving them to grasp at the remnants of their shattered defenses."

Phoenix's smile was predatory, gleaming like a blade's edge. "Let them dance upon the threads of their delusions while we compose their downfall, note by note."

In tacit concord, Vuarus and Phoenix turned their focus to the tendrils of shadows that ensconced them, preparing to entwine destinies in ways that Ong, Keisha, and their compatriots could scarcely fathom. The proscenium was in place, the players poised at the precipice, every movement leading inevitably to a final, explosive crescendo.

As they met the sovereign's eyes, gratitude radiated from Keisha and Ong, woven into their gazes. "Your Majesty, your support and the Alliance you offer are invaluable," Keisha conveyed, her voice laden with gratitude.

A regal nod of affirmation graced King Manard's countenance, an amalgamation of conviction and optimism. "Our realms have endured the crucible of suffering, yet united, we shall stand firm against the abyss that hungers for our lands."

"We shall not falter," Ong's declaration held the tenacity of unyielding iron, his gaze unwavering.

As they rose from their seats, an exchange of parting words echoed between the trio and King Manard, an unspoken harmony they now forged under the banner of shared purpose. The chamber, the palace, Crystal Vale itself – they receded into the annals of memory as the group ventured forth. Each stride brought them nearer to the zenith of their objective.

Beyond the city gates, Ong turned to Keisha, his demeanor pensive. "Our next destination should be E'vahona. The council must be informed about the events in Goldmoor and our accord with King Manard."

Keisha's agreement was a testament to their synergy. "Perhaps within the council's chambers, we shall unearth knowledge of allies that may march beside us in this impending battle."

Their path stretched before them, a tapestry of uncertainty woven with threads of peril and hope. With each step, their thoughts traversed the maze of forthcoming challenges. The murmur of the forest, a symphony of whispers, seemed to reverberate with their resolve – a subtle reminder that their journey was not solitary.

E'vahona beckoned from the horizon, and an unspoken covenant was sealed in the exchange of glances between Ong and Keisha. The road ahead held dangers, sharp as thorns, yet their spirits were undaunted. They strode forth their hearts aflame with an unquenchable determination, committed to safeguarding their realms and unveiling the shrouded machinations of the Dark Dominion.

Chapter 15

Shadows Unveiled: Veiled Afflictions

Back within the sanctuary of E'vahona, Ong and Keisha embraced familiarity after their tumultuous exploits. The moon, a celestial sentinel, adorned the heavens with its argent radiance, casting a silvery caress over the Eladrin city. They tread through the labyrinthine streets in the gentle glow of its ethereal light, their steps weaving an intricate choreography guided by the night's embrace. The late hour had painted the surroundings in a symphony of muted hues, and the city responded in kind by adorning itself with myriad luminous threads. These threads created a tapestry of soft luminescence, transforming E'vahona into a realm that transcended the earthly plane.

Ong's voice, an embodiment of both relief and the weariness of battles fought, found resonance in the night's tranquility. "I am glad we are home," he mused, his eyes flitting to Keisha, his beautiful wife by his side – weary yet resolute.

Keisha nodded, the soft crescent of her lips etching a fleeting smile. "Indeed, a haven where our words can weave without fear of eavesdroppers."

Crossing the threshold of their home, tranquility lingered like an old friend, wrapping its comforting arms around them and gently easing away the remnants of tension. Preceding them, Pumpkin – a graceful embodiment of loyalty – settled with a passive stretch and a contented rumble, the panther's presence a soothing melody.

Her fingers wove through Pumpkin's sleek fur, and Keisha addressed the feline with a hushed endearment. "You too, dear friend, have journeyed through the shadows."

Perched upon a nearby chair, Ong exhaled a sigh of satisfaction. "Lyra has become a puppeteer of shadow, her strings deftly tangled in this tapestry. That she could relay our conversations to Phoenix speaks of her cunning and treacherous allegiance."

Keisha's features, a canvas of contemplation, bore the weight of concern. "The knowledge that every whisper is intercepted is disquieting. Yet, it signals they perceive our actions as a threat."

As the night embraced them and the embers of the hearth flickered in a quiet cadence, their words became a ritual of recounting – a ritual that transformed the room into a sanctum of revelation. The trials and tribulations of the days shared voice, a symposium of minds navigating the enigmatic currents of fate. And amidst their dialogue, the topic pirouetted towards the enigmatic Shadow Wraiths, the clue of their association with Kadona's fall taking root.

"Do you envision a possibility," Keisha's thoughts wandered like ephemeral whispers, "that the Shadow Wraiths could be wielded as weapons against Kadona?"

Ong's countenance shaded with contemplation, a cloud passing over the moon. "A shadow of doubt looms. If even a sovereign like Queen Jeanne could be trapped by their terror, Kadona, formidable though she is, might not be impervious to their touch."

"Indeed," Keisha's voice resonated with a melancholic undertone. "The preservation of Kadona's shield becomes a crucial stratagem. She stands as one of E'vahona's stalwart guardians." Ong's agreement held the gravity of a solemn vow. "Let this night embrace us, then.

Tomorrow, we shall face the council and lay bare the tapestry of our revelations."

Keisha acknowledged his suggestion with a nod, the tendrils of weariness inching into her bones. "A rest well earned. We tread a path of challenges, and our steps must be sure."

Harmony found them as they surrendered to the sanctuary of rest, E'vahona enfolding them within its mystical aegis. Unbeknownst to them, the loom of destiny continued to weave as shadows converged to carve their next chapter.

They slumbered in the cocoon of night, embracing dreams as ephemeral as moonlight. And with the dawn's tender caress, Ong and Keisha arose, their spirits invigorated, ready to face the sunlit canvas of a new day adorned in hues of gold and rose. Their journey had not waned; it had only gathered further momentum.

The ensuing day unfolded like a tapestry of intent. Ong and Keisha headed toward the heart of E'vahona, the city resonating with a symphony of purpose, its winding avenues ushering them to the sanctum of Eladrin power. The council chambers, a realm of opulent elegance, welcomed them. Lord Karrenen, the council's venerable presence, acknowledged them with a nod steeped in somber empathy.

"Ong, Keisha," Lord Karrenen's voice held the wisdom of ages and the resolve of leaders who grappled with dire truths. "Your return has not gone unnoticed. The council stands ready to hear of your trials and revelations."

Keisha's response bore a blend of appreciation and readiness. "We are grateful for this audience, Lord Karrenen. Our quest bears the weight of our realms' future."

Lord Karrenen's visage bore the lines of sage concern. "The council's gathering is a tapestry of intentions. The discussion awaits, but I suggest you find rest in the interlude. Your fortitude is a beacon in these trying times, and E'vahona is your shield and sword."

With the council's blessings resonating in their hearts, Ong and Keisha navigated the hallowed streets of E'vahona. As they retreated, the city whispered its assurances, a silent pact between realms and the champions who stood as their guardians.

With a glance that held a wealth of unspoken understanding, Ong and Keisha responded to Lord Karrenen. "Your counsel is valued," Ong conveyed, his words laced with respect. "After the trials, we've endured, the prospect of rest is indeed welcomed."

Lord Karrenen's presence receded like a guardian spirit, leaving the duo to contemplate the forthcoming council meeting that loomed like a crossroads. As the council's intentions hung in the air, Ong and Keisha emerged from the chamber, embracing a rare moment of stillness amidst the disruption of their lives.

"Rest sounds like a gift," Keisha mused, her voice carrying the weight of their endeavors. Ong's hand found hers, a silent reassurance of their unity in uncertainty. "Before we return, what do we say we find solace in E'vahona's gardens? Amidst the petals and whispers of nature, we might discover the serenity we seek."

Keisha's eyes sparkled with appreciation, mirroring the promise of their upcoming rest. "That's a wonderful idea."

Thus, they departed the council chambers, temporarily liberated from their responsibilities. Their steps carried them to the sanctuary of E'vahona's gardens, a realm where time seemed to slow, and the burdens of their quest could be momentarily set aside. In this sanctuary of blooms and tranquility, Ong and Keisha found a haven that embraced them, a space where the troubles of their world could pause, if only for a while.

Beneath the morning sun's gentle caress, they ventured toward the heart of E'vahona, where the sprawling gardens unfolded like an artist's masterpiece. A symphony of colors and fragrances greeted them as they entered, and the delicate music of trickling streams serenaded their senses. Towering trees adorned with leaves that shimmered in many hues created a cathedral of nature's splendor, the essence of Eladrin craftsmanship.

Keisha's eyes widened in wonder, the garden's beauty leaving her breathless. "Ong, it's like stepping into a dream," she whispered, her voice touched by reverence.

Ong's smile held the warmth of shared memories. "The gardens have always held a special place in E'vahona, a refuge for the soul."

Hand in hand, they wandered the winding paths, surrounded by a tapestry of blossoms that seemed to dance harmoniously with the wind's gentle caresses. Crystal-clear streams meandered through the garden, forming shimmering pools mirroring the flora's vibrant palette. Their journey led them to a grand tree, its branches an invitation to seek shade and contemplation.

Seated upon the verdant grass, Ong's gaze met Keisha's. "Here, amidst this tranquil symphony, we can momentarily release the weight of our burdens."

Keisha's smile was gratitude, a fleeting moment of peace in her eyes. "You've found a haven within E'vahona's embrace, Ong, and now we share it."

In the haven of nature's grace, Ong and Keisha lingered, allowing the garden's serenity to envelop them. Amidst the blooms and the whispers of leaves, they found solace, a rest before the storm that awaited them beyond the garden's tranquil borders.

In the enchanting haven of E'vahona's gardens, Pumpkin, the spirited companion, danced amidst the blooms with a vitality that seemed to infuse the air. Her ebony coat shone like polished obsidian beneath the sun's caress as she pursued a nimble squirrel, her lithely coordinated movements displaying raw grace. Ong and Keisha, observers of her exuberant ballet, couldn't help but be enchanted by her infectious joy, finding solace in her unadulterated delight.

Ong's gaze shifted toward Keisha, softened by the playfulness before them. "Amid shadows and uncertainties, these moments remind me of the essence we safeguard."

Keisha's eyes met his, mirroring the depth of his sentiment. "Our realm's essence, the promise of a better tomorrow – they're causes that render every struggle meaningful."

As if to underscore their connection, Ong leaned in, his lips brushing against Keisha's in a gesture that transcended words. In that fleeting kiss, the world seemed to dissolve, leaving only the intertwining of their souls and the garden's tranquility. Their closeness lingered as he embraced her, exuding security and tenderness. Together, they observed Pumpkin's triumphant return and tail aloft like a banner of victory.

Ong declared, his voice unwavering as the strength of his convictions. "Naia amin evarinya, nauva thaurënya." (With unity, we'll eclipse this darkness.)

Nestling into his embrace, Keisha's heart found a haven, her worries eased by his nearness. "Le melme nauva aldae, elen siluva lyenna." (Yes, united we stand, like stars shining together.)

Amidst the garden's tapestry of hues and the cocoon of their connection, Ong and Keisha found rest, a sanctuary of stillness in an unraveling world. Aware that trials loomed on the horizon, they clung to this tranquil juncture, drawing from it not just rejuvenation but also the steadfast assurance that their bond was a beacon that could guide them through the darkest of times.

Phoenix's agitation was palpable, manifesting in the restless pacing reverberating through the shadows around him. His fury smoldered like a suppressed blaze, the air thick with the weight of his anger. Ong and Keisha's return to E'vahona had ignited a tempest within him, an exasperating obstruction he couldn't seem to dissolve.

"Unfathomable!" The words hissed past his clenched teeth, the venom in his voice underscored by the gleam of malice in his eyes. "How do they always evade us? How do they conjure barriers to shield themselves from our reach?"

Lyra focused on deciphering the enigmatic intricacies of the Whispering Shadows and shifted her attention toward Phoenix. A sardonic smile toyed at her lips, a spark of amusement dancing in her eyes. "Ah, dear Phoenix, not even our shadowy servants can infiltrate a realm hidden from inquisitive eyes."

The intensity of Phoenix's glare could have withered a forest, his ire unrelenting. "Spare me your mockery, Lyra."

With a soft chuckle that bordered on rudeness, Lyra tilted her head. "Of course, my lord.

Merely pointing out the inevitable."

Vuarus, a spectator to this volatile exchange, interjected with a measured tone that commanded attention. "Enough, both of you. Squabbling serves no purpose. We need to recalibrate to lay a new foundation for our ambitions. Ong and Keisha may have eluded us temporarily, but our dominion is expanding, and there are avenues we can exploit more effectively."

Phoenix's scowl etched deeper lines onto his face, but he yielded a reluctant nod. "You're not wrong, Vuarus. We must look ahead."

Vuarus surveyed them both with a composed, discerning gaze. "Lyra, continue your investigation into the Whispering Shadows. Their potential has yet to be fully harnessed. Phoenix, we must revisit our strategies for dominion and recruitment. Our network is a web to be spun, its threads manipulated to suit our purposes."

With a begrudging submission, Phoenix turned away from the curved shadows that mirrored his frustrations, his mind already weaving new strands of hostility designed to undermine Ong, Keisha, and those aligned with them.

As they submerged themselves in their wicked schemes, unbeknownst to them, E'vahona's protective veil was not the sole actor in this intricate choreography of power and destiny. Forces hidden in the labyrinthine folds of reality were stirring, casting their shadows upon the tapestry of their aspirations.

The sanctum of the Eladrin Council stood as a bastion of elegance and authority within the heart of E'vahona. Its interior was adorned with exquisite craftsmanship, and the walls were adorned with murals depicting the realm's storied history. At the center of this ornate chamber lay a grand circular table, its surface etched with intricate patterns that seemed to shimmer with a faint, ethereal glow. The council members, distinguished in their bearing and attire, took their positions around the table, a confluence of wisdom and power that bespoke their roles in shaping E'vahona's fate.

Among them, Lord Eldrion held a position of venerable authority, his age manifested in the silver strands of his hair and the lines etched upon his features. When he finally spoke, his voice carried the weight of time itself, a resonant echo of past ages.

"Esteemed council members," Lord Eldrion's voice was a soothing yet commanding presence, "we are summoned here in a time of turmoil when shadows stretch across our realm and beyond. The tidings we bear are grave, casting a pall over our lands and those that lay adjacent. Crystal Vale and Goldmoor have been trapped in the clutches of darkness."

A glimmer of concern manifested in the raised hand of Lady Seraphina, her empathetic nature and perceptive insights well-known among her peers. Her inquiry was soft-spoken yet carried weight. "Ong, Keisha, if you would, share with us the firsthand account of your experiences. What horrors did you witness?"

Keisha and Ong stood as sentinels before the council, their demeanor resolute as they recounted the grim tableau of destruction that had unfolded in Goldmoor and Crystal Vale. Their words wove a vivid tapestry of despair, of ominous forces unfurling in the wake of the Dark Dominion's evil designs. Lady Isadora, her vibrant spirit tempered by astute intuition, directed her gaze toward Keisha, her query as piercing as her eyes.

Keisha nodded somberly, her expression conveying the gravity of the matter. "Indeed, Lady Isadora. These entities are Shadow Wraiths, exuding fear and darkness, cloaking their surroundings in despair."

The council's collective thoughts seemed to materialize in the gaze of Lord Karrenen, his mastery over magic making him a beacon of curiosity and intellect. Leaning forward, his inquiry was measured but urgent.

"And the architects of this malevolence, Phoenix and Vuarus—have their ambitions been laid bare to you?"

Ong's countenance tightened, a reflection of his resolve. "They are amassing a dominion, drawing upon forces that emerge from the depths of the Abyss, weaving a sinister tapestry to bring their dark aspirations to fruition."

The council members exchanged wary glances, their concerns echoing like ripples across a pond. Lord Thaldir, with his countenance of ancient wisdom and beard that flowed like a cascade, interlaced his fingers thoughtfully.

"Our enemies are strategic and relentless," Lord Thaldir's voice carried the weight of experience and wisdom. "We must remain vigilant and prepare ourselves accordingly."

Lady Elowen, a skilled diplomat renowned for her insight, leaned in, her eyes reflecting concern and determination. "But how can we counteract their growing influence? What actions can we take to safeguard our realm?"

Lord Galadon, a seasoned warrior known for his bravery on the battlefield, spoke with unwavering conviction. "Our defenses must be fortified, Alliances forged, and our unity must remain unbreakable against the encroaching darkness."

Lady Lythia, the council's empathetic healer and comforter, interjected with compassion. "And let us not forget the innocent victims trapped by the terror of the Shadow Wraiths. We must extend our aid and solace to those who have suffered."

Lord Alaric, the master strategist whose mind navigated the complexities of warfare, offered his perceptive insights. "Striking at the heart of the Dark Dominion necessitates both strength and cunning. We must delve into their vulnerabilities to undermine their nefarious plans."

Lady Mirabelle, a sorceress whose enchantments held an air of mystique, added her magical perspective. "Could we seek out potential allies from other realms, those who share our concerns and are willing to join our cause?"

The council deliberated an intricate web of perspectives, a tapestry of knowledge and strategies woven with urgency. Each member's unique expertise painted a mosaic of possibilities and challenges while the impending threat loomed large in their collective thoughts.

Amidst the discourse, Keisha's heart stirred for the victims whose lives had been ravaged by the malevolent Shadow Wraiths. Her hand rose slightly, seeking Lady Lythia's compassionate attention. "Excuse me," Keisha's voice was tinged with concern, "is there anything within our power to aid those who have suffered from the Shadow Wraiths' affliction? We've witnessed their devastating influence firsthand – even the Queen of Goldmoor succumbed to their grip."

Lady Lythia, the embodiment of empathy and solace, regarded Keisha somberly. "We will endeavor to ease their pain, Keisha. However, the wounds inflicted by the Shadow Wraiths run deep, leaving scars upon the heart and spirit that are not easily healed."

Keisha nodded, her empathy a bittersweet companion. "I understand. It's heart-wrenching to witness the innocent bearing the weight of these evil forces."

Lady Seraphina, the embodiment of wisdom among the council members, shared her illuminating thoughts. "In our realm resides magic and knowledge, forces that possess the potential to alleviate even the gravest suffering. Let us unite our talents, weaving them into a tapestry of hope to counteract the encroaching darkness."

While the council's discourse flowed like a river of ideas, Keisha's gaze remained steadfastly fixed upon Lady Lythia. Her eyes conveyed a silent plea, an unspoken yearning for a way to alleviate the torment of those trapped by the evil grip of the Shadow Wraiths.

Amidst the ebb and flow of deliberations, Ong's attention turned to two council members renowned for their martial prowess and strategic insight – Lord Galadon and Lord Alaric. With a subtle raise, he sought a moment to contribute his insight. "Forgive my interruption," Ong's voice resonated with steadfast determination, "I wish to remind the council that our Alliance extends to good and neutral dragons. Their strength and wisdom could become the cornerstone of our resistance against the encroaching threat of the Dark Dominion."

Lord Galadon, a figure whose valor was matched only by his combat skills, nodded with a firm agreement. "Ong speaks the truth. The dragons' presence alone is a beacon of hope and courage, casting a light that can pierce through the shadows of despair."

Lord Alaric, the orchestrator of strategies in the realm's defense, wove his insights into the discourse. As he spoke, the flickering torchlight in the council chamber cast shifting shadows upon the walls, emphasizing the gravity of his words. "In addition to their might, the dragons introduce a strategic advantage. The Dark Dominion may not have foreseen the alignment of such powerful allies in our cause."

Lord Karrenen, a paragon of magical mastery, offered a measured response, his eyes glinting with the ethereal luminescence of his arcane expertise. "You may be correct but let us not forget that they could have the alignment of the evil dragons."

Keisha felt her heart stir with newfound hope, a spark ignited by recognizing their Alliance's strength. The majestic and potent dragons held the potential to sway the balance of power and illuminate the path toward victory in the face of the looming darkness. Their words resonated like beacons of hope in the dimly lit chamber, casting their light upon the intricate tapestry of strategies and Alliances woven to confront the encroaching threat.

Continuing their deliberations, Lord Karrenen, a paragon of magical mastery, redirected the discourse to a topic that had been approached with cautious restraint—the looming threat posed by the enigmatic Shadow Wraiths upon Kadona, the revered guardian of E'vahona.

His voice, laden with solemnity, echoed through the council chamber, drawing the attention of all present. The grand chamber, adorned with ancient tapestries and illuminated by the soft radiance of enchanted sconces, seemed to hold its breath in reverence for the council's discussion. The polished marble table at its center bore ornate carvings of protective sigils, a testament to the chamber's purpose.

"There lies an inquiry we must confront, one that pertains to safeguarding Kadona," Lord Karrenen began, his gaze laden with gravity. The high-vaulted ceiling above him stretched toward the heavens as if seeking divine guidance. "The Shadow Wraiths have unveiled their potency as formidable adversaries, orchestrators of fear even within the heart of Goldmoor's Queen. Though Kadona wields unparalleled might, the prospect that these wraiths might attempt to assail her cannot be disregarded."

Lady Seraphina, an embodiment of sagacity and grace, offered her voice to the discussion. Her words resonated like a soothing melody in the chamber's hallowed air. "Indeed, Lord Karrenen's wisdom is paramount. Kadona is a sentinel of E'vahona, pivotal in maintaining the realm's equilibrium. Should the wraiths exploit her vulnerabilities, the ramifications could prove disastrous."

Lord Eldrion, the venerable sage, wove his insights into the conversation. His voice carried the weight of centuries of knowledge, and his words were like ancient runes etched into the annals of time. "Let us not belittle the Shadow Wraiths' aptitude for manipulating the very tapestry of emotions. Fear, a primal sentiment, wields remarkable power, capable of subduing even the most formidable beings." The council chamber's ambiance grew taut as the weight of the potential threat settled like an impenetrable mist.

Keisha's heart clenched, a disruption of worry storming within her, her thoughts a cascade of concern for Kadona's security. The prospect they grappled with was unsettling, yet it was a reality they could not afford to dismiss—a truth that compelled them to face the disquieting reality of their guardian's potential vulnerability.

Lord Karrenen's gaze swept over his fellow council members, his tone steadfast. "We must stand prepared to shield Kadona at any cost. Through the tapestry of enchantments, strategic placements, or other potent methods, we shall forge an impenetrable bulwark against the wraiths' designs upon her." The council, a symphony of united resolve, nodded in concordance. The path ahead loomed treacherous, yet their commitment to fortifying E'vahona's defenses and safeguarding its guardians held steadfast, resonating within the very bones of the chamber itself.

Amid the ongoing discourse, Keisha's thoughts raced, weaving threads of strategies and enchantments that could strengthen Kadona against the encroaching shadows. Her mental tapestry was complex, threads of magic and protective wards intertwined in a delicate defense dance.

Ong's brows knit together in a tapestry of concern as he voiced a question woven through his thoughts. "Considering the cloaking enchantments that veil E'vahona, might it not be wisest for Kadona to remain within the city's protective embrace? The Shadow Wraiths have yet to penetrate its clandestine location."

Lady Elowen, a diplomat of exceptional skill, graced the discourse with her insights. Her words were like the gentle flutter of leaves in a forest, carrying the weight of diplomacy and foresight. "Indeed, the veiled sanctuary of E'vahona offers a layer of security, but we must not confine our considerations solely to that aspect. Should the Dark Dominion's grasp extend to unveil E'vahona's whereabouts, the repercussions could prove catastrophic."

Lord Galadon, the brave warrior renowned for his unyielding bravery, brought his perspective to the assembly. His words were like the clash of swords in battle, resolute and unwavering. "And let us not overlook the broader threat posed by the dominion between Phoenix and Vuarus. Their collective strength could manifest in formidable attack strategies."

Ong nodded, acknowledging the intricate balance they sought to strike. "Therefore, our course is to fortify Kadona's defenses while diversifying beyond E'vahona's concealment." The council's discourse persisted, weaving an intricate tapestry of strategies and safeguards to protect Kadona.

Each council member, bearing their distinct expertise, wove threads of wisdom into the fabric of their discussions. Bound by their dedication to safeguarding both the realm's sentinels and its very essence, they navigated a labyrinth of possibilities.

As the meeting neared its close, Keisha's heart swelled with appreciation for the council's unwavering determination. In the face of formidable trials, their unity and resilience cast a radiant light amid encroaching shadows. The chamber, adorned with ancient tapestries and shimmering enchantments, seemed to resonate with the council's resolve, a sanctuary of hope amidst the looming darkness.

As the discussions gradually wound down and the weight of their deliberations hung heavily in the chamber, Lord Karrenen's gentle yet commanding voice rose again. His words were like a soothing melody, offering respite to weary souls. "Esteemed colleagues, this day has been long and rife with endeavors. I propose we adjourn, for now, granting ourselves the much-deserved reprieve. We shall gather anew tomorrow, embarking on our deliberations with renewed vigor."

A chorus of nods, a symphony of agreement, swept through the assembly—a visible echo of the shared weariness present. The council members, their faces etched with the gravity of their responsibilities, yearned for the solace of rest.

Lord Galadon's gaze lingered momentarily, his unwavering spirit palpable as he addressed his peers. His words were like a rallying cry, infusing the chamber with resolve. "May rest enfold you, dear companions. Our horizons beckon with myriad considerations, and we shall carve our path with an indomitable spirit."

As the council meeting gradually concluded, the footsteps of departing Eladrin council members painted a soft symphony upon the grand chamber's marble floor. The weight of their responsibilities momentarily lifted, replaced by the anticipation of a new day and fresh strategies. Lord Karrenen, a repository of wisdom and mastery over magic, lingered beside Ong and Keisha, his presence a beacon of assurance. His words carried the reassurance of a sage. "Your reports have unveiled crucial insights, and I foresee that Lord Galadon's discourse tomorrow may unveil a potential remedy for our mounting apprehensions."

Keisha's nod bore the weight of her gratitude, momentarily eclipsing her weariness with a glimmer of hope. "We are indebted for your counsel, Lord Karrenen."

Ong echoed Keisha's sentiments with heartfelt appreciation. "Your support and the council's resolve in confronting these tribulations are deeply valued."

A reassuring smile played upon Lord Karrenen's lips as he inclined his head. His parting words held the promise of a new day. "Laivasse melme, yondo ammelda"

(Rest well, both of you.) "Galu nîn le melin enni" (We shall meet again on the morrow.)

As the chamber slowly emptied, Ong and Keisha stepped beyond its confines, guided by the ethereal radiance of E'vahona's enchanting lights. Beyond its walls, the moon retained its gentle luminescence, enfolding the city in a tranquil embrace. Side by side, Ong and Keisha navigated the pathways, their silhouettes cast in the moonlight, a testament to their shared purpose interwoven with the council's commitment.

Returning to their abode, the serenity of E'vahona seemed to infuse the air, granting them a reprieve from the tumult beyond its borders. Pumpkin, their steadfast companion, awaited them with a contented purr, a living reminder that life held moments of unabridged joy even amid the encroaching shadows.

Settling into their bed, Ong and Keisha embraced the sanctuary that E'vahona provided—a sanctuary that encapsulated both enchantment and security. As they closed their eyes, their thoughts danced upon the threshold of the trials ahead, the Alliances they were weaving, and the answers they fervently sought. On the morrow, the sun would herald a new tapestry of revelations, propelling their journey forward into the uncharted expanse.

Amidst the stillness of the night, E'vahona enfolded its stalwart protectors while stars cast their vigilant gaze upon their slumber. And in the realm of dreams, whispered promises of uncertain destinies, intertwined fates, and the looming specter of shadows painted a prelude to the days yet to come.

Chapter 16

Shadows Unveiled: Secrets of Ardinia

In the tender cradle of their abode, Ong and Keisha roused from their slumber, greeted by the caress of dawn's initial rays. The window welcomed the sun's gentle touch, imbuing the room with a honeyed radiance that painted everything in hues of warmth. The soft, amber light streamed through the curtains, casting intricate patterns on the tapestries that adorned the walls. Emerging from the embrace of dreams, their senses gradually reintroduced them to the realm of the conscious, and amid this transition, a familiar and comforting rumble reached their ears. It was the melodic purr of Pumpkin, their devoted panther companion. Her eyes, the color of green shimmered with a wordless invitation that held a bond deeper than speech.

Ong swung his legs over the bed's edge with a grin that carried the cadence of understanding, stretching as the remnants of sleep dispersed like morning mist before a rising sun. "Seems someone is eager to greet the day," he mused, his voice infused with a chuckling harmony that resonated in the air.

Keisha, entwined with Pumpkin's eager gaze, nodded in accord. "I believe she longs for play, to dance in the hours ahead."

In response, Pumpkin released a gentle puff, her tail tracing an anticipatory rhythm. The invitation hung in the atmosphere, irresistible as a siren's call. Yielding to the pull, Ong descended to the floor on all fours, a willing participant in this dance of camaraderie. Laughter burgeoned like a spring breeze as Pumpkin executed swift darting maneuvers and playful swipes, her motions a testament to the finesse of her feline grace. The room came alive with their joy, every leap and twist reflecting the vibrant spirit of the morning.

When the impromptu ballet concluded, Ong's hand found refuge amidst Pumpkin's fur, offering an affectionate ruffling. "Enough frivolity, dear friend. The sun now calls us to sterner endeavors."

Keisha drew near, her touch a gentle melody as she graced Pumpkin's sleek coat with her fingers. "A significant moment awaits us, a convergence of purpose."

Pumpkin, contentment tinging her final purr, nestled nearby, her luminous eyes ever watchful. Silent understanding flowed between Ong and Keisha, a symphony of glances, before they rose from the floor, their movements bearing the weight of destiny. The room held its breath, aware of the profound journey ahead.

"To the council chambers, then," Ong proposed, his words a blend of resolve and anticipation that hung in the air like a prelude to a grand aria. The weight of responsibility etched upon his face, softened only by the spark of determination in his eyes.

Keisha's affirmation came as a nod, her energy akin to the kindling of stars within her gaze. "Let us glean the wisdom of Lord Galadon, for his insights may illuminate the path ahead." Her voice held the promise of discoveries waiting to unfold, like ancient scrolls revealing forgotten knowledge.

With preparations concluded, Ong and Keisha embarked upon the labyrinthine streets of E'vahona. The city, a tapestry woven with enchantments, greeted them with its timeless allure, now enhanced by the gentle morning luminescence. Life pulsed like a river, the rhythm of the Eladrin's existence resonating harmoniously, yet beneath it all flowed a current of unity, a shared destiny that united them.

As they trod the cobblestone thoroughfares, E'vahona unfurled its wonders around them, a realm of dreams manifested, whispers of magic breathed into being. The buildings, adorned with intricate carvings and ivy-covered archways, seemed to whisper secrets of ages long past. And within this realm, Ong and Keisha strode with purpose, poised to embrace the counsel of the ages, for within the embrace of their city, adventures yet untold awaited their touch

Their path brought them to the hallowed precincts of the council tower, an architectural marvel that stood as a testament to the sagacity and might enshrine within its walls as they traversed the threshold of its grand entrance, a palpable aura of anticipation wrapped around them, as if the very stones had eavesdropped on the gravity-laden discourse that awaited within.

The cadence of their footfalls resounded along the corridor, a harmonious echo that accompanied Ong and Keisha on their journey toward the council's inner sanctum. Here, amidst the tapestried halls, lay the crucible wherein the enigmatic truths of Ardinia were poised to unveil themselves. With each advancing step, their determination congealed, threads of connection intertwining the fiber of their being with the companions old and new who shared their plight.

The door to the council chamber yielded beneath their touch, a gateway to the threshold of a narrative yet unwritten. The room seemed to pulse with an ancient power, its walls adorned with shimmering crystals and intricate murals depicting the history of their realm. Council members were engrossed in animated exchanges within the chamber's embrace, their voices weaving together like the diverse strands of a tapestry wrought with strategy and aspiration.

Amidst this symphony of discourse, the words of Lord Galadon rang forth, resonating like a chime of promise, heralding the potential for an Alliance that could reshape the destiny of their beleaguered lands. The prospect of enlisting the Nymphs' mastery over the elements gleamed as a luminous beacon, illuminating pathways hitherto obscured. The council chamber held its breath, aware that within these discussions lay the seeds of hope that could bloom into a new era for Vacari.

Ong and Keisha found their seats at the council's sacred dais, their mere presence a living testament to the unity forged amidst disparate realms, an agreement drawn together by a singular adversary. The dais was a masterpiece of intricate carvings, each symbol representing a different realm, a reminder of the bonds formed.

Lady Seraphina, her demeanor one of grace and command, addressed the assembly with a voice that bore the weight of anticipation. Her words hung in the air like a delicate tapestry, woven with threads of hope and determination. "As we tread this path forward, let us not forget that our bonds—forged through trials shared, history etched, and aspirations kindled—are the bedrock upon which our collective resilience is built."

Lord Karrenen, his aura one of gravitas, stood with a gesture that claimed the chamber's attention, his gaze ablaze with determination. His presence felt like the cornerstone of their collective resolve. "Our era of contribution has dawned. The Nymphs of Ardinia present an avenue we must explore, leveraging our mastery and grit to pursue triumph."

The enthusiasm of Lady Isadora's spirit sparkled as she added her voice to the discourse, her words akin to the sparkle of stars against a nocturnal canvas. Her optimism was a beacon in the room, piercing through the shadows. "Though our adversaries wear the veil of shadows, we stand united as luminous beacons that shall pierce through the very heart of their obscurity."

And so, in the heart of that council chamber, where the currents of resolve, unity, and foresight converged, Ong and Keisha took their place as pivotal players in a narrative woven with threads of courage, strategy, and the conviction that even in the darkest of times, light could be kindled by the flames of fellowship.

Lord Thaldir's voice, a timbre that carried the weight of centuries, resonated like a resonant bell, casting ripples of ancient wisdom upon the air. His words were a bridge to the past and a beacon to the future. "Our might is not solely in the strength of arms, but in the unbroken tapestry of our unity. Let us stand as a beacon, igniting hope that shall kindle the spirits of our realms and reach the distant echoes of Vacari."

Guided by the compass of Lady Elowen's diplomatic finesse, the discourse flowed with the grace of a river carving through time. Her words were like the gentle current that carried them forward. "Our choices today are etched upon the scrolls of destiny. As we approach the Nymphs, may our words be imbued with earnestness and reverence, conveying the urgency of our shared tribulation."

In the heart of the council's deliberations, Ong and Keisha found themselves enveloped in a symphony of resolve, where every uttered sentiment was a note woven into the harmonious melody of unity. The gravity of each uttered syllable pressed upon them, bearing both the mantle of responsibility and the wings of boundless potential. Their sojourn, marked by a cascade of trials, had led them unerringly to this nexus, a crossroads where destiny met with the choices they would inscribe upon its fabric.

Within the council's sanctum, energy surged like a current of purpose, infusing the air with a charge that transcended mere discourse. Ong's gaze met Keisha's in a silent exchange, an unspoken vow that bound them to this sacred mission. The Nymphs of Ardinia, whispers of legend, now beckoned as the harbinger of transformation. This key could reforge the course of their struggles and unshroud the veiled forces of nature that had slumbered in obscurity.

As the deliberations meandered toward their closure, a collective sense of purpose, weighty yet invigorating, descended upon the chamber. Lord Galadon, the guardian of wisdom, locked eyes with Ong and Keisha, an unspoken covenant forged within their shared glance. The council had spoken, the tapestry of their way forward now unrolled with clarity. Emboldened by the council's sagacity, Ong and Keisha recognized that the path leading to Ardinia's core would test their courage and determination as never before. Amidst the tapestry of time, they stood poised to inscribe their names as champions, bearing witness to the tapestry of destiny as it unfurled its secrets before them.

The cadence of their footsteps wove another stanza of resonance within the corridor as they emerged from the council chamber. The door swung shut behind them, an echo of finality that encapsulated the aura of shared purpose and unity. The crossroads had been reached, a threshold crossed; it was time to step beyond the familiar into the veiled sanctum of Ardinia. The corridor, dimly lit by softly glowing sconces, seemed to stretch endlessly ahead, mirroring the path they now trod into the unknown. Within the embrace of secrets and potential, Ong and Keisha set their sights on the Nymphs, seeking their Alliance to turn the tides of Vacari's destiny. Every stride they took resonated with the gravitas of their mission, the hopes of realms manifold resting upon their shoulders, as profound as the starlit sky.

As the sun's final rays cast long shadows, Lord Galadon and Lord Karrenen arrived at Ong and Keisha's haven. Their expressions danced between resolve and eager anticipation, carrying the weight of a choice's consequence. In the wake of their council's resolution, a new path had been etched—one that guided them to Ardinia's heart, to the elusive Nymphs who held the power to reshape the tapestry of their war-torn world.

Ong and Keisha greeted their visitors in the haven's sheltering embrace, a tranquil refuge amid the maelstrom of uncertainty. The room's soft, ambient light added a touch of serenity to their meeting. Lord Galadon's gaze flickered with the spark of anticipation as he began to weave his words. "Ong, Keisha, our research into the Nymphs of Ardinia has unveiled a tale of wondrous and primal power. These beings are the threads that bind to the very essence of nature, conduits of its elemental forces."

Beside him, Lord Karrenen nodded in affirmation, his eyes ablaze with unwavering intensity. "Their mastery aligns with specific facets of nature—the aqueous flow, the sylvan verdure, the currents of air—all drawn beneath their unparalleled dominion. Their pledge of allegiance to our cause is equivalent to wielding the titanic forces of nature against the Abyssal Dominion."

Leaning closer, Keisha's curiosity spiraled like the curling tendrils of incense smoke. "Yet, how do we weave our appeal? The Nymphs guard their realm, enigmatic and reclusive." Her voice carried the undertones of a question that had been echoed by countless before them, a puzzle waiting to be unraveled.

A knowing smile curved Lord Galadon's lips, his eyes alight with sagacity. "Indeed, Keisha. We've devised a stratagem to align their compass of duty and custodianship with the fragile balance of Vacari. A looming threat to this equilibrium, a powerful artifact coveted by the Abyssal Dominion, stands as our enigmatic ally. We believe the Nymphs' intrinsic bond to nature will compel them to preserve this harmony by aiding our cause."

Ong's brow furrowed in contemplation. "A promising strategy, but the path to Ardinia—does it harbor challenges akin to the sentinel guardians of the dragons?"

With a confirming nod, Lord Karrenen affirmed Ong's concern. "Indeed, barriers akin to those protecting the dragons shield Ardinia from the uninvited. Yet, insights have been unveiled; a ritual that pairs enchantments and artifacts, a key to surmounting these barriers, if only temporarily."

Lord Galadon's gaze bore the gravity of the cosmos, reflecting the seriousness of their endeavor. "Arming you with these artifacts and the arcane wisdom, you will traverse these barriers. Thus, within the heart of Ardinia, you shall find yourself amidst a realm unmatched in its majesty and enchantment."

Keisha and Ong exchanged a resolute glance, their determination akin to the steadfastness of mountains. "Whatever trials await," Keisha declared, "we stand prepared to conquer them and secure the Alliance of the Nymphs. The fate of our realm and others hinges on this crucial endeavor."

The baritone of Lord Karrenen's voice resonated with a fatherly pride. "In your unwavering dedication, Vacari finds a symphony of valor. Faith finds root in your conviction. The unity you've woven can tip the balance in our favor, a balance that sways on the fulcrum of shared purpose."

As the council members spoke, Ong and Keisha found solace in their words, as if kindling reawakened their purpose, a fire rekindled against the darkness of uncertainty. The path they embarked upon was formidable, yet not insurmountable, for they bore not only the knowledge and artifacts bestowed by Lords Galadon and Karrenen but also the unyielding tenacity that coursed through their very beings, a current of resilience to brave the storm.

With an unspoken understanding, the symposium concluded, its echoes fading like the vanishing of a whispering breeze. With Lords Galadon and Karrenen's departure, Ong and Keisha stood amid the afterglow, ignited by urgency and anticipation. The once ephemeral notion of journeying into Ardinia had crystallized into a tangible pathway, its cobblestones of destiny ready to bear their footsteps. In the dimly lit haven, their resolve burned brighter than ever, casting aside the shadows of doubt as they prepared to venture into the heart of Ardinia, where the Nymphs held the key to a new chapter in the unfolding epic of Vacari's destiny.

As the door sealed behind the departing council members, Ong and Keisha exchanged glances, their twin orbs reflecting determination and a glint of expectation. The time had come to prepare for their odyssey into Ardinia, an expedition into the unknown, a quest for the Nymphs' benediction. Guided by the council's wisdom and bolstered by their indomitable spirits, they were poised to unveil the arcane enigmas nestled within Ardinia's sanctuary. This venture marked the inception of a fresh chapter in their relentless campaign against the Abyssal Dominion, etched with the ink of courage and embossed with the seal of hope.

Amidst the fervor of preparations, a familiar question arose in Ong's mind. Casting a contemplative gaze toward Keisha, he broached the topic. "Pumpkin—what of her? Should she venture with us, or do we leave her to the comforts of home?"

Keisha took a moment to consider, her lips curling into a soft smile. "The idea of having Pumpkin accompany us might prove brilliant. The Nymphs' rapport with nature could be mirrored in her presence—a symbol of loyalty that may beckon their goodwill."

Ong's nod echoed in agreement. "Indeed, she's more than just a companion. She embodies the essence of our affinity with the natural world."

And so, the verdict was settled. They ensured Pumpkin was well-prepared for the journey, tending to her every need. They gathered supplies, enchanted artifacts, and knowledge to navigate the mystical barriers that shield Ardinia. With Pumpkin by their side, the trio stood at the precipice of an uncharted expedition, their determination forging the binding link to the Nymphs' Alliance—a union poised to rewrite the destinies intertwined with the tapestry of their realm. As they embarked on this quest, their hearts beat in unison with the rhythm of nature, ready to face the challenges and revelations ahead.

Amidst the rhythmic cadence of their preparations, a luminous apparition manifested—the form of Kadona, radiant and ephemeral. Her presence held an aura of sagacity, her essence a harmonious blend of wisdom and vigor. The urgency in her voice, an echo from realms beyond, bore the weight of an imperative message. "Ong, Keisha, are you traversing the path to Ardinia? There is a truth you must wield. In discourse with the Nymphs, share the desolation wrought by the Abyssal Dominion upon our verdant sanctuaries here in E'vahona."

Keisha's countenance softened into contemplation, her brow a canvas of thought. "But, Kadona, what relevance lies within this revelation?"

Kadona's eyes held a mosaic of melancholy and resolution. "The Nymphs—wardens of nature—are the elemental sentinels of our sylvan realms. Their fates are woven with the lifelines of our forests. By unveiling the magnitude of the wounds inflicted by the Abyssal Dominion, you evoke the resonant call for their aid, a plea to restore equilibrium where it has been shattered."

A nod underscored Ong's agreement. "This plea is not limited to our realm alone. It extends as tendrils connecting every realm interlaced by the darkness of the Dominion."

In response, Kadona's visage was graced by a smile, an embodiment of reverence. "Indeed. Your quest eclipses provincial boundaries, embracing a symphony that harmonizes the very essence of Vacari."

Keisha and Ong bowed in homage, words a cadence of gratitude. "We treasure your counsel, Kadona. Your illumination guides us through the shadows."

With a final gesture, Kadona's luminosity receded, leaving a palpable sense of solace and fortitude. Laden, with both their preparations and Kadona's counsel, Ong and Keisha embarked from E'vahona, resolute in purpose. Their passage would transcend boundaries, unravel secrets, and seek the Alliance capable of reshaping the tale of their unrelenting struggle against the Abyssal Dominion. As they ventured forth, their hearts carried the weight of their realm and the hopes of countless others, and the echoes of Kadona's wisdom resonated in their minds like a guiding star in the darkest of nights.

Beneath the aegis of Lord Galadon's and Lord Karrenen's wisdom, the trio—Ong, Keisha, and Pumpkin—braced themselves for the odyssey to Ardinia. The day to journey into the heart of the mystical forest had unfurled like a parchment unrolling to a long-anticipated tale. Amidst the gathering of supplies and satchels' fastening, a sense of mingled anticipation and trepidation took root within them, a symphony where every note was imbued with the resonance of the uncharted journey ahead.

Under the sovereign dominion of the sun, its golden scepter casting ethereal light, they embarked from E'vahona, threading their way into the depths of the empyreal woods that enfolded their city. The atmosphere pulsed with life with every stride, an orchestra of verdant voices bearing the cadence of nature's secrets. As the foliage enveloped them, the tapestry of existence seemed to harmonize, an intricacy that only deepened as they neared the veil that demarcated E'vahona from the realm of Ardinia.

In reverence, they halted at this juncture, their gazes transfixed by the diaphanous threshold. There, where the foliage quivered and the air quivered with enchantment, stood the boundary—an ephemeral boundary endowed by Lord Galadon's counsel, a barrier that sifted truth from deception, fidelity from feigned intent. Its luminous aura was both guardian and guide, the nexus where their purpose would be weighed against the measure of sincerity.

Beside Keisha, Pumpkin padded with a soft whine, her eyes aflame with an unspoken allegiance. Keisha, in response, knelt to stroke her, her touch a reassurance woven of tenderness. "Are you prepared, dear Pumpkin?"

Ong, his gaze unwavering and harboring an ember of steadfastness, met Keisha's eye. "We shall prevail."

A fortifying breath accompanied a nod of agreement from Keisha. As artifacts dangled from their grasp and incantations clung to their tongues like secrets yearning for release, they embraced the boundary. The realm's heartbeat seemed to pulse as one, the resonance of leaves stirring a symphony of anticipation as if the very forest held its breath in anticipation of their step.

Thus, positioned on the threshold between realities, Ong, Keisha, and Pumpkin were poised to articulate the chants that would part the veil. Ancient and potent words would forge the conduit that bridged two worlds. With outstretched hands and unwavering voices, they stood at the precipice of a chapter anew, awaiting to engrave their names upon the arcane annals of Ardinia—a narrative sung by winds, composed by leaves, and whispered within the labyrinthine wisdom of the woods. The echoes of their journey resonated in the air, a symphony of anticipation, as they readied themselves to step into the unknown.

Chapter 17

Shadow Unveiled: Veil of the Nymphs

Ong, Keisha, and Pumpkin embarked upon the threshold of Ardinia, a realm as enchanting as a dream woven by the fingers of nature's weaver. As they crossed over from their world into this mystical expanse, a symphony of wonder enveloped them, embracing them in the enchanting beauty of this magical realm.

Imagine towering ancient trees, their gnarled branches reaching high into the sky, standing like silent guardians over the landscape. The leaves, an iridescent mosaic of vibrant greens, formed a shimmering canopy overhead. The sun, casting its golden tendrils through the trees, painted a tapestry of warm light on the forest floor. Meandering streams, crystal-clear and sinuous, flowed like liquid melodies through the emerald tapestry.

In vast meadows, wildflowers painted the landscape with a kaleidoscope of colors. Each bloom is a testament to nature's vibrant palette. The air itself was an elixir, a fragrant blend of blooming flowers and earthy aromas. Above, the boundless cerulean sky stretched out majestically, a brilliant backdrop contrasting with the lush greenery below.

In this realm of unparalleled beauty, Ong, Keisha, and Pumpkin felt themselves entranced by the heartbeat of creation. Here, the land remained untouched by the shadow that gripped their world, a living testament to the resilience of life. It was more than just geography; it embodied life's vitality, a canvas where every stroke spoke of nature's enduring spirit.

Ong's heart surged with renewed purpose as their gazes drank in the panorama. Here, the Nymphs were not merely allies but sentinels, guardians of a realm that encapsulated their ideals. These Nymphs served as protectors of Ardinia, safeguarding its magic and natural beauty. This revelation kindled their determination anew, an inferno stoked by a breath of resolve. And thus, armed with revitalized intent, they embraced the landscape and advanced deeper into Ardinia, their souls aflutter with eagerness to greet these revered guardians of a realm where magic and nature converged. They walked a path woven with the threads of beauty and magic, their hearts aligned with the symphony of Ardinia's enchanting embrace.

As Ong, Keisha, and Pumpkin strode further into Ardinia's embrace, they were engulfed in a panorama that painted awe across their hearts. Colossal arboreal sentinels soared, bridging the realms of earth and sky with their verdant arches, a testament to the silent wisdom of the ages. These ancient trees stood tall as guardians, their branches connecting the terrestrial and celestial realms. Streams of crystalline purity snaked their way through the landscape, bearing whispers of their journey from distant sources, each eddy and swirl a reflection of the azure sky above, as if sharing secrets from the heavens.

Yet it was the residents of Ardinia who held them captive in their awe—a spectacle that defied the boundaries of imagination. Here, creatures of legend and enchantment resided amid the splendor of nature's creation. The presence of unicorns graced the land, their alabaster coats aglow with the radiance of moonlight as they moved with a grace akin to ethereal ballet. These unicorns were not just beautiful beings but also symbols of innate nobility and grace, a living testament to the regal spirit of Ardinia.

Above, the sky itself was painted with wonder as Pegasus—creatures of celestial wings and glistening plumage—etched their silhouettes against the canvas of the sky. Their flight was a ballet of freedom, each movement a whispered symphony that stirred the winds. And beneath the verdant canopy, fairies wove trails of luminescence, ephemeral beings who danced upon the cusp of reality and dreams. Their presence was like a magic brushstroke on an enchanting scene, adding an ethereal quality to the realm.

As they ventured deeper into this realm, Ong, Keisha, and Pumpkin couldn't help but feel like interlopers in a living tapestry of fantasy and beauty. The boundaries between the ordinary and the extraordinary blurred, and they found themselves humbled by the majesty of Ardinia, a realm where reality and dreams intertwined, and legends walked among them.

As if guided by the unseen threads of destiny, butterflies painted in iridescent hues appeared as if conjured by the very heart of Ardinia. Their delicate wings unfurled like vibrant whispers, a ballet of curiosity that encircled Pumpkin in a dance of ethereal intrigue. Each butterfly seemed to carry a message of enchantment, a part of the living magic of Ardinia.

The air itself resonated with a symphony of life—a harmony conducted by myriad creatures, each note distinct, each voice an offering to the sanctity of Ardinia's embrace. The forest echoed with the sounds of nature's chorus, and the land seemed to respond to their presence.

Her eyes were wide with wonder. Pumpkin reveled in this dance of fleeting phenomena. Her rumbling purr merged with the melody of the land, an ode to delight that reverberated through the forest. Ong and Keisha exchanged glances, their eyes kindled with shared amazement. The realm they now traversed was a living mosaic, untouched by the shadow of darkness, a sanctuary where nature's marvels thrived.

With hearts brimming with reverence and respect for the realm's residents, they ventured forth, their footsteps guided by the very rhythm of the land. While the journey ahead promised trials, at this moment, they were entranced by the splendor that Ardinia had unfurled—a symphony of the extraordinary, an ode to the arcane.

Every step they took echoed with the delicate pulse of nature, as if the very earth acknowledged their presence and welcomed them as honored guests. The kaleidoscope of life around them continued its enchanting performance. In this realm of wonder, they walked as witnesses and participants, a part of the living tapestry that was Ardinia."

Amidst the shroud of secrecy, within the veiled heart of their clandestine sanctum, Vuarus seethed with frustrated agitation, a storm of vexation etched upon his countenance. His features, cast in shadows, contorted into a sinister scowl that bespoke of simmering discontent. Vuarus, a mastermind of shadowy schemes, brooded over the unsettling reports in the dimly lit chamber. "Reports have trickled in—a fleeting glimpse of Ong and Keisha, they say, like phantoms revisiting Crystal Vale," he hissed, his words edged with an acidic ire that lingered in the air. "And yet, as swiftly as they emerged, they vanished again, slipping through our grasp like mist between fingers."

Across the chamber, Phoenix stood like a monument carved from wrath. His hands balled into fists of incensed fury. His piercing gaze, alight with dangerous intensity, fixated upon the depths of shadow. Phoenix, a relentless enforcer of their dark intentions, seethed with frustration. "They are a whisper that eludes our ears, a mirage that defies our reach," he snarled, the resonance of his voice an undertone of impending disruption. "It's as though they possess an uncanny talent to dissolve beyond the boundaries of our pursuit."

Vuarus reclined into his seat, an air of brooding contemplation enfolding him. The contours of his face played host to the maelstrom of his thoughts, an intricate interplay of vexation and strategizing. "The enigma of their vanishings gnaws at our designs," he mused, his words disquieting. "Our resolve must be absolute, for their fugitive waltz only serves to nourish the sapling of their alliance. With every fleeting moment, they amass strength and camaraderie."

A sardonic grin graced Phoenix's lips, an emblem of his sinister intentions. "Trust me, Vuarus, the sands in their hourglass are diminishing. They grasp futilely at the reins of destiny, ignorant of the certainty we wield," he proclaimed, his tone dripping with malice. "Their resistance shall bow, and soon enough, they will be ensnared by the web we've woven."

Vuarus and Phoenix united, a dark intent duet woven through their plotting threads. Their sinister camaraderie was underscored by ambitions that resonated with the ominous echoes of dominion. A brittle dominion held them, a tenuous equilibrium between shared purpose and whispered betrayal. In their concealed lair, hidden from the world's gaze, shadows birthed secrets, and the eternal conflict for supremacy waged on.

Within the concealed heart of their lair, Vuarus and Phoenix plotted with the precision of shadowy architects, their malevolent symphony composing the unsettling overture of their dark designs.

Deeper into the heart of Ardinia's ethereal realm, Ong, Keisha, and Pumpkin ventured into a world painted with hues that defied mortal comprehension. Towering sentinels of nature, majestic and grand, breached the canopy, their outstretched arms cloaked in leaves that glinted like a myriad of emeralds and gilded coins. The sunlight, an artist's brush, painted the forest floor in dappled splendor, casting a kaleidoscope of greens and glistening golds. Every footfall upon the verdant carpet reverberated with a whispered promise of magic.

The air bore witness to the symphony of nature—an orchestral display composed of trilling birds and the hushed susurrus of leaves as they exchanged secrets with the wind. The very atmosphere seemed alive, embracing them with the vibrant pulse of Ardinia. Each breath inhaled was a draught of rejuvenating vitality, infusing them with the essence of this mystical realm.

A crystal-clear stream meandered into view, a liquid ribbon of diamonds in the sunlight's embrace. Keisha's laughter unfurled like a songbird's melody as she dipped her hand into the water, ripples cascading from her touch. Ever the mischievous companion, Ong retaliated with a cascade of liquid, eliciting playful squeals from Keisha. Pumpkin, their panther ally, joined in the aquatic revelry, her inky paws dancing upon the water's surface. In this moment of joy and camaraderie, they were not just explorers but kindred spirits, intertwined with the magic of Ardinia.

Their laughter, a tapestry woven with joy, painted the air, capturing the essence of this enchanted realm. As the waters of the stream became a canvas for their playful spirits, the weight of their mission momentarily dissolved, leaving only the rapture of the present. In Ardinia, the world emerged anew—a realm untouched by the tendrils of darkness that clawed at their lands.

The air seemed to shimmer with otherworldly visitors, delicate fairies with wings of iridescent opulence, dancing upon the tapestry of nature. Amidst a nearby meadow, a unicorn, its countenance noble and radiant, grazed with an aura that whispered of ancient mystique. These magical beings were not mere observers but part of the living magic surrounding them.

With the sun's descent, the land was embraced by a warm, golden glow—a farewell caress that bathed Ardinia in a tapestry of colors. Ong, Keisha, and Pumpkin rested on the grassy bank, their limbs weary but hearts alight. The laughter gave way to contented sighs as they gazed upon the heavens, where clouds painted an ever-shifting panorama of hues, the sky a canvas of blush and tangerine.

"Such a remarkable place," Keisha mused, her voice a delicate breath from the breeze.

Ong's serene nod echoed her sentiment. "Ardinia stands in stark contrast to the darkness we battle—a sanctuary untouched by the blight that engulfs our realm. In moments like these, we find solace and strength."

Pumpkin, a living shadow stretched beside them, emitted a contented rumble, her eyes heavy with the weight of satisfaction. Amid the splendor of Ardinia, the burden of their mission waned, replaced by the sublime beauty of the present.

Like a loyal sentinel, her presence added to the feeling of security in this magical realm.

As the sun yielded to Twilight's embrace, Ong and Keisha exchanged a shared smile—an unspoken affirmation of their bond forged through laughter. Yet, even in the arms of this paradisiacal haven, the specter of their mission loomed, casting shadows upon the tranquil tapestry—an ever-present reminder that their odyssey remained far from its conclusion. Their smiles carried a mixture of joy and determination, reflecting the complexities within them.

With the soft rustle of leaves and the gentle murmur of the stream as their lullaby, Ong and Keisha found a secluded glade bathed in the quiet, golden light of the fading day. There, beneath the protective canopy of ancient trees, they lay down, their bodies cradled by the verdant earth. Pumpkin, their loyal companion, nestled beside them, purring like a soothing melody harmonizing with the forest's serenity.

As the twilight deepened, the trio succumbed to the embrace of slumber, their dreams interwoven with the mysteries of Ardinia, their hearts, and souls at one with the enchantment surrounding them. In this ethereal realm, where time flowed like a tranquil river, they found respite from their arduous journey, recharging their spirits for the challenges ahead. They glimpsed visions of unity and hope in their dreams, reflecting the magic that permeated Ardinia's essence.

As daylight surrendered to twilight and the sky's canvas transformed into a tapestry of stars, Aeliana's contemplative gaze remained fixed. Reports of the strangers' actions had evolved into a song of hope, igniting a flicker of curiosity within the guardian's heart. The duty of safeguarding Ardinia was both an honor and a burden, a bond to the very essence of the land. With each passing moment, Aeliana became increasingly open to the possibility that these outsiders might be kindred spirits rather than intruders.

The winds' currents, the melodies of avian choirs, and whispers of the strangers' presence reached Aeliana's ears—a tale of curiosity, laughter, and interaction with Ardinia's inhabitants. Each report cast Ong, Keisha, and Pumpkin in a different light—friends of the land, admirers of its magic, and guardians of its balance.

It was a tale of stark contrast, for Aeliana had long been the shield against those who would exploit or harm Ardinia. Yet, the newcomers possessed an air of reverence, treading softly upon the earth and acknowledging the sanctity of the realm. And so, Aeliana maintained her vigil, her contemplative gaze a shroud of mystery as she observed their actions and considered the evolving tapestry of Ardinia's destiny.

With the first gentle rays of dawn painting the heavens with hues of gold and blush, Ong and Keisha stirred from their slumber within Ardinia's embrace. The radiant beauty of their surroundings greeted them, infusing their spirits with tranquility. Silent understanding passed between them—a recognition that their journey was far from its conclusion. It was a mission driven by purpose and the need to safeguard their realm from the encroaching darkness.

Renewed in purpose, they continued their odyssey, their footfalls gentle upon the soil. The ancient sentinels of the forest whispered ancient secrets to the wind, and the crystal-clear streams murmured tales of ageless magic. Their senses harmonized with the rhythms of Ardinia, a symphony woven from the threads of nature's melodies. Each step was a testament to their connection to this mystical realm, a bond that strengthened with every heartbeat.

Amidst the verdant expanse of Ardinia's enchanted embrace, Ong, Keisha, and Pumpkin ventured deeper, unaware that their steps were woven into the very fabric of the realm's consciousness. Aeliana, the guardian entrusted with the mystical realm's preservation, had not disregarded their arrival. Vigilant and cautious, Aeliana's ethereal form glided through the woodlands, her watchful gaze ever attuned to the delicate symphony of nature that enveloped Ardinia. She sensed the newcomers' purpose and connection to the land, and her curiosity mingled with a sense of duty as she continued observing their journey.

Ahead, the heart of Ardinia unfurled like a dreamscape—a realm where nature was painted with unrestrained artistry. It was a sanctuary where the air was a symphony of fragrant notes, a fragrant overture conducted by blooming flora that swayed in harmonious choreography. This verdant panorama trapped Ong and Keisha, their senses intoxicated by the heady perfume of blossoms intertwined with the gentle breeze. Delicate petals brushed their skin like whispered caresses, and the song of birds filled their ears with nature's melody.

Unbeknownst to the trio, the guardian of Ardinia, Aeliana, remained a silent sentinel, a spectral presence that merged seamlessly with the dappled canopy above. Her form, an ethereal echo of the forest's splendor, dissolved into the tapestry of leaves and sunlight, a testament to her kinship with the land. Her eyes, ancient orbs of knowing, bore witness to the strangers who stepped onto her hallowed domain. She sensed their presence and intent with every rustling leaf and chirping bird.

Aeliana's awareness was not solely a matter of vision but a communion with the very essence of Ardinia. She gathered insights into the newcomers, from bird songs' cadence to the breeze's whispers. They stood apart from those who had ventured here before—individuals who radiated a reverence for the realm's splendor unlike the past intruders. Their steps were a delicate dance, a rhythmic waltz that seemed to harmonize with Ardinia's enchanting denizens. Aeliana recognized this harmony, a connection woven into the very fabric of Ardinia's existence, and she watched, her curiosity piqued by these kindred spirits who had entered her realm.

With each step Ong and Keisha took deeper into the heart of Ardinia, the threads of destiny wove their gazes with Aeliana's vigilant watch. Time held its breath, a moment suspended in the tapestry of existence. The guardian's presence exuded an aura of enchantment and regal wisdom, embodying the ancient magic that coursed through the very veins of the land. It was as though the forest itself had taken form in her.

In a fluid motion, Aeliana emerged from the living tapestry surrounding her. Her form materialized as if woven from the essence of the forest, a being of ethereal grace and earthly strength. It was as though she had always been there, an integral part of Ardinia's splendor. The air around her shimmered with a soft luminescence, casting an otherworldly glow upon her presence. Her voice, a sonorous symphony, drew its notes from the babbling brooks and the rustling leaves, resonating with the pulse of the land.

"Greetings, wanderers, in Ardinia," her voice carried an enchanting cadence that was a testament to her deep connection with the land. It seemed to echo from every forest corner, embracing Ong and Keisha in its ethereal embrace. "I am Aeliana, steward of this realm. I sense your purpose here. Speak, and let your intentions unfurl."

Ong and Keisha exchanged a mutual glance, their eyes reflecting a medley of awe and respect. In the presence of Aeliana, the air seemed to shimmer with magic, and the very earth beneath them pulsed with anticipation. Stepping forward, they acknowledged the privilege bestowed upon them—standing before Aeliana, the venerable and otherworldly guardian of Ardinia.

With a respectful nod shared between them, Ong stepped forward, embodying the resilience of Crystal Vale. "I am Ong, a ranger of Crystal Vale, and at my side stands Keisha, a sorceress of elven lineage."

Aeliana's perceptive gaze settled upon Keisha, her eyes a wellspring of gentle curiosity. "An Eladrin in Ardinia," she murmured, a smile tugging at the corners of her lips. "Though your form speaks of an elf, your presence bears the grace and essence of an Eladrin."

Keisha met Aeliana's gaze with a nod, her smile a reflection of the reverence she held. Her heart swelled with the unique connection she felt in this mystical place. "Your insight is keen, Guardian Aeliana. Indeed, I am an Eladrin, and the privilege of standing in your presence is an honor beyond words."

The guardian's ethereal demeanor seemed to shimmer with approval. "The honor is mutual, Keisha, sorceress of the Eladrin. You both are welcomed guests in Ardinia, and your presence here is destined for more than chance encounters."

Her attention then shifted back to Ong, her eyes attentive to his words. "We journey with a plea for alliance, Guardian Aeliana," Ong spoke, his voice a steady river of respect. "Our realms teeter on the edge of oblivion, threatened by encroaching darkness that hungers for dominion. In the unity of Nymphs and our kindred realms, we envision a bulwark against this evil force."

As Ong wove the tapestry of their dire situation, Aeliana's gaze balanced ancient wisdom and compassionate concern. When he described the ravaged forests, a trace of sorrow flitted across her eyes like a shadow that passed through a sunlit glade. The weight of their plight settled upon her heart, and she felt a profound empathy for the suffering of their realms.

With a graceful motion, Aeliana beckoned to the air itself, and two fairies materialized as if woven from the very threads of nature. These radiant fairies hovered nearby, their wings a symphony of delicate motion. In silent communion with Aeliana, they conveyed the somber tidings they had gathered. Through the subtle language of light and gestures, they communicated the dire state of the forests and the encroaching darkness that threatened their existence. A nod from the guardian signaled their retreat, their presence melding with the whispers of the land once more.

Aeliana returned her focus to Ong and Keisha, her voice bearing the weight of epochs. "The echoes of the shadow have reached even the ears of Ardinia. The eerie transformation of the Purplefire and Emeraldwood forests resonates as a haunting change within the heart of this realm."

Aeliana's radiant aura absorbed the echoes of sorrow that emanated from Keisha's words. Her unwavering gaze held the weight of ages, her expression a tableau of empathetic understanding. "To witness such eerie transformation is to feel the land's heartbeat weep," she whispered, her words a gentle breeze that carried the weight of the world, rustling the leaves and causing the nearby flowers to sway in response.

Ong's grasp on Keisha's hand conveyed unspoken solace, a silent pledge of unity in their mission to restore balance. He spoke, his voice a conduit for their shared dedication. "We do not merely seek an alliance against the encroaching darkness; we also entreat your guidance and assistance in restoring the equilibrium sundered by this cataclysm. We recognize the Nymphs of Ardinia as stewards of elemental forces, a potent bulwark against the evil alliance that threatens to engulf us."

Aeliana's gaze shifted between Ong and Keisha, her eyes mirroring the intricate thoughts weaving through her essence. "The malevolence of Vuarus has left its mark on Ardinia, known to us as Azeron, a being whose inclinations have forever brushed the edges of shadowed realms."

Keisha's brows furrowed in remembrance. "Azeron... The name echoes with ancient darkness." Aeliana's ethereal form flickered with the resonance of a memory's echo. "Indeed, and it is a memory seared into Ardinia's consciousness. The alliance you propose bears the power to pivot the axis of nature itself, a deed that ripples through every realm, including Ardinia."

Ong's solemn nod sealed their commitment. "This is why we stand before you, Guardian Aeliana, with humility, seeking an alliance that will mend the breach and stand as a bastion for the sanctity of life."

Aeliana's gaze melded approval with caution, her ancient eyes revealing the gravity of the challenge she presented. "Your plea resonates with unwavering truth. The ability to sway the heart of Ardinia's guardian is a challenge entrusted to you. Through unswerving dedication, demonstrate your intentions, and you shall unearth the alliance you seek."

With those words, the destiny of their mission hung suspended, balanced on the edge of decision as Ong and Keisha faced Aeliana. Their purpose solidified against the consuming shadows that encroached. Ong's nod echoed their steadfast pledge, a wordless covenant embracing the forthcoming trial.

As their plea lingered, Aeliana's luminous form seemed to waver momentarily, as if the profoundness of their words rippled through her very being.

"The Heart of Twilight," Aeliana's voice whispered, an exhalation of astonishment. Her radiant presence shimmered, briefly faltering before resuming its ethereal equilibrium. "Such an artifact holds a resonance that echoes beyond realms. Its potency is not to be wielded without heed."

Keisha shared a knowing glance with Ong, sensing the depth of Aeliana's response. "It possesses the capacity to mold destinies, to shape the interplay between light and shadow," she ventured cautiously, her words carrying a reverent weight.

Aeliana's gaze, once distant in contemplation, locked onto Keisha with a piercing focus. "The Heart of Twilight is pivotal in the symphony of realms. Its purpose and might have echoed through the corridors of time, a guiding light or shrouding darkness, contingent upon the hands that grasp it."

Ong's brows knitted in introspection, and he spoke with a profound realization. "It forms the crux of the Abyssal Dominion's ambitions. They believe its potency will solidify their dominion." Aeliana's luminous form seemed to ripple with the profundity of knowledge she bore. "The heart wields a capricious nature, both in its intrinsic essence and the intricate consequences it may weave. Before we proceed with your trial, revelations must be unveiled, and comprehension must be nurtured."

Keisha bowed her head with respect. "We come as pupils, eager to comprehend and demonstrate our commitment to restoring harmony."

Aeliana's gaze balanced wisdom with concern. Her ethereal form seemed to shimmer with an otherworldly elegance, her luminous presence a testament to her insight. "Initially, I shall impart the wisdom you seek to unravel the Heart of Twilight's essence and the far-reaching repercussions of its might," she began, her voice a vessel for the weight of eras.

Ong and Keisha exchanged another meaningful glance, their resolution unwavering. Ong's eyes reflected a profound readiness, while Keisha's expression blended anticipation and reverence. "Our minds are prepared for the lessons," Ong affirmed resolutely, his sincerity resonating in his words.

Aeliana's voice infused the air, and the very forest seemed to hush in reverence, eager to absorb her words. "Very well, seekers of stability. Take heed, for the Heart of Twilight conceals a saga that spans dimensions and eons."

As Aeliana's words unfurled like the delicate petals of a mystical flower, Ong and Keisha tuned in, their hearts and thoughts receptive to the profound knowledge she was poised to bestow.

Aeliana began weaving history and magic, unfurling a vibrant tableau of the Heart of Twilight's origins and profound relevance. "The Heart of Twilight isn't confined to a mere artifact of might," Aeliana commenced, her voice a symphony of cosmic wisdom. "It serves as a living vessel for the intricate equilibrium binding luminescence and obscurity, life and demise, creation and obliteration. Forged by the primordial forces that etched the very fabric of existence, its essence unfailingly upholds harmony amidst realms."

Keisha's eyes gleamed like twin stars, reflecting a blend of reverence and wonder. "Thus, it transcends being a mere instrument of power. It embodies the essence of balance itself."

Ong inclined his head, his demeanor solemn, acknowledging the gravity in the air. "The looming darkness casts a shadow over our lands, threatening not only the realms but the very essence of nature itself. We intend to shield our domains and uphold the sanctity of the natural world."

Aeliana's radiant presence seemed to shimmer with a subtle change, as if touched by the depth of Keisha's resolve. Her gaze bore into them a wellspring of comprehension transcending spoken language. "The alliance you propose reverberates beyond mere agreements, touching upon the intricate equilibrium of Ardinia. Before I extend my blessing, I must delve deeper into your motives and the depths you are willing to plumb."

Keisha locked eyes with Aeliana, and her resolve chiseled in stone. "Guardian Aeliana, the significance of this alliance is etched into our understanding. We stand resolute, prepared to embark on whatever odyssey is demanded to safeguard our realms and mend the ruptured harmony."

Aeliana's form ignited with an intensity that shimmered like starlight. "So be it, Ong and Keisha. Let your intentions be as clear as the light and your hearts as unwavering as the roots that intertwine with the earth. The pact you seek binds you not solely to the Nymphs but to the very heartbeat of Ardinia."

With these words, the meeting had only glimpsed the horizon, and the journey that unfolded would scrutinize the depth of Ong and Keisha's commitment, the resilience of their realms, and their ability to kindle a spark of affinity within Ardinia's sentinel heart.

Keisha's voice hung like a storm on the horizon, her words laden with determination and emotion, carrying a somber weight. "The obscurity veiling our domains is masterminded by Phoenix Shadowwalker—an embodiment of malevolence who has conspired with Vuarus. In their dominion's sinister embrace, they've unshackled venomous serpents and wraiths born of shadow, instigating havoc and leaving a wake of eerie transformation."

A tremor danced within Keisha's voice, betraying the strain of her words. She closed her eyes briefly, a solitary tear traversing her cheek, a glistening testament to the agony of witnessing rampant destruction. The image of once-thriving woodlands reduced to ashen remnants bore down upon her heart, an unspoken lament etched in her gaze.

Aeliana's nod shimmered like the majestic dance of constellations, a cosmic affirmation of their quest's significance. "Indeed. Across generations, its guardianship has been entrusted to those who comprehended its true essence. Yet, as time unfurled its tapestry, the knowledge of its existence and purpose fragmented and warped."

Ong's brow furrowed in contemplation. "And now, the Abyssal Dominion hungers to exploit its might for malevolent aims."

Aeliana's luminous gaze harbored a wellspring of sorrow, the weight of ages bearing down on her ethereal form. "The forces of disarray perennially seek to manipulate the most potent wellsprings of power. The Heart of Twilight, if misappropriated, holds the sway to tilt the equilibrium irrevocably toward darkness. My sacred mandate is to ensure such a cataclysm remains a distant prospect."

Keisha's voice bore a tinge of urgency, her determination palpable. "Hence why we've sought your counsel, Aeliana—to fathom the heart's puissance and its tether to existence."

Aeliana's form seemed to resonate with approval. "In your pursuit of enlightenment, you exhibit both humility and determination. Before the trial unveils itself, I shall impart the incantations that part the veils to the heart's core. Yet, be forewarned—the heart's enigma is far from facile. Its riddles demand more than intentions; they require profound comprehension to unfurl."

Ong and Keisha exchanged a steely gaze, fortified by the resolve to confront any crucible that lay in wait. "We stand prepared to validate our resolve and cognizance," affirmed Ong.

Aeliana's ethereal form pulsated with a symphony of ancient sagacity and latent potency. "And so, the trial commences. To demonstrate your worthiness, you must traverse the Veil of Whispering Dreams—a realm birthed from the heart's core. Here, the boundary between reality and dreams wavers, discernible solely by those who harbor unflinching intent."

Keisha's gaze ignited with determination. "We are poised for this, Aeliana."

With a flourish of her luminous hand, Aeliana beckoned them, guiding them toward a gossamer curtain quivering in twilight's hues. "Cross the Veil of Whispering Dreams and let your motives light your path. May your hearts remain resolute, for this trial shall unveil the authenticity of your purpose."

Ong, Keisha, and Pumpkin exchanged a final glance—an unspoken covenant of unity and indomitable will. With their hearts as guides, they entered the diaphanous divide into the Veil of Whispering Dreams. In this realm, reality melded with dreams, their commitment unwavering and their destiny uncertain.

Chapter 18

Shadow Unveiled: Trials of Twilight

Keisha's voice, tinged with determination, cut through the mist. "Ong, in this realm where dreams intertwine with reality, our every move must be deliberate. Our bond and trust in one another will be our guiding lights."

Ong's agreement was committed as he felt the weight of their journey intensified. "We navigate a terrain as much within as it is without. Our resolve must match the challenges that arise."

As they ventured deeper into the Veil, their senses became attuned to the subtle shifts around them. The mist seemed to murmur secrets, and the shadows danced in an intricate choreography. Their steps were synchrony, a testament to their unity and shared purpose.

The trials concealed within the Veil remained veiled themselves, mysterious and unpredictable. But Ong and Keisha embraced the uncertainty, recognizing they would only uncover the answers they sought by confronting the enigmas. With every step, they traversed a tangible landscape and an inner realm, delving into the heart of their grit and devotion.

In the Veil of Whispering Dreams, time and space seemed to meld, forming a surreal and ethereal realm. Ong and Keisha moved as if suspended between reality and the figments of imagination. Raindrops glistened like liquid diamonds in the faint light that filtered through the mist, and the air was heavy with a sense of anticipation.

Ong's hand reached out, finding Keisha's fingers and intertwining them. Their connection was a lifeline, grounding them in the shifting expanse. "Keisha, in this realm, where the boundaries blur, our unity is our strength. We tread where others might falter."

Keisha's response was a whispered affirmation, her voice carrying the weight of their shared purpose. "Ong, as we journey through this veil of uncertainty, know that our bond is a beacon guiding us through the storm."

Together, they pressed on, their steps echoing in the mist-shrouded silence. The Veil held its secrets close, and as they advanced, Ong and Keisha embraced the challenge with steadfast hearts and unyielding spirits. Through obscurity, they forged a path to unravel the enigma that would reveal the depths of their intentions and the authenticity of their alliance.

Trial 1: Confronting the Past

As they forged ahead, the mist began to thin, revealing a scene that struck Ong with haunting familiarity. Before him unfolded a tableau straight from his past—a vivid and unsettling image. In this spectral vision, Keisha teetered on the back of a dragon, her expression etched with raw fear. The reality was tangled with illusion, for in the real world, Ong had managed to avert her fall, saving her from a dangerous descent with the aid of Kimras. Yet, here, trapped within the web of this dream, Ong was powerless to change the course of events.

"Keisha!" Ong's cry echoed through the misty landscape, his heart hammering against his chest. He surged forward, his steps laden with a burden that felt otherworldly—a resistance as if the very air thwarted his advance. His arms stretched toward her, fingers straining to bridge the gap, his very being desperate to rewrite the tragedy unfolding before him.

The words she had once spoken echoed like a guiding refrain: "Falling is easy, Ong. The hard part is learning to trust that someone will be there to catch you."

His outstretched hand came agonizingly close, grazing Keisha's fingertips. But the scene shifted again, contorting into an enigmatic whirl. The surroundings were warped, complexity and confusion intermingling. Suddenly, Ong was anchored to solid ground, but Keisha was absent.

"Keisha?" Ong's voice broke, his plea swallowed by the damp murkiness around him.

Desperation clawed at his chest. A gnawing uncertainty mirrored the relentless rain.

Then, emerging from the shadows, Keisha appeared—a mirage of herself, her eyes vacant, empty of recognition. She regarded Ong with a hollow gaze as if adrift within the currents of a fragmented reality.

Ong's heart clenched, his steps tentative yet purposeful. He moved toward her, voice a gentle balm. "Keisha, it's me. Ong."

But she remained wrapped in her reality, a temporary captive within this dream's labyrinth. The weight of the trial pressed upon Ong—a stark reminder of the bonds that tethered them, the shared memories that defied mere illusion.

Drawing strength from the tapestry of their journey, Ong tenderly clasped Keisha's hand, entwining their fingers with a respectful touch. Eyes closed, he delved into their shared experiences, the challenges they had conquered, and the moments that cemented their unity. Within his heart, a glow ignited—a luminescence that waged war against the dream's encroaching darkness.

A brilliant light blossomed, a sanctuary within the nightmarish realm. As the light encompassed them, the dream's contours shifted once more. The mist withdrew, unveiling a tableau of breathtaking splendor. Ong and Keisha stood on a precipice overlooking an expanse unfurled in panoramic grandeur. Raindrops had ceased their descent, replaced by sunlight that fractured through parting clouds, gilding the horizon in shimmering gold.

Keisha turned toward Ong, her eyes gleaming with newfound recognition and profound gratitude. "Thank you," her words were a whisper, laden with the weight of their shared journey.

Ong's smile radiated warmth, his spirit buoyed by her presence. "Keisha, together we brave these trials. Always."

And thus, as if touched by some ethereal magic, the dream's tendrils untangled, the Veil of Whispering Dreams relinquishing its grasp. Ong and Keisha stepped forth, freed from the depths of the trial's illusion. They emerged with a shared triumph and a rebirth of their connection—an unspoken vow that their unwavering unity had fortified.

Unbeknownst to them, the trials they had triumphed over were a prelude to what awaited them. A tapestry of challenges lay ahead, each thread woven with increasing complexity, designed to stretch their grit and resilience to their utmost limits. Yet, regardless of the trials that lay concealed within the depths of the

Veil, they held to the unshakable belief that united, they could conquer the most formidable adversaries.

The journey through the Veil of Whispering Dreams had unveiled more than the mysteries of their past and the depths of their connection. It had revealed the indomitable spirit that resided within them—a spirit that would not falter in the face of darkness and would rise to the occasion when the realm's balance hung in the balance. And as Ong and Keisha stood at the threshold of the unknown, their hearts entwined in shared purpose, they were prepared to face whatever challenges the realm had prepared for them, ready to reshape destiny.

Trial 2: Battle of Shadows

In the second trial's enchanting realm, Ong and Keisha were trapped by a symphony of shadows and mist, their surroundings a dance of obscurity and illusion. The air held a mystic weight, an anticipatory tension that permeated every fiber of their beings.

Amidst the ethereal mists, a horde of evil figures materialized, their sinister intentions evident in their menacing gazes and ominous countenances. Ong and Keisha's instincts surged with adrenaline as they drew their weapons—the lines between reality and the dreamlike battleground blurred.

Side by side, they moved in perfect harmony, their steps synchronized with unspoken understanding. They confronted the encircling adversaries, the clash of steel against steel echoing through the eerie mist. The dance of combat unfolded, a ballet of skill and strategy as Ong and Keisha wove their blades with seamless precision. In the chaos, a familiar presence emerged from the shadows—Pumpkin, their loyal companion, leaped into the fray with fierce determination.

The trio's unity became their greatest strength, a force that pushed back the tide of darkness. Adversaries fell before their combined might, their movements resembling a symphony of courage and unity. Yet, as their foes vanished, the mist's embrace dissipated, revealing a vast, empty void that seemed to stretch into infinity. There, in the heart of the void, they stood, the echoes of their battle still reverberating, their breaths ragged.

But their victory was followed by a new challenge—a wounded Pumpkin lay before them, her paws bruised, her form haggard. Keisha's heart ached as she knelt beside their faithful panther, her gentle touch offering comfort against the pain. Ong joined her, his hands steady as he tended to Pumpkin's injuries. At that moment, they transitioned from warriors to caregivers, their bond deepening as they shared concern for their beloved companion.

Keisha's determination shone in her eyes as she met Ong's gaze, silently vowing to mend what was broken. Their actions mirrored their journey, where unity had transformed adversity into strength. As they cared for Pumpkin's wounds, they became not just healers but living embodiments of their shared resilience, protectors of the bond that had withstood trials in both reality and dreams.

Pumpkin's breathing steadied under their care, and Ong and Keisha embraced her, their touch tender and unwavering. Their shared connection was reflected in how they held one another and their loyal companion, united in their commitment to face the trials ahead.

Ong wiped away a tear that glistened on Keisha's cheek with a wistful yet warm smile. "Our journey has never been easy, but it's brought us closer," he confessed, his voice carrying the weight of their shared experiences.

Keisha's gaze met his, her eyes shimmering with gratitude and determination. "No matter the challenges, we've always found a way through."

With one final touch to Pumpkin's sleek fur, they rose as one, their unity stronger than ever. Pumpkin trotted beside them, a living testament to the unbreakable bonds they had forged. Facing the mist of the Veil once more, Ong and Keisha exchanged a meaningful glance, conveying their unwavering resolve. Hand in hand, they stepped into the veiled unknown, a realm that promised trials as enchanting as they were perilous. Together, they ventured forth in unity, love, and unwavering courage, ready to confront whatever shadows and dreams the trials might unfold.

Trial 3: Facing Doubt and Darkness

Into the heart of Trial 3, Ong and Keisha ventured, the veil of mist concealing the path ahead. The air held its breath, hushed in weighty anticipation as they stepped further into the shrouded realm, an enigmatic labyrinth unfurled. It was a winding maze lined with mirrors that reflected their appearances and the echoes of their innermost doubts and insecurities.

The mirrors stood like sentinels, beckoning them to confront the shadows within their souls. Each reflection held a profound moment of vulnerability, each scene a testament to the battles they had fought, not only with external foes but also with the doubts that could erode the strongest bonds.

Keisha's breath caught as a mirror revealed her image, surrounded by an uncontrollable magic storm. Her eyes were wide with fear as the storm raged, the chaos of her power threatening to consume her. Another mirror unveiled her struggling to harness her magic, a cloak of self-doubt casting a shadow over her potential. Then, a reflection depicted her standing alone, arms outstretched, a plea escaping her lips as she begged Ong not to abandon her for another.

Ong's gaze was drawn to a mirror that mirrored his struggles with a bow and arrow, each shot missing its intended mark, frustration etched upon his face. Another reflection unveiled him standing on the outskirts of an Eladrin gathering, the sense of isolation almost tangible. He moved closer to Keisha, the sight of himself from the past leaving a bitter taste in his mouth as he walked away from her. The image ignited a surge of anger against his uncertainties.

As they navigated the labyrinth's twists, the mirrors encircled them, their reflections magnifying the doubts in their minds. Keisha's hands grew clammy, and Ong's fists clenched, but they shared a glance, a silent reminder that they were united in their journey. With a shared resolve, they approached a mirror that encapsulated their combined fears.

Keisha lifted her hand, weaving a measured thread of magic that danced gracefully around her fingertips. Her reflection transformed, the raging storm morphing into a gentle breeze that caressed her hair.

Ong stepped forward, his focus on the bow in his grasp. As he drew the string, the arrow found its mark precisely, shattering his image of doubt. The reflections wavered, the grip of fear weakening.

With steadfast steps, they neared the moment of Keisha's plea and Ong's inner struggle. Her voice, though tremulous, was laced with conviction. "I trust you, Ong. I believe in us."

Ong met her gaze, his voice unwavering, "And I will never forsake you, Keisha. Our unity is unbreakable."

Their words resonated through the labyrinth's expanse, a harmonious declaration that shattered the mirrors' illusions. The mist receded, revealing a tranquil clearing bathed in sunlight. Keisha's tears were no longer born of fear but liberation, and Ong's once-vexing uncertainties were replaced by newfound resilience. In a tender embrace, they reveled in the triumph over their inner demons.

As they emerged from the labyrinth, hand in hand, they carried the lessons etched in their hearts. The trial had gifted them the strength to confront their vulnerabilities, forging a love fortified by trust and resilience. Each step onward was imbued with the labyrinth's teachings, preparing them for the uncharted paths.

Trial 4: The Garden of Unity

As the trio of Ong, Keisha, and Pumpkin crossed the threshold into the Sacred Grove, a profound serenity embraced them. The air bore a fragrance of tranquility, and the gentle susurrus of leaves weaved a lulling melody. They found themselves standing amidst a resplendent arboreal sanctuary, each plant a testament to nature's artistry, each more enchanting than the last. Keisha's eyes widened, pupils dilating with wonder as she beheld the magnificence around her. Her voice, scarcely louder than a breath, carried a palpable awe, "This place is nothing short of enchanting."

In tacit agreement, Ong inclined his head, his gaze marked by a hushed reverence. "Indeed, it is a testament to the boundless power of the natural world."

Embarking upon an exploratory journey through the verdant tapestry, they soon discerned that this garden was no haphazard assembly. Instead, the plants wove intricate patterns, each bloom, tendril, and tree entwined in a symphony of interdependence. The garden pulsated with an energy that resonated with the essence of unity and equilibrium.

Pumpkin, their steadfast panther companion, navigated the surroundings with cautious curiosity, her movements as graceful as the breeze that rustled through the leaves. It was as though even she acknowledged the sacredness woven into the fabric of this place.

Keisha lowered herself gracefully beside a patch of flowers, her fingers tracing the petals with a touch as delicate as a whisper. "There's an undeniable connection here, a harmony between all these living beings."

In quiet accord, Ong nodded, his eyes kindling with contemplation. "I believe this trial is an invitation to seek that same harmony within ourselves and our partnership."

The journey of discovery continued, revealing that some plants yearned for nurturing. Some wrestled with adversity, their growth stunted, while others thrived with vibrant splendor. A realization gradually unfurled—their role within this haven was to restore the equilibrium, much akin to their mission of revitalizing balance across their realms.

"This garden mirrors our endeavor to ally," Keisha mused, her gaze shifting towards Ong, a silent connection between them.

He returned her sentiment with a gentle smile, a profound understanding of her words illuminating his features. "Just as every plant possesses a purpose within this garden, we each contribute something unique to our alliance."

In this tranquil glade, amidst the lush embrace of nature's embrace, Ong, Keisha, and Pumpkin became part of a living tapestry, intertwining their roles, strengths, and destinies. As the Sacred Grove whispered its lessons, they gleaned that unity was not merely a goal to aspire to—it was the fabric of their journey.

Shoulder to shoulder, they embarked on nurturing the garden's essence. Ong's sinewy strength was a fitting counterpart to Keisha's gentle finesse. Their combined efforts wove a tapestry of profound growth and rejuvenation—a symphony of skill and sensitivity that mirrored the realm's magic.

With each tender touch and care-filled gesture, a thread of unity wove between them, transcending mere collaboration. It resonated as a living testament to their shared purpose and intertwined destinies, a tangible manifestation of the bond they'd cultivated through trials and tribulations.

As the finishing touch was bestowed upon a bud, the garden radiated with a soft luminescence as if acknowledging their shared effort. Then, like an ethereal whisper brushing their minds, a harmonious and melodic voice unfurled its melody, reverberating through their souls. "In unity lies strength, and in partnership blooms harmony. This garden thrives as a reflection of your alliance." In the exchange of a glance, a silent acknowledgment passed between Keisha and Ong, their eyes aglow with newfound wisdom. They understood that their journey wasn't about the external alliance they sought and the union they'd cultivated within them.

The garden shimmered with a serene approval, its tendrils swaying in a gentle, approving breeze. A quiet satisfaction settled upon them, the culmination of their labor and learning. Armed with the insight that unity and accord were their guiding stars, they walked forth, feeling the mantle of accomplishment wrapped around their shoulders. They were poised to embrace the forthcoming challenges, steadfast in the realization that unity was the beacon that would light their way through the shadows that besieged their realms.

With hearts emboldened and spirits alight, they left the Sacred Grove, the memory of the harmonious garden seared into their consciousness. Their final trial awaited, a culmination of their journey, and with each step, they carried with them the profound understanding that unity was the beacon that would light their way through the shadows that besieged their realm.

Trial 5: The Crucible of Choices

In the ever-shifting tapestry of mist and dreams, Ong and Keisha were trapped in separate trials, each confronted by an ordeal that tested the very core of their beings.

In Ong's vision, he stood upon the jagged edge of a precipice, the world beneath him a vortex of molten fire and ominous red glow. Keisha was suspended perilously over the searing abyss, caught in the clutches of unseen forces that threatened to relinquish her into the fiery inferno below.

His heart reverberated within him, torn between two realms of anguish. To save Keisha, his partner and beloved, he must divulge the secret of E'vahona's hidden sanctuary. Yet, his soul was bound to a sacred oath to safeguard the realm that had chosen him as its guardian.

"Ong, please!" Keisha's anguished plea resonated in the air, her gaze locking onto his with a desperate plea for deliverance.

A tumultuous upheaval of conflicting emotions surged within him as he grappled with an unenviable choice. Love waged war against duty, two titans vying for supremacy within his soul. The weight of Keisha's fear bore heavily upon him, and the realization that he held the power to end her torment tormented him mercilessly.

Yet, amidst the turmoil, a quiet resolve began to unfurl like the wings of an ancient bird. A determination rooted in the solemn oath he had pledged to E'vahona—a pact that transcended even the most profound love. With a heavy heart, Ong closed his eyes, his hands curling into fists as he found strength in his conviction. Slowly, he turned away from the precipice, Keisha's anguished gaze, and from the allure of relinquishing the realm's safeguarded secrets. He walked resolutely from the edge, each step weighed by a sorrowful decision that would forever echo in his soul.

In the ever-shifting tapestry of mist and dreams, Ong and Keisha were trapped in separate trials, each confronted by an ordeal that tested the very core of their beings.

In Keisha's dream, the air held its breath in anticipation of an impending cyclone. Amidst the eerie stillness, she was trapped within a moonlit clearing, her wrists bound to a weathered post. A sinister ring of Druchii archers encircled her, their malevolent grins and cruel jests casting a chilling shadow over the scene. Their bows were drawn, arrows aimed at the defenseless figure of Ong, who shared a similar fate.

"Keisha, it's me! Don't yield to them!" Ong's voice reverberated through the charged atmosphere, a symphony of urgency and earnest request.

Tears glistened in Keisha's eyes as she confronted the heart-rending dilemma. On the one hand, she could safeguard Ong—the keeper of her heart—by surrendering the enigmatic truths of E'vahona. Conversely, she held a sacred duty as an Eladrin, an entrusted guardian of the realm that had woven its essence into the very fabric of her being.

Her gaze oscillated between Ong's imploring eyes, brimming with an unspoken affinity, and the looming presence of the Druchii archers, poised to unleash their lethal arrows. The struggle within her was visceral, a vortex of devotion and obligation that tugged at her soul. Ong's desperation, his vulnerability, resonated deeply within her.

Yet, as a testament to her unwavering loyalty, Keisha inhaled a trembling breath and shifted her gaze away from Ong's anguished expression. She chose to close her eyes to the agony of the decision, to turn her back on the love that beckoned. Her bonds with E'vahona were unbreakable, an unyielding responsibility she could not forsake. Each step she took away from Ong was a shard of her heart shattering, the echo of her choice reverberating in the silent realm of dreams.

The resonances of their choices lingered like fading echoes, and an ethereal hush settled over the dreamscape. A serenity, both eerie and profound, replaced the earlier tension. Ong and Keisha stood apart, each heart burdened by the gravity of their decisions. Their souls had brushed against the precipice of sacrifice, the depth of their bond now veiled in an even more profound understanding.

The voice, soft as a breeze yet resonant as distant thunder, broke the stillness. "The trials are concluded," it declared, the timbre carrying a weight of finality. Slowly, the veils of mist began to retreat, revealing the glorious panorama of Ardinia once more.

The landscape unfolded like a breathtaking tapestry, the vibrant hues of Ardinia's beauty awash with the warm embrace of sunlight. Still separated by their choices, Ong and Keisha silently contemplated the world. The trials had reshaped their bond, forging a connection that transcended even the most profound love rooted in duty, loyalty, and sacrifice.

In the distance, the silhouette of Aeliana appeared, bathed in a radiant light that seemed to emanate from her very being. She approached, her presence a soothing balm to their weary souls. "Your choices have been made, and your commitment tested," Aeliana intoned, her eyes reflecting the wisdom of ages. "Through these trials, you have demonstrated the strength of your alliance and the depth of your devotion. You have found the path to safeguard your realms in unity and purpose."

Ong and Keisha exchanged glances, their eyes meeting with an unspoken understanding. The trials had revealed that their love, while profound, was but one facet of their connection. Their unity was founded on something more profound—an unbreakable bond forged through shared trials and sacrifices.

Aeliana continued, "As guardians of your realms, you now possess the strength and wisdom to confront the hostility threatening your lands. The heart's secrets shall remain veiled, but your alliance has been fortified, and your resolve steeled."

As they passed through the portal, leaving behind the dreamscape of trials, they carried the lessons learned—the value of duty, the strength of unity, and the enduring power of their love. The journey ahead would be fraught with challenges, but they were prepared to face them as guardians, allies, and soulmates.

And in the realm of Ardinia, where their hearts beat as one, they would rise to meet whatever darkness threatened their beloved lands, bound by a unity that could not be broken.

Keisha's eyes gleamed with unyielding determination. "Beyond the realm of E'vahona, our alliance shall remain veiled, a secret woven into the fabric of time."

Aeliana's smile, a whisper of ethereal grace, curved gently. "Your discernment is a testament to your wisdom." With her words, an unspoken covenant seemed to settle in the air—an agreement that transcended mere speech, rooted in their shared purpose.

Beneath the dappled tapestry of sunlight that filtered through the verdant canopy, Aeliana beckoned with a gracious gesture, guiding Ong and Keisha along a path that led deeper into the heart of Ardinia. The landscape around them bore an almost sentient aura, a symphony of beauty that hummed with latent magic, secrets poised on the cusp of revelation.

With each step, their feet seemed to press into layers of mystic knowledge beneath the soil. Aeliana's voice, carrying the timbre of ageless wisdom, wove a delicate harmony with the rustling leaves. "You have confronted your innermost fears and embraced the essence of Ardinia's magic," her words resonated, infusing the air with an aura of significance. Her gaze, a fusion of sagacity and compassion, regarded both Ong and Keisha.

"Before we move forward," she spoke, her words akin to whispered incantations, "there is a gift I wish to bestow upon you." Aeliana paused, allowing the weight of her intent to find its mark. "It is a bond of connection, a medium through which we may commune when the threads of destiny entwine our paths."

Heavy with curiosity and anticipation, a shared glance passed between Ong and Keisha. What Aeliana extended transcended mere spoken words—an intangible tether, a connection spanning time and distance.

Aeliana extended her hand, and a gossamer thread from her palm emerged with a gentle, iridescent luminance. It bore the essence of Ardinia's magic, a testament to its origin. She shifted her gaze to Ong. "For you, Ong of Crystal Vale, a connection rooted in the age-old strength of the earth."

With a touch of reverence, Ong extended his hand, allowing the ethereal thread to entwine his wrist. The moment it settled, a soothing warmth unfurled within him as though the pulse of the land had merged with his very being.

Aeliana's focus shifted to Keisha, a moment pregnant with anticipation. "And for you, Keisha of E'vahona, a connection interwoven with the very essence of the elements."

Keisha extended her hand, her breath held in wonder as a second thread emerged. Its luminous hues danced and flickered akin to the mesmerizing play of flames. The thread wound around her wrist, imbuing her with a surge of vitality, like the raw power of the elements themselves flowing through her veins.

Aeliana's tender yet resolute voice conveyed an ancient authority undertone as she explained, "These threads shall serve as conduits across distances when the need arises. Place your trust in their magic, for they are a tangible extension of the enchantment that binds Ardinia."

Ong and Keisha nodded a harmonious agreement between them, manifesting gratitude and unwavering determination. Their expressions bore the weight of understanding, the profound significance of this bestowed gift—a manifestation of the alliance they had nurtured with Ardinia.

With each step they took, Aeliana's words resonated in the air, an unspoken promise that threaded their hearts together. The path ahead remained veiled in enigma, yet they carried with them the means to traverse any gaps that might try to separate them.

Bound by threads woven by destiny, they embraced Aeliana's guidance, poised to confront any trials destiny chose to lay before them. Her words flowed like a river of wisdom. "The trials have unveiled the depth of your bond," she stated, her gaze unwavering, imbued with a knowing that transcended time. "However, for the time being, the bond you share and the alliance it signifies must remain hidden—especially beyond the boundaries of E'vahona."

Ong and Keisha nodded solemnly, comprehending the gravity of the secrecy that their alliance demanded. "Rest assured," Ong affirmed, his voice carrying the weight of commitment.

With a tender curve of her lips, Aeliana's grace continued to illuminate the scene. "Before you embark on your next path, I have one final offering." With a fluid gesture, her hand extended, and from its center emerged a small crystal, its surface intricately carved.

She presented it to Ong, the weight of anticipation filling the air. "This crystal bears the resonance of a unique magical pocket within Ardinia. When the time aligns—when you seek us, or we seek you—channel your intentions through it. It shall act as a compass, guiding your presence to one another."

Keisha, in turn, received a crystal akin to Ong's, their fingertips brushing the artifacts, and in that connection, a temporary energy passed, marking their unity.

"Gratitude fills my heart," Keisha voiced, her words woven with sincerity.

Aeliana's gaze mirrored both ancient sagacity and the spark of aspiration. "Now, go forth, embrace the road that beckons, and remember that the radiance of Ardinia accompanies you."

With her farewell resonating in the air, Ong, Keisha, and Pumpkin commenced their departure, retracing their steps from the core of Ardinia and into the midst of veiled mists. As their journey continued, Aeliana's voice lingered on the breeze, echoing a reminder, "Hold steadfast to this understanding: the core of this alliance is founded not merely on might, but on the bonds of empathy and trust that intricately entwine your destinies."

With a graceful gesture, Aeliana summoned a shimmering portal that beckoned them back to their realms. Ong and Keisha stepped forward, their hearts and souls intertwined in a new understanding of their partnership.

With each stride, the mists shrouded them, and the realm of Ardinia gradually dissolved from view. Their destination lay in the world beyond—a reality brimming with challenges. Yet, they bore within them the realization that solitude was a myth. Allies and the ember of hope thrived even amidst shadows.

Emerging from the enshrouding mist, they stood once more at the precipice of their world. A mutual glance between Keisha and Ong conveyed a profound, unbreakable rope between them. The crystals, touched by their fingers, silently bore witness to a pact—an unspoken commitment to shield their realms, to stand as one against the impending darkness, and to champion a future where light and optimism triumphed.

Their journey remained an unfinished tapestry, each footfall propelling them forward with renewed vigor, fortified by the fusion of timeless and newfound alliances.

Chapter 19

Shadows Unveiled: Reporting back to the Eladrin Council

Emerging from the ethereal embrace of the portal, Ong and Keisha found themselves reacquainting with the familiar tapestry of E'vahona—the night sky unfurled above them, a vast canvas painted in celestial hues. The moon's argent countenance hung low, casting a gentle, silvery sheen over the city below. Its radiance shimmered on cobblestone streets, turning them into rivers of quicksilver. Like distant lanterns, stars pierced the indigo canopy, their soft glow lending an otherworldly charm to the surroundings.

Their footfalls resonated through the enchanting streets, each step a connection between the extraordinary and the ordinary. The air bore a gentle, comforting whisper, as if the very city welcomed them back into its embrace. Buildings adorned with intricate carvings stood as silent sentinels, their architecture an ode to E'vahona's rich history.

Amidst the tranquil serenade of the night, Lord Karrenen approached, his presence an embodiment of E'vahona's legacy. He wore robes that mirrored the night sky, adorned with intricate patterns that caught the moonlight. His gaze held a genuine warmth as he welcomed them. "Welcome back," his voice carried, a soothing symphony of camaraderie. "News of your return reached me. How fared your journey?"

A shared glance between Ong and Keisha spoke volumes, a silent conversation laden with the echoes of challenges overcome. "Adventure would be an apt description," Ong responded, his tone carrying a hint of fatigue underscored by an undercurrent of gratitude.

A nod of comprehension accompanied Lord Karrenen's smile. "I can only imagine," he conceded, his voice a mingling of empathy and recognition. "However, considering the late hour, I recommend that both of you seek rest. Tomorrow morning, the council chambers shall be prepared for your debriefing."

Keisha stifled a yawn, her exhaustion surfacing with an undeniable force. "You're right, Lord Karrenen. Rest sounds like the most enticing proposition right now."

"Indeed," Ong affirmed with a nod. "We shall convene with the council to share our experiences come dawn."

As they began their retreat toward the embrace of their home, Pumpkin scampered ahead, her vitality a testament to her delight in familiar surroundings. With a graceful curl, the panther nestled into her chosen corner, her rhythmic purring a lullaby of contentment.

Seated in the peaceful ambiance of their dwelling, Ong and Keisha faced each other, and their gazes interlocked in the half-light. "What a journey," Keisha commenced, her voice an admixture of wonder and fatigue. "From the opulence of Ardinia to those trials that tested our very core, I still find it hard to believe all that we've traversed."

A nod of agreement accentuated Ong's response, his eyes mirroring the weight of experiences etched upon his soul. "Indeed, the breadth of our discoveries and the deepening of our bond are remarkable. Yet, the trials—particularly the final—laid bare our vulnerabilities and compelled us to contemplate the choices that might await."

Keisha sighed, the fatigue of emotional upheaval evident on her shoulders. Her eyelids, heavy with exhaustion, momentarily drooped. "Confronting those visions was an emotional ordeal, but it also crystallized my emotions toward you and our shared purpose."

His hand reached out, encompassing hers within its gentle grasp. Their fingers interlocked, a symbol of their unbreakable connection. "You're not alone in that sentiment, Keisha. As arduous as it's been, our journey has woven an unbreakable bond between us."

A brief silence ensued, during which the weight of unspoken thoughts hung heavy. Against this backdrop of contemplation, Pumpkin's tranquil snores painted a tableau of comfort. Eventually, Ong punctuated the stillness with a voice that held both tenderness and resolve. "Tomorrow, we stand before the council to unveil our alliance with Ardinia. We must be ready to convey every aspect of our journey, the trials, the growth, and the profound connections we've forged."

Keisha's nod radiated resolute determination, her eyes alight with unwavering purpose. "Our task extends beyond recounting the journey," she affirmed, her voice carrying the weight of responsibility. "We must impress upon the council the necessity of safeguarding our newfound alliance until it's indispensable. The veil of secrecy is our strongest armor against the Abyssal Dominion's knowledge."

Ong's hand provided a reassuring squeeze, his touch a silent affirmation of their shared cause. "Precisely. The sanctuary of our realm hinges upon our discretion and timing."

In perfect accord, they drew closer, their spirits aligning as they exchanged an affectionate kiss—an unspoken pact sealed with the warmth of their lips. "Rest is a necessity," Ong recommended, his words a gentle murmur painted with affection. "As the sun graces us with a new day, our purpose shall guide us toward untrodden paths. There is much to be done."

As the night's velvety shroud enveloped them in its tranquil fold, Ong, Keisha, and Pumpkin nestled into a cocoon of much-needed repose. Their slumber became a tapestry interwoven with reflections of battles waged and victories seized, a dreamscape where their thoughts intertwined with the tapestry of their shared journey.

Unbeknownst to them, the dawn heralded fresh trials, pivotal decisions, and revelations that would etch their following Odyssey chapters. The world of Vacari awaited, and within it, their alliance with Ardinia was a beacon of hope, a light to pierce the shadows that threatened their realms.

Within the concealed recesses of the Abyssal Dominion's hidden chambers, an air of palpable tension clung to the surroundings like a shroud. Phoenix, a figure aflame with restless energy, paced ceaselessly across the dim expanse. His footsteps echoed ominously in the dimly lit chamber as fiery eyes brimming with vexation flickered like embers in his frustration. "How can they vanish so adeptly? Have they truly mastered the art of evasion?"

Lyra, the embodiment of a shadow's subtlety, leaned casually against a wall that embraced her presence. The soft, dim light cast eerie shadows upon her features, and a wry grin played upon her lips, amusement and annoyance mingling seamlessly in her demeanor. "Phoenix, darling, expecting our adversaries to cater to your schedule is an exercise in futility."

Phoenix's gaze shot daggers at Lyra, his irritation palpable. His voice carried a sharp edge as he responded, "I expect them to be where we can track them down."

Vuarus, usually the embodiment of contemplative calm, bore a furrowed brow as a troubling realization etched lines upon his features. His voice carried the weight of unease as he spoke, "There is a more profound enigma at play, Phoenix. The ancient tomes we've sought with enthusiasm have inexplicably vanished. It's as though they've been snatched from our grasp."

Phoenix's pacing ceased abruptly. His attention snapped to Vuarus as if drawn by an unseen force. "Are you insinuating that they've acquired the texts we've yearned for?"

Vuarus' nod was solemn, his eyes aflame with an unsettling concern. "It's a possibility—one we cannot afford to dismiss. And if they possess the secrets concealed within those scrolls, they have an arsenal of our past transgressions."

Beneath Phoenix's veneer of frustration, a simmering anger emerged, tangible and charged. "Their newfound knowledge could be a weapon, a potent tool to bend us to their will."

Lyra's laughter, a velvety ripple of sound, intertwined with the ominous atmosphere of the room. "Isn't it fascinating, Phoenix? The infamous Abyssal Dominion—the epitome of power—is governed by leaders who harbor mistrust even in their unity."

Vuarus' expression hardened, his voice stern as steel. "This isn't a matter of jest, Lyra. If Ong and Keisha have delved into the depths of our history, they could expose our weaknesses and manipulate us from within."

Phoenix's agitation morphed into a veneer of chilling calm, an unsettling stillness radiating from him. "Then we must brace ourselves. If they intend to challenge us, they will witness the full force of our dominion."

As the trio stood amidst shadows, a silence fell—an almost tangible weight that underscored the gravity of their predicament. The Abyssal Dominion, a volatile union bound by ambition, dominance, and mutual suspicion, rocked upon the precipice of transformation. Ong and Keisha's actions had ignited a chain of events poised to reshape their fates. In the twilight of uncertainty, their destinies hung suspended, awaiting the hands that would shape their narrative.

From the shadows that clung to the chamber's corners, Qellaun emerged—an embodiment of stealth and surveillance, his very presence weaving an uncanny tapestry of enigma. His form seemed to flicker in the dimness, casting an otherworldly aura that heightened the eerie ambiance. His voice, a mere susurration, pierced the air like a whispered secret. "Mighty lords, my watchful gaze has been cast over Crystal Vale and Goldmoor. Yet, Ong and Keisha have not visited either realm since their last encounter. It's as if they've dissolved into the ether."

Phoenix's eyes, a volatile interplay of irritation and curiosity, ignited with enthusiasm. "Vanished? Such an act eludes their capabilities."

Qellaun's nod held a weight of acknowledgment, his words veiled in shadows. "I've tracked their habitual routes and interactions. They might be delving beyond our immediate vicinity, perhaps in pursuit of alliances that transcend our immediate scope."

Lyra, a confluence of shadow and disdain, responded with a scoff, her voice dripping with cynicism. "Alliances? Unless they summon allies from the nether, their existing circle appears exhaustive."

Vuarus' patience, once unwavering, waned as he turned his gaze toward Lyra, his voice edged with frustration. "Enough, Lyra. Spare us your acerbic wit and channel your energies toward the task. We're endeavoring to uncover the Heart of Twilight. Remember, failure won't spare you or your brother from the repercussions—your titles within the alliance will be ruthlessly stripped."

Lyra's response was measured, each word an incisive blade honed with precision. "The Heart of Twilight's shrouded sanctuary resists easy revelation. Its secrets are veiled beneath layers of enigma."

Phoenix's patience, too, wore thin, his fist colliding with a table in a burst of pent-up anger. "Find it, and we shall. Regardless of the toll it exacts."

Within the chamber, a silence descended, the air thick with unresolved tension. The Abyssal Dominion teetered upon a precipice, suspended between a future of dominion or desolation. In the interplay of determination, ambition, and submerged conflicts, they navigated an intricate dance that could seal their fates in glory or doom.

In the wake of their tense deliberations, the members of the Abyssal Dominion dispersed—each carried away by the gravity of their aspirations and designs. Amidst the fading echoes, the chamber stood as a testament to the intricate interplay of their collective destinies, a symphony of power and intrigue that echoed into the heart of a world on the brink of change.

Amidst the explosive exchange that engulfed the ranks of the Abyssal Dominion, Talleoss stood as an observer—a silent sentinel shrouded in a veneer of amusement and cynicism. His presence threaded through the air like a phantom's whisper, a figure adept at quiet contemplation and astute analysis. As the dissenting voices clashed and the tendrils of discord unfurled, his lips curled with a knowing amusement that danced upon the precipice of mockery.

A mirthful murmur escaped his lips in the ancient Draconic tongue, the words winding forth like serpentine coils. "Iilthun aluska, lythareth morik," (How these individuals squabble and brawl).

Talleoss, a master of secrets and a harbinger of clandestine intentions, had cultivated a life veiled in shadows—a realm of solitude where he navigated the currents of information without raising a ripple. As the bickering voices echoed within the chamber, he couldn't suppress a soft chuckle that resonated like a cryptic melody in the heart of the night.

"Malurin jukris," he breathed, a wry smile gracing his lips. (Such folly).

Amidst the grand tableau of power plays and personal vendettas, Talleoss remained steadfast in his convictions. Loyalties were unspoken. He harbored his allegiance beyond the Abyssal Dominion's reach. Despite the crystal prison that ensnared his form, his spirit retained its indomitable essence—a flame of resilience untouched by captivity. Beneath the veneer of impassivity, he had forged a pact shrouded in secrecy—a solemn vow made to Kadona, a harbinger of light amid encroaching shadows. Together, they had woven a clandestine narrative, a promise to join forces against the surging tide of darkness.

His thoughts swirled with a wise determination, a clandestine pact woven with threads of secrecy. "Iilrithas tashira, veltharn Kadona," he mused to himself. (I shall remain the silent sentinel, an unseen ally). His gaze, sharpened by sagacity, held an unspoken oath. "Santhar veska, aklar saesh." (When the hour aligns, destiny's truth shall be revealed).

Vuarus's gaze, sharp and calculating, locked onto Phoenix. "Remember our original plan, Phoenix. Capturing Keisha is our optimal course. Her Eladrin lineage and potent magic make her a coveted prisoner. Her panther companion presents an additional layer of complexity."

Phoenix's nod was a sinister dance of shadows and intentions. "Indeed, Vuarus. She could be wielded as a potent weapon against her kin by bending her will." Their voices dipped into hushed secrecy as they embarked on a whispered strategy session, crafting the most covert approach to ensnare Keisha without rousing the suspicions of their adversaries.

The threads of their dark machinations wove a perilous tapestry, one they hoped would bind the elusive Eladrin to their evil designs.

Amidst their plotting, Lyra's voice broke through with an air of cynicism. "Capturing Keisha might prove more intricate than your confidence implies. She's demonstrated resourcefulness and tenacity. Let's not overlook her alliance with Ong, who's no easy adversary."

Vuarus's withering stare bore down on Lyra. "I am well aware of their prowess. That's why precision in our plan is paramount. Errors are a luxury we cannot indulge." Phoenix leaned closer, his words dripping with vicious intent. "Once she's within our grasp, we shall dismantle her resistance. She'll watch her ties to E'vahona, and her people crumble desperately."

Lyra rolled her eyes but begrudgingly acquiesced. "Fine, fine. I pray your 'precise plan' doesn't backfire spectacularly."

Vuarus's gaze frosted as it settled on Lyra. "It won't, provided everyone adheres to their assigned roles. And, for clarity, Keisha isn't just allied with Ong—she's wed to him." His voice dipped into a chilling whisper as he muttered, "Keisha is vital for my plans, and I will ensure that no one, including Phoenix, dares to interfere."

The revelation hung like a dark omen, and a malicious smile ghosted across Phoenix's lips. "All the more reason to exert control. Her vulnerability is more potent than we imagined." In the wake of their discussions, an unsettling tension lingered.

The Abyssal Dominion's ambitions stretched like tendrils of night, poised to snare their unsuspecting targets in a labyrinth of deceit and maleficent intent.

Morning's embrace bathed E'vahona in a radiant golden light, setting the Eladrin city aglow with ethereal beauty as Ong and Keisha approached the grand council edifice. The architecture soared with an elegance that whispered of ages past, its spires reaching for the heavens, a testament to the enduring legacy of the Eladrin civilization. Lord Karrenen's presence inside the council chamber seemed to weave a spell, his magical aura palpable in the air, as he graciously welcomed the duo. The remaining council members, a gathering of wisdom and authority, assembled around the majestic circular table, their faces a reflection of both anticipation and curiosity.

With a nod of consent from Lord Karrenen, Ong and Keisha embarked on their account. Ong's voice resonated with a reassuring timbre, each word painting vivid images of their journey through the enchanting realm of Ardinia. He spoke of majestic landscapes and encounters with enigmatic beings, his words weaving a tapestry of wonder and intrigue. Keisha's gentle yet unwavering voice seamlessly intertwined with Ong's, her narrative adding depth to their shared experiences, especially their interactions with Aeliana, the Guardian of Ardinia, and their forged alliance.

As their narrative unfolded, Keisha's voice tapered into a poised pause. A shared glance between her and Ong conveyed a profound unity, and Ong cleared his throat, his gaze steady as he addressed the council directly. "Before we proceed further, we wish to discuss a matter of utmost significance. Aeliana, the Guardian of Ardinia, has genuinely requested that the knowledge of our alliance with her realm remains in secrecy for now."

The council members listened intently, their expressions shifting from curiosity to somber contemplation as Ong and Keisha recounted their journey through Ardinia. The vivid descriptions and shared experiences painted a rich tapestry of their time in the mystical realm.

When Ong addressed the matter of secrecy regarding their alliance with Ardinia, the council members exchanged glances, their brows furrowing in consideration. Lord Karrenen, the figurehead of their council, leaned forward, his voice carrying the weight of leadership. "This alliance with Ardinia is a development of great import, and we appreciate the trust you've placed in us by sharing it. However, the need for secrecy is clear. We shall honor Aeliana's request and safeguard this knowledge within the confines of our council."

A murmur of agreement rippled through the chamber as the council members pledged to keep this secret close. It was evident that the council recognized the delicate nature of this alliance and the potential dangers that could arise if it became widely known.

Ong and Keisha exchanged a relieved glance, grateful for the council's understanding. With the matter of secrecy addressed, they continued to share their experiences and insights gained during their journey, painting a more comprehensive picture of the alliance's potential and significance in the face of looming threats.

Lord Karrenen's arched brow revealed his curiosity, prompting Ong to continue. "We have acceded to her plea, and thus, we propose that only the esteemed members of this council be entrusted with this revelation. We intend to unveil this alliance at the opportune moment—a move that could deliver a devastating blow to the Abyssal Dominion."

Lord Galadon, renowned for his strategic brilliance, leaned forward, his eyes reflecting contemplation. "A prudent strategy, indeed. Concealing the presence of such a valuable ally until the right moment may indeed prove to be a formidable weapon against our mutual adversaries."

A nod from Lord Karrenen affirmed his agreement. "Agreed. We shall honor Aeliana's wishes and safeguard the secrecy of this alliance."

A palpable wave of relief washed over Keisha, and her eyes sparkled with gratitude as they traversed the council assembly. Ong's reassuring grip on her hand conveyed their shared satisfaction and the soundness of their decision.

Lady Elowen, a diplomat of unparalleled skill, added her voice to the discussion. "The bond forged between our realms will bolster our united resistance against the encroaching darkness. Ong and Keisha, your wisdom and discretion are valued beyond measure."

Lord Thaldir, the repository of ancient wisdom, offered his sage perspective. "In these intricately woven bonds, I perceive the strength and the promise of a force without equal."

Lord Galadon reclined with a confident smile. "With this pact, our preparations continue unabated. Armed with ancient knowledge and mystic allies, the Abyssal Dominion shall soon face a challenge they could never have anticipated."

Having secured the council's unanimous endorsement, Ong and Keisha exchanged glances imbued with a sense of accomplishment. As they left the grand council edifice, a renewed sense of purpose settled upon them. While the road ahead remained daunting, they journeyed not as solitary figures but as champions, encouraged by the presence of allies in their quest for triumph.

Chapter 20

Shadows Unveiled: Kadona's Oceanic Guidance

In the mystical realm of E'vahona, the tendrils of dawn reached through the delicate drapes of Ong and Keisha's abode, painting the room with a gentle, golden embrace. Stirring from their slumber, they felt a subtle undercurrent of something otherworldly grazing their senses. It was as if the very essence of dreams had woven itself into the fabric of their reality.

And then, as if summoned from the ethereal realm, Kadona, the Luminary Goddess and guardian of the Eladrin Elves, manifested before them. Her presence was a luminous tapestry of celestial radiance, a breathtaking vision that defied mortal comprehension.

Her voice, a symphony of warmth and urgency, rippled through the air like a melody that resonated with the very heartstrings of the universe. "Keisha, Ong," each syllable she uttered was a resonating chord, "a matter of utmost significance demands your presence."

Keisha and Ong shared a silent communion, their spirits harmonizing in the presence of such divine luminance. They knew that this moment was destined, that their fates were entwined with the Goddess's purpose.

"Goddess Kadona, your radiance graces our humble home," Keisha spoke, her words infused with reverence. "How may we be of aid?"

Kadona's gaze, like stardust caught in a moonbeam, danced between them, her eyes holding the wisdom of ages. "From the mystical realm of Coraluna, the domain of the merfolk, a message has come to me. The threads of destiny waver, and alliances must be woven to counter the encroaching shadows. I implore you to voyage to Coraluna and secure their pact."

Ong's affirmation was unwavering, his voice resonating like the solid foundations of the earth. "As you command, Goddess Kadona."

But the Goddess's message was far from complete. "Another purpose unfurls like delicate petals in the breeze. Both luminary and shadow may covet the Heart of Twilight, an artifact of potent secrets yet concealed. Lysander, the Ancient of Seas, guards the cartography to its hidden sanctuary. Seek him amid the enclaves of Coraluna."

A revelation blossomed within Keisha's eyes, akin to the unfolding of a starlit tapestry. "In Lysander's depths, the riddle to unveil the Heart's sanctum may lie, like a treasure hidden beneath the azure waves, waiting for those with the courage to seek it."

Kadona's voice gathered like a crescendo, her words a herald of unshakable resolve, resonating through the room like a sacred proclamation. "Wise and hoary, Lysander's insight is a compass in the most turbulent waters. Remember, your shoulders bear not the burdens of a singular realm. Fates myriad rest upon your odyssey. Nerissa, Keeper of the Heart of Twilight, is Lysander's aegis, a sentinel to its sanctity."

Locked in a steadfast accord, Ong and Keisha exchanged glances, their commitment echoing like a harmonious duet, their voices filled with unwavering determination. "Goddess Kadona, we grasp the mantle of your charge. To Coraluna, we shall voyage, and within Lysander's lore, the path shall be unveiled."

Kadona's countenance remained aglow, an embodiment of solace itself. "As you tread the paths of destiny, let the luminance guide and fortify your journey. As allies rally amidst shadows, may their strength burgeon. Fare thee well, and know that my watchful gaze shall ever be upon you."

With Kadona's ethereal aura fading like a sigh in the wind, Ong and Keisha surged from their resting place, reborn with a renewed flame of purpose. The voyage to Coraluna beckoned—an odyssey entwined with promises of comradeship, veiled enigmas, and trials that held the sway to the world's destiny.

Locked in a shared resolve, Ong and Keisha's eyes conversed silently. After the conversation with Kadona, the mantle of their journey bore the sigil of Shimmering Coast, an oceanic sanctum where the merfolk's kinship awaited. Here, the accord must be woven against the gathering dark, and the fabled harbinger of the abyss—the Heart of Twilight—must be unraveled in Lysander's presence.

Yet, their perception bore the weight of awareness. The Abyssal Dominion, tendrils of malevolence cast wide, sought to shadow their every step, thrusting the merfolk into unbidden peril.

"Lord Karrenen might proffer counsel," Ong ventured, shattering the hush. "He could illuminate a path to Shimmering Coast that eludes the gaze of our foes."

Keisha concurred with a nod, her eyes reflecting her consent in the language of her permission. "Agreed. The merfolk's safety hinges upon our discretion."

With their resolve steeled and their purpose clear, Ong and Keisha embarked on their journey, guided by the radiant light of Kadona's wisdom and the hope of forging alliances that would shape the destiny of E'vahona and beyond.

Thus resolved, Ong and Keisha left their haven and went to the council's hallowed hall. Lord Karrenen, the venerable sage, was found within, deeply engrossed in the ancient chants that filled the chamber with mystic resonance. Lord Karrenen's gaze lifted as they entered, and his eyes welcomed them with a genial embrace.

"Hail, Ong and Keisha," his words wove a tapestry of warmth. "Pray, how might my wisdom serve you?"

Ong's stride bore purpose, his intent clear and unwavering. "The shores of Shimmering Coast beckon. A pact with the merfolk, an audience with Lysander—the crux of our design."

Lord Karrenen's demeanor shifted to sobriety as he considered their words. "A noble and paramount pursuit, given the pall that shrouds our days."

Keisha took up the discourse, her voice a vessel for their shared apprehension. "Yet, the relentless pursuit of the Abyssal Dominion threatens to unveil our steps prematurely. We must shield the merfolk from untimely jeopardy."

Lord Karrenen's beard was brushed in contemplative strokes as he mulled over their predicament. "I comprehend your plight. And within the annals of antiquity, a solution resides—an arcane portal that veils passage to realms afar, shielding your traverse from prying eyes."

Ong and Keisha exchanged glances that shimmered with intrigue, as if they held a whispered conversation in the language of anticipation. "A portal of enchantment?" Keisha ventured, the cadence of her voice a dance of curiosity.

Lord Karrenen's affirmation was a gesture of sage wisdom. "Indeed, a portal woven from the strands of magic itself. It's a lattice of transit that casts no trace upon the threads of existence, a conduit that shall bear you to your chosen sanctuary. Like shadows dissolving in the night, you shall vanish from one realm and reemerge in another, all unseen by watchful eyes."

Ong's countenance ignited like the first starlight piercing Twilight's cloak. "A beacon of hope in the murk. How might this conduit be summoned?"

A tender glimmer played at Lord Karrenen's lips, as if he held the key to a harmonious secret. "Such a weave is intricate, born from the harmonics of distinct essences. I shall assemble the necessary facets and compose the incantations. Once the tapestry is poised, you shall traverse the threshold and find yourselves in Shimmering Coast."

Gratitude, pure and resonant, was etched into Keisha's gaze. "Lord Karrenen, your generosity shall not be forgotten. Your guidance gifts us solace."

He acknowledged their sentiments with a regal incline of his head. "To aid you is an honor graced upon me. I shall weave the strands, and when the skein is whole, I shall summon you."

"With the council's chambers gradually retreating behind them, Ong and Keisha embraced renewed hope, an aura akin to a gossamer shroud that wrapped around their hearts. The prospect of traversing to Shimmering Coast, veiled from the relentless pursuit of the Abyssal Dominion, brought them closer to the merfolk's embrace and the enigma-bound Heart of Twilight's secret unveiling.

The passage of time bore witness to Ong and Keisha's unwavering resolve as they prepared for the imminent journey to Shimmering Coast. Their abode, a sanctuary of tranquility, was filled with the subdued hum of anticipation. Their belongings, carefully selected for their voyage, were arrayed in precise order. The panther, Pumpkin, moved with an innate understanding, her presence a testament to their unbreakable bond.

Ong's soft and measured voice wove a protective spell around their preparations. "The portal will soon be ready. Lord Karrenen's wisdom shall guide our path."

Her eyes reflecting the ethereal dawn, Keisha met Ong's gaze with unwavering determination. "The merfolk await, and the Heart of Twilight beckons. We shall unravel the shadows that seek to engulf our realms."

As they donned their traveling attire, adorned with enchanted trinkets and amulets, they bore the weight of their purpose with grace. The portal's imminent summoning filled the room with quiet anticipation, a melody of promise harmonizing with the beating heart of E'vahona."

"Within the abyssal heart of the Abyssal Dominion's hidden sanctum, a disruption of vexation hung heavy, casting shadows as palpable as ink upon the air. Phoenix, a figure cloaked in obsidian wrath, traversed a path of agitation. His eyes, twin infernos, smoldered with incensed fury.

"Unacceptable!" he spat, each syllable a venomous dagger. "How can this be, that whispers of the Heart of Twilight and the mythic merfolk city evade our grasp?"

Lyra, a bearer of steel resolve against the maelstrom of Phoenix's wrath, now stood disarmed by his palpable disappointment. She had scoured the recesses of ancient chronicles, plumbed the abyssal deeps of forbidden knowledge, and summoned shadows to her counsel. Yet, the void of her findings stared back with a chilling emptiness. Anxiety knotted her once unyielding demeanor, and her voice tinged with a rare uncertainty as she faced Phoenix's smoldering gaze.

"Every resource, every conduit of my arts, I have exhausted, Phoenix," her words held the strain of her exertion. "Yet, the threads remain elusive. These enigmas are shrouded, concealed beyond the touch of even our most twisted endeavors."

Vuarus, a sentinel of taciturn composure, found voice amidst the charged stillness. "Perhaps, Lyra, we must tread a path anew. A fresh vantage could unveil our quarry, obscured as it is. The Heart of Twilight and the merfolk's realm seem locked in shadows too deep, unfathomable even to our network's treacherous reach."

Phoenix's hands clenched in the cyclone's hold, a silent proclamation of his discontent. "No room for errors, Vuarus. The Hearts might bind the realms; the alliance of Eladrin and enigmatic merfolk could sway the tides against us. We must secure them."

Vuarus, his gaze unyielding, met Phoenix's storm. "Urgency begets wisdom, yet haste births folly. Perhaps Lyra should divert her talents elsewhere. Pursuing a sole quarry in obscurity may court our undoing. By diversifying our pursuit, we might unveil other veiled founts of power."

Lyra found strength anew as if the darkness itself imbued her with resolve. "Indeed, Phoenix. The realms are vast and ageless. The trail to revelation is not singular. If we stray our hunt to myriad secrets, we might unearth a symphony of truths, orchestrating a melody that guides us to our desired crescendo."

Phoenix's visage contorted in a mosaic of frustration, a sculpted mask of thwarted ambition. In the aftermath of his vexation, a surge of expelled air bore witness to his restraint. "Very well," he acceded, though the weight of his words held the gravity of unspoken consequences. "But heed me, Lyra. The realm of defeat is naught but an abyss we cannot fathom. The truths concealed must be unearthed ere the Eladrin weave them to their advantage."

In the shadowed recesses of their sanctum, the agents of the Abyssal Dominion embarked on a new path, their ambitions undiminished, their pursuit relentless, as they sought to unravel the secrets hidden within the tapestry of E'vahona.

As the tension coiled in the room, the leaders of the Abyssal Dominion contemplated their strategy. Their quest for dominion and supremacy continued, and the unknowns ahead fueled their determination. They understood that to control the shadows was to control their destiny, and they would stop at nothing to achieve it.

Vuarus, the contemplative one among them, sat in thought, considering a plan. "Phoenix, I have been pondering a strategy. Keisha's connection to Ong and her panther companion poses a challenge. To break her defenses, we must separate her from their unwavering unity."

Phoenix's eyes burned with ambition, reflecting his conniving intent. "Exactly. But how can we create a division between them? Their bonds are strong, and that panther possesses a wisdom we shouldn't underestimate."

Vuarus nodded, ready to conduct their evil symphony. "Indeed, we need a diversion—a discord that will draw Ong's attention away and make Keisha vulnerable enough to consider seeking our aid."

The Abyssal Dominion's sinister plans continued to take shape as Phoenix and Vuarus delved deeper into their machinations. Phoenix's fingers moved with a vicious rhythm, and his smile exuded wickedness as he proposed using the Heart of Twilight as a weapon. The room filled with the ominous air of their plotting, and they were determined to exploit their adversaries' weaknesses, even if it meant disrupting E'vahona's delicate balance.

Vuarus's eyes glinted with dark fascination as he contemplated the possibilities. "Creating illusions that unravel their bonds, sow doubts in their sacred union, and perhaps even make Keisha believe that Ong has somehow betrayed her. However, we must fully understand the Heart's capabilities to wield such mastery."

In the depths of their secret council, the Abyssal Dominion's malevolent designs took shape, their intent to wield the power of the Heart of Twilight as a weapon against the unity of Ong, Keisha, and their enigmatic companion. The shadows of E'vahona grew darker still as their machinations unfolded.

Phoenix nodded, a predator considering its quarry. "Precisely. Their dynamics, their vulnerabilities, must be discerned. We must unveil chinks in their armor, the fault lines we may exploit."

Vuarus ascended from his throne, his very stance exuding unwavering resolve. "Our spies shall shadow their every gesture. Insights shall be culled, and a stratagem hewn to sunder their alliance, all while we remain veiled in obscurity."

Phoenix arose, darkness swirling around his form. His eyes were aflame with wicked intent. "Once Keisha stands solitary, desperation shall bind her to our puppet strings. The illusion of salvation we shall weave, her solitary beacon of hope."

Vuarus's smile was wicked, a precursor of malevolence. "And Ong, in his valiant pursuit, shall wander straight into our snare."

With shared malevolence and the communion of sinister understanding, the two architects of darkness perpetuated their scheming. Their plans coalesced, driven by an insatiable thirst for dominion and the yearning to fracture the unity between Keisha, Ong, and their newfound compatriots.

In the shadowy depths of their hidden sanctum, the Abyssal Dominion's sinister web of intrigue continued to spin, casting its dark threads across E'vahona, threatening to unravel the very fabric of the world.

In the tranquil realm of E'vahona, Ong and Keisha stood once more in the presence of Lord Karrenen. The council chamber had gathered its constellation of Eladrin, a spectrum of expressions dancing between hope and trepidation. The time of action loomed, Kadona's guidance etching its mark upon their destiny.

The mission to court the merfolk's alliance, an act of weaving alliances across realms, beckoned with a cadence of urgency.

Lord Karrenen's voice, a conductor's wand in the air, cut through the atmosphere, resonating with authority. "Before the portal opens to Shimmering Coast, a final query begs an answer. In the echoing caverns of the merfolk's realm, how shall your voices reach their ears?"

Keisha's gaze converged with Ong's, a silent exchange of understanding rippling between them. Her voice, a clarion of resolve, unfurled in response. "My lord, the tapestry of friendship embraces Adrianna and me—a mermaid of Shimmering Cove. Our paths converged in past sojourns, and I trust this bond will lead us to the merfolk's council. Adrianna can pave the way for an audience with their leadership."

A nod from Lord Karrenen, deliberate as a sign of wisdom. "Indeed, Adrianna—a mermaid whose name is whispered by the currents. A worthy harbinger for this venture. Upon arriving, seek her counsel, yet veil your pursuits with shadows. The Abyssal Dominion's tendrils are insidious, and caution must be your guide."

With a flourish of his staff, the ether embraced Ong, Keisha, and their feline companion, Pumpkin. The boundary of reality shimmered and quivered, relinquishing the sanctuary of E'vahona and ushering in the ethereal allure of Shimmering Coast.

Upon the cove's sandy shores, a tableau of enchantment unveiled itself, captivating Keisha's heart with the heady symphony of anticipation and urgency. She met Ong's gaze, and her nod conveyed their unspoken accord. "Swiftly, we must find Adrianna," her voice, like a whispered incantation, carried the weight of destiny. "Our cause's foundation lies in her aid. Together, we shall map the journey to Coraluna and sow the seeds of allegiance."

Ong's touch, a soothing breeze of reassurance, caressed Keisha's shoulder. "Remember Karrenen's counsel, my love. The shadows conceal and protect. Our steps must be whispered to evade the prowling darkness. Let us advance with the wariness of phantoms and unearth Adrianna's counsel."

Ong and Keisha embarked along the shoreline with Pumpkin, their steadfast guardian, trailing beside them. Their eyes traced the labyrinthine weave of waters, vigilant for the merfolk's presence. The quest ahead, a crossroads of trials, beckoned them forward—a narrative written by resolve, penning alliances in ink of unity against the encroaching tides of night.

In the tranquility of Shimmering Coast's embrace, Keisha's thoughts raced like a galloping steed, charting their course amid the currents of fate. A familiar touch brushed her skin as her fingers combed her pack—a smooth conch shell nestled within her belongings. Recognition surged, a phoenix ascending within her mind. The shell, a friendship bridge, held the key to their advance. Adrianna's gift, bestowed to summon aid when needed, now rested in Keisha's grasp, a conduit pulsating with their connection to the merfolk. With the shell clutched close, Keisha was poised on the precipice of a chapter yet unwritten, her heart thrumming with anticipation—the embrace of a destiny interwoven with friendship, power, and the rising crescendo of a symphony bound by unity.

Amid the tranquil embrace of Shimmering Coast's sanctuary, Keisha and Ong wove their cautious steps, their footfalls whispered a lullaby upon the hallowed earth. Beneath the verdant canopy, they found solace in the sheltering shadows. Keisha's fingertips embarked on a dance of purpose, seeking the conch shell nestled amongst her belongings—a symphony of anticipation spiraling within her very touch. Triumph alighted upon her lips, a smile carving the path of victory as the shell's contour met her grasp.

A profound purpose burned in her gaze as she lifted the shell to her lips. A mellifluous murmur emerged, a symphony crafted solely for merfolk ears and, more specifically, Adrianna's. Ong, a question on his brow, bore witness to this silent serenade, yet Keisha's playful smile was a balm to his curiosity.

"We summon a dear friend," she disclosed, her voice a tender secret as her gaze lingered upon the tranquil waves. "Adrianna shall heed."

Their message cast, they sought refuge within the dappled shade, their awareness attuned to the embrace of the iridescent waters that stretched before them. The ocean's tender caress played a gentle symphony upon the shoreline—a cadence of patience in the tapestry of their vigil. Their eyes converged, a silent oath etched upon their souls—an understanding that their odyssey was at its threshold and that a symphony of secrets danced within their fate.

Amidst the hush of the ocean's breath, a subtle transmutation of water's embrace seized Keisha's attention. Before her, the aqueous canvas erupted with life as Adrianna emerged—a graceful and splendid sea nymph. Her golden hair cascaded like liquid sunlight, her sea-green eyes a reflection of boundless depths, and her mermaid tail enveloped in a tapestry of regal purples. An embodiment of ethereal beauty, Adrianna's presence was as if the sea had whispered her into existence.

"Adrianna!" Keisha's delight surged forth, her countenance an incandescence of joy.

"Keisha, your presence blesses the tide," Adrianna's voice was a tranquil harmony, an invocation of solace.

The reunion of friends marked a new chapter in their journey, as the mermaid Adrianna, a beacon of wisdom and allyship, stood ready to guide them through the labyrinthine waters of the merfolk's realm, Coraluna.

In an embrace as warm as a sunbeam's touch, Keisha conveyed their purpose for seeking Shimmering Coast's embrace and their plea for a merfolk alliance. Adrianna nodded in solemn comprehension, her sea-green gaze an empathetic pool mirroring the tides of challenges ahead.

"We stand as allies, Keisha," Adrianna's voice, a soothing murmur, bore the weight of her pledge. "Yet the sunlit shores are fraught with peril. Creatures of myriad realms patrol this realm during daylight's reign. Bide your time amidst the shelter of these trees. Night's mantle shall unveil a safe path."

Keisha and Ong, guardians of shared resolve, exchanged a silent dialogue before granting their ascent. They delved deeper into the emerald heart of vegetation, embracing nature's cloak to conceal their presence. Here, beneath the verdant canopy, they nestled in a secret niche—a sanctuary veiled from the sun's vigilant gaze. Adrianna's reassurance lingered in their thoughts as she vanished beneath the waves, her departure a fluid farewell.

"We shall prepare while the twilight veils us," Keisha's voice held a calm eagerness, a symphony woven with anticipation. "This rest is our canvas; let's craft it to our advantage."

Ong's nod was a silent affirmation, a sentinel's vow to guard their chosen sanctuary. Beside them, Pumpkin, the guardian of shadows, found reprieve—a panther's gaze shimmering with the flicker of impending adventure. As the day unfurled its chapters, they surrendered to Shimmering Cove's embrace—a symphony of beauty and mystery that whispered tales of newfound alliances and secrets unknown, a realm poised for their discovery.

As the shroud of night unfurled its ebony tapestry upon Shimmering Coast, Adrianna returned—a beacon of ethereal radiance that thrived in darkness. By her side stood Aqilus, her mate, a guardian of the watery depths, his mermaid tail adorned in a symphony of azure hues that cascaded like liquid sapphire in the moon's luminescence. Sea-green eyes converged with resolute purpose, his physique a testament to his role as sentinel within the merfolk's realm.

With an artful ballet, Adrianna and Aqilus embarked upon their approach, a tandem of elemental grace converging with the awaiting adventurers. Bound by the gravity of their undertaking, Keisha and Ong exchanged glances—the weight of their mission reverberating like a melody within their souls. Adrianna's voice, reminiscent of the tranquil sea, cleaved the silence. Keisha's explanation was a symphony of purpose, painting their quest with the brushstrokes of her words. Adrianna's nod bore empathy and understanding, her sea-green eyes like pools of empathy and resolution.

Aqilus turned, the current of his gaze commanding the spotlight. His words were measured, a compass guiding urgency while tracing the contours of their strategy. With a gentle smile, Adrianna presented a gift of incalculable value—the seaweed that would grant them passage through the depths. Their fingers embraced this lifeline, sharing its magic with Pumpkin, ensuring her guardianship within their venture.

As the enchantment of the seaweed woven its spell, Aqilus's counsel lingered—an unspoken understanding that time's river flowed with urgency. With synchronized determination, they treaded toward the water's edge, the sea's incredible allure beckoning with its siren song. Moonlight kissed their forms, finally embracing the land they relinquished. Keisha and Ong descended into the aquatic abyss, their silhouettes vanishing beneath the glistening surface. A chapter unwritten, bound to the enigma of Coraluna, embraced them in its tide. The symphony of their quest unfurled anew, submerged in mysteries as vast as the ocean's expanse.

Chapter 21

Shadows Unveiled: Journey to the Mystic City of Coraluna

Beneath the enigmatic caress of the ocean's depths, a realm of untold marvels unfurled its secrets before the eyes of Keisha and Ong. Coraluna, the legendary Underwater Kingdom spoken of in hushed tales, emerged as a realm born from dreams and spun with threads of unparalleled beauty. A palette of hues, as if drawn from the imaginations of artists and poets, painted the sprawling corals that adorned the ocean floor. Vibrant blues, like shards of cerulean dreams captured in liquid form, seemed to capture the essence of the boundless sea. Radiant purples whispered of twilight mysteries, their depths hinting at secrets hidden in the abyss. Deep pinks and mesmerizing oranges mirrored the hues of a surreal sunset, casting an ethereal glow upon the underwater landscape. Like a living tapestry, each coral formation swayed in an eternal dance with the currents, their delicate tendrils entwined harmoniously.

A mesmerizing cavalcade of life, akin to a symphony of colors, filled the watery expanse. Schools of fish, their scales adorned with shades more vivid than the most inspired artist's canvas, glided with ethereal grace through the liquid realm. Among these aquatic wonders, the enchanting sea horses paraded, their forms slender and adorned with intricate patterns that seemed chiseled by the hands of celestial artisans.

Their colors, a respectful homage to the corals, formed a living tapestry that graced the underwater sanctum. Like prima ballerinas of the ocean, sea flowers pirouetted in graceful unity with the gentle currents, unfolding their petals in an elegant ballet that seized the senses. The aqueous sunlight, filtering through from the world above, cast an iridescent embrace, illuminating every crevice and corner of this submerged paradise.

As the tandem of Keisha and Ong descended further into the heart of Coraluna, their very souls became awash with the vibrant crescendo of colors and life enveloping them. Even their companion Pumpkin, ordinarily exuberant and brimming with playfulness, moved with a newfound reverence, darting amid the corals and sea flowers as if partaking in a sacred ritual of exploration.

"By the gods," Keisha's voice escaped her lips in a hushed whisper, a testament to the overwhelming awe that gripped her. Her words, carried by the gentle undertow, mingled with the ambient currents. "This beauty... it outshines even the grandest tapestries of imagination."

Ong, his eyes wide like windows into the cosmos, nodded in silent agreement as he drank in the breathtaking spectacle before him. "It's as though we've stepped into the realm of dreams, where reality and fantasy harmonize in breathtaking unity."

Adrianna, a guide bathed in the essence of the ocean, graced them with a warm smile, her sea-green eyes mirroring the hues surrounding them. "Coraluna, my dear friends, is a realm where magic and beauty hold court, where the hand of nature paints its most vibrant strokes. Yet, as enchanting as the surface may appear, there are depths to this kingdom that remain concealed. Join me and let us traverse onward to the heart of this realm's mysteries."

Guided by the wisdom of Adrianna and the graceful presence of Aqilus, the trio pressed further into the tender embrace of Coraluna's depths. The very essence of the sea enveloped them, weaving a tapestry of wonder and intrigue that drew them ever more profound. With each passing heartbeat, the allure of this aquatic sanctuary seemed to amplify, ensnaring Keisha and Ong in enchantment as irresistible as the siren's call.

As the intrepid quartet—Keisha, Ong, Adrianna, and Aqilus—pressed deeper into the heart of Coraluna, their path unfolded before them like pages from an enchanted story. The ocean floor, a canvas woven from dreams and adorned with nature's finest brushstrokes, bore many coral formations. Some were as delicate as whispered secrets, intricate in their design, while others stood tall and imposing, their presence a testament to the grandeur of the underwater realm. Amidst this living tapestry, a kaleidoscope of marine life thrived, each species a testament to the boundless creativity of the ocean's depths. Fish, adorned in palettes too bold for mere reality, flitted and danced among the corals, painting a living mosaic of colors that pirouetted before the observers' wide eyes.

Their journey led them to encounters with creatures of profound elegance—dolphins, the very embodiment of grace, moved through the waters in harmonious pods. As if attuned to the newcomers' presence, the dolphins approached with a curiosity that bridged the gap between their worlds. Echoes of their playful clicks and lyrical whistles resonated throughout the aqueous realm, a symphony that embraced the senses and whispered tales of connection.

Further still, the enigma of an ancient civilization emerged from the depths, a phantom from the annals of time itself. These ruins, draped in the embrace of coral, held stories etched into their time-worn pillars that lingered like forgotten melodies. Intricate carvings adorned the weathered stone, a cryptic language hinting at legacies now submerged in the currents of memory. Nature had claimed its dominion over the remnants of this underwater city, with sea plants and creatures weaving their narrative of life's unyielding spirit amidst the echo of forgotten lives.

With a voice that carried the weight of reverence, Adrianna shared her wisdom, revealing the secrets of the past. "Behold these ruins, remnants of a civilization that once flourished here, a testament to the merfolk's ancient ties to the sea. The ebb and flow of time leaves its mark, yet our roots are entwined with the very currents that cradle us."

Aqilus's tone, a blend of contemplation and wisdom, added his voice to the conversation. "Time may obscure the physical remnants, but the sea remains the keeper of memories. We must honor those who forged our path and, in doing so, safeguard the delicate equilibrium of this realm."

Keisha and Ong, captivated by the echoes of history and the depth of connection, listened with rapt attention. Amid the echoes of time and the vibrant chorus of sea life, they found themselves linked to the ocean's embrace—a connection that whispered of mysteries yet unveiled and the limitless possibilities that danced within the currents.

With the continuing steps of Keisha, Ong, Adrianna, and Aqilus, the saga within Coraluna's enchanting depths took shape. They found themselves amidst scenes of breathtaking beauty, each more mesmerizing than the last. Corals, sculpted by nature's hands, adorned the expanse in a mesmerizing display of hues and forms that defied earthly imagination. Colors mingled and clashed, choreographing an aquatic ballet, while a lively symphony of small and grand fish filled the depths with their graceful presence.

In her curiosity, Pumpkin flitted and twirled between the corals and sea flowers, an embodiment of wonder amidst the tapestry of Coraluna's wonders. Tiny fish, shimmering like living gemstones, danced in the sunlit patches that filtered through the water, casting a spell of light and shadow that painted the underwater world with a touch of magic.

Deeper into the heart of Coraluna, the group's journey carried them into a realm where coral formations rose like towering monuments, evoking a sense of awe that resonated with every breath they took. Amid this grandeur, the dolphins emerged as ethereal dancers, their movements mirroring the currents that embraced them. Their presence was an enchanting addition to the underwater symphony, a testament to the seamless harmony of life in the ocean's embrace.

Yet, amidst this captivating beauty, Ong's inquisitive nature stirred, giving voice to a question that had lingered like a shadow. His gaze turned to Aqilus, a wellspring of knowledge and experience. "Aqilus," he ventured, his voice laced with curiosity and concern, "as mesmerizing as this realm is, do hidden dangers lurk beneath its captivating surface?"

Aqilus responded with a solemn nod, his sea-green eyes shimmering with both the light of wisdom and the shadow of caution. "Indeed, Ong, Coraluna's allure is not devoid of peril. While beauty thrives here, so do creatures that have evolved to navigate its intricacies, often wielding adaptations that might challenge those who venture here."

He gestured toward the vibrant tapestry of sea life around them, his words carrying a weight of truth. "Some of the residents of these corals wield venomous defenses or potent toxins designed to safeguard their territory. The currents, while enchanting, can be unpredictable and swift, a challenge even for the most skilled swimmers. Even though the dolphins are known for their friendliness, the sea holds territorial beings that might perceive outsiders as intruders."

Adrianna's voice, a blend of caution and camaraderie, added her insight. "Ong, it's a realm woven with balance. An intricate tapestry of beauty and wonder exists in tandem with the dangers. It's the eternal rhythm of life beneath these waves."

Keisha and Ong, absorbing the wisdom shared by Aqilus and Adrianna, found themselves imbued with profound reverence for the fragile equilibrium that sustained this submerged domain. Coraluna stood as a realm of paradoxes—where perils and marvels coexisted in a delicate choreography, an embodiment of the sea's enigmatic mysteries, as boundless as they were capricious.

Deeper still, the trio—Keisha, Ong, and their steadfast companions—delved into Coraluna's heart, the essence of enchantment flowing through their veins. Corals, wrought by nature's masterful hands, took on forms that defied imagination, each shape a testament to the boundless creativity that flowed beneath the waves. Colors intertwined like verses of a forgotten song, and exotic creatures glided gracefully, their scales shimmering as though sewn from stardust.

Guided by the seasoned wisdom of Adrianna and Aqilus, their passage continued, a mesmerizing dance toward Coraluna's inner sanctum. Keisha's heart swelled with an intoxicating blend of awe and anticipation, her senses alive to every nuance of this submerged world. With her curiosity, Pumpkin wove through the corals, embodying the realm's natural cadence. Her sleek and agile form became an extension of the very currents that embraced her—a reminder that even amid the unknown, a profound sense of belonging thrived within the heart of this underwater realm.

As their journey through the depths continued, Keisha's curiosity could no longer be contained. "Have you ever crossed paths with the Heart of Twilight?" she inquired, her words carrying the weight of wonder.

Her mermaid form gliding with the grace of ocean currents, Adrianna turned her gaze toward Keisha, her eyes reflecting the depth of the sea's mysteries. "The Heart of Twilight?" she echoed, her voice a gentle cadence akin to the murmurs of the waves upon the shore. "Throughout my existence, I've heard echoes of such a legend, whispered in fragments of tales and rumors that dance upon the sea breeze."

Aqilus, a sage presence among them, added his insights. "The Heart of Twilight remains enigmatic even among our kind," he affirmed. "To find answers to such ancient riddles and arcane knowledge, one would be wise to seek counsel from King Oceanous himself. He is a repository of wisdom spanning eons, a custodian of truths hidden beneath the tides."

Ong's gaze met Keisha's, their shared curiosity finding a voice. "Would King Oceanous be open to sharing his wisdom with those from the world above?" he pondered.

Adrianna's smile held a comforting reassurance. "King Oceanous values the bonds that bridge our worlds," she revealed her words as a gentle reassurance. "If there is one who can illuminate the shadows surrounding the Heart of Twilight, it is he. I shall gladly guide you to his presence."

Keisha and Ong swam forth with newfound resolve, their companions by their side. The castle of Coraluna beckoned as a sanctuary harboring secrets that could potentially tip the balance in their struggle against the encroaching darkness.

In the watery depths of Coraluna's embrace, Keisha, Ong, Adrianna, and Aqilus pressed onward, and the world seemed to transform around them. The corals took on an almost otherworldly glow, radiating an inner luminescence that cast a soft, mystical light upon their surroundings. Swarms of iridescent fish choreographed intricate ballets, weaving ribbons of vibrant color through the liquid expanse.

Then, around the curve of a coral ridge, a breathtaking vista unfolded—an image that left Keisha and Ong awestruck. At the heart of Coraluna lay a sight of magnificent wonder. A castle, a jewel of resplendence, stood as the fulcrum of a vast clearing amidst the corals. Its walls, crafted from the purest glass, were transparent veils that invited sunlight to dance through, infusing the underwater chambers with a warm, golden radiance.

The castle, encircled by a tapestry of interlocking corals, exuded a regal presence and an air of protection. Like nature's sentinels, these formations surrounded the court in a loving embrace, bestowing it with a fortified elegance. Keisha couldn't help but be spellbound by the ingenuity and aesthetic brilliance of the merfolk's architectural marvel.

Aqilus, a gentle guide through this aquatic realm, swam alongside them, his gaze tender as he observed their reactions. "Welcome to the heart of Coraluna," he announced, carrying the weight of ancestral pride. "This is the Luminous Keep, our castle—a testament to artistry and enchantment, hewn from the very gifts of the sea."

Drawing closer to the resplendent Luminous Keep, Keisha's eyes fixed upon a grand gate, a sentinel of entry, standing ajar like a welcoming gesture. Flanking the entrance stood merfolk sentries, their watchful gazes unwavering, a testament to their vigilant duty. Adrianna glided with a regal grace toward the gate, a silent communication passing between her and the sentries, granting passage without a word.

Within the castle's embrace, the interior unfolded like a realm from dreams: an ethereal luminescence suffused every recess, an inner glow woven into the very fabric of the walls. Intricate and vibrant mosaics graced the floors with scenes that told stories of marine marvels, Merfolk history's tapestry, and the oceanic realm's unyielding beauty. Graceful arches and corridors beckoned, an enchanting labyrinth leading deeper into this aquatic palace's heart.

Adrianna turned to her companions, her voice a soothing caress. "Welcome to the Luminous Keep, the pulsating heart of our realm. King Oceanous awaits, his wisdom ready to greet you. Let us not prolong his anticipation."

Keisha and Ong followed Adrianna with hearts thrumming with eagerness, their steps echoing in harmony with the corridors. A cadence matched their excitement. They journeyed through the grand chambers of the Luminous Keep, poised to stand before the enigmatic sovereign—a meeting that held the promise of revelations and a key to unlocking the very secrets that kindled their quest.

And so, as Keisha, Ong, Adrianna, and Pumpkin crossed the threshold into the grandeur of the Luminous Keep's throne room, their senses were flooded with a sight that held them momentarily spellbound. King Oceanous, the venerable ruler of Coraluna, sat upon a coral throne that radiated an aura of majesty. His mermaid tail, an intricate canvas of colors, undulated with the fluid grace of waves in constant motion. A golden trident, symbolic of his dominion over the seas, gleamed with a divine luminescence, an artifact of sovereignty intertwined with the essence of the ocean.

As their presence neared, King Oceanous greeted them with a warm smile—a smile etched with eons of wisdom and the tenderness of a compassionate heart. His eyes shimmered like the depths, reflecting the sea's mysteries and secrets. The spirited splashes of Pumpkin, a sprite in the presence of royalty, seemed to amuse the king, and his laughter resonated like a flowing melody within the aquatic expanse. This harmony bridged their worlds and whispered unity.

"Welcome to the heart of Coraluna," he intoned, his voice a timeless echo resonating through ages spent beneath the unfathomable depths. "I've sensed your arrival and extend my welcome, eager to offer you the embrace of our hospitality."

Keisha and Ong exchanged glances, their souls kindled with exhilaration and reverence. This was the juncture of destiny, a crossroads where alliances were to be forged, and the tapestry of their quest could be woven with the threads of hope and unity.

King Oceanous continued, his gaze a conduit connecting them to realms unseen. "I've gathered that you seek an alliance with Coraluna—a covenant that carries the weight of oceans and stars. Our bond with the sea transcends time and is sacred. Nevertheless, I am open to a discourse on this matter."

A contemplative pause followed, his visage etched with the wisdom of oceans. "Yet, it's paramount to recognize that while I wield dominion within Coraluna, a higher presence guides our course—the deity of our realm, Lysander, the God of the Sea. The ultimate decision rests within his currents."

Keisha nodded her demeanor, a portrait of respect for their ways. "Your words are heard and honored, King Oceanous."

The merfolk sovereign inclined his head, a gesture laced with regality and understanding. "For the present, let us weave the fabric of hospitality. Adrianna, my daughter, I ask you to guide our esteemed guests to chambers befitting their stature."

Adrianna dipped in a respectful bow. "Without hesitation, Father."

As Adrianna led the way, Keisha, Ong, and Pumpkin followed the mermaid through the labyrinthine passages of the Luminous Keep. The air held a sense of anticipation, a symphony of unspoken conversations yet to unfold, and every step was a dance with Coraluna's revelations and enigmas. Meanwhile, King Oceanous beckoned Aqilus to his side, entrusting him with a sacred task—to journey to Lysander's dominion, the realm of the God of the Sea, and relay the tale of the visitors who sought the presence of the deity himself. An endeavor that held the promise of destiny's ripples spanning the depths of realms.

As the sun's tender light filtered through the veils of water, infusing the depths with a luminescence born of dreams, the destiny of the pending alliance lay like an offering at the altar of the enigmatic God of the Sea.

With purpose coursing through his veins, Aqilus navigated the aquatic pathways with swift determination. His journey carried him to the grand citadel of Lysander, a realm where the currents spoke of divine majesty. Arriving at the imposing gates, guardians of this sacred domain, Aqilus, was recognized, a gesture that granted him passage. Guided by attendants, he was led through labyrinthine corridors, each step propelling him toward a meaningful encounter with the figure of unparalleled power—Lysander, God of the Sea.

Lysander's gaze, the deep hue of ocean abysses, settled upon Aqilus with an intrigue that stirred the waters of curiosity. "What tidings ride the waves from Coraluna, Aqilus?" His voice, a resonance of authority, carried the weight of tides.

With humility woven into his stance, Aqilus bowed his head. "Greetings, Lord Lysander. King Oceanous extends his respect. He conveys those visitors, hailing from the surface, seek an audience with you."

A single eyebrow ascended upon Lysander's brow—a movement that echoed thunderous currents of thought. "And who are these visitors, and what purpose propels them to my realm?"

Aqilus hesitated briefly, navigating the delicate currents of his words. "One among them is an Eladrin, my lord. Keisha, a soul sheltered by Kadona's grace."

At Kadona's name, a shifting current of emotion passed through Lysander's countenance. His visage softened, a glimmer of recognition like a distant star in his gaze. "Kadona's lineage, you say? That alters the tides of fate."

Aqilus acknowledged this shift, his gaze unwavering. "Indeed, my lord. King Oceanous seeks an audience for these visitors, a request he humbly places before you."

Reclining upon his coral throne, Lysander's bearing became that of contemplation—a figure entwined with the essence of the sea itself, and moments ebbed before he spoke again, his words resonant as crashing waves. "Very well. Convey this message to King Oceanous. An audience is granted, but it shall unfold within my sanctum."

With an understanding nod, Aqilus absorbed the decree. "Thank you, my lord. Shall I depart to carry this news?"

Amusement played within Lysander's eyes—a gleam akin to moonlight upon waves. "Indeed, inform King Oceanous of my accord. Additionally, tell him to bring his daughter, Adrianna. This confluence of destinies pertains to her as well. As my emissary, you shall be present at this encounter, Aqilus."

Acknowledging the privilege bestowed, Aqilus offered another bow before departing. He swam back toward Coraluna, his heart buoyed by Lysander's favorable response. With every stroke through the waters, he carried not just tidings but a revelation that the journey ahead held significance beyond the horizon—for Keisha, Ong, and the very tapestry of their submerged world, woven within Lysander's fathomless currents.

Aqilus's mission was fulfilled as he located King Oceanous within the grand chamber, where the regal ruler's eyes shimmered with anticipation and the spark of curiosity ignited.

"Aqilus, what tales do you bear?" King Oceanous inquired, his voice a cadence of ocean whispers carrying wisdom.

With an obeisant inclination, Aqilus conveyed his message. "My liege, I bring the breath of Lysander's words. An audience is granted, yet it shall unfurl within the confines of his sanctum. He seeks your presence, along with Adrianna and my own."

King Oceanous nodded, his visage a tapestry woven with threads of approval and contemplation. "Thus, shall it be. The mandates of divinity must be acknowledged. Summon our kin and spread the tidings of our imminent voyage. At the break of day, we shall embark upon the journey to Lysander's realm."

Aqilus's words became a herald, setting in motion a dance of preparation among the merfolk. During fervent excitement, an undercurrent of tension lingered—a reminder that destiny's embrace is often intertwined with the unknown. Keisha and Ong, observant and intertwined in thought, exchanged glances, both sensing the gravitas that lay ahead.

Amidst the flurry of preparations, Keisha and Ong found themselves seated by the tranquil waters—a haven where their reflections merged with the ripples of anticipation. Ong's grasp enveloped Keisha's hand, an anchor of reassurance in the face of uncertainty. "Nerves are natural, but remember, we've navigated the currents of adversity before. At this moment, let us rest. Tomorrow, we confront the tides as one."

Keisha's lips curved into a gentle smile, her fingers entwining with Ong's—a tapestry woven with shared conviction. "You're right. We now immerse ourselves in repose and trust that the voyage will unveil truths."

A shared nod conveyed their accord, and they surrendered to the cradle of the underwater realm's tranquility. The rhythm of the waves, the kaleidoscope of marine life, and the promise of the enigma awaiting them within Lysander's realm merged into a soothing balm.

A cascade of gold and amethyst hues painted the waters as the sun dipped beneath the horizon. Keisha and Ong's weariness became a tide that gently washed over them, cradling them within Coraluna's embrace. Amidst the realm's splendor, their hearts found equilibrium, each other's presence a sanctuary of solace.

And so, beneath the serene canopy of Coraluna's domain, they surrendered to rest—unaware of the tapestry of trials and revelations that awaited them in the depths of Lysander's realm. The silent realm of dreams became their haven, a prelude to the symphony of destiny about to unfold.

Chapter 22

Shadows Unveiled: Realm of the Abyssal Sovereign

Emerging from the grand embrace of the Merfolk castle, Ong and Keisha felt an intricate tapestry of emotions woven within them—a potent blend of eagerness and trepidation. Before them stood King Oceanous and Aqilus, their presence a fortress of guardianship, their words a reminder of the duality that thrived within Lysander's realm. King Oceanous commenced, his voice a deep resonance that traversed the currents, "Beyond the surface allure lies a splendid and treacherous domain. Immense sharks, guardians of these waters, roam with instincts sharpened by survival and guardianship."

Aqilus, his aura radiating an authoritative calm, continued the cautionary tale. "Staying within our sphere is paramount, for these waters conceal perils as much as beauty. Coraluna's magnificence conceals the ocean's forged defenders. Our guidance shall be your compass, but unity and caution shall be your armor."

In the exchange of a single glance, Keisha and Ong acknowledged the gravity that hung between them. The allure of adventure danced hand in hand with the understanding that the depths harbored trials unlike any they had confronted. With Ong's grip upon the trident, a tangible excitement coursed through them as they followed King Oceanous and Aqilus, embarking upon the heart of Lysander's realm. Here, secrets lay veiled, and revelations dared to reshape their quest and the destinies of kingdoms under their protective wings.

King Oceanous led their expedition, his tail an iridescent crescendo of colors as he guided them through the labyrinthine paths of underwater corridors. Aqilus swam nearby, his presence an embodiment of their hosts' vigilant guardianship. Gratitude blossomed within Keisha, a flower of appreciation for the merfolk's steadfast guidance. Beside her, Ong's grip upon his spear tightened, his senses attuned to the currents of potential danger.

Sleek and commanding forms darted within their peripheral vision—a congregation of sharks, formidable denizens of the abyss, patrolling the coral perimeters. The sight elicited a symphony of emotions within Keisha—an orchestra of awe, caution, and wonder. Aqilus's counsel echoed in her memory, an anchor that urged her to remain close to their united front. A glance exchanged with Ong, and she gripped the trident that Aqilus had entrusted her—a symbol of readiness and resolve.

Pumpkin, a feline vessel of curiosity, swam in elegant synchrony with Keisha, her watchful gaze oscillating between the vibrant fauna and the shadows crept by the sharks. Keisha's hushed murmurs formed a bond of camaraderie with her feline companion, a whispered covenant to remain alert and steadfast. Pumpkin's eyes shimmered with a blend of exhilaration and wariness, mirroring Keisha's sentiments, her lithe form a graceful presence within the aqueous tapestry.

As their expedition unfolded toward Lysander's domain, the symphony of Coraluna unfurled its grandeur. Sunlight painted a celestial ballet upon the water's surface, casting kaleidoscopic hues upon coral canvases. The undulating grace of seagrass and the rhythmic choreography of currents merged into a harmonious cantata that resonated with the ocean's soul.

Yet, beneath the tranquil veneer of Coraluna, a knowing pulse echoed—an understanding of Lysander's dominion, a majestic and formidable realm. Between Ong and Keisha, unspoken bonds solidified, their journey emblematic of their resolve and courage. With each fin's stroke, they approached a juncture that held the power to redefine their odyssey, to rewrite the narrative of realms hanging in the balance, and to carve their legacy into the very bedrock of the ocean's memory.

A new chapter in their odyssey shimmered on the horizon in the embrace of coral gardens and the mysteries unfurling within the ocean's depths. The realm of the Abyssal Sovereign loomed, a threshold for secrets and revelations poised to sculpt their comprehension of the world and the crucible of trials that awaited them.

Within the expanse of the underwater tapestry, their expedition became a symphony of movement and purpose. King Oceanous's words lingered as ethereal echoes woven within the currents that cradled them. "Lysander's dominion is ruled by equanimity, yet veiled beneath lies a tempestuous nature," King

Oceanous intimated, his tone an infusion of reverence and caution. "In his presence, approach with veneration and humility; therein lies the potential to stir his favor."

The sage advice settled upon Keisha and Ong like morning dew, the gravity of their impending audience deepening as they ventured farther into the enigmatic depths. Aqilus accompanied them, his presence akin to a steadfast beacon amidst the shifting tides. His sea-green eyes held an understanding gleam, a repository of wisdom as he contributed, "His trident, forged by the very currents upon his ascension as the God of the Sea, is a vessel of raw power and emblematic of his sovereignty. It demands respect for the artifact and the deity wielding it."

The weight of these truths layered upon them—a mantle of significance—as they pressed onward, unfurling a journey within the ocean's embrace. Around them, the aquatic world danced with vibrancy—a canvas adorned with coral dioramas, a cavalcade of darting fish, and the regal presence of awe-inspiring sea creatures. Beneath the ebb and flow of beauty lay an undercurrent of tension—an unspoken accord with the challenges that awaited in Lysander's realm. Guided by King Oceanous's wisdom, anchored by Aqilus's watchful guidance, and encouraged by the trident clutched in Ong's grasp, they navigated onward. Their hearts, an intertwining of excitement and trepidation, surged as they inched closer to their imminent rendezvous with the enigmatic Abyssal Sovereign.

Delving deeper into the heart of Lysander's dominion, the serenity of the aquatic paradise transformed into an ominous tapestry tinged with foreboding. In a sudden surge, a squadron of sleek, formidable sharks emerged from the shadows, their primal instincts incited by the intrusion of outsiders. The water churned in their wake, a tempest brewing as their predatory precision directed them toward their quarry. The ocean's embrace, once tranquil, now bore the weight of impending peril, their movements executed with lethal grace.

The command resonated like a decree etched in the currents as King Oceanous's voice rang out, a sonorous directive that cut through the water's depths. "Prepare yourselves!" His words held authority, a rallying call in the face of danger. "Adrianna, wield your magic to shield us!"

Adrianna's sea-green gaze ignited with an ethereal luminescence, the embodiment of her conjured powers. With a flourish of her will, she erected a protective bulwark—a barrier of shimmering energy that embraced the group in its iridescent cocoon. The magical veil pulsed, its effervescent glow a testament to her formidable skills. Yet, the sharks persisted, their strategy synchronized as they encircled the enclave, patience guiding their lethal dance.

Keisha's heart quickened, the pulse of anticipation echoing in her veins. Amidst the orchestrated ballet of predators, her consciousness melded with her innate magic, merging her energies with Adrianna's defense. Strengthening the arcane lattice, she fortified the barrier—a manifestation of their collective resilience.

Beside her, Ong wielded the trident as an extension of his purpose. The weapon was an emblem of his mettle, each deft movement a tribute to his warrior's prowess. His eyes gleamed ferociously, his stance unwavering as he thwarted the sharks that dared to infringe upon their sanctum.

Aqilus, a fierce force tempered by mastery, engaged in a balletic conflict beneath the waves. His spear became an extension of his will—a symphony of calculated strikes that intercepted the predators before they could breach the mystical shield. Each parry conveyed a resolute message—an unyielding challenge they were prepared to meet.

Even Pumpkin, a panther amidst the tides, played her part. Her lithe form navigated the aquatic currents gracefully, a dance of evasion that eluded the sharks' attempts. Armed with her natural weaponry, her movements mirrored the might of the tides, her resilience a testament to her seasoned spirit.

As the skirmish persisted, a symphony of defensive magic and skilled combat wove through the water—a pulse of unity against primal menace. Slowly, a retreat began, acknowledging the united front they faced. Their predatory instincts met a collective defense that swayed the tide in favor of the defenders. With a final testament to their unyielding resolve, the sharks yielded to the depths, their departure leaving a trail of triumph entwined with lingering apprehension.

An exhale, a shared release, echoed through the aqueous realm. Within the haven of Adrianna's ward, the group reconvened, their eyes reflecting the aftermath—a blend of victory's rush and the enduring shadow of their recent trial. Keisha's gaze met Ong's, and within that silent exchange thrived an understanding—a reminder of the perils they braved and the grit that anchored them amidst the embrace of allies and the abyss.

As their odyssey carried them deeper into the heart of Lysander's dominion, a panorama of breathtaking magnificence unfurled before their eyes. Ong and Keisha exchanged incredulous glances, their very breath caught in the awe-inspiring spectacle of Lysander's castle. Rising from the abyssal depths like a regal gem sculpted by the ocean's embrace, the castle's walls shimmered with iridescent glass, capturing and refracting light in an enthralling dance. Embedded gemstones, each a vibrant hue, adorned the walls in a mosaic of kaleidoscopic brilliance as if the very essence of the sea had been woven into the structure.

The coral formations encircling the castle evoked a symphony of enchantment, the coral's vivid palette a testament to nature's artistic ingenuity. Keisha's gaze traced the contours of the coral sculptures, their intricate forms adorned with sparkling gemstones that emitted a luminous glow. Statues of merfolk graced the entrance, their poised figures embodying the fluid grace of the underwater realm.

A pair of formidable merman sentinels heralded the visitors' approach. Their tridents crossed in an imposing display of authority, their unyielding expressions a tangible deterrent to the uninvited. Passage into Lysander's inner sanctum was no casual affair.

However, the atmosphere shifted as King Oceanous and his retinue neared the entrance. With seamless synchrony, the sentinels elevated their tridents in tandem, forging a path granting guests access to the monumental gateway. Thus, Ong, Keisha, King Oceanous, Adrianna, and Aqilus traversed into the awe-inducing realm of Lysander—the God of the Sea.

Within the splendid antechamber of Lysander's castle, an undercurrent of anticipation swirled, almost palpable. The hall itself was a tapestry of intricate coral sculptures and glistening gems, each facet reflecting the luxury of the underwater kingdom.

Their guide, a merman of regal bearing, navigated with determined grace toward the threshold of the throne room. Extending a respectful nod to the guardians stationed there, he entered the sanctum and exchanged hushed words with Lysander. The god's resonant voice reverberated through the hallway, issuing instructions to his emissary.

"Grant them entrance," Lysander's pronouncement cascaded like an ocean's surge, bearing the weight of his dominion over the sea. The merman emissary affirmed his master's mandate with a nod, beckoning the guests to proceed. An amalgamation of excitement and trepidation gripped them, propelling them toward the yawning expanse that led to the very heart of Lysander's realm—the throne room.

The colossal doors yielded with a flourish, unveiling the glorious majesty of Lysander's domain. Ong, Keisha, King Oceanous, Adrianna, and Aqilus tread the threshold of the throne room, their collective gaze converging upon the towering figure seated on the throne. Lysander, the God of the Sea, emanated an aura of authority that pulsed like a tidal surge, a living embodiment of the ocean's immeasurable might.

Toweringly impressive, Lysander occupied the throne room with an air of majesty that transcended mere mortal presence. His towering stature and cobalt-blue eyes, each brimming with the profundity of eons, radiated a pearl of timeless wisdom. His athletic and sculpted physique bore witness to his dominion over the sprawling expanse of the ocean. Beside his resplendent throne lay his prized trident—a symbol of his sovereignty and mastery, adorned with golden filigree and gem-encrusted embellishments glittered as if holding fragments of the sea's very essence.

In measured approach, the group neared Lysander, their footsteps resonating softly in the chamber's hallowed hush. Lysander's intelligent and perceptive gaze swept across each visage, his scrutiny acute and discerning. It was Keisha, however, who drew his focal point. His address directly threatened her essence, his voice reverberating with a resonance that wove a connection through her soul.

"You are the Eldarin of whom Aqilus spoke," Lysander's voice carried a timbre that unfurled like the waves' embrace. Keisha acknowledged with a respectful nod, her gaze reciprocating the blend of reverence and intrigue mirrored within his gaze.

Then, like a shifting tide, Lysander's attention turned to Ong, his scrutiny evaluating and sizing up the warrior from Crystal Vale who had bound his fate to Keisha's. Ong's affirmative nod accompanied the mention of their union, Lysander's unwavering gaze an inquisition that reached depths beyond the tangible.

But Lysander's gaze did not linger solely upon the humans; it alighted upon Pumpkin, the feline companion who had traversed the watery realm by their side. An unexpected yet genuine smile brushed his lips, an enigmatic warmth unfurling—an unexpected display of emotion from a deity known for mercurial temperament.

Resuming his focus on Keisha and Ong, Lysander's demeanor became intent, his eyes vivid with purpose as he directed his attention to them. "Your pursuit of an alliance carries unusual significance, particularly considering Kadona's proclivities. Such overtures have been scarce in the annals of history. Speak to me of why she treads this path now."

A shared exchange between Keisha and Ong transpired—a silent accord that resonated with unity and trust. Gathering resolve, Keisha drew a steadying breath, her words poised and deliberate. She began the intricate tapestry of their predicament, weaving a narrative that unveiled the inexorable rise of Phoenix, the nefarious designs of the Abyssal Dominion, and their brave endeavors to thwart the evil force encroaching upon their realms. With unwavering conviction, they recounted their confrontation with Vuarus, the being once known as Azeron, and his profound connection to ancient prophecies that cast shadows upon their fate.

A fleeting recognition flitted across Lysander's visage as Azeron's name resonated within the throne room. Yet, the transformation that overcame him was nothing short of a disruption. His eyes, once serene, now ignited with tempestuous turmoil, and his voice erupted with an unexpected tempest. "Azeron, you say? The very one who was entwined with the Dragon Council? That betrayer dares to intrude upon these realms?" His words carried a fusion of ire and wounded loyalty, a betrayal at the heart of their shared history.

His focus, once diffuse, laser-focused upon Keisha, his gaze plumbing her depths as though uncovering cryptic layers of her soul. "There lies an unspoken depth to this saga, does there not?" Keisha acknowledged his perception with a gravely composed nod, bracing herself before divulging the existence of the Heart of Twilight—a relic poised to tilt the balance between luminescence and shadow. The gravity of her revelation lingered, hanging in the air like an unvoiced anthem, as an immutable silence descended upon the chamber.

Lysander's countenance drifted into the tapestry of contemplation for a fleeting heartbeat. His unmoored gaze traversed a realm of introspection as he grappled with the weight of their disclosure. Without averting his eye, he summoned a merman attendant, a directive issuing like a thunderclap. "Summon Nerissa," his command resounded, an imperious decree that admitted no contradiction.

As the merman hastened to fulfill Lysander's mandate, the Sea God returned his scrutiny to Keisha and Ong. "Nerissa, the guardian of the Heart of Twilight," he proclaimed, his words now tenderly wreathed in reverence for her sanctified charge. "She alone shoulders the mantle of safeguarding its potent might and enshrouded enigma."

The imminent arrival of Nerissa permeated the air, a prophecy of revelations awaiting to be unfurled—an impending destiny that opened itself before them like the unfurling waves of the sea.

In tandem with the air's electric charge, the opulent curtains that concealed an archway across the chamber's expanse stirred, giving passage to a figure enigmatic yet elegantly poised. Nerissa, her mermaid tail adorned in a cascade of sapphire depths, glided with an elegance born of purpose. Like the sea's most profound depths, her eyes reflected both the wellspring of her rational soul and the gravity of her sacred duty. She traversed the expanse with graceful determination, a living testament to her role's solemnity.

Lysander's once tempestuous countenance now radiated warmth and approval as he witnessed Nerissa's entrance. A fraction of elevation graced his posture as he gestured toward Keisha and Ong. "Nerissa, allow me to present Keisha and Ong—brave souls who have journeyed from distant realms in pursuit of alliance and sanctuary."

Nerissa's gaze, a reflection of wisdom and acknowledgment, first settled upon Keisha and Ong before returning to Lysander—a silent salute to his summons. Lysander, a beacon of regality and weighty purpose, then directed his words toward her, the cadence of his speech carrying both gravitas and an undertone of urgency. "Nerissa, these visitors bring tidings of the utmost consequence. They speak of the Heart of Twilight, an artifact with boundless potency and untapped potential. Their plea for alliance is inextricably interwoven with this artifact's essence." In the symphony of moments that followed, Nerissa's demeanor wove threads of curiosity and understanding, her eyes flitting between Keisha and Ong as though tracing the lines of their destiny. Granted permission by Lysander's silent consent, she extended a graceful gesture that beckoned them forth—a silent promise of her intent to listen, understand, and partake in the discourse to come.

The ensuing conversation, an interplay of voices that harmonized thoughts, ideas, and revelations, carried an ethereal weight—a weight further anchored by Nerissa's insights as the revered guardian of the Heart of Twilight. Within the tapestry of dialogue, she illuminated the artifact's ageless origins, enigmatic power, and role as a fulcrum that balanced the opposing forces of luminance and shadow. As Keisha and Ong unraveled the fabric of their encounters and struggles, Nerissa emanated an aura of profound empathy. This attuned resonance affirmed the authenticity of their shared quest, leaving an unspoken question in the air, a mystery of who the Heart of Twilight's original owner, Talleoss, indeed was.

When the crescendo of dialogue peaked, Lysander's gaze pivoted toward Keisha and Ong, his eyes enunciating a fusion of unwavering resolve and discernment. "An alliance is scribed into the annals of fate," he proclaimed, his voice resonating with the solemn weight of his pronouncement. "Yet, prudence must be our guide.

If Azeron, now shrouded as Vuarus, has knitted himself to Phoenix's cause, the shadows have allied with a force of staggering might."

Lysander's countenance dimmed after his declaration, casting a solemn pall over the room's ambiance. "Azeron, since epochs past, relegated merfolk as mere figments of myth. Your presence, the alliance forged, serves as testimony to the tidal shifts of destiny itself. Understand this path is not without its tribulations. The dark forces relentlessly advance, forging labyrinthine obstacles fraught with peril."

Amid this solemn chamber, where the weight of the ocean's depths seemed to press upon them like a relentless tide, Keisha and Ong stood resolute. Lysander's countenance, once stormy with anger, had transformed into a portrait of unwavering resolve. Like the boundless expanse of the sea, his cobalt-blue eyes bore into Keisha's, their depths revealing the turbulent currents of his emotions.

The atmosphere hung heavy with purpose, as if the air had been charged with the weight of their impending destiny. Lysander's words, uttered with a cadence that resonated like a sacred chant, reverberated through the grand chamber, weaving an invisible tapestry of commitment that bound them together.

Undaunted by the formidable presence of the God of the Sea, Keisha took a deliberate step forward. Her movements were a testament to her unwavering determination, and her gaze, an unyielding flame of conviction, locked onto Lysander's. In that charged moment, their connection transcended mere words, becoming an unspoken commitment that pulsed through the currents of their shared purpose.

"But find solace in unity," Lysander's voice, now an invocation, echoed in the chamber, its resonance a clarion call to stand as one against the encroaching shadows. Like a beacon in the night, his unwavering gaze offered them solace and strength amidst the encircling darkness. The chamber itself seemed to hold its breath, as if acknowledging the weight of the covenant etched into the fabric of their destinies. This covenant would guide them through the trials ahead and safeguard the delicate balance of their interconnected realms.

In this pivotal moment, the grandeur of Lysander's realm bore witness to the forging of an alliance that transcended the ordinary. The currents of destiny surged forward, carrying with them the hope of a united front—a force that could defy the abyss.

"Lysander," Keisha's voice carried the earnestness of her plea, bridging the realms with the power of her words, "there is an aspect that merits your awareness—one veiled in obscurity, even from Kadona's far-reaching sight. A nefarious compact has been woven between Vuarus and Phoenix—an unholy alliance threatening Kadona's essence. Phoenix's pledge to Vuarus harbors a sinister promise: the erasure of her presence, casting an eclipse of uncertainty over her well-being and the equilibrium she nurtures."

As Keisha's words wove a tapestry of revelation, the emotions on Lysander's countenance shifted like the ever-changing sea. Curiosity gave way to a rising tide of outrage, and each shade of his reaction reflected the tempestuous facets of the ocean itself. The tranquil currents of his demeanor fractured, giving way to the fiery furnace of his realm's indignant wrath. His trident, a symbol of his authority and dominion, seemed to amplify the tension in the chamber. Its glorious gold and jewel-studded tracery contrasted starkly with the knuckles that clenched it in a vice grip. A rumbling growl emanated from Lysander's throat, an echo of his booming voice that pierced the chamber with a gust of raw emotion. "Kadona," he bellowed, his voice a titan's outcry, resonating against the walls like a storm unleashed. "A paragon of trust, a sentinel of luminance, imperiled by the audacity of the abyss. How dare Vuarus seize such arrogance?"

The symphony of his words conducted an ensemble of fury intermingled with the melody of a guardian's honor, a testament to Lysander's unwavering reverence for Kadona, the beacon of light that spanned the tapestry of realms. His eyes, now embodying an elemental tempest, ignited with a ferocity that sought to scourge the shadows and lay bare the truth, his gaze boring into Keisha as though seeking veracity.

Keisha met his intensity with a conviction forged in steel, her gaze an un-yielding tether amidst the surging storm of emotions. "We stand prepared to combat whatever difficulties arise, to shield Kadona from the machinations of darkness. In this alliance, woven from realms known and concealed alike, we yield the potential to thwart even the most insidious designs."

A transformation rippled across Lysander's tempestuous visage—a fusion of anger and determination that ignited the forge of resolve within him. "You do not err in your proclamation," he responded with a symphony of smoldering rage and unwavering intent. "The scope of this threat transcends its origins—a malignant blight that seeks to consume the essence of our cherished realms."

Inhaling deeply, the storm within him found a modicum of restraint, a maelstrom gentling into a gale of conviction. "Kadona's luminescence shall not be dimmed by the shadows' hand. Our ramparts shall fortify, our strengths interlace, and we shall stand as bastions against the encroaching void striving to sunder our domains' harmony."

Keisha's acquiescent nod, a symbiotic communion of understanding, affirmed the pact forged amidst turmoil and purpose. In Lysander's vow, an accord was cemented—an alliance that transcended the mundane, pledging defiance against the obscurity that dared assail the sanctity of their worlds.

In the symphony of moments that followed, Nerissa's demeanor wove threads of curiosity and understanding, her eyes flitting between Keisha and Ong as though tracing the lines of their destiny. Granted permission by Lysander's silent consent, she extended a graceful gesture that beckoned them forth—a silent promise of her intent to listen, understand, and partake in the discourse to come.

The ensuing conversation, an interplay of voices that harmonized thoughts, ideas, and revelations, carried an ethereal weight—a weight further anchored by Nerissa's insights as the revered guardian of the Heart of Twilight. Within the tapestry of dialogue, she illuminated the artifact's ageless origins, enigmatic power, and role as a fulcrum that balanced the opposing forces of luminance and shadow. As Keisha and Ong unraveled the fabric of their encounters and struggles, Nerissa emanated an aura of profound empathy. This attuned resonance affirmed the authenticity of their shared quest, leaving an unspoken question in the air, a mystery of who the Heart of Twilight's original owner, Talleoss, indeed was.

When the crescendo of dialogue peaked, Lysander's gaze pivoted toward Keisha and Ong, his eyes enunciating a fusion of unwavering resolve and discernment. "An alliance is scribed into the annals of fate," he proclaimed, his voice resonating with the solemn weight of his pronouncement. "Yet, prudence must be our guide. If Azeron, now shrouded as Vuarus, has knitted himself to Phoenix's cause, the shadows have allied with a force of staggering might."

With each step they took away from the chamber, their hearts reverberated with the resonance of their purpose—a potent chord of unity capable of harmonizing even the most sinister of machinations. Within the realm of the abyssal sovereign, an unwavering stance had been carved—an emblem of defiance that would resonate across the undulating seas and the tapestries of disparate domains, etching a legacy of illumination in the ceaseless shadow's embrace.

Emerging from the grand chamber, the air still pregnant with the electric residue of their discourse with Lysander, a merman awaited them. He extended a vibrant coral, a living relic whose hues danced like a kaleidoscope beneath the fractured light. Ong accepted the coral, its rich colors contrasting with the watery surroundings, feeling like a piece of the sea's soul in his hand. His touch was a bridge to the depths from which it had been plucked, tangibly connecting their worlds. His gaze gravitated towards the waiting merman, a sentinel of their alliance's call, whose eyes held a depth of purpose that matched the weight of their commitment.

The merman's voice, a resonant echo, conveyed the weight of their shared commitment. "This coral shall serve as Lysander's edict," he intoned his words, each syllable carrying the solemnity of their pact. "When the currents of adversity surge, break this coral, and our aid shall hasten to your side." The coral seemed to pulse with a life of its own as he spoke, a living testament to the bond they had formed.

Ong's fingers coiled around the coral, its resilience a tangible reminder of their interwoven destinies. Its surface was smooth and cool to the touch, symbolizing their unity amidst the ever-shifting tides of fate. He nodded in acknowledgment, silently accepting the lifeline woven between their worlds, a bond kindled amidst shared purpose.

Beside him, Keisha observed the exchange, a fire of determination igniting her gaze. Like the coral, her eyes held a kaleidoscope of emotions, reflecting the depth of their journey and the weight of their mission. Her attention then shifted to King Oceanous, a pillar of support within the merfolk realm. Gratitude radiated from her eyes, a testament to the profound impact of his solidarity, like the shimmering surface of the sea reflecting the sun's warmth. "King Oceanous, your alliance is a beacon of hope," she said, her words carrying the weight of their collective appreciation.

King Oceanous's smile, an illumination, harbored a camaraderie that bridged the expanses of ocean and land. Like the endless depths of the sea, his eyes held a wisdom that transcended time. "Consider yourselves intertwined within our extended kin, dear ones," he responded, his voice an undertone of shared purpose. "Side by side, we shall fortify our bastion against the encroaching shadows, resolute in our stand against the impending tempest."

As they turned, the merman's gesture beckoned another figure from the periphery—an ethereal merman carriage adorned with the grandeur of the sea emerged from the depths. It glided towards them, its form bathed in the luminescent embrace of aquatic sunlight. The carriage seemed almost otherworldly, straddling the line between reality and myth. The merman extended an arm with an air of reverence, a signal of invitation for them to embark on this oceanic vessel, a sacred conduit between realms.

"We shall return you to Shimmering Coast with utmost swiftness," the merman intoned, his words a testament to the gravity of their mission and the urgency that underscored their journey. The carriage seemed to shimmer with anticipation, as if it, too understood the weight of their quest and the need for haste.

As Ong, Keisha, and Pumpkin boarded the carriage, they were greeted by a plush interior adorned with cushions that cradled them with a gentle embrace. The sea horses, majestic and graceful, stood at the ready, their eyes holding a spark of knowledge as they prepared to carry the trio back to their realm. The surroundings were a testament to the luxury of the underwater world, a realm where beauty and purpose intertwined seamlessly.

As the carriage began to move, gliding gracefully through the aqueous expanse, the trio cast a final gaze upon the realm of Lysander. Vibrant corals adorned the landscape, their colors a vivid testament to the sea's artistry. Gemstones glittered like stars in the sea's depths, casting a mesmerizing glow. Statues and vigilant sentinels stood as silent guardians, their watchful eyes seeming to follow the departing travelers with a solemn understanding.

Their thoughts converged into a harmonious symphony of resolute determination fueled by the unity they had forged across realms. The path ahead may have veered into the unknown, a labyrinth of uncertainty and danger. However, with allies like Lysander and the merfolk, they confronted the shadows with a potency sourced from the bonds they had so unwaveringly established.

And as the merman carriage gracefully carried them through the aqueous expanse, bound once again for Shimmering Coast, the rhythm of their resolve resonated in tandem with the ebb and flow of the tides—an allegory for the eternal cadence of hope and unity, tethering them amidst the impending storm.

Upon their return to Shimmering Coast, Ong, Keisha, and Pumpkin disembarked with hearts brimming with gratitude, their minds entwined with the weight of their purpose and the alliance they had solidified. The waters shimmered in consonance, mirroring the unity that now thrived between them and the merfolk. The play of light on the sea's surface seemed to dance to the rhythm of their shared commitment, a visual testament to the bond they had forged beneath the waves.

However, the transition from the Shimmering Coast to the familiar terrain of Vacari unveiled a scene starkly contrasting the underwater realm's magnificence. A lamentable tableau awaited them—a poignant departure from the once-lustrous flora. The aftermath of decay and corruption etched somber marks on once-vivid foliage. Once stalwart and regal, trees now bore scars inflicted by sinister magic, their leaves languishing in desolation. Once filled with the sweet scents of blooming flowers, the air now carried a heavy pall of decay, a lament for the land's lost vitality. An expanse of dismay surged through Keisha, Ong, and Pumpkin as they confronted the harrowing transformation that had occurred in Vacari. In their zealous pursuit of power, it was undeniable that Vuarus and Phoenix had unleashed the storm of darkness upon the land, sowing seeds of discord and desolation. The ground beneath their feet seemed to resonate with the sorrow of the land, a testament to the hostility that had taken root.

"We must make haste to E'vahona," Keisha's voice trembled with urgency, her words desperate to restore the land they loved. Her distress was mirrored by Ong, whose determination burned brightly in his eyes, a steadfast resolve to confront the darkness that threatened to engulf their home. "Whatever they're orchestrating is contaminating our homeland."

Ong nodded with unwavering determination, and his jaw set firmly, a silent vow etched upon his features. "Unchecked, this darkness will consume everything. We must rally our allies, fortify our defenses, and cast back this evil tide."

Pumpkin, a steadfast presence, stood by their side, her senses attuned to the pervasive unease that permeated the air. Her fur bristled with concern and readiness as she scanned the once-familiar landscape, now transformed into an eerie and foreboding realm. With every stride they took, the forest, once an oasis of serenity, now exuded an ominous aura. Their realm's very heart was under siege, and it was their indomitable spirit that would defy the encroaching shadows.

Through the labyrinthine woods, their resolve deepened, the alliance etched with the merfolk serving not merely as a safeguard for Coraluna but as an emblem of unity in the face of unfathomable peril. Approaching the borders of E'vahona, their steps carried a weight of solemn determination. The journey ahead promised trials, but the tendrils of alliance, determination, and unyielding strength held within their grasp guided them toward reclaiming their realm from the clutches of darkness.

As they neared the thresholds of E'vahona, their hearts remained heavy with resolve. They understood that the battle for Vacari was far from its culmination, but this shared commitment would cast a beacon of light in the encroaching darkness. In unity and determination, bolstered by the strength of their forged alliances, they would rise to meet whatever awaited, inscribing their defiance upon the looming shadows. The path ahead was shrouded in uncertainty, but they would navigate it together, drawing strength from their forged bonds and the purpose that burned within them.

Chapter 23

Shadows Unveiled: Abyssal Dominion Schemes Unveiled

Amidst the enigmatic depths of the Merfolk kingdom, Keisha and Ong embarked on a journey, their hearts blissfully unaware of the impending enigma that unfurled its veiled tendrils. The iridescent coral reefs adorned with vibrant sea anemones stretched like a mesmerizing tapestry beneath them. Schools of exotic fish darted through the crystal-clear waters, their scales shimmering in a mesmerizing dance of colors. Sunlight pierced the surface in ethereal shafts, casting enchanting patterns on the ocean floor, where vibrant corals swayed to an ancient, unending rhythm.

Meanwhile, within the clandestine chambers nestled deep within the heart of the Abyssal Dominion's fortress, Phoenix and Vuarus stood locked in a tense encounter. Their expressions were as unyielding as the obsidian walls surrounding them, mirroring the gravity of the sinister plans they were weaving. The air seemed to hold its breath, laden with the weight of their evil machinations.

Phoenix's eyes gleamed with an insatiable hunger, reminiscent of a ravenous beast pursuing dominion over all that lay before it. They were twin flames of malevolence, burning with the desire to conquer. In contrast, Vuarus's gaze emanated an aura of calculated intelligence, akin to a master strategist poised to unravel an intricate puzzle that could reshape the very fabric of Vacari. In a voice that slithered like the whisper of a serpentine secret, Phoenix addressed Vuarus, his words dripping with vicious intent, "The time has come, Vuarus. Vacari must be compelled to reckon with our formidable might. Their state of blissful ignorance has endured for far too long."

A sardonic smile tugged at the corners of Vuarus's lips as he replied, his voice a cunning murmur that seemed to echo through the shadows, "Indeed, Phoenix. The fusion of our forces has birthed an exponential surge in our power. The moment has arrived to unveil the gravity of their folly in opposing us."

Phoenix's fingers danced with an aura of sinister energy. This macabre ballet accentuated his words, each movement sending ripples of dark power through the chamber. "We shall unleash bedlam upon their tranquil realm, sow the seeds of discord among their unsuspecting residents, and lay bare the insignificance of their resistance. Their audacity to stand against us shall exact a price they cannot evade."

Vuarus's eyes gleamed with a maleficent fervor, igniting a spark of wicked intent within them. They were like twin orbs of abyssal energy, radiating an otherworldly malevolence that sent shivers down one's spine. He added, his voice a sinister whisper that seemed to crawl through the very shadows, "Yet, let us not unveil our arsenal all at once. Like artisans of dread, we shall offer them fleeting glimpses of our supremacy. We shall keep them teetering on the precipice of uncertainty, their minds consumed by apprehension regarding the extent of our dominion."

Phoenix's grin manifested sheer malevolence as he concurred, his teeth gleaming like the jagged edges of a blade in the dim light of the chamber. "Indeed, Vuarus. We shall allow them to glimpse the fringes of their vulnerability and perceive the lurking shadows of our maleficence. But we shall shroud the depths of our abyss in mystery, leaving them trapped within the tendrils of our ominous enigma."

As the two sorcerers wove their sinister tapestry of strategies, the shadows surrounding them seemed to thicken, embodying their malicious intent. The aspirations of the Abyssal Dominion were on the cusp of a haunting metamorphosis, an insidious turn that would soon cascade like a chilling symphony, its echoes reverberating through the realm of Vacari and beyond.

Phoenix's eyes glinted with a wicked delight, the essence of an evil revelation swirling within the labyrinth of his twisted thoughts. "Vuarus," he intoned with a calculated cadence, his voice resonating with the impending darkness, "the time has come for us to assert the might of the Abyssal Dominion before the eyes of the Eladrin. We shall mark their forests with the weight of our presence, and the very heart of the Purplefire Woods shall feel the shadow of our impending power."

Vuarus's lips curled, mirroring Phoenix's sinister enthusiasm. "A choice both cunning and foreboding. Let them bear witness to the relentless advance of our dominion—a prelude to the sovereignty we shall claim."

Addressing Lyra, who stood poised with fervor, Phoenix's voice dripped with a dark, honeyed malevolence, an evil harmony that resonated with his intent. "Lyra and Qellaun shall be the harbingers of our wrath. Descend upon Goldmoor, for it is under your vigilant gaze that the fires of reckoning shall be stoked."

Lyra's lips curved into a wicked crescent, a cauldron of excitement bubbling beneath her facade. Her eyes, like twin embers of chaos, blazed with anticipation. "Consider it etched in destiny, Phoenix. Goldmoor shall become an epitaph to the cacophony of chaos we orchestrate." As Phoenix directed his minions, his voice echoed like an incantation infused with the essence of shadow and power. "Take wing, my devoted servants, and etch upon the firmament the symphony of defiance met by our might."

With an uncanny swiftness, the minions responded, their forms unraveling like obsidian tendrils into the ephemeral tapestry of air. Lyra and Qellaun melted into the shadows, shadows that embraced them with a dreadful tenderness—a prelude to their nefarious mission.

Vuarus's laughter swirled through the chamber like a malevolent breeze as he beheld Phoenix. "A new era unfurls its wings over Vacari—a disruption of dread and disorder. Our reign shall stretch like shadows, all-encompassing and unassailable."

Phoenix's grin matched Vuarus's, a mirror reflecting their shared malevolence as he proclaimed, his voice carrying the weight of impending doom, "Let the Eladrin quiver and let cities crumble as offerings upon the altar of our ascendancy. Behold the overture of a symphony of devastation and know that this is but the prologue."

In the throes of motion, the forces of darkness choreographed their macabre ballet, weaving their sinister intentions into tangible form. As their designs took shape, the Purple Forest and Goldmoor awaited their impending fate—a tableau of torment that whispered of the yawning abyss they had unwittingly beckoned forth.

Vuarus's eyes glimmered with a cold and calculated brilliance, his thoughts dancing upon the edge of Phoenix's design. "Why restrict ourselves solely to the embrace of our minions?" he mused aloud, his voice carrying the weight of a strategist steeped in hostility. "Let our dark dragons partake in this symphony of chaos. Their presence shall etch an indelible mark of futility upon the tapestry of resistance."

Phoenix's grin stretched into the contours of a sinister crescent, a spark of wicked intent kindling within his gaze. "Your insight knows no bounds, Vuarus. Let the heavens witness our dominion as the sky becomes an orchestra of fire and shadow, and the earth quivers beneath the thunder of our might."

Shifting his focus to a colossal obsidian orb throbbing with an inky vitality, Vuarus unfurled the tendrils of his power, weaving them into a delicate web that bridged the gap between his consciousness and the dark dragons: an ethereal conduit formed, a bridge of thought and purpose. The dark dragons, ancient and evil, awaited their master's command, their eyes aflame with a hunger for chaos and destruction.

"O' dragons born of the abyss," Vuarus's voice carried the resonance of ancient conjurations, a melody of darkness that pierced the veil between realms. It echoed like a mournful dirge through the chasm of worlds. "Cast aside the veil that separates our realms and heed our summons. Join us, serpents of darkness, in the grand unraveling of Vacari's realms. Let the winds bear your wings, and the earth tremble beneath your talons. Let them feel the tumultuous storm when they dare to challenge our dominion."

As the connection solidified, Vuarus felt the dragons' malevolence swell and intertwine with his own, a symphony of maleficent harmony born from their shared thirst for destruction. Their eagerness brewed like an electric charge gathering amidst the portentous sky, a storm on the brink of revelation.

Phoenix's incantation resonated through the chamber, each word a thread woven with shadows and power, binding the dragons to their evil purpose. "Soar, brethren of the Abyss," he intoned, his voice a command that swirled like the currents of a Stygian sea, "etch your darkness upon the canvas of the heavens. Unleash the thunder of our might and let the world beneath you quiver with a fear they can scarcely comprehend."

The obsidian orb pulsed again, relinquishing its hold over the dark dragons. As forgotten legends sprung to life, the dragons ascended, their sinuous forms weaving through the skies. Each scale glowed with unnatural radiance, embodying the malevolence that surged within.

Their roars reverberated through the air, each echoing an incantation of dread as they unleashed torrents of shadow, fire, and entropy upon the world below.

The Purplefire Woods, once a sanctuary of vibrant life, now bore the scars of destruction—scorched groves and smoldering remnants of what once flourished. The heavens wept flames, and the air pulsed with power as ancient as the void. Yet, amid the devastation, pockets of resilient life clung to existence, their tenacious spirit a testament to the enduring magic of the realm.

Similarly, Goldmoor plunged into a nightmarish abyss. The dark dragons circled above, their shadows blotting out the sun, casting a pall over the city's grandeur. Stone and wood succumbed to the onslaught, consumed by the flames of destruction. Streets became rivers of fire, and the city's proud spires crumbled like forgotten dreams, swallowed by the all-encompassing chaos of the Abyssal Dominion's malevolent symphony.

Vuarus observed the culmination of his designs with grim and chilling satisfaction, his eyes glittering with a sinister rapture. The chamber seemed to resonate with the weight of finality as he spoke, each word a decree of doom. "This," he murmured, his voice laden with the weight of despair, "is the toll of defiance—a requiem of suffering and the herald of an era draped in the mantle of our mastery."

Phoenix's laughter, an eerie chorus of malevolence, swirled through the chamber like a symphony of chilling dissonance—an anthem to the chaos they had unshackled. "Let their gaze be drawn to the inexorable truth," he proclaimed, his words a cold embrace of certainty, "that in the clutches of darkness, even hope shall find no sanctuary. The dominion of Vacari shall be eclipsed beneath our shadow."

Thus, the combined forces of the Abyssal Dominion, forged anew by the fury of the dark dragons, unfurled their wings of devastation across the canvas of Vacari's realms. Landscapes quivered, their foundations trembling beneath the deluge of evil might, a tempest invoking the harrowing reality of power beyond reckoning.

Amidst a desolate expanse, where the borderlands between the mortal realm and the Abyss coalesced into an enigmatic weave, Phoenix and Vuarus took their stand. Their presence was an amalgamation of sinister energy—a nexus where the boundaries of reality and unreality blurred, a tether between the mundane and the eldritch.

Phoenix extended his hand with a flourish akin to a maestro summoning a symphony of shadows. Obsidian tendrils spiraled, merging into a nebulous sphere of stygian darkness. With a flick of his wrist, he released the globe, a harbinger of destruction that found its mark amidst a grove of trees. The impact ignited a fire unlike any other—a conflagration that devoured with an unnatural hunger, its flames casting macabre silhouettes that danced with a semblance of malevolent sentience.

Beside him, Vuarus became a conduit for the arcane energies of the Abyss. His eyes, twin beacons of ethereal luminescence, summoned forth the spirits of an abyssal netherworld. These spectral entities emerged, grotesque embodiments of existential paradox, contorted forms that spat in the face of the natural order. A wave of Vuarus's hand propelled them forth, a maleficent mandate that sent them scouring the land with a promise of pandemonium.

Born from the primordial depths, these avatars of chaos moved with a sinister elegance, ripping through soil and space alike, transgressing the very essence of reality. Their touch was a malediction—inflicting decay and corruption upon the tapestry of existence, rending vibrant life into desiccated echoes. As their hostility unfurled, the world quivered in agony, a tumultuous symphony of despair and entropy.

In their wake, the very earth trembled—a heartbeat in synchrony with the pulse of their potency. The atmosphere grew leaden, an amalgam of palpable dread that hung heavy in the air. Above, the heavens recoiled, their once-azure expanse smothered beneath the pall of malevolence that pervaded every nuance of the scene.

Phoenix's laughter reverberated, a dissonant melody that reverently accompanied his unfurled chaos. "Bear witness to the Abyss incarnate," he taunted, his words imbued with cruel triumph, "for its force transcends the limits of comprehension, and all that dares oppose us shall wither in its wake."

Vuarus's voice, a whisper from the abyssal chasm, underpinned Phoenix's proclamation. "Creation bends to the cadence of our maleficent chorus," he intoned, his tone chilling as the void, "and even the tapestries of gods shall fray before the torrential onslaught of our dominion." The desolation that encircled them underwent a sinister transformation, transmuting into a realm of terror that bore testament to the unfathomable might they harnessed. The earth beneath their feet fractured and fragmented, birthing billowing columns of malefic energy spiraling toward the heavens. Reality itself twisted and wavered as if the skeins of existence were unraveling, and the veils separating dimensions grew perilously tenuous.

At the zenith of this chilling spectacle, Vuarus and Phoenix turned their gazes upon each other, their eyes aflame with an infernal fervor—a reflection of the abyssal forge within their souls. In eerie accord, their voices converged, a chorus of profane incantations woven with strands of Abyssal essence. The words rippled through the air like an ominous dirge, casting tremors into the hearts of any witnesses who dared glimpse upon this unsanctified rite.

The potency they commanded inspired awe and invoked terror—an explosive power capable of forging worlds anew in their sinister image. Cloaked in the embrace of the Abyss, the Abyssal Dominion emerged as a colossal threat—a force of darkness poised to engulf all that dared stand in its path. The fabric of Vacari's realms quaked in terror as they heralded a malevolent epoch, and the world held its breath in anticipation of the impending cataclysm.

As the lingering echoes of their joint incantation faded, Phoenix and Vuarus exchanged a knowing look—an unspoken acknowledgment of their dominion over the arcane abyss that answered their beckoning. The exhibition of supremacy had served its purpose, imprinting indelibly upon the annals of history that their mastery of darkness transcended mere ambition. Empowered by this newfound wellspring of might, they were poised to unleash chaos upon the world, a symphony that would crescendo into a cacophony of submission.

Vuarus stood at the threshold of the Purple Forest, a vortex of Abyssal energy coalescing around him—an aura that pulsed with the cadence of malevolence. Beside him, Phoenix's eyes gleamed with the anticipatory luster of a malevolent architect, his very being resonating with the impending birth of their most vile creation: the Wraithbound. This eldritch entity, born of malice and ethereal shadows, reveled in the sanguine banquet of stolen life force—an entity that cast naught but desolation and death in its wake.

With a dark verse uttered in solemn invocation, Vuarus summoned the Wraithbound forth from the recesses of its prison, nestled deep within the abyssal abyss. A frigid breeze, pregnant with an otherworldly chill, swept through the air, causing the verdant sentinels of the Purple Forest to quiver in a wretched dance. Emerging from the veil of shadow, the Wraithbound manifested—a shape-shifting specter with tendrils of stygian ink unfurling like voracious talons. Its eyes smoldered with an unquenchable craving, a hunger that rumbled through the void of its soul as it cast its gaze toward the realm of Goldmoor.

"Unleash it," Phoenix commanded, his voice a blade honed in the crucible of intent—a tone that bore the gravity of certainty, a cold embodiment of calculated resolve.

Vuarus's palm ascended in a gesture that reverberated through the tapestry of the arcane. The Wraithbound, trapped within his command, became a harbinger of doom, propelled towards Goldmoor. However, Vuarus was no reckless puppeteer; he had woven constraints into the entity's fabric—a temporal leash tethering its unleashed malice. With a sage understanding of its value and the need for tactical restraint, he ensured the creature's rampant fury was a calculated gambit, a card to be played wisely in their shadowy arsenal.

As the Wraithbound descended upon Goldmoor, its malefic aura spread like a contagion—a virulent plague that bore witness to its dreadful presence. Peace, once a familiar embrace, became an elusive memory as life withered in its icy grasp. The entity's sinister touch heralded an exodus of panic, a fleeing symphony traversing the city's veins as souls were siphoned with each malevolent contact.

Lyra and Qellaun, the harbingers of darkness, reveled in the bleak ballet that unfolded before them. The once-proud city convulsed, metamorphosing into a grotesque dreamscape of despair. Structures crumbled in a desolate waltz while the cobbled streets seemed to bleed shadows, an ink-black tide that sought to devour every vestige of illumination.

As the ebbing sands of predetermined time flowed, the Wraithbound's ethereal form quivered, its potency waning as if the symphony of doom was drawing to its inevitable coda. Vuarus observed with a measured satisfaction, an architect of calculated cruelty, as the entity's malefic influence receded like a retreating tide. Goldmoor, scorched by the ordeal, had tasted the void within the Abyssal Dominion's dominion—a haunting prelude of the abyss that awaited should they dare stand in its way.

With a final edict spoken in the command language, Vuarus summoned the Wraithbound back to its Abyssal origin, its brief existence once more merging with the shadows from whence it was birthed. The tableau left in its wake was one of desolation and despondence—an unspoken testament to the alliance's dreadful might, a tapestry woven from the loom of their hostility, a stark reminder of the storms they could unleash upon the world. The world of Vacari, once vibrant and full of life, now bore the scars of their malice, a landscape forever changed by the maleficent symphony they had composed.

Amidst the ruins that had once been Goldmoor, the tendrils of the Abyssal Dominion's influence unfurled like serpentine shadows. The city, grappling with the aftermath of the Wraithbound's calamitous embrace, was trapped by a creeping darkness that whispered of the malefic power that had wreaked havoc upon its streets.

Phoenix stood like an eerie sentinel amidst the sad aftermath, his lips curving into a perverse semblance of a smile. The city, once alive with vitality, now lay in ruins, a canvas tainted by strokes of desolation and despair—a testimony to the dark forces obedient to his command.

A flourish of Phoenix's hand birthed an orb, an embodiment of somber energy that thrummed with latent malevolence. His magic, a whisper lost to the wind, imbued the orb with an insidious message—a prophecy of doom. Its trajectory was guided towards the palace of King Alex, a course that culminated in a shattering burst of dark flames. Within the conflagration, the very visage of Phoenix emerged—an ephemeral effigy of dread, etching itself upon the city's psyche like a mark of impending twilight.

A spectral cadence rippled through the chamber, a ghostly messenger borne of Phoenix's design. The voice that emerged was a chilling resonance, a haunting vessel that carried the weight of ominous revelation. "King Alex, sovereign of Goldmoor," the voice pronounced, each syllable dripping with a vicious undertone. "Regard this as a mere sliver, a fleeting glimpse into the abyssal wellspring that the Abyssal Dominion commands. Shadows merge, and the surge of darkness shall quell all defiance. Heed this forewarning."

With the fading embers of the orb's inferno illuminating his retreating figure, Phoenix's gaze lingered for a heartbeat before he rejoined Vuarus. The symmetry of their malevolent partnership had accomplished its purpose, a symphony of dread that echoed in the hearts of those who bore witness. This crescendo instilled trepidation and laid bare the abyssal fury they could unleash upon a world unprepared.

In the depths of Afor, their sanctum of stratagem and shadow, the two figures exchanged accolades, a silent homage to their choreographed victory. Around them, shadows undulated in a spectral ballet, weaving a tapestry of conquest and darkness. "Goldmoor," Vuarus hissed with satisfaction, his eyes twin orbs aglow with triumph, "shall emerge as a parable, a cautionary tale for those who dare defy the inexorable tides of our dominion."

Phoenix's grin unfurled like a shadowed crescent moon, and his gaze was ensnared by the undulating tendrils of the Abyss that enveloped them. "Indeed," he intoned, a herald of their looming reign, "let them cower in the wings of obscurity, for the Abyssal Dominion, forged in the crucible of shadow, shall cascade as a tempest, and the very earth shall shudder beneath our might."

In the heart of Afor, Phoenix's attention veered toward an imperative task, and his strides imbued with resolute purpose. He navigated the labyrinthine expanse, descending into the underground abyss that harbored a cryptic chamber—a place of tenebrous expectancy designed to incarcerate a prisoner of paramount consequence. Within the confines of this underground abyss, Phoenix orchestrated an intricate ballet of chains and wards, each sigil aglow with baleful energy—a symphony of containment forged from malevolent potency. With a calculating smile, he surveyed his handiwork, a fortress of darkness that defied any glimmer of escape. Content with the manifestation of his sinister craftsmanship, Phoenix turned away, his mind already spiraling into the following intricate threads of his sinister narrative.

Meanwhile, in a shadowed alcove of the underground sanctum, Vuarus sought out his high priest, Malrik. The sinister sorcerer had a question that gnawed at the edges of his evil thoughts, which carried the potential to sow discord within the hearts of their adversaries. With calculated intrigue, Vuarus leaned in and asked, "Malrik, my trusted servant, we have witnessed the havoc we've unleashed upon these lands. But what of the elf, Keisha, and her unique connection to the forests? How would the destruction we just unleashed affect her?"

Malrik, a repository of dark knowledge, considered the query with an arched brow. After contemplating for a moment, he began to expound on Keisha's unique connection to the forests. "Master," he began, his voice laced with the authority of his insight, "an elf's bond with the forests is indeed profound, an intertwining of spirit and nature that shapes their very being. However, Keisha's connection is unlike any we have encountered before. It's as if she shares a bond and a symbiotic fusion with the woods. The devastation we've wrought will do more than unsettle her; it will strike at the core of her existence. It shall weaken her physically and spiritually, like a rift tearing through the very soul of the forest itself, and, in turn, her soul. The threads of her connection to the woods will not just fray; they will unravel, leaving her vulnerable and ripe for capture."

Vuarus's eyes gleamed with an evil delight as he absorbed Malik's response. With a sly, knowing grin, he added, "Perhaps, Malik, we have found a way to capture her, to trap her in a web of darkness she cannot escape. The forests she holds dear will become her prison, and she shall be our prisoner. However," he continued, his tone taking on a more contemplative note, "we must not underestimate her. Keisha is always accompanied by her husband, Ong, and their loyal panther, Pumpkin. They would put her safety as their top priority. Still, it's an idea worth exploring. If we can find a way to separate her from them or if the destruction weakens her enough, we may succeed."

With a cunning glint, Vuarus leaned closer to Malrik and whispered, "But remember, Malrik, this is information we shall guard closely. Do not divulge our plans to anyone else. The element of surprise is our ally, and we shall keep our intentions shrouded in darkness until the opportune moment arises." Malik nodded in understanding, fully aware of the need for secrecy in their evil scheme.

Chapter 24

Shadows Unveiled: Alliance Assembled and Secrets Revealed

Amid the alluring splendor of the Hidden Isles, a mystic realm ensconced within Vacari's embrace, the atmosphere hums with electric enthusiasm. It's as if the air crackles with anticipation, a palpable sense of destiny on the cusp of unfolding. Within the heart of this enigmatic haven, the grand hall stands as a testament to the realm's profound magic. Ornate tapestries, handwoven by old sorcerers, depict dragons intertwined with the very essence of starlight. Each thread seems to shimmer with a celestial glow, telling tales of cosmic unions.

Shimmering crystals hang like suspended galaxies from the hall's vaulted ceiling, casting prismatic constellations upon the chamber's walls. As they sway gently, refracted beams of light create a mesmerizing dance of colors that sweep across the room, painting the scene with otherworldly hues. At the room's center rests a grand round table, a polished relic of antiquity that has witnessed the birth and fall of civilizations. Its surface gleams like a mirror, reflecting the collective hopes and fears of those gathered. Encircling it are chairs, each exquisitely carved with intricate designs that whisper tales of forgotten times. The grain of the wood tells stories of ancient forests, while the craftsmanship hints at the artistry of a bygone era.

Each chair cradles a representative from a unique realm, a confluence of worlds united by an impending cataclysm. Their attire speaks of their origins: flowing robes of crystal-threaded silk, suits of enchanted armor, and regal garments adorned with symbols of their homelands. Each face carries the weight of responsibility, and their eyes, a mix of hope and trepidation, search for common ground amid the diversity of their assembly.

Among these luminaries stand the majestic dragons, noble creatures whose presence evokes awe and reverence. Their massive forms, adorned with scales that glint like gems, occupy a sacred enclave within the hall. Their eyes, gleaming with ancient wisdom, survey the assembly with regal regard, their sheer existence a living testament to the gravity of the gathering. They are not mere spectators but participants in a cosmic drama that could shape the fate of entire realms.

Keisha and Ong, bearers of a destiny yet to be fully revealed, stand as beacons of purpose at the forefront of this congregation. Lord Eldrion, a figure of dignified curiosity intermingled with hints of worry, gestures for them to commence the proceedings. With a breath drawn from the depths of resolve, Keisha emerges from the shadows cast by the dragon motifs, her voice a steadfast melody that resonates through the hall's foundations.

"In this nexus of existence, where realms intertwine, we stand united by the threads of fate," Keisha begins, her words weaving a spell of unity. "With heartfelt gratitude, we extend our appreciation to all gathered here. Our venture into the enigmatic realm of Coraluna has borne fruits of consequence."

At Keisha's side stands Ong, a guardian of unyielding strength. A silent assurance bolsters their shared purpose, a bond formed through trials and tribulations. The representatives lean in, their eyes gleaming with an anticipation akin to gazing upon a fabled tapestry's final, climactic reveal.

Keisha unfurls the canvas of their journey, weaving a tale that dances with the brilliance of moonlit waves. She recounts their encounters with merfolk, beings of aquatic grace, and speaks of discourse exchanged beneath the tranquil depths of Coraluna's hidden oceans. The alliance formed through shared purpose and mutual respect is the linchpin to thwarting the looming shadow cast by the Abyssal Dominion.

In this symphony of revelation, King Alex, a monarch whose scepter commands respect, acknowledges the gravity of the newfound alliance. His regal and affirming nod encapsulates the shared understanding that this unity is a beacon of hope for Goldmoor's salvation. Aqilus, a sovereign of dignified presence and resolute countenance, lends his voice to the unfolding tale, embellishing the merfolk's contribution with the eloquence of a bard's poetic verses.

He paints a vivid tableau of the undersea realm, an ethereal garden of coral king-doms and phosphorescent wonders that kindle the fires of imagination within every heart present. As his words flow like a soothing current, the audience is transported to the depths of Coraluna, where bioluminescent flora sway to a silent, enchanting melody, and aquatic creatures of unparalleled beauty glide through cerulean waters. It is a world of wonders, a realm worth preserving, and the assembly can't help but be swept away by the vivid imagery painted by Aqilus's words.

The grand hall of the Hidden Isles, with its celestial tapestries, shimmering crys-tals, and an assembly of diverse realms, has become the crucible of a new alliance, a glimmer of hope against the encroaching darkness of the Abyssal Dominion. In this moment, destiny hangs in the balance, and the threads of fate are woven ever tighter, binding these realms together in a common cause.

Adrianna, an embodiment of serene grace, stands at the heart of the gathering, her presence a beacon of tranquility amid the swirling currents of discourse. Her gaze, deep pools of tranquil wisdom, mirrors the endless expanse of the sea's embrace, a silent testament that beyond the immediate lies a canvas yet to be painted with the hues of possibility.

As the tapestry of discourse unfurls, other representatives, each a sovereign of dis-tinct dominions, add their threads to the intricate weaving. With voices as varied as the myriad hues of a peacock's plumage, they outline the riches, strengths, and strategies their realms shall bring to the burgeoning alliance. The dragons, potent as the primordial forces that sculpt mountains and carve rivers, lend their vocal resonance to this crescendo of unity, their rumbling harmonies an affirmation that they stand as indomitable pillars in this struggle against the encroaching dark.

In the heart of the grand hall, as the symphony of voices swells, a tapestry of resolve is woven. Threads of hope and purpose interlace into a fabric that defies the very fabric of impending doom. Each word, each gaze, and each breath evokes an enchantment that solidifies the assembly's shared commitment. Amidst dragon motifs that seem to come to life in the play of light and luminescent crystals cast-ing ethereal glows, the Hidden Isles' fate takes root in the hearts of the gathered, a fragile but determined bud in the face of adversity.

Amidst the contemplative currents of discourse, Keisha and Ong weave a tapestry of recounted events, a narrative laden with a sense of urgency that casts a shadow over the gathering. Like melodies carrying the weight of a mournful dirge, their words elicit grave nods and furrowed brows from those who bear witness. King

Manard, a ruler marked by the etchings of concern, wears a map of worry on his furrowed brow. The dragons' noble eyes, harboring a solemn understanding, exchange glances heavy with the gravity of the Abyssal Dominion's nefarious machinations.

In the symphony of voices, Keisha's tone transforms, her words woven with threads of compassion and a touch of vulnerability. "During our journey within the merfolk's realm, we unveiled the depths of darkness to which the Abyssal Dominion would descend. The Purple Forest and Goldmoor suffered their ruthless onslaught, and the scars of their malevolence mar the very fabric of our lands." The room, a collective witness to the tale, stiffens in the grip of emotions as diverse as the colors of a kaleidoscope. The atmosphere ranges from a wave of explosive anger, like a stormy sea crashing against rocky shores, to an unwavering resolve that kindles like a solitary star in the vast night sky, burning with the promise of a new day.

King Alex, a monarch whose grip tightens into clenched fists, mirrors the sentiments woven into the tapestry of his kin. The dragons, possessors of an ancient fury that dances beneath the surface of their scales, emit low growls that resonate like thunder within a storm-clouded sky. Knowledge of the encroaching darkness, its tendrils extending to brush against the very boundaries of their dominions, unites the assembly in a vow to stand persistent against the rising tides of malevolence.

As the discourse continues its winding path, the warp and weft of conversation reveal a shared purpose and an alliance forged not merely through necessity but through hearts entwined by the threads of camaraderie. The Hidden Isles, lush in their secretive beauty, bear witness to this unbreakable bond, their fauna and flora echoing the unity that blossoms within their midst.

Thus, within the embrace of the Hidden Isles' enigmatic embrace, the ages meld—old alliances rekindle their fires while new bonds crystallize in the heart of adversity. Amidst the murmurs of strategy and the cadence of contemplation, the leaders peer through the chasm of uncertainty, each mind a beacon aglow with the fire of determination. For within their collective gaze lies the unshakable vow to reclaim the stolen light, to banish the encroaching shadows back to the depths from whence they crawled.

As the symphony of discourse paints its vivid tableau within the hall, a moment of profound stillness descends, a tapestry of thoughtfulness woven by the threads of contemplation. King Manard, a voice that carries the weight of curiosity tinged with respect, lifts the veil of silence. His brows, etched with interest, quiver slightly as he addresses the merfolk's representatives, his words cautious yet genuine.

"Pardon my curiosity, a reflection of my limitations. Within your realm beneath the waves, what are the treasures you bear? How shall your abilities ripple through the waters of our alliance?" The question hangs in the air like a pearl waiting to be plucked from the ocean's depths, a testament to the shared curiosity that binds these diverse realms in their quest to confront a familiar foe.

Aqilus, an embodiment of regal splendor and contemplative wisdom, rises like a sentinel, and the room falls into a hushed reverence, their collective gaze fixed upon him. He meets King Manard's gaze with a nod of acknowledgment, a silent acknowledgment of the importance of the question.

"Your query is one deserving of understanding, King Manard," Aqilus begins, his voice a melodic dance that captures the attention of all present. His words flow like the gentle caress of ocean waves against the shore. "Within the vast expanse of the ocean, the merfolk are endowed with a mastery that transcends the mundane. The power that courses through the waves is our birthright, wielded with finesse and precision."

Aqilus's voice, a cadence like the rhythmic heartbeat of the sea, ensnares the room's collective focus, an audience entranced by the arcane knowledge that spills forth. "In embracing the ocean's depths, we command the currents, shaping their vigor and direction at our whim. Like loyal sentinels, tides heed our call, rising and falling in orchestrated harmony. Our affinity extends to the creatures that dwell within the depths, each finned and scaled denizen an extension of our will."

King Alex and his fellow leaders gaze unblinking, like stars suspended in a vast night sky, absorbing the revelation with awe, befitting the unveiling of long-lost secrets. With a serene authority, Adrianna adds her voice to the unfolding symphony. "Furthermore, our communion with the ocean's magic allows us a means of distant discourse. The resonance of the sea's whispers becomes our conduit, transmitting messages through the ether of water, crossing lands and realms expeditiously."

Aqilus, a custodian of ancient bonds, continues the tale with a reverence that imparts a sense of mysticism. "Our relationship with the God of the Sea, Lysander, intertwines our fates. His sagacity and the weight of his ancient understanding bestow insights into the veiled enigmas of the aqueous realm and the unseen forces that choreograph our existence."

In the backdrop of the hall, Adrianna, her gaze a reflection of her realm's devotion, contributes with unwavering resolve. "The synergy of our strengths, an orchestration of currents harnessed, distant voices carried upon the ocean's breath, and the knowledge granted by Lysander's benevolence culminate to mold us into a force that defies common reckoning. The expanse of the sea, a tapestry woven with the threads of might, stands as a testament to our pledge to this alliance."

The significance of the merfolk's prowess takes root within each leader's heart. Their expressions transform from initial curiosity to a reverence that kindles the embers of respect. The tapestry of unity, woven with threads of distinct abilities, assumes new vibrancy as the realm's guardians recognize their true strength. Beneath the tapestry's backdrop, the dragons, noble guardians of ages past, lend their resonant voices, a basso hum that accompanies the convergence of powers and the crystallization of unwavering determination. At this moment, with all its enigmatic beauty, the Hidden Isles bears witness to the birth of an alliance that may yet turn the tide against the encroaching darkness.

In the sanctum of the Hidden Isles, where the veil between realms thins and the pulse of destiny echoes through the air, the leaders of disparate dominions glean the depth of the merfolk's enigmatic gifts. With each revelation, a tapestry of bonds intricately woven gains added layers of color, affirming their shared purpose in the face of encroaching darkness. The very essence of the room seems to resonate with the harmony of their unity. As discussions unfurl their multifaceted threads, strategies bloom like petals beneath a rising sun, and an unwavering resolve to combat the consuming shadow ignites a conflagration of determination, relentless in its pursuit of an unbroken dawn.

Amidst the whirl of words and the forging of futures, Keisha senses a seam in the fabric of conversation, an opportunity to retreat discreetly from the council's embrace. She navigates the currents of the hall until she finds a secluded nook, where the symphony of voices subsides, and her thoughts form a bridge that stretches beyond realms. The tendrils of her consciousness reach out to Aeliana, Guardian of Ardinia, a connection borne from shared purpose and a thread of destiny that intertwines their fates.

Aeliana's response traverses the currents of thought, a testament to her serene resolve amidst uncertainty. Keisha's request finds acceptance in her words, a melody of understanding that harmonizes with the chorus of destiny. The exchange is a symphony in the ether, a subtle agreement that resonates with the weight of shared purpose.

With the understanding secured, Keisha retraces her steps to the heart of the council hall, where the tides of discourse reach a cresting point. The door's sweep marks Aeliana's entrance, an embodiment of presence that transcends mere physicality. Accompanied by Keisha, she steps into the midst of the gathered leaders, her arrival akin to a moonlit breeze that carries a hint of the unknown. The assembly's collective gaze turns toward her, recognizing her as a new figure in this intricate dance of fate, a guardian with her part to play in the unfolding symphony of unity.

King Alex, a monarch whose mantle is woven with respect and sagacity, offers his reverence through a nod that speaks volumes of acknowledgment. "Aeliana, Guardian of Ardinia," he intones, a voice that carries the weight of recognition. "We stand humbled by your presence, a manifestation of wisdom in these uncertain times. Your name resounds with tales of courage, and we seek to understand the unique strengths your realm can offer to this tapestry of unity."

Aeliana, her demeanor a reflection of tranquility that dances within her gaze, steps into the spotlight with an air that is both commanding and inviting. Her words, like whispers woven into a gentle breeze, paint portraits of her realm's connection to the essence of nature. "King Alex," she begins her voice a chime of lyrical clarity, "Ardinia's heart beats in tandem with the earth's pulse. Our bond with the land is profound, granting us the power to shape the ground we tread and manipulate flora and fauna. Our warriors are tuned to the symphony of the natural world, channeling its raw vitality to safeguard our realm."

The words linger, like the fragrance of petrichor after a cleansing rain, leaving an imprint in the air and an understanding that the tapestry of unity is more intricate and vibrant than they could have imagined.

King Manard's inquisitive gaze shines with a gem-like curiosity, a glint of light amidst the tapestry of his regal demeanor. He leans forward, an embodiment of focused attention, and with words as carefully chosen as the brushstrokes of a master artist, he poses his question. "And amidst the threads of fate, what binds you to the Heart of Twilight?"

Aeliana, a paragon of unwavering poise, stands firm in the spotlight, her gaze a steady reflection of the moon's tranquil glow. Her response is a river of conviction, flowing unbroken by hesitation. "The Heart of Twilight, a beacon that bridges realms, is the very lifeblood of Ardinia. Within its essence, the symphony of light and shadow entwines, their harmonies giving birth to magic that courses through our veins. Our kinship with this enigmatic power is the cornerstone of our strength, a force that guided us through tempestuous tides. And now, as we embrace unity, we offer the heart's radiant embrace to our shared cause."

Each sovereign's leaders absorb Aeliana's revelations with a quiet reverence. In this chamber, where destiny is forged, a hushed symposium of contemplation takes hold, an interlude punctuated by the murmurs of the dragons' silent approval. It is a pivotal moment where the threads of each realm's essence are intricately woven, creating a symphony of power and resolve that resonates within the Hidden Isles' core.

With the Guardian of Ardinia's presence now etched into the fabric of their alliance, a new strand of determination takes root. Amidst the ongoing discourse, like alchemists refining a potent elixir, the leaders mold their plans, fashion their visions of unity, and foster the burgeoning awareness that the encroaching shadows cannot endure the brilliance of their combined might. In this chamber of destiny, the leaders stand united, their hearts and realms entwined in a symphony of purpose that will shape the very fate of their worlds.

As the cadence of conversation approaches a crescendo, it is Ong who steps into the limelight, his voice a pillar of unwavering authority that demands attention. His gaze, an all-seeing sentinel, sweeps across the assembly, a look that traverses the landscape of those who share this clandestine council. "Before the tapestry of our deliberations unfurls further," Ong's words emerge as a command, a resonance that halts the flow of discourse, "I offer a proposition of discretion. I propose that the knowledge of the merfolk's involvement and the synergy of Ardinia's power within this alliance should remain confined to the ears present in this very chamber."

Like ripples upon a tranquil pond, his words find attentive ears, and a collective hum of agreement murmurs through the assembly. Ong's gaze narrows with a focus akin to a hawk's as his attention settles upon King Alex, a figure he has come to esteem deeply. "Your Majesty," he addresses the ruler of Goldmoor with a blend of deference and urgency, "I am acutely aware of the intricate tapestry your realm weaves. Yet, I pray you, in the labyrinth of shadows we navigate, let this knowledge be a secret whispered only among us. Your queen's state of being demands an undivided focus, unburdened by the weight of our trials."

King Alex's countenance remains serious, his gaze locked with Ong's in a moment of unspoken accord. Between them, a river of understanding flows, unburdened by words. King Alex assents to Ong's plea with a nod as solemn as an oath sworn in the moonlight. "Your concerns echo in the depths of my heart, Ong. The well-being of my queen stands paramount. The secrets woven within this alliance shall remain shrouded, a guardian to her tranquility."

Once enveloped in a tension as taut as an archer's bowstring, the chamber exhales in a symphony of relief. The cloak of discretion is drawn close, and an understanding is now shared like an unbreakable bond. The leaders, united by the threads of their shared knowledge, navigate the labyrinthine corridors of their decisions, veiling their intentions to protect loved ones and cherished realms. The covenant of unity deepens each member as a guardian of dominions and hearts intertwined within the Hidden Isles' embrace. In this moment of mutual understanding, the assembly stands as a bastion of trust and solidarity, fortified by their shared resolve to face the encroaching shadows.

Ong's gaze, an anchor of unspoken understanding, flits briefly to Lord Karrenen, and within that glance, a river of shared resolve courses. Lord Karrenen, like a sentinel summoned forth, rises from his seat, his presence once again commanding the room's attention. His voice, rich with the weight of conviction, resonates through the air, casting a mantle of gravity upon the gathered assembly.

"Fellow leaders," his words are both a clarion call and a hushed confessional, "our discourse has cast a radiant light upon the tapestry of potential, yet even within this brilliance, we must acknowledge the looming specter of shadows that hungers to engulf us. The Abyssal Dominion's stratagems as insidious as the softest whisper of poison, would ensnare our vulnerabilities and shape them to their sinister designs. Kadona, a beacon of unyielding resilience and radiant light, stands as a potential target, a gem set within the enigmatic expanse."

A shiver, imperceptible yet profound, courses through the assembly. The implications of Lord Karrenen's words ripple like tendrils of smoke, a truth that curls around their collective consciousness. King Manard's brow furrows, etched with concern, his fists clenching in a proclamation of his resolve. "Were Kadona's realm, E'vahano, unveiled to those who would harness its power for ill, the tapestry of equilibrium she safeguards could unravel like a fragile thread, casting our realms into a chasm of chaos."

Keisha's heart tightens at the thought, the moment's urgency threading through her thoughts. Adrianna's sea-green eyes burn with a fierce determination that mirrors the merfolk's commitment. "The fate of E'vahona must remain veiled, hidden from the eyes that would exploit its strength. We stand united to protect Kadona and safeguard the secret of E'vahona's existence, for in it lies a key to power and vulnerability."

The leaders acknowledge the duality of their mission within the sanctum's embrace, where destiny is etched like ancient runes upon the walls of time. To guard Kadona is to shelter the very essence of their realms, but to shield the existence of E'vahona is to fortify the walls that protect them all from an onslaught of darkness. In this unspoken understanding, they find themselves on the precipice of a battle that transcends the physical, a symphony of unity that stretches across realms, binding them together as guardians of light against the encroaching night. The Hidden Isles, a realm shrouded in mystery, stands as their sacred stage, destiny, and guiding conductor.

Within the chamber's enigmatic embrace, where destinies interlace like threads of silver and gold, the leaders stand united in their resolve. The Hidden Isles witness this union as a symphony of shared purpose and unbreakable bonds reverberates within their verdant heart.

A solemn murmur, like an echo of the wind through ancient corridors, threads through the assembly. Ong's voice, a bastion of unwavering resolve, rises like a steadfast beacon, his gaze traversing the sea of determined faces surrounding him. "Amidst the tapestry of our unity, there lies an unshakable truth—the sanctuary of Kadona demands our guardianship. Our decisions shall not waver, nor shall our commitment falter. As the guardians of our realms, we stand shoulder to shoulder, an unyielding shield against any harm that seeks to befall her."

A chorus of agreement, expressed through the shared language of fervent nods, weaves a spell of unity across the room. Within these hallowed walls, their souls align as leaders and bearers of an oath to the Goddess who guides their destinies. As the shadows of uncertainty lengthen, they take refuge in each other's resolve, the embodiment of an alliance as unbreakable as the earth they stand upon. The symphony of unity reaches its zenith within the chamber, a crescendo of purpose that transcends the boundaries of their realms and unites them in their quest to safeguard the light.

As the river of discourse flows, a voice emerges that commands attention, the rumble of its power mirrored in the glint of its eyes. Kimras, the majestic Gold Dragon, his wings a resplendent mantle, breaks through the current of discussions with a presence that carries the weight of ages. His voice, deep and resonant as an ancient cavern's echoes, calls the room's attention.

"From the vantage point of my vigilant watch," Kimras begins, his voice a harmonious blend of authority and sagacity, "I have observed and cataloged the unfolding events. The dragons that scarred the forests and Goldmoor were not bound by mere draconic flesh; they were ancient entities from the abyss, creatures sequestered within the heart of darkness. Phoenix and Vuarus have tapped into the arcane channels to manipulate these abyssal forces, bending their will to serve their evil design."

A collective gasp, like a breath stolen by the wind, sweeps through the assembly, eyes widening as the gravity of Kimras' revelation unfolds. King Manard, a figure of regal determination, absorbs the knowledge with eyes as sharp as the sword's edge, his fingers curling into fists that hint at the storm of his emotions. "The reins of abyssal power rest within their grasp, a mastery over forces that dance with malevolence. It portends a connection that reaches beyond our mortal realm, an alliance with darkness itself."

A shadow, like a shroud cast by a passing storm cloud, descends upon the gathering, a tangible echo of the gravity of the revelation. Aeliana, a beacon of unyielding strength, retains her composure though her eyes gleam with the fire of resolve. "The tendrils of the Abyssal Dominion's influence reach further than we dared assume. The command over these abyssal forces threatens to unleash an explosive torrent that could unravel our lands and the fabric of reality itself."

In this chamber of unity and shared resolve, where destinies are forged, the leaders grapple with the stark truth that shadows seek to consume all they hold dear. Their strength and alliance now stand as a bulwark against the abyssal tide, a testament to their unwavering will to stand against the forces that seek to destroy their worlds.

Kimras' noble head dips solemnly, his gold eyes aflame with a shared trepidation. "Beware the treacherous depths of their mastery over the abyss. A power fueled by chaos and the taint of corruption, it is a force that now turns its malevolent gaze upon us. In this dangerous hour, we must stand united, our realms a bulwark against the abyss's insidious grasp."

A renewed current of purpose sweeps through the chamber, an unseen tide that knits their souls into an unbreakable weave of intent. No longer a mere coalition against an adversary, their alliance now manifests as a beacon, a citadel of hope against the relentless tide of encroaching darkness. Resolute glances pass among the leaders, unspoken promises sealed in the depths of their eyes as they pledge to combat the formidable specter that looms before them.

King Alex's countenance dims, his gaze heavy with shadows as he addresses them, his voice a vessel of the burdens he bears. "Esteemed companions, I stand before you with a heart burdened by sorrow. Goldmoor, beleaguered and bruised, lies in the wake of tremendous suffering. The very woods that have been our sanctuary are destroyed, and our city's walls have crumbled. Our people face dire straits, desperate for sustenance and solace."

Around the assembly, empathy weaves a tapestry of shared concern across faces etched with understanding. Lord Manard, a pillar of compassion, nods solemnly. "We bear witness to the gravity of your plight, King Alex."

A shadow of thought touches Lord Karrenen's visage, brows knit in contemplation. "In the realm of magic, a boon may yet be bestowed. Supplies could traverse realms in a heartbeat through an intricate web of portals. A humble gesture, a lifeline offered freely in this hour of dire need."

A glimpse of relief sweeps across King Alex's stance, gratitude a cloak that drapes his weary shoulders. "From the very core of my soul, I extend my gratitude to you all. Your camaraderie is a salve beyond measure."

But amidst the discourse, Keisha's voice emerges as a bastion of unwavering compassion. "King Alex, our response pales compared to the trials Goldmoor has withstood. United, we confront this darkness, forging an unbreakable alliance to overcome all adversities."

With a measured rise, Lord Karrenen's presence claims the room, an embodiment of command and wisdom. "For the present, let us adjourn this gathering. But pay attention—they echo through these hallowed halls. Be vigilant against the Abyssal Dominion's ominous threat. Our strength forms a shield, an impenetrable defense against the darkness that yearns to devour us."

With those final words, the leaders of their realms disperse, determination and unity lingering like an echo in the air. Each return to their territory, charged with a renewed dedication—an unyielding pledge to safeguard their provinces, to wield unity as an invincible weapon, and to triumph against the tide of encroaching shadows that seek to shroud their lands.

Chapter 25

Shadows Unveiled: Dark Designs on Keisha

As Phoenix leaned forward, his eyes filled with evil intent, a dark tension filled the room. His proclamation cut through the air like a poisoned blade, sending shivers through those gathered.

Lyra, known for her strategic mind and pragmatic approach, furrowed her brows in deep contemplation. "Seizing Keisha won't be an easy task," she cautioned, her words carrying the weight of challenges. "Her will is strong, bound to her purpose. She won't abandon her allies or yield to the idea of Ong's betrayal."

Phoenix's cruel grin remained, his features twisted with calculated malice. "Whether she joins us or stands in defiance matters little to me," he retorted, his words dripping with venomous disregard. "My interest lies in one thing—vengeance. A reckoning for her obstructions, her rebellions, every stumbling block she has thrown in our path."

Lyra's brows knitted further, her meticulous nature driving her to emphasize the importance of a flawless plan. "Our plan must be airtight. Failure is not an option," she declared, resonating with urgency.

In this shadowed chamber, where sinister plots and dark ambitions simmered, the stage was set for a high-stakes confrontation, where Keisha's fate hung in the balance, and the forces of darkness conspired to achieve their nefarious goals.

"Indeed," Phoenix's affirmation was a steel-edged whisper. "We must exploit her frailties, unveil chinks in her armor, and torment her fears. Once she is trapped, her allies' fate shall dangle in our hands."

Lyra's gaze remained frigid and calculating, a glacier of intent. "What if she endures unyielding?"

As Phoenix's pupils darkened, his determination swallowing the light, he declared, "Then she meets her demise. No one is beyond replacement." Vuarus, aware of Phoenix's vengeful intentions, smiled slyly, recognizing that Phoenix was playing right into his hands. "Phoenix is right," he affirmed.

In that chamber filled with tension, the architects of the Abyssal Dominion plotted their sinister schemes, fueled by Phoenix's vendetta and their desire to exact vengeance for the barriers Keisha had placed before them.

Vuarus leaned forward, his voice a sinister whisper that echoed like a serpent's hiss. "We've prepared a special place for her, a hidden underground cell where she'll be isolated and powerless. The essence of her being, tied to the pulse of nature as an elf, will be our instrument of isolation. The depths of the earth will sever her connection to the living world, and the weight of solitude will break her spirit. No one will be able to find her, and by the time they realize her absence, it will already be too late for both her and her realm."

Lyra's eyes gleamed with approval, her predatory instincts assessing the situation. "A fitting fate for someone who has dared to challenge us," she remarked, her tone laced with satisfaction.

Phoenix's lips curled into a cold smile, reflecting his merciless resolve. "Indeed. Let her taste the bitterness of captivity and the emptiness of isolation, her efforts rendered meaningless in the face of our dominion."

In this chamber of hostility, the Abyssal Dominion's dark plans unfolded like a tapestry of darkness, with Keisha as their unwitting prey.

A sinister symphony of strategies unfolded in the heart of the Abyssal Dominion's planning chamber, each noting a chord of vengeance and cruelty that echoed through the shadows.

With unsettling resolve, the members of the Abyssal Dominion delved deeper into their clandestine discourse, each hushed utterance giving birth to evil designs that were laden with deceit and malice. Their plots unfurled like the shadowy wings of a ravenous creature, driven by their insatiable thirst for dominion and retribution.

Qellaun's voice cut through the tension like a blade honed by practicality. "We must remain mindful that the absence of Keisha will not go unnoticed, especially by Ong and the Eladrin. While they may be incapable of pinpointing her location, her vanishing will not escape their vigilant eyes. We mustn't underestimate their resolve to safeguard their own."

Phoenix's gaze honed to a razor's edge, contemplating Qellaun's counsel. "Indeed, we must orchestrate diversions and disturbances across various domains, a tapestry of chaos that might lure their attention away from Keisha. Within the storm of confusion, we can enact our designs."

Vuarus, the precursor of shadows, affirmed with a nod. "By plunging realms into discord, we might cloud their perceptions, affording us the precious window to ensnare her."

Their strategies took shape in this chamber of darkness, an evil symphony that sought to cast the realms into turmoil and conceal their sinister intentions.

Lyra's gaze shifted among her co-conspirators, an orchestrator of dark melodies. "Remember, our ultimate aim is to shatter her resolve, to twist her into a weapon against those she holds dear. Her captivity is but the prologue to our grim symphony."

Vuarus glared at Lyra, his expression carrying an air of amusement. "No, my dear Lyra, we are not concerned about turning her into a weapon, as that would never happen."

As their ominous discourse unfolded, an aura of malice hung like a shroud, a testament to the unholy unity that bound their wicked pact.

Lyra leaned forth, her fingers tracing contemplative patterns upon the table's surface. "Can we not craft a web of slumber to ensnare both Keisha and her panther? Enchanted flora, woven with subtlety, is akin to nature's hand. Thus, they would be lulled into unconsciousness, oblivious to our mastery."

Vuarus exchanged an enigmatic glance with Phoenix before returning his attention to Lyra's proposition. "While your suggestion bears merit, I fear such finesse might not align with our goals. We seek not just their surrender, but their surrender beneath the weight of our supremacy, to realize the futility of resistance against us."

In the dark heart of their alliance's conclave, strategies of malevolent artistry took root, entwining the souls of the architects in a wicked symphony, each noting a chord of darkness that resonated with their insidious purpose.

Phoenix's solemn agreement resonated like a dark omen, his words a chilling echo in the chamber. "Subtlety is not our aim, but rather an exhibition of our power. We seek to imprint upon them the depths of our might and inscribe upon their hearts the unassailable truth that escape is a fleeting fantasy. Their fear-stricken gaze, the bitter comprehension that their guardianship falters – that is the essence we wish to evoke."

Lyra, a shadowed strategist, reclined contemplatively, her mind weaving intricate patterns. "Indeed, I concede the point. It was a mere pondering, an avenue of thought. However, you are correct; our message's clarity is paramount."

Vuarus leaned into the gathering, his eyes gleaming with a sinister gleam like the waning moon's evil gaze. "Rest assured, Lyra, and we shall etch our declaration onto the tapestry of their realms. Keisha's capture shall be the resounding testament to our dominion, a proclamation that none can defy."

Lyra's assent was resolute, her gaze unwavering. "Then let our proclamation thunder with unwavering force, leaving no doubt in their hearts."

Amidst the crystallizing designs, the alliance's tendrils of power tightened, their intent to ensnare Keisha fueled by a hostility that eclipsed even the darkest shadows.

A sinister smirk danced upon Phoenix's lips as he contemplated Lyra's idea. "Your proposition, Lyra, may not conform precisely to our initial intention. Yet, a twisted echo could resonate. I want Ong to witness Keisha ensnared within our grip, powerless and defenseless. The guttural cry of desperation, the anguish etched in his gaze – that will be a wound through his very soul, a cruel reminder of his inability to safeguard her."

Vuarus leaned back, a sinister amusement in his gaze. "Your thoughts have a certain allure, Phoenix. For in this, it's more than mere capture; it's the breaking of their spirits, the destruction of hope."

Lyra's curiosity found a voice through a raised eyebrow. "But what if Ong retaliates, consumed by fury?"

Phoenix's grin broadened, and a predator's satisfaction revealed. "Let his rage be kindled. We shall stand ready. His futile assault to liberate her shall only solidify our dominion, a defiant testament to his powerlessness."

As the sinister undercurrents of their strategy deepened, their collective resolve solidified, driven by a thirst for vengeance and the intoxicating belief in their supremacy.

Vuarus leaned into the conspiratorial air, his words like honeyed poison, laced with unyielding assurance. "Rest assured, Lyra. Our clutches will conceal Keisha from prying eyes. Shrouded in the deepest magic's embrace, our chambers are impervious to even the sharpest senses. Ong will hunt for her alone, a solitary quest where we hold dominion. The more his desperation deepens, the more his struggle shall echo as a hollow symphony of futility."

Lyra's understanding bloomed like a dark flower, her gaze sharpening with new-found insight into the intricate web they spun. "We shall let him chase phantoms while our grip tightens around the realms. His futile dance will etch the truth of our might upon his heart."

"Exactly," Vuarus echoed, his eyes luminous with the prospect. "When Keisha is secured in our clutches, his spirit shall fracture, his hopes dashed to naught."

A devious light danced in Vuarus' eyes as he leaned forward, his tone a calculated whisper of malevolence. "Now, consider this twist. Should she be a stubborn ember, we shall present Eladrin and Ong with a compelling illusion of choice."

Phoenix's curiosity ignited like a flicker in the dark. "A choice? But I hold no desire to release her."

Vuarus raised a reassuring hand, his voice like silk brushing over steel. "Bear with me, Phoenix. 'Tis but a ruse, I propose. Picture this: We seize Keisha, a puppet, over the abyss. A threat poised to plunge her into its depths unless they disclose E'vahona's exact sanctum."

Phoenix's objection subsided, intrigue sparking anew. "Continue."

Vuarus' grin unfurled like a hidden dagger's glint. "Even should they yield the secret, and we concede temporary freedom, the twist reveals itself. As their eyes bear witness, the abyssal dragons shall ascend, claws seizing her from the heavens."

Malevolent amusement danced in Phoenix's gaze. "We shall claim what we covet—the location of E'vahona."

Vuarus' laughter dripped like venom. "Indeed. The revelation shall mirror their folly, realization dawning as they surrender the realm's heart while losing her forever, a double-edged fate where their cherished Kadona shatters alongside her."

Phoenix's laughter reverberated through the chamber like a haunting melody. "Very well, Vuarus. Your plan might add a little more spice to this game."

Lyra's voice cut through the conversation, her tone laced with skepticism. "You do realize, Phoenix, that she won't break under pressure, don't you? This is more about your revenge for every time she's interfered with your plans."

Phoenix's laughter filled the chamber again, a chilling symphony of dark amusement. "You've got me there, Lyra. I don't have any illusions about her suddenly joining our cause. But the game, the theatrics—those are essential. And in the end, when we send her to the abyss, it won't just be about silencing her. It'll be about establishing our rule, showing them we are unstoppable. No one will ever dare cross us again." The malicious satisfaction in his voice was palpable, and the alliance of darkness contemplated the depth of their machinations.

Vuarus's laughter joined Phoenix's, the two sharing a moment of dark camaraderie. He turned to Phoenix, a twisted smile on his face, and offered his praise. "Well played, my friend. A plan so maliciously intricate, it's a symphony of chaos."

Vuarus regained his composure with a nod, his gaze sweeping over the gathered figures. "Enough of this for now. Let us return to our work to show the realms how formidable we've become. If you have further ideas about capturing our dear Keisha, please bring them to Phoenix or me. But remember, our immediate focus is on spreading our dominion."

Their meeting dissolved, each member of the Abyssal Dominion dispersing to carry out their nefarious tasks, the air heavy with anticipation of the impending storms their plans would unleash upon the realms.

Vuarus glanced at them and smirked. "Well played, Phoenix. Your desire for revenge played perfectly into my hands." The alliance of darkness embraced their ominous pact, driven by their thirst for power and vengeance.

Chapter 26

Shadows Unveiled: Wrath of the Malevolent Dragons

They converged with the evil dragons in the heart of Afor, Vuarus, and Phoenix under their sinister command. The atmosphere seemed to pulse with impending chaos, an eerie tension that hung thick in the air, while the dragons' eager eyes gleamed with anticipatory malevolence.

Zylron exhaled torrents of scorching flames that wove through the air, a fearsome dance of fiery supremacy. His scales shimmered like molten copper, radiating the infernal heat that fueled his power. It was as if the very essence of fire had taken physical form in the sinuous coils of his body.

Beside him stood Glaciera, a white dragon whose icy breath could freeze the essence of courage in its tracks, a stark contrast to the chilling aura that enveloped her. Like crystalline glaciers, her scales glistened with an otherworldly frost, and her cold, azure eyes betrayed no hint of mercy.

Drakthor, the embodiment of cunning and ruthlessness, flexed his obsidian-scaled wings, casting a haunting shadow over the assembly. His form was a symphony of darkness, a predatory silhouette that exuded a sense of foreboding. His eyes, obsidian orbs devoid of warmth, held a fathomless depth of malevolence.

Venfyr, the green dragon, regarded the proceedings with a twisted smile, his eyes gleaming with malice as he reveled in the discord he would soon sow. His green scales shimmered with an unnatural vibrancy, a reflection of the poison that coursed through his veins, and his body coiled with an eerie grace.

Thundria's formidable presence, manifested through the Topaz Dragon, seemed to amplify the evil energy that crackled in the air. Her scales were a brilliant, gem-like yellow, radiating an unnatural radiance that felt almost blinding. Her eyes held an electrifying intensity, a harbinger of the storms she could conjure.

Vuarus grinned, his voice a velvet-edged blade that dripped with promises of destruction. "My loyal brethren, the time has come for us to unleash the power within. The lands of Emeraldwood shall be our canvas, and our hostility shall be our brushstroke." His crimson eyes burned passionately, reflecting the wicked delight courting his being.

Phoenix's eyes glowed with the zeal of a fanatic; his dark intentions mirrored in the dragons' menacing gazes. "Zylron, Glaciera, you shall lead the way. Show them the fire and ice of our dominion. Drakthor, Venfyr, and Thundria bolster their efforts with your unique talents. Let the world tremble before the might of the Abyssal Dominion." His voice held the weight of impending doom, a harbinger of the calamity they were about to unleash upon the unsuspecting realm.

With a cacophony of triumphant roars, the dragons launched themselves into the sky, their mighty wings carrying them toward the lush expanse of Emeraldwood. As they neared their destination, the once serene forest was bathed in a crimson and frosty glow, an ominous prelude to the impending devastation. The air seemed to tremble with foreboding as the dragons descended upon their unsuspecting prey.

Zylron, a creature of infernal majesty, unleashed torrents of flames that engulfed the towering trees, reducing them to charred remains. His fiery breath painted the sky with a mesmerizing yet horrifying dance of destruction, leaving behind a trail of smoldering ruin in his wake.

Nearby, Glaciera, a vision of frozen malevolence, let loose her icy breath, transforming the landscape into an otherworldly spectacle of frozen foliage and glittering crystalline formations. Her frosty touch encased once-vibrant flora in a deathly embrace, turning them into grotesque statues of cold, lifeless beauty.

The other dragons contributed their powers to the infernal display with equal fervor. Drakthor's shadows deepened the gloom, his dark aura swallowing patches of sunlight, plunging the forest into an abyss of darkness and despair.

Venfyr reveled in chaos, inciting turmoil among the forest creatures with whispers of deception. His sinister influence sowed discord among the inhabitants of Emeraldwood, turning them against one another in a nightmarish frenzy.

Thundria's topaz brilliance intensified, electrifying the air and conjuring violent storms that raged overhead. The symphony of elemental power echoed through the land, a prelude to the calamity that the Abyssal Dominion had set in motion. Thunder boomed and lightning lashed out, illuminating the chaos below with brief, blinding flashes.

Emeraldwood quaked beneath the weight of evil might, its once lush heart now resounding with anguished cries and the lamentations of the dying. The Abyssal Dominion reveled in the infernal spectacle, their chilling laughter intertwining with the tumultuous upheaval. They were the harbingers of doom, and as the forest writhed in agony, they watched with satisfaction, trapped in a vortex of their own making—a vortex of doom.

Amid the unrelenting devastation, the evil dragons exulted in their boundless power, their sinister cravings unfurling like wings in the abyss. The forest's plaintive pleas for mercy were met with thunderous roars that reverberated through the very soul of Emeraldwood, drowning out nature's lament with cruel, malevolent glee. The once-vibrant heart of the forest wilted under the relentless onslaught, its beauty twisted into grotesque forms by the dragons' insatiable hunger.

Amidst the chaos, the Abyssal Dominion observed their designs for dominion reaching apexes of hostility with a perverse delight. With each sundered tree and every creature's desperate flight, the alliance's grip upon the realms constricted further—a testament to the irresistible might of their sinister forces. It was a symphony of malice, a dark crescendo that echoed through the very fabric of reality.

As the sun dipped beneath the horizon, casting an eerie twilight over the desolated panorama, the dragons finally began their retreat, and a cruel satisfaction was attained for the moment. The once-vibrant woodland stood scarred and fractured, a somber testimony to the ravaging might of the evil dragons and the shroud of darkness they had draped upon the earth. Their odious mission was fulfilled, and their evil laughter lingered like a haunting echo.

The Abyssal Dominion observed their homecoming with a sardonic satisfaction, knowing that the calamitous power they had harnessed was a preview of the terrors yet to be unleashed. As the shadows deepened and night enshrouded the realm, the evil dragons ascended as harbingers of chaos, their reign of dread only at dawn. The world trembled in anticipation of the horrors that awaited, for the Abyssal Dominion's thirst for dominion and vengeance knew no bounds.

An unsettling tension threaded through the heart of E'vahona, the realm of the Eladrin. The enchanted woods that encircled them trembled with an intangible disturbance, their once-peaceful canopy now quivering with disquieting energy. Whispers of distress rode upon the wind, a haunting melody of nature's anguish that resonated within the hearts of the Eladrin.

Intricately entwined with the natural world's rhythms, Keisha detected the disquiet with acute sensitivity. Her affinity for the forests ran deep, allowing her to sense their jubilations and sorrows. A profound sadness settled upon her, intensifying as the disharmony in the atmosphere surged.

Compelled by the burgeoning turmoil, she departed from the sanctuary of their abode, traversing the otherworldly beauty of E'vahona. Her footsteps echoed with hesitation, mirroring the uneasiness that thrummed through her. The vibrant hues of the landscape seemed to pale in brilliance, veiled by an unseen shroud of ominous anticipation, as though the very heart of E'vahona itself held its breath, awaiting an impending storm.

Ong, ever attuned to her emotions and ever vigilant as her protector, perceived her absence and traced her path through the ethereal beauty of E'vahona. His heart constricted upon finding her beside a cascade that shimmered like liquid starlight. Tears glistened in her eyes as she gazed into the distance.

Without a word, he approached and enfolded her in a cocoon of solace, his strong arms wrapping around her in a tender embrace. She leaned into him, drawing strength and comfort from his resolute presence. "Ong," her voice quivered, "one of the forests is in agony. I can sense it—the anguish, the devastation. Yet, I cannot discern which forest is afflicted."

Ong held her gently yet securely, sharing in her sorrow. He had witnessed the profound depth of her bond with the natural world and understood the torment she now endured. "We'll confront this together," he murmured with unwavering support. "We shall uncover the truth and find a way to alleviate this destruction."

Keisha nodded, her tears staining his shoulder as she clung to him. "I know," she whispered. "But the pain—it's overwhelming. The forests are an extension of my being, and their suffering is unbearable."

He kissed her temple tenderly, his touch a balm to her wounded spirit. "We shall safeguard them, whatever the cost. For now, let us concentrate on gathering information. Our companions have sensed a similar disturbance. By uniting our insights, we may untangle this enigma and uncover a means to remedy it."

Their embrace kindled a shared resolve, an unspoken pact forged amid the tumultuous echoes of destruction. The devastation that had struck a chord within their hearts served as a clarion call, a reminder of the encroaching darkness that menaced their realms. In this moment of uncertainty, their unwavering love and steadfast determination emerged as a radiant beacon, illuminating the path of resistance and unity they must undertake.

In the heart of E'vahona, an aura of tension enveloped the air, bearing witness to Keisha's profound distress. Her intimate link with the natural world had gifted her an acute sensitivity to the tremors of ruin that rippled through the land. The Eladrin city was a tableau of wary anticipation, its denizens clustering in somber groups, their countenances reflecting the bewilderment and sorrow that gripped their collective spirit.

Amidst the gathering, Lord Karrenen, his age-old eyes reflecting the moment's gravitas, approached Keisha and Ong. His presence exuded a soothing wisdom, a haven of assurance amidst the fierce currents of uncertainty. "Lady Keisha," he spoke, his voice a steadying force, "I comprehend the anguish that weighs upon you. The echoes of destruction have penetrated even the sanctum of our city."

Keisha's gaze held sorrow and frustration, mirroring her inner turmoil. "But which forest, Lord Karrenen? Which of them falls victim to this onslaught?" Her voice trembled with grief and determination, seeking answers to the forest's cries for help.

Lord Karrenen's voice carried the echoes of ages past, each syllable resonating with the accumulated wisdom of centuries. "The anguish that courses through you, Lady Keisha, binds us all who hold the natural realm dear. Yet, for the present, let us tend to your well-being. Your strength, poised to rise against this encroaching shadow, is a vital cornerstone."

Keisha yielded to the counsel with a sigh that released a cascade of emotions. "You speak true. At this moment, rest is the most prudent path. But, Lord Karrenen, I pray you, once the veil of uncertainty lifts and the forest's suffering is revealed, do inform me."

The venerable elf nodded in solemn agreement. "Certainly, my lady. You shall be the first to know when we unmask the afflicted woods."

Lord Karrenen's gaze, like the first light of dawn, softened with empathy, casting a warm glow on the gathering. It was a beacon of understanding that illuminated the tense atmosphere in the room. "We are laboring ceaselessly to pinpoint the exact locus, my lady," he spoke with a voice as soothing as a babbling brook. "The task is formidable, given the vastness of your senses' reach and the expanse of our forested lands. Be assured that we shall not relent until the answer is laid bare before us."

Ong's touch, a comforting presence upon Keisha's shoulder, spoke volumes of solidarity in uncertainty. His hand was like the roots of the ancient trees, grounded and unwavering. "Keisha, Lord Karrenen is right," he said, his words as gentle as a breeze rustling through leaves. It reminded them of unity and that they were all in this together. "You must gather your strength, for when we discern the location, your readiness for action will be crucial."

Keisha's nod was tinged with tension, her expression a vivid tableau of emotions as she grappled with the dueling desires to unearth the truth and seek solace. Like pools of swirling emotions, her eyes reflected the turmoil within her. "You're right, Ong," she whispered, her voice as fragile as a butterfly's wings. "It's just... the not knowing is a torment that gnaws at me, like a hungry beast lurking in the shadows."

As Keisha and Ong navigated the ebb of the assembly, Lord Karrenen's gaze trailed their departure. His eyes, a blend of concern and optimism, followed them with unwavering consideration. Even during the impending darkness, their unity remained unwavering, casting light upon their indomitable spirit in the face of adversity. However, beneath his stoic exterior, a gnawing worry festered – a fear that the Abyssal Dominion had sensed Keisha's unique connection to the forest and was poised to exploit it for their nefarious purposes.

Amidst the core of the Abyssal Dominion's clandestine sanctum, a place shrouded in darkness and foreboding, Phoenix's aura of malevolence encased as he penned his ominous missive. The chamber seemed to cower in his presence as if aware of the sinister power emanating from him. His words, sculpted with meticulous calculation on a parchment that absorbed the very essence of his intent, bore an unmistakable air of lofty supremacy. They were a declaration of dominance woven with threads of arrogance, each stroke of his quill resonating with an eerie authority. A mere twitch of his fingers and the message was dispatched, the shadow of his influence slithering across the vast expanse of the realms like a viper in the night.

With the passage of days, the realm's responses materialized, delivered by obedient couriers who dared not question the edicts of their formidable masters. The message from King Alex, sovereign of Goldmoor, bore an ember of defiance beneath its veneer of formality. His voice resounded through the message, an enthusiasm of rebellion that coursed like wildfire through his words. "The Abyss shall turn to ice before I bend the knee to your ilk," he proclaimed, his defiance burning brighter than the fieriest star.

Conversely, King Manard's reply bore the polish of measured diplomacy, a well-crafted tapestry of words refusing submission while veiled in civility. His missive exuded a steadfast commitment to his realm's integrity and the welfare of his people. Skillfully declining Phoenix's offer, it maintained the delicate dance of decorum even in the face of impending conflict.

Phoenix absorbed the contents of the messages with a grin that radiated self-assurance, his dark eyes dancing over the indomitable words of King Alex and the graceful yet unwavering response from King Manard. The parchment felt like a trophy in his hands, a testament to his power and the fear he instilled in those who dared to oppose him.

His attention shifted to Vuarus, his kindred harbinger of shadows, and a sarcastic chuckle erupted from him, echoing through the dimly lit sanctum. "As expected, their retorts," he mused, his voice dripping with smug satisfaction. "They cling to their empires and pride like bulwarks against our power, but little do they know that those very bulwarks shall become their downfall." Vuarus nodded, a sinister glint illuminating his obsidian eyes as they shared a profound understanding. "Stubborn they are, these monarchs," he replied, his voice a whisper of darkness. "Yet, their tenacity shall herald their downfall. Their pride will blind them to impending doom."

Phoenix's grin broadened, the predatory glint in his eyes undiminished. "Indeed," he agreed, his voice carrying the weight of impending doom. "Let their pride be their anchor, a weight that shall ultimately pull them under the tide of their ruin. And now, let us forge on with our endeavors, for the realms are poised to quiver before the unrelenting supremacy of the Abyssal Dominion."

Against the backdrop of skies painted in fiery crimson hues, the ominous silhouette of Dread Spire loomed with a sinister grandeur. Having quenched their thirst for destruction in the heart of Emeraldwood, the evil dragons soared back to their foreboding citadel. Their ebony wings cast somber shadows over the desolation they had wrought upon the realm, a grim reminder of the darkness that had taken root in the hearts of those who dared to defy the Abyssal Dominion.

Within the shadow-shrouded depths of Dread Spire, Zylron, Glaciera, Venfyr, and their draconic kin congregated, their eyes ablaze with a blend of satisfaction and eager anticipation. The potency bestowed upon them by the Abyssal Dominion had unfurled devastation upon the once-verdant forest, kindling an intoxicating primal exhilaration within their fiery hearts.

Zylron's scales, still aglow with smoldering embers, resonated with a resonant, throaty laugh that reverberated through the vast cavernous hollow. His laughter was like the crackling of burning timber. "Did you witness the enthusiasm with which the trees succumbed to our flames?" he boomed, his voice echoing in the chamber. "The very heart of the woodland ablaze, a sight to behold!"

Glaciera, her wintry breath still lingering in the air, nodded with a regal air of agreement. Her voice was like the chill of a frozen wasteland. "And the delicate tapestry of frost and snow that adorned all, as if the very essence of winter had heeded our summons."

Venfyr's eyes danced with a mischievous glint as he contributed, a sly grin on his draconic visage. "Ah, and the fleeing residents of the woodlands! Their panic and trepidation, a harmonious melody that resonated pleasingly in my ears."

Thundria, known as the Topaz Dragon, emitted a deep rumbling purr of contentment, her satisfaction tangible. Her purr was like the rumble of distant thunder. "Our supremacy is unassailable, our devastation undeniable. The Abyssal Dominion's boon has given us the power to mold this realm in our image."

Amidst their revelry, a deep voice cut through the cavern, drawing their attention. Phoenix, his presence a blend of fire and shadow, stood before them with a calculating smile. His aura was like a flickering flame in the abyss. "My loyal dragons, you have performed admirably. The forests tremble at your might, and the realms of light are on the brink of despair."

Zylron, the red dragon, lowered his massive head in respect. His eyes were like burning coals. "Our loyalty to you and the Abyssal Dominion knows no bounds, Phoenix."

Phoenix's eyes glinted with vicious delight. "Excellent. Your deeds have not gone unnoticed, and they serve as a reminder to those who would dare oppose us."

Glaciera's icy gaze locked onto Phoenix. "But what about our next move, Phoenix? Will we continue to bring chaos to the realms?" Her voice was as cold and calculating as the deepest winter night.

Phoenix's smile widened, revealing the depths of his hostility. "Indeed, my dear Glaciera, our work has only just begun. The chaos we've sown is but a prelude to the grand symphony of destruction we shall orchestrate. The realms shall be our canvas; we shall paint it with the darkest shades of despair."

Drakthor, the embodiment of darkness, hissed in approval. His voice was like the whisper of shadows. "Let us plunge them deeper into the abyss, where hope is a distant memory."

Venfyr, the green dragon, chuckled with wicked glee. His laughter was like the rustling of poisonous leaves. "The discord we sow shall be their undoing, and the realm shall bow before our dominion."

Thundria's voice resonated with thunderous authority. Her words were like a tempest's roar. "We shall remind them of their powerlessness with each storm we conjure. The realms will tremble at the mere mention of our name."

Phoenix's eyes sparkled with dark amusement. "Yes, my loyal dragons, we shall cast a deep shadow so it shall blot out the very sun. The Abyssal Dominion's supremacy is inevitable, and the realms shall kneel before us, or they shall crumble into oblivion."

As the dragons basked in their evil purpose, the darkness of their intentions hung heavy in the air, a palpable reminder of the impending doom they would unleash upon the unsuspecting realms.

Phoenix's grin widened, a mixture of malice and cunning. His eyes glinted like twin fires in the darkness. "Oh, indeed. But now, my dear dragons, we turn our attention to a new endeavor that will strike fear into the hearts of our enemies. We will capture the Eladrin Keisha, and in doing so, we will shatter their hopes and tear any semblance of unity asunder they possess."

The dragons exchanged knowing glances, their eyes gleaming with anticipation. The thrill of destruction had ignited a hunger within them, and the promise of capturing a powerful adversary only fueled their dark desires. As they listened to Phoenix's plan, a sinister aura enveloped Dread Spire, a testament to the evil alliance between the dragons and the forces of darkness.

Talleoss, the ancient and enigmatic figure who resided within the intricate design of the dragon-shaped staff, stood in the shadows of a chamber within Dread Spire. The staff, a conduit of his magic and connection to the divine realm, was a constant companion—an artifact of immense power that bound him to his true allegiance.

As Phoenix addressed the dragons, Talleoss listened intently, his keen senses absorbing every word. The news of the destruction of the forest weighed heavily on his heart, a bitter reminder of the price being paid in the name of the Abyssal Dominion's power.

Though his visage remained concealed in the shadows, his thoughts conflicted. Talleoss was not a servant of the Abyssal Dominion; he had chosen to stay loyal to Kadona, the true goddess of the realm. The destruction of nature, which he held so dear, was a painful reality he had to endure for the sake of his mission.

Yet, as the conversation continued, Talleoss knew he had to keep his true feelings in check. His presence within Dread Spire was a delicate balance, a high-stakes game of deception. If he showed any sign of dissent, he would betray himself and risk exposure to the evil forces surrounding him.

Talleoss's heart weighed heavy with the knowledge of the impending threat to Keisha and the realms she symbolized. It was a burden he bore solemnly, a reminder of his duty to protect the natural order and the true goddess, Kadona.

As the dragons and Phoenix continued their discussions, Talleoss focused on his internal resolve. He was a guardian of the proper order, a dragon bound within the staff, a beacon of light in the shadows. And though he walked a dangerous path, he was determined to navigate it with wisdom and courage, all to preserve the realm from the clutches of darkness.

His staff pulsed with suppressed magic, symbolizing his connection to the divine realm and unwavering commitment to the cause. Talleoss knew that his time would come, that he would play a crucial role in thwarting the plans of the Abyssal Dominion and protecting the realm he loved.

He remained hidden in the shadows, a silent sentinel biding his time, ready to rise when the decisive moment arrived.

The somber news washed over E'vahona like a shroud of melancholy, its weight settling heavily upon the hearts of the Eladrin. Whispers of the tragedy wound through the city's winding passages, igniting an intricate dance of sorrow and simmering anger. It wasn't until later that the location of the devastation was definitively confirmed: Emeraldwood Forest, one of their most cherished sanctuaries, had been violated and defiled.

In the peaceful embrace of the chambers, Keisha and Ong received the confirmation that ignited the anger that had festered within them since the first tremors of destruction reached their senses. Lord Karrenen's voice carried the gravity of the news, his words etching a somber path into their minds. "Emeraldwood Forest indeed suffered the assault. We have learned that Phoenix has extended his dark hand, sending messages to King Alex and King Manard, demanding their surrender to his will."

Ong's jaw set in an unwavering line, his grip on Keisha's hand tightening as if to anchor himself. The responses from the two kings were resolute, echoing the strength that flowed through their realms. King Alex's fiery defiance, however, managed to pierce the weight of the situation with a touch of reluctant amusement. His words resounded with unwavering spirit, proclaiming that even the depths of the Abyss would freeze over before he yielded to Phoenix's command.

Keisha's laughter, tinged with a bittersweet undertone, danced through the air. The irony of King Alex's response momentarily lit up the oppressive atmosphere, allowing a flicker of amusement to break through their grim contemplations. "Well," she managed to quip, a mixture of wistfulness and humor in her tone, "at least we can be certain that King Alex won't surrender without putting up a fight."

Ong nodded in agreement, his gaze focused on the message before him. "Absolutely. But this is far from the end. We must be prepared for what lies ahead."

Stepping out of the council chambers, a sense of urgency propelled their every step. The destruction of Emeraldwood Forest was a dire proclamation of the Abyssal Dominion's intent, and their threat loomed ominously on the horizon. Ong and Keisha exchanged a meaningful look, their eyes reflecting the unwavering resolve that burned within them. They understood the weight of their responsibility—their duty to shield their realms and allies from the evil forces that sought to engulf their world in darkness.

Shadows of uncertainty obscured the path before them, yet their determination remained unyielding. The ruin of Emeraldwood Forest had ignited a fierce flame within their hearts, one that would illuminate their actions as they ventured into the heart of the abyssal storm. With every stride, they inched closer to unraveling the enigma that cloaked their adversaries' true intentions.

And so, as Ong and Keisha embraced the challenges ahead, they held onto the promise of hope that guided their journey. With Emeraldwood Forest and Crystal Vale as their destinations, they embarked on a treacherous odyssey, bolstered by the belief that their old and new alliances would stand unwavering against the storm that threatened to engulf their realms. Theirs was a path fraught with danger, but their determination and the bonds they forged would be their greatest weapons in the battle against the Abyssal Dominion.

Chapter 27

Shadows Unveiled: Ripple Effects - Reactions from Coraluna and Ardinia

Coraluna's Ripple Effects and Response

An unsettling turmoil cast its shadow in the heart of Coraluna, a realm beneath the waves where serenity usually reigned supreme. The ethereal glow of the coral threw eerie patterns on the ocean floor, usually a place of tranquil beauty. Adrianna and Aqilus, revered as the guiding lights of the merfolk domain, detected a peculiar anxiety among the residents of these crystalline waters. Once-joyful fish now darted with frantic haste, their iridescent scales flashing like panicked stars. The once-graceful sea horses appeared skittish, their manes flowing wildly, as if a concealed disturbance had shattered the tranquil equilibrium that had enveloped their world.

Adrianna's eyes, the hue of the deepest sea, narrowed in shared concern with Aqilus. There was a silent symphony of apprehension in their gaze, a wordless exchange that conveyed their unease. It was evident that something had awoken in the sanctum of the ocean depths, and a duty, woven into their very beings, beckoned them to unravel this enigma. Their fluid forms wove through coral tapestries, their tails a symphony of graceful movements that conducted the aqueous ballet. With each sweeping motion, they ventured further into the heart of Coraluna, an anticipatory pulse guiding their path.

As they descended into the hidden chambers of the realm, an undertone of unease murmured like a hidden melody, swirling within the currents that enveloped them. The gentle rhythms of the sea now bore an unfamiliar cadence, like a ballad sung in a strange key. And yet, this regal merfolk navigated the shifting tides with an unswerving determination, a dance of purpose amidst the mounting disquiet.

Arriving at a sacred coral haven where kaleidoscopic fish had once woven their intricate tapestries, they now moved in disjointed, scattered patterns, avoiding their customary formations. The coral, once a vibrant mosaic of colors, now seemed to pale compared to the merfolk's troubled hearts. With her connection to the mystic sea, a birthright intertwined with her essence, Adrianna reached out to commune with the aqueous realm. Beneath her touch, she sensed an echo that chilled her to the core, a dissonance within the symphony that Coraluna thrived upon.

Aqilus, his stalwart tail a rudder of swift propulsion, glided to Adrianna's side, his presence a bastion of support amidst the shifting currents. His voice, a deep resonance reverberating through the aqueous expanse, bore the weight of their shared apprehension. "Adrianna, do you feel the unease that gnaws at the heart of our realm?" His words hung in the water like a solemn prophecy, echoing through the depths of Coraluna as they prepared to confront the unknown.

With a solemn nod, Adrianna's cascading locks of blonde hair danced like sunlit tendrils in the current, an ethereal caress of the depths. Each strand moved with a life of its own, a testament to the ancient bond between Merfolk and the ocean. "Indeed, Aqilus. The currents of Coraluna bear witness to a profound unrest. The very pulse of our realm falters, and the coral creatures heed its call."

Guided by purpose and steadfast resolve, they pressed onward, venturing into the labyrinthine abyss that cradled Coraluna's secrets. Along their odyssey, they bore witness to creatures unshackled from their gentle natures - animals of the deep showing signs of untamed aggression and audacious denizens retreating into the embrace of unseen sanctuaries. The realm's disquiet spread like tendrils, entwining even the most resilient inhabitants within its unsettling grip.

Their journey reached an apex as they converged upon a coral tableau of glorious hues, an opulent mosaic woven by nature's deft hand. Adrianna's senses heightened, attuned to the whispers of the aqueous realm. She reached out, her touch a communion with the very fabric of the sea. In that brief instant, a torrent of images cascaded into her consciousness - visions of the verdant Emeraldwood Forest, consumed by voracious flames and the sorrowful tableau left in their wake.

Aqilus's perceptive gaze caught the turmoil that swirled within Adrianna's eyes, a storm of emotions that threatened to consume her. He steadied her trembling form with a touch as gentle as the whisper of a breeze. "What glimpses unfolded in the sea of your mind?" His voice, a soothing murmur, carried the weight of genuine concern.

Adrianna's words trembled upon her lips, a delicate dance of vulnerability. "Emeraldwood Forest... Ruthless flames beset its ancient boughs. The heart of the Eladrin realm, ablaze."

Aqilus's countenance, once a canvas of serene wisdom, now bore the shades of ominous contemplation. "But how could such strife traverse from the earth to the ocean's depths?"

Adrianna's gaze, as deep and unfathomable as the abyss itself, met his with an epiphany that rippled across her features. "The threads of fate bind Emeraldwood and Coraluna more profoundly than we knew. The forest's suffering resonates through the very waters that cradle our realm. An unholy symmetry, Aqilus, as the forest weeps, so do our seas."

Determination surged through Aqilus's ligaments, his fingers coiling into fists as he embraced the newfound purpose that beckoned. "Then let the tides of fate bear witness. We shall delve into the heart of this calamity and sunder its malevolent source. We cannot abide as our kingdom wanes beneath this encroaching darkness."

Galvanized by a shared resolve transcending their existence, Adrianna and Aqilus embarked on a quest to unravel the enigma that tainted Coraluna's waters. Each stroke of their tails propelled them further into the azure depths, a tandem echo of unity and purpose. Time was their adversary, its unyielding current a reminder that the tides of destiny were in motion, and the realm's equilibrium hung in a precarious balance.

As they delved into the unfathomable chasms, a labyrinthine tapestry woven from mystery and trepidation, the merfolk monarchs knew their pursuit was a race against the relentless march of time. The harmonious undercurrents of Coraluna had been fractured, and their quest to mend this symphony of existence became an endeavor carved from necessity. The very essence of their realm depended on their unwavering determination to restore what had been lost beneath the waves.

With unwavering determination kindling within their souls, they delved deeper, daring to uncover the very nexus of disruption that had affixed its dark tendrils upon their realm. The shadows of uncertainty gave way to the luminous beacon of purpose, propelling them through the aqueous abyss. For within the heart of their quest lay the fate of Coraluna and the delicate interplay between land and sea, where the destinies of Eladrin and merfolk were eternally bound. Beneath the shimmering embrace of Coraluna's crystalline waters, Aqilus and Adrianna toiled with unwavering resolve, weaving intricate spells amidst the iridescent currents that wove their realm together. Their brows knitted in focused determination as they endeavored to unveil the elusive nature of the encroaching darkness that had cast a pall over the sea creatures' once harmonious symphony.

Around them, the denizens of the deep swam with an undercurrent of unease, their once jubilant pirouettes now hesitant, burdened by the unsettling echoes of an impending threat. Adrianna's touch, as gentle as the ocean breeze, brushed against the sleek flank of a passing dolphin, a fleeting connection that rippled tranquility through the uncertainty.

"The origins of this shadow must be revealed," Aqilus voiced with frustration and determination, his words like echoes that resounded amidst the cerulean expanse. "Coraluna, a realm bedecked in serenity and beauty, should never be shrouded in such unnatural discord."

Adrianna's gaze met his with an unyielding resolve that mirrored his own, a testament to their shared commitment to safeguarding their aquatic haven. "A shield must be forged, Aqilus, to safeguard our realm from the malevolent touch that seeks to fray its tapestry."

Aqilus exhaled a heavy sigh, his gaze drifting across the shifting ebb and flow of the currents around them. "Perhaps we should seek the counsel of King Oceanous, ruler of the depths. His bond with the sea and its myriad creatures might offer insights to pierce this enigma."

Adrianna's agreement resonated as a nod, a shared understanding that their unity alone might not suffice against the encroaching darkness. "You're right, Aqilus. King Oceanous's wisdom might illuminate our path. Let's pray for his guidance."

Through the ethereal fabric that knitted their world, Aqilus and Adrianna pooled their magic, creating a mystical communication bridge traversing the ocean's embrace. Soon, King Oceanous, a figure of regal majesty whose presence resonated like the resonant chords of an age-old song, manifested before them. His aura bore the weight of eons, a testament to his dominion over the deep.

"Greetings, Aqilus, Adrianna," King Oceanous's voice, as resonant as the ocean's tide, greeted them with a nod of recognition. "The disturbance in Coraluna has stirred my senses. A matter of concern, indeed."

Adrianna's response held a sense of both trepidation and urgency, her voice like the susurrus of waves on a moonlit shore. "Your Majesty, the encroaching darkness has cast its shadow upon us. We labor to unearth its source and quell its influence, but we need your sagacious guidance."

King Oceanous regarded them with a contemplative gaze, the depths of his eyes reflecting the mysteries that dwelled beneath the waves. "I shall lend my insight to your cause and seek counsel from Lysander, the Sea God, whose knowledge spans the ocean's breadth and depths."

Unspoken gratitude danced between Aqilus and Adrianna, their glances a shared symphony of appreciation for the aid they were receiving. "Your Majesty, your wisdom and the prospect of Lysander's counsel offer us hope," Aqilus expressed with the respect that resonated in his voice.

With a regal inclination of his head, King Oceanous's form began to wane, his presence an ephemeral visage amidst the watery currents. "I shall reach out to you once I have communed with Lysander. We shall weave a tapestry of insight and magic to protect Coraluna's sanctuary."

As the shimmering projection of King Oceanous dissolved into the depths, a renewed sense of purpose thrummed within Aqilus and Adrianna. With unity and the promise of allies yet to be summoned, they resolved to stand as the bastions of Coraluna, guardians of the sea's fragile equilibrium against the encroaching tide of darkness.

As the spectral connection with King Oceanous ebbed away, Aqilus and Adrianna returned to their task with hearts fortified by the knowledge that they were not alone in their struggle. The alliance they had forged, like a tapestry woven from unity and resolve, granted them strength in this hour of darkness.

In the realm of ethereal hues that Kadona inhabited, her essence radiated like a cascade of starlight against a midnight sky. Amid the tranquil luminosity, she extended her energy, reaching out across the expanse of the boundless ocean to connect with Lysander, the Sea God. Their communion was a dance of points, their essences intertwining with the ebb and flow of the endless tides, forming a connection that transcended the confines of their separate realms.

Lysander, a figure draped in the cerulean majesty of the deep, emerged before Kadona, his form towering like a pillar amidst the aquatic currents. A nod of acknowledgment greeted her. "Kadona, your presence is a rarity. To what do I owe the honor?"

Kadona's voice, like the melodic whisper of the ocean's breath, resonated with urgency. "Lysander, The Abyssal Dominion's evil forces have unfurled their darkness upon the sacred lands of Emeraldwood Forest. This encroaching shadow threatens the realm of land and the seas under your guardianship."

A shadow crossed Lysander's serene countenance, a storm of concern momentarily eclipsing his typically tranquil manner. "Emeraldwood Forest... I sensed its turmoil, but the source eluded me."

The luminosity of Kadona's form intensified a beacon of determination within the nebulous expanse. "Vigilance is paramount, Lysander. The forces of darkness may seek to extend their dominion into the seas, unraveling the delicate harmony you uphold."

A steeliness infused Lysander's gaze, his resolve a fortress carved from the bedrock of his purpose. "Your counsel is received, Kadona. The safety of the ocean is my unwavering charge. I am grateful for your warning."

With a parting of ethereal currents, their exchange concluded, and Kadona issued her final counsel. "Stand vigilant, Lysander, and remember that the Eladrin shall stand shoulder to shoulder with you. Against The Abyssal Dominion's encroachment, unity shall be our beacon."

As Kadona's luminous presence waned, Lysander's towering form began to fade, a seamless transition into the depths he called home. Soon, King Oceanous, a figure radiating an aura of regal authority, emerged to take Kadona's place.

"Greetings, Lysander," King Oceanous addressed the Sea God with a respectful nod. "I have been apprised by my daughter, Adrianna, and her companion, Aqilus. They were the bearers of grave tidings regarding the evil forces laid siege to Emeraldwood Forest, a threat extending its talons to our watery domain."

Lysander's voice resonated with a resonance that mirrored the depths he governed. "I am not ignorant of this development, King Oceanous. Kadona herself has just conveyed the same concern to me. The darkness must not be permitted to spread further."

King Oceanous nodded, his gaze a beacon of unwavering determination. "A proposal, Lysander. Let us unite our energies and weave a barrier near Emeraldwood Forest. A ward that shall serve as a temporary bastion against The Abyssal Dominion's influence. Yet, we must act swiftly, for its potency shall wane, and the encroaching tide must be met head-on."

A gleam of concurrence illuminated Lysander's eyes, an agreement forged in the crucible of shared purpose. "A barrier is a wise strategy, King Oceanous. However, our efforts must extend beyond our dominions. The alliance of Eladrin and other kindred spirits must unite in the face of this darkness."

With a nod of understanding, Lysander extended his trident towards the sea, its prongs shimmering like the scales of ancient sea dragons. A brilliant radiance erupted from its tip, a symphony of light that transformed the waters around Emeraldwood Forest. The waves, usually a testament to their capricious dance, transformed into a swirling vortex of energy, a shimmering curtain that sparkled like liquid sunlight, heralding the birth of a barrier forged from unity and shared purpose.

Upon the canvas of the sea, the tower of the barrier stood, a shimmering testament to the collective might of King Oceanous, Adrianna, and Aqilus. As the waves whispered their rhythmic secrets, King Oceanous, the ruler of depths, summoned his words through the conduit of the sea's connection, their resonant echoes unfurling within the minds of the merfolk leaders.

"Adrianna, Aqilus," his voice, like the haunting melody of oceanic currents, permeated their consciousness. "Be vigilant, for Aegis now enfolds the seas that embrace Emeraldwood Forest. Observe with unwavering watchfulness, attuned to the currents of any disturbance or stirrings of malevolence. Should shadows intrude, notify me without delay."

Adrianna and Aqilus acknowledged the message with a resonance that mirrored the sea's depths, their thoughts melding with its currents. The mantle of responsibility draped over them, a weight as profound as the ocean's embrace. Their commitment to protecting their realm from the encroaching darkness burned with the zeal of undying devotion.

Ardinia's Ripple Effects and Response

Within the realm of Ardinia, a tapestry woven from enchantment and magic, a disquieting murmur stirred the very essence of existence. Aeliana, a luminous

Nymph Queen whose wisdom flowed like the rivers that embraced her realm, felt the tremors of unease ripple through the land she cherished. Where once harmonious melodies resonated, a haunting undertone of fear now echoed, casting shadows upon the once-vibrant tapestry of her domain.

Aeliana's emerald gaze, a reflection of the lush foliage surrounding her, surveyed the expanse stretching like an emerald ocean. Her heart, a compass of empathy, weighed heavily with concern for her beloved realm. The ancient trees, their gnarled branches reaching skyward in an old dance, seemed to murmur in hushed tones, sharing secrets known only to the verdant sentinels. Once swept by zephyrs of carefree delight, delicate petals now shrank as if recoiling from a nebulous menace. Even the creatures that roamed this sacred expanse, animals that once met her gaze with warm curiosity, now tread cautiously, their instincts awoken by an unseen malaise.

Aeliana's connection with Ardinia was as profound as the roots that threaded through its soil, and the whispering wind conveyed its distress to her very core. Her resolve, a pillar of strength that stood amidst uncertainty, spurred her into action. With a regal bearing and a grace that mirrored the coursing rivers, she beckoned her trusted companions - the fairies, radiant beings of ephemeral light who embodied the very essence of the natural world.

Gathering in a glen embraced by dappled sunlight, the fairies assembled in a display of luminescence that painted the air with radiant hues. Aeliana, her gaze a convergence of concern and determination, addressed them with a voice that carried the weight of her realm's plight. "Beloved ones, Ardinia, our sanctuary of life and wonder, quivers in turmoil—the heart of our land beats in discord, an unfamiliar and unsettling rhythm. I implore you to take wing and embark upon a quest to unveil the source of this disruption. Be our eyes and ears in the depths of our realm and unveil the truth that shadows our existence."

The fairies, their wings shimmering like spun moonlight, nodded with solemn resolve. With a symphony of delicate yet determined flutters, they took to the sky, each carrying a fragment of Aeliana's concern as they departed on their whispered mission. Through moonlit glades and starlit streams, they navigated the labyrinthine beauty of Ardinia, their luminous forms casting trails of brilliance across the verdant expanse.

Within the ethereal weave that connected them, the fairies communed, sharing their discoveries as they ventured deeper into the heart of their realm. They unveiled clearings suffocated by an oppressive silence, where once-thriving life recoiled from an unseen malevolence. The air carried an uncanny chill, a reminder that a malign force had usurped the sun's embrace. Fragments of whispers reached their sensitive ears, tales of intrusion and disruption that had unbalanced the delicate equilibrium that danced between predator and prey, flora and fauna, life and magic within Ardinia.

The passage of hours in the realm of Ardinia marked a diligent pursuit by the fairies, threading through every hidden enclave and sunlit glade with meticulous care. Upon their return to Aeliana, the Nymph Queen, their expressions bore the weight of the tidings they carried - a symphony of solemnity and concern resonating within their luminous gazes. Each word they spoke echoed like distant whispers, unveiling tales of darkness slithering along the fringes of Ardinia, insidiously wilting foliage and coaxing creatures to vanish from sight.

Aeliana, the harbinger of wisdom in a realm where nature's rhythms converged, listened unwaveringly, absorbing the weight of the sad news unearthed. Her heart, a wellspring of empathy, embraced the realm's turmoil as if it were hers. Gratitude as profound as the roots that anchored her realm flowed from her lips as she thanked her fair companions for their unwavering diligence.

With a gaze that held the intensity of sunlit emerald, she resolved, "We shall not permit this shroud of darkness to shackle Ardinia's spirit. We stand united, steadfast against the unknown, and we shall journey to uncover the hidden origins of this dissonance that threatens our world. The harmony that beats in the heart of our realm shall be restored."

The fairies, a constellation of determined lights, mirrored Aeliana's enthusiasm with a shared nod, a pledge woven into the fabric of their collective will. As the Nymph Queen surveyed her realm, a land that unfolded like a living tapestry before her, she understood the path ahead would be fraught with challenges. Yet, her unwavering resolve, a beacon of hope and strength, bloomed like a rare flower amidst the turbulent winds.

Aeliana, regal in her bearing, recognized the urgency that coursed through the veins of Ardinia. In the solemn embrace of twilight, she summoned her most trusted fairies, their forms resplendent with wings that captured the hues of dawn's earliest light. As they gathered in a glen illuminated by starlit luminescence, her voice unfurled like an enchanting melody.

"Within our sanctuary, an ominous darkness thrives," Aeliana intoned, her voice a musical river that flowed through the silent glen. "With your ethereal grace and innate connection to the elements, I pray for your journey beyond our boundaries into the enigmatic heart of Vacari. Seek the origin of this disquiet, but remember, caution shall be your constant companion."

The fairies, their determination a constellation of unwavering lights, acknowledged their queen's charge with a blend of grit and apprehension. The perils that lurked beyond Ardinia's borders were known to them, yet their loyalty to the realm's essence and their monarch's cause kindled the enthusiasm within their hearts.

With a gentle wave, they launched into the velvety night, their wings carrying them like spectral fireflies into the unknown. In unity and harmony, their quest echoed the rhythms that infused Ardinia's breath, their flight a testament to their resolve and the realm's enduring spirit.

Guided by instincts honed by eons of symbiosis with the natural world, the fairies ventured beyond the realm's embrace, venturing into Vacari's depths. The forest of Emeraldwood received them like long-lost kin, yet even its vibrant beauty bore a shadow that sent tremors down their delicate spines.

As they moved deeper into the heart of the woodland, the fairies felt the palpable presence of malevolence that Aeliana had spoken of. A stifling darkness permeated the air, draping the verdant majesty of the forest in a shroud of haunting despair. The creatures that danced among the trees, usually luminous in their innocence, now sought refuge from the foreboding force that lingered.

With silent determination, the fairies traced the web of darkness that tainted the realm's essence, each flicker of intuition guiding them toward a focal point where the corruption was most concentrated. The revelation that awaited them held sorrow and despair within its heart - the very core of Emeraldwood bore the scars of an evil energy that sought to unravel its sacred spirit.

With hearts heavy as rain-laden clouds, the fairies gathered the essence of this corruption, tangible evidence of the darkness insidiously entrenched within Emeraldwood's embrace. They recognized the importance of conveying this somber truth to their queen, a fact that held the key to understanding the realm's precarious plight.

Returning to Ardinia, their luminescent presence an echo of the moon's embrace, the fairies unveiled the evidence before Aeliana, their expressions a kaleidoscope of sorrow and resolute purpose. Aeliana's gaze met the darkness embodied, her heart an altar of empathy for the suffering that clung to the very essence of their world. At that moment, she understood the gravity of the connection that bound the realms together and the importance of unity in the face of encroaching shadows.

"Even our sacred haven is not invulnerable to the reach of darkness," Aeliana murmured, her voice an elegy for the harmony that had been tarnished. "Vacari's essence is unsettled, and it extends its tendrils into the very heart of Ardinia. We are more than a realm; we are a tapestry woven from alliances and bonds, and together, we shall stand strong."

A determined resolve ignited within Aeliana's emerald gaze as she surveyed the realm that sprawled beneath her, a living canvas of life and magic. The fairies gathered around her, their wings shimmering like constellations against the darkness. Within their collective determination, an oath was sealed - to safeguard their realm, to rekindle the harmony that the shadows sought to extinguish, and to forge an unbreakable alliance that would fend off the encroaching darkness, no matter the trials that awaited.

In the realm of Ardinia, Aeliana, the Nymph Queen, had gathered her ethereal kin - the wood, forest, and air nymphs. A somber pall draped over the air, a testament to the gravity of the situation that had unfurled within Emeraldwood Forest. The nymphs, connected to nature's essence, exchanged glances that spoke of the shared understanding of the looming peril.

An invocation of determination emanated from Aeliana's voice. Each syllable was etched with unwavering resolve. "A fate intertwined with Ardinia's falls upon us. To shield our realm from this advancing darkness, we must unite."

The nymphs, their eyes a symphony of elemental luminescence, nodded in unison, their energies like threads woven into the fabric of reality. A cadence of power converged, a harmonious fusion of wood, forest, and air, their essence kindled into a coruscating tapestry of magic. The conjured veil, an embodiment of life's vitality and air's ethereal touch, merged into existence, encircling the realm that had become a sanctuary.

Within Aeliana's gaze danced relief and gratitude as the barrier congealed, a guardian born of combined essence. The nymphs, their duty fulfilled, stepped back, their ethereal forms reverberating with the triumph of their magic. With a newfound purpose, their attention shifted to their queen.

A forest nymph offered counsel, her voice a susurrus of rustling leaves. "Our actions safeguard Ardinia for now, Aeliana. But remember, in this struggle, solitary battles will falter. Our strength lies in unity against the looming darkness, as an alliance poised against The Abyssal Dominion."

Aeliana's agreement manifested as a determined nod, a regal acknowledgment of the wisdom within their words. "Indeed, we cannot stand as lone sentinels. Our steps shall tread in harmony with those of Vacari, for unity shall be our shield against the encroaching abyss."

With their shared purpose firmly entrenched, the nymphs dispersed, each ethereal form melting into their respective domains. Aeliana lingered amidst the vibrant hues of Ardinia, her heart heavy yet resolute. The journey ahead was rife with peril and uncertainty, but within her, the unyielding commitment to safeguard her realm and allies from the encroaching darkness burned with the intensity of a thousand suns.

E'vahona's Reactions

Within the heart of E'vahona, an aura of anxiety settled like a shroud of whispered concerns. Lord Karrenen, a figure of regal stature, stood amidst the radiant tapestry of their realm, his contemplative gaze directed towards the horizon. The air, laden with the fragrance of nature's symphony, seemed to hold a murmur of unrest, a distant whisper of turmoil that tugged at the edges of his thoughts.

Yet, before he could delve further into the labyrinth of his musings, Lady Mirabelle, a vision of grace reminiscent of moonlight's dance, approached him. Her eyes, twin pools of ancient wisdom, shimmered with a light that bore the weight of knowledge as she met his gaze.

"My lord," her voice, like the gentle cadence of a celestial aria, spilled forth with a delicate concern. "Through the intricate threads of magic that bind us to the realms, I perceive an unsettling tremor. Darkness awakens, its tendrils weaving a shadowed tapestry across Ardinia and Coraluna."

Lord Karrenen turned to her, his intuition resonating with her revelation's harmonious chords. "I, too, have sensed the ripples, Lady Mirabelle. Nature's essence seems to quiver as if foretelling a fierce storm on the horizon."

Mirabelle's gaze, a deep well of solemn understanding, met his. "The equilibrium falters. Our allies, they stand at the precipice of dire straits."

With a thoughtful inclination, Karrenen acknowledged the gravity of her words. "We must convene the council and apprise Keisha and Ong of this unsettling development. The unrestrained and malevolent darkness must be met with unwavering resolve."

A heavy mantle of responsibility settled upon them, its weight sinking into their souls as they exchanged this solemn acknowledgment. In E'vahona, where the cadence of nature's melody was revered as a sacred hymn, the encroaching darkness arrived like a discordant note in a once-harmonious symphony. It served as a stark reminder of their realm's fragile existence, a clarion call that reverberated through the fibers of their being, rallying them to arms to protect their allies, their realms, and the very essence that wove the tapestry of their reality.

As the council's urgent summons reached the ears of Ong and Keisha, the air seemed to thicken with an unspoken urgency, pressing upon their senses like a palpable presence. A storm of emotions swirled within her, and Keisha felt the tremors of unease ripple through her like a quivering echo. She descended to her knees. A humbling gesture mirrored her soul's turmoil as the intensity of the sensation threatened to engulf her.

Swift, purposeful footsteps approached, and Ong materialized at her side, his visage etched with concern and unwavering determination. Gently, he extended his hand, a lifeline in the face of her inner tempest, aiding her rise from her temporary surrender to the embrace of the earth itself. "Keisha, what ails you?"

Her eyes, twin pools of worry and resolve, met his, reflecting the depths of her concern. "Ong, the very fabric of existence frays before us. Darkness... it encroaches, its ominous shadow extending even into the sanctity of E'vahona."

Ong's grip on her hand tightened, a silent vow etched in his resolute nod. It affirmed their unity in the face of adversity, an unspoken promise that they would confront this encroaching darkness together, side by side, standing steadfast against the relentless tide of hostility.

Guided by Ong's unwavering presence, Keisha regained her footing with renewed determination. Her resolve flared to life, like a dormant ember reignited by a breath of purpose. Together, they embarked on their journey to the council chamber, where the solemn expressions of their fellow Eladrin echoed the gravity of the hour. Lord Karrenen, a beacon of authority and resolve, awaited at the head of the chamber, poised to address his assembly.

"Comrades," he commenced, his voice a rich tapestry woven with concern and solemnity. "We have been touched by the encroaching darkness that casts its ominous shadow upon our allies in Ardinia and Coraluna. Keisha, Ong, I understand that this darkness has not eluded your perception."

Keisha nodded, her bearing resolute, her gaze unwavering. "Indeed, Lord Karrenen. The sensation was an inundation, akin to an evil force attempting to rend the veil that delineates our realms."

Ong's grip on her hand tightened, his resolve etched into the lines of his countenance. "Inaction is not an option. Our destinies are irrevocably interwoven with theirs; the darkness's dominion over them could also breach the sanctum of E'vahona."

The council members exchanged silent glances, their expressions a fusion of unwavering determination and shared concern. Lord Karrenen's timbre, firm and commanding, resonated throughout the chamber. "Then let us entwine our strengths, forging a unity born of shared purpose. Bound by more than mere magic, our realms are knitted together by a common cause. We shall confront this encroaching darkness and guard the symphony that sustains our worlds."

Within the hallowed recesses of the council chamber, the Eladrin's collective determination resounded like an oath sworn by the very elements. The looming darkness had become the catalyst for an indomitable bond, a clarion call that transcended the confines of their realms. In solidarity with their brethren in Ardinia and Coraluna, the Eladrin stood poised to lend their courage, ready to unveil their dormant strengths to counterbalance the encroaching shadows.

Lord Karrenen's gaze swept the assembly, his voice a compass guiding their resolve. "To stand against this darkness, to safeguard our allies and the realms we cherish, we must look to those whose wisdom is steeped in the tapestry of ages. Ere we embark on our quest to Emeraldwood Forest, let us first pilgrimage to the Hidden Isles' enigmatic shores."

His proclamation lingered in the air, an unspoken understanding that cascaded between the council members. Keisha and Ong exchanged a wordless accord, their nods a declaration of alignment. "Your words hold wisdom, Lord Karrenen," Ong affirmed. "The dragons of the Hidden Isles bear knowledge and insights that could illuminate our path."

Keisha's grip upon Ong's hand tightened, a blaze of determination kindling in her eyes. "Time is of the essence, and our resolve shall not waver. Delaying is a luxury we cannot afford in the face of this looming threat."

Embracing their shared purpose, the council members arose from their seats, their collective energy pulsating with unswerving intent. Lord Karrenen's voice, an embodiment of authority and guidance, brought the discourse to a resolute close. "And so be it. Ready yourselves for the odyssey ahead. Together, we shall seek the counsel of the dragons, forging an alliance that shall meld our strengths and cast light upon the encroaching darkness."

As the Eladrin elves dispersed, each embarking upon their requisite preparations, the resounding echoes of their determination reverberated through the hallowed halls of E'vahona. Lord Karrenen, watching their determined departure, held a lingering concern within his heart. He leaned closer to the remaining council members. He quietly shared his suspicions, "I fear the Abyssal Dominion's sinister design may be to sever Keisha's special bond with the forests, using the destruction as a weapon against us. I am thankful that Ong is her anchor, for their unity may prove our greatest strength."

Chapter 28

Shadows Unveiled: Abyssal Dominion's Sinister Remaking of Emberwood

Vuarus and Phoenix loomed like dark titans within the heart of Dread Spire, their malevolent presence a palpable force that seeped into every shadowy crevice of the chamber. Their mastery over the arcane arts of darkness cast an eerie aura, like a shroud of malice hanging in the air. A sinister alliance bound them together, their ambitions twisted and forged in the crucible of wicked intent. The chamber itself seemed to shiver under their ominous voices, their whispered discussions a chilling symphony that echoed through the room as they delved into the extent of their sinister capabilities.

"Is it not a lamentable irony," Lyra's voice chimed in, her demeanor calm, "that the lush forests defy your dominion?" Phoenix turned his gaze to Vuarus, a spark of curiosity dancing in his eyes. Vuarus returned the look with a knowing smirk, his words pregnant with insinuation.

An evil grin spread across Phoenix's face. "And where, I wonder, shall we exert our influence?" he mused aloud.

Vuarus's eyes gleamed with sinister anticipation, a plan unfurling before them like a tapestry woven with evil intent. "Emberwood," he declared, his voice carrying a sharp edge. "Near Old Flameford, its transformation will serve as a potent proclamation."

Lyra's laughter rippled through the chamber like a discordant melody, her amusement mirroring the unfolding malevolent design. Once a thriving forest teeming with life, Emberwood now stood on the precipice of being twisted into a sinister reflection of their nefarious ambitions.

Amidst their calculated plotting, Phoenix's voice pierced the shadows with a chilling resonance. "Zylron," he intoned, his words hanging like a dark decree.

From the stygian recesses, Zylron emerged, the red dragon an avatar of malefic power. His scales glistened ominously in the dim light, his presence an embodiment of impending dread. Zylron's eyes shimmered with an eerie luminescence as he lent an ear to Phoenix's directives. His grim satisfaction was evident in the growing, predatory grin that stretched across his maw.

"Consign the arboreal splendor to the embrace of infernal fire," Phoenix instructed, his tone dripping with evil intent.

Zylron's lips peeled back, unveiling rows of glinting teeth in a sinister grin. "With elation," he hissed, his voice a confluence of eager anticipation and devilish delight. The pact of the Abyssal Dominion set its nefarious design into motion as the once-vibrant forest of Emberwood teetered on the precipice of transformation, about to be etched into an ominous tale of malevolent dominion.

With the ominous command given, Zylron unfurled his mighty wings and ascended into the heavens, the essence of Dread Spire's malevolence coalescing around him. A sinister aura enveloped the red dragon as he soared towards the sky, his form a manifestation of the potent darkness that surged within him. The destiny of Emberwood Forest teetered on a precipice as Zylron readied himself to unleash a torrent of destructive power upon the once-thriving expanse. Above Emberwood Forest, the sky underwent a dreadful metamorphosis. Voluminous clouds of smoke and ash mushroomed from the canopy, their ashen tendrils casting an ominous pall over the once-celestial heavens. The fire's rage that Zylron had ignited had set ablaze the very heart of the forest, reducing age-old trees to smoldering husks and vibrant blossoms to charred remnants. The symphony of life that had once flourished within its embrace had been silenced, replaced by an eerie and unsettling stillness.

Upon alighting amidst the aftermath, Zylron's draconic visage twisted into a sinister grin, his molten eyes blazing with the infernal glee of chaos wrought. With an imperious sweep of his gaze, he took stock of the destruction he had wrought—a desolate wasteland at his feet. The forest's grandeur had been eclipsed, replaced by the grim testament to the Abyssal Dominion's malevolent might.

Meanwhile, the harbingers of doom, Vuarus and Phoenix strode forward amidst the ravaged expanse, their presence a contagion that fed the atmosphere of dread. Vuarus's sorcerous might wove through the air, the very fabric of reality yielding to his dark designs. Sinister trees sprouted from the desecrated ground, their grotesque forms akin to skeletal appendages reaching out with twisted intent. Each tree pulsed with an aura of malice, an insult to the natural order.

In contrast, Phoenix's conjured power took on a different guise, an insidious beauty that masked treacherous intent. Foliage emerged, benign yet laden with subtle menace. Vines adorned with thorns entwined themselves around tree trunks, an intricate web ready to trap any unsuspecting soul. Flowers, with petals as delicate as silk, concealed venomous barbs—luring victims with false allure, only to trap them in a deadly embrace.

Together, in a sinister symphony, Vuarus and Phoenix molded their twisted vision upon the remains of Emberwood. A once-vibrant realm, teeming with life and beauty, had metamorphosed into a manifestation of their evil desires. The air reverberated with their ominous laughter, an eerie chorus that heralded the dawn of a new age—one tainted by the seeds of corruption they had sown.

Amid this newly wrought landscape, Glaciera, the bearer of icy dominion, descended from the heavens. Her wings cast a frigid breeze, her presence heralding a numbing chill slicing through the once-still air. As she descended, a cascade of snowflakes began to fall, each delicate crystal blanketing the scorched earth in a pristine layer of white. The ashen remnants of devastation were enshrouded by the ethereal touch of her wintry sovereignty, a poignant reminder that nature's beauty and rejuvenation could emerge even in the darkest throes of malevolence.

The arboreal creations birthed by Vuarus now bore the mark of Glaciera's frosty embrace, their once-twisted forms now adorned with delicate frost crystals and shimmering icicles. Each branch glistened with an ethereal allure, a stark juxtaposition against the lingering air of dread that clung to the forest. Emberwood had been transformed into an enchanting and treacherous realm where beauty and danger danced hand in hand, interwoven in an intricate tapestry of nature's duality.

With precision and purpose, Glaciera directed her commanding magic toward the waterfalls that once cascaded with vitality. At her mere beckoning, the water ceased its downward journey, frozen in mid-fall. Once teeming with life's vibrancy, the liquid streams became transient ice sculptures, capturing the suspended motion's essence. The once-lively waters now stood as silent sentinels of the otherworldly spell that had befallen the forest.

Amidst the snow-dusted expanse, Vuarus and Phoenix observed the culmination of Glaciera's power with satisfaction. Emberwood's transformation was complete—a realm now dominated by frigid shadows and enigmatic allure. A sense of betrayal hung in the air, a forewarning of the peril masked beneath the beguiling facade. The evil alliance had successfully turned the forest into a manifestation of their dominion, a mirror reflecting the depths of their corrupted prowess.

Bound by their nefarious intent, Vuarus and Phoenix delved into the heart of Emberwood, their merged forces reaching deep within the earth's bosom. Their sorcery beckoned forth the very essence of darkness and malice, shaping stone and soil into an intricate labyrinth of twisting caves and winding tunnels. These underground passages defied natural norms forged by the Abyssal Dominion's will to craft an environment that resonated with shadows and fear.

The cavern walls bore the etchings of sinister sigils and intricate glyphs, glowing with an eerie luminescence that pulsed with malefic energy. Within the depths, shadows danced, casting unsettling silhouettes that possessed an uncanny autonomy. The air itself carried an undercurrent of foreboding, a chilling embrace that defied the laws of nature, leaving an indelible mark of their dominion upon every inch of the labyrinthine depths.

In the shadowed aftermath, a malevolent symphony played out between Vuarus and Phoenix, their gazes exchanging a sinister affirmation. Emberwood Forest, once a realm of serenity, had now metamorphosed into a canvas of nightmares. Every element, every essence of this once-enchanted expanse had been irrevocably tainted by the insidious touch of their dark sorcery. The forest stood as a testament to their dominion over both the tangible world and the ethereal forces of darkness that lay beyond.

As architects of malice, they savored their triumph, beholding the embodiment of their sinister desires. The once-vivid and enchanting tapestry of nature had now been contorted into a grotesque reflection of their Abyssal Dominion, an emblem of their mastery over both the light and the shadow.

Content with their malevolent masterpiece, Vuarus, and Phoenix withdrew from the corrupted forest, leaving a realm shrouded in dread, designed to unsettle the hearts of those who ventured into its depths.

Having wrought their initial transformation, Vuarus and Phoenix channeled their dark energies anew, summoning forth creatures from the nethermost reaches of the Abyss. A portal, wrought from shadows and sinew, yawned open, bridging the chasm between the worlds and allowing a horde of vile and twisted entities to surge into Emberwood Forest.

From the abyssal depths emerged a grotesque procession of creatures, each more nightmarish than the last. Ethereal and malevolent shadow wraiths slithered forth, their forms ever-shifting between existence and nonexistence, embodying the uncanny. Sinister serpents, their scales like obsidian mirrors, slithered through the underbrush, their malevolent gaze hinting at a malefic intelligence that brooked no mercy.

An eerie cacophony now shattered Emberwood's once-pervasive silence. The whispers of the shadow wraiths and the serpentine hisses coalesced into a haunting melody emanating from the heart of darkness itself. As the apparitions danced with an ethereal elegance, leaving trails of shadow in their wake, the serpents glided with the fluidity of malevolence incarnate, weaving through the ominous undergrowth with a silence that mirrored the abyssal depths from which they emerged.

As the grotesque inhabitants propagated throughout Emberwood Forest, the air grew oppressive, weighed down by an aura of malice. The atmosphere was tainted by the cloying scent of decay, intertwining with the sinister orchestration that had transformed the serene landscape into a realm of perpetual gloom and terror. The unholy alliance of the ominous trees, venomous foliage, and these vicious denizens forged an environment that struck terror deep into the hearts of any who dared draw near.

Amidst this desolation, Vuarus and Phoenix stood as architects of their nightmarish reality, watching with sardonic satisfaction as their malevolent creation flourished. Emberwood Forest, once a realm of vibrant life, now lay trapped in eternal night. Darkness had conquered, and the forces of the Abyss reigned supreme. This once beautiful land was forever marked by the Abyssal Dominion's indelible stain, an eternal testimony to the darkness within their souls.

Undeterred by their derisive laughter, Lyra turned her gaze from the transformed forest to meet the eyes of Vuarus and Phoenix. A glint of determination shone within her, unwavering despite the chilling atmosphere. "As you wish," she replied, her voice tinged with resolve. "I have delved into ancient tomes and consulted scholars from realms near and far. Though concrete proof eludes me, I've uncovered whispers of a realm concealed beyond the known seas."

Vuarus's eyebrow quirked, genuine intrigue flaring in his eyes. "Whispers? Pray, tell us more." A nod of affirmation from Lyra. "Indeed. Legends whisper of an enigmatic underwater kingdom, veiled even from the ken of merfolk. A realm submerged beneath the depths, brimming with untold wonders and ancient sorcery. Yet these tales are fragmented, woven into the tapestry of various cultures and histories."

Phoenix leaned forward, his skepticism momentarily eclipsed by curiosity. "And what do these fragments hint at concerning the location of this hidden domain?"

Lyra's contemplation led to a thoughtful expression. "It remains elusive, their threads intertwining in ambiguity. Some speak of uncharted waters beyond the known seas, while others hint at mystic portals as gateways to this hidden realm. But the Heart of Twilight is a common thread through these narratives."

Vuarus exchanged a silent glance with Phoenix before turning back to Lyra. "The Heart of Twilight, the artifact we seek, harnessing the dual forces of light and shadow."

Lyra affirmed with a nod. "Indeed. The tales reveal its ability to unveil gateways to realms concealed from the mortal gaze. If any path to the Mer kingdom exists, it lies through the Heart's power."

Phoenix's skepticism remained palpable. "And do you genuinely put faith in these legends?"

Lyra locked eyes with Phoenix. Her resolve is a steadfast flame. "I trust in the potency of knowledge, in the concealed truths that yearn to be unveiled. The Abyssal Dominion may hunger for ultimate dominion, but genuine strength emanates from our comprehension and mastery of the universe's enigmas."

Vuarus's laughter, though soft, resounded with amusement. "Truly a singular spirit, Lyra. Your enthusiasm for research is commendable, even if the prospects sometimes appear fruitless."

Lyra's lips curved into a wry smile, a mixture of determination and defiance. "Futile or not, it's the path I tread. And one day, the labyrinth of my research may unravel the key to the Mer kingdom or some other forgotten enigma capable of tilting the scales in our favor."

Phoenix's smirk held an air of self-assuredness. "For now, let us focus on the strength we already command."

A reverent hush settled among the trio, allowing Lyra to immerse herself in her insatiable thirst for knowledge. Her thoughts danced amid the pages of tomes and scrolls, ferreting out fragments of secrets that might shape their unfolding destiny.

Vuarus and Phoenix exchanged a knowing look, a subtle interplay of amusement and contemplation. The road they walked was fraught with peril and unpredictability, yet each fragment of information carved into their grasp molded the intricate tapestry of their ambitions. With every piece acquired, the dominion of darkness they aspired to wield drew ever closer, a shadowy canvas poised for their mark.

Phoenix's contemplative gaze shifted back to Lyra, their silent connection a harbinger of unfolding intrigue. "Speaking of secrets, what say you of our designs concerning Keisha? Will her fortitude crumble under duress?"

Lyra's hands paused above the ancient text. Her brow furrowed in thought. "I doubt it. Keisha is stubborn and fiercely devoted. She'll endure our cruelties with an unyielding spirit, a captive harboring steadfast silence."

Phoenix's lips curled into a sinister smile. "Excellent. Her captivity becomes a weapon we can employ. Once Ong or the Eladrin relinquish E'vahona's location under duress, we shall torment her with the illusion of liberation... only to deliver her unto the Abyss."

An intrigued eyebrow raised by Lyra, curiosity like a coiled serpent within her. "A vicious twist indeed. Yet do you believe she'll yield, even in the face of her life's tether snapping?"

Phoenix's laughter cascaded through the chamber like chilling notes of a haunting symphony. "No, I have no such illusions. That is our intention. We shall shatter her resolve, exhibit the futility of her rebellion, and unfurl the Dominion's unremitting might. I never intended for her to yield."

Vuarus's solemn nod mirrored Phoenix's sentiment. "A plot nestled in layers of strategy. Her capture is a tool for manifold advantages. Once E'vahona becomes naught but a name, our supremacy shall remain unchallenged," he intoned, his eyes gleaming with a calculated fervor. "Furthermore, with control of E'vahona, we gain the means to unravel Kadona's reign and extinguish her luminous presence from this world. Keisha's spirit will be broken, and Ong will watch her fall into the abyss." Vuarus whispered, "There, her spirit will be free for me to use for my benefit."

A flicker of satisfaction danced within Phoenix's eyes. "Precisely. Now, words have run their course. Let us return to our respective pursuits and, in doing so, weave the narrative that unfurls the Abyss's dominion."

With unspoken unity, Vuarus and Phoenix shifted their focus, embracing the task. The dialogue concerning Keisha and the shadows of their plotting melted into the periphery of their concentration. The dominion they forged was one woven from darkness, steeped in fear, and infused with the insatiable hunger for supremacy. As the tapestry of their evil ambitions continued to unfurl, the realms upon which their sinister designs cast a looming shadow remained ignorant of the impending storm that would irrevocably alter their destinies.

Chapter 29

Shadows Unveiled: Seeking the Dragons' Council

Deep within the heart of E'vahona, a sacred enclave nestled between the Emberwoods and the Emeraldwoods, the Eladrin Council had gathered. Each member of this illustrious assembly bore the weight of concern upon their visage, etched in lines of unwavering determination. The centerpiece of their congregation was a circular table, a masterpiece of Eladrin craftsmanship, adorned with intricate carvings that told the stories of generations past.

Representatives from diverse Eladrin clans, their colorful robes and regalia a testament to their unique lineage, encircled the table. Their gaze converged upon Ong and Keisha, who stood firmly at the forefront. Flanking them was their ever-vigilant companion, Pumpkin, a graceful feline whose emerald eyes remained fixed upon the momentous proceedings.

Within the chamber, an electric air of anticipation crackled like magic. It was a silent prelude to the pivotal discussions about to unfold. Lord Karrenen, a venerable figure of authority and wisdom, initiated the discourse. His voice resonated through the room like a clarion call to action, unyielding, yet tinged with an underlying apprehension that mirrored the concern on their faces.

"We find ourselves standing upon the precipice of an unprecedented challenge," Lord Karrenen declared, his words carrying the weight of centuries of knowledge. "The encroaching darkness casts its ominous shadow over our homes and the essence of our existence. In this dangerous juncture, we must seek counsel from those who have confronted adversities like ours."

As his words hung in the air, they were not just a statement but a solemn promise of resolution. Keisha exchanged a significant glance with Ong, their shared determination forming an unspoken pact that transcended the confines of language. The gravity of their responsibilities pressed upon them, forging a resolve that surpassed mere words. They understood the path ahead would be arduous and uncertain, yet their hearts remained unwavering in their commitment to safeguard their cherished world.

Ong's voice resonated throughout the chamber with unwavering clarity like a powerful invocation. "Our destined journey leads us to the Hidden Isles," he proclaimed, his words echoing with an unshakeable conviction and an urgency that ignited the room. "The dragons, ancient and venerable beings who have borne witness to the emergence of the Abyssal Dominion, possess an understanding of the imminent peril that confronts us. Their timeless wisdom holds the potential to illuminate our path in this hour of dire need."

The council members nodded in unison, their somber expressions attesting to the gravity of the situation. The prospect of seeking counsel from the ancient and majestic dragons bore significance beyond measure. The dragons, beings of awe-inspiring power and insight, held within them a repository of knowledge that transcended mortal comprehension. As the deliberations unfolded, Keisha found herself enveloped by the reassuring embrace of nature's essence, a quiet affirmation that their course of action was in harmony with the world they held dear.

"Our realm's intrinsic connection with the tapestry of nature empowers us to sense even the subtlest shifts in the world around us," Keisha articulated, her voice a harmonious blend of unwavering determination and empathetic insight. "However, the dragons' perspective promises to allow us to transcend the confines of our immediate boundaries."

A unanimous consensus echoed through the council chamber, a collective agreement that the path before them was resolute and irrevocable. With meticulous care, the intricate dance of preparations commenced, orchestrating the gathering of essential supplies and the invocation of potent magic. Guided by the currents of mystic energy, the assemblage found themselves transported to the sun-kissed shores of Hidden Isles. The realm of the dragons stretched forth, an ethereal landscape adorned with breathtaking vistas and populated by creatures that embodied both awe and majesty.

As their feet met the sandy shores, the heavens above witnessed the descent of the dragons, their colossal forms casting imposing shadows upon the land. Among the distinguished creatures was Kimras, the golden embodiment of wisdom and grandeur, whose regal demeanor was accompanied by a nod of recognition.

"Greetings, Eladrin," Kimras spoke, his voice a resonant rumble carrying the weight of eras gone by. "Your presence within our realm is acknowledged with gravity. Share the tale of the darkness that casts its shadow upon your world." The air seemed to vibrate with the profoundness of the moment, as the Eladrin prepared to unveil the dire threat that had brought them to the dragons' doorstep.

Ong and Keisha exchanged a resolute glance, a silent affirmation of their commitment to the task. As the narrative unfurled, Keisha's voice took on a storyteller's cadence, recounting the chronicle that had transpired since their return from the Merfolk kingdom. With vivid detail, she painted the portrait of the Abyssal Dominion's rise, the tragic demise of Emeraldwood Forest, and the imminent peril that had compelled them to seek the counsel of the revered dragons.

"Our world's equilibrium hangs in precarious balance," Ong supplemented his voice, echoing Keisha's sentiments. "We have embarked on this quest, believing that the wisdom of the dragons can serve as a beacon guiding us through the tempestuous darkness that seeks to undermine the very foundations of existence."

Kimras listened with a measured solemnity, his gaze unwavering and penetrating. As the narrative reached its culmination, a profound silence descended upon the assembly, pregnant with the weight of contemplation. In a language that transcended spoken words, the dragons communicated amongst themselves, their thoughts echoing like distant thunder, inaccessible to mortal ears.

Following this enigmatic discourse, Kimras turned his gaze back to the Eladrin. "The Abyssal Dominion is a peril of grave magnitude," he began, his words reverberating with a resonance that seemed to resonate with the echoes of time. "The tendrils of its malevolence have been sensed within the very currents of magic itself, a dire omen that we, too, recognize and acknowledge. Our commitment to thwart its ambitions is unwavering. Your quest finds solidarity within our hearts, and together, we shall endeavor to illuminate the shadows that threaten your world's essence."

"The pursuit that led you to our realm is a profound testament to the depth of your commitment," Kimras continued, his voice resounding like the echo of an ancient truth. "We shall summon the Dragon's Council—a grand assembly that transcends the boundaries of realms. Within this assembly, we shall weave the fabric of a committed plan to stand against the encroaching darkness that seeks to shroud us all."

Keisha and Ong exchanged an unspoken understanding, the dragons' unwavering resolve intertwining seamlessly with their own. Empowered by the alliance forged, they were now armed with the guidance they had sought. Their spirits were encouraged to face the formidable adversities on the horizon.

With rapt attention, the council of majestic dragons listened as Keisha and Ong unraveled the tapestry of dire circumstances threading through their realms. Kimras, the golden embodiment of wisdom, acknowledged their words with a subdued rumble, his luminescent eyes reflecting a profound comprehension of the gravitas they carried.

"The encroachment of the darkness upon Coraluna and Ardinia has not escaped our vigilant gaze," Keisha's voice reverberated, unwavering in its steadiness despite the gravity of her proclamation. "Both realms have erected ethereal bulwarks to hold back the advancing tide. Yet, the temporal nature of these defenses casts a shadow over our resistance."

A quiet ripple of thoughts passed through the dragons, a symphony of unspoken understanding and interconnected wisdom transcending verbal discourse. Kimras directed his gaze back to Keisha, words rippling like ripples in a vast pond. "We share your insight into the struggle set upon your realms. The determination to defend one's realm is a noble endeavor, and the alliances fostered shall serve as the bedrock upon which we shall forge a united shield against the Abyssal Dominion."

As one, the dragons bore witness to the symphony of determination that emanated from the gathered assembly. Their collective consciousness illuminated the shared purpose that bound them together, a realization that unity held power to eclipse even the most formidable of shadows.

"In the tapestry of unity woven since our first encounter," Kimras pronounced with a sense of gravity, "we shall find the threads that can fortify our resolve. With these threads, we shall intertwine the strengths of dragons, Eladrin, merfolk, and nymphs, creating a luminous shield to stand against the encroaching darkness."

Ong's posture radiated unyielding conviction as he stepped forward, his voice carrying the resonance of a vow. "As we traverse the path before us, we understand that the journey shall be treacherous. But with hearts united and resolve unwavering, we shall navigate these trials to safeguard our realms and the world within our hearts."

The weight of the dragons' gaze encompassed the entirety of the Eladrin Council and the steadfast couple before them. In this reverent moment, a symphony of resolute souls stood united, their collective strength woven into a tapestry that would be remembered through the annals of time.

"We shall summon the Dragon's Council," Kimras declared, his voice resonating with the weight of ancient authority. "Across the realms, our kin shall convene to weave a tapestry of strategy that intertwines our collective strengths and boundless wisdom. But, understand this, noble Eladrin: the path ahead is shrouded in peril, and the ledger of sacrifice may be called upon." The gravity of the dragons' commitment hung in the air, a reminder that their alliance came at a price, but one they were willing to pay to defend their cherished world.

Keisha and Ong exchanged a knowing glance, their resolute eyes reflecting the solemn truth in Kimras' words. In the impending confrontation with the Abyssal Dominion, the currency of challenge would demand payment, yet their resolve remained unswayed.

"We stand prepared to confront the trials that await us," Keisha asserted, her voice an unwavering echo of her steadfast conviction. "As a united front, we shall forge a barrier against the encroaching darkness."

As the sun dipped below the horizon, casting its final hues upon the Hidden Isles, dragons and Eladrin bore witness to an unspoken covenant—an oath to defend their sanctuaries and comrades from the looming shadows. The council of dragons had convened the symphony of their intentions, weaving intricate strategy patterns. Amidst the enigma of what lay ahead, a beacon of optimism radiated, fueled by the unity of varied forces coalescing under a shared banner.

Keisha's gaze held hope and apprehension as her inquiry resonated through the council of dragons. "Once the insidious advance of the Abyssal Dominion is halted and the sanctuary of our realms restored, will there be a way to mend the wounds? Can we resurrect the splendor of places like the Emeraldwood and the Purplefire Woods?"

Kimras regarded Keisha with a measured gaze, comprehending the depth of her query. "The scars inflicted upon these lands are profound, Keisha. The shame of darkness runs deep, and rekindling their vitality is a task of intricate complexity. Yet, there exists a glimmer of hope."

He allowed his words to linger, each syllable resonating in the hearts of the assembly. "The essence of Eladrin magic, particularly that borne of nature's embrace, wields an unparalleled potency. Restoration becomes a reality when woven in concert with the timeless magic of the Nymphs. However, this endeavor hinges upon eradicating the Abyssal Dominion's hostility."

Keisha absorbed Kimras' pronouncement with a nod, the weight of his insight finding its place within her thoughts. "So, the pivotal step is to sever the darkness that encroaches upon our realms."

"Indeed," Kimras affirmed, his gaze unwavering as he met Keisha's eyes. "The union of might and purpose that we have woven stands as our beacon against the abyss. Together, we shall kindle the fires of reclamation, purging the corruption that plagues the land and restoring its vitality to its rightful state." The dragons and Eladrin had set their course, with hope and determination lighting the path ahead, even in the face of daunting challenges.

A renewed current of purpose surged through Keisha as her gaze swept over the assembly of Eladrin and the majestic dragons. The path ahead was formidable, yet their unity and unwavering resolve held the promise of quelling the insidious advance of the Abyssal Dominion and mending the wounds it had inflicted upon their world.

Stepping forward, Ong's voice resonated with steadfast determination. "With our focus set on halting the Abyssal Dominion's onslaught, we shall march forward, understanding that the reclamation of our lands awaits us upon victory."

Kimras, the venerable gold dragon, nodded in unison with Ong's sentiment. "The Dragon's Council shall stand as your unwavering allies, committed to the same purpose that unites us."

With their commitment solidified, the assembly of dragons and Eladrin cast their collective gaze towards the horizon, a shared purpose lighting their way through the enigmatic labyrinth of the days to come. The path was strewn with obstacles, yet it shimmered with the promise of renewal, a beacon of hope against the shrouding darkness.

Kimras shifted his attention, focusing on Ong and Keisha, a reflective quality in his wise eyes. "Consider this, Ong and Keisha, for it could offer insights into the tactics of the Abyssal Dominion. It involves a journey to the remnants of Emeraldwood to witness firsthand the aftermath of their evil influence."

Ong's agreement manifested as a nod, his eyes finding a steadying connection with Keisha's. "Indeed. Unraveling the Dominion's methods demands an understanding forged in the crucible of confronting their devastation head-on."

Though Keisha's posture held a hint of tension, the storm of her emotions brewed within her eyes. "I comprehend the necessity, yet the prospect of witnessing such ruination upon a once beautiful realm is daunting."

Kimras acknowledged her hesitance with a solemn inclination of his draconic head. "You bear a heavy burden, Keisha. The scars etched by the Dominion upon Emeraldwood testify to their dark power. Nonetheless, the importance of gathering firsthand knowledge is paramount."

His gaze turned to Ong. "Ong, stand as her steadfast support in this endeavor. The emotional toll of confronting such devastation is profound. And do not overlook the potential remnants left by the Dominion, a trove of clues that may yet be revealed."

Ong's gaze held an unwavering tenderness as it met Keisha's, an unspoken vow of solidarity. "Together, we shall confront the shadows that haunt Emeraldwood, for no burden is carried alone, Keisha." Their bond and resolve remained unbroken as they prepared to face the trials.

Steeling herself, Keisha drew a deep breath, her determination kindling into a fierce flame. "You're right, Ong. We can't let their actions go unchecked. Our path leads to Emeraldwood, where we'll gather every fragment of information available."

Kimras' approval resonated with a dignified nod. "Excellent. Bear in mind that the unwavering strength of both Eladrin and dragons stands beside you. The road ahead may be treacherous, but we shall emerge victorious through our unified purpose."

Locked in shared resolve, Ong and Keisha embarked on their journey, guided by purpose and curiosity. The quest to uncover the truth held within Emeraldwood was a tapestry woven with challenges and revelations, each thread an essential part of their realm's salvation. As they ventured forth, they carried with them the collective yearning of their people and an unyielding determination to stand firm against the advancing darkness.

However, a cloud of melancholy contemplation cast a shadow over Kimras as he spoke again. "Yet, the crux of our endeavor lies deeper still. Vuarus, formerly known as Azeron, serves as the Abyssal Dominion's conduit—a rope through which their nefarious energies flow."

Keisha's brow furrowed in deep thought. "Severing that connection is paramount, but it sounds daunting. How can we achieve such a feat?"

Kimras' gaze bore the gravity of ages. "Extricating Vuarus is no trifling matter. His newfound might is formidable, and his mastery over the Abyss's gifts makes him a formidable adversary. Then there is Phoenix, who derives his strength from the Abyss."

Ong's jaw clenched in silent acknowledgment, his gaze mirroring Keisha's. "We've witnessed the extent of their power firsthand. Overcoming them won't come without great challenges."

The dragon's response was solemn and resolute. "Indeed, it will not. Yet, for the liberation of our realm, it is a trial we must surmount."

Keisha's eyes narrowed, a spark of ingenuity lighting her gaze. "Phoenix's power—can't we target that directly?"

Kimras' reply echoed with patient wisdom. "Phoenix's power is entwined with Vuarus, an extension of the conduit itself. While Vuarus remains tethered to the Abyss, Phoenix's prowess shall persist. To sever one link is to sever both." The challenges ahead were immense, but the determination of the Eladrin and the dragons remained unbreakable as they confronted the dark forces threatening their world.

Lord Karrenen leaned in with measured determination in the heart of their council chamber, his voice carrying the weight of unwavering purpose. "We are left with no alternative. Our path lies in unbinding Vuarus from his connection to the Abyss, thereby fracturing the Dominion's grip upon our world."

In solemn agreement, Kimras, a figure of ancient wisdom, nodded his colossal head. "You grasp the essence of our endeavor. However, let me clarify: Disentangling Vuarus from the Abyss is no feat accomplished through simple combat. His bond runs deep, perhaps demanding sacrifices and strategic finesse beyond our current understanding."

Keisha's gaze edged with steely determination, met the look of her allies. "We cannot flinch in the face of adversity. Our realm cannot forever languish under the oppressive veil of the Abyssal Dominion."

Kimras' commanding presence filled the chamber as he spoke, his words resonating with an authority drawn from centuries of existence. "Let the truth be acknowledged among us. Our objective is steadfast. We shall untether Vuarus from the Abyss, freeing our world from its grasp. The path is laden with thorns, and sacrifices may become our currency, yet we harbor a glimmer of hope within the unity of purpose and the might of our resolve."

Within the chamber's confines, the Eladrin and Ong shared determined glances, understanding the gravity of their undertaking. As they faced the challenges ahead, they bore the weight of a destiny intertwined with the evil forces threatening their world. Their commitment remained unshaken, and they stood united in their resolve to confront the Abyssal Dominion and secure the future of Vacari.

Amid their council's deliberations, Silvara, a silver dragon whose regal presence had thus far remained silent, finally lent her voice to the discourse. Her words flowed with a lyrical cadence, carrying the weight of ancient wisdom. "Were Talleoss among us, his potent might could have sufficed to sever the connection between Vuarus and the Abyss. His bonds with the elemental forces are profound, and his unique energy might counteract the shadows woven by Vuarus' malice."

Keisha's gaze took on a contemplative hue. "Yet, Talleoss' whereabouts elude us, leaving us without a certain solution."

In Silvara's eyes, a glimmer of sorrow danced momentarily. "True, he vanished under enigmatic circumstances, veiling his current destination."

Ong's countenance grew resolute. "We cannot anchor our hopes solely on a shrouded prospect. We must seek another avenue."

Kimras' gaze, a blend of respect and comprehension, settled upon them. "Indeed. We must exhaust all paths within our reach. The convergence of Eladrin's and dragon's strengths shall serve as our beacon throughout this journey."

Silvara's nod affirmed their stance. "Though Talleoss' absence casts a shadow, we possess within our realm entities of formidable power, capable of stepping forth to meet this challenge."

With Keisha's determination palpable, her resolve rippled outward. "Then let our strategy center on severing the ties binding Vuarus to the Abyss, dismantling the grip of the Abyssal Dominion upon our world."

In unison, the dragons nodded, a solemn accord solidifying their dedication. The proceedings pressed on, blueprints materializing, tactics coalescing. Amid the discussions, an intangible cohesion and determination filled the atmosphere of Hidden Isles. The union between the Eladrin and the dragons stood unshaken, a beacon of hope guiding them as they braced themselves to face the encroaching darkness. The path ahead remained uncertain, but their unity and resolve remained unwavering.

A moment of gratitude and determination filled Keisha as she rose to express her profound appreciation to the dragons for their unwavering aid. However, before she could utter her words of thanks, a sudden disquiet swept over her, like an icy wind cutting through her. Her heart raced, and her senses sharpened in vigilant alertness. Her fingers clenched the table's edge, and a gasp caught in her throat.

Her legs gave way in that fleeting moment of trepidation, and she crumpled. Swiftly, Ong was by her side, his concern evident as he enveloped her in his arms. The attention of the council members and the dragons shifted from Keisha to the young dragon who had ventured uninvited into their midst.

The young dragon's words tumbled forth, an urgent torrent of apology, as he revealed the shocking transformation of Emberwood. Once a place of ethereal beauty and tranquility, the forest had been twisted into a realm of sinister phantasms and foreboding shadows.

Within the charged sanctum of the room, Kimras retained his regal bearing, a stalwart presence in the face of unforeseen turmoil. As Ong's support steadied Keisha, her breathing gradually returned to its normal rhythm, and a profound silence settled over the chamber, underscoring the gravity of the situation.

In due time, Kimras' voice cut through the hush, a sonorous tapestry woven with concern and unwavering determination. "The unfolding events before us are undeniably disconcerting. If the Abyssal Dominion possesses the power to twist an entire woodland into such a grotesque visage, our concerns must expand beyond our initial estimations. We are compelled to unearth a method to counterbalance their evil influence, to thwart the relentless corruption of our realm." The new revelation added an even more urgent dimension to their mission, and the council began considering how to confront this escalating threat.

Keisha's determination rekindles a fire forged in the crucible of challenge. "We dare not suffer their darkness to propagate unbridled," her voice resounds with unwavering resolve, infusing each word with a tempered steeliness. "The groves, the seas, all that constitutes our cherished sanctuary, dangles precariously upon the precipice."

The tangible union enveloping the assembly is palpable. The resolution shared between the Eladrin Council, Ong, and the dragons is as undeniable as blood coursing. Kimras appraises the congregation, the moment's gravity etched into his gaze.

"It stands as unequivocal that action beckons. Our sagacity and resources must intertwine, birthing stratagems to countermand the Abyssal Dominion's influence and unearth the chinks in their sinister armor. The fate of our domains and staunch allies' dominions sway precipitously upon this dangerous course of action."

As the council gathering draws to a close, and the dragons and their guests disperse to contemplate the monumental challenge before them, the destiny of their lands and the alliances they've forged hangs in the balance. With unwavering determination, they prepare to face the looming storm that threatens to plunge their world into unrelenting darkness.

In the aftermath of the deliberations, amidst the gradual dispersal of companions, Kimras, the embodiment of regality, subtly signals Ong to linger. Ong strides forth, making his way to the presence of the golden dragon, his demeanor a mix of curiosity and nuanced concern.

In the surreal stillness of the evening, Kimras' voice rises, resonating like an ancient elven ballad. It carries a weight that feels as old as the stars themselves. "Ong," he begins, each word bearing the weight of centuries, "your deep dedication to our sacred charge has not gone unnoticed. And I see how the very essence of your soul is entwined with Keisha's."

With a wisdom that mirrors the ages in his eyes, Ong acknowledges Kimras, his every gesture reflecting the grace of an elder receiving a profound revelation.

"Keisha is not merely a resident of our realm; she resonates with its heartbeat, attuned to its subtlest vibrations—a rare and revered gift," Kimras continues, his gaze distant as if traversing the annals of time. "The evil metamorphosis overtaking Emberwood Forest, with its creeping darkness, will seek to eclipse her radiant spirit. Therefore, I implore you to be her shield, her sanctuary, as she grapples with these shadowed times."

Ong's response is palpable, an unwavering foundation of resolve shaped by time-less dedication. "Your words are heard, wise dragon. I pledge to be her guiding light through ever-twisting mazes and shadowed paths, to guide and guard her against the encroaching darkness."

Their exchange culminates in a profound bow, echoing the sacred oath between two destined allies. "Such a bond," Kimras intones with a voice shimmering with awe, "shall rise as an unyielding pillar against the gathering storm. While the challenges may cast vast and foreboding shadows, your allies will rekindle hope, illuminating even the most suffocating voids." The alliance between Ong and Keisha is fortified, a beacon of hope amid the impending darkness.

As they part ways, an unspoken promise lingers, a bond forged in destiny's cru-cible. The Eladrin Council embarks on the mystical path to E'vahona, their every step heavy with the anticipation of an impending clash of fates. Meanwhile, Ong, Keisha, Pumpkin, and the young dragon messenger of dire warnings set their sights on the heart of what was once the lush Emeraldwood.

The journey ahead is a tapestry woven from threads of enigma and destiny, fraught with challenges and revelations. But they advance, their spirits unyield-ing, guided by the enduring glow of their shared purpose, ready to confront the encroaching darkness that threatens to engulf everything they hold dear.

Their separate paths converge on a singular destiny, and the symphony of their unity resonates through the realms of Vacari. The tale of their courage and deter-mination will be etched into the annals of history, a beacon of hope amidst the shadows that seek to obscure their world. After the departure of Ong, Keisha, and the others on their respective missions, Lord Karrenen, the wise leader of the Eladrin Council, sought a private moment with Kimras.

Concern etched lines into Karrenen's aged features as he spoke to the majestic golden dragon. "Kimras," Lord Karrenen began with a voice heavy with appre-hension, "I cannot help but worry about the Abyssal Dominion's motives. Their ability to corrupt entire forests, as they did with Emberwood, is troubling. It seems as though they possess knowledge of the threat we pose to them and the vulnerabilities we hold, especially Keisha's unique connection to our world."

Kimras regarded Lord Karrenen with a profound wisdom that belied his age. "Your concerns are not unwarranted, Lord Karrenen. The Dominion's actions are calculated and malevolent. They are not to be underestimated. Keisha's gift, her deep connection to our realm, has made her a target, and they seem to understand the significance of disrupting that connection."

Lord Karrenen nodded, his expression grave. "We must remain vigilant and prepare for further assaults on our realm and people. The unity of Eladrin and dragons is our greatest strength, but it is also what the Dominion fears. We must use that unity to protect our world and those who call it home."

Kimras' golden eyes shimmered with determination. "Agreed, Lord Karrenen. Together, we shall stand as a bastion against the encroaching darkness, defending our lands, people, and Keisha's radiant spirit. The Dominion may scheme and plot, but they will find no easy victory while we breathe."

With their shared resolve reaffirmed, Lord Karrenen and Kimras parted ways, ready to face the challenges ahead and protect the realms of Vacari from the relentless ambitions of the Abyssal Dominion

Chapter 30

Shadows Unveiled: Investigating the Destruction of Emeraldwood Forest

Ong and Keisha, accompanied by their steadfast companion Pumpkin, embarked on a perilous journey through the winding terrain that led them deeper into the enigmatic depths of the Emeraldwood Forest. With its towering sentinels cloaked in an eerie shroud, the forest cast a formidable, foreboding silhouette that loomed ominously over their path. Its vast expanse bore the weight of enigmatic events, secrets whispered through the rustling leaves and entangled branches that seemed to reach out like gnarled fingers.

As they ventured deeper into the heart of the forest, an unsettling unease crept over Ong like a shadowy specter, causing him to clasp Keisha's hand with a grip forged by protective instincts. Keisha, her eyes a wellspring of reassurance, bestowed upon him a tender smile that carried the warmth of their shared history. "You need not bear the weight of worry alone, Ong. Together, we have faced trials aplenty."

Ong's smile in response held the essence of his concern, a silent testament to the palpable unease that hung in the air like a heavy mist. "I know, Keisha, but this darkness has seized the forest. It chills me to the core."

With an affectionate lean, Keisha nestled her head upon Ong's shoulder, finding solace in his steadfast presence. "We shall confront whatever challenges lie in wait, just as we always have. Remember, we have Pumpkin with us."

Pumpkin, their loyal companion, trotted joyously at their side, her ebony fur a stark contrast to the shadowy depths around them, her tail an exuberant metronome of agreement as if assuring them that together, they would face whatever mysteries and dangers awaited in the heart of the Emeraldwood Forest.

Upon the forest's edge precipice, Ong drew a deep breath, his thoughts drifting like ephemeral echoes to the distant Crystal Vale. "Thoughts of Crystal Vale consume my mind. How does this turmoil affect it?"

With a comforting hand on his arm, Keisha offered solace in the face of his unspoken concerns. "Answers will come in due course. For now, our mission is to uncover the secrets of this forsaken place and find a way to quell its hostility."

They stood at the threshold of the forest, the gnarled and fractured trees looming overhead like grotesque sentinels. The atmosphere hung heavy with a disturbing silence, the feeble rays of sunlight struggling to breach the thick canopy. Ong's grip on Keisha's hand tightened, his resolve unwavering. "You speak the truth. Let us unravel the mysteries that dwell within."

And so, with unwavering determination, they readied themselves to penetrate the forest's heart, prepared to confront the enigma hidden within its shadowy depths.

As Ong and Keisha ventured deeper into the forest's core, the landscape descended into a nightmarish tableau. Once-proud arboreal giants now lay broken and charred, their twisted forms casting grotesque specters upon the forest floor. Some stood frozen in spectral ice, while others had withered to mere skeletons, their vitality drained. The earth beneath their feet bore witness to the relentless devastation strewn with debris and ash, a testament to the explosive forces ravaging this once-thriving realm.

Pumpkin, their loyal and vigilant companion, trod in the wake of Ong and Keisha, her feline senses acutely attuned to the shifting currents of the forest. A peculiar aura seemed to have trapped her, compelling her to keep closer to her human companions. The atmosphere hung heavy with an intangible malevolence. This spectral energy sent ripples of disquiet coursing through their very bones, as if the forest held its breath in anticipation of their presence.

Keisha's heart ached as she beheld the spectacle of nature's desolation. "To witness the natural world in such a woeful state rends my spirit. This forest, once a bastion of vibrant life..."

Ong, his visage etched with solemnity, concurred with a nod. "Indeed, Keisha. It's as if a nefarious trespass befell a sentient entity, and its essence now lies in tatters."

Pumpkin emitted a soft, foreboding growl, her fur bristling like a sentinel of the wild, steadfastly guarding her companions. Her keen instincts sensed an unseen presence poised to reveal itself.

As they delved deeper into their quest for answers, they unearthed eerie remnants: scorch marks like dark scars etched upon the trees, frostbite's icy grip, and other unnatural phenomena that had left indelible marks upon the forest's canvas. Keisha knelt beside a charred tree, her brow furrowed as she examined the scorched bark. "This devastation transcends the mere wrath of dragons. A malevolence lingers, a darkness that surpasses the elemental forces of fire and ice."

Ong joined her in contemplation, his gaze narrowing as he surveyed the surroundings. "You speak the truth, Keisha. It is as though the very spirit of the forest has been tainted."

Pumpkin, a steadfast sentinel, emitted a low growl, her eyes fixated on a distant corner of the forest, signaling that she had detected something of profound import.

Keisha arose, instincts honed to a fine edge. "Pumpkin senses an enigma. We should heed her guidance."

With Pumpkin as their guide, they embarked on an odyssey deeper into the forest's heart, relentlessly seeking to unearth the wellspring of the evil energies that had cast a shadow upon this once-thriving realm.

As Pumpkin led them further into the forest's heart, her ears perked, and her nose quivered, detecting a peculiar fragrance wafting through the air. She paused, her fur standing on end, and then proceeded with deliberate caution, her movements akin to a feline stalking its prey. Keisha and Ong trailed behind her, their senses alive with anticipation, until they beheld the enigmatic sight that had captured Pumpkin's unwavering attention.

Amidst the contorted arboreal sentinels and blighted flora, they came upon a congregation of beings that had once epitomized ethereal beauty. Yet, the evil taint of dragon fire and destruction had rendered them grotesque parodies of their former selves. Once the very embodiment of the forest's grace and elegance, these creatures now wore the shroud of abomination.

Keisha's heart trembled as her gaze fell upon these unfortunate beings. Once luminous and enchanting, they had become unrecognizable, their forms twisted, and their countenances marred by the pervasive darkness that had engulfed the forest. Delicate wings that once soared in pristine splendor now hung in tatters, and their vibrant hues had dulled into a somber pallor. Tears welled in Keisha's eyes, a fusion of grief and righteous anger surging within her. "This is an affront to nature... they were once an integral part of this forest's enchantment, and now they stand defiled."

Ong's visage hardened, his fists clenching in simmering rage. The weight of the devastation bore upon his shoulders, and his anger radiated like a palpable storm. "The dragons' actions have left an indelible scar upon this land. These creatures are unfortunate victims of their hostility."

Pumpkin issued a low growl, her fur bristling as she observed the creatures warily. It was as if even she, in her feline wisdom, could sense the unnaturalness that had befallen them. Keisha's compassion for these tormented beings swelled, and her determination to thwart the Abyssal Dominion intensified. "We must bring an end to this darkness. We cannot allow them to continue trashing the beauty of our world."

Ong nodded resolutely. "You speak true. Our duty extends beyond our realm, encompassing all its residents. We must unearth a means to rectify this calamity and restore the equilibrium that has been sundered."

Pumpkin let forth a resounding roar, her gaze fixed upon Keisha and Ong as if imploring them to take decisive action. With a shared purpose that burned like an unquenchable flame, they pressed deeper into the forest, their determination undiminished despite the harrowing sights surrounding them. A singular goal now propelled them forward: to unveil the truth behind the Abyssal Dominion's evil designs and extinguish the encroaching darkness that threatened to devour their world.

Ong and Keisha forged ahead with trepidation, their footsteps carving a cautious path through the desolation that cloaked the once-lustrous forest. With each stride, the unrelenting scope of devastation unfolded before them. Skeletal trees stood as mournful sentinels, their charred limbs reaching out like supplicating specters. Frozen foliage glistened with an eerie, icy allure, a cruel juxtaposition against the erstwhile vibrancy that once thrived in this realm.

Their breaths caught in their throats as they arrived at a modest river or babbling stream that wended through the forest's forsaken heart. Once crystalline and pure, the water lay veiled in shadowy murkiness, vastly different from the pristine flow they had remembered. Keisha knelt by the water's edge, her fingers tracing its surface, only to be met with a frigid chill that sent a shiver through her soul.

Ong crouched beside her, his countenance etched with disquiet. "This water... It's unnatural.

It's as though the darkness has infected even the very elements themselves."

Keisha nodded solemnly, her heart weighed down by the gravity of the revelation. "This is how it began in Coraluna. The encroachment of darkness must have originated here, poisoning the waters that eventually tainted the sea."

Pumpkin, ever alert, approached the tainted liquid, her inquisitive nose twitching as she sampled the corrupted essence. Abruptly, she emitted a low growl, her instincts prickling with an unsettling unease. She retreated from the water's edge, picturing Ong and Keisha with eyes that harbored a mixture of caution and concern.

Keisha's brow furrowed as she watched Pumpkin's reaction. "What troubles you, girl? What have you sensed?"

Ong, now standing, placed his hand on the hilt of his sword. "Whatever it may be, it's wiser not to tarry here. There's a palpable hostility as if the very essence of this place has been irrevocably tainted."

Keisha concurred, her gaze still trained on their vigilant companion. "Let's continue our journey. We must unearth the intricate connections between this devastation and the Abyssal Dominion's evil designs."

Guided by Pumpkin's unwavering resolve, they pressed onward, navigating through the desolation that clung to the land like a lingering curse. The air bore witness to the weight of sorrow and despair, starkly contrasting the vibrant and teeming forest they had once known. As they plunged deeper into the heart of desolation, the sinister forces at play unfurled their tendrils with ominous clarity.

Ong, Keisha, and Pumpkin journeyed more profoundly into the ravaged forest, their senses assailed by the otherworldly sights and sounds that enveloped them. The air seemed to echo with the murmurings of the dark power that had laid waste to the land.

In a somber clearing, they stumbled upon the remnants of a once-majestic tree, now reduced to a scorched and pitiful stump. Surrounding it lay grotesque remains of what had once been vibrant flora, their elegance twisted into unnatural deformities. Keisha's heart plummeted as the full extent of the tragedy that had befallen this thriving ecosystem unfurled before her.

Pumpkin's growls grew more frequent, her keen senses attuned to the disturbances in their midst. It was as if the shadows had gained malevolent sentience, shifting and murmuring with ominous intent. Ong maintained a vigilant grip on his weapon, his eyes ceaselessly scanning the surroundings for any warnings of impending danger.

Keisha quivered, a mélange of dread and anger coursing like wildfire through her veins. "The Abyssal Dominion... they've defiled this sanctuary, rendering it a grotesque caricature of its former splendor."

Ong's voice, imbued with a coiled fury, resounded like the distant rumble of thunder. "We cannot permit their sinister shroud to prevail. We must unearth their designs and explore any means of reclamation."

Pumpkin, the ever-watchful sentinel, suddenly halted in her tracks, her ears erect like vigilant sentinels, focused on an enigmatic presence lurking in the distance. With a sharp growl, she drew the undivided attention of both Ong and Keisha. Tracking her gaze, they discerned a shadowy figure weaving amidst the contorted arboreal sentinels.

Keisha's grip tightened around her staff. "Who goes there?"

From the obscurity emerged the form of a creature, once a paragon of elegance and grace in the shape of a deer, now perverted into a grotesque nightmare. Its eyes gleamed with an unnatural crimson luminescence, and its movements manifested as dissonant and erratic.

Ong advanced cautiously, his blade unsheathed, though the anguish etched upon his features was palpable. "What manner of abhorrence has befallen you?"

The corrupted creature unleashed a chilling, lamenting sound that sent icy tendrils of disquiet slithering down Keisha's spine. Pumpkin, undaunted, stood vigilant, her fur bristling as she regarded the creature with wary vigilance.

Keisha's voice quivered, a confluence of sorrow and unwavering resolve imbuing her words. "This is the adversary we confront, Ong. We cannot allow their reign of chaos to persist."

Ong nodded gravely, his unwavering gaze fixed upon the corrupted creature. "You speak true, Keisha. This is a stark reminder of why our quest to halt the Abyssal Dominion is paramount."

As the forest, twisted and tormented, whispered its sinister secrets and the corrupted apparition continued to haunt their path, the unwavering resolve of Ong and Keisha crystallized. They understood that unraveling the riddles of this desecrated realm was an irrevocable step in quelling the evil forces that aspired to plunge their world into perpetual darkness.

Keisha's heart throbbed with an ache for the once-majestic forest, now trapped in the coils of malevolence. A surge of unwavering resolve welled within her as she extended her hands, invoking the latent power of her elemental magic. Her eyelids fluttered closed, surrendering herself to the realm of mystic energies. She honed her focus, intertwining her essence with the magic that flowed through her like a coursing river.

As her magic unfurled, she perceived the heartbeat of the land, the delicate threads of life weaving together all living entities. Her consciousness plunged deeper into the forest, and with each passing heartbeat, she bore the burden of the corruption that gripped this once-verdant realm.

Her magic whispered secrets to her, unveiling the extent of the devastation. It was not merely the trees and flora that had borne the brunt; even the very earth itself had succumbed to the touch of evil energies. The corruption had permeated the same fabric of the land, akin to a festering wound poised to spread its venom.

Yet, amid the shadows of despair, her magic unearthed a disturbing truth. The corruption had tendrils extending beyond the forest, reaching an ominous horizon. With a sinking heart, Keisha discerned that the darkness had ensnared the nearby waters, encroaching upon the realm of Coraluna.

Her eyes fluttered open, locking onto Ong's concerned gaze. "The corruption... it spreads, Ong. It has breached the sanctity of Coraluna's waters."

Ong's countenance solidified, his grip on his sword assuming an unyielding determination. "We are compelled to thwart this malevolence. We shall not permit it to engulf more of our world."

Pumpkin emitted a low, echoing growl, a visceral echo of their shared resolution. Keisha lowered her hands with a weighty sigh, the gravity of their task settling upon her shoulders. They could not afford to falter, not when the very essence of their world hung in the balance.

Ong's voice rang with unwavering commitment. "Let us persist in our investigation. We must fathom the Abyssal Dominion's machinations and unearth the means to undo the havoc they have sown."

As they ventured further into the shadowed heart of the corrupted forest, the oppressive darkness inched ever closer, a constant reminder of the evil forces that conspired against them. Yet, Keisha and Ong pressed onward, their bond and shared purpose illuminating the path through the obscurity.

After hours of systematic exploration, Keisha and Ong emerged from the corrupted forest, their hearts burdened by what they had witnessed. In a clearing, they found solace, the silvery moonlight piercing through the tenebrous canopy above.

Keisha leaned against a weathered tree, her eyes cast towards the distant horizon, lost in contemplation. "It feels as though their destructive acts serve no purpose other than to display their malevolent might," she murmured, her voice tinged with a potent blend of anger and sorrow. Ong nodded gravely, his visage a mirror to her sentiments. "Yet, a glimmer of hope exists,"

he asserted firmly. "If we can thwart the Abyssal Dominion, perhaps we can uncover a means to mend the damage they have wrought. The dragons alluded to the potential for healing the land through the magic of our allies."

Sensing their somber spirits, Pumpkin pressed affectionately against Keisha's leg. Keisha rewarded her loving husband with a tender smile. "You're right. Surrendering is not an option. Our world is a treasure worth defending."

Ong drew closer, his hand finding Keisha's, their fingers intertwining like a symbol of their shared resolve and profound affection. "We shall discover a way, Keisha. We shall end the Abyssal Dominion's rule of darkness."

Keisha tightened her grip on his hand, drawing strength from her protective husband's unwavering resolve. "Thank you, Ong," she whispered. "Having you as my loving husband grants me the courage to confront whatever challenges lie ahead."

The moonlit clearing held them in its tranquil embrace, a brief respite from the trials ahead. The road they walked was fraught with danger, their mission daunting. Yet, as they stood hand in hand, Ong and Keisha found strength in their unity. They were bound by love, purpose, and a shared commitment to their realm. Together, they would face the encroaching darkness and uncover the truths beneath its shroud.

Renewed in their determination, Ong and Keisha left the corrupted forest behind and ventured toward Crystal Vale. This time, the journey proved shorter, yet as they approached the familiar lands of the Eladrin realm, their hearts weighed heavier than ever. They discerned the inescapable truth that the darkness had touched even these sacred grounds and harbored a sense of foreboding regarding what awaited them.

The signs of encroaching darkness were undeniable as they entered Crystal Vale. The vibrant landscape colors had dulled, the atmosphere bore an unnatural chill, and calm dialogues and anxious glances had supplanted the once-joyous laughter of the citizens.

Ong and Keisha traversed the realm, their steps slowing as they absorbed the grievous transformations. The river waters, once pristine, had turned murky and devoid of life, the majestic trees had surrendered their luster, and even the resilient flowers seemed to struggle in their efforts to bloom.

Keisha's heart ached in resonance with the land, her innate connection with nature enabling her to feel the anguish of the very earth itself. She knelt by the riverbank, submerging her fingers in the tainted waters. "The situation is graver than I had anticipated," she uttered softly. "The darkness has seeped even into the heart of Crystal Vale."

Ong stood steadfastly beside Keisha, his hand resting gently on her shoulder. "Fear not, Keisha," he vowed with unwavering resolve. "We shall find a way to quell the Abyssal Dominion and breathe life and beauty back into our beleaguered realm."

Ever watchful, Pumpkin's senses tingled, prompting a low growl to escape her. Ong and Keisha shared an instinctual glance, their senses heightened, attuned to the enigmatic disturbance that had ensnared Pumpkin's notice.

In the wake of Pumpkin's guidance, they arrived at a gathering within Crystal Vale, where King Manard stood amidst a cluster of concerned citizens. King Manard, bearing a grave countenance, addressed the assembly. Keisha and Ong approached, their gazes met by King Manard's eyes, which reflected both anxiety and unwavering resolve.

"Keisha, Ong, your timely return is a source of solace," he acknowledged, his voice heavy with the gravity of the situation. "Even our most hallowed sanctuaries have not been spared by the encroaching darkness. We toil to reinforce our mystical defenses, but our strength is finite."

Keisha nodded somberly, her heart burdened by the weight of the moment. "We exert every effort to thwart the Abyssal Dominion," she declared. "Our journey led us to Emeraldwood Forest, where we bore witness to the extent of their devastation."

Understanding flowed silently between them as King Manard's gaze lingered on Ong and Keisha. "Then we must brace ourselves for the trials that lie ahead," he proclaimed with conviction. "Our people are resolute, unified in their readiness to safeguard our realm."

In unison, Ong, Keisha, and King Manard comprehended that their world teetered on the brink of a conflict that would mold the destiny of all they cherished. The shadow of darkness had fallen upon their lands, but the unwavering light of their determination burned ever brighter. Amidst the creeping obscurity, they drew strength from their collective unity and clung to the unshakeable belief that they could surmount any adversity.

With shared determination, Ong and Keisha turned their attention to King Manard. "Our path leads us back to E'vahona," Keisha stated resolutely. "We are responsible for relaying our findings to Lord Karrenen and the Eladrin Council."

King Manard acknowledged their resolve with gratitude and hope in his eyes. "Your tireless efforts are deeply appreciated," he expressed. "May the resilience of the Eladrin and the indomitable spirit of Crystal Vale see us through these challenging times."

Ong and Keisha exchanged a silent nod with King Manard, their mutual understanding transcending words. They pivoted, retracing their steps away from Crystal Vale, bound for E'vahona. The path that lay ahead remained cloaked in uncertainty, yet they carried with them the knowledge that they did not walk alone in this arduous battle. They faced the weight of their mission side by side, upheld by the hope that their endeavors would forge a brighter future for all. However, as they ventured away from Crystal Vale, a faint, mystical transmission brushed against their thoughts—a message imbued with urgency. Keisha and Ong exchanged a knowing look before Lord Karrenen's voice of concern and anticipation resonated within their minds. "Ong, Keisha," Lord Karrenen implored, "we have received disquieting reports from Emberwood Forest. Before you return to E'vahona, we implore you to investigate the full extent of these changes. The

Abyssal Dominion's grip appears to be tightening, and we must ascertain the full scope of their evil influence."

With the newfound urgency of their mission, Ong and Keisha quickened their pace. The path ahead remained shrouded in enigma, yet each step was fueled by their unwavering resolve to unearth the truth and quell the evil forces that threatened their realms.

Chapter 31

Returning to Emberwood Forest

Deep within the heart of Emberwood Forest, an evil presence stirred, its essence a swirling vortex of shadows and maleficent intent. It coiled and writhed, forging a sinister entity that seemed to meld seamlessly with the very fabric of the ancient trees and the earth itself. This abominable creation bore the unmistakable mark of the Abyssal Dominion, a living sentinel crafted to guard their newly conquered territory.

Once a realm of lush beauty and tranquility, the forest had been irrevocably altered. The once proud and vibrant trees now stood as gnarled sentinels, their once-lush leaves replaced by a ghostly, sickly pallor. The earth beneath their feet felt cursed, as if the ground recoiled from the touch of malice that now permeated it.

Meanwhile, on the forest's fringe, Ong, Keisha, and their loyal companion, Pumpkin, ventured cautiously through the surrounding wilderness. The air hung heavy with an eerie hush, broken only by the distant whispers of the wind. The once-vibrant tapestry of colors adorned the forest had surrendered to a somber, ominous palette. Shades of deep purple and ashen gray dominated, contrasting the vibrant greens and blues of days long past.

Even from a distance, the scars of devastation were palpable, etched into the land by the cruel hands of dragon fire and ice. The trees bore the marks of searing flames and frostbite, their branches twisted in agony. The very earth witnessed the horrors that had unfolded, with jagged cracks and fissures marring its once-smooth surface.

Unbeknownst to the intrepid trio, the evil entity observed their every move with an unblinking, predatory gaze. Its connection to the Abyssal Dominion strengthened with each passing heartbeat, and it eagerly awaited the moment when it could fulfill its dark purpose.

As they ventured deeper into the forest's heart, their path meandered towards the once-pure stream that flowed with crystalline waters. Now, it was a tainted, inky ribbon, radiating an aura of disquiet that sent shivers racing down their spines. The water's surface seemed to writhe with hostility, as if unseen forces conspired to corrupt its essence. Pumpkin's instincts were acutely attuned to the ominous atmosphere, and she hesitated at the water's edge, emitting a low, guttural growl that mirrored her profound unease.

Little did they fathom that their presence had not eluded the notice of the evil entity, whose presence lingered like a malignant shadow, poised to sound the alarm at the slightest provocation. It watched, patient and unrelenting, as the trio pressed on, unaware of the dangerous web of darkness that had trapped them within Emberwood's evil grasp.

Deep within the accursed heart of the Abyssal Dominion's fortress, an eerie whisper reverberated through the dim corridors, as if the walls bore witness to the vicious schemes that unfolded within. As the sinister entity observed the unwitting intruders, it transmitted its findings to its malevolent creators, Vuarus and Phoenix.

Vuarus and Phoenix, two dark overlords of the Abyssal Dominion, exchanged a knowing, malevolent glance as the unsettling information reached their ears. Vuarus's voice dripped with venomous amusement as he contemplated their next move. "It appears we have unwelcome guests trespassing in our newly conquered domain," he mused. "Shall we grant them a glimpse of the darkness they so audaciously seek to challenge?"

Phoenix's grin widened, a sinister glint dancing in his eyes. "Indeed, my malevolent comrade.

Let us unveil the true, unforgiving might of the Abyssal Dominion."

With dark incantations and gestures, they began to weave their sinister enchantments, drawing forth the shadowy depths of Emberwood Forest with a shared malevolent intent. Their dark influence spread like creeping tendrils, entwined with the essence of the evil entity lurking in the shadows.

Empowered by the Abyssal Dominion's dark magic, the entity obediently executed their twisted wishes. It contorted and warped the forest's surroundings, crafting an unsettling illusion meant to confound the senses of Ong, Keisha, and Pumpkin. In this haunting mirage, the forest's sounds became distorted echoes, and distances stretched and folded in on themselves, leading them astray into the heart of deception.

As the trio ventured deeper into the forest's enigmatic heart, they encountered phantom dangers, illusions designed to test their mettle and resolve. Trees whispered dark secrets, their branches twisting with malevolence. The ground beneath their feet shifted like quicksand, and eerie shadows danced at the edges of their vision. Every step they took became a more profound journey into the abyss, a treacherous game orchestrated by the evil minds of the Abyssal Dominion. The fabric of reality seemed to conspire against them, entangling them further within the web of darkness their malevolent adversaries had weaved.

Unbeknownst to Ong, Keisha, and Pumpkin, they were on the cusp of experiencing the full depths of the Dominion's cruelty as their passage through the forest metamorphosed into a nightmarish ordeal aimed at breaking their spirits and extinguishing their hope.

The Abyssal Dominion, in their sadistic anticipation, reveled in the impending confusion and desperation of their unsuspecting prey, eager to savor every moment of their torment. The evil overlords watched from their dark fortress, their cruel satisfaction growing with each passing moment as the trio's plight deepened.

In Emberwood Forest, Ong, Keisha, and Pumpkin pressed onward, their footsteps crunching through the pristine snow that blanketed the forest floor. The atmosphere bore a frigid, unnatural cold that seemed to seep into their very bones. With her elven sensitivity to the balance of nature, Keisha felt the harshness of the cold more acutely than most.

As they continued their journey, the bitter chill intensified, the air becoming a piercing, icy embrace that threatened to freeze their souls. Keisha shivered involuntarily, her breath materializing in visible puffs of frost. She instinctively wrapped her arms around herself in a futile attempt to ward off the biting cold. Ong, his concern etched across his features, glanced in her direction, his body fighting the numbing cold.

"Pumpkin," Keisha whispered through chattering teeth, her voice strained by the cold, "we need warmth."

Sensing her distress, the loyal panther pressed closer to Keisha's side, her thick fur radiating a comforting heat that offered some respite. Yet even Pumpkin's presence couldn't entirely banish the relentless cold surrounding them, an icy reminder of the evil forces that held sway in the forest's heart. The elements seemed to conspire against them, as if the Abyssal Dominion's grasp extended not only into the shadows but also into the very essence of Emberwood itself.

As if in eerie response to Keisha's desperate plea, the evil presence lurking in the shadows seemed to hone in on her vulnerability. The biting cold intensified with a sinister twist of its dark power, becoming an icy tempest of relentless proportions. Once a gentle blanket, the snowfall grew heavier and denser, transforming into a furious blizzard that obscured their vision and turned every step into an arduous battle against the elements.

Keisha's breath caught in her throat, and her once-determined stride faltered as the merciless snowflakes clung to her eyelashes and the tips of her hair. Her world became a disorienting maelstrom of swirling whiteness, a frozen abyss that threatened to swallow them whole. Ong's voice was a faint whisper amidst the howling gales, his struggles evident as he fought to maintain forward momentum.

"Pumpkin, stay close!" Keisha's voice, though strained, carried an unwavering determination. Pumpkin's warm and steadfast presence pressed against her leg, offering solace amidst the frigid storm. With renewed resolve, Keisha compelled herself to take another step and then another, her fists clenched to steady her trembling hands. The relentless onslaught of snow and cold sought to erode their willpower, but they clung to their purpose, driven by a fierce determination to overcome this evil trial.

However, it became evident that the Abyssal Dominion demanded more from their trial. The snowfall intensified alarmingly, rising from their ankles to their knees until they found themselves wading through a sea of white. Keisha's elven senses struggled to penetrate the blizzard's veil, and her heart raced within her chest as the tendrils of panic threatened to overwhelm her. The elements conspired against them, pushing the boundaries of their endurance as they forged deeper into the heart of the hostility that held sway in Emberwood Forest.

But even as the evil illusion sought to break their spirits, Ong's voice rang out, a rock of steadfastness amidst the chaos. "Keisha, stay with me. Together, we shall find our way through this."

His words served as an anchor, grounding her amidst the storm's fury. Aware of Keisha's vulnerability to the cold, Ong pulled her close, wrapping his arm protectively around her. The warmth of his body offered a respite from the relentless cold that threatened to consume them. Pumpkin, the loyal panther, nuzzled against them, her presence a source of comfort amidst the freezing storm.

With Ong's unwavering presence and Pumpkin's reassuring warmth, Keisha mustered the strength to continue, each step a hard-fought victory against the unseen forces that sought to unravel them. Ong's protective embrace provided physical warmth and emotional support, reminding her they were in this trial together, their bond unbreakable.

As the snowfall persisted and the forest around them transformed into a frozen labyrinth, Keisha clung to the knowledge that the strength of their bond would guide them through this malevolent trial. Unbeknownst to them, the Abyssal Dominion watched with perverse satisfaction, savoring their struggle and relishing the despair they had sown. The cruel overlords reveled in the torment they inflicted, unaware that the trio's determination and unity were powerful weapons against the darkness that surrounded them.

Yet, little did the Dominion realize that their efforts to crush the spirits of Ong, Keisha, and Pumpkin only fortified their resolve and cemented the unbreakable bond that bound them together against the encroaching darkness.

Within the heart of the swirling blizzard, Ong, Keisha, and Pumpkin pressed onward, their determination unyielding in the face of the Abyssal Dominion's relentless illusions. The snow-covered forest appeared as a shifting maze, each step leading them further into the labyrinthine unknown.

After an eternity of battling through the unrelenting snow, their progress stopped. The path they had been following vanished into a wall of thick, frost-covered trees. Keisha's brow furrowed in bewilderment as she turned to survey the way they had traversed, only to find it obscured by the ceaseless snowfall.

"Now what?" Ong's voice, tinged with frustration, cut through the frigid air, his frosty breath emphasizing the question that hung heavily in the wintry expanse.

Keisha's elven eyes scoured their wintry surroundings, her keen senses watchful for a glimmer of hope. It was then that her perceptive gaze captured a flicker of movement, a tantalizing glimpse of something concealed just beyond the reach of the gnarled trees. Her heart quickened as she blinked, and there it was—an entrance to a cave, a sanctuary promising shelter from the relentless storm.

"Ong, look!" Keisha's voice rang out with newfound optimism as she pointed toward the fleeting vision. "A cave, just there. Let's make for it!"

Driven by this beacon of hope, they pushed onward through the dense underbrush, their footsteps muffled by the thick snow beneath. The cave's mouth drew them closer, a beckoning call promising warmth and respite. Yet, as they closed in on the spot where it had appeared, the cave melted away like a mirage, leaving them surrounded by nothing more than gnarled trees and the relentless dance of falling snow.

Confusion melded with exasperation as they regrouped, attempting to fathom the perplexing phenomenon. Keisha's voice betrayed her frustration. "It was right there, I swear."

Ong's perceptive eyes scanned their surroundings, his expression pensive. "Let's not give up just yet. We might have missed something."

As the trio faced this bewildering twist in their harrowing journey, their determination burned brighter than ever. The malevolent illusions of the Abyssal Dominion might test their resolve. Still, they remained unyielding in their quest to navigate the treacherous heart of Emberwood Forest and uncover the secrets hidden within its frozen depths.

They forged ahead again, spotting another fleeting glimpse of a cave entrance slightly to their right. Renewed determination spurred them onward, the promise of respite fueling their efforts. Yet, once more, as they reached the precise spot where the cave had beckoned, it dissolved, leaving them entwined in the same unforgiving forest.

Keisha's vexation mounted with each elusive illusion. "This can't be mere coincidence.

Something is distorting our perception."

They persevered in their quest, confronting two more elusive cave entrances that proved equally ephemeral. With each disappointment, their resolve waned, and the relentless blizzard's onslaught seemed to amplify.

Standing there, catching their breath and grappling to understand the situation, Keisha's revelation struck like a bolt of clarity. "Ong, I believe these visions deliberately attempt to mislead us. They want us to wander pointlessly."

Ong's furrowed brow mirrored his contemplation. "What's our next move then?"

Keisha's gaze hardened, determination rekindled within her eyes. "We fall back on our instincts, Ong. We trust what we know, not these deceitful apparitions."

With a revitalized resolve, they turned away from the beguiling visions, retracing their steps to the original path. The blizzard's fury seemed to relent as if acknowledging their steadfast determination. As they pressed on, the forest remained stubbornly unaltered, the snowfall relentless, yet the path ahead felt clearer, guided by their instincts rather than the Abyssal Dominion's treacherous illusions.

A subtle transformation stirred within the frozen labyrinth as they persevered, as though their defiance resonated with the very essence of the forest, lessening the blizzard's intensity and gradually yielding to their determined spirits.

Amidst the storm's relentless assault, Ong, Keisha, and Pumpkin pressed forward, their connection unyielding, their resolve indomitable. Finally breaking free from the dense woods, their eyes alighted upon the entrance to a cave, untouched by the wiles of distortion and deception.

With a renewed sense of purpose, they crossed the cave's threshold, leaving behind the beguiling illusions and treacheries woven by the Abyssal Dominion. The path ahead might be fraught with peril, but their unity, unwavering trust, and relentless determination would serve as guiding lights through any challenges that lay ahead.

Stepping into the cave, Ong, Keisha, and Pumpkin breathed a sigh and felt relieved the outside world was left behind, replaced by an eerie stillness that enveloped them. Within the dimly lit cavern, walls adorned with icicles glinted like crystalline shards. Keisha's breath hung in the air, her heart still racing from the bewildering illusions they had recently faced.

As they ventured deeper into the eerie stillness of the cave, Ong couldn't help but notice Keisha's lingering shivers, a testament to her unfamiliarity with the biting cold. He pulled her closer, wrapping his arms around her to share his body heat. Keisha leaned into his embrace, her gratitude evident in her eyes as she whispered a heartfelt "Thank you."

Ong nodded, his voice soft but determined. "I know you're not used to this cold, my love. I'll do whatever it takes to keep you warm and safe." Their bond, forged in the face of adversity, remained unbroken, a source of strength and comfort during the Abyssal Dominion's malevolent trials

Little did they fathom that the Abyssal Dominion's sinister designs were far from complete. Unbeknownst to them, Vuarus and Phoenix had taken note of their entrance into the cave and decided to orchestrate a twisted game of psychological torment.

As Ong and Keisha ventured deeper into the cavern, the walls began to shift and warp, casting eerie shadows that danced in the muted light. Keisha's footsteps faltered as the twisted visages of her friends and loved ones appeared before her, their expressions twisted in pain and terror. Her heart hammered in her chest, and she staggered backward, attempting to shake off the disturbing visions.

Ong's grip on his weapon grew taut at her side as shadowy figures enveloped him, each hissing taunts and sowing seeds of doubt in his ears. His breath quickened, his thoughts spiraling as the illusions preyed upon his deepest fears and insecurities.

Ever vigilant, Pumpkin released a low growl, her eyes narrowing as she sensed the evil energy that hung heavy in the air. She positioned herself between Ong and Keisha, her instincts sounding the alarm that something was amiss, ready to defend her companions from any unseen threat.

Unaware of the torment assailing them, Keisha and Ong exchanged concerned glances, each recognizing the unease in the other. Undeterred, they pressed forward relentlessly, their determination unyielding as they sought to uncover the truth and overcome the trials that loomed before them.

As they delved deeper into the cave, the illusions escalated. Keisha glimpsed fleeting images of her homeland, E'vahona, cloaked in darkness, her heart heavy with profound loss. Meanwhile, Ong was besieged by haunting memories of battles lost, failures endured, and defeats suffered. These apparitions exploited their vulnerabilities, fanning the flames of their fears and doubts.

Yet, even in the face of this psychological onslaught, their unwavering bond remained their anchor, a source of strength that helped them distinguish reality from illusion. Together, they pressed onward, determined to unravel the evil tricks of the Abyssal Dominion, and emerge from this ordeal with their spirits unbroken.

Unbeknownst to them, Vuarus and Phoenix observed the unfolding events with a malicious satisfaction that glinted in their malevolent expressions. Their twisted amusement thrived as they witnessed the torment they had inflicted, their illusions warping reality itself.

However, as the illusions intensified, so did the resolve of Ong and Keisha. They clung to each other, drawing strength from their unbreakable bond and steadfastly refusing to surrender to the Abyssal Dominion's cruel machinations. Just when the illusions consumed them entirely, an inner surge of indomitable fortitude propelled them forward.

With a fiery determination, Ong and Keisha confronted the illusions head-on, dispelling them with unwavering resolve. The cave's walls ceased their eerie shifting, the oppressive shadows withdrew, and the tormenting visions dissolved like ephemeral mist.

Pumpkin let out a triumphant growl, her tail flicking with satisfaction as the oppressive energy lifted from the cave's confines. Ong and Keisha exchanged a resolute glance, their shared strength as their guiding beacon through the harrowing ordeal.

The Abyssal Dominion's twisted game had ended. Their unity, resilience, and the unwavering bond between them had emerged victorious over the darkness that had sought to rend them apart. As they continued their journey deeper into the cave, they were aware that whatever challenges awaited them, they would confront them together, their unbreakable spirit a testament to their enduring love and determination.

As Ong, Keisha, and Pumpkin ventured deeper into the cave, the atmosphere grew increasingly taut. The air seemed to constrict, and an unspoken foreboding settled upon them. Unbeknownst to them, the Abyssal Dominion had concocted another sinister trial to test their mettle.

Suddenly, as they advanced, the ground beneath them gave way with a nauseating lurch. Ong and Keisha were sent plummeting into separate cavern chambers, the sudden descent leaving them disoriented and gripped by panic. They landed on the cold, uneven ground, their senses reeling from the impact.

Pumpkin's presence was felt beside Ong, her low growl echoing his unease. Ong could barely discern his surroundings in the dim light, the shadows dancing and shifting around him, concealing the true nature of the chamber's depths.

In the cave's depths, Keisha had been deposited in an entirely different area, far from Ong's reach. Her heart raced within her chest as she struggled to regain her footing, surrounded by an oppressive aura that sent dread cascading down her spine.

As both Ong and Keisha ventured to explore their separate and bewildering environments, it became painfully evident that the Abyssal Dominion had conjured yet more excruciating illusions to torment their souls. Ong stumbled upon a twisted tableau of his past, reliving moments fraught with doubt and failure. The echoes of battles lost, and the weight of his responsibilities bore down on him, threatening to crush his resolve.

Conversely, Keisha was entangled in a haunting mirage of E'vahona, now utterly consumed by malevolent darkness. The once-vibrant trees lay withered, the skies were shrouded in an inky blackness, and her beloved homeland crumbled before her very eyes. A profound sense of loss gripped her heart, and she fought against the tears that threatened to spill forth.

Amid these tormenting visions, Ong and Keisha were besieged by perilous phantoms—shadowy creatures writhing and twisted before them, their forms undergoing eerie, unnatural transformations. These nightmarish entities lunged at our heroes with malevolence blazing in their eyes, forcing Ong and Keisha to rely on their instincts and battle-honed skills to evade the deadly attacks.

Pumpkin, their unwavering companion, remained vigilant, her senses keenly attuned to the presence of these illusory fiends. Fueled by fierce determination, she leaped into action, her lithe form darting and weaving as she engaged in a fearsome combat dance alongside Ong. Her claws and teeth found their marks, striking down illusionary foes with uncanny precision.

Ong and Keisha's survival instincts kicked into high gear as the illusions and phantom adversaries assailed them from all sides. Tempered by shared trials, their bond was a beacon of hope in this nightmarish labyrinth. It is a testament to their unyielding spirit and determination to conquer whatever challenges the Abyssal Dominion could conjure.

Meanwhile, Keisha harnessed her elemental magic, summoning barriers of wind and fire to fend off the relentless onslaught of the illusions that threatened to engulf her. Her heart raced as she called every ounce of strength, her very essence a blazing counterforce against the encroaching darkness.

Yet, as she battled on, a creeping realization gnawed at her soul. The destructive forces unleashed by the Abyssal Dominion had taken their toll on the natural world around her. The once-vibrant energies of Emberwood Forest, which had fueled her elemental magic, now waned in their potency. Though valiant, her barriers of wind and fire flickered and faltered, their brilliance dimmed by the devastation surrounding her. It was a grim reminder that the Dominion's malevolence had left no corner of their world untouched.

Ong and Keisha fought with unwavering ferocity as the illusions and phantoms continued their relentless assault. Their determination and the indomitable bond that united them provided the strength to confront the torment head-on.

And then, as abruptly as it had begun, the torment ceased. The shadows withdrew, the illusions dissipated, and the imaginary creatures evaporated into thin air. Ong and Keisha stood victorious within the eerie silence of the cave once more, their breaths ragged and their spirits shaken but unbroken.

Pumpkin's triumphant purr echoed through the cave, her warm presence a soothing balm to Ong's and Keisha's wearied souls. With a glance exchanged between them, they shared an unspoken recognition of the indomitable strength they had unearthed within themselves and their enduring bond.

The Abyssal Dominion's cruel attempts to shatter their spirits again faltered. Their unwavering resilience, unity, and unbreakable connection had carried them through the oppressive darkness that had sought to drive a wedge between them. As they forged onward through the winding cave, they brought with them the certainty that whatever trials lay ahead, they would confront them together, side by side, their connection unyielding.

Within the shadowy sanctums of the Abyssal Dominion, Vuarus and Phoenix observed the unfolding events in the cave with a mix of fascination and vexation. As the illusions crumbled and Ong and Keisha emerged victorious, a scowl marred Phoenix's countenance. "They should have crumbled by now. Why do they persist in defying us?"

Vuarus, his gaze steady and contemplative, turned to his counterpart. "Perhaps because they harbor knowledge we have overlooked."

Phoenix's eyes narrowed as he regarded Vuarus with a hint of begrudging respect. "And what knowledge might that be?"

Vuarus gestured towards the scene before them. "They understand that they will inevitably reunite no matter the distance that separates them. Their bond is unassailable, and they leaned upon that connection to navigate the torment."

Phoenix's frustration simmered beneath his surface, yet a grudging comprehension crept into his expression. "So, their unity is their strength."

Vuarus nodded, a glint of admiration in his eyes. "Indeed. Their unity, trust, and love for one another—a force we cannot easily dismantle."

Though Phoenix's fists clenched in frustration, a begrudging respect momentarily overshadowed his anger. "We shall see. We'll find a way to exploit their vulnerabilities."

Vuarus remained composed, his gaze fixed upon the fading vision of the cave. "By all means, we can try. But remember, they are resourceful. They adapt, they learn, and they grow stronger. Underestimating them could prove difficult."

In the shadowy depths of their realm, the Abyssal Dominion contemplated their next move, knowing that Ong and Keisha's unbreakable bond remained a formidable obstacle to their dark ambitions.

With these words echoing in the depths of the Abyssal Dominion, the evil forces prepared for their next move, knowing that Ong and Keisha's resolve remained unshaken, a beacon of hope in the ever-encroaching darkness.

As the ethereal scene dissipated into the shadows, Phoenix's lingering frustration was overshadowed by the undeniable truth of Vuarus's words. The bond shared by Ong and Keisha was a force to be reckoned with, a strength that had emerged triumphant in the face of the Abyssal Dominion's torments. Though the Dominion had devised the trials, the couple's shared resilience became their most potent weapon.

Deep within the foreboding heart of their shadowy realm, Vuarus and Phoenix watched, their malevolent minds plotting the next move. The battle was far from concluded, and as they schemed and hatched their dark designs, an unsettling awareness gnawed at them—an understanding that Ong and Keisha were no ordinary adversaries.

Lyra, a shadowy presence lurking nearby, her voice steeped in a cold and calculating tone, broke through the oppressive silence to address Phoenix. "Keep in mind, one of your tactics is to seize Keisha, to place her where Ong's protective reach cannot find her. To manipulate her as a pawn, a vulnerability he cannot ignore. Eventually, she becomes the offering, the sacrificial pawn to the Abyss."

Phoenix shifted his gaze to Lyra, a curious mix of intrigue and irritation dancing in his eyes. "And what is the point of your counsel, Lyra?"

Lyra's unwavering gaze met his, a relentless determination in her eyes. "My point is this: you intend to exploit their bond, to sunder them by employing what they cherish most against them. But you underestimate the might of their love. Such actions may fracture them, but they won't bend to your will. Ong and Keisha's connection is not a vulnerability easily manipulated."

A faint sneer tugged at the corner of Phoenix's lips. "You sound almost concerned for their welfare, Lyra."

Lyra's countenance remained a mask of calculated detachment, her words void of emotion. "I am concerned with equilibrium, Phoenix. Their bond is a testament to the forces you and Vuarus have perpetually underestimated: love, tenacity, and unity. Your attempts to sever it might kindle a fire of resolve beyond your anticipation."

Phoenix's pent-up frustration simmered beneath the surface, his fingers drumming a steady rhythm on the armrest of his ominous throne. "They cannot elude us forever, Lyra. We shall discover a means to exploit their bond and turn it into their undoing."

Lyra's unyielding gaze held fast, an intensity unbroken. "And while you scheme, remember that even in the deepest abyss, a glimmer of light persists. Ong and Keisha's love and unity might be the barrier between your Dominion and their ultimate triumph."

With a final, contemplative look, Lyra retreated into the shadows, leaving Phoenix with profound words resonating like distant echoes within the darkness. As he resumed his sinister machinations, a subtle tremor of uncertainty gnawed at the fringes of his consciousness, reminding him that even the formidable power of the Abyssal Dominion might falter compared to the bonds forged through shared trials and tribulations.

From the concealed recesses of the shadowy domain, Vuarus's voice slithered forth, as sharp as the keenest blade. "Lyra, while you ponder the strength of their love, do not disregard that love can also be a double-edged weapon. Ong's unwavering commitment to safeguarding Keisha might become his undoing. Should he falter in her rescue, the burden of guilt and self-blame could drive a wedge between them."

Lyra shifted her gaze back to Vuarus, her eyes narrowing in contemplation of his sinister counsel. "You propose that manipulating their emotions could erode their bond."

A malicious smile curled upon Vuarus's lips. "Precisely. If Ong believes he has failed Keisha, guilt and self-doubt could cloud his judgment. He may even begin questioning his abilities and worthiness. In this fragile state, he would be ripe for manipulation."

Lyra's countenance remained pensive, her thoughts entwined in intricate possibilities. "So, you advocate for a more subtle approach—exploiting the existing fractures rather than directly assaulting their connection."

Vuarus's eyes glimmered with evil intent. "Indeed. As Ong wrestles with his inadequacies, Keisha may perceive a growing rift between them. Seeds of doubt could take root, and the ropes of their bond stretched to the limit. It's merely a matter of time before their unity crumbles."

Lyra's unwavering gaze remained fixed, her contemplations delving into the depths of possibility. "Yet you underestimate the resilience of their bond. Even amidst doubt and guilt, their love possesses the potential to prevail."

Vuarus's chuckle carried an undertone of mockery. "We shall witness, Lyra. Emotions are fragile and susceptible to manipulation. They can be molded and twisted to our advantage."

With a final enigmatic gaze, Vuarus melded back into the shadows, leaving Lyra with the chilling repercussions of his words lingering in the air. As the intricate game unfolded, the equilibrium between love and manipulation hung precariously on the precipice of darkness.

Amid the forest's eerie ambiance, Vuarus's voice reverberated with cruel delight. "Shall we indulge in one final game, my dear adversary? A game that will leave you irrevocably divided."

Keisha's heart raced like a wild stallion as the once-dormant vegetation around her abruptly appeared, their green tendrils unfurling with sinister intent. Once a tranquil haven, the forest transformed into a nightmare before her eyes. Thick as serpents, Vines slithered toward her with malice in their every twist and turn. Ong reacted swiftly, his blade gleaming in the dappled sunlight that pierced through the dense canopy.

"Pumpkin, lend your strength!" Ong's voice reverberated with an undercurrent of desperation as he grappled with the relentless verdant assailants. Pumpkin, his loyal feline companion, sprang into action. Her lithe form became a blur of feline grace as her formidable jaws snapped relentlessly at the encroaching vines.

However, they multiplied like shadowy phantoms, thwarting her every attempt to subdue them.

Amid the chaos, Keisha's heart pounded like a trapped bird within her chest as the malicious flora tossed her about like a mere puppet. She strained to hear Ong's impassioned cries and Pumpkin's defiant snarls, but their voices were distorted and remote, drowned by the claustrophobic embrace of the insidious undergrowth.

Ong's veins pulsed with newfound vigor as he freed himself from the vegetal shackles, his eyes aglow with unwavering resolve. He surged forward, slashing at the relentless tendrils that ensnared his beloved Keisha, his every movement a manifestation of fury and trepidation. His blade flashed like a comet's tail, cutting through the living bonds that sought to claim her.

Yet, these verdant adversaries possessed an eerie sentience of their own, their grip refusing to relent. Keisha's world swam in a blurry whirl as she was forcibly hurled to the unforgiving ground, her fragile form subjected to the cruel embrace of the unyielding undergrowth. An encroaching darkness threatened to consume her senses.

"No!" Ong's anguished cry reverberated through the forest, his indomitable will driving him onward as he grappled through the treacherous thicket. He waged an arduous war against the ensnaring tendrils, his desperation lending him an almost supernatural strength.

Finally, with a final, thunderous sweep of his blade, Ong cleaved through the last of the voracious plants that had imprisoned Keisha. He cradled her limp and battered form in his arms, her vulnerability a stark reminder of the peril that loomed around them. Her once vibrant spirit now seemed fragile, like a delicate blossom in danger of wilting.

"Pumpkin, we must depart," he murmured through gritted teeth, his voice a turbulent blend of fury and profound concern. He cast a fiery glare into the shadow-draped recesses of the forest, where Vuarus's malevolent presence appeared to linger like a venomous serpent in the darkness.

With the weight of Keisha's unconscious body cradled in his arms, Ong ventured forth through the gnarled and twisted trees of the sinister forest. Each step was fraught with an unwavering determination that challenged the very essence of the woodland, an oppressive presence that clung to his heart like a shadowy shroud. Once a place of enchantment, the forest had revealed its true, evil nature. Ong and Pumpkin now carried Keisha's fragile form through this living nightmare, their resolve unyielding in the face of overwhelming darkness.

Finally, he chanced upon a modest clearing where the moon's ethereal light bathed Keisha's form in an otherworldly glow. Tenderly, he lowered her to the ground, his eyes fixed upon her with a potent mix of gentleness and anguished concern. The moonlight painted a silver halo around her, casting an almost ethereal aura upon her as if she were a lost celestial being in the heart of the abyss.

Through the night's passage, the whispered cadence of the wind rustled through the trees, a harbinger of the chilling truth that the Abyssal Dominion's cruel games had left indelible marks. Doubts and discord now festered within the very core of their unyielding bond. The forest bore witness to their trials, its ancient trees sighing with the weight of secrets and sorrows.

As the night's curtain lifted, Keisha's eyelids trembled and parted, her gaze struggling to focus on the worried countenance of Ong. A faint smile graced her lips, her voice but a fragile whisper. "Hey..."

Relief washed over Ong's features as her eyes met his. He settled beside her, a tender sweep of his fingers brushing aside a stray strand of hair from her visage. "Hey there."

Summoning her strength, Keisha propped herself up on her elbows, though a hint of discomfort danced across her features. "I guess we managed to escape their little game."

Ong's gaze remained locked onto her, a fusion of lingering concern and concealed turmoil simmering beneath the surface. "I couldn't shield you from the clutches of those plants. I couldn't ensure your safety..."

With a growing tenderness in her smile, Keisha reached out to cup his cheek, the warmth of her touch a soothing balm against his skin. "Ong, you found me. Despite all odds, you never wavered. You fought relentlessly to bring me back."

His lips curved into a subtle smile, a glint of gratitude and affection shimmering in his eyes. Leaning nearer, he bestowed a tender kiss upon her lips. "Mae ammelda, Keisha. Hantale nai (I love you, Keisha. Thank you)."

Moved by his words, Keisha's heart surged with emotion. She delicately traced her fingers along the contours of his jawline, her gaze locking onto his. "Mae ammelda enyárë, Ong. Meldo nin (I will always believe in you, Ong. You're my hero).

Beneath the moonlit canopy of the forest, their bond deepened, its resilience unshaken by the Abyssal Dominion's relentless assaults. They clung to one another, discovering strength and solace in the enduring love that anchored them through the trials ahead.

With a tender nod, Ong assisted Keisha in finding a more comfortable position, enfolding her in his protective embrace. The soft murmur of leaves rustling overhead and the distant forest's nocturnal symphony crafted a soothing lullaby. Pumpkin, their loyal companion, nestled close, radiating warmth and security.

As the night unfolded, Keisha's breathing steadied, exhaustion finally overtaking her. Ong regarded her with a medley of emotions dancing in his eyes. With a tranquil sigh, he relaxed, finding solace in the peaceful embrace of the forest and the woman who held his heart. Daunting challenges loomed on the horizon, but united. They remained steadfast against the encroaching shadows.

The night faded away, punctuated by the gentle rhythm of their breaths, embracing the respite offered by slumber in each other's arms. In the heart of Vacari's mystical realm, they found strength not just in their love but in the enduring beauty of the world around them, a testament to the indomitable spirit of their bond.

Chapter 32

Shadows Unveiled: Returning Home with Echoes of Darkness

The morning sun painted the forest with a gentle warmth, starkly contrasting with the previous day's icy trials. Shafts of golden light filtered through the leaves, creating a mosaic of dancing patterns on the forest floor. Dewdrops glistened like scattered diamonds on every blade of grass, while the air carried a fresh, invigorating scent that promised a new beginning.

Ong stirred from his slumber, his senses awakening to the world's transformation. His gaze immediately found Keisha nestled beside him, her form bathed in dawn's soft, ethereal glow. The weight of their recent ordeals lingered in his mind, urging him to hasten their return to E'vahona. "Keisha," he whispered, tenderly brushing a stray strand of hair from her face. She shifted, her eyes fluttering open to meet his concerned gaze.

"Morning," she murmured, a soft smile gracing her lips. Like emerald pools, her eyes mirrored the serene beauty of the forest awakening around them.

"Good morning," he replied, his voice subtly urgent. "How are you feeling?" The forest held its breath, waiting for her response, as if the trees were attuned to her well-being

She nodded, though the shadows of weariness clouded her eyes. "I'm a bit tired, but I'll manage." Her words were like the gentle rustling of leaves in the morning breeze, a testament to her resilience.

Ong's hold on her tightened as he leaned in, pressing a gentle kiss to her forehead. It was a kiss filled with affection and determination, a silent promise of protection. "We must make our way back to E'vahona," he insisted, his tone brooking no argument. "You need proper rest."

Keisha's smile warmed as she regarded him. "Always watching over me," she whispered, her voice a soft melody harmonizing with the forest's awakening chorus.

"Always," he affirmed, offering a reassuring smile. He carefully extricated himself from her embrace and rose to his feet, extending his hand to help her. The forest, a witness to their every movement, seemed to nod in agreement, as if acknowledging the strength of their bond.

Pumpkin, their loyal panther companion, stretched and yawned, her graceful form unfurling beside Keisha. Her obsidian fur shimmered with hints of amber in the morning light, a living embodiment of the forest's mystical allure. The trio shared a silent moment, their unspoken bond transcending words.

"Let's head home," Ong said, his hand entwined with Keisha's as they began their journey back to E'vahona. With its secrets and enchantments, the forest whispered its farewell, promising that even in the face of adversity, love and resilience would always find their way back to the light. As they retraced their steps through the outskirts of Emberwood Forest, Ong and Keisha exchanged a silent yet knowing glance. The memories of their previous journey in this forest were still vivid, etched in their minds like a dark painting. The scars of dragon-induced destruction were a stark reminder of the peril that lurked within these ancient woods, a threat that extended to the forest and the realms beyond its borders.

This time, they opted to skirt along the forest's edges, treading cautiously on the familiar yet unnerving terrain. The air hung heavy with an unsettling presence that sent ripples of unease down their spines. Their steps, though vigilant, were accompanied by a tangible sense of foreboding. Their faithful feline companion, Pumpkin, remained ever close, her senses keenly attuned to the environment.

"We'll find our way," Ong murmured, his voice a beacon of resolve amid the encroaching shadows. Like a mantra, his words sought to dispel the lingering ghosts of their past encounters in this haunted forest.

Keisha nodded in agreement, her grip on his hand tightening. "Yes, we will," she affirmed, her gaze fixed on the path ahead. Her determination was unwavering, a testament to her courage in the face of the unknown.

They continued their journey in determined silence, each step a testament to their unwavering commitment to push forward, regardless of the persistent darkness. The forest whispered its ancient secrets, a haunting chorus of rustling leaves and creaking branches that bore witness to their every move. It was as though the trees held their breath, waiting to see if these two intruders could defy the ominous aura that clung to the woods.

Suddenly, Pumpkin's ears pricked up, and she emitted a low growl, her sharp eyes locked onto a distant figure retreating deeper into the forest's heart. Ong and Keisha exchanged cautious looks before following the panther's gaze. There, amidst the twisted trees and concealed underbrush, they glimpsed a fleeting silhouette vanishing into the murky gloom.

Their instincts ignited, and without a word, they pursued, stepping with care as they trailed the elusive figure. The forest, in response, seemed to tighten its grip around them, its presence suffocating and oppressive. Yet, propelled by an unyielding determination to unearth the truth, they pressed on, their footsteps echoing through the dense undergrowth.

The elusive figure continued to elude their grasp as they ventured deeper into the shadowy heart of Emberwood Forest. It was as though the very shadows conspired to deceive them, distorting their perceptions, and rendering it impossible to pinpoint the source of their pursuit. Ong's concern for Keisha grew with each passing moment, and an uneasy sensation gnawed at his core, warning him that they might be walking directly into a trap set by forces they had yet to comprehend.

"Keisha," Ong began, his voice tinged with unease, "I think we should consider turning back.

It's not safe here, and I can't bear the thought of risking—"

Keisha halted him with an unwavering gaze. Her eyes were fixated on a patch of darkness pulsing with unnatural energy, a swirling shadow of shadow amidst the forest's subdued hues. "Ong, I can sense it. There's something significant here, something we can't ignore."

He sighed, torn between the instinct to protect her and his admiration for her unwavering determination. He nodded reluctantly. "Very well, but let's proceed with caution. Stay close, and if anything feels amiss, we exit immediately." His words were a solemn pact, a promise to safeguard their well-being.

Their cautious exploration persisted, every step underscored by the rustling of leaves and the echoing hush of their surroundings. Pumpkin remained steadfast at their side, her senses attuned, her presence a comforting anchor amidst the palpable uncertainty.

As they advanced, the forest grew denser, the air thickening with ominous energy. Keisha's instincts guided her, an unyielding sense of urgency propelling her onward. She couldn't shake the conviction that they were drawing near, that whatever they sought was within their grasp, the forest itself guiding them like a spectral compass.

Then, abruptly, they stumbled upon a small clearing, the moon's soft radiance filtering through the trees, casting an eerie luminescence upon the scene. At the clearing's heart stood an enigmatic obsidian altar adorned with cryptic symbols, an ancient relic lost to time. The atmosphere around it crackled with otherworldly power, and an unmistakable sense of foreboding washed over them like an icy shroud.

Keisha's heart quickened as she approached the altar, her instincts affirming that they had found their objective. "Ong, take a look at this," she murmured, her voice scarcely audible amid the forest's hush.

Ong joined her, his attention fixed upon the altar. He furrowed his brow as he scrutinized the symbols, a disquieting feeling settling deep within him. "This doesn't feel right," he murmured, his hand instinctively reaching for the hilt of his sword, his fingers trembling with a mixture of apprehension and curiosity. The forest had revealed its secrets, and they now stood at the precipice of an enigma that defied easy comprehension.

Before they could react, the earth beneath their feet trembled, and a surge of dark energy radiated from the altar. Shadows converged, manifesting into a form that was both ethereal and menacing. The entity that materialized before them exuded an aura of malice, its eyes gleaming with a sinister intelligence, like twin orbs of obsidian reflecting the abyss.

"You've come in search of answers, have you not?" the shadowy figure hissed, its voice a frigid whisper in the night, a voice that seemed to echo from the depths of a haunted crypt.

Keisha's grip on Ong's hand tightened, her eyes a blend of fear and determination. "Who are you? And what is this place?" Her voice quivered, but her resolve remained unbroken.

The figure's lips curved into a sinister grin. "I am but a servant of the Abyssal Dominion, a precursor of shadows and secrets. This altar, a conduit of our power, unveils the enigmas concealed within the darkness." Its words carried an otherworldly weight, like cryptic verses from an eldritch tome.

Ong's muscles coiled with tension, his protective instincts springing to life. "We have no interest in participating in your games. We seek only to comprehend and defeat the darkness that haunts these lands." His words declared their unwavering purpose, a defiance against the hostility that threatened to trap them.

Laughter erupted from the enigmatic figure, its echoes rippling through the clearing and sending an eerie chill coursing down their spines. "Ah, the unrefined defiance of mortals. Very well, if you hunger for answers, then prove your mettle. Survive the trials we shall lay before you, and perhaps we shall bestow upon you the knowledge you seek."

The figure's presence dissipated before they could react, leaving an ominous silence like an oppressive mist that closed around them, suffocating and heavy.

Keisha and Ong exchanged a wary glance, their hearts throbbing in their chests. The decision before them was crystal clear, yet the path they were about to tread was fraught with peril and uncertainty, which led deeper into the heart of darkness itself.

As Keisha and Ong advanced cautiously, the ambiance around them transformed. The air grew thick with foreboding, the atmosphere carrying an unsettling weight that sent shivers rippling through their spines. Shadows deepened, concealing their surroundings and making it increasingly difficult to discern what lay ahead, as if the very forest had become a sentient entity, conspiring with the evil presence that awaited them.

Ever vigilant, Pumpkin moved in tandem with them, her senses razor-sharp. Her instincts mirrored those of her companions, and she assumed a protective stance, her ears perked, and her muscles primed to react at the faintest hint of danger. In the heart of this ominous realm, they would rely on their unwavering bond and indomitable spirit to face the trials that awaited.

Their journey led them deeper into the forest's heart, and the darkness pressed in with each stride. Keisha clutched Ong's hand, every faculty on high alert. Every rustling leaf and the distant sound carried a sinister weight, as if the very forest had come alive with evil intent.

Ong's sword remained unsheathed, its gleaming blade contrasting with its op-pressive shadows. His sharp eyes scanned their environment for movement, a sentinel against the encroaching peril. The tension in the air was palpable, an energy that pulsed with menace and provocation. He forged onward, his resolve unwavering, though the disturbing sensation of being watched gnawed at him like unseen claws.

Overhead, the forest canopy blocked out most of the moon's illumination, cast-ing the forest floor into an even more bottomless abyss of shadow. The trees appeared to warp and contort unnaturally, their branches assuming grotesque angles that reached out like bony fingers, as if the forest were mocking their intrusion.

With each advancing step, the enigmatic darkness grew more profound, an in-escapable shroud that intensified the eerie sensation of being under scrutiny, as if evil eyes watched their every move from the shadows. Keisha's heart raced, her instincts urging her to retreat. Yet, her insatiable curiosity and unyielding resolve propelled her onward, a defiant response to the encroaching fear that threatened to consume them.

As they ventured deeper into the ominous abyss, a guttural growl reverberated in the distance, sending a visceral chill down their spines. Pumpkin's ears pricked, her feline instincts acutely aware of impending danger. She inched closer to Ong and Keisha, her unwavering gaze fixated on the elusive shadows that seemed to frolic just beyond their peripheral vision, her growl an ominous harmony to the forest's dark symphony.

Ong's fingers tightened around the hilt of his sword, his vigilant eyes darting from side to side as he endeavored to discern the origin of the ominous noise. The oppressive presence of unseen watchers only added to the heavy tension in the air. Their hostile scrutiny felt like an evil weight upon their shoulders.

"Keisha," he murmured, his voice scarcely audible, "we must be prepared for anything. Stay close to me and remain vigilant."

She nodded, her pulse racing in her veins. The path ahead was dangerous, and they had no alternative but to advance. Guided by Pumpkin's vigilant stance and determination, they forged onward, unacquainted with the challenges ahead or the concealed mysteries yet to be unveiled. The ever-conspiratorial forest drew tighter around them, its enigmatic shadows collaborating to obfuscate their course. But Ong, Keisha, and Pumpkin were resolute, not to be easily dissuaded. With each stride, they stood ready to confront the unknown darkness, their unwavering determination relentless in the face of uncertainty, determined to uncover the truth that lay hidden in the heart of the abyss.

When Keisha, Ong, and Pumpkin finally emerged from the dense undergrowth, they found themselves in a vastly altered clearing compared to the forest they had traversed. The once faint glimmer of moonlight had entirely surrendered, leaving the expanse veiled in impenetrable obscurity. The shadows coalesced in a dense and unyielding embrace, as though the very essence of the night had gathered at this exact point, a convergence of darkness that defied the moon's feeble attempts to pierce it.

Ong's instincts flared, his senses acutely attuned to potential danger. An unsettling sensation crept up the nape of his neck, signaling the presence of concealed threats. His grip on his sword tightened, the blade gleaming faintly amid the scant illumination that pierced the darkness, a beacon of steel in the shadowy abyss.

"Stay close," he whispered to Keisha, his voice a mere breath in the oppressive silence, a vow to protect her from whatever evil forces lurked in the void. Pumpkin moved with the grace of a shadow beside him, her obsidian eyes mirroring the enigmatic ambiance. Every fiber of his being screamed for vigilance, urging him to be prepared for the unseen peril that encircled them.

Though the clearing appeared devoid of life, Ong couldn't shake the troubling notion that they were under surveillance. He scrutinized the shadows, each subtle sound magnified in the oppressive hush. The forest withheld its breath, poised for an impending moment, as if time itself had slowed to witness their plight.

Keisha inched nearer to Ong's side, her heartbeat echoing the rapid cadence of his own. The ominous aura weighed upon them like a tangible force, the darkness an oppressive shroud that sought to engulf them. She believed in Ong's instincts, understanding that his experience and intuition were their guiding beacons in this impenetrable abyss.

Pumpkin's ears twitched, her heightened senses acutely attuned to any movement. She crouched low, her sinewy muscles coiled and ready for action. Whatever lurked within the shadows, she was unwavering in her commitment to safeguard her companions, a guardian of the night.

Ong's vigilant gaze darted around their surroundings, a hunt for any trace of motion. He sensed the hairs on his neck stand on end, a shiver coursing down his spine. The disquieting unease burgeoned, the unsettling conviction of their not being alone intensifying with every passing moment.

Inexplicably, a faint murmur of sound reached his ears, a subtle rustling emanating from all directions. It was as if the atmosphere teemed with concealed activity, a whisper of malice that encircled them. Whatever entities lurked nearby were deliberate and cunning, masters of concealment, their intentions hidden within the inky depths of the night.

His thoughts raced, endeavoring to assemble the puzzle of their environment. The darkness toyed with his senses, distorting reality and rendering the familiar into an eerie and unsettling semblance, like a nightmarish canvas painted with strokes of uncertainty and dread.

"Something is awry," Ong murmured, his voice taut with apprehension, the words a reluctant admission of the inexplicable. "Remain vigilant. We share this domain with unseen cohorts."

Keisha acknowledged with a nod, her senses acutely alert. The encroaching darkness pressed upon them like a heavy shroud, an inescapable presence that resisted explanation. She watched and listened in this realm of concealed enigmas and looming peril, sensing that they were trapped within a labyrinth of shadows and mysteries, where threats hid themselves beyond their perception, like ghosts haunting the edges of their reality.

A guttural growl from Pumpkin cleaved through the silence, a stark warning that electrified Keisha and Ong. The black panther's obsidian gaze remained fixed on a point just ahead, her lithe form poised for a swift assault, a living embodiment of their collective resolve to confront the unknown.

Ong's knuckles whitened around the hilt of his sword, his eyes narrowing as he concentrated on the exact location. Something stirred there, a fleeting motion amidst the obscurity. As his vision adjusted, a faint silhouette emerged, a form that seemed to merge from the very heart of the shadows, like a specter materializing from the void.

His instincts clamored for action, compelling him to defend against the impending threat. Yet, the figure stood motionless, its countenance obscured by the night's embrace. It was as though it challenged them, beckoning them to draw nearer, a silent invitation into the heart of their enigmatic world.

A dense silence enveloped the clearing, the tension tangible and oppressive. Ong and Keisha remained poised, their heightened senses attuned, awaiting the next move from the enigmatic figure. The secrets in this forest were on the verge of revelation, and the lurking shadows were poised to unveil their authentic nature, like a curtain about to rise on a macabre stage where the truth would be revealed in its most unsettling form.

Ong's focus was abruptly commandeered by Keisha's sudden, forceful pull, a violent jerk that sent shivers coursing down his spine, causing his grip on her to waver. His heart thundered in his chest as he turned sharply in her direction, but his searching gaze met naught but vacant space – she had eluded his grasp. In that disorienting instant, her initial cry hung in the air, a haunting echo that slowly dissolved into an oppressive silence, enveloping Ong's mind in a suffocating blanket of apprehension.

"Keisha!" His voice tore through the oppressive darkness, tinged with raw panic and a desperate urgency reverberating through the murky void. His heart pounded, eyes darting wildly through the impenetrable abyss surrounding him. Yet she remained elusive, a phantom in the night, and a creeping dread clutched at Ong's chest as he grappled with many dire possibilities, each more chilling than the last.

"Pumpkin, find her!" Ong's voice quivered as he beseeched their steadfast companion. The sleek, usually swift, and sure-footed panther now seemed disoriented, struggling to navigate the obsidian shroud that enveloped them, her obsidian fur blending seamlessly with the surrounding darkness.

"Keisha!" Ong's desperate cry pierced the stillness once more, his trembling hands clutching his sword, poised for a battle against an unseen foe. Fear swelled within him, a relentless tide threatening to consume his resolve. He couldn't bear losing her in this realm of shadows and enigma, his very soul yearning for the return of her presence.

As Ong's anguished calls hung in the air, time stretched into an agonizing eternity, his cries rebounding off the invisible walls of the void. But there was no response, no sign of Keisha. It was as if she had been devoured by the darkness, leaving him alone in this harrowing abyss, a solitary figure confronting the overwhelming unknown.

"Pumpkin, where is she?" Ong's voice quivered once more, each passing second amplifying his mounting anxiety. The stifling cloak of helplessness descended upon him, its weight heavy on his shoulders, his heart a leaden burden, a relentless reminder of his inability to protect the one he loved.

Amid the enigmatic clearing, a haunting silence reigned, broken only by the relentless rhythm of Ong's racing heart. His thoughts raced, chasing after the dreadful specter of losing Keisha, swallowed by the unforgiving shadows that clung to their world, which had become a labyrinth of despair.

"Keisha, please," he murmured, his voice a fragile plea laden with unbridled emotion. But the oppressive darkness remained steadfast, holding her fate close, indifferent to his anguished plea, like a cruel and relentless adversary.

As time stretched into a disheartening eternity, Ong's fear transmuted into an unwavering resolve. Despair was a luxury he couldn't afford. He pledged to unearth her, to extract her from the abyss that had swallowed her whole. With Pumpkin as his steadfast companion, he steeled himself to scour every inch of the forest to unearth its arcane secrets and retrieve the woman he loved from its insidious clutches, his love and determination kindling a fire within him that would burn through the darkest of nights.

And so, armed with his sword and aided by Pumpkin's fierce loyalty, Ong plunged deeper into the oppressive void, propelled by an unyielding determination to rescue Keisha and lead her back into the warm embrace of the light, no matter the cost, no matter the trials that lay ahead.

Ong's heart thrummed, his veins coursing with adrenaline as sinister laughter tore through the stagnant air. The sound reverberated like a macabre symphony, its malevolence unmistakable—an unsettling reminder of Phoenix's presence. Ong's grip on his sword tightened, the weapon trembling in his hand, a potent cocktail of anger and fear coursing through him, a tempest of emotions swirling within him like a raging storm.

And then, as if conjured from the depths of the encroaching shadows, a form materialized—a menacing figure standing alongside the fiery silhouette of Phoenix. Ong's gaze sharpened, his teeth grinding together as he recognized the man at Phoenix's side. An aura of malice radiated from him, sending ripples of dread coursing down Ong's spine. It was Vuarus, the embodiment of darkness and chaos, a harbinger of despair.

But what seized Ong's attention, drawing forth an agonizing torrent of emotions, was the sight that pierced his heart—a helpless figure atop a crimson-scaled dragon. Keisha. His gut twisted painfully, a tempest of anguish and fury storming through his veins. There she was, vulnerable and bound, trapped in the clutches of the forces they had vowed to defy, a damsel in distress in the most dire sense.

"Keisha!" Ong's voice cracked a cacophony of desperation and rage echoing through the shadowed clearing. His sword quivered in his grip as he stepped forward, his eyes locked onto the harrowing tableau before him. Every fiber of his being cried out for him to charge ahead, to wrench her from their evil grasp. Yet he knew, deep in his soul, that the odds were overwhelmingly stacked against him, that this was a confrontation fraught with peril.

Phoenix's laughter, like venomous serpents, slithered through the air, its cruel notes a sinister reminder of the treacherous game they were trapped in. "Let her go!" Ong's voice reverberated, a defiant battle cry infused with the fierce intensity of his love and unwavering determination. His eyes, aflame with defiance, locked onto Phoenix's fiery gaze, confronting the evil warlock responsible for his love's plight. This confrontation would test the very limits of his strength and resolve.

Vuarus, the embodiment of darkness itself, harnessed the shadows surrounding him, the inky tendrils curling and swirling at his malevolent command. Ong's knuckles whitened as he clutched his sword, every muscle in his body coiled with tension, bracing for the unleashing of the evil sorcery that loomed on the precipice of eruption. His heart raced, his thoughts whirling in desperation and unyielding resolve, a warrior ready to face the darkest adversaries.

Phoenix, his eyes dancing with wicked delight, finally ceased his laughter, an evil grin stretching across his face. "Ah, young lovers," he mused, his voice dripping with malice. "How you've vexed my plans with your meddling. But fear not, dear Ong, for you shall bear witness to your beloved's suffering. Revenge is a dish best served in the most agonizing of ways." His words hung like a curse, casting a foreboding shadow over the already treacherous confrontation, a confrontation that would test the very bonds of love and courage.

With a sinister flourish of dark energy, the dragon bearing Keisha upon its back began its ascent into the ominous sky. Ong's heart plummeted, a gut-wrenching blend of panic and grief constricting his chest. "Keisha!" he bellowed once more, his voice a raw cry of agony reverberating through the shadowy clearing, a cry that pierced the very heavens.

Beside him, Pumpkin emitted a low, threatening growl, her form crouched and ready, mirroring Ong's inner turmoil. However, the distance between them and the airborne dragon stretched, and Ong's resolve crystallized. He couldn't let them take her; he couldn't allow Keisha to be lost to the unforgiving embrace of the darkness. With a steely determination burning in his eyes, he knew he had to act, to defy the odds and fight for the woman he loved with every fiber of his being.

Determined, he took a bold step forward, his resolve solidifying. He couldn't stand idly by while his love was torn away from him, not when there was a glimmer of hope, no matter how faint, that he could reach her. But as he moved, Vuarus's dark magic surged, conjuring a swirling vortex of shadows that rent at the very fabric of reality, an evil force determined to block his path, to thwart his valiant efforts to save Keisha. Ong's steps faltered, his sword quivering in the face of the overwhelming power that manifested before him, a power that sought to challenge his very existence.

As the vortex expanded, Ong's vision blurred, and the edges of his consciousness began to fade. He reached out, his fingers barely grazing the tips of Keisha's bound hands, an agonizing near-miss. Then, in a cruel twist of fate, the insidious vortex swallowed her whole, leaving Ong grasping at emptiness, his heart heavy with despair, a crushing sense of powerlessness overwhelming him.

"No!" Ong's anguished cry reverberated through the void, his heartache and despair resonating within the very essence of his being. Every fiber of his being felt like it was being torn apart by the relentless magic that swirled around him. He fought against the inexorable pull, his mind a chaotic storm of fury, grief, and unshakable determination, a warrior refusing to yield even in the face of overwhelming odds.

And then, as suddenly as it had begun, the all-encompassing darkness receded, leaving Ong alone in the desolate clearing. His chest heaved with the tremendous effort of resisting the abyss that had threatened to consume him. His eyes burned with fierce resolve, and when it finally emerged from his torment, his voice was a thunderous declaration that echoed through the silent forest, a vow to confront the darkness that had stolen Keisha from him.

"Phoenix!" As he shouted into the empty, shadowed expanse, Ong's voice cracked with fiery rage. "If you so much as lay a finger on Keisha, if you harm her in any way, I swear by all that is sacred, your life will be the price you pay!" His words were a solemn oath, a promise etched in the depths of his soul, a warning to the evil forces that dared to challenge his love.

Ong crumpled to his knees, a heart-wrenching cry escaping his lips, his sword abandoned and left to clatter against the unforgiving ground. The immense weight of his failure bore down on him, an unbearable burden that he couldn't escape. He hadn't been able to protect Keisha, to save her from the encroaching darkness that had torn her from his grasp, a bitter taste of defeat gnawing at him.

Ever loyal Pumpkin approached him with concern and devotion, her sleek form a comforting presence. Yet Ong's gaze remained fixed on the void that had replaced the vibrant company of Keisha. Her laughter and the warmth of her touch felt like distant echoes now, haunting reminders of what had been stolen from him, a haunting absence that tore at his soul.

Amidst the desolation surrounding him, Ong's heart ignited with an unquenchable fire—a burning determination to rescue Keisha from the forces that had dared to separate them. He rose from his knees, fists clenched in unwavering resolve, his eyes focused on the horizon, a hero prepared to embark on a dangerous quest.

"I'll find you, Keisha," he vowed, his voice a fierce whisper, a promise to the woman he loved more than life itself. With Pumpkin steadfastly at his side, he turned away from the bleak clearing, his path set with the guiding lights of love and the lingering echoes of darkness that had taken her, a journey into the unknown that held both danger and hope.

Ong couldn't afford to be consumed by grief and despair. Keisha was out there, somewhere, held captive by the relentless clutches of the Abyssal Dominion. He knew he had to act, to embark on whatever difficult journey lay ahead to bring her back, a hero on a quest to rescue his beloved from the depths of darkness.

Emerging from the forest depths, they returned to the familiar surroundings of E'vahona. The city, once a haven of towering trees and intricate architecture, now bore the weight of doubt and fear that had been cast upon it. The shadows lurking in every corner were a stark reminder of the trials that awaited them, a realm that darkness had touched.

Amidst the bustling Eladrin city, its citizens oblivious to the turmoil that had gripped Ong's world, he moved with a sense of determination that belied the darkness that weighed on his heart. His jaw was set in resolve, each step purposeful as he made his way to the city's heart. The grand chambers of the Eladrin Council awaited him, and he understood the grave responsibility that rested upon his shoulders—to inform the realm's wisest and most influential leaders of the tragedy that had befallen them, a solemn duty he could not shirk.

Within the ornate chamber, the members of the Eladrin Council had assembled—sages and rulers who had dedicated their lives to safeguarding their realm and its people. Lord Karrenen, Lady Mirabelle, and the rest turned their attention to Ong as he entered, their expressions a blend of curiosity and concern, their eyes fixed on the bearer of dire news.

Ong's voice remained unwavering as he recounted the harrowing events of the previous day—the dangerous encounter with the insidious Abyssal Dominion, the treacherous trap concealed within the forest's depths, and the cruel theft of Keisha from his side. He spared no details, his words infused with the raw, unfiltered emotion of a man who had witnessed the love of his life being cruelly torn away, a painful story told with unwavering honesty.

As his narrative came to an unhappy conclusion, a weighty silence enveloped the chamber. Lord Karrenen's visage bore the gravity of their predicament, his furrowed brow a testament to the depth of their collective concern. "Indeed, this is a dire situation," he murmured, his voice reflecting the shared anxiety that loomed large, a leader who understood the gravity of the challenge ahead.

Lady Mirabelle stepped forward, her eyes filled with empathy and determination. "Swift action is imperative," she declared, her words carrying an unwavering resolve. "The Abyssal Dominion may wield formidable power, but we possess strength and unity. We shall marshal our forces, devise a comprehensive strategy, and embark on a mission to bring Keisha back to us," a leader who refused to yield to despair.

Ong nodded solemnly with deep gratitude and a fire of determination burning in his eyes. He was acutely aware that this quest was not one he could undertake alone; his people's strength and unwavering support were indispensable. "I am committed to doing whatever is necessary to rescue her," he vowed, his voice resonating with unshakable resolve, a hero ready to face the darkest challenges.

Lord Karrenen's hand rested reassuringly on Ong's shoulder, a touch that conveyed both empathy and resolve. "We stand as one, Ong. Keisha is not just your beloved; she is one of us. We will not cease our efforts until she safely returns to our embrace," a leader who understood the importance of unity in the face of adversity, a promise of unwavering support.

The Council's unwavering assurance gave Ong a renewed sense of purpose. He knew the path ahead was fraught with peril and uncertainty but armed with Pumpkin's loyalty and bolstered by the steadfast support of his people, he was prepared to pursue the elusive echoes of darkness that had stolen Keisha away.

Exiting the council chambers, Ong was acutely aware of the emotional storm raging within him. Despair loomed like a specter, but he refused to be engulfed by it. Keisha's absence weighed heavily on his heart, a constant reminder of the danger she faced, a love tested by the shadows.

He was briefly alone before Lord Karrenen emerged, his commanding presence tinged with compassion. As he approached Ong, his somber expression hinted at the gravity of the situation, a leader who shared in the burdens of his people.

"Ong," Lord Karrenen began in hushed tones, "I fear the Abyssal Dominion will attempt to contact either you or me. They may exploit Keisha as leverage, demanding the location of E'vahona, threatening to lay siege to our realm," a leader who foresaw the potential dangers that loomed ahead.

Ong's brow furrowed, haunted by the memory of his vision in Ardinia. The image of Keisha being used as a pawn in the hands of darkness gnawed at his conscience. "I swore an oath to protect E'vahona's secret," he said with a trace of frustration, "but I cannot stand idle while Keisha's life hangs in the balance," a guardian torn between duty and love.

Lord Karrenen's hand found its way to Ong's shoulder again, his gaze unwavering and steady. "You bear the weight of E'vahona's safeguarding, Ong. But remember, you are not alone in this fight. You have allies who stand resolute, ready to defend Keisha's well-being," a reminder of the strength that could be found in unity.

Meeting Lord Karrenen's gaze, Ong felt his determination rekindled. Protecting E'vahona's secret was paramount, yet he recognized that, in dire circumstances, sacrifices for the greater good might be necessary. With Keisha's fate hanging in the balance, he was willing to confront the darkness head-on.

"Thank you, Lord Karrenen," Ong said, his voice a blend of gratitude and determination. "I will exhaust every resource to ensure Keisha's safe return," a promise forged in the crucible of love and loyalty.

Lord Karrenen nodded, his expression a blend of concern and confidence. "Remember, Ong, you do not stand alone. We shall stand as one to meet this challenge head-on," he assured Ong, his voice filled with unwavering determination. With a resolute look, Karrenen drew a small, intricately designed scroll from his robes, its surface adorned with ancient symbols that could only be deciphered by the dragons. He held it out to Ong, the scroll pulsating with an otherworldly energy.

"As a sign of our unwavering commitment," Karrenen continued, "I will send this message to the dragons immediately. It bears the urgency of our situation and the plea for their aid in the rescue of Keisha. Trust in the bond we share with the dragonkin, Ong. Together, we shall bring her home."

In that shared moment, their words hung heavy in the air—a silent pact to protect, fight, and reclaim Keisha from the clutches of the Abyssal Dominion. With allies at his side and an unwavering love fueling his resolve, Ong was ready to confront whatever darkness lay ahead. As Lord Karrenen turned to leave, Ong watched him go, the weight of their shared commitment lingering in his heart.

With that, Lord Karrenen turned to a secluded area within E'vahona, where the ancient bond between the Eladrin and the dragons was kept alive. The dragons, including Kimras, had always been the guardians of the natural world, and their instincts had sensed the impending threat of the Abyssal Dominion long before it had become manifest.

Karrenen unfurled the scroll, and as he read its sacred words, an ethereal connection was forged between him and Kimras, the wise and ancient dragon. In the heart of the forest, Kimras sensed the urgency and responded to the call, his massive wings unfurling as he prepared to take flight. The dragons, protectors of the realm, were ready to heed the plea for aid, for they knew that the balance of nature itself hung in the balance.

He watches as Lord Karrenen heads off to send the message, a silent acknowledgment of the path ahead and the challenges they would face together, and then looks down at Pumpkin, who stood faithfully by his side. Ong couldn't help but feel a profound connection with his loyal companion. He gently ran his fingers through her sleek fur, whispering words of determination and reassurance.

"We will find her, Pumpkin," he murmured, his gaze steady and unwavering. "And when she returns home, I swear I will exact vengeance upon Phoenix for the pain he has wrought."

Pumpkin let out a soft, almost imperceptible growl, echoing her agreement with Ong's vow. Her fierce protectiveness was a testament to their bond, which extended beyond words and into unspoken understanding.

With Pumpkin by his side and a fire of determination burning within him, Ong knew the path ahead would be challenging and treacherous. But he was prepared to face whatever obstacles the Abyssal Dominion threw his way, all to bring Keisha back to the safety of their home.

As the sun began to set, casting long shadows across E'vahona, Ong stood there with Pumpkin, his heart filled with resolve. The echoes of darkness had taken Keisha from him, but he was determined to silence those echoes and bring her back into the light.

Chapter 33

Shadows Unveiled: Victory Celebration in Afor

Beneath the oppressive, starless expanse of Afor's ebony heavens, Keisha was trapped in an evil waltz with Zylron, a sinister partner. His wicked grin cast a chilling omen upon the scene, etched in the feeble glow of the moon's sickly light. Nearby, the enigmatic Phoenix loomed like a spectral presence, his unyielding gaze fixated upon Keisha. Within those piercing orbs swirled a macabre melody of triumph and cruelty, crafting a sinister tune reverberating through the encroaching shadows.

"Where shall we deposit Keisha, Phoenix?" Zylron's voice slithered through the oppressive silence, his tones dripping with a vicious edge.

In response, Phoenix's voice emerged from the cold depths of his indifference, "Take her to the foreboding tower. And then summon the others. The hour of revelry has arrived."

As Keisha's heart raced within her chest, she was held firmly in Zylron's unyielding grip. Her fragile form struggled to move, her legs barely touching the gnarled path beneath her as she dangled helplessly. She refused to surrender to the abyss that threatened to engulf her. Throughout her disorienting journey, her gaze remained locked onto the looming figure of Phoenix. He stood as a sentinel, his predatory eyes never wavering as he observed her every faltering movement—a silent conductor orchestrating a twisted and surreal symphony of darkness.

Zylron's malevolent sneer left a bitter imprint before he melded into the enigmatic obscurity of the shadows. Keisha's fingers clenched into resolute fists, her spirit ablaze with unwavering determination. The flames of her resolve burned brighter than ever, for she knew she must remain unyielding, not only for herself but also for Ong, her beloved.

As Phoenix, the precursor of malevolence, prepared to depart, his cruel laughter rippled through the air like a venomous serpent's hiss. Undaunted, Keisha's voice, a beacon of defiance, cleaved through the oppressive darkness. "You shall not shatter my spirit, Phoenix. Regardless of your dark designs, I shall unearth the strength to defy your sinister machinations."

Phoenix turned to face her again, his evil smile curling like a thorned vine. "Time shall be the judge, Keisha. Time shall reveal the truth of your resolve."

With those ominous words, Phoenix dissolved into the shroud of shadows, leaving Keisha to confront the murky depths of Afor's abyss. Heavy with the impending challenges, her heart resonated with the weight of her unwavering determination.

Meanwhile, at the heart of the Dread Spire, Phoenix's triumphant laughter echoed through the winding corridors as he crossed the imposing threshold of the sinister fortress. His predatory eyes locked onto Lyra, who stood there, an indomitable presence amidst the shadowed gloom. A sarcastic smirk graced his lips, the satisfaction of his recent conquest etched upon his countenance. "Well, Lyra," he purred, "I have proven your doubts wrong. We have successfully trapped the elusive Keisha."

Lyra's visage remained stoic, but a smoldering anger flickered within her unwavering gaze. "Capturing her may be one feat, Phoenix. But breaking her spirit, that is another battle entirely."

With a dismissive wave, Phoenix brushed off her concerns. "Oh, have no fear. We possess methods most potent." He leaned in closer, his voice dripping with malice like poison. "In the end, she will submit to our dark dominion."

Lyra's unwavering gaze bore into Phoenix's soul as she retorted, "Time shall reveal the veracity of your words."

Further into the shadowed abyss of the Dread Spire, Phoenix ventured. From the obsidian veil, Vuarus emerged with a wicked grin adorning his lips. He advanced towards Keisha, who remained captive near the towering spire. With a sarcastic bow, he extended a gloved hand toward her, his demeanor mocking. "My dear, a celebration would be incomplete without your presence. Shall we partake in the festivities?"

Keisha's eyes blazed with a fiery mixture of anger and defiance as she met Vuarus's evil gaze. She steeled herself against the urge to lash out, understanding that her true strength resided in her unyielding resolve. Her jaw clenched as she begrudgingly accepted his offered hand, surrendering herself to be led deeper into the heart of the Dread Spire, where the ominous revelry awaited, cloaked in the chilling embrace of the night.

The grand hall of the Dread Spire was bathed in an ominous, flickering light. The wavering torches lined the walls, casting elongated, eerie shadows that danced like evil spirits across the chamber. A palpable aura of foreboding anticipation clung to the air like a shroud as the sinister assemblage of the Abyssal Dominion congregated to commemorate their triumphant capture of Keisha.

Keisha, her ethereal presence now marred by the dark cuffs imprisoning her wrists, stood defiantly at the heart of the chamber. These sinister restraints, pulsating with evil energy, clamped onto her, their sinister grip choking the life from her magical abilities. Her eyes, twin beacons of indomitable will, burned with unyielding defiance, even as her mystical essence lay trapped within the insidious fetters. Around her, the Dominion's members reveled in her vulnerability, their cruel laughter and mocking gazes like a vicious chorus that sought to pierce her spirit.

Into this shadowed maelstrom, Keisha, Phoenix, and Vuarus made their entrance, their smirks mirroring the darkness of their surroundings. Vuarus, bearing a new set of cuffs in his evil grasp, approached her with a wicked grin that widened as his eyes met hers. "My dear Keisha," he cooed, "we simply cannot afford the inconvenience of your troublesome magic during our revelry, can we?"

With a swift, almost hypnotic motion, he snapped the cuffs onto Keisha's wrists, sealing her magical essence within their dark embrace. Like the echo of a lurking predator, a sinister chuckle escaped his lips. Phoenix joined in, his laughter intertwining with Vuarus's as they savored their triumph, the room's eerie light flickering in cadence with their shared malevolence.

Keisha's jaw clenched with steely resolve as the cruel cuffs constricted around her wrists, their dark magic pressing down like a relentless boulder upon her soul. The oppressive weight of her suppressed powers bore heavily upon her spirit, yet she quelled the fiery urge to lash out, to shatter the chains that imprisoned her.

Instead, she locked her unwavering gaze with the cold, evil eyes of Vuarus and Phoenix, her determination a blazing ember that refused to be extinguished.

Vuarus, the precursor of her captivity, emitted a sinister chuckle that rippled through the air like the echo of a demonic incantation. He gestured with a mocking flourish towards a nearby chair. "There you go, my dear. A throne fit for a captive guest of honor."

With a heart racing like a wild stallion, Keisha reluctantly complied, taking her seat with a defiant chin uplifted. She knew all too well that she occupied a precarious perch, surrounded by enemies who delighted in her torment. Yet, she harbored no intention of revealing weakness, denying them the satisfaction they so eagerly sought.

Amidst the discordant symphony of laughter and revelry that swirled around her, Keisha's thoughts raced with genuine purpose. She knew, deep within the core of her being, that she must find a pathway to escape the clutches of the Dominion to be reunited with Ong, her beloved. With each fleeting moment, her determination surged, her resolve to combat the encroaching darkness that hungered for her unwavering and unyielding.

As the night's festivities continued to unfurl like a tapestry of shadows and secrets, Keisha's vigilant gaze remained steadfastly affixed to the sinister recesses of the room. Her agile mind worked tirelessly, weaving threads of strategy and hope into the darkest tapestry, a testament to her indomitable spirit in the face of hostility.

Phoenix's cruel grin stretched wider, revealing a malevolence piercing the air as he drew near Keisha. His voice, a serpent's hiss, dripped with the venom of his intent. "You see, my dear, we have fashioned a unique abode just for you—a subterranean cell etched with ancient runes, carefully crafted to imprison your magic and shatter your spirit."

Vuarus's laughter resonated through the grand hall in unholy harmony, its eerie echoes reverberating off the cavernous walls. "A bleak, lightless abyss, where even the faintest glimmer of illumination would dare not intrude. A desolate sanctuary, wherein the only company you shall know is your desolation."

Like a captive bird, Keisha's heart fluttered in her chest as their words pressed upon her, the grim reality of her impending confinement descending like a shadowed curtain. A shiver trailed down her spine as she envisaged the icy, suffocating void that awaited her in that subterranean dungeon.

Phoenix's eyes gleamed with a sadistic amusement that sent shivers through the very marrow of her bones. He continued, each word a chilling incantation. "To heighten your stay, we have imbued the cell with the essence of the Abyss itself. Prepare yourself for a tapestry of... intriguing visions as you languish below."

Vuarus, leaning closer, his breath a spectral chill against her ear, whispered with cruel intimacy, "And as for any notions of escape, my dear, do abandon them. The cell is ensorcelled, fortified by enchantments that would confound even the most cunning of trackers. If you manage to find it, your sleep will be haunted by these visions, and thus, you shall never know a moment's peace."

Keisha's hands clenched into unyielding fists, her nails sinking into her palms as she waged a silent battle to preserve her composure. She was resolved—resolute in her determination not to allow her tormentors to glimpse the trembling heart beneath her stoic facade.

Amidst the suffocating shroud of their laughter, Keisha's gaze remained steadfast, an unbroken beacon of defiance. Her mind churned ceaselessly, formulating plans of escape, and clinging to the indomitable strength of her bond with Ong. Their reunion was a certainty she clung to, a light in the darkest of dungeons.

The encroaching darkness seemed to press in, a relentless adversary intent on smothering her hope. Yet, within the depths of Keisha's spirit, an unquenchable flame blazed a testament to her unyielding resolve. No matter how far into the abyss they sought to plunge her, she vowed to rise above, to defy the looming shadows that hungered to trap her.

Keisha's voice pierced the frigid air with unwavering defiance, a proclamation of her unbroken spirit. "No matter your cruelty, my spirit shall remain unbroken."

Vuarus, turning to Phoenix, wore a sinister smirk, his eyes glittering with wicked intent. "How shall you respond, dear brother?"

Phoenix's laughter, as chilling as the breath of the abyss, reverberated once more. He closed the distance between himself and Keisha, his fingers gripping her chin, forcing her to meet his evil gaze. "Ah, such determination," he mused, a cruel glint in his eyes. "I sincerely hope we don't break you, not out of concern for your strength, but rather because I relish the torment you shall endure before we offer you as a sacrifice to the insatiable hunger of the Abyss."

Keisha's jaw remained resolutely clenched, her steely gaze locked onto Phoenix's evil eyes, refusing to betray even a hint of fear. She was acutely aware of their sadistic desire—to witness her spirit crumble beneath the weight of their cruelty. Yet, she harbored an unwavering determination, a vow etched in the core of her being. No matter the horrors they concocted, she would endure, resist, and stand as a testament to unyielding defiance.

Amidst the raucous celebration, enveloped by the gloating members of the Abyssal Dominion, Keisha's resolve blazed brighter than the torches that illuminated their vile revelry. She refused to permit the encroaching darkness to consume her. Instead, she kindled the fires of resistance, anchoring herself in the hope of escape and the promise of reuniting with Ong.

Vuarus's sardonic smirk deepened, and his words dripped with venomous satisfaction as he redirected his attention to Keisha. "Is it not a peculiar twist of fate, my dear? Your father met his demise within the Abyss, and now, you shall tread the same path. However, the distinction is stark. He found release in death, while you shall endure eternal torment—a poetic irony, would you not agree?"

He circled her like a prowling predator, his gaze locked onto her, relishing her distress like a sumptuous feast. "You may harbor hopes of rescue from your beloved Ong or your Eladrin allies, but they would need to divulge the location of their concealed sanctuary. We both know they would never do that. Hence, my dear, acquaint yourself with the notion that our hospitality shall endure for an extended sojourn."

Keisha's fists remained clenched at her sides, her resolve unyielding, even as Vuarus's cruel taunts cut close to the bone. She drew strength from the memory of her father, his selfless sacrifice etched into her soul. She met Vuarus's gaze with unwavering determination. "I shall not beg for mercy nor yield to your threats. Torment me as you will, but my spirit shall remain unbroken."

Vuarus's laughter, chilling as the breath of the Abyss, reverberated through the chamber, its sinister cadence echoing eternally within the obsidian shadows. "Oh, my dear, we shall see. True darkness thrives not in the absence of light but in the relentless persistence of despair. And that, dear Keisha, is a force that even your most cherished memories and hopes may not shield you from."

Keisha's jaw remained locked in an unyielding vice. Her unwavering resolve was a beacon of defiance amidst the encroaching darkness. She clung to the belief that, somehow, she would uncover the path to resist, endure, and break free from this suffocating abyss.

Lyra's voice, dripping with perverse amusement, sliced through the oppressive atmosphere like a poisoned dagger. "Oh, Keisha, you remain blissfully unaware of the horrors we have meticulously crafted for you. The cell we have designed is a masterpiece of evil enchantment. It shall sever your bonds with all you hold dear – your comrades, your beloved husband, and even the essence of nature coursing through your elven veins."

Keisha's eyes blazed with an indomitable defiance as she locked her gaze onto Lyra's cold, calculating eyes. "You may endeavor to sever me from the world, but you shall never break my spirit. I shall unearth a way to resist, endure, and conquer each torment you hurl upon me."

Lyra's chuckle, laced with condescension, echoed through the chamber like a haunting melody. "How noble of you to harbor such beliefs. However, let me assure you we wield centuries of expertise in breaking spirits, shattering wills, and plunging souls into the gaping maw of despair. Your determination, dear Keisha, shall crumble before the might of our malevolent mastery."

Keisha's heart thundered within her chest, a fierce storm of anger and determination raging. She was resolute, an unbreakable bastion despite their evil designs. No matter the depths to which their cruelty sank, she clung to the cherished memories of her loved ones, the unshakable bond she shared with Ong, and the unyielding power of her connection to nature. In the suffocating abyss that threatened to engulf her, she remained steadfast, her spirit aflame with the unwavering belief that she would summon a guiding light.

Qellaun, sinister and evil, approached Keisha, his smile a grotesque mockery, his eyes gleaming with malice and sadistic satisfaction. "You may cling to the fragile hope that your precious Ong will mount a heroic rescue, but allow me to enlighten you, my dear. He shall not find you. The cell we meticulously fashioned is a concealment and arcane artistry masterpiece. Even if he were to breach the fortress's defenses, the cell's location shall forever elude his grasp."

Keisha's unyielding gaze met Qellaun's, a fierce determination blazing within her eyes. "You underestimate the power of love and the indomitable strength of our bond. Ong will embark on an unrelenting quest to find me, and he shall not rest until he has unearthed a path to liberate me from your clutches."

Qellaun's laughter, cold and cruel, reverberated through the chamber, a dissonant symphony that chilled to the bone. "Love, my dear, is a feeble ember, easily smothered by the encroaching darkness that now envelops you," he taunted, his voice laced with mockery. "A sentiment easily dismissed, as your mother once demonstrated."

Keisha's heart sank at the mention of her mother, an Eladrin archer who had, in her pursuit of vengeance against those who had taken Keisha's father from her, abandoned her daughter. It was a wound that had festered for years, and now, Vuarus's words cut like salt upon it.

"And as for your dear Ong," Qellaun continued, his tone dripping with spite, "even if he infiltrates the heart of our fortress by some chance, the cell's insidious magic shall veil its existence from his senses. He shall be adrift, and you shall remain trapped in this realm of eternal torment." Keisha's fists clenched with a tenacity born of defiance, a resolute bulwark against the encroaching despair that sought to consume her. She would not yield to their cruel taunts; her spirit remained unbroken. No matter how dire the circumstances grew, she clung steadfastly to hope, a beacon amidst the encircling shadows that thirsted for her light.

As they neared a bland expanse of stone, dread welled within her as Vuarus began a chant in a language foreign to her comprehension. Suddenly, tendrils of inky energy wove themselves into the very essence of the stone, weaving intricate and sinister patterns. The air crackled with evil magic, casting sinister shivers down her spine.

Before them, the wall underwent a grotesque transformation as the final rune shimmered with an unholy luminescence. Keisha's heart sank as she beheld what lay beyond—a chilling portal to her impending captivity. The chamber that yawned before her was eerie and desolate, bathed in the pallid glow of an other-worldly luminescence. The atmosphere was heavy with an oppressive melancholy, as if the walls had absorbed the suffering of countless souls trapped within, and an unnatural cold, particularly biting for an elf, gripped the chamber in a frigid embrace.

Vuarus, with a cruel push, propelled her forward, her wrists still trapped by the evil cuffs of dark magic, while Phoenix, his grin twisted and malicious, followed suit. Keisha stumbled into the cell, her unbroken gaze fixed on the open doorway. It was as if the very energy of the runes etched into her clinging to her, forging chains that bound her irrevocably to the bleak destiny that awaited.

A sinister transformation took place in the dimly lit cell of Vuarus's evil design. The air grew heavy with dark magic as Vuarus raised his hands, conjuring arcane energies that swirled around the cell. Keisha, her once-vibrant magic brimming with life, felt an icy shiver crawl down her spine as the sinister sorcerer's spell took hold.

Vuarus's magic latched onto Keisha's own, like a predatory vine trapping its prey. As the spell settled in, it began its insidious work, siphoning away the very essence of Keisha's power. The first time she was thrust into this maleficent prison, her magic dwindled drastically, rendering her powerless against the sinister duo of Vuarus and Phoenix.

Unknown to Keisha, Vuarus secretly funneled the stolen magic into a malevolent rift, a direct conduit to the Abyss. It was a dark and hidden gambit that would further their nefarious designs and keep Keisha in the dark about her actual predicament. For now, her magic was stolen, her powers diminished, and the abyssal forces grew stronger by the day, all in the shadows of the Dread Spire.

"Now, my dear Keisha," Vuarus sneered, his voice dripping with contempt, "welcome to your new abode. A place where your magic shall wither, starved and unspent, and your indomitable spirit shall be ground to dust beneath our relentless heel."

The cuffs that once bound her, symbols of her helplessness, were now redundant. Her magic, the source of her strength, was the true captive, held hostage within the cell. And with each passing day in this accursed place, it weakened further, a stark reminder that time was no ally in this grim realm. The evil plot to drain her powers and channel them into the Abyss remained concealed from her, a sinister secret that only deepened her plight.

Keisha's fingers slipped up to caress the necklace that Ong had given her out of love, and she had never taken it off since then. She touched the circlet, which brought some relief to her even now. Unbeknownst to her, Phoenix's evil eyes had been fixated on the glimmering necklace. He summoned dark magic in a twisted act of spite, his fingers tingling with sinister energy. With a cruel flick of his hand, he shattered the beautiful circlet into three distinct pieces. As the necklace splintered, one of the gemstones popped out, rolling to the ground like a fallen star. Phoenix chuckled sinisterly, his voice dripping with malice.

"Such sentimentality," he sneered, watching Keisha's horrified expression. "I find it utterly distasteful."

As the silver circlet necklace lay in ruins before her, Keisha couldn't contain the rush of tears that welled up in her eyes. Her trembling fingers instinctively reached out, but nothing was left to hold onto. The symbol of her love for Ong, shattered and scattered like her hopes, left her heartbroken and vulnerable in her grim captivity. She wept, her sobs echoing in the cold, dark cell where she was imprisoned, the loss of the necklace magnifying the ache of separation from the man she loved more than anything in the world.

Vuarus, standing nearby, waved his hand subtly, directing the gemstone and the broken pieces to a specific location hidden along Keisha's future path as she remained imprisoned. Unbeknownst to Keisha, the remnants of the shattered necklace would become a critical clue in Ong's relentless search for her, a symbol of their love enduring even in the face of darkness.

Phoenix's laughter, a chilling symphony, reverberated through the suffocating silence as he added his taunting refrain, "Remember, my dear Keisha, there is no escape, no soul to heed your anguished cries, and no glimmer of hope for rescue. You are bound to us, an eternal captive, just as your beloved Ong failed to shield you from our grasp."

Keisha's heart drummed with frantic intensity as they turned away, the entrance melding seamlessly back into the unforgiving stone wall, leaving her trapped in unending darkness. Alone in the abyss, she waged a silent battle against tears, unwavering in her defiance and determined not to grant them the satisfaction of witnessing her fear. Her fingers instinctively reached for the necklace Ong had gifted her out of love—a necklace that no longer adorned her neck, shattered into pieces by Phoenix. She surveyed the frigid, desolate cell that would be her solitary realm.

Amid the vast sea of despair, a flicker of determination ignited within her. She couldn't permit herself to be broken after enduring all she had. She clung fiercely to her inner resolve, a defiance that blazed like a bed of witnessing her defeat.

With a deep, steadying breath, Keisha cast her gaze about the confines of her bleak chamber, her eyes locking onto the etched runes that adorned the walls. These runes exuded a sinister energy, a testament to the malevolent artistry of her captors. Yet, she refused to allow them to shackle her spirit. Somewhere within the intricate web of these symbols, there had to be a vulnerability, a weakness that might pave the path to her escape.

Seated upon the unyielding coldness of the stone floor, Keisha turned her unwavering focus to the runes, her mind racing with thoughts of liberation. Whatever dire fate the Abyssal Dominion had contrived for her, she was steadfast in her resolve to defy their expectations.

She was no helpless pawn; she was a warrior, a wife, and a guardian of nature. No matter how daunting the shadows appeared, she would unearth the means to illuminate them and defy her captors.

Within the oppressive hush of her cell, Keisha's ironclad resolve began to show its first cracks.

The weight of her situation, the crushing isolation, and the unrelenting darkness bore down upon her, suffocating her like a heavy shroud. She struggled to hold back the tears, to maintain her unyielding strength, but the unsettling specter of dark minions lurking in the corners shattered her composure.

Her tears flowed freely, mingling with the all-encompassing despair that trapped her. The visions, born of her fears and doubts, twisted and writhed around her, a cruel chorus of mockery and taunts. Amidst this torrent of anguish, a fragile whisper escaped her trembling lips, carried forth on the breath of her plea.

"Ong, please..."

The name hung in the still, chilly air, a desperate plea pulsating with the depth of her love, fear, and boundless desperation. In that fleeting moment of vulnerability, her once unyielding strength lay stripped away, leaving only a profound ache that resonated within her heart.

As the oppressive darkness closed in, Keisha clung tenaciously to that whispered invocation—a small yet potent declaration of her enduring love and unwavering determination to find her way back to the light, no matter the formidable challenges ahead.

In a realm distant and detached from the abyss that held Keisha captive, Ong felt a faint, distant echo—a thread of connection that reached out and tugged at his heart. He could not discern whether it was a figment of his imagination or something more profound. Still, he clung to it with a fierce determination, for it served as a lifeline of hope amidst the encroaching shadows that threatened to consume them all.

Tears welled in Ong's eyes, his heart heavy with the weight of Keisha's distant plea. His voice trembled as he called out to the heavens and the loyal companion who had stood by his side throughout their journey.

"Pumpkin, my faithful friend," he whispered, his voice quivering. "We must find her. We must bring her back to the light."

Chapter 34

Shadows Unveiled: The Search Begins

In the heart of the mystical realm of E'vahona, Ong, a figure of unwavering resolve, stood in the presence of Lord Karrenen, his visage bearing the indelible mark of determination. His fingers, clenched into taut fists, betrayed the intensity of his emotions while he summoned the essence of courage with a profound inhalation before addressing his esteemed lord.

Around them, E'vahona's ethereal beauty unfolded like a living tapestry. Trees with silver-barked trunks reached toward a shimmering canopy of leaves that seemed to sing in a breeze only they could perceive. The air carried the faint scent of blossoms that glowed with an otherworldly radiance, their petals casting a gentle, multi-hued rain upon the land.

"I must embark upon a quest to locate her, Lord Karrenen," Ong declared, his voice a steadying force amid the turbulent sea of his apprehensions. "I cannot bear to languish idly while she remains ensnared in their sinister clutches."

Lord Karrenen, a sage of empathy and caution, regarded Ong with compassion and prudent concern. His eyes mirrored the wisdom of ages, and his presence drew strength from the very essence of E'vahona itself. "Indeed, Ong," he responded, his words measured like a tapestry woven with wisdom. "Your love for Keisha is evident but heed me well: Charging recklessly into peril will not serve her nor you. It might entangle you further within the treacherous web."

A ripple of tension traversed Ong's chiseled jawline, and for a fleeting moment, he averted his gaze, grappling with the internal turmoil that raged within. He knew that Lord Karrenen spoke truths, but the unbearable image of Keisha's suffering refused to be exorcised from his thoughts. The forest around them seemed to hold its breath, as if waiting for Ong's decision to resonate through the very heart of E'vahona.

"I cannot remain inactive," he whispered, his voice tinged with the desperation of a heart that refused to surrender.

Lord Karrenen extended a steadying hand, resting it reassuringly upon Ong's sturdy shoulder. The touch conveyed physical comfort and a deep understanding of Ong's torment. "I empathize with the storm of emotions within you," he murmured. "Yet, let us not forget that Keisha possesses a spirit as unyielding as your own. To safeguard her, we must tread this difficult path with wisdom and strategy."

Ong, his gaze returning to Lord Karrenen's with an unwavering intensity, pledged his solemn resolve. The forest exhaled a collective sigh of recognition, leaves rustling in quiet approval. "I shall start by gathering intelligence, seeking the faintest trace of her existence," he declared firmly. "But I vow, Lord Karrenen, that Keisha shall not suffer a moment longer than fate dictates."

A nod of solemn agreement passed between them, a silent pact etched in the annals of their shared purpose. The forest, in its timeless wisdom, bore witness to their commitment. "Your passion shall be your guiding star, Ong," Lord Karrenen affirmed. "In this undertaking, you shall not walk alone."

Ong, infused with gratitude and fortified by his newfound determination, nodded in acknowledgment. In his heart, an unbreakable promise was forged. He would unearth the whereabouts of Keisha, employing cunning and caution, for they ventured into enchantment where recklessness courted peril and wisdom was the most faithful ally.

Ong's strides carried a sense of unwavering purpose as he ventured once more into the embrace of Emberwood Forest. The memories that clung to this place were a poignant blend of beauty and sorrow, the forest's splendor forever tainted by the evil shadows that had taken root. The ancient trees loomed overhead like sentinels, their branches adorned with leaves that whispered secrets of the past.

At his side, Pumpkin, his loyal companion, moved with a grace that belied her predatory instincts, her every sense finely tuned to the lurking perils of their surroundings. Her obsidian fur rippled with an almost supernatural sheen, absorbing and reflecting the dappled sunlight that filtered through the canopy.

As they arrived at the clearing where the ominous altar had once loomed, Ong's heart sank like an anchor in despair. The spot that had once harbored a sinister artifact now lay barren, devoid of any vestige of its infamous past. His brow furrowed with frustration, his eyes scanning the ground for any signs of recent disturbance.

"Pumpkin," he murmured, his voice laced with a palpable sense of disappointment that seemed to echo around them. "It's as if they've obliterated all traces of their presence here."

A low, rumbling growl emanated from the black panther, her green eyes shimmering with shared frustration and an unyielding determination. She gently nuzzled Ong's hand, a silent reassurance that together, they would uncover an alternative path.

Ong released a weary sigh, his fingers running through his tousled hair in exasperation. He had hoped to discover some semblance of a clue, a faint whisper of the Abyssal Dominion's nefarious machinations or a cryptic breadcrumb leading to Keisha's whereabouts. Yet, as he stood there, it became painfully evident that their elusive foes possessed a mastery of evasion, perpetually staying one step ahead, leaving no trace for him to follow.

With a heart as heavy as the ancient oaks surrounding him, Ong turned away from the lonely clearing, his loyal feline companion trailing close behind. Surrender was not an option; Keisha's life hung in precarious balance, suspended in the clutches of malevolence. He persevered until he uncovered the elusive trail that would lead him to Keisha and usher her back to the sanctuary of safety. With its silent wisdom, the forest seemed to whisper that it would aid him in his quest, its ancient spirits standing vigilant against the encroaching darkness.

Vuarus and Phoenix, the sinister architects of darkness, stood within the heart of their shadowy sanctum, their eyes fixed upon a scrying mirror that unraveled the unfolding scene in Emberwood Forest. Like shadowy specters, they observed Ong's mounting frustration as he scoured the land for any vestiges of the once-ominous altar that had cradled their malevolent artifact.

The mirror's surface seemed to ripple with malefic intent as it displayed Ong's determined quest. Phoenix couldn't help but release a low, evil chuckle, his lips twisting into a sarcastic smirk. "Behold him, Vuarus," he taunted, reveling in a newfound overconfidence. "So fervently desperate to uncover a clue, yet blissfully unaware that we are the puppeteers, forever manipulating the strings of fate."

Vuarus, his eyes gleaming with evil delight, nodded in macabre accord. "Indeed, my dear friend," he whispered, savoring the taste of impending victory. "He dances upon our chessboard, a pawn unknowing."

As Ong's silhouette grew smaller in the distance, Vuarus returned to the sinister mirror. "The altar may have vanished, but the seeds of confusion and doubt it sowed in his heart remain," he murmured, his voice dripping with vicious satisfaction. "He shall question every stride he takes, haunted by uncertainty."

Phoenix, an air of self-assuredness about him, leaned casually against a darkened table, his arms folded in an arrogant display. "Precisely our intention. His desperation will shroud his judgment, and in his frenzy, he shall stumble into grievous errors."

Vuarus's lips contorted into a sinister, triumphant smile. "Errors that shall inexorably draw him deeper into the abyss of despair. And when he ultimately unravels the truth, it shall be a revelation far too late."

Phoenix's eyes gleamed with a sinister fervor. "He shall pay for his boldness, for defying us, for everything he's done to us."

Vuarus, his mind plotting dark stratagems, spoke with a contemplative air. "But for the present, let us savor his mounting frustration. Let him comb the world from zenith to nadir while we, like vipers in the shadows, tighten our grip upon Keisha."

Phoenix's grin widened, sinister and predatory. "Indeed, and when the celestial clock strikes the opportune hour, we shall execute our moves with such precision that Ong shall remain utterly bewildered."

As the scrying mirror continued to reveal Ong's unwavering search, Vuarus and Phoenix exchanged a chilling, evil laugh. The intricate web of deceit they had woven ensnared Ong, and he unknowingly struggled to break free while they remained concealed in the darkest recesses, orchestrating his downfall. The echoes of their malevolent laughter seemed to reverberate through the very fabric of their dark domain, a haunting reminder of the impending darkness that loomed over all.

Within the heart of her dim, forlorn cell, Keisha sat upon the frigid stone floor, her very being quaking with an all-consuming terror. The sheer isolation of her confinement seeped into her bones, an oppressive stillness that stifled her breath. The only respite from this desolation came in soft, eerie whispers that seemed to emanate from the walls, a cruel reminder of the malevolent evil surrounding her. In the cruel tapestry of the Abyssal Dominion's dark machinations, these were the moments when their insidious mind games truly began to take their toll.

Before her eyes, apparitional visions danced, a nightmarish tableau of twisted memories from her past and the grotesque phantoms of her present fears. She was forced to witness her father's death, the harrowing scene unfolding in agonizing detail—the flames devouring him, the desolation etched upon his anguished countenance. The searing heat of the inferno enveloped her, choking smoke filling her lungs as she futilely sought to rescue him.

Yet, these tormenting visions showed no mercy, unfurling before her like a relentless storm. The faces of cherished friends and loved ones morphed grotesquely into mocking, accusing specters. Her homeland now languished in the tenacious grasp of shadow and decay, every detail etching itself into her soul. In the heart of this malevolent reverie, she stood alone, a solitary figure in a world bereft of vitality and hope.

Clutching her head in agony, her eyes squeezed shut to escape the cruel torment that threatened to consume her. She whispered words of defiance, struggling to remind herself that these were but illusory phantasms, her spirit more significant than the malevolent projections. Yet, these apparitions persisted, burrowing their insidious roots into her besieged mind.

Amidst the cacophony of her fractured thoughts, a familiar, soothing voice broke through the darkness—her father's say, a beacon of solace and strength. "Stay resolute, my beloved daughter. Within you lies the power to defeat this abyss."

Tears welled up in Keisha's eyes, the lifeline of her father's words a fragile thread of hope amidst the abyss of despair. But the shadows pressed in, smothering her, submerging her in a chilling sea of dread and remorse.

In her feeble state, Keisha's whispers devolved into anguished sobs. She curled into a pitiful ball upon the frigid stone, her fingers clawing at the unforgiving floor as if attempting to tether herself to reality. The ceaseless deluge of visions showed no mercy, each cruel tableau a stark reminder of her profound vulnerabilities.

Unbeknownst to Keisha, the Abyssal Dominion reveled in her torment, their sinister laughter reverberating through the labyrinthine corridors of her fragile psyche. They bore witness as her spirit wavered, as her resilience crumbled beneath the weight of their relentless torment. With each tear she shed, with every instant of despair, they chalked up another sinister triumph in their ruthless game of darkness and anguish.

While Ong's unyielding resolve guided him back to the enigmatic altar nestled within Emberwood Forest, a clandestine assembly unfolded in the concealed sanctuaries of the Hidden Isles. Kimras, the venerable gold dragon and leader of the dragons' council, addressed his kin with a sense of urgency deep within their ancient lair's core.

"Drakonshaar ala Hidden Isles," Kimras began, his draconic words reverberating through the immense cavern, "Keisha ui etched irsa wer bekiwilti chambers di hesi gra'kuli." (Dragons of the Hidden Isles, Keisha is etched within the deepest chambers of our hearts.) "Jaciv slathalina valiantly alongside udoka, kagh jaka, jaciv languishes persvek wer garnilti di straits." (She fought valiantly alongside us and now languishes in dire straits.)

The dragons, their immense forms exuding an aura of majestic attention, listened with rapt intensity, their draconic senses acutely attuned to the profound concern threaded through Kimras' tone. In a voice that resonated with solemn determination, Kimras pressed on, "Wer grip di wer dargru dominion extends coita sinister vrelveli grover kagh kous, jashir jacioniv zi whaisinw mrith asta wielga aproploklexi." (The grip of the Abyssal Dominion spreads its sinister talons far and wide, concealing her very presence with their fell sorceries.) "Oli yth zklaen ti remain passive observers." (But we mustn't remain passive observers.) "Yth nishka unite hesi arcaniktok prowess kagh marshal hesi resources ekess shirr wer yothi'haic batobot shroud jacioniv wyogale." (We shall unite our magical prowess and marshal our resources to rend the veils that shroud her location."

A silent, collective understanding passed among the dragons, their influential minds forging a connection with their leader's unspoken thoughts. Kimras, his eyes gleaming with unwavering resolve, acknowledged their silent accord with a nod. "Si mi familiar di hesi formidable relekihl, kagh vuarus vraexic onkquo jedarkic." (I am familiar with our formidable challenge, and Vuarus wields potent forces.) "Nevertheless, yth re indebted ekess Keisha ui|ulph unwavering navnik, kagh yth nishka jaseve thric inhelk unturned." (Nevertheless, we are obligated to Keisha's steadfast spirit, and we shall leave no stone unturned.)"The dragons rumbled in unanimous agreement, the resonance of their collective determination manifesting like an ethereal tempest. They grasped the gravity of the situation and were poised to contribute their mystical might to the cause. Kimras extended his grand wings, and, at last, he ascended, his voice resounding like a celestial proclamation.

"Origato coi qe vucat batobot hesi janik emerges de hesi unity." (Let it be known that our might emerges from our unity.) "Yth nishka focus hesi arcanik, interweaving coi mrith ir voga ui|ulph merkran, endeavoring ekess pierce wer vuirash shroud batobot jashic Keisha." (We shall focus our magic, interweaving it with one another's essence, endeavoring to pierce the obsidian shroud that conceals Keisha.) "Ulnaus, yth nishka scour wer grikori, kagh persvek tirir zyak, yth nishka tiichi wer unbreakable tonoparic yth tepoha akuecha." (Together, we shall scour the realms, and in doing so, we shall honor the unbreakable bonds we've forged.)

As the dragons raised their noble heads and allowed their magic to intertwine in a breathtaking display of radiant light and formidable power, their unified call reverberated through the cosmos. With every heartbeat, their determination swelled, a testament to their unwavering bond with Keisha and their steadfast commitment to her deliverance from the clutches of darkness. Kimras, their stalwart leader, bore a weight of concern that mirrored the stormy skies above, for Keisha was more than a comrade—she was their cherished friend, and her peril ignited a fire within their mighty hearts that would not be quenched until she was reclaimed from the abyss.

"Within the dim and ominous recesses of the Dread Spire, Zylron, a sinister dragon cloaked in shadows, stood amidst the gathering of the Abyssal Dominion. Like twin shards of obsidian, his eyes flickered with an unease that reverberated through the marrow of his being. Amidst the din of the ongoing celebration that surged around them, he leaned in, his voice a shrouded whisper that bore the gravity of caution.

"Listen well, my brethren," Zylron commenced, his utterance a subdued murmur that resonated with the weight of their clandestine discourse. "The forces of light, the benevolent dragons, possess strength beyond reckoning and an unwavering connection to Keisha, our prized captive. We must acknowledge the looming threat they present."

His compatriots exchanged wary glances, the veneer of glee melting away to unveil the grave expressions etched upon their faces. Nearby, Vuarus, an enigma shrouded in malevolence, quirked an eyebrow in contemplative intrigue. Zylron pressed on, his words laden with somber intent.

"We dare not underestimate their resolve nor their capacity for intervention," he admonished, his voice now carrying an air of grim sobriety. "Our salvation lies in sowing the seeds of discord amongst them, guiding them along divergent paths that fragment their efforts to locate our precious prize."

In the chill of the Dread Spire's confines, the sinister council of the Abyssal Dominion forged a nefarious plan designed to thwart the inevitable intervention of the benevolent dragons. Shadows deepened, and malevolent whispers took flight, a testament to their unwavering commitment to maintaining their ironclad grip on Keisha, even as the forces of light plotted her salvation.

An evil smile tugged at the corner of Vuarus' lips, the embodiment of cunning. "Ah, Zylron, your insight is as sharp as obsidian. Distraction, indeed, is a potent weapon." He turned to the sinister assembly, his gaze a commanding force. "Let us choreograph a symphony of chaos, a cacophony of discord, to divert their vigilant eyes away from our most treasured possession. We shall keep them entangled in a web of uncertainty, sapping their strength across fragmented fronts."

Zylron, the precursor of caution, offered a solemn nod. "Precisely," he affirmed. "And regarding our defenses, Vuarus, let us fortify the wards surrounding the captive's cell. We dare not afford even the slightest lapse or misjudgment. Her stolen magic is a potential bane, a weapon they could wield against us."

In the shadowed heart of their dark domain, the council of the Abyssal Dominion conspired with whispered promises of deception and guile, their sinister intentions unfurling like the inky tendrils of an abyss. With a calculated blend of strategy and sorcery, they would confront the impending storm of light and resistance, determined to safeguard their evil dominion and the fragile threads that bound them to their captive, Keisha.

Vuarus' eyes gleamed with approval, acknowledging Zylron's insight. "You're right, Zylron. We can't afford any chinks in our defenses. "Let us strengthen the barriers and ensure her powers are siphoned away to the Abyss, leaving her powerless within the cell." He turned to the others. "Spread the word; make sure this is implemented immediately."

"As Lyra descended into the dimly lit chamber where Keisha was imprisoned, a sinister anticipation coursed through her veins. She reveled in the vulnerability of her captive, her malicious intent palpable in every calculated step she took. The air grew heavy with the weight of spite as she approached Keisha, her presence casting an ominous shadow over the room. When she spoke, her voice dripped with cruel satisfaction."

"Ah, dear Keisha," Lyra sneered, her words a venomous caress. "How does it feel to be at the mercy of the Abyssal Dominion? To have your light extinguished and your spirit broken?"

Keisha, though weakened by her captivity, met Lyra's gaze with a defiant glimmer in her eyes. She refused to show weakness in the face of her tormentor, even as Lyra circled her like a predator toying with its prey.

Lyra's laughter, a chilling symphony of cruelty, echoed through the cell. She raised her hand, fingers crackling with dark energy, and with an evil gesture, she sent a surge of pain coursing through Keisha's body. The captive elf gasped in agony, but she refused to cry out, her spirit unbroken.

As the torment continued, Keisha's resolve remained unshaken. She clung to the memories of her loved ones and the promise of freedom, determined to defy her captors at every turn. The battle of wills between the captive and her tormentor raged on, a testament to the strength of the light that refused to be extinguished in the heart of darkness.

Lyra's cruel words and malevolent presence hung like a dark cloud over Keisha's confinement. Each day in the Abyssal Dominion's grasp brought new trials and torments. Still, Keisha clung to her unyielding spirit and the memories of her loved ones like a lifeline in the suffocating darkness.

Vuarus, watching from the shadows, observed the torment with a cold satisfaction. He knew the Abyssal Dominion had forged Keisha into a formidable adversary in their relentless pursuit of power. Yet, they were determined to break her, to extinguish the spark of resistance that still burned within her.

As the days turned into weeks, Keisha's isolation and the relentless barrage of torment began to take a toll on her physical and emotional well-being. Her once-vibrant spirit felt like the unending cruelty of her captors was slowly wearing it down. Yet, she refused to succumb to despair, drawing strength from the love and memories that anchored her.

Vuarus and the Abyssal Dominion continued plotting and scheming in the shadows, their evil intentions shrouding in darkness. They believed they could break her and extinguish the light within her. Still, Keisha's spirit remained unbroken, a testament to the resilience of the Eladrin and the power of love and determination.

The battle between Keisha and her tormentors raged on, a clash of wills determining her fate. In the heart of the abyss, a flicker of hope remained a small but unyielding light that refused to be extinguished, a light that burned with the promise of freedom and the strength to defy the darkness.

"Keisha felt the insidious drain on her magic, like a relentless tide pulling her power away. It was as if an unseen force was siphoning her essence, leaving her feeling increasingly powerless and vulnerable within the confines of her dark prison."

The realization struck her with a profound sense of dread. Not only were they tormenting her, but they were also dismantling the very source of her strength and connection to her father's legacy. The evil spell cast by Vuarus had become an instrument designed to sever her ties to the magic that had once been her ally and a part of her very identity.

Despite the overwhelming darkness that surrounded her, Keisha's spirit remained unbroken. She knew that her magic reflected her inner strength, and she would fight to retain it, even as the Abyssal Dominion sought to drain it from her. The battle for her freedom had taken a sinister turn, but Keisha was determined to defy the odds and emerge victorious, holding onto the flicker of hope that still burned within her.

Keisha's defiance burned brighter than ever as she faced the daunting challenge of the cursed cuffs that drained her magic. The fear that had briefly gripped her heart gave way to a steely resolve. She refused to be a helpless victim in this vicious game orchestrated by the Abyssal Dominion. Instead, she embraced her inner warrior, drawing on her resilience and strength.

With every breath, she focused her thoughts, determined to find a way to resist the relentless siphoning of her magic. Her father's legacy, her connection to the essence of nature, and her indomitable spirit were sources of power that couldn't be quickly extinguished. She knew there was a glimmer of hope even in the darkest times and would hold onto it with unwavering determination.

As the oppressive weight of the evil spell threatened to smother her abilities, Keisha's inner fire burned brighter, a beacon of resistance against the encroaching darkness. She was ready to face whatever challenges lay ahead, for she was a warrior, and warriors didn't surrender to despair. Within the dimly lit chamber of despair, Vuarus took a deliberate step back, his eyes fixating upon Keisha's with a chilling blend of amusement and malevolence. His gaze was like icy tendrils that crept through the freezing air, settling upon her like a shroud of darkness. "And now, my dear Phoenix," he mused, addressing his sinister ally, "shall we indulge her longing and amplify her suffering?"

Phoenix's grin widened, his eyes ablaze with a sinister ardor that mirrored the fires of damnation itself. The room seemed darkened as if the shadows were drawn to his malice. "Indeed," he responded, his voice dripping with a macabre exhilaration that hung heavy in the stifling atmosphere. "Let her taste the bitter remnants of her darkest memories—the anguish of irreplaceable loss, the haunting specter of despair, and the inescapable realization that her struggles are but a futile wisp in the face of our darkness."

Keisha's heart raced as the dreadful truth crystallized before her. The torment she had already endured had been excruciating, but now they were poised to push her to the precipice. It felt as though the very walls of the chamber were closing in, delving into the abyss of her psyche to unearth her most agonizing memories. The room seemed to pulse with evil energy, like a living entity conspiring with her captors to wield her past against her.

Phoenix leaned in closer to Keisha, his voice a venomous whisper that dripped with malice. As his words hung in the dimly lit chamber, the air thickened with malevolence. "You see, dear Keisha," he hissed, his breath cold against her ear, "your cherished Ong is a frail human. Humans, as history has shown, are fleeting and fickle creatures. They tire easily, especially when burdened by the darkness that has eclipsed his life. It's only a matter of time before he abandons his futile search for you and seeks solace in the arms of another. Perhaps someone prettier, someone unencumbered by the shadow of your existence." An evil chuckle escaped his lips, a chilling sound reverberating through the oppressive silence. His eyes fixated on Keisha's anguished countenance. "And then, my dear, what will become of your forlorn hopes?"

As Phoenix and Vuarus turned and departed from the cell, their sinister laughter lingered like a noxious aftertaste, a cruel reminder of the torment they reveled in inflicting. In their wake, the oppressive shadows pressed in, enveloping Keisha in a suffocating shroud. The torment resumed, and an unrelenting storm swirled before her eyes like a nightmarish tapestry.

Before her, the faces of lost loved ones materialized, their ethereal visages a haunting specter of her past. She felt the searing sting of past failures, the cruel lash of moments scarred by heartbreak and despair. Each memory carved anew, a fresh wound that bled the agony of her suffering, an unending reminder of her unyielding pain.

Keisha's jaw clenched with a determined resolve as she fought valiantly against the relentless emotions. The encroaching darkness sought to engulf her, to submerge her in an abyss of agony and despair, but she remained resolute. She pushed back with every fiber of her being, summoning the memories of hope, love, and unwavering determination that had carried her through even the most harrowing trials.

As the tormenting visions persisted, Keisha drew upon her inner well of strength, adamantly refusing to let them shatter her indomitable spirit. She declined to grant Phoenix and Vuarus the satisfaction of witnessing her crumble. At her core, she was a warrior, a fighter who would endure. As long as a glimmer of light flickered within her, she passionately believed she could conquer even the darkest torments.

Yet, the visions weighed upon her heart, a relentless torrent that threatened to drown her resolve. She clung desperately to her inner strength, struggling to defy the encroaching darkness that sought to consume her. The cruel words of her captors echoed incessantly in her ears, and the mere mention of Ong, her beloved husband, struck a painful chord deep within her.

A rush of doubt surged through Keisha's soul, a fear that Phoenix's sinister words held a sliver of truth. Tears welled up in her eyes, her breath trembling in the face of her inner turmoil. "Ong," she whispered, her voice a fragile thread amidst the chaos of her besieged thoughts. His name stood as a lifeline, a connection to the light in her heart. With clenched fists, she struggled to refocus on her love for Ong, striving to find the inner strength necessary to combat the encroaching doubts that threatened to overwhelm her.

As Ong distanced himself from where the sinister altar had once loomed, an undercurrent of frustration surged within him like a relentless tide. He glanced downward, meeting Pumpkin's earnest gaze, her bright eyes attuned to the turbulence coursing through his veins. Kneeling beside his loyal companion, he tenderly caressed her fur, his touch a complex symphony of solace and melancholy.

Once a place of mysterious wonder, the forest around them now felt like a labyrinth of shadows and unanswered questions. Ong's heart ached with the absence of Keisha's guiding presence, her light no longer illuminating the path ahead. But he refused to succumb to despair, drawing strength from the memories of their love and the unwavering loyalty of his furry friend. "Thank you, girl," he murmured, his voice reflecting the emotions swirling within. "You and Keisha, you've been my family. We're not giving up, Pumpkin. I'll scour every inch of this forest, leaving no stone unturned for even the faintest clue." His fingers tightened around her fur, drawing strength from their bond.

Pumpkin nuzzled against him, a silent pledge of unwavering support that carved a small, bittersweet smile upon Ong's lips. Their connection, born of love and shared trials, was a beacon in the encroaching darkness. He harbored no illusions about the formidable challenges ahead, but his determination burned unyielding. With a resolute nod, he rose to his feet, a rekindled resolve shining in his eyes. Hand in paw with Pumpkin, he embarked on his relentless quest, determined to uncover any fragment of hope that might guide him back to his beloved wife.

Together, they ventured deeper into the enigmatic heart of Emberwood Forest, where the trees whispered ancient secrets, and the very earth held the key to Keisha's fate. Ong's unwavering love and Pumpkin's loyal companionship became their most potent weapons in uncertainty and darkness, forging a bond that would withstand even the darkest trials.

Chapter 35

Shadows Unveiled: Ong's Pursuit-Unraveling the Shadows

Ong's heart pulsed with mounting frustration, an insidious beast gnawing at his soul as he limped away from the oppressive embrace of Emberwoods. The enigma of Keisha's disappearance clung to him like a relentless shadow, a weight that seemed to grow heavier with each futile step. Like a cunning specter, the Abyssal Dominion had woven an impenetrable cloak of secrecy around her, and it infuriated him to no end.

As he wandered through the labyrinthine woods, Ong's worry deepened, his mind a tumultuous sea of unanswered questions. How could the Abyssal Dominion, those dark sorcerers of the abyss, be so elusive, so maddeningly skilled at obscuring their tracks? He knew that his love, his precious Keisha, was trapped in a web of evil intrigue, and he could not bear the thought of her suffering in the clutches of those shadowy malefactors.

And then, as if guided by a flicker of inspiration from the cosmos, a revelation struck him with the force of a celestial lightning bolt. Fel Thalor, the ancient city of the Druchii, whispered in the annals of history as a place where secrets danced like phantoms in the moonlight. It was a den of treachery, where deceit was an art, and malevolence coursed through the very stones.

Ong's resolve ignited like a starburst in the night sky. Fel Thalor held the key to the puzzle that haunted him, the key to unraveling the tendrils of darkness that had ensnared Keisha. If anyone knew of the Abyssal Dominion's twisted machinations, it would be the residents of this accursed city, beings who had once reveled in the heart of shadows.

With newfound determination, Ong altered his course, his footsteps becoming a symphony of urgency and hope. Every heartbeat was a drumroll of desperation, driving him forward. Fel Thalor was no ordinary place; it was a tainted, malevolent essence that clung to the very air. As the ominous city loomed closer, its towering spires of obsidian, each one darkened by centuries of corruption, stretched skyward like fearsome sentinels of the abyss.

Stepping foot into the accursed city felt like an unholy descent into the depths of a waking nightmare. The air seemed to thicken with an unsettling tension, as if the very stones beneath his feet remembered, with haunting clarity, the countless atrocities whispered within the shadowed recesses of their walls. Ong ventured forth, his every sense primed to the point of hypersensitivity. It was a dangerous gambit, but he would wager his soul if that's what it took to rescue Keisha.

In Fel Thalor, the moonlight was spectral, casting eerie, elongated shadows that danced with malice. The city's architecture, once grand, now bore the scars of dark enchantments, with obsidian spires twisting like sinister talons into the night sky. Draped in shadowy robes, Sinister figures moved through the narrow alleys like wraiths, their eyes gleaming with secrets that seemed to slither like serpents in the gloom.

Every step Ong took felt like a journey deeper into the abyss itself. The air was thick with an oppressive aura, and he could almost taste the palpable malevolence that hung like a shroud over the city. As he ventured further into the heart of Fel Thalor, he knew that he was stepping into a world of treachery, where deception and darkness were the currency of survival.

The city's cobblestone streets, worn smooth by centuries of wicked footsteps, resonated with an eerie silence that absorbed even the faintest whisper. Ong's heart pounded in his chest, a constant reminder of his chosen dangerous path. Yet, for Keisha, he would brave this forsaken realm, confront the enigmatic Abyssal Dominion, and unearth the secrets that would lead him to her.

With each passing moment, Fel Thalor's secrets whispered to him, promising answers and dangers in equal measure. Ong steeled himself, for he knew that within these shadowed streets, his destiny and Keisha's salvation awaited, intertwined like the darkest threads of fate.

Amidst the suffocating gloom, he combed through the labyrinthine alleys and concealed passages, each step a dangerous dance with the hostility that permeated every corner of Fel Thalor. The city breathed an ominous breath, and he listened intently. With hushed words, he questioned the whispers of the wind, seeking answers hidden within the very stones of this ancient and sinister city. He reached out to the forsaken spirits, those lost souls bound to Fel Thalor, hoping they might offer enlightenment.

Time seemed to stretch to infinity as Ong delved further into the unfathomable depths of Fel Thalor. Along the way, he stumbled upon fragments of history, echoes of dark rituals, and cryptic mentions of forbidden alliances. The city held its breath as if the very stones themselves anticipated his arrival, eager for him to uncover the chilling secrets that had festered in the bowels of this forsaken place.

As the sun dipped below the horizon, casting elongated shadows across the twisted architecture of Fel Thalor, Ong's determination grew ever more resolute. He had managed to unearth elusive hints of a sinister presence, like fleeting echoes of malevolent laughter dancing at the fringes of his perception. Piece by agonizing piece, he assembled a nightmarish puzzle that hinted at an ancient and wicked entity lurking in the depths of this city.

Yet, with every revelation, the haunting truth grew clearer—his quest was far from its conclusion. Fel Thalor was a labyrinthine web of secrets, each strand leading him further into the abyss. Ong knew that he courted danger with each step in this shadowy realm, but the alternative, the thought of Keisha in the clutches of the Abyssal Dominion, was unfathomable.

Amidst the relentless pursuit of answers, Ong's thoughts invariably drifted to Keisha. The memory of their love, an unbreakable bond, fueled the fires of his determination. He swore to unveil these sinister shadows, to expose the Abyssal Dominion's darkest secrets, and to bring her back.

Ong's resolve, an unyielding flame, remained unwavering as the first stars twinkled in the night sky. His path was fraught with peril, but he understood that only within the darkest shadows of Fel Thalor lay the truth he so desperately sought.

Deep within the heart of the Dread Spire, their laughter resonated like a chilling, cacophonous melody—a symphony of darkness that heralded their triumph over Ong's indomitable determination. In this nightmarish theatre of shadows, the puppet masters held the strings, and the stage was set for their wicked game to unfurl.

The Dread Spire was a nightmarish fortress, a testament to their evil power. Its spires reached upward like the gnarled fingers of a monstrous entity, casting long shadows that seemed to writhe and slither across the floor. Torches flickered with eerie green flames, illuminating the grotesque tapestries that adorned the walls, depicting scenes of suffering and betrayal.

Vuarus and Phoenix revealed their roles as architects of Ong's torment within this accursed stronghold. The chamber they occupied was a twisted sanctuary of dark sorcery, where their plans were meticulously woven like a tapestry of despair. The air thrummed with unholy energy as if the sheer walls of the Dread Spire itself were complicit in their evil designs.

As they plotted and schemed, the sinister duo could almost taste the sweet victory within their grasp. The pursuit of Ong, the unraveling of his hope, and the inevitable descent into the treacherous volcanic region outside Fel Thalor were all part of their grand symphony of cruelty. The shadows that clung to them seemed to writhe with delight, for in this dance of deception, they were the masters, and Ong was but a pawn in their wicked game.

Within the icy confines of her lonely cell, Keisha endured a nightmarish existence, her spirit relentlessly assaulted by haunting visions that clawed their way from the abyss. Each intrusion felt like a relentless torment, a glimpse into the unfathomable void of darkness and despair. The oppressive weight of the abyss bore down upon her, threatening to swallow her whole. The visions twisted and writhed, revealing grotesque scenes of unimaginable suffering that etched themselves into her soul.

As if to compound her misery, the temperature in her cell plummeted even further, plunging her into an arctic abyss of bone-chilling cold. The already frigid air took on a severe edge, manifesting in visible puffs of her breath. Keisha shivered uncontrollably, her body wracked by violent tremors as the cold seeped into her marrow.

Glaciera, the white dragon, wielded her sorcery with a cruel flourish, intensifying the cold until it bordered on unbearable. Keisha's body ached, her skin prickling with frost, and she huddled in the corner of her cell, clutching her arms around herself in a desperate attempt to preserve any vestige of warmth.

Vuarus and Phoenix, malevolent puppeteers of her suffering, observed with twisted amusement as Keisha's torment deepened. To them, it was a perverse game, a sadistic gambit aimed at shattering her spirit, at bending her will to their sinister designs. They reveled in her anguish, in the cruel knowledge that she was entirely at their merciless mercy.

"Are you enjoying your accommodations?" Phoenix sneered, his voice dripping with vicious satisfaction.

Keisha's teeth clenched together as she shot them a defiant glare, her eyes ablaze with unyielding spirit even in the face of such brutal torment. She refused to capitulate. She would not grant them the grim pleasure of seeing her crumble.

Yet, as the relentless visions assailed her psyche and the cold bore into her, Keisha's resolve was stretched to its absolute limit. She clenched her fists, determined to hold fast, to resist the tears that threatened to betray her steely determination.

Deep within the labyrinth of her despair, Keisha clung to the memory of Ong's voice, the warmth of his touch, and the enduring embrace of his love. They provided a feeble flicker of strength in the bleakest moments—a fragile beacon of hope amidst the encroaching shadows. It whispered to her in the silence, a yearning to be cradled in Ong's arms, to find solace in his unwavering love again. A tear welled up in her eye, unbidden and unrestrained, as she longed for the comfort of his presence.

Yet, Keisha summoned an ironclad resolve even in her yearning and vulnerability. She would not yield to the tormentors who sought to break her. Instead, she clung fiercely to her defiance, holding onto the essence of her spirit with unwavering determination. She whispered her longing for home and Ong's embrace in the depths of her being, allowing the tears to fall as a silent testament to her strength before she steeled herself for the battle ahead.

Ong pressed onward, his frustration a relentless storm swelled with each labored step. The trail he had pursued, once harboring the promise of answers, had metamorphosed into a maddening wild goose chase. It had fooled him, leading him deep into the labyrinthine folds of volcanic mountains, a landscape that did not care for the hearts and hopes of those who dared tread its treacherous terrain.

The atmosphere grew rarefied with every ascent as if nature conspired to withhold its breath. Once stable, the ground beneath his boots crumbled beneath his determined stride. The path, an unruly serpent, coiled steeply and without mercy while jagged rocks, like malevolent sentinels, lurked to trip him at the slightest misstep. Ong's teeth clenched in stubborn resolve, his determination the sole lodestar guiding him. He could not falter, not when Keisha's life dangled precariously in the balance, a fragile thread that connected their fates.

The wind, a mournful wail that echoed the essence of foreboding, howled around him. Instincts honed by adversity whispered that he was trapped, led astray, a mere pawn in a sinister game orchestrated by the Abyssal Dominion. Yet, even as doubt gnawed at his resolve, he couldn't banish the haunting feeling that he must persist. Somewhere amidst these unforgiving peaks, he believed, lay the key—a crucial clue that would unfurl the path leading him to Keisha.

As Ong continued his relentless ascent, time seemed to warp and stretch, hours stretching into an eternity. Like a storm within his mind, his thoughts churned with a maelstrom of emotions. He couldn't help but drift into a cherished memory that had etched itself into the core of his being—a moment of luck in the Purplefire Woods, where the threads of fate had woven their intricate tapestry.

The Purplefire Woods had come alive with a surreal vibrancy in that memory. The trees, their leaves aglow with ethereal hues, seemed to whisper secrets to the breeze. Shafts of dappled sunlight pierced the canopy, gently warming the forest floor. Birds serenaded the world with melodic tunes, and the air was imbued with enchantment.

Yet, even amid this enchantment, Ong's heart had raced with a mixture of excitement and trepidation. He first glimpsed Keisha in these woods, her eyes like twin stars in the twilight. The memory of their chance encounter filled him with a profound sense of destiny—a belief that their love was not mere luck but a force of nature, as unyielding as the roots of the ancient trees.

In the present, Ong clung to that memory like a lifeline, a reminder that love and determination could pierce the darkest shadows amidst the harshest trials. It was a beacon that lit his way through the unforgiving terrain, a promise that he would not rest until he held Keisha in his arms once more.

In that vivid flashback, Keisha appeared like an ethereal nymph, her silhouette dancing in the shimmering embrace of a crystalline stream. Her laughter had rung like music in the forest's embrace as she reveled in the cool, rejuvenating waters, oblivious to Ong's entranced gaze. He remembered how she had cast a playful scowl upon discovering his quiet observation, her fiery spirit manifesting even in those tender moments. The memory drew a wistful smile from him, a testament to her indelible mark on his heart.

And then, as if prompted by the memory of their first encounter, he couldn't help but reminisce about another pair of watchful eyes. Pumpkin, the faithful feline companion who had entered his life on that fateful day in the woods, had mirrored his fascination for Keisha. The bond forged in those shared moments was a testament to the unpredictable beauty of twists and turns.

With Keisha's image crystallized in his thoughts, her strength and unwavering spirit a luminous beacon, Ong found solace and determination in those cherished memories. They became the pillars of his resolve, the steadfast companions on his arduous journey, illuminating the path forward as he pressed on, driven by the enduring love they shared.

As the sun dipped below the horizon, painting the heavens with a mesmerizing palette of orange and purple, Ong ascended to the pinnacle of one of the volcanic peaks. There, amidst the desolation that stretched before him, his heart sank like a stone in the turbulent waters of despair. He had been lured into a relentless wild goose chase, a siren's song leading him astray. No clue graced this unforgiving landscape, and no sign heralded Keisha's whereabouts.

Frustration and anger churned within him, boiling like molten lava in a cauldron. He couldn't fathom how he had fallen prey to their deception and been trapped in their dark machinations. Clenching his fists until his knuckles turned as white as the snow-capped peaks, he wrestled to harness the storm of emotions threatening to consume him. Control was his lifeline, and he couldn't afford to lose it now. Keisha's fate hung in the balance; he was her unwavering protector.

Inhaling deeply, Ong pivoted to descend the jagged mountain. He was not defeated, far from it. This setback, this cruel twist of fate, only kindled the flames of his determination. It fueled the relentless drive within him to unearth the truth, to break the chains that bound Keisha to the clutches of the Abyssal Dominion. He would search, fight, and not rest until he cradled her safely and, in his arms, again.

Down the volcanic slopes, he strode, his frustration simmering beneath the surface, a storm waiting to erupt. He knew that regrouping and reassessing his strategy was imperative. Returning to the ominous embrace of Fel Thalor, his thoughts gravitated to the place where Keisha had received her vision of her father—a fragment of hope in the dark tapestry of their trials.

The Druchii city, eternally draped in shadows and foreboding, greeted him with its twisted, enigmatic architecture, casting elongated shadows that mirrored the depths of his mood. With each purposeful step, memories of his prior time spent here resurfaced—the battles fought alongside Keisha and her loyal companions, a testament to their indomitable spirit.

Eventually, Ong arrived at the sacred ground where Keisha had endured the heart-wrenching vision of her father's ethereal apparition. The atmosphere here held the weight of her sorrow, a palpable aura of anguish that had seared itself into the very stones. As he surveyed the site, his heart ached with the profound sadness and concern he had felt for her on that fateful day.

In his mind's eye, he recalled the vivid memory of Keisha's face, etched with pain and vulnerability as she had witnessed her father in that spectral form. Her eyes had brimmed with tears, her soul laid bare, and she had turned to Ong for solace, the anchor that would keep her from being swept away by the storm of emotions.

He remembered how he had held her close, his arms a fortress against the despair that threatened to engulf her. She had cried like raindrops in a storm, and he had whispered words of comfort, assuring her that he would be there and face whatever trials lay ahead together.

Now, standing at the very place where her world had shattered, Ong yearned to convey that unyielding message once more—to tell her, in the language of his heart, that he was still in relentless pursuit, that he would never waver, never abandon her to the persistent shadows that sought to tear them apart.

As Ong stood in contemplation, ensnared by the tendrils of memory, something stirred in the periphery of his vision. A small, glistening sphere, bathed in the feeble ambient light, beckoned him with a beguiling allure. Curiosity, as old as time itself, surged within him, prompting him to extend a hand and grasp the mysterious orb.

In his palm, it rested—a creation unlike anything he had ever encountered, a fragile globe that seemed to pulsate with an otherworldly vitality. Its surface shimmered with an ethereal luminescence as if it harbored secrets of distant realms waiting to be unveiled.

Ong's gaze transfixed upon the enigmatic sphere, and without a conscious thought, he focused on it. In that fleeting moment, the world around him seemed to fade away, eclipsed by the emergence of haunting images swirling within the fragile orb.

Before him, the poignant scenes of Keisha's torment played out like a tapestry of despair. He witnessed her countenance etched with agony and suffering, subjected to the relentless machinations of the Abyssal Dominion. Her memories unfurled like spectral wisps—her father's death, a haunting specter from her past, and the persistent fears and doubts that gnawed at her very soul.

As the visual symphony of her suffering unfurled, Ong's heart convulsed with an intensity that eclipsed mere emotion. It was an unrelenting torrent of anger, a storm that surged within him, driven by a profound fury unlike any he had ever experienced. His rage was aimed at the Abyssal Dominion, those malevolent architects of her torment, and at himself for not shielding her from this cruel fate.

In an uncharacteristic surge of rage, he did not merely release the sphere from his grip; instead, he hurled it with all his might. The orb collided with a nearby rock, a symphony of glassy shards that echoed his seething anger. The shatter of the fragile object was a visceral release, a physical manifestation of his tumultuous emotions, as he stood there, chest heaving, staring at the fragments that now lay scattered at his feet.

With his chest heaving and his heart a storm of emotions, Ong cast his gaze heavenward and unleashed a primal scream that rents the air. "Phoenix!" His voice, a thunderous declaration of wrath and resolve, reverberated through the desolate, foreboding streets of Fel Thalor, its echoes carrying his anger and frustration to the very corners of the city.

At that moment, he knew that the evil eyes of the Abyssal Dominion were upon him, their ears tuned to the declaration of his unwavering determination. He wanted them to understand that he would be an unyielding force, an indomitable tempest that would not be quelled until he had snatched Keisha from their clutches. The cost was of no consequence; he would ensure that Phoenix could never again inflict harm upon his beloved.

As Ong's thunderous fury reverberated through the unforgiving terrain of the volcanic mountains, deep within the dread-infused heart of Afor's ominous Dread Spire, Phoenix, and Vuarus exchanged knowing glances that dripped with malicious amusement. Their icy and devoid-of-empathy laughter cut through the oppressive atmosphere, starkly contrasting the turmoil gripping Ong's soul.

Our dear friend Ong possesses quite a fierce spirit," Vuarus remarked, a wicked curve gracing his lips as he savored the unfolding drama.

Phoenix's eyes glittered with a sinister amusement that mirrored his counterpart's sentiment. "Indeed, he burns with a temper that rivals the very fires of the volcano. I wonder how long it will take before his unwavering resolve crumbles into despair."

Vuarus, casually leaning against a somber stone pillar, folded his arms across his chest with a sardonic grin. "Not long, I'd wager. With each fruitless search, his frustration will only deepen into his very being."

In sinister unison, they both erupted into laughter once more—a mocking chorus that resounded through the cavernous, shadowed corridors of the Dread Spire, a symphony of triumph that celebrated their malevolent game and the puppet they had skillfully manipulated.

Within the dim and oppressive confines of the cell, Vuarus summoned forth a malevolent creation—an eerie tapestry woven not of warmth and comfort but of shadows and unspeakable torment. He and Phoenix advanced upon Keisha, their malicious grins casting grotesque shadows as they unveiled their innocuous offering.

Vuarus leaned in, his voice a sibilant whisper as he explained to Phoenix the sinister purpose of their creation. "This, my dear companion, is no ordinary blanket. It is a shroud of darkness, an instrument of suffering. When draped upon her, it will sow the seeds of despair within her soul, each thread carrying the weight of her darkest fears."

Phoenix's eyes gleamed with wicked anticipation as he observed the diabolical craft. "Ah, the exquisite cruelty of it. To see her spirit wither beneath the weight of her nightmares. Vuarus, you have truly outdone yourself this time."

Together, they presented their nefarious creation, their smirks reflecting the perverse satisfaction they derived from their malevolent artistry as they closed in on Keisha with their innocent offering.

"Here, dear Keisha," Phoenix taunted, his voice a honeyed venom, dripping with a false sympathy that curdled in the oppressive air of the cell. "We thought you might feel chilly in your desolate corner."

Keisha's wary gaze locked onto the offered blanket, her instincts screaming a dire warning of its evil nature. She hesitated, her inner turmoil a storm of indecision. A fierce internal debate raged within her, pitting the wisdom of her instincts against the numbing cold that had permeated her very bones. In the end, the chilling embrace of the cell compelled her to extend her trembling hand and accept the offering.

As soon as she wrapped the "blanket" around her shivering form, the world around her fractured and gave way to a maelstrom of nightmarish visions. Her surroundings dissolved into oblivion, replaced by a surreal landscape fashioned from the raw fabric of her deepest fears and agonizing memories. With harrowing clarity, she bore witness to her father's fall, the forest consumed by merciless flames, and Ong's face contorted in anguish—each vision a relentless plunge into the depths of her despair.

Desperation fueled her frantic attempts to wrench the suffocating blanket away, but it clung to her like an insidious vice, its grip tightening with every futile struggle. The visions intensified an unyielding onslaught that threatened to shatter her spirit. Within the dismal confines of her cell, her anguished cries echoed, a haunting chorus of torment heard only by her tormentors, who reveled in her suffering.

Phoenix and Vuarus stood as cruel puppeteers, their eyes alight with sadistic glee as they bore witness to Keisha's torment. Each agonizing twist and turn of her suffering only fueled their amusement, their evil hearts finding perverse pleasure in the depths of her despair. They reveled in their dominion over her, intoxicated by their wielding power.

"Such a pitiable sight, wouldn't you agree?" Vuarus mused, his voice dripping with a sinister satisfaction that mirrored the wicked grin etched upon his lips. "To be ensnared within the very nightmares you have so valiantly battled."

He circled Keisha, his movements like a vulture circling its prey, relishing the aura of hopelessness that enveloped her. Then, in a voice that oozed with malicious delight, he revealed the malevolent truth concealed from her.

"You see, dear Keisha," Vuarus continued with a chilling revelation, "the magic you once wielded, the very essence of your power, now flows like a river into the veins of the denizens of the abyss. Your suffering feeds them, fuels their darkness, and grants them strength beyond measure."

As the words hung in the air, Keisha's eyes widened with horror and realization. The truth was a bitter pill to swallow, a cruel twist in the already torturous narrative of her captivity.

Keisha's tortured gasps and anguished sobs were the sole testaments to her torment, and her voice was rendered impotent in the face of a mental battleground where anguish and despair waged relentless warfare. The twisted "blanket" that enveloped her continued to constrict, its tendrils of torment congealing with each desperate movement she made, ensnaring her ever deeper within its cruel web of suffering.

Left in harrowing solitude amidst the unforgiving crucible of her nightmarish torment, Keisha instinctively curled into a tight ball, her wretched form trapped by the cursed blanket's relentless grip, an ever-constricting vise that defied all hope of escape. The ceaseless onslaught of visions redoubled its ferocity, mercilessly assaulting her senses with an unyielding barrage of pain, fear, and despair.

In the dimly lit corners of her shattered psyche, the echoes of her voice, crying out in agony, reverberated like haunting echoes of a soul in torment.

Tears streamed down her face, and she pressed her trembling hands against her temples as though, through sheer willpower, she might fend off the invasive images that relentlessly tore through the fragile fortress of her mind. Her breaths came in ragged gasps, each one a desperate struggle for air, her heart a relentless drum that beats in time with the frantic cadence of her thoughts. She clung to her sanity with a tenacity born of sheer necessity in this darkness.

The visions seemed to revel in her torment, their malevolent tendrils weaving her deepest fears and profound regrets into a nightmarish tapestry of suffering. She bore witness to herself, isolated and empty amid a desolate wasteland that stretched to the horizon—an eerie tableau that mirrored the ruins of E'vahona, its haunting remnants surrounding her like specters of lost hope. In this phantasmal trance, she beheld the image of Ong. His once-loving gaze now transformed into a visage of disappointment and betrayal. And as the haunting montage continued, she was forced to relive the heart-wrenching moment when her father had fallen to his death, the anguish etched in his eyes forever seared into her memory.

Amidst the relentless tide of visions, Keisha was caught in the merciless undertow of another painful memory. She watched herself as a child, standing in a dimly lit room, her eyes pleading with her mother not to leave. "Don't go, Momma," she whispered, her voice a fragile plea that echoed through the corridors of time. But her mother's resolve remained unshaken, her footsteps receding into the shadows as she embarked on a quest for vengeance. The memory became a poignant tableau that Keisha had long tried to bury—a memory of her mother found lifeless later, torn by the quest that had torn their family. It left Keisha adrift in a world where she had lost her mother and her father, a forsaken soul wandering the desolate landscape of her despair.

Tears flowed freely down Keisha's cheeks, the ceaseless weight of the visions pressing upon her like an unrelenting vice, threatening to crush her spirit. In the suffocating abyss of her torment, she clung tenaciously to the fragments of hope she could muster, summoning memories of Ong's radiant smile, his unwavering faith in her, and the comforting warmth of his touch. These cherished recollections, her last vestiges of solace, were slowly but inexorably consumed by the voracious shadows that enveloped her.

Time became an enigmatic blur as Keisha weathered the relentless assault, the fragile boundary separating reality from illusion steadily eroding with each agonizing heartbeat. The pervasive darkness insinuated itself into the very fiber of her being, whispering insidious doubts and sowing the seeds of fear within the recesses of her mind. Yet, amidst the turmoil and despair, a stubborn spark of defiance persisted—a small but committed voice that refused to be silenced.

As the visions crescendo into a cacophony of torment, a faint yet unmistakable glimmer of light pierced through the oppressive darkness. It was a memory—a poignant moment of connection and profound love—that she clung to with every ounce of her remaining strength. She fought back against the suffocating weight that threatened to engulf her, uncurling her trembling form and rising to her feet.

In that fleeting moment of resilience, a startling vision unfolded before her. Amidst the tumultuous sea of torment, she glimpsed fragments of her elemental magic—a radiant energy that had been her constant companion throughout her journey. Yet, this time, it was different. Her magic pulsed like a brilliant beacon, glowing radiantly into the abyss.

But to her horror, the residents of the abyss, grotesque and shadowy figures, reached out with clawed hands, greedily grasping at her elemental magic as if it were a lifeline. They consumed it with insatiable hunger, their forms twisting and contorting as they absorbed the very essence of her power.

Keisha's heart pounded with fear and desperation as she witnessed her magic being devoured by the denizens of this nightmarish realm. It violated her very being, a theft of the elemental energy that had defined her. She knew that she couldn't let this continue and that she had to break free from the tormenting visions and the evil grasp of the abyssal residents. With renewed determination, she pressed on, her inner strength a flickering flame in the abyss's consuming darkness.

"I won't be broken," she whispered, her voice quivering but resolute, the words a fervent oath that transcended her weakened state. "I won't give them the satisfaction."

Despite the frailty of her body and the relentless battering of her spirit, Keisha summoned her innermost reservoirs of resilience. With unwavering determination and the memory of Ong's steadfast love as her guiding light, she defied the encroaching shadows that sought to consume her. In that act of unwavering defiance, she unearthed a glimmer of hope—a fragile ember that she vowed to nurture and protect, regardless of the depths to which her captivity plunged. And as her whispered words hung in the stifling air, she added another, even softer plea: "Ong, please find me."

Ong, having recently departed Fel Thalor in search of guidance, arrived home in E'vahano to seek out Lord Karrenen, and pressed onward through the treacherous landscape, his frustration a relentless storm swelled with each labored step."

Lord Karrenen's countenance remained grave, his thoughts hidden behind a mask of solemnity as he regarded the mysterious sphere. "Ong," he intoned, his voice a steady stream of counsel, "I empathize with your anguish and your enthusiasm to liberate Keisha from her torment. However, heed this caution: heedless haste, devoid of a well-devised plan, may usher in dire consequences that neither of you can escape unscathed."

Ong's fingers clenched into tight fists, his emotions a tempestuous maelstrom that roiled within him, threatening to erupt in a torrent of frustration and despair. "I understand the need for caution," he muttered through gritted teeth, "but with every passing moment, they torment her with these visions, seeking to destroy her. I can't allow that to happen."

Lord Karrenen's eyes softened with empathy as he spoke, "I do not ask you to abandon your quest, Ong, for your love and determination are unwavering. Instead, I implore you to temper your resolve with wisdom. Seek allies, gather knowledge, and prepare yourself for the trials. There are ancient forces at play, and the Abyssal Dominion is a formidable adversary. To confront them, you must be as prepared as possible."

Ong nodded, his frustration slowly giving way to a steely determination. "I will do whatever it takes, seek out every ally, and gather the knowledge needed to rescue Keisha. Time may not be on our side, but I will make every moment count."

Lord Karrenen placed a hand on Ong's shoulder, a gesture of solidarity and support. "Then, let us work together, my friend. We will uncover the secrets within this sphere, gather the strength of allies, and forge a path to confront the Abyssal Dominion. Keisha's fate rests in your hands, and together, we shall strive to free her from the shadows that trap her."

Lord Karrenen's gaze softened, his hand resting reassuringly upon Ong's shoulder. His voice offered solace and wisdom like a guiding beacon in the storm. "Your determination, Ong, is a beacon of light amidst this encroaching darkness. However, we must navigate this treacherous path with care. The Abyssal Dominion has revealed its formidable power and willingness to go to any length to assert its control. We need a meticulous strategy to ensure Keisha's safety and the eventual defeat of our enigmatic adversaries."

Ong nodded, his resolve unshaken but tempered by the sagacious counsel of Lord Karrenen. "You are right, my friend," he admitted, his voice steady. "I cannot allow my emotions to blind me. I will wait, I will plan, and I will endure. But never doubt, I shall not rest until Keisha is liberated." Lord Karrenen's gaze dwelled on a blend of respect and compassion, acknowledging Ong's unwavering commitment. "I have no doubt, Ong. Keisha possesses a strength matched only by the depth of her love for you. We shall forge a path to bring her back to our embrace. But we shall do so with the utmost care, for she knows that you are fighting for her, and that knowledge shall be her steadfast anchor in this stormy sea of trials."

Lord Karrenen's gaze held a thoughtful glint as he contemplated the enigma that was the Abyssal Dominion. He leaned in slightly, his voice hushed but brimming with concern. "Ong, I must share something with you, a suspicion gnawing at my mind. I believe the Abyssal Dominion may possess knowledge about Keisha's magic, its connection to the forests, and its elemental nature. It's possible that their destruction of these sacred woods was not merely cruel but a calculated move to weaken or sever her connection to her elemental magic."

Ong's brow furrowed as he absorbed Lord Karrenen's words, the gravity of the revelation sinking in. "You think they knew about her connection to the forests and used it against her?" he asked, his voice tinged with concern and anger.

Lord Karrenen nodded solemnly. "It's a possibility we cannot ignore. The Dominion's actions seem too deliberate to be random acts of destruction. If they knew of this connection, it would explain their relentless pursuit of her, their determination to break her spirit by tearing apart the very essence of her power."

Ong's fists clenched in frustration, his determination burning even brighter. "If they thought they could weaken her by destroying the forests, they underestimated Keisha's strength and resilience. We will find a way to restore her connection to the elemental magic and defeat the Abyssal Dominion, no matter the odds."

Their resolve solidified, and Ong and Lord Karrenen continued to shape their plan, their determination unwavering in the face of this new revelation.

In the ethereal realm that cradled Talleoss, the imprisoned dragon fiercely loyal to Kadona, a glimmer of light flickered to life within the crystalline confines of his prison. Summoning every ounce of his willpower, he strained against the iridescent bounds of his crystal prison, extending the twisted tendrils of his consciousness far beyond its boundaries to reach out to Kadona. Like a wisp of breath upon the wind, his ethereal touch brushed against her mind, transcending the boundaries that separated them across the vast realms.

"Kadona," Talleoss's voice resonated in her thoughts, imbued with a palpable urgency and unwavering determination.

Startled and momentarily taken aback by the unexpected presence, Kadona, who had been deeply immersed in her endeavors within the enigmatic Hidden Isles, halted her tasks. She recognized the familiar touch of Talleoss's consciousness, and with a mixture of astonishment and relief, she responded, her thoughts a delicate echo in the tapestry of their connection. "Talleoss? Is that truly you?"

"Yes," Talleoss affirmed, his mental presence growing more substantial. "I have managed, albeit briefly, to pierce the formidable barriers of my imprisonment. You must know something of great import that could tip the scales in our battle against the insidious Abyssal Dominion."

Kadona's curiosity surged, her focus honing in on Talleoss's words with unwavering attention. "Tell me, Talleoss. Do not keep me in suspense."

And so, Talleoss embarked on a haunting narrative, recounting the grim tale of Keisha's capture, her relentless torment, and the fragments of insight he had gleaned from his brief connection to her. "Phoenix," he conveyed, "seldom carries the staff with him, a significant detail that may aid us. But I require your assistance pinpointing the precise location where they hold Keisha."

She queried with urgency, "Is there anything more, Talleoss? No matter how seemingly insignificant, even the tiniest detail could prove pivotal."

Talleoss's mental presence carried a palpable aura of frustration as if he were striving to convey even more than words could contain. "I deeply regret that my knowledge is limited," he responded, his regret etched within their shared connection. "Yet, I shall continue to lend my ears to the echoes of Keisha's anguish, striving to gather any information that may aid her liberation. She deserves nothing less than freedom from this harrowing torment."

Kadona's profound gratitude coursed through the ethereal channels of their mental bond, a heartfelt expression of appreciation that resonated deeply within their shared connection. "Thank you, Talleoss," she conveyed, her voice imbued with the weight of their shared purpose. "Your tireless efforts are immeasurable, and together, we shall find respite only when Keisha is freed, and the Abyssal Dominion's sinister machinations are thwarted."

Talleoss's voice, though fading, echoed with a solemn promise. "Rest assured, Kadona, I remain ever watchful, ever attuned to the threads of fate. Our connection shall be rekindled when the stars align and the moment is right."

As Talleoss's presence gradually receded, it returned to the crystalline prison that held him captive. Kadona, now alone with her thoughts, harbored a potent mix of emotions—an unwavering determination to rescue Keisha, an undercurrent of profound worry for her safety, a flicker of hope that burned bright within her heart, and a simmering frustration at the confines of her divine role. Keisha's abduction had escalated the conflict, but with stalwart allies like Talleoss, they would continue their relentless battle against the Abyssal Dominion, their resolve unwavering as they sought to reclaim what had been stolen.

"Please, don't let me lose this guardian as I did her father," Kadona whispered to the wind, her voice heavy with the weight of responsibility and love. "She is precious to me, especially to her husband and people." In her plea, she revealed a tender side—a ruler who cared deeply for her subjects and the bonds they shared. Yet, she couldn't help but resent the restrictions imposed upon her divine nature, yearning for the freedom to act more directly in times of crisis.

Seated on the porch steps of their cherished home, Ong cast an introspective gaze toward the firmly closed door. His mind, a storm of worry and frustration, weighed heavily upon him like a looming storm threatening to unleash its turmoil. Beside him, Pumpkin, his steadfast and loyal companion, lay at his side—a silent sentinel, providing a comforting presence amidst the maelstrom of his thoughts.

In the wake of the recent events that had unfolded over the past few days, Ong's spirit had borne the weight of his relentless determination to uncover Keisha's whereabouts. The counsel he had received from Lord Karrenen in the council chamber played like a haunting refrain in his mind. The Eladrin leader's words had been a soothing balm for his impulsive instincts, a reminder of the importance of patience and strategic deliberation, of refraining from heedless forays into the jaws of danger. Though aware of the wisdom in Lord Karrenen's advice, Ong found himself torn as the relentless absence of Keisha continued to gnaw at his very soul, a wound that refused to mend.

His eyes remained fixed on the tower that had been their sanctuary—a home of their creation, nestled amidst the enchanting embrace of E'vahona's ethereal beauty. Memories, as vivid as the present, surged like the gentle breeze that rustled the leaves of their cherished garden. In those recollections, the symphony of their life together played on—an orchestra of laughter, tender conversations, and shared moments of unspoken understanding.

They had found solace and joy in their home, crafted with care and adorned with crystals that seemed to capture and radiate the very essence of their love. The gardens, an oasis of vibrant colors and fragrant blooms, had been Keisha's sanctuary, her oasis of serenity amid the chaos of their adventures. Hues of purple and blue had painted the landscape, a reflection of her enduring affection for those shades.

Yet, the memories that held Ong in their thrall were a bittersweet testament to the strength of their bond, a bond now strained by the agonizing void left in Keisha's absence. This void seemed to grow with each passing moment as if the fabric of their world longed to be woven back together.

Pumpkin, his steadfast and ever-faithful companion, stirred from her rest, her instincts attuned to the subtle shifts in her master's emotions. With a gentle nudge and an unwavering gaze, she conveyed an unspoken understanding and deep concern that transcended mere words. Her dark, soulful eyes mirrored the turmoil that consumed Ong's heart, a mirror into the depth of their unspoken connection.

In response to Pumpkin's comforting presence, Ong heaved a sigh, his fingertips tracing a soothing path behind her velvety ears. His touch, though tender, was burdened with the weight of his distracted thoughts, his focus scattered by the relentless ache of Keisha's absence.

"We'll find her, girl," he whispered to his loyal companion, his voice a solemn vow laced with unyielding determination. "No matter how many stars must pass before she returns to our side, I will not relent in my quest."

With resolve hardening his features, Ong rose from his perch on the porch steps, his eyes briefly returning to the closed door that guarded the home they had lovingly built together. An inner conflict played upon his countenance, the temptation to seek solace indoors warring with his unwavering commitment to the pursuit of Keisha. Yet, with a resolute shake, he turned his back on the door, his gaze returning to Pumpkin—an unspoken promise between them that their journey to reunite their family would endure, no matter the trials ahead.

With the porch steps beneath him and Pumpkin by his side, Ong's gaze lingered on the closed door that guarded the sanctuary of their home. The memories etched within those walls whispered to him, tempting him to seek solace within their familiar embrace. Yet, his heart remained resolute, his steps tethered by an unspoken oath.

He knew that entering their home without Keisha would only amplify the emptiness that consumed him. The absence of her laughter, warmth, and presence within their shared haven would be a painful reminder of what he longed to reclaim. So, he remained on the porch, a sentinel in waiting, his heart determined to reunite their family before crossing the threshold into their cherished abode.

"I can't go in there until she's back," he murmured, his voice carrying the weight of his devotion and the depths of his longing. Each word he uttered was the essence of his unwavering love and unyielding resolve. "It just... it doesn't feel right."

As he whispered those words, a faint voice, laden with tears, seemed to echo in the air, carried by the gentle breeze. "Ong, please find me," it pleaded, a haunting reminder of Keisha's enduring torment. His reaction was immediate; his breath caught in his throat, and his heart pounded with hope and desperation. It was as though Keisha's voice had reached out from the depths of her suffering, a fragile thread connecting their souls across the vast expanse that separated them.

Pumpkin, the loyal companion, acknowledged his decision with a nudge and a soft whine, her understanding deep and unspoken. Ong found solace in her silent support, a reminder that he was not alone in this relentless pursuit. Their bond had formed during the tumultuous days of their first battle in Goldmoor. Keisha had ventured to confront a dragon, leaving Pumpkin by Ong's side to aid him in his daring mission to free the King and Queen of Goldmoor.

"I'm heading to Old Flameford," Ong declared, his voice firm and resolute. "There might be something there, some clue, anything that could lead us to her. Let's go, girl."

With Pumpkin at his side, he embarked on the journey ahead, carrying the weight of his determination, the enduring memories of their shared battles, and the strength of their unbreakable bond. The path ahead remained uncertain, but within his heart, a spark of hope blazed, lighting the way through the darkest times.

Chapter 36

Shadows Unveiled: The Council's Concerns

Ong stormed through the ruins of Old Flameford, his frustration growing with each step. The once-thriving village had been reduced to rubble, a haunting reminder of the destructive power of the Abyssal Dominion. He had hoped to find some clue, some sign of where Keisha might be, but his search had yet to yield anything. His heart weighed heavy with worry, and anger burned as he thought of Keisha's captivity.

Amidst the debris, Ong's keen eyes caught a glimmer of something metallic. He rushed over and found a twisted piece of metal that seemed out of place among the ruins. As he picked it up, he realized it was a fragment from Keisha's circlet necklace, a piece he recognized instantly. His heart skipped a beat, hope mingling with the dread that had settled in his chest.

Tracing the necklace fragment lovingly with his fingertips, Ong closed his eyes and tried to sense any trace of Keisha's magic. It was a long shot, but he was desperate. He reached out with his senses, feeling the ebb and flow of the surrounding energy. There was a flicker, a faint trace of Keisha's magic, but it was fleeting, like a distant echo.

Frustration gnawed at Ong as he realized that the trace was too faint, too distant to be of any immediate use. He clenched his fists, his nails digging into his palms as he fought back the surge of anger and helplessness. He couldn't let despair consume him, not when Keisha's life was on the line.

Ong's frustration boiled over, his anger directed at the unseen puppeteer orchestrating this cruel game. He knew in his heart that Phoenix was behind this, that the twisted sorcerer had broken Keisha's necklace and scattered its fragments as a sadistic taunt. The knowledge fueled his determination even further; he would find Keisha and make Phoenix pay for every ounce of suffering he had inflicted upon her. With newfound resolve, Ong pressed on through the ruins of Old Flameford, determined to uncover any clue that would bring him closer to his beloved Keisha.

Taking a deep breath, Ong pocketed the pendant fragment and looked around. He knew he couldn't stay here forever. He had to regroup to find a way to strengthen his connection to Keisha's magic and track her down. But for now, he had no choice but to leave Old Flameford behind.

As he walked away from the ruins, Ong's determination burned brighter. He would find Keisha, no matter the cost. He would unravel the shadows that had taken her, piece by piece, until he brought her back to his side.

Meanwhile, in E'vahona, a sense of unease hung in the air. Lord Karrenen and the Eladrin Council gathered in the Great Hall, their expressions grave. Karrenen stood before them. His voice was laced with concern as he spoke about Ong's relentless search for Keisha.

"We cannot ignore the toll this is taking on him," Karrenen said, his gaze somber. "His desperation grows with each passing day, and we must consider the impact it could have on our people, particularly those who have come to rely on Keisha's strength and guidance. She has been a symbol of hope for many, and her absence weighs heavily on their hearts."

One of the council members spoke up; her voice was soft but persistent. "We cannot underestimate the bond between Ong and Keisha. It is a powerful force that has carried them through countless challenges. But we must also be realistic. It has been months, and our efforts to locate her have been in vain."

Karrenen nodded, his expression pensive. "I fear for Ong's well-being. His relentless pursuit could lead him to dangerous paths."

Another council member offered a suggestion. "We should contact our allies and seek their aid in locating Keisha. We cannot let Ong shoulder this burden alone."

Karrenen's eyes flashed with determination. "You are right. We have allies in many realms, and Keisha's plight affects us all. Let us send them word, share our information, and ask for their assistance," he declared, a firm resolve in his voice. "I know that the dragons are using their magic and knowledge to help locate Keisha, and we must rely on the strength of our connections to find her and bring her back."

The council members nodded in agreement, their unity a testament to their determination to aid Ong and bring Keisha home. In the face of adversity, they would stand together, drawing upon their alliances and resources to rescue their beloved friend and protector from the clutches of the Abyssal Dominion.

As the council members deliberated, Ong's determination continued to guide him. He would search every corner of their world, leaving no stone unturned until he found Keisha. And as time passed, the shadows that enshrouded her would be unveiled, one by one, until he brought her back to the light.

In a secluded chamber deep within the heart of Hidden Isles, the dragons convened to discuss their progress in locating Keisha. Kimras, his golden scales glinting in the soft light, cleared his throat and addressed the group. "We've been pooling our magic and knowledge, yet we've encountered unexpected roadblocks in pinpointing Keisha's exact location."

Silvara, the sleek silver dragon, nodded thoughtfully. "It's as if a shroud of darkness obscures our vision. Our powers seem to be diminished when trying to find her."

Amara, the amethyst dragon, said, "I sensed a dark presence interfering with our efforts. It's almost as if someone is actively trying to thwart our search."

Kimras rumbled in agreement, his eyes narrowing. "We cannot discount the possibility that Vuarus, the Abyssal's master of shadows, might be using his magic to create these obstacles. He could be masking Keisha's presence from our senses."

The dragons exchanged knowing glances, a sense of unease settling in their hearts. The thought that the Abyssal Dominion was actively trying to hide Keisha's location from them only fueled their determination to break through the barriers and find her.

Amara's eyes gleamed with newfound hope as she absorbed the information that had just reached her. "I have news," she began, her tone carrying a sense of urgency that drew the attention of the gathered dragons. "One of our young crystal dragons returned from patrol around the Abyss and reported seeing some construction atop the volcanic mountains. It could be related to the Abyssal Dominion's activities."

Silvara's scales shimmered as she considered this latest information. "If they're investing their resources there, it might be an opportunity for us to gather more information or even disrupt their plans."

Kimras nodded, his expression resolute. "Indeed. Let's focus our efforts on investigating this construction. We may be able to uncover some clues that will lead us to Keisha."

With renewed determination, the dragons turned their attention to devising a plan to approach the volcanic mountains and gather intel about the Abyssal Dominion's activities. The possibility of finding a lead to Keisha's whereabouts ignited a spark of hope within them, driving them forward in their quest to bring her back.

Kimras cleared his throat, a glint of mischief in his eyes. "We can make it even more difficult for them. I suggest that one of our dragons keeps targeting and destroying whatever they build on those volcanic mountains. Let's make their task so frustrating that they'll have no choice but to station guards to protect it."

Amara's gaze brightened at the suggestion. "That's a clever strategy. We can exploit their weaknesses and force them to divert resources from other endeavors."

Silvara nodded approvingly. "It's a risky move, but if we can keep them occupied and on the defensive, it might buy us more time to locate Keisha. We can keep this up until they reinforce their defenses."

As the dragons began to disperse, Kimras, the golden dragon, couldn't help but speak to himself in a low, contemplative voice. "Why didn't we destroy Vuarus when he turned to darkness when he was Azeron? Is this our fault?" His words lingered in the air, a heavy burden of regret weighing on his heart.

Talleoss continued his vigil in another realm, his ethereal presence reaching out in search of any fragment of information that could aid Keisha's rescue. The crystalline confines of his prison were an ever-present reminder of his limitations, but his determination remained unwavering. He would not rest until he played a pivotal role in Keisha's liberation, his loyalty to Kadona, and the bonds they shared driving him forward in this relentless quest.

In the heart of Afor, within the shadowed halls of the Dread Spire, Phoenix and Vuarus stood side by side, their eyes gleaming with evil intent. Their voices resonated with an eerie harmony as they looked out over a darkened crystal.

"It's time to strike again," Vuarus hissed, his fingers tracing the map before them. His eyes gleamed with an evil intent that sent shivers down the spines of those in the room. "But not just any strike. This time, let's bring devastation to the heart of Purplefire Woods again, for the second time. When we're done, nothing will be left to recognize."

Phoenix's lips twisted into a malicious grin. "Agreed. Let the flames of destruction dance through the trees, consuming everything in their path."

As they plotted their sinister course of action, Lyra, a skilled sorceress within the Abyssal Dominion's ranks, stepped forward, her expression thoughtful yet deferential. "Might I suggest, Masters, that we place a surveillance device in Keisha's cell? This way, she can witness the destruction of Purplefire Woods, adding to the pleasure of our triumph."

Phoenix and Vuarus exchanged knowing glances, the idea of savoring the devastation through Keisha's eyes appealing to their twisted desires. Phoenix nodded, his voice a low, chilling murmur. "An excellent suggestion, Lyra. Prepare the device, and make sure Keisha is aware of its purpose. We shall indulge in her despair as we watch her forest crumble."

"In the dimly lit cell, Keisha's heart sank as Phoenix and Vuarus entered, a sinister device in their hands. Fear clawed at her as she watched them approach, her voice shaking with desperation.

Phoenix and Vuarus stood before Keisha. Their faces twisted with malice. Phoenix leaned in, his voice dripping with malice as he explained, 'This device, dear Keisha, is a conduit of destruction. We will use it to unleash an explosive force upon your beloved Purplefire Woods. The flames will devour everything, and the forest will be reduced to ashes.'

Tears welled up in Keisha's eyes, and her voice quivered with anguish as she pleaded, 'Please,' she begged, her eyes wide with terror, 'don't destroy Purplefire Woods. You can do whatever you want to me but spare my Purplefire Woods. I beg you!'

Phoenix and Vuarus exchanged a wicked glance, their laughter echoing cru-elly through the cold, stone chamber. Their amusement sent shivers down Keisha's spine, and she realized that her pleas had fallen on deaf ears.

With a shared, malevolent nod, they began to chant dark incantations, their words woven with eldritch power that reached out to the very essence of the forest. Keisha's heart ached as she watched the first tendrils of fire flicker to life in the distance, and a sob escaped her lips. She was forced to watch in helpless horror as her beloved forest began to crumble and burn, her heart breaking with each passing moment."

The ground trembled violently, and tendrils of shadow erupted from the earth, surging through the land like a relentless, malignant force. Once teem-ing with life, trees twisted and convulsed in agony as the corruption spread like a vicious plague.

The air grew thick with an acrid, foul stench as the once-vibrant foliage shriveled into grotesque, ashen forms. The very heart of Purplefire Woods, a sanctuary of vibrant life and ancient wisdom, was now a grotesque tableau of despair and desolation. It was an absolute nightmare, and Keisha could scarcely believe the cataclysmic horror unfolding before her.

Their cruelty knew no bounds. In the skies above, they summoned Shadow Wraths, grotesque abominations born of shadows and malice, to patrol the borders of their targeted areas. These spectral sentinels were harbingers of dread, their presence enough to make even the bravest souls think twice before attempting to cross the boundaries of the Dominion's influence.

But that was just the beginning. Vuarus, a master of malevolence, conjured forth a Serpent of shadow and fire, a guardian that slithered between realms with a sinister grace. Its mere presence struck terror into those who dared to tread near, and its haunting hiss echoed through the air like evil magic, pro-claiming that the path was not just forbidden but a gateway to unfathomable suffering.

As he gazed over their malevolent handiwork, Phoenix's laughter melded with the howling wind, a discordant symphony of cruelty reverberating through the tortured forest. "Let them feel the crushing weight of our insur-mountable power. Let them know that resistance is futile and a choice that invites torment beyond imagination."

Vuarus's eyes glittered with sadistic pleasure, his dark satisfaction palpable. "And as they cower before our unparalleled might, they'll never suspect the depths of depravity that lurk within the shadows of their doom."

Their maleficent plans set in motion, they withdrew from the crystal's view, leaving behind a scene of destruction and despair that would forever haunt the memories of those who witnessed it. The echoes of their cruel laughter lingered like a chilling and ominous warning, a haunting prelude to the horrors yet to come.

With their malicious display of power concluded, Phoenix and Vuarus released their cruel grip on Keisha, allowing her to sink back into her cell's cold, unforgiving stone floor. As the remnants of their eldritch magic lingered in the air, Phoenix turned to her, his laughter dripping with sadistic glee.

"You see, dear Keisha," he taunted, his voice a venomous melody, "Purplefire Woods is just a shadow of its former self. And all because you couldn't resist pleading for its salvation." Phoenix laughs. Vuarus glances at Keisha and smirks. "It would seem this particular forest was special to her." Phoenix laughs again. "Well, it is gone now."

"Keisha's heart ached, and her eyes welled up with tears as the weight of their cruelty settled upon her. Purplefire Woods had been more than just a forest to her; it was a place of sacred memories, a testament to her love for Ong, and the site where they had exchanged their vows. The thought of it being desecrated tore at her soul.

Their laughter echoed through the dimly lit cell, a cruel symphony of torment that reverberated in Keisha's ears long after they had departed. She was left alone in the aftermath of their malice, her heart heavy with despair, and she couldn't help but curl up into a tight ball. Tears streamed down her face as she cried in agony, the pain of seeing a place so dear to her heart ravaged and destroyed.

As Phoenix and Vuarus withdrew from the crystal's view, leaving behind a scene of destruction and despair, Vuarus turned back, a wicked smile on his lips. He whispered to himself, barely audible but filled with sinister delight, 'Little did she know, every tree we burned, every leaf we withered, shattered another piece of her soul.' His eyes gleamed with malice as he acknowledged the psychological torment they had inflicted on Keisha through their actions."

Her voice carried her plea, a desperate and frantic call to the one person she longed for in her darkest moments. "Ong," she whispered, her voice trembling with sorrow and longing, "please, hold me. This place, where we exchanged our vows and became one, it feels like they're tearing apart our love itself and erasing the sacred memories we created here."

But in the cold, oppressive cell, her cries were ignored, unheard by anyone but the merciless shadows that enveloped her. Keisha's grief was palpable, her anguish profound as she grappled with the desecration of a place that held.

Amidst the serene beauty of E'vahona, Lord Karrenen's keen senses detected a subtle but disquieting shift in the magical currents that coursed through the realm. A dissonance in the harmonious symphony of nature's magic raised the hair on the back of his neck, and his Eladrin eyes, vibrant with age-old wisdom, narrowed with concern.

Once a bastion of tranquility and enchantment, the realm had been irrevocably altered by Keisha's absence. Her guiding presence had been a beacon of hope, and the domain mourned her loss. The very land seemed to grieve. Its verdant heartache was mirrored in the muted colors of its flora and the mournful songs of its ethereal creatures.

But now, something else stirred beneath the surface, an undercurrent of unrest that troubled Lord Karrenen's soul. He couldn't ignore it, not when the stakes were so high. Keisha's vanishing act had already cast a dark cloud over their once-pristine world, and this new disturbance threatened to unravel the fragile tapestry of E'vahona further.

Lord Karrenen extended his senses determinedly, reaching out through the connections that bound his people to the land. He sought to bridge the gap between himself and Ong, the guardian of Purplefire Woods, whose connection to the forest was an unbreakable bond.

"Ong," he called out through their ethereal connection, his thoughts carrying the weight of his unease, "I sense a disturbance in our realm's magic. Something is amiss, and I fear it may be linked to Keisha's absence. Can you feel it, too?"

"Yes," Ong's voice resonated in Lord Karrenen's thoughts, laced with worry and determination. "I've felt it too, my lord. It's as if the very essence of the forest mourns Keisha's absence, and now, another disturbance ripples through its magic. I'm on my way to Purplefire Woods to investigate. Together, we'll uncover the truth behind this unsettling shift."

Memories flooded Ong's mind as he traversed the now-dreary landscape. This was where they had held their wedding ceremony, where vows of love and devotion had been exchanged beneath the vibrant canopy of the woods. The memory of that day, with Keisha's radiant smile and the soft rustling of leaves, weighed heavily on his heart.

As he ventured deeper into the woods, dread intensified, and his steps grew heavier. It was as if the very essence of the forest mourned Keisha's absence, its magic tainted by the evil forces at work. Ong knew something dire had transpired here, threatening the forest and his beloved Keisha.

Suddenly, a faint voice reached his ears in the eerie silence—filled with tears and desperation. "Ong, please... just hold me."

His heart ached at the sound, and he knew he had to press on to find Keisha and end the torment that had befallen their beloved woods. With his sword in hand and a fierce determination burning in his eyes, he ventured deeper into the heart of the corrupted forest, ready to confront the darkness that threatened everything he held dear.

Tears welled up in his eyes as he called out, "Keisha! I'm here! I'm coming for you!" His voice echoed through the darkened trees, carrying his determination and love into the forest's depths.

As Ong ventured deeper into the heart of the devastated Purplefire Woods, the air seemed to seethe with sorrow and anger. He could feel the weight of the forest's suffering, its anguish manifesting in the twisted and withered remains of once-vibrant life.

The corrupted trees cast grotesque shadows, their gnarled branches reaching out like skeletal fingers as if desperately trying to grasp onto the life they had lost. The charred ground crackled beneath his boots, and the acrid scent of scorched earth and decaying foliage filled his senses.

Amidst this desolation, the mournful howls of the Shadow Wraths haunted him, their spectral forms flickering like dark flames. Their eerie whispers echoed the forest's lament, a dissonant symphony of despair.

And then, the Serpent of shadow and fire, a monstrous guardian of malevolence, slithered forth with its sinister presence. Its eyes blazed with an unholy fire, and the ground trembled beneath its ominous coils. Ong couldn't help but shudder, knowing this destruction was no accident. It was a deliberate act of cruelty, and he was determined to uncover its source and end it.

With anger burning in his eyes, Ong couldn't contain his frustration any longer. He turned

to his allies with a voice that carried the weight of his emotions. "This is enough! The Dominion has gone too far by targeting Purplefire once again. We must find out how they orchestrated this and stop them, whatever it takes!"

His words resounded with a fierce determination, a fiery resolve to protect what he held dear. The destruction of Purplefire Woods had unleashed a storm within him, and he was prepared to confront the tempest head-on.

As Ong's boots crunched through the desolation of the once-vibrant Purplefire Woods, his mind swirled with a maelstrom of emotions. The pain of imagining Keisha's heartache at the sight of her cherished woods reduced to ruin gnawed at him. Anguish and rage rose within him, creating an unquenchable fire of determination.

He couldn't let this grievous offense against nature and his beloved Keisha go unanswered. With every step he took, he felt the weight of responsibility press upon him, urging him to confront the hostility that had brought about this destruction.

Surveying the twisted landscape, Ong vowed solemnly that he would not rest until he uncovered those responsible for this heinous act. The memory of Keisha's deep love for this place, where they had forged their bonds and shared their dreams, fueled his unwavering resolve. He knew he would do whatever it took to bring justice and retribution to the shadowed forces that sought to snuff out the light of their world. With determination burning in his eyes, he embarked on his quest to confront the darkness and restore the beauty that had once thrived within these hallowed woods.

Malrik, the Chief Priest of Vuarus, stood expectantly in the dimly lit chamber deep within the underground temple. The flickering candlelight cast eerie, dancing shadows upon his gaunt face, etching reverence and a touch of madness into his features as he gazed upon the dark, foreboding altar before him. "My Lord Vuarus," he intoned, his voice quivering with sincere devotion, "our unwavering loyalty to you has garnered us many blessings, yet the true depths of the power we seek still elude us."

Vuarus, the embodiment of shadows, materialized from the abyss of obscurity, his presence manifesting as piercing red eyes that bore into Malrik's very soul. An otherworldly intensity radiated from him as he inquired, "Speak, Malrik, and share your thoughts. What proposal do you bring before me?"

Malrik lowered his head further, his words a whispered prayer. "My Lord, we have been graced with the presence of the Eladrin woman, Keisha. Her connection to the natural world is formidable, and her essence holds the potential to amplify your power to unprecedented heights. Sacrificing her, I believe, may hold the key to unleashing the full dominion of shadows."

Vuarus contemplated Malrik's fervent words, his features enshrouded in shifting shadows. "You perceive potential in her sacrifice, Malrik?"

The priest nodded with unshakable zeal, his eyes wide and fanatical. "Yes, my Lord. Your strength would become unparalleled with her life force coursing through the abyssal channels. The very realm of shadows would bend to your inflexible will, and all those who dare to oppose us would be swept aside like insignificant grains of sand."

Vuarus's lips curled into a sinister smile, the venom in his gaze intensifying. "Your loyalty and vision are commendable, Malrik. Be assured the plans to offer Keisha's life to the Abyss are already in motion. Her torment will serve as the wellspring of my boundless power."

Malrik bowed even more profoundly, his devotion unwavering. "As you command, my Lord.

Your dark wisdom guides us upon the inevitable path toward absolute darkness."

With an unsettling hiss, Vuarus's form dissolved into tendrils of shadow, his presence retreating from the chamber, leaving a lingering aura of malevolent anticipation. "Ensure the preparations are made, Malrik. The culmination of our efforts draws ever closer."

As Malrik remained alone in the chamber, the emotional fire in his eyes burned brighter. The impending sacrifice of Keisha was destined to be a harbinger of the Abyssal Dominion's ultimate ascendancy. He understood with unwavering certainty that by offering Keisha to the abyss, his master, Vuarus, would attain unparalleled strength and power. This sacrifice was not merely a cruel whim but an essential step toward realizing their evil ambitions.

Malrik could feel his power growing as he stood there, fueled by the dark rituals and the impending offering. The thought of Keisha's torment becoming the wellspring of his master's might fill him with a sinister thrill. This sacrifice would tip the scales irrevocably in favor of the Abyssal Dominion, and Malrik relished the prospect of the chaos and devastation they would sow.

However, a dark cloud of frustration settled over his features as he discovered the altar had been destroyed. The carefully laid plans were disrupted, and Malrik's fury grew. His fingers clenched into fists as he stared at the broken remnants of the altar. Despite the setback, his determination remained unshaken. He would rebuild it and strengthen the enchantments; this time, it would take more work to dismantle.

As the time for sacrifice drew near, Malrik knew he had a crucial role to play. The altar must be ready, and the offering must be delivered. The Abyssal Dominion's power depended on it, and he would not allow any obstacles to deter their grand design.

Chapter 37

Shadows Unveiled: Veiled Ambitions

In the shrouded recesses of the chamber, Lyra, concealed within a cocoon of shadows, had surreptitiously observed the clandestine exchange unfolding between Malrik and Vuarus. Her intrigue danced like a firefly's light, illuminating her every thought as she contemplated the enigmatic conversation. As the fleeting specter of Vuarus dispersed into nothingness, leaving only a lingering trace of shadowy essence, Lyra shed her concealment. It moved forth, her dark, penetrating eyes fixed upon the enigmatic figure.

"It was always your design, wasn't it?" Lyra's voice, velvet-soft but tinged with admiration and amusement, dripped like honey into the dusky atmosphere.

Vuarus turned to meet her gaze, his countenance an inscrutable mask carved from obsidian. "Indeed, Lyra. The die was cast for Keisha when she stumbled into our clutches."

Lyra's voice, a haunting whisper that seemed to resonate with the secrets of ages past, broke the stillness of the chamber once more. "No, Vuarus, not when Keisha fell into our clutches but from the very inception of your sinister plan. This was your intention, was it not?" Her words carried the weight of revelation, as if she had uncovered a concealed puzzle piece in their evil game.

Vuarus's eyes, pools of abyssal mystery, bore into Lyra's as if daring her to delve deeper into his abyss. "Indeed, Lyra. The tapestry of her destiny was woven with threads of darkness from the beginning."

Lyra's gaze remained unwavering, her knowledge of Vuarus's machinations adding layers to her intrigue. "And the Eladrin guardian, Kadona? Does she not possess the power to thwart your design?"

Vuarus chuckled again, a chilling, melodic cadence resonating with an unsettling finality. "Ah, Kadona. She is bound by an unbreakable decree that restricts her from intervening in our affairs. Even the gods must obey certain cosmic laws."

Lyra's curiosity now burned like an unquenchable fire, her eyes aflame with a relentless quest for understanding. "And what of the power you seek to gain from this sacrifice, Vuarus? What dark ambitions fuel your insatiable hunger for it?"

A devilish grin curled upon Vuarus's lips, its malevolence casting shadows within shadows. "I intend to harness it, my dear Lyra, for myself alone. In the realm of gods, an unquenchable thirst for power courses through my veins. With it, I shall transcend all that is mortal and ascend to the realm of the divine."

As the murky tendrils of shadow converged around Vuarus, casting him into an eerie shroud of malevolence, Lyra couldn't suppress a shiver that coursed through her like an icy breeze. The clandestine union she had thrust herself into concealed secrets and ambitions far more intricate than she had ever fathomed.

Lyra's lips curled into a sly smirk, her eyes glinting with a mischievous spark akin to a fox reveling in a cunning ploy. "Yet, in breaking her, in witnessing her spirit crumble, you found delight. Why, I wonder?"

Vuarus's gaze remained transfixed upon some distant, ethereal horizon, his voice a sultry, ominous murmur that resonated with ancient, forbidden knowledge. "As Keisha's spirit wanes and fractures, it becomes pliable, malleable to my will. Her fractured essence shall nourish my power, rendering her servile for the impending ritual."

Lyra raised a curious eyebrow, and her curiosity further ignited like a spark in the night. "And what of the vengeance you promised for Ong?"

Vuarus's lips twisted into a frigid smile, his eyes gleaming with a vicious satisfaction that could freeze the heart. "Ong dared to defy my dominion, to question my authority. Breaking his beloved is a subtle retribution, a cruel reminder of his powerlessness.

A sinister chuckle escaped Lyra's lips, resonating through the chamber like a haunting melody. "So, her sacrifice serves a dual purpose – power and vengeance?"

Vuarus's gaze turned piercing, and his voice was imbued with the very essence of shadowy deception. "Indeed, Lyra. And when Ong stands witness to her sacrifice, the sweetness of vengeance shall be nectar to my soul. Even if he divulges the secret of E'vahona's location, Keisha's fate is inexorably sealed."

Lyra's smirk deepened, her head tilting in acknowledgment, her eyes locked in a mesmerizing dance with Vuarus's. "Truly, you are a master of your dark art, my Lord."

Vuarus's enigmatic smile deepened his schemes, unfurling like the sprawling wings of an encroaching abyss. "I am the architect of destiny, Lyra. And the dominion of shadows stands poised to reshape the world in its dark image."

As Lyra dissolved into the shadows, her laughter reverberated through the chamber like an ethereal echo. Vuarus watched her departure with an unyielding gaze, his ambitions intertwining with the fabric of existence itself.

"In a moment of chilling introspection, Vuarus whispered, 'Her sacrifice is the linchpin, essential to unlocking the full extent of my dark ambitions. With her spirit offered willingly and her connection to the forests torn asunder, I shall ascend to unparalleled heights of power, and none shall possess the strength to challenge me.' Yet, deep within the shadowed recesses of his mind, a truth remained concealed—a truth known only to him. Revenge was a tantalizing prospect but a pawn in the grand scheme. What he truly desired was Keisha herself, and the unique power she held. Revenge served its purpose in keeping Phoenix in check and creating a favorable opportunity to seize what he coveted most."

From the inky depths of the shadows, Vuarus's form coalesced, an ephemeral wraith emerging as Lyra's haunting laughter faded into the obscurity of the night. He turned to find Phoenix, his fellow harbinger of the ever-encroaching darkness, regarding him with an enigmatic glint in his eyes.

"Ah, Phoenix," Vuarus greeted, his voice an ethereal symphony of the realm beyond. "I presume you've managed to find some amusement for yourself."

Phoenix responded with a sarcastic smile, the flickering flames within his gaze mirroring a profound darkness that dwelled within. "Amusement might not be the precise term, but matters have been evolving as planned."

Vuarus inclined his head, the nebulous tendrils of intrigue swathing him like a cloak of shadows. "Evolving indeed. I have engaged in discourse with Malrik, the high priest. He shall assume command over the sacrificial altar."

Phoenix raised a quizzical eyebrow. His curiosity alighted like a spark in the gloom. "And what were his sentiments regarding this arrangement?"

A smug smile danced upon Vuarus's lips. "He expressed enthusiasm, to put it mildly. He perceives Keisha's impending sacrifice as the herald of the Abyssal Dominion's inevitable ascension."

Phoenix's laughter echoed, tainted with the dark undercurrent of amusement. "Ah, the intoxicating allure of dominion and mastery. Mortals, how easily they succumb to the siren's song of power."

Vuarus's gaze flickered, a shadow of amusement veiling his eyes. "Indeed, their desires make them predictable pawns in our intricate game. Nonetheless, a minor complication has arisen in our meticulously woven plot."

Phoenix's interest flared, his eyes ablaze with intrigue, like flames consuming ancient parchment. "Pray tell, Vuarus. What has disrupted our carefully crafted scheme?"

Vuarus's smile held a trace of vexation. "It appears that the altar we intended to employ has been obliterated. The selfsame altar was meant to serve as the conduit for channeling sacrifices into the Abyss."

Phoenix's laughter resounded, a haunting melody that harmonized the realms of shadows and flames. "How... ill-fated. Perhaps we underestimated the need to safeguard it."

In response, Vuarus's eyes gleamed with a veiled challenge. "It holds little significance. We shall reconstruct it, fortified by layers of safeguards. No further disruptions will be tolerated."

Phoenix's grin broadened, a fierce resolve kindling within his fiery gaze. "Agreed. We shall rebuild the sacrificial altar, forging it to withstand intrusion."

As the two enigmatic harbingers of the lurking shadows exchanged their stratagems, their ambitions intertwined like intricate threads of darkness. Unbeknownst to the world, it quivered under their sway, utterly oblivious to the impending cataclysm that their dominion would soon unleash.

Phoenix's eyes glimmered with evil delight as he continued their conversation within the realm of shadows. "And let us not forget the brilliance of siphoning her magic, Vuarus. Transferring it to the abyss's denizens has stripped her of power and multiplied the torment she endures. A masterstroke, I must admit."

Vuarus nodded in agreement, his inscrutable expression holding a hint of satisfaction. "Indeed, Phoenix. Her magic, once a source of strength and hope, now fuels the forces of darkness that seek her destruction. It is a cruelty beyond measure and serves as a testament to our ingenuity."

"In the depths of their shadowy chamber, where the sinister symphony of their plans played out, Phoenix and Vuarus reveled in the knowledge that their carefully laid schemes were bearing fruit. Keisha's spirit withered, her will crumbling, making her the perfect candidate for the sacrifice they needed."

Phoenix nodded in solemn agreement, silently acknowledging the darkness that bound them both. "She is on the precipice, Vuarus, teetering on the edge of surrender. It won't be long now."

Vuarus's lips curled into a semblance of a smile, but it was born of the abyss. "No, Phoenix, it won't be long. And when the time is right, we shall harvest her fractured spirit and bask in the intoxicating power it shall yield. The dominion of shadows awaits its ultimate triumph."

Phoenix's smirk curled like a wisp of dark magic, a shadowy riddle in his eyes. "Perhaps it's high time we paid a visit to our captive. The blanket has served its purpose, wouldn't you agree?" Vuarus's lips arched into a sly smile, a mastermind orchestrating a clandestine opera. "Indeed, my dear Phoenix. But fret not. I have yet another little surprise in mind."

With a quirked eyebrow, Phoenix inquired, "A new amusement for our cherished Keisha?"

Vuarus's chuckle dripped like midnight honey. "Exactly. And this particular trinket promises to offer her an exquisite journey into the depths of despair."

A malevolent spark danced in Phoenix's eyes as Vuarus conjured forth an intricate crystal of silvery luminescence. "Ah, a crystal. You do possess a unique talent for amusement, Vuarus."

Vuarus's fingers delicately traversed the crystal's surface, an aura of evil energy oozing from its core. "Indeed, but this crystal is no ordinary plaything. It possesses a unique property – the capacity to simultaneously inflict agony and ecstasy, an intricate dance of sensations that shall prove irresistible."

Phoenix's laughter resonated softly, a symphony of shadowy amusement. "You do relish your creations, Vuarus. Let us not prolong our guest's anticipation any further."

With solemn purpose, they departed the chamber, their echoing footsteps resonating through the Dread Spire's twisted passages as they descended into the unfathomable depths where Keisha languished.

The journey through the labyrinthine, shadow-choked corridors of the Dread Spire was swift, every footfall ringing with the weight of anticipation. As they drew near the entrance to the underground cell, Vuarus's fingers brushed the enchanted door, and it swung open as if obedient to his very will, revealing Keisha huddled within, her eyes wide with dread and despair.

Her once-vibrant eyes, now dulled and etched with haunting despair, flickered toward the approaching specters. As Vuarus and Phoenix entered her cell, their presence cast a suffocating veil that intensified the surrounding darkness.

"Well, well, Keisha," Phoenix purred, his voice dripping with amusement and cruel delight. "Have you yearned for our company?"

While he spoke, Vuarus stooped to remove the tattered blanket that had been her sole comfort for the past agonizing three months. The biting chill immediately embraced her, sending shivers racing down her fragile form.

Vuarus couldn't help but smile as he witnessed her shivering, the cruel satisfaction dancing in his eyes. He leaned closer to Phoenix and whispered, "Her Eladrin heritage has never known such cold. Let us use it to break her even further, my dear Phoenix. The abyss delights in her suffering." Phoenix nodded with a sinister grin, acknowledging Vuarus's suggestion. He raised his hand and beckoned Glaciera, an elemental entity bound to their will, who had the power to control the temperature within the cell.

"Glaciera," Phoenix commanded with cold authority, "increase the cold. We want our dear Keisha to feel the full embrace of despair."

As if responding to his malevolent request, the temperature in the cell plummeted even further, causing Keisha to tremble uncontrollably in the icy grip of her tormentors.

Keisha's voice emerged as a fragile whisper, marked by weariness and indomitable defiance. "I will never submit to you, no matter the torment you devise."

Vuarus chuckled softly, his eyes gleaming with a malevolent luster as he unveiled the silvery crystal. "Ah, my dear Keisha, your resistance adds flavor to this endeavor. You see, we've prepared a little surprise for you."

With a subtle flourish, Vuarus raised the crystal, its radiant presence captivating Keisha's gaze with a potent blend of trepidation and curiosity. A surge of energy emanated from the crystalline artifact, tendrils of shadow reaching out to touch her skin. The sensations unfurled like a symphony, entwining pain and pleasure into an overwhelming duality that sent shivers racing down her spine.

Keisha's breath caught, her body tensing in response to the conflicting sensations that surged through her. Gritting her teeth, her eyes squeezed shut as she bravely attempted to endure the relentless assault on her senses.

"Ah, the exquisite dance of torment and delight," Phoenix mused, his voice a velvety whisper that hung heavy in the air. "Do you feel it, Keisha? The interplay of suffering and ecstasy, the boundaries between them dissolving like the mists of a dream."

As the sensations intensified, Keisha's will remained unbroken, her defiance a beacon of strength amidst the darkness that sought to consume her.

Vuarus's unwavering gaze remained fixated upon Keisha, his countenance a twisted tableau of perverse satisfaction. "You see, Keisha, even the most resolute souls can be fractured, and you offer us something extraordinary in your vulnerability."

Keisha's determination faltered in the throes of the crystal's inexorable influence, her grasp on control slipping like sand through her fingers. Despite her valiant efforts, an involuntary gasp of torment escaped her lips, an agonizing testament to the crystalline artifact's relentless power.

Phoenix couldn't help but steal a fleeting glance at Keisha, discerning the undeniable marks of sleepless nights in the shadows beneath her eyes. He chuckled lightly, his voice dripping with teasing insinuation. "You ought to consider a bit more rest, Keisha, though it might only invite more shadows."

Drawing nearer, Phoenix's eyes sparked with a mischievous glint, an unmistakable predatory aura enveloping him. "So, my dear Keisha," he continued, his voice lowering to a beguiling whisper, "shall we embark on the captivating journey of discovering how much longer you can endure?"

Vuarus and Phoenix exchanged an unspoken, knowing glance, and their mirthful amusement was palpable. They departed the cell in tandem, the ponderous door sealing her within, trapped in the swirling sensations and shadows. As they withdrew, leaving behind the forsaken confines of Keisha's cell, the sad echoes of her anguished cries rippled through the labyrinthine corridors of the Dread Spire. It was a haunting symphony, an ominous resonance that wove itself into the very fabric of the shadows.

As the crystal's influence deepened, Keisha's resistance waned further, her spirit straining against its very limits. Amidst the torment, a fleeting image of Ong's face flickered in her mind, an enduring reminder of the love and resilience that resided within her. With a trembling breath, she steeled herself, resolute in her resolve to withstand the Abyssal Dominion's evil machinations. But beneath the surface of her determination lurked shadows of another kind, darker and more haunting. Keisha's thoughts were plagued by long-buried fears and anxieties, remnants of a past she had tried to forget. The memory of her mother's abandonment, the feeling of being forsaken and alone, resurfaced with relentless intensity. The crystal that Vuarus had crafted seemed to tap into those buried emotions, amplifying her deepest fears.

Amid her torment, Keisha's voice shattered the oppressive darkness, a trembling and desperate whisper that bore the weight of her ceaseless yearning and relentless suffering. "Ong...," she uttered, the fear in her voice palpable, her weariness evident as she confessed her dread of sleep, her exhaustion, and her unwavering longing for the presence of Ong.

As Ong knelt amidst the desolation, his thoughts turned to the painful realization that Keisha's absence wasn't the only source of sorrow that had befallen their realm. He couldn't ignore that the darkness that had tainted Purplefire Woods ran deeper than the surface corruption. It had tapped into something within him, a wellspring of emotions and fears that were now bubbling to the surface.

Memories of his fears and doubts surfaced, like lingering shadows cast by the evil forces ravaging their beloved woods. The haunting whispers of his current fear—the fear of failing Keisha—loomed large in his mind, a relentless burden that weighed on his every step.

As he continued to trace the scars on the earth, his hands trembled with a mixture of grief, anger, and an overwhelming sense of vulnerability. The pain from his past, long suppressed, had resurfaced in the wake of the current crisis.

Ong knew that to heal the land and save Keisha, he had to confront the external forces threatening their world and the internal demons that haunted him. The journey ahead was not merely about restoring the beauty of Purplefire Woods; it was about finding the strength within himself to face the darkness, both within and without.

As Ong knelt, a bitter sense of helplessness washed over him. The enormity of the destruction weighed heavily on his shoulders, and anger bubbled up within him towards those who had wrought such devastation upon this sacred place. Purplefire Woods had been deliberately targeted by malevolent forces, and Ong was determined to uncover the truth and thwart their wicked plans.

Rising to his feet, he felt a spark of renewed determination ignite within him. His eyes scanned the desolate landscape, taking in the haunting remnants of what once was. The corrupted trees cast grotesque shadows, their gnarled branches reaching out like skeletal fingers, as if desperately trying to grasp onto the life they had lost. The charred ground crackled beneath his boots, and the acrid scent of scorched earth and decaying foliage filled his senses.

Each step Ong took carried the weight of a promise: to restore the woods, to protect the people he cared for, and to face whatever darkness lay ahead. The journey would be arduous, but he would not falter. The land, Keisha, and his own soul demanded nothing less.

Amidst this desolation, the mournful howls of the Shadow Wraths haunted him, their spectral forms flickering like dark flames. Their eerie whispers echoed the forest's lament, creating a dissonant symphony of despair.

But Ong was not alone. He could feel the presence of allies and kindred spirits who shared his determination to confront the darkness and restore the beauty that had once thrived within these hallowed woods. With their support and his unwavering resolve, he would uncover the source of this hostility and end it—for the sake of Purplefire Woods and for Keisha, whose memory fueled his determination to press forward into the heart of the corrupted forest.

Ong's eyes, attuned to the magical energies around him, caught a faint glimmer beneath the filth. His heart quickened as he recognized the unmistakable shape of the jewel—a heart, the same hue as Keisha's eyes and as vivid as his love for her. He carefully retrieved the jewel with wonder and determination, brushing away the dirt and dust. Despite its tarnished appearance, its inner brilliance still shone through, a testament to the enduring love he sought to rekindle.

Clutching the heart-shaped jewel in his hand, Ong couldn't help but feel a renewed sense of hope. This small, cherished fragment of Keisha's necklace was another step closer to reuniting with her, a symbol of their enduring love even in the darkest times.

As Ong rose, his jaw set in unwavering resolve. He refused to allow the dominion's malevolence to obliterate every trace of Keisha's essence from this world. He vowed to find her, unravel the dark forces that had trapped her, and rekindle her light, no matter the peril or the trials ahead.

With a final, poignant glance cast back at the woods that had once served as a sanctuary, Ong pressed onward, fueled by an unquenchable fire that refused to be doused. The path that stretched before him was shrouded in uncertainty, yet one thing remained resolute in his heart: he would undertake whatever trials lay ahead to reunite with Keisha.

As Ong turned his back on the lonely remnants of what had once been the thriving heart of the Purplefire Woods, a heavy sigh escaped his lips. The burden of frustration bore down upon him, a constant companion that reminded him of the countless hours spent scouring the forest, seeking any trace, any hint that might draw him nearer to Keisha.

His gaze lowered to Pumpkin, his steadfast companion who had unwaveringly stood by his side throughout this arduous journey. With a mixture of sorrow and unwavering determination, he murmured, "We seem no closer to finding her than we were months ago, my loyal friend. I'm lost, unsure of where else to turn."

Just as he was on the cusp of taking another determined step, a delicate whisper, like a spectral wisp, seemed to materialize on the wind, bearing a haunting resonance of his name. Ong's head snapped upright, his heart thundering in his chest as he strained to capture the elusive sound. Could it be? Could Keisha's voice truly bridge the chasm that separated them?

"Ong..."

His natural and ethereal name danced upon the breeze, sending electric shivers down his spine. But there was something more in that voice—something he had never heard. It was a deep and primal fear that shook him to his core. Keisha had always been fearless and solid, but this... this was different.

His heart hammered relentlessly within his chest as he closed his eyes, as though seeking to sharpen his senses, better to attune them to the faint, ghostly sound. "Keisha?"

In that charged moment, Ong felt a surge of hope wash over him, mingled with a tinge of fear that Keisha's voice might be an illusion, a cruel trick of the forest that had tormented him for so long. But one thing was undeniable—the fear in her voice had shaken him as he had never known her to be that afraid until now.

Before he could comprehend the unfolding events, an incandescent brilliance engulfed him, a force of such intensity that it defied all logical explanation. Ong staggered backward, his senses thrown into disarray, as the very fabric of his surroundings blurred and shifted, the once-familiar embrace of the woods and the presence of Pumpkin slipping away like the fading vestiges of a dream.

When the radiant maelstrom finally relented, Ong stood amidst the all-too-familiar environs of E'vahona. Confusion intermingled with frustration surged within him, and he clenched his teeth, jaw locked in sheer determination. "No," he muttered, his voice carrying the weight of defiance. "Not now."

He had been forcibly wrenched from his ceaseless search, torn away from the solitary place where a glimmer of hope had managed to endure. As the crushing reality of his abrupt displacement settled in, he could not dispel the nagging sensation of time slipping through his grasp, like the relentless trickle of sand in an hourglass.

With a sigh heavy enough to shake his very core, Ong cast one final, longing glance back toward the woods, his heart aching for the path he had been compelled to abandon. Though he stood once more in the heart of his people within E'vahona, his thoughts remained firmly tethered to Keisha, an unwavering beacon amid the ever-lengthening shadows.

As he turned to retrace his steps toward the heart of E'vahona, the uncertainty of the future weighed down his strides, and he could not shake the feeling that destiny had yet to reveal its full hand.

Beneath the surface of his simmering frustration, Ong harbored a determination that smoldered with intensity as he traversed the grand arches of E'vahona. He was prepared to confront the Eladrin Council about this unexpected summons that had torn him away from the relentless pursuit of Keisha. With an expression as tempestuous as the storm-tossed sea, he strode into the council chamber, his gaze unwavering as it locked onto Lord Karrenen.

"Why have I been summoned back?" Ong's voice sliced through the air like a blade, tinged with a palpable discontent that mirrored his reluctance to be torn from the ceaseless hunt for answers.

Karrenen met Ong's unyielding gaze with a demeanor that balanced empathy and steely resolve. "There is news, Ong. The dragons have returned with their discoveries, and we deemed it imperative that you be present."

A furrow etched Ong's brow, a tapestry of curiosity and a restless impatience as the mere mention of dragons pricked his interest. Yet, beneath it all, the yearning to return to the embrace of the Purplefire Woods gnawed at him. "What have they found?"

Karrenen's unwavering gaze bore into Ong's, and his words hung heavily in the air, sinking into the core of Ong's consciousness. "They have stumbled upon an altar, perched atop one of the volcanic peaks—an altar that harbors ominous intent, hinting at a dark ritual."

The gravity of those words settled like a leaden shroud over Ong. Sacrifice... The dominion's relentless hunger for power had guided them along a path fraught with unfathomable cruelty, and Keisha's life lay at the epicenter of their sinister designs.

"An altar?" Ong's voice trembled with urgency. "Where is it? Which mountain?"

Karrenen's expression bore a touch of sympathy as he answered. "The volcanic range to the north, not far from the territories of the Emberwood Forest and Fel Thalor."

Ong's heart constricted at the mere mention of the forest that had once been Keisha's sanctuary, where they had woven the tapestry of their memories and sought refuge from the world's tumult. The insidious tendrils of the dominion's malevolent influence lay ensnared it. He vividly recalled that it was the place Keisha had been cruelly snatched months ago, leaving an indelible void in his soul.

As he pondered the forest's fate, he could only begin to fathom the evil energy concealed within that ominous altar. This cryptic enigma whispered of Vuarus and Phoenix's sinister intentions for a place so intricately intertwined with their shared past.

This once-hallowed forest stood in grim proximity to Fel Thalor and Old Flameford, the ancestral cities of the Druchii and Phoenix, respectively. Now, it had morphed into a grotesque caricature of its former self, a haunting testament to the dominion's ceaseless and unforgiving encroachment upon the world.

"I should've been there," Ong murmured, a heavy mixture of self-blame and anger toward the dominion weighing on his words.

Karrenen, his touch a comforting anchor on Ong's shoulder, offered words of reassurance. "You are here now, Ong. Your presence is more crucial than ever. This discovery may be key to unveiling the dominion's intentions and ultimate goals for Keisha."

Ong's jaw set, his determination crystallizing into resolve. He would not permit Keisha to become another pawn in the dominion's evil game. "Then let us gather all the information we can about this altar. It might be the very key to finding her."

In agreement, Karrenen nodded solemnly. "We will dispatch scouts to delve deeper into this matter. I understand your frustration, but remember. You do not stand alone in this ordeal. We are here beside you every step of the way."

Ong's eyes met Karrenen's, a potent blend of gratitude and unwavering determination shimmering within their depths. Together, they vowed to unmask the dominion's shadowy machinations and wrench Keisha from the Abyss's cold embrace.

"Ong," Karrenen began, his tone measured but tinged with sorrow, "I must share with you that the dragons acted swiftly upon discovering the altar. They obliterated it before it could be fully activated."

Relief cascaded over Ong, intermingling with a profound gratitude for the dragons' intervention. The mere thought of Keisha being subjected to a dark ritual sent shivers down his spine. "Thank the gods," he whispered, his voice scarcely rising above a breath.

Karrenen nodded, his countenance solemn. "Indeed, but we must not let down our guard. The dominion will undoubtedly reinforce their efforts, fortifying the area to prevent further interference."

Ong's gaze transformed into a steely determination, a glint of resolve that shimmered in his eyes. "Then we must be relentless, Karrenen. We will gather every fragment of information about the dominion's intentions, their sinister designs for Keisha."

Karrenen's unwavering support shone in his gaze, affirming their shared mission. "You speak true, Ong. Each second we seize is a step nearer to wrenching her from their clutches. We shall make their journey to achieving their evil goals as difficult as can be."

Within the chamber, tension hung heavy, a palpable reminder of the delicate equilibrium they tread. Despite the temporary respite provided by the altar's destruction, both men were acutely aware that it was but a fleeting victory. The dominion's ominous intentions loomed like a haunting specter, a perpetual menace that cast its shadow over every action they took.

Ong's jaw clenched, his unwavering determination etched into his features. "We shall continue to rally allies, fortifying our cause. In their wicked schemes, Keisha's life is not a pawn to be trifled with."

Karrenen regarded Ong with a blend of admiration and empathy. "She is blessed to have your unwavering loyalty, Ong. We stand by you, offering every measure of support within our grasp."

Ong's gaze met Karrenen's, his eyes holding a profound sincerity. "No, Karrenen," he replied with a conviction that rang like a vow, "I am the one who is blessed. I didn't know what I was missing the day I met Keisha until she came into my life. I will move heaven and earth to find her and to extinguish those who have inflicted pain upon her."

Ong hesitated momentarily, his voice carrying a heavy burden as he confided in Karrenen, "I've found a piece of her necklace, Karrenen, along with the jewel I gave her during our engagement ceremony. It's as if Phoenix deliberately broke it, knowing that it would taunt me and remind me of the pain Keisha endured when she was captured."

Karrenen's expression darkened, mirroring Ong's own emotions. "It is a cruel act, indeed. Phoenix's malevolence knows no bounds. But take heart, Ong. We shall use every shard and piece as a reminder of our determination to free Keisha and end the dominion's darkness."

As they stood shoulder to shoulder, united in their shared purpose, the weight of the world's shadows bore down upon them. Time became their most treasured commodity, each passing moment inching them closer to the dominion's ultimate schemes and the impending reckoning that would decide the fate of their world.

Ong's voice quivered its tremor, a testament to the depth of his emotions. "Karrenen, please... convey my deepest gratitude to the dragons. Let them know... let them know that I am profoundly sorry for misjudging them at the outset. I have realized that there are noble and virtuous dragons, just as those tainted by darkness."

Karrenen nodded, his expression one of understanding and solidarity. "I shall ensure your message reaches them, Ong. They will comprehend and appreciate your acknowledgment."

Ong's gaze dropped, a blend of thankfulness and regret tugging at his heart-strings. "Especially Kimras... and the council he guides. They are true allies, willing to stand unwavering against the relentless tide of darkness. I am deeply grateful for their unwavering presence in this harrowing struggle." His voice quivered, emotions long kept in check now threatening to overflow. "Karrenen, there were moments when I teetered on the precipice of despair. But witnessing the dragons' unyielding efforts has rekindled a spark of hope, a reminder that we are not solitary in this difficult fight. That Keisha is not alone."

Karrenen's gaze softened, a comforting hand resting gently on Ong's shoulder. "Your heart bears a heavy burden, my friend, and it is a weight you bear justly. But remember, you are not traversing this difficult path in solitude. We stand together, committed against the dominion's relentless grasp. Keisha's strength is your strength, and your unwavering determination resonates within all who hold her dear."

Ong's chest constricted, and for a fleeting moment, he sensed the storm of emotions within him, teetering on the brink of eruption. He cleared his throat, summoning the strength to steady his voice. "Thank you, Karrenen. Thank you for being my guiding light when I waver."

Karrenen's smile radiated warmth, a testament to his steadfast support. "It is an honor to stand by your side, Ong. Together, we shall confront this looming darkness and guide Keisha to embrace the light."

Yet, as he moved away, a lingering recollection tugged at the edges of his consciousness, compelling him to halt and pivot back to face Karrenen once more.

Ong's voice quivered, his words uncertain and fragile as he ventured into unknown territory. "Hold on," he began, pausing to gather his thoughts. "Before I left the woods, there was something... I heard something. It was like a whisper, a fleeting echo in the breeze, but it sounded like Keisha."

Karrenen's demeanor shifted from contemplation to rapt attention. "What did you hear, Ong?"

Ong's eyes held a delicate balance between hope and apprehension. "It was her voice, Karrenen. It sounded as though she was in pain."

Drawing nearer to Karrenen, Ong's earnestness shone through. "And you see, it hasn't been just once," he confessed in a hushed tone, "I've heard her voice on multiple occasions as if it were echoing through the very depths of my thoughts."

The Eladrin lord's brow furrowed, his gaze a reflection of both empathy and profound comprehension. "It is entirely possible, Ong. Keisha may attempt to reach, communicate, or call out for you."

Karrenen's words lingered in the air, resonating with a sense of connection that transcended the confines of the present moment. They hinted at a more profound and mysterious bond, one where Keisha's voice resonated through the shared experiences of Ong and Keisha.

Karrenen observed the anguish etched into Ong's features, the glimmer of unshed tears in his eyes betraying the depths of his torment. Ong's voice quivered with the heavy burden of his emotions as he revealed, "Karrenen, the last time I heard her voice, it was drenched in fear and agony, barely more than a fragile whisper. The memory haunts me, and I cannot rid myself of this unsettling feeling that something is dreadfully amiss. I'm consumed by worry, Karrenen, a fear for her like I've never known."

Karrenen's gaze held a distant, reflective look as he continued, "You know, Ong, there was one other time in Keisha's life when she felt that same fear that her voice now carries. It was when she lost both her parents, and for a while, she believed she was utterly alone in the world. The fear of isolation and helplessness is something she's carried with her since that time. Perhaps, in some way, Keisha is experiencing that same feeling now."

Ong's eyes widened with empathy as he absorbed Karrenen's revelation. The depth of Keisha's experiences and fears drew them closer, forging a stronger bond. He nodded solemnly and replied, "Karrenen, I had no idea Keisha had such a difficult time. It only reinforces our commitment to bringing her back, to ensure she never has to feel that kind of isolation. We'll find her, Karrenen. Together, we'll make sure she knows she's loved and never alone."

Karrenen, his heart heavy with empathy, paused momentarily as he reflected on Ong's impassioned words. He understood the profound bond between his friend and Keisha and was deeply moved by it. With genuine gratitude in his voice, he responded, "Ong, your unwavering dedication to her is truly commendable. I feel fortunate to have a friend like you who cares so deeply. We'll stand steadfastly by her side, facing whatever challenges may arise. We shall ensure she knows she's not alone in her tribulations."

He looked directly into Ong's eyes and continued, his voice tinged with a newfound seriousness, "Be prepared, Ong. If you hear her voice again, please inform us immediately if that connection returns. It might be a sign, a way for us to reach out and offer her aid."

Ong nodded resolutely, a fire of determination burning in his eyes. "I promise I won't ignore it if I hear her again. I'll do whatever it takes to help her, no matter what."

Karrenen's hand on Ong's shoulder was both grounding and reassuring. "Good. We are all in this together, Ong. Remember that."

As Ong left the chamber, the echoes of Keisha's whispered cry lingered in his heart. A renewed sense of purpose surged within him. He would be vigilant, listening for her voice in the wind, ready to respond if she reached out across the vast chasm that separated them. In the face of the dominion's darkness, their unyielding resolve would be the beacon of hope that would guide them to Keisha's side.

After Ong had left the council chamber, Karrenen turned to the assembled members, his gaze thoughtful. The chamber, adorned with intricately carved stone walls that bore the history of the Eladrin realm, exuded an air of solemnity. Sunlight filtered through tall, arched windows, casting dappled patterns of light and shadow across the long, polished table where the council members sat. The atmosphere was one of gravity and introspection as Karrenen began to speak.

"I believe we owe Ong an apology," he began, his voice carrying a touch of regret, echoing within the chamber's hallowed walls. The flickering torches on the walls cast dancing shadows that underscored the weight of his words. "In the beginning, many of us doubted his suitability for Keisha. We allowed our prejudice to blind us, to make judgments based on his human heritage."

He paused momentarily, letting his words sink in, the silence accentuating the moment's gravity. "But Ong has proven time and again that love knows no boundaries. He has shown unwavering dedication, not only to Keisha but to our cause as well. It's a reminder that we should never underestimate the power of love, especially in the face of darkness."

Karrenen's gaze swept over the council members, his expression of solemn resolve amplified by the chamber's ambiance. The intricate tapestries that adorned the walls depicted heroic Eladrin figures in epic battles, their rich colors brought to life by the flickering torchlight. "Especially me," he added, his voice carrying the weight of his realization, the words reverberating in the cavernous space. "I've come to consider Keisha a daughter, and I owe Ong an apology for my initial doubts."

He paused, his eyes scanning the faces of those seated around the table, each one a representative of the Eladrin realm. The polished marble table, adorned with ornate carvings of mythical creatures, gleamed beneath the torchlight. "His determination to find and bring her back to us speaks volumes about his character."

Karrenen's expression grew more determined, his voice steady with conviction, and the torches' flickering flames mirrored the unwavering resolve in his gaze. "We misjudged him, blinded by the biases we held. We deemed him inadequate because he was not one of us. And yet, who among us could claim to be doing more for Keisha? Who would go to such lengths, endure such trials, for the one they love?"

He let the weight of his words settle over the council, a silence enveloping the chamber as the truth of his words resonated, the very stones of the chamber seeming to bear witness to this moment. "Ong's actions should serve as a lesson for us all. We must remember that one's origin does not determine worth but by the choices one makes, the love one shows, and the sacrifices they are willing to make. Let us not repeat the mistake of underestimating others due to preconceived notions."

A sense of unity filled the room, an unspoken agreement to heed Karrenen's words. The council members exchanged knowing glances, each one recognizing the importance of setting aside biases and embracing the depth of character that could exist within anyone, regardless of their background.

With a final nod, Karrenen concluded, "Ong's devotion to Keisha should inspire us all to be better judges of character, to see beyond the surface, and to recognize the potential for greatness in unexpected places." The echoes of his words lingered in the chamber, a profound shift in perspective and purpose settling over those who had gathered there.

Karrenen, however, remained behind, lost in his thoughts as a tumultuous sea of introspection washed over him. He gazed out the chamber's arched window, offering a breathtaking panorama of E'vahona's ethereal beauty. Beyond the window, the city's spires and bridges seemed to float amidst the forest's ancient trees, bathed in the soft, silvery light of the Eladrin realm. The world outside reflected the wonder and magic that filled their lives but also held the lingering absence of one they cherished.

His mind drifted to Keisha, the young woman who had become entwined with their destinies, her strength and resilience shining as a beacon in the darkest times. Her absence weighed heavily on his heart, and he could not shake the feeling that he had failed her, that they all had.

In a soft, contemplative tone, Karrenen spoke to himself, his words carrying the weight of his newfound understanding. "When Keisha returns," he murmured, his gaze distant as he watched a gentle breeze rustle the leaves of trees in E'vahona, "I must make amends. From this day forth, I shall tell her that she is my daughter in every sense. She should never feel orphaned, never believe she has no family, no one who cares."

His commitment to rectify his past misjudgments and heal the wounds of neglect grew stronger with every passing moment. "Ong, her devoted husband," he continued, his voice filled with conviction, "has cherished her as if she were the most precious and special soul in all the realms, and I shall support him in breaking the chains of solitude that have bound her for too long. Together, we shall be the family she has longed for, and she shall never question her place in our hearts again."

With that solemn vow, Karrenen turned away from the window, his resolve unwavering. The time for redemption and healing had come, and he was determined to ensure that Keisha would never again feel alone in a world filled with those who cherished her. The chamber seemed to resonate with the profound shift in his determination, and the ethereal beauty of E'vahona bore witness to his heartfelt commitment

Chapter 38

Shadows Unveiled: Echoes of Torment

In the dim, frigid cell that had become her wretched abode, Keisha crouched in a desolate corner. Her once-glorious locks now resembled a tangled thicket, and her tattered garments clung to her skeletal form like a shroud of misery. With each passing day, her inner fire dwindled, threatened by the oppressive shadows that enveloped her. As she cast her eyes longingly upon the minuscule, iron-barred window high above, a glimmer of hope, faint yet persistent, clung to the recesses of her weary soul.

Beyond the confines of her prison, in the cold, light-starved corridor, Lyra and her evil brother Qellaun moved with arrogance and cruelty that defined their Druchii nature. They approached bearing a pitiful offering—a tarnished plate laden with remnants of unidentifiable sustenance and a thick, inky substance that oozed like malevolence itself.

Lyra's eyes narrowed to malicious slits as she neared Keisha's cell, her lips curving into a sardonic smile. "Well, well, what a fortunate day for you, dear Keisha," she purred, her voice dripping scornfully. "We've graced you with a banquet, as you can see."

Qellaun, his visage contorted into a cruel grin, added, "Indeed, Keisha. Do you realize your great fortune that we're even bothering to feed you?"

With deliberate cruelty, they placed the plate just beyond Keisha's grasp, allowing the noxious aroma of the unappetizing morsels to assault her senses. Qellaun scrutinized her with suspicion, his eyes narrowing. "It appears she hasn't shown much interest, Lyra."

Lyra responded with a derisive chuckle, using her foot to nudge the plate closer to Keisha, causing its contents to slosh ominously. "Well, Keisha," she taunted, "the choice is yours. You can partake in this exquisite feast or starve. Not that you have many choices left to make."

Keisha, weakened but unbroken, pushed the plate away with trembling hands, a spark of defiance igniting in her weary eyes. Qellaun shot her an evil glare, his patience wearing thin.

With a voice dripping with malice, he snatched the plate from the ground and thrust it toward Lyra. "Perhaps the beasts will appreciate it," he spat, his frustration palpable. "I've had enough of this." He then turned to his sister, a sinister glint in his eye. "I'll be relieved when she's offered to the abyss."

Lyra laughed cruelly in agreement, nodding her head. "Yes, there's hardly anything left of her. Her husband wouldn't recognize her now. Although," she added with a wicked grin, "perhaps he'll find a new interest once she's gone. Who knows, maybe he'll turn his attention to me."

As the heavy cell door slammed shut behind them, the siblings exchanged a wicked laugh, fully aware that Keisha's fate was sealed. The echoes of their heartless jests resonated through the desolate corridor, leaving Keisha alone once more. The mention of her husband's interest in Lyra gnawed at her, a seed of doubt planted in her heart amidst the relentless cruelty she had endured throughout her agonizing months of captivity.

In the murky depths of a dimly lit chamber, Vuarus and Phoenix loomed, their evil intentions entwining in a sinister ballet, their thoughts coiling like serpentine tendrils of inky darkness. All around them, the dominion's nefarious power pulsed, as if it were a sentient force in harmony with their wicked desires.

With a cruelty that glittered in his eyes like shards of ice, Phoenix murmured, "I yearn for Ong to bear witness to her torment, to taste the bitter fruits of her anguish as if they were his own soul's torment."

A frigid smile, like frost spreading across his visage's dark canvas, slithered onto Vuarus's lips. "Indeed," he hissed, his voice dripping with malice like venom from a serpent's fang. "The Eladrin must share in her agony on the deepest level. For far too long, they have hoarded secrets, concealing the truth of E'vahona. This shall be the toll they pay, their suffering."

An insidious inspiration ignited within Vuarus, his deft fingers weaving dark magic into a crystalline sphere. "This shall capture the very essence of her suffering," he declared, his words laced with a chilling undertone.

As the sphere took form, Vuarus's sorcery intertwined with it, forging a sinister conduit to channel Keisha's torment. He handed the malevolent creation to one of the dominion's shadowy minions. "Place it within her cell," he instructed.

The crystal sphere pulsed faintly within Keisha's cell, its magic attuned to her suffering. Unseen and unfelt by her, it began its nefarious work, a vile vessel designed to trap the echoes of her anguish—pain, fear, and desperation. It morphed into a sinister conduit through which her torment would flow like a cursed river.

Meanwhile, Phoenix cradled a second crystal sphere in another hidden corner of the dominion. Innocuous and empty, it held a menacing promise, poised to unveil a nightmarish truth.

Phoenix sent the sphere on a silent journey through the shadowy tendrils of his power. It materialized within Ong's reach, the human warrior's fingers brushing against its cold surface, oblivious to the abyss it concealed. As Ong's fingers closed around the orb, his heart sank at the sight of something attached to it—a fragment of Keisha's necklace, a poignant reminder of her torment and captivity.

The cruel irony cut at Ong's heart, as he clutched the necklace piece and the orb, both bearing the weight of his love's suffering. It was a haunting symbol of the lengths to which Phoenix would torment them. Ong vowed to rescue Keisha with determination, burning anew, no matter the darkness threatening to consume them.

Ong returned to E'vahona with a leaden heart, a burdensome weight pressing upon him as he clutched the ominous crystal sphere. As he presented the enigmatic artifact before the council, Karrenen's brow furrowed in apprehension. "What is this, Ong?"

"It's a window into Keisha's torment," Ong replied, his voice tinged with sorrow, a river of empathy coursing through his words. "Phoenix and Vuarus have sent it, hoping we bear witness to the depths of her suffering."

A council member chimed in, their voice laced with concern. "But what of the necklace piece, Ong? Why would they send that as well?"

Ong's voice broke, and tears welled up in his eyes as he answered, "It's a cruel reminder that they hold her and that they have the power to break her. We must act swiftly to save her from this nightmare."

The council members exchanged solemn glances, a palpable gravity settling over their assembly. Karrenen voiced the lingering uncertainty that hung in the air, his words laced with doubt. "Should we activate it? Unveil its contents?" A murmur of agreement resonated through the council, and at last, Karrenen concluded, "Let us bide our time and choose when the moment is ripe."

Thus, the crystal sphere remained dormant, a vessel harboring secrets untold as moments turned into hours and days; anticipation within the council burgeoned, a volatile mixture of dread and determination fueling their unwavering resolve. The specters of suffering loomed ominously over Keisha and those who dared defy the dominion's evil grasp, their fates entwined in the shadows of despair and hope.

Ong's words hung heavy in the air, weaving a grim tapestry of understanding among the council members. The mere glimpse he had caught of the sphere's contents had ignited a furious tempest within their hearts. In silent unity, they pledged to brace themselves for the harrowing truth, aware that their righteous mission risked becoming entangled in the snares of vengeance. The line between duty and emotion blurred with each passing moment, and the shadows that clung to Keisha whispered of darkness that threatened to consume them all.

The council's decision weighed heavily upon them, a grim reminder of their treacherous path to rescue Keisha and defy the dominion's malevolence.

Vuarus and Phoenix returned to Keisha's cell, an ominous tension thickening the air. Unbeknownst to her, Vuarus activated the crystal sphere he had secretly placed earlier, its enchantment awakening with malevolent vigor. Within the chamber, an eerie glow suffused the surroundings, and the shadows seemed to writhe maliciously as if the very darkness conspired against them.

Keisha's body tensed, a palpable shiver coursing through her as though the embodiment of her deepest fears materialized in the chamber. Unseen, spectral hands seized her heart, squeezing it in an icy vise. Her eyes widened, wrought with a potent mixture of confusion and unbridled dread as the cruel spectacle of torment unfurled before her.

Whispers of cruel and relentless taunts and echoes of anguish reverberated through the chamber, an invasive malevolent storm that assaulted her psyche.

The spectral manifestations of her most dreaded fears took form, their presence an unyielding assault on her senses. The weight of hopelessness bore down upon her, a relentless pressure threatening to extinguish any vestige of her resilience.

Vuarus's voice, bereft of empathy and as frigid as the abyss, resonated within the confinements of her tormented mind. "You, Keisha, harbored the audacious notion that you could defy us," he sneered, his words laced with vicious cruelty. "You dared to believe your love could be an impenetrable shield against the relentless tide of encroaching darkness. How naive you are. The ever-encroaching shadows can cruelly extinguish even the most radiant flames."

With a chilling satisfaction that mirrored his malevolence, Vuarus added, "And let it be known, I was ingeniously meticulous in designing your cell, Keisha. Every facet of its torturous existence was crafted to hasten the erosion of your spirit. Oh, and by the way," he taunted, his voice dripping with sadistic glee, "your magic, the very essence of your being, has been siphoned away to the denizens of the abyss. They shall put it to use for the darkest of purposes."

Phoenix's laughter, tinged with sadistic amusement, intertwined with the cacophony of torment. "You are naught but a mortal, Keisha, trapped in a world of our design. Your struggles, in all their zeal, are futile."

As Keisha's vision blurred, tears of both physical and emotional anguish streamed down her face. The grotesque images shifted and evolved, each projection more nightmarish than the last. The crystal sphere, an unholy vessel, captured every nuance of her suffering, distilling it into a haunting spectacle that would be witnessed by those who dared to challenge the dominion.

The malevolent echoes of torment continued to resound, a grim testament to the relentless cruelty of her captors, and the unyielding spirit of Keisha was tested in the crucible of this nightmarish ordeal.

With the sphere now activated, the Eladrin council had assembled to witness Keisha's torment. Their expressions painted a mosaic of anger and empathy. Ong's knuckles whitened as his fists clenched, the sight of her anguish igniting a fiery determination within him.

Karrenen's eyes carried the weight of both sorrow and unwavering resolve. The echoes of Keisha's torment etched themselves into the very fibers of his heart. In response to Vuarus's comments about her magic, Karrenen's voice quivered with anger and sorrow. "You monsters," he muttered, his fists clenched at his sides.

As the crystal sphere continued its ghastly unveiling, the dominion's malevolence cast its ominous shadow over all who dared to stand in its path, a formidable force of darkness and despair that threatened to engulf them all.

Keisha's surroundings shifted once more, the spectral grasp of the Shadows Wraiths transporting her into another macabre reverie. This time, she found herself amidst the heart of a bustling city, the atmosphere heavy with the intoxicating scent of foreign spices and the hum of unfamiliar conversations. Faces, hazy and indistinct, swept past her like fleeting phantoms. She caught a glimpse of Ong among the crowd, yet his presence felt distant, his laughter a mere echo of its former warmth.

Phoenix's voice resonated in her consciousness, entwining with the illusory tableau. "Do you perceive it, Keisha? Your beloved husband, Ong, continues his life in your absence. He has moved forward, finding solace in another to warm his bed and heart."

Keisha's heart ached as the illusion played out before her, and tears rose. The torment of seeing Ong move on without her was too much to bear. Yet, deep within, a spark of resilience remained, a testament to her unwavering love and determination to endure this nightmarish trial.

Keisha's heart ached painfully within the confines of the illusion, an anguish she struggled to bear. She observed as Ong strolled arm in arm with another woman, their laughter chiming like a cruel melody. Doubt gnawed at the corners of her mind, and for a fleeting moment, the shadows of despair threatened to engulf her.

Yet, buried within her indomitable spirit, a spark of defiance ignited. She clenched her fists, her voice breaking through the illusion. "No... I refuse to accept this."

Phoenix's laughter reverberated around her, dripping with sadistic satisfaction. "Oh, but Keisha, can you truly deny the potency of these visions? The relentless torment of reality? He is but human. He will inevitably move on in time, leaving you behind, as you have always been alone, adrift in the unyielding sea of despair."

Keisha's resolve wavered, her vision blurred by tears that cascaded down her cheeks as she battled against the relentless onslaught of haunting images—yet, buried within the depths of her anguish, a desperate plea escaped her lips, a whispered request that hung in the air like a fragile, ethereal wisp. "Ong, please don't leave me," she implored.

But amid her torment, she clung to the memory of Ong's unwavering love like a lifeline, a beacon of radiant light piercing through the suffocating shroud of darkness. She closed her eyes, gripping that cherished memory with all her strength, a fierce determination that would not yield to the cruel machinations of the Shadows Wraiths.

The spectral vision began to dissipate, the suffocating grip of the Wraiths slowly relinquishing their hold. Keisha's voice, though frail, resonated with an unyielding resolve. "No matter your illusions, I hold fast to the truth. Ong's love for me is unwavering, and I shall not allow you to distort it."

As the imaginary world crumbled around her, Keisha found herself back in her grim cell, the oppressive weight of the shadows still clinging to her very being. Yet, within the crucible of torment, a spark of indomitable defiance glimmered, a reminder that love and unshakable truth could withstand even the darkest manipulations. Crumpling to the cold stone floor, she released a flood of tears, a release of the emotions that had been held captive for far too long.

While Keisha endured the malevolent visions conjured by the Shadows Wraiths, Ong's anguish manifested elsewhere, a storm within the hallowed chamber of E'vahona's council. Frustration and helplessness surged through him, erupting like a furious storm. His knuckles whitened as his fists clenched at his sides, and his eyes blazed with a wave of unrelenting anger, a burning testament to his determination.

"You will halt this madness at once!" Ong's voice thundered through the council chamber, each word a resounding declaration that pierced the very heart of the room. "Should any of these accursed visions bring her harm, if you so much as lay a finger upon her again," he seethed, his voice laced with a cold fury, "my arrows will find their mark in your heart, Phoenix!"

His chilling threat hung in the air, an echoing storm of anger and desperation that swept through the assembly. Council members exchanged startled glances, Karrenen's eyes reflecting concern and empathy. Ong's heart bled for Keisha, his love for her coursing through his veins like an unyielding torrent. He could scarcely bear the thought of her enduring such torment.

As the echoes of his righteous indignation reverberated, Ong's gaze softened, his voice descending to a mere, almost whispered, murmur. "Keisha, my beloved, wherever you may be, understand this—no matter the fabrications they weave or the cruel attempts to sunder us, my love for you shall forever endure. You are my heart, my soul," he confessed, his words' vulnerability contrasting with the anger that had ignited them. "And I shall find you, regardless of the cost."

With those solemn words, Ong's rage began to wane, supplanted by a quiet but resolute determination. He turned away from the council chamber, each step heavy with the weight of his emotions. Keisha's suffering had kindled a fire within him that would fuel his unwavering quest, an unyielding resolve to reunite with her.

A peaceful atmosphere enveloped the council chamber, where council members exchanged meaningful glances, their collective concern deepening. Amidst the heavy air, Karrenen's gaze gravitated to the crystalline sphere resting solemnly on the table, its ominous presence a haunting reminder of the torment Keisha endured. He observed Keisha's visage inside the globe, her eyes no longer ablaze with the spark of her spirit but instead reflecting a profound, desolate emptiness. "Did you witness the depth of her despair?" Karrenen's voice quivered, his words thick with both sorrow and guilt, his eyes never straying from the haunting image held within the sphere. He whispered to himself but loud enough for those nearby to hear, "I am sorry, Keisha.

I should have revealed that you were my daughter when you lost your parents. I failed you. I will find a way to make amends."

The council members followed Karrenen's gaze. Their collective focus is trained upon the haunting image of Keisha within the crystal sphere. "Indeed," Lady Seraphina remarked softly, her voice carrying a weighty concern. "Her eyes appear empty, as though the very spark of her spirit has been cruelly extinguished."

As the council members focused on the unbearable image of Keisha within the crystal sphere, Lady Seraphina's empathetic gaze settled on Lord Karrenen. She gently interjected, "Karrenen, it wasn't just you. We all bear the weight of this failure. We sent her on missions, indeed, but as a council, we collectively failed to embrace her as we should have. We let her down," she admitted, her voice carrying the weight of responsibility. Her gaze encompassed the council, a sad reminder of their shared guilt. "Now, it falls upon each of us to make amends, to ensure she never feels alone again."

Lord Thaldir's countenance darkened, the weight of a grim revelation settling heavily upon him. "The Dominion," he said, "is not merely seeking to break her physically. They are engaged in the insidious task of eroding her spirit, extinguishing the very essence of who she is."

Ong's hands clenched into tight fists, his knuckles stark against his skin. "We cannot allow this to persist," he declared, the urgency in his voice cutting through the air like a blade. "She has endured three months of their torment, damn it. Three months is an eternity. They will obliterate her if we do not act."

A solemn consensus rippled through the council, a shared understanding of the pressing need for intervention. The dominion's cruelty transcended the corporeal, infiltrating the very core of Keisha's being. The room hung heavy with their shared sense of helplessness, but it was also charged with an unshakable determination to rescue her, to wrest her from the clutches of malevolence.

Karrenen's gaze remained unwavering, affixed to the crystal sphere, his voice resonating with unyielding resolve. "We will locate her, Ong. We will bring an end to this nightmare. And we will ensure that the dominion pays for the suffering they have inflicted upon her."

The council members nodded, their collective determination filling the chamber with an unwavering resolve. As the echoes of Keisha's torment reverberated within the crystal sphere, they understood that time was of the essence. The dominion's malevolence had surpassed a grievous threshold, and their patience had grown thin. The battle against the encroaching shadows was far from over, but the flame of their resolve burned brighter than ever before.

Ong's gaze remained fixed upon the harrowing image of Keisha, her anguished form etched indelibly into his mind. In a sudden surge of fury, he hurled the crystal sphere across the room, where it collided with the wall and shattered into a thousand fragments, a visceral symbol of their unyielding determination to end her suffering.

Ong's chest heaved with the disruption of his emotions, an intricate tapestry woven with threads of anger, desperation, and grief that threatened to consume him. He turned to face the council, his voice quivering with the raw intensity of his convictions. "I recognize that we're exhaustively striving to liberate her from that wretched place, but I can no longer abide watching her endure such torment. They savor her agony, revel in her suffering, and I, for one, refuse to bestow them with that satisfaction."

Karrenen's gaze brimmed with empathy, his voice a harmonious resonance of shared understanding. "Ong, your frustration and anguish resonate with each one of us. Each passing moment she endures is a blade thrust into our very hearts. We shall retrieve her and ensure that they pay dearly for their hostility."

With a solemn nod, Ong pivoted and strode purposefully toward the exit of the council chamber, each step infused with restless energy, a genuine need to take immediate action. The heavy door closed behind him, leaving the council in a somber silence.

Lord Thaldir, his countenance etched with gravity, shattered the calm. "I would not envy Phoenix when Keisha is once more in Ong's embrace. I fear that Ong's thirst for vengeance may devour him entirely." He glanced meaningfully at his fellow council members and added, "Though I suspect he might not be alone in seeking vengeance. Vuarus deserves the same retribution as Phoenix, if not more."

The council members exchanged knowing glances, their collective resolve honed to a razor's edge. The dominion's cruel grasp had shattered Keisha's body and spirit, but in doing so, it had also forged an unbreakable resolve within those who loved her. The disruption of their retribution gathered strength, and when it finally unleashed its fury, the dominion would confront the relentless storm of their suffering.

Within the dimly lit confines of Keisha's wretched cell, an evil aura hung heavy in the air as Vuarus and Phoenix lingered. Vuarus summoned yet another ethereal creation, a grotesque amalgamation of darkness and despair, with a deft flourish of his hand. He positioned it strategically within Keisha's field of vision, a cruel specter that taunted her, a relentless reminder of the unending torment she endured even in their absence.

A sinister smile played upon Phoenix's lips as he reveled in her suffering. "A small token to keep you company during our absence," he jeered, his words dripping with sadistic glee.

Keisha's gaze fell upon this fresh manifestation of her agony, her eyes now empty of the fiery determination that had once burned within them. Their malice pressed down upon her, breaking her spirit further with each passing moment. It felt as though every ounce of hope and strength within her was being mercilessly stripped away, leaving naught but a hollow, lonely shell in its wake.

As Vuarus and Phoenix exited, their departing footsteps echoing ominously through the cold, oppressive cell, Keisha's resistance crumbled. Her emotional fortress gave way to an onslaught of anguish and fury, and she let out a scream that sliced through the air like a dagger, her voice an instrument for the profound agony she had been forced to endure.

Tears flowed freely down her cheeks as her sobs reverberated within the unforgiving walls of her prison. Her cries eventually devolved into incoherent whispers, fragmented echoes of her shattered heart reaching out in a desperate plea for solace. Then, with a voice so faint the surrounding shadows nearly consumed it, she uttered his name—a fragile, heartfelt plea that carried the immense weight of her yearning. "Ong, where are you? Please, hurry. I am not sure how much more I can take. Please, find me." She curled up in a small ball on the cold floor, her spirit crushed by the unrelenting cruelty of her captors.

Chapter 39

Shadows Unveiled: Whispers in the Shadow

In the dimly lit chamber of E'vahona, Ong stood solitary, his heart heavy with worry, and the haunting echoes of Keisha's anguished cry still reverberating in his ears. The encroaching shadows seemed to converge upon him, mirroring the darkness that had taken root within his soul. The chamber, carved from the living rock of E'vahona, held an eerie stillness, broken only by the faint flicker of bioluminescent moss clinging to the walls. It cast a pale, ethereal glow, revealing the intricate patterns of ancient symbols etched into the stone.

The council's discussions and strategic planning felt distant and muted, overshadowed by the relentless torment that held his thoughts in an iron grip. The councilors, cloaked in the subtle luminescence of their ceremonial robes, appeared as mere specters in the dim light, their voices fading into the background like distant echoes in the abyss.

Observing the abrupt change in Ong's typically resolute demeanor, Karrenen, his keen eyes attuned to the subtleties of his friend's distress, wordlessly approached Ong. His mere presence was a silent testament to their shared concern. Karrenen's steps were hushed, his boots barely making a sound on the smooth, polished floor of E'vahona.

Ong's gaze remained fixed on an undefined point in space, lost amidst the haunting resonance of Keisha's voice. His voice quivered, a palpable blend of anguish and frustration coloring his words. "Karrenen, did you hear that?" His voice broke, his fists clenched with unrestrained emotion.

Karrenen's brow furrowed as he tried deciphering the cryptic message within Ong's words. "Hear what, my friend?"

"It was her," Ong's voice trembled with emotion, his knuckles white against the turmoil within. "I heard her voice. She called out to me, asking where I was and pleading for me to hurry." His words were laden with a profound agony, and he continued, "Her voice was barely above a whisper, Karrenen. It sounded like she was crying, in pain, or perhaps both."

Karrenen's heart constricted at Ong's revelation, the gravity of the situation sinking even more profoundly. He gently rested a reassuring hand on Ong's shoulder, his determination unwavering. "Ong, she's reaching out to you, even in the darkest moments. It signifies that she's still fighting, still holding on."

Ong's gaze locked with Karrenen's, a potent mix of desperation and determination burning brightly in his eyes. "I can't remain idle any longer. I won't let her suffer while I stand by and do nothing."

Karrenen nodded resolutely. "We are employing every resource to rescue her, Ong. She will not remain trapped by the Dominion." The chamber seemed to pulse with their shared determination, the bioluminescent moss responding to their resolve by casting a stronger, more vibrant light, pushing back the shadows that had threatened to consume them.

A heavy silence enveloped them, the weight of their mission and the relentless torment Keisha endured hanging palpably in the air. The chamber of E'vahona seemed to close around them, the walls bearing witness to their shared resolve. The very stones, etched with the history of their people, whispered their support in the stillness.

Ong's clenched fists slowly relaxed, and his resolve hardened once more. "We will rescue her, Karrenen. No matter what it takes, we'll bring her back."

Karrenen offered Ong's shoulder a supportive squeeze. "We stand by your side, Ong, every step of the way."

Yet Ong's gaze dropped to the ground, his voice heavy with self-blame. "But I've already failed her, Karrenen. I failed to protect her from being captured, and now I'm failing to rescue her." His fists clenched at his sides again. Frustration was palpable in every movement. "I promised to keep her safe, to protect her, and yet..."

Karrenen's expression softened, empathy radiating from his features. He gently cupped Ong's cheek, coaxing his gaze to meet his own. "Ong, you are doing everything within your power. None of this is your fault. The Dominion's influence is vast, their reach insidious. You are not failing her. You are fighting for her with every fiber of your being."

Ong's eyes searched Karrenen's for reassurance and found it in the unwavering support he saw there. "I just can't bear to think of her suffering, Karrenen. I can't bear to hear her voice, filled with pain."

Karrenen's grip on Ong's shoulder tightened, manifesting their shared determination. "Then let that pain be your strength, Ong. Allow it to fuel your unwavering resolve to rescue her. We're close, Ong. We are unearthing their plans and identifying their weaknesses. And when the opportune moment arises, we will strike with all the might at our disposal."

A renewed fire kindled in Ong's eyes, a poignant blend of grief and determination. "You're right, Karrenen. I won't let her suffer any longer. I will do whatever it takes to bring her back."

Karrenen nodded resolutely, a fierce resolve mirrored in his gaze. "We are with you, Ong. We shall confront this encroaching darkness together and restore her to the light."

In that shared moment, a silent oath passed between them, a solemn promise forged in despair. The haunting echoes of Keisha's torment seemed to wane in the face of their unwavering determination. In that instant, they transcended being just Ong and Karrenen, becoming the embodiment of hope in a world shrouded in shadows. The heart of E'vahona, the hidden sub-realm within Vacari, bore witness to their unwavering resolve, its ancient stones echoing their determination.

Lyra's eyes flickered with annoyance and begrudging admiration in the Dread Spire as she observed the scene unfolding before her. The chamber, carved from obsidian stone, exuded an eerie, oppressive aura. Jagged shadows danced along the walls, casting sinister silhouettes that mocked the very concept of hope. Sinister runes etched into the floor pulsed with evil energy, serving as a dark backdrop to the unfolding drama.

Once a paragon of strength and defiance, Keisha now stood as a mere shadow of her former self, her spirit shattered and her will utterly crushed. The Dominion's ruthless methods were undeniably effective, and the evidence lay before Lyra, though she refused to accept their apparent victory without challenge.

"She may be broken, but she will never bow to you," Lyra's voice carried a defiant undertone, her words a steadfast testament to Keisha's enduring strength.

Vuarus turned his gaze toward Lyra, his lips curling into a knowing smile that sent shivers down her spine. His presence distorts the air, making it harder to draw breath. "Bow to us? My dear Lyra, such gestures are unnecessary. We seek the complete breaking of her spirit, for a shattered spirit is far more malleable and useful."

Lyra's brow furrowed, a complex blend of unease and understanding clouding her expression. The chamber's walls closed around her, amplifying her unease. "You intend to mold her into your instrument, to wield her as a tool?"

Vuarus's eyes gleamed with an unsettling combination of amusement and malice. Shadows seemed to writhe in the chamber's corners as if responding to his evil aura. "Exactly, Lyra. A spirit shattered and meticulously restructured becomes a potent force. Keisha's suffering will serve as the foundation for our Dominion's ascent, as I have explained to you previously."

Lyra's gaze remained fixed on Keisha, her internal struggle evident in the depths of her eyes. While she harbored no affection for the Dominion, she couldn't deny the effectiveness of their strategy. She had witnessed Keisha's transformation first-hand—the gradual erosion of her resilience and the rise of a fragile vulnerability. The chamber seemed to echo with the ominous resonance of their conversation as if the very stones bore witness to the struggle between light and shadow.

As Vuarus and Phoenix continued their conversation, Lyra's thoughts drifted to the profound implications of their actions. The Dread Spire, their sinister sanctuary, seemed to pulse with evil energy, the walls absorbing the darkness that permeated the room. The air grew heavier, laden with the weight of their malefic intentions. Lyra couldn't help but contemplate the grim mosaic that Keisha's once-unyielding spirit had become.

Keisha's spirit, once a blazing beacon of resistance, had been reduced to fragmented shards by the Dominion's cruel methods. While Lyra bore no love for the Dominion, she couldn't help but acknowledge the grim brilliance of their approach. They had achieved what the Druchii had been unable to do thus far, leaving a trail of despair in their wake.

Vuarus turned back to Lyra, his gaze penetrating and intent. "But do not forget dear Lyra, what we intend to do with her after breaking her spirit is the most critical aspect. Her role will be pivotal in our grand design."

Lyra's eyes narrowed, curiosity and apprehension swirling within her like a turbulent vortex. She had always been enigmatic, torn between her loyalty to the Dominion and her desires. Vuarus's words hung heavy in the air, leaving her to ponder what role Keisha would play in the Dominion's sinister plans—a position that transcended the mere breaking of a spirit.

Vuarus's smile deepened, his eyes ablaze with anticipation. The shadows in the room seemed to converge as if drawn by his dark charisma. "Indeed, Keisha's torment and transformation are only the inceptions. Her shattered spirit will serve as a guiding light, leading us toward the culmination of our ambitions. The Dominion's reign is imminent, and Keisha's suffering shall herald its advent."

The Dread Spire itself seemed to resonate with Vuarus's words as if it had been waiting for this moment. The runes etched into the obsidian walls pulsed with evil energy, a grim reminder of the darkness that threatened to engulf their world. In that chilling moment, Lyra realized the true extent of the Dominion's sinister plot, and the weight of her choices hung heavily upon her.

Phoenix's lips curled into an evil smile, his eyes shining with a twisted sense of satisfaction. "Revenge is a dish best served cold, my dear Vuarus. I yearned for her downfall, for her to suffer as she made me suffer. This is nothing short of perfect." His voice held a chilling edge, and a shadowy glint danced in his eyes, not just for Keisha but also for another target. "And as for Ong, the thought of his anguish adds another layer of delight to this intricate tapestry of torment. The time for reckoning draws near, and I relish the prospect of watching them both crumble."

Vuarus's gaze bore into Phoenix. His approval was evident. "Ah, the sweet taste of vengeance, my dear Phoenix. It is a sensation like no other. As for our next target, let us cast our ominous shadow over the realm of Goldmoor. Its inhabitants shall tremble beneath our influence, and the very foundations of the land shall quiver at the Dominion's touch."

In that chilling moment, the two figures shared an unsettling unity of purpose; their intentions aligned with the evil forces that propelled them forward. In their wake, chaos would flourish, and the Dominion's power would weave its insidious influence throughout the tapestry of the world, leaving no corner untouched by its dark grasp. The impending doom they heralded hung heavy in the air, a harbinger of despair.

Malrik's voice crackled through the enchanted communication, a mixture of anxiety and determination palpable in his words. "My Lord Vuarus, I must convey that we have encountered unforeseen delays in our efforts to reconstruct the abyssal altar. The necessary resources, especially the rare metal crucial for its assembly, have proven elusive."

Vuarus responded with swift authority, his voice commanding the situation. "Delays are impermissible, Malrik. The very fate of the Dominion hinges upon the completion of that altar. We can ill afford any setbacks."

Malrik hurriedly sought to alleviate his master's concerns. "Rest assured, my Lord. I have identified a potential source for the elusive metal we require. The realm of Goldmoor boasts extensive deposits of the very metal we seek. If we lay claim to it, the reconstruction of the altar could be expedited."

Vuarus's lips curled into a sardonic smile. "Goldmoor, you say? Very well, Malrik. Our path is now clear. We shall cast our ominous shadow over Goldmoor and ensure it becomes another piece in our grand design's intricate puzzle."

As the communication ended, Vuarus's gaze turned distant, his thoughts weaving the intricate threads of chaos that would soon ensnare Goldmoor. The Dominion's relentless march extended everywhere, sparing no realm from its ominous reach. Goldmoor, once a bastion of hope, would soon witness the darkest days as the Dominion's insatiable hunger for power drove it to consume all in its path.

In the shadowy and desolate confines of her cell, Keisha's eyes were drawn to the peculiar device left behind by her captors. Its surface shimmered with an otherworldly iridescence, casting an eerie, soft glow across the room. She reached out with trembling fingers, her touch hesitant, as if anticipating the device's recoil at her contact.

As her fingers brushed against the device, a surge of magic pulsed through her, and suddenly, her surroundings seemed to shift and twist. Visions materialized before her eyes, phantom threads weaving a tapestry of memories and emotions.

She saw her childhood home, bathed in the golden hues of a setting sun. Laughter echoed in the air as she played in the yard, the warmth of family wrapping around her like a comforting embrace. But then, the scene shifted, and the once-familiar faces contorted into grotesque masks of darkness and despair, leaving her alone and abandoned.

Tears welled up in Keisha's eyes as the images continued to unfold. She saw herself walking in Purplefire Woods, a radiant bride, her heart brimming with hope and anticipation. But the joy gave way to an overwhelming sense of loss, a gut-wrenching pain that left her breathless.

The scenes shifted again, showing moments of happiness and love with Ong. Their shared laughter, the gentle touch of his hand, and the look of adoration in his eyes rushed back to her, piercing her heart with a bittersweet ache. And then, as if the tapestry threads were being pulled apart, the moments unraveled into shards of darkness.

Keisha's grip on the device tightened as her vision blurred with unshed tears. The images shifted once more, revealing her torment since her capture. The pain, the fear, and the relentless cruelty surged to the surface, threatening to drown her in a sea of despair.

But amidst the darkness, a spark of defiance flickered within her. She remembered Ong's promise to find her no matter the cost. A surge of determination coursed through her veins, pushing back against the suffocating weight of her captors' malevolence.

As the visions slowly faded, leaving Keisha breathless and shaken, she clung to that spark of defiance like a lifeline. The device had given her a glimpse into her past, pain, and love. It illuminated the depths of her suffering and ignited a flicker of hope.

With renewed strength, Keisha whispered, "I won't be broken. I won't let them win." And as the shadows of her cell closed around her, she held onto that glimmer of hope, a beacon of light in the encroaching darkness. Once saturated with despair, the room seemed to echo with the resonance of her determination, a testament to her unyielding spirit.

Under the shadow of E'vahona's protective canopy, Ong stood alongside Karrenen, the weight of his emotions etched deeply into his visage. The mere whisper of Keisha's voice had fractured the fragile composure he had managed to maintain. He nodded solemnly as Karrenen elucidated their plans, his heart heavy with apprehension and determination.

"Ong, we're assembling a team of skilled elves and ethereal nymphs to embark on an expedition into the volcanic regions surrounding Emberwood and Fel Thalor," Karrenen explained, his eyes holding a depth of understanding. "Our mission is to scout for concealed Dominion activities, gather vital intelligence, and assess the situation."

Ong's gaze met Karrenen's, his determination unwavering. "I must be part of that team, Karrenen. I cannot remain idle while Keisha is in peril."

Karrenen placed a reassuring hand on Ong's shoulder. "I comprehend your resolve, my friend. Your unwavering dedication is admirable, and your presence
will undoubtedly fortify our mission. We depart at the break of dawn. Make the
necessary preparations."

As the first rays of dawn painted the sky with gilded gold and delicate pink hues,
Ong found himself amidst a group of seasoned elves and ethereal nymphs. Their
purpose was crystal clear—to navigate the treacherous terrain of Emberwood and
Fel Thalor, seek out any concealed Dominion activities, and, if possible, uncover
clues that might lead them to Keisha.

The arduous journey through the volcanic terrain tested their resilience, every
step an ordeal as they ventured deeper into the fiery heart of the region. The air
clung to them, thick with the acrid scent of ash and sulfur, a ceaseless reminder
of the lurking danger beneath the earth's surface. The ground beneath their feet
was treacherous, an unforgiving landscape of jagged rocks and uneven terrain,
mirroring the tumult that had befallen their world.

As they neared the outskirts of Fel Thalor, an overwhelming sense of foreboding
descended upon the group. The city, once a thriving beacon of civilization, now
lay in ruin, its architecture defiled by the evil touch of the Dominion. The
devastation surrounding them served as a stark and sorrowful testament to the
insidious presence of the Dominion.

Amongst the wreckage, the group moved cautiously, their senses heightened, and
their instincts finely tuned to detect any lurking danger. The elves' keen eyes
and the nymphs' ethereal connections to the natural world proved invaluable
as they meticulously scoured the area for concealed secrets. Ong's heart raced
with anticipation and dread, every step taking him closer to the elusive truth he
fervently sought. Like an ethereal whisper carried on the wind, Keisha's voice
lingered in his mind, a haunting reminder of the mission's dire urgency.

As hours stretched into days, their unwavering determination propelled them
forward through the unrelenting passage of time. Each discovery and a cryptic
clue they unearthed brought them nearer to unraveling the Dominion's sinister designs. Amidst the charred remnants of Fel Thalor, they stumbled upon a
chilling revelation—an altar, its construction left incomplete, yet its malevolent
purpose unmistakably evident.

Ong's jaw clenched as he surveyed the altar, a maelstrom of anger and sorrow
churning within him. He could only fathom the unspeakable horrors that would
transpire upon this darkened platform. This twisted monument bore the hall-

mark of the Dominion's cruelty and malice, a testament to the hostility that sought to engulf their world.

Karrenen's voice sliced through the oppressive silence. "We must dismantle this abomination and ensure it never sees completion."

Nods of agreement coursed through the group as they set to work, disassembling the accursed altar stone by stone. Each strike, each piece removed, was a resounding defiance against the Dominion's ever-reaching grasp, symbolizing their unwavering resolve to defy the encroaching darkness.

As the last stone was cast aside, a profound sense of satisfaction mingled with their collective weariness. Their mission had yielded results, unearthing the Dominion's vile intentions and disrupting their sinister progress. However, Ong's thoughts remained steadfastly fixed on Keisha. His determination to rescue her now heightened to an unyielding fervor. Looking back at the dismantled altar was a stark reminder that their pursuit must now be hastened; they had to find her before the Dominion could rebuild and carry out its nefarious purpose.

With the altar reduced to rubble, the group embarked on their journey back to E'vahona, their burdensome discoveries weighing heavily upon their hearts. The path ahead remained uncertain, the pervasive darkness still looming, but they had struck a resounding blow against the Dominion's oppressive reign. And amidst the chaos and uncertainty, Ong's resolve shone brighter than ever—his commitment to reuniting with Keisha, liberating their world from the Dominion's evil grasp, and forging a future free from the taint of shadows was an unquenchable flame that burned within him. Each step they took was a testament to their unwavering determination, a declaration that they would not rest until Keisha was free and their world was rid of the Dominion's malevolence.

Veiled beneath shrouds of ethereal darkness, Vuarus and Phoenix, the precursors of malevolence, led their sinister horde into Goldmoor—a city once teeming with vitality and hope, now reduced to a wretched tableau of devastation and chaos. The once-majestic buildings lay in shattered disarray, their former inhabitants fleeing in terror or huddling in quivering fear. A thick haze of despair hung heavy in the air, infused with the acrid scent of smoldering timber and the anguished cries of the wounded.

Amidst this nightmarish wasteland, Vuarus's eyes gleamed with perverse satisfaction as they wove through the harrowing ruins. "What a lamentable spectacle, would you not agree? A kingdom once held high in pride and prosperity now lies broken amidst the ashes."

Phoenix's sardonic grin darkened, his lips curling into an evil smile. "Yet, the true lament lies in the fate of the queen. Still trapped within the clutches of our shadow wraiths, she shall remain oblivious to the grand spectacle of her beloved city's demise."

Their callous laughter echoed cruelly, a haunting accompaniment to their inexorable march of destruction. Their vile minions scoured the lonely streets, looting with reckless abandon—seizing any trace of metal, whether it was a precious artifact or a mundane tool, and pillaging the remains of once-elegant dwellings, ruthlessly wrenching away metal embellishments, weaponry, and implements.

As they advanced further into the heart of the despoiled city, Phoenix's predatory gaze fell upon a solitary figure standing resolute amidst the wreckage. It was King Alex of Goldmoor, his countenance etched with a formidable mix of anguish and unwavering determination. His eyes bore into Phoenix's, an unquenchable ember of resolve gleaming within.

Phoenix's cold smile deepened as he approached the indomitable king. "King Alex, how poetically fitting it is to encounter you here again amidst the remnants of your kingdom. Your pride has led you to this precipice."

The king's voice rang with an ironclad resolve. "You may have reduced our city to ruins, but our unwavering spirit remains unbroken. Goldmoor shall rise anew."

Vuarus pivoted with an evil smirk, his lips curling in cruel amusement. "Ah, you speak of rising again, just as the Eladrin Keisha did, do you not?" His voice dripped with mockery, like venomous honey. "Full of spirit and determination, yet she languishes in our clutches, shattered and tormented."

King Alex's fists clenched, his visage distorted by anger. "You shall face the consequences of your actions, Vuarus."

Vuarus's eerie laughter reverberated through the crumbling ruins. "Ah, the hunger for vengeance, how quaint. But let us not rush ahead of ourselves. Your city has fallen, and your kingdom shall follow suit."

With a final derisive glance, Vuarus melted into the shadows, leaving behind a city in ruins and a king's unwavering resolve to reclaim his realm, regardless of the price to be paid. The darkness of their malevolence clung to Goldmoor, but the ember of hope still smoldered within the hearts of its resilient people.

King Alex sighed in relief after Vuarus and Phoenix left Goldmoor, but he couldn't shake the lingering unease that Vuarus's cryptic words about Keisha had stirred within him. He found it hard to believe she could be in their hands, but the uncertainty gnawed at him. He knew he needed to find a way to contact Ong to discuss this matter.

Meanwhile, Karrenen received troubling news that Goldmoor had been attacked once again. However, there was a peculiar twist to this assault; unique materials and metals had been taken from the city. Concern etched across his face, Karrenen turned to Ong, his voice tinged with urgency. "Ong, you need to go to Goldmoor. It has been attacked again, but this time, something unusual happened. Special materials and metals were stolen from the city."

Ong furrowed his brow. "That sounds ominous, especially the theft of the metals. I will journey to Goldmoor immediately and speak to King Alex." With a determined nod, Ong turned and set forth on his journey.

Upon his arrival in Goldmoor, Ong's presence was swiftly relayed to King Alex. The king came out of the palace to meet Ong, his expression a mix of relief and apprehension. King Alex locked eyes with Ong, his gaze intense, and wasted no time addressing the pressing matter. "Ong, what did Vuarus mean about Keisha? What has befallen her?"

Ong's heart weighed heavy, recognizing that King Alex remained unaware of Keisha's capture and suffering. He drew a deep breath, and his voice is laden with sorrow. "King Alex, I deeply regret that you had to learn of this in such a manner. The Dominion, led by Vuarus and Phoenix, has abducted Keisha. They've subjected her to unimaginable torment, breaking her spirit."

King Alex's eyes widened in shock and fury. "No... This cannot be. We must rescue her, Ong."

Ong nodded, his resolve unwavering. "We shall, King Alex. We're expending every effort to bring her back. We shall not allow them to annihilate her."

King Alex's jaw clenched, his fists firm. "I pledge any aid I can offer, Ong. Goldmoor shall stand by your side in this battle."

Ong's grip on his bow tightened, a fusion of gratitude and sorrow shimmering in his gaze. "Thank you, King Alex. We shall require every ally we can muster."

Amidst the ruin and devastation, a bond formed between the two leaders united in their relentless quest to rescue Keisha. The shadow of the Dominion may have loomed large, but the light of their determination burned brighter than ever.

With resolve etched into every line of his countenance, Ong set his thoughts on the solemn duty ahead. He knew he must convey the grim tidings of Keisha's capture and the evil designs of the Dominion to King Manard and the merfolk leaders. His journey took him first to Crystal Vale, a city resplendent in crystalline beauty but now marred by the heavy burden he bore.

Upon his arrival, Ong was guided to the grand hall where King Manard awaited, an aura of surprise emanating from the monarch as he sensed the urgency in Ong's presence. "Ong, what brings you to our halls with such a grave demeanor?" inquired the king.

Ong's voice was solemn as he began to relay the dire message. "King Manard, I bear grievous tidings. Keisha, my beloved wife, has been seized by the vicious hands of Vuarus and Phoenix. They subject her to indescribable torment, with dark rituals planned in her name."

Shock and concern mingled in King Manard's features, his heart heavy with the gravity of the revelation. "This is a matter of utmost gravity. We shall not permit their nefarious designs to come to fruition. Crystal Vale shall stand unwaveringly by your side, Ong."

A profound sense of gratitude swelled within Ong's chest as he nodded appreciatively. "Thank you, King Manard. We require all the allies we can muster." The bond of unity between land and sea deepened as they resolved to face the encroaching darkness together.

Departing from Crystal Vale, Ong's path led him to the gleaming shores of Shimmering Coast. Here, he sought the audience of Aqilus and Adrianna, esteemed merfolk leaders, understanding the significance of their involvement. As he approached, he found them conversing near the tranquil waters, their graceful presence reflecting the depths of their aquatic realm.

Ong initiated the discourse with an urgent tone. "Aqilus, Adrianna," he began, his voice resounding with distress.

Both merfolk leaders pivoted to face him, their expressions a blend of curiosity and anticipation. Aqilus, with a measured tone, voiced the question that hung in the air. "Ong, what brings you to our shores?"

Drawing a deep breath, Ong acknowledged the weight of the news he bore. "Keisha, my beloved, has been seized by Vuarus and Phoenix. They intend to employ her in a dark and sinister ritual. I felt it imperative that you both be apprised of this dire development."

Aqilus and Adrianna exchanged a meaningful glance, their concern mirroring the gravity of the situation. Adrianna, with empathetic resolve, expressed their solidarity. "This is indeed a grave predicament, Ong. The merfolk shall unite with you in this endeavor. We shall do all that lies within our power to assist."

Ong nodded, his heart warmed by their unwavering support. "Thank you, both. We are formulating a plan to liberate her, but the strength of your allies is paramount to our success."

As Ong conveyed the harrowing news of Keisha's capture to Aqilus and Adrianna, the merfolk leaders absorbed the grim tidings with profound concern. However, when Ong's words began to unveil the extent of Keisha's suffering, it was Adrianna who, in a vulnerable moment, could no longer contain the anguish that welled within her. Tears welled in her eyes, glistening like the ocean's surface under the moonlight, and her voice quivered as she spoke.

"Ong," Adrianna began, her tone breaking with emotion, "you must understand that Keisha is not just an ally; she is a cherished friend. Our friendship was woven into the fabric of our lives when we were both young and full of dreams. We have shared secrets, laughter, and moments of joy. The thought of her enduring such torment... it rends my heart. We shall stand beside you as allies and kindred spirits who have known Keisha's light." Like silver droplets, her tears fell to the shimmering sands of Shimmering Coast, a testament to the depth of her bond with Keisha and her unwavering commitment to their shared cause.

As Ong departed from the shores of Shimmering Coast, his heart carried a newfound hope. Having shared the grim tidings with those who needed to be informed, he found solace in knowing he was not alone in this difficult struggle. United with allies spanning the diverse realms, he clung to an unwavering determination to rescue Keisha from the vile clutches of the Dominion and to extinguish their malevolent reign, like a hero venturing forth on an epic quest, driven by a burning desire for justice and the strength of unity.

In the dimly lit chambers of their malevolent dominion, Vuarus's temper flared like a fiery storm as Malrik delivered the news of the altar's destruction once again. His crimson eyes blazed angrily, and his voice hissed through clenched teeth, "Put guards around the area. No one is to approach unless they have my explicit permission."

Malrik, bowing deeply, struggled to contain his apprehension. "Yes, my Lord. It shall be done." As Malrik retreated, Phoenix, Vuarus's ever-present confidant, approached with a wry smile.

"You looked ready to incinerate him, my Lord. The destruction of the altar seems to vex you."

Vuarus's gaze remained unyielding, the roiling frustration simmering beneath the surface. "It's an inconvenience, nothing more. But this time, we shall ensure the area is secured."

Phoenix's grin widened, reflecting the dark humor often dancing in his eyes. "Speaking of inconveniences, did you see the shock on King Alex's face when you mentioned Keisha?"

Vuarus's eyes flickered with a momentary satisfaction. "Indeed. It seems the king was unaware of her fate until now."

Leaning closer, Phoenix adopted a conspiratorial tone. "Is there a way we can show her state to everyone? A little visual demonstration of what she's going through. That might break their spirits further."

Vuarus's gaze turned contemplative as he considered Phoenix's suggestion. "An intriguing idea. We possess the means to create illusions and manipulate perception. It could serve our purposes well. But we must ensure that Keisha doesn't perceive it as a sign of hope or rescue."

Phoenix nodded eagerly, his grin widening like a crescent moon on a sinister night. "Of course, my Lord. We'll craft it to align perfectly with our agenda."

Vuarus's lips curled into an evil smile, revealing teeth as sharp as daggers. "Very well. Let us proceed with this plan. A glimpse into her torment might be the final nail in their coffins."

As the two evil figures walked away, the echoes of their sinister intentions reverberated through the shadowed corridors of their dominion, setting the stage for a new level of psychological warfare that would leave their enemies in the throes of despair.

Amidst the hallowed halls of their sinister enclave, Lyra's voice cut through the heavy atmosphere like a blade, causing Vuarus and Phoenix to pause in their stride. They turned their attention to her, and her audacity earned her an arched eyebrow from the evil pair. "Forgive my curiosity, my Lords," she began, her voice measured and laden with intrigue, "but why is taking hold of E'vahona so imperative to our cause beyond it simply belonging to the Eladrin?"

Vuarus, ever the master of secrets and hidden knowledge, responded with a knowing smile, his dark eyes locked onto Lyra's. "E'vahona holds more than just political significance, my dear Lyra. It is a wellspring of ancient magic, a place where the very fabric of reality is interwoven with power. This realm is a convergence of energies, a nexus of arcane forces that can be harnessed and controlled."

Phoenix chimed in with an air of excitement, his voice carrying the undertones of a forbidden desire. "And let's not forget Kadona, the guardian of E'vahona. She has a unique connection to this place; her presence adds another layer of potency to its magic. With E'vahona under our Dominion, we can bend its magic to our will, amplifying our powers and reshaping reality itself."

Lyra's eyes glittered with newfound intrigue as she absorbed their words. "So, E'vahona is not just a conquest but a wellspring of unimaginable power."

Vuarus's smile deepened, his tone laced with anticipation. "Indeed. And once we have it firmly in our grasp, the Dominion of Shadows will become an unstoppable force, rewriting history and shaping the world according to our desires."

As the weight of their ambitions settled in the air, they continued down the dim corridor, their plans entwined with the essence of E'vahona itself—a realm whose magic and secrets promised to reshape their destinies and the world they sought to dominate.

Vuarus and Phoenix eventually retreated to a more secluded area, away from prying eyes and ears. The flickering shadows cast dancing patterns across their features as they delved deeper into their conversation, the corridors of their enclave bearing witness to the sinister schemes that would shake the world to its core.

Phoenix's gaze remained fixed on Vuarus, a question gleaming in his eyes like a dagger. "You mentioned earlier that breaking Keisha's spirit is crucial for the sacrifice. Why is that my Lord?"

Vuarus's voice took on a condescending tone in their shadowed sanctuary, his patience tested by the need for repetition. "Pay attention this time, as this is the last occasion I shall elucidate. Her spirit, once shattered, becomes malleable, pliable to the will of the Dominion's magic. When the time comes for the sacrifice, her essence will be imbued with a darkness that will amplify the potency of the ritual. Her pain, despair, and suffering will all coalesce into a surge of power that I can direct as I see fit."

Phoenix's brows furrowed as comprehension dawned. "Her broken spirit becomes a channel for the Dominion's influence, allowing you to wield it more effectively."

Vuarus nodded, his eyes gleaming with dark anticipation. "Precisely. A broken spirit is akin to a fractured vessel, and I will pour the might of the Dominion into it, shaping her essence into a force that will empower me beyond measure. It is a culmination of her torment and her fate."

Phoenix's lips curled into a cold, calculating smile. "And revenge against Ong plays its part as well."

Vuarus's smile mirrored Phoenix's, a chilling blend of vindictive satisfaction and calculated ambition. "Indeed. Ong's helplessness and despair at seeing his wife sacrificed will be the sweetest revenge. He will know that his defiance, his attempts to thwart me, were all in vain."

As the shadows seemed to deepen around them, the two dark figures stood united in their evil purpose, their plans aligning with the destiny they aimed to reshape. Keisha's plight continued to be the linchpin in their intricate machinations.

Phoenix's gaze glinted with a sinister idea, a smirk tugging at the corners of his lips. "Perhaps we should extend an offer to Ong and one of the Eladrin for a chance to negotiate a deal. A clever manipulation to buy us more time."

Vuarus's laughter, like the sinister echo of shadows, filled the air. "Ah, my dear Phoenix, the art of deception suits you well. Let's present them with an illusion of negotiation, a mirage of compromise. It will keep them guessing, doubting their course of action."

As they shared a moment of dark amusement, the intricate web of intrigue and betrayal they were weaving grew more elaborate, more delicate. The Dominion's power ebbed and flowed, its agents moving like chess pieces on a malevolent board. And in the center of it all, Keisha's fate hung in the balance, her spirit broken and her essence a pawn in their grand design.

In the dimly lit temple of the Dominion, Vuarus sat upon a twisted obsidian throne, his presence exuding an aura of evil power. As he contemplated the intricate threads of his dark plans, Malrik, his Chief Priest, entered the temple with a respectful bow.

"My Lord Vuarus," Malrik began, his voice reverent, "I request a moment of your time in private."

Vuarus regarded Malrik with a cool, calculating gaze and nodded, signaling them to proceed. Together, they walked deeper into the temple, where the shadows grew denser, obscuring their conversation from prying ears.

Once they were alone, Malrik spoke with reverence and trepidation. "My Lord, I have conducted extensive research into the upcoming sacrifice, and I bring news that I believe will please you."

Vuarus arched an eyebrow, intrigued by Malrik's words. "Go on, Malrik. I'm listening."

Malrik's voice was laced with a hint of anticipation. "The sacrifice of Keisha, the Eladrin, will fulfill the requirements necessary for you to retain your godhead."

Vuarus's lips curled into a satisfied smile. "Ah, excellent news. So, that means I have another four years before I must find another sacrifice."

Malrik shook his head, a knowing look in his eyes. "Not quite, my Lord. Keisha's sacrifice is unique. Her connection to nature, elemental magic, and the potency of her essence have made her a compelling offering. By sacrificing her, you will gain another two centuries before you must seek another."

Vuarus's eyes gleamed with malevolent satisfaction as he absorbed this information. The prospect of gaining an additional two centuries of godhood sent a dark thrill coursing through him. He imagined the boundless power he would wield over the realms, the dominion he would exert over the hearts and minds of mortals. But another aspect that delighted him even more was the extended duration of Keisha's torment.

A cruel smile played on Vuarus's lips as he contemplated the implications. The knowledge that he could prolong her suffering, increase the depths of her despair, and break her spirit more thoroughly brought him an insidious joy. He relished the idea of watching her spirit crumble under the weight of her agony, knowing that he had the time to shatter her resolve, bit by bit meticulously.

Turning away from Malrik, Vuarus's thoughts were consumed by the possibilities that stretched before him. Keisha's sacrifice would not only secure his godhood for centuries but also grant him the perverse pleasure of inflicting even more profound suffering upon her. The Dominion's grip on her soul would tighten, and her anguish would become his source of power, a twisted symphony that would resonate through the ages.

Chapter 40

Shadows Unveiled: The Realms In Shock

The Abyssal Dominion's Cruel Intent

In the heart of the Abyssal Dominion, shrouded in the murk of secrecy, Vuarus, and Phoenix concealed themselves within the shadowy veil of their sinister intentions. Like eerie echoes from the netherworld, their voices mingled in a sinister symphony, plotting the unveiling of their malevolent might. This revelation would reverberate through the very foundations of Keisha.

In the dimly lit chamber of darkness, Phoenix's lips curled into a macabre grin as he spoke, his words a venomous whisper that seemed to emanate from the darkest recesses of his soul. "It is time, my friend, to reveal to the denizens of Keisha the depths of suffering we have inflicted upon her, the abyssal shroud we've cast over her very spirit."

Vuarus, his eyes gleaming with sinister anticipation, nodded in agreement. "Indeed, dear Phoenix. Yet, we must also unveil the grim transformation she has undergone—a once-vibrant soul now reduced to a mere shadow of her former self. That will send shivers down their spines."

Their eyes locked, a malevolent understanding passing between them like an unholy covenant. This was no mere confrontation; it was a choreographed ballet of power and manipulation, a performance orchestrated to sow the seeds of fear and doubt across the realms.

With mastery over the very essence of darkness itself, Vuarus and Phoenix wove their ominous message in the gloom. It was a revelation that would cascade like an ink-black tide, spreading its evil tidings everywhere, connecting the realms through the intricate threads of magic that bound them.

Vuarus, his voice dripping with malice, whispered the damning truth, like a serpent's hiss, "Four months—four long, torturous months in our cruel captivity."

Phoenix's grin twisted into something even more wicked, embodying malevolence. "Let the realms tremble as they digest this morsel of information. Let them ponder the fate of the once-defiant Eladrin, now entangled in our nightmarish web."

Their nefarious message echoed through the shadowy corridors of the Abyss, a revelation that set the realms ablaze with hushed rumors and foreboding speculations. The Dominion had made its move, and the domains teetered on the precipice of disbelief, caught in the sinister dance of deception and despair.

Torture by the Abyssal Dominion

Imprisoned within the nightmarish abyss, Keisha remained utterly oblivious to the sinister machinations unfurling beyond the grim confines of her cell. Her existence had become an unending tapestry of torment and desolation, each day a relentless cascade of suffering that crushed her soul. Amidst the eternal twilight, spectral shadows writhed and whispered, their sinister murmurs tormenting her with grotesque apparitions tearing at her sanity's fragile fabric.

Within this surreal prison, the boundaries between reality and delusion grew thin, and the shadows seemed to breathe, to pulsate with their evil life force. Ethereal specters, the ominous Shadow Wraiths, danced around her, their touch as cold and invasive as death's icy grip. As they enshrouded her, Keisha's vision fragmented into a kaleidoscope of haunting images, each flickering before her eyes like the fevered visions of a tormented dreamer.

In one poignant instant, she stood at the heart of E'vahona, the city basking in the radiant embrace of the sun's golden light. Laughter, as sweet as the melodies of forgotten realms, reverberated through the air, and the comforting warmth of camaraderie embraced her very being. But then, the idyllic tableau twisted, the luminous brilliance faltering, and the once-familiar light succumbed to the haunting darkness. The city, once radiant, crumbled into ruin, its streets echoing with desperate cries and sorrowful pleas, a symphony of despair that shattered Keisha's heart into countless shards.

Tears welled in Keisha's eyes, her heart heavy with an ineffable sorrow as she bore witness to the heart-rending devastation that unfolded before her. She reached out, yearning to touch the memories slipping through her grasp like an elusive mist. Still, the relentless Wraiths held her captive, guiding her through a haunting procession of visions that burdened her spirit with insurmountable grief.

In the embrace of Ong, Keisha found solace, his steadfast arms offering both strength and comfort. Their shared laughter harmonized with the gentle rustling of leaves, a harmonious symphony beneath the timeless canopy of Emberwood's ancient trees. But as swiftly as a gust of wind through the forest, the scene transmuted the once-warm atmosphere, giving way to an ominous chill. Ong's form flickered and waned, his eyes turning vacant and remote. A cry of despair welled within Keisha's throat as she reached out to him, yet he dissolved into the ether like a specter, leaving her stranded in the frigid void.

Keisha's reactions mirrored the emotional turmoil of these visions, her heart torn between joy and sorrow, hope and despair, as the cruel Shadow Wraiths subjected her to this vicious psychological assault.

The Wraiths, relentless in their torment, weaving an intricate web of illusions, each strand a cruel distortion of the cherished reality she had once known. Keisha's heart ached beneath the crushing weight of longing and loss, her spirit battered by the ceaseless waves of anguish. As the sinister visions swirled around her, a haunting whisper reverberated through her mind, carrying the essence of despair.

Amidst this unending torment, Keisha's voice emerged as a fragile whisper, a delicate wisp carried away by the shadows that held her captive. Once radiant beacons of life's vitality, her eyes now mirrored the inky abyss that enveloped her. Yet, within the profound abyss of suffering, a flicker of her indomitable spirit endured—a resilient spark of defiance that stubbornly refused to be extinguished completely.

Keisha's breaths tore from her chest in ragged gasps, the relentless onslaught of torment finally relenting. She felt utterly spent, her spirit battered and bruised, the aftermath of the cruel assault on her senses. In her despair, a sad, feeble whisper escaped her lips like a fragile wisp carried away by the shadows that imprisoned her.

"Ong... help me, please," she murmured, her voice quivering with a poignant blend of desperation and aching longing. With a final shudder, she curled into a protective ball, seeking refuge from the harrowing specters that enveloped her.

Unbeknownst to Keisha, her desperate plea was not ignored. Vuarus and Phoenix stood vigilant, their malevolent grins mirroring the cruelty of their actions. With a sinister flourish of dark magic, they seized Keisha's whispered request, their sinister power weaving it into a perverse thread that would stretch far beyond the confines of her grim prison.

And thus, those haunting words, "Ong... help me, please," reverberated through the very shadows themselves, resonating with a malevolent resonance that sent sinister ripples coursing through the interconnected realms, bearing the heavy burden of Keisha's anguish and despair.

The relentless Wraiths continued their cruel charade, each illusion a perverse mockery of the world she had once known. Keisha's heart throbbed with the crushing weight of yearning and grief, her spirit buffeted by the ceaseless on-slaught of torment. Amidst the haunting visions that danced around her, a mournful whisper echoed within her mind, carrying the essence of desolation.

Within the crucible of anguish, Keisha's voice emerged as a mere whisper, a fragile thread entwined with the shadows that held her captive. Once radiant with life's vitality, her eyes now mirrored the Stygian darkness that engulfed her. She was yet buried deep within the unfathomable abyss of suffering; a faint ember of her indomitable spirit persisted—a stubborn spark of resistance that refused to yield to utter destruction.

As the boundaries of her perception blurred and shifted, the shadows themselves assumed an eerie sentience. The spectral forms of the Shadow Wraiths swirled around her, their glacial touch invasive and cruel. They enveloped her, causing her vision to fragment into a tumultuous whirlwind of images that flickered before her eyes like fevered phantasms.

It was a symphony of torment, a cacophony of despair, and Keisha was the unwilling audience, trapped in a nightmarish theater where her suffering played out before her. The Wraiths reveled in their malevolent performance, each vision designed to break her spirit further and shatter her resolve. Yet, within the depths of her agony, Keisha clung to a sliver of hope, a fragile whisper of her true self that refused to be extinguished.

In Ardinia

Amidst the enchanting realm of Nymphs and fairies, the radiant Queen Aeliana took her place in her ethereal subjects, their presence as delicate as the petals of the most elusive flowers. The news of Keisha's capture had reached their celestial ears, casting a shadow over their otherworldly haven.

A palpable concern etched itself onto the exquisite features of these luminous beings as they exchanged troubled glances, their iridescent eyes mirroring the collective worry that hung heavy in the air like a gentle mist. Queen Aeliana, her essence interwoven with the very heart of the natural world, summoned her nymphs and fairies to her side.

She implored them to witness the distressing images of Keisha's suffering in a voice as lyrical as the song of a thousand birds. Their realm was renowned for its profound connection to the natural world, pulsating with vibrant energies, and the sight of Keisha's torment pierced their hearts like a thorn. "Look upon her," Queen Aeliana prayed, her voice trembling with an unmistakable sorrow that seemed to resonate with the elements around them. "The fire that once burned so brilliantly in her eyes when she graced our realm has been quenched, almost extinguished. We must unite, my dear subjects, against this encroaching darkness, not only for Keisha but for the salvation of all realms." Like a haunting melody, her words resonated with poignant clarity, igniting a shared determination among her subjects—a resolve to confront the evil force that threatened to snuff out Keisha's indomitable spirit.

Queen Aeliana's voice remained a gentle yet unwavering current as she addressed her people, her regal presence infusing them with a renewed sense of purpose. "Throughout the annals of our realm's history, we have faced and conquered darkness. Keisha shines as a radiant beacon, and we shall not permit her light to be extinguished."

The Nymphs and fairies nodded in solemn accord, their delicate forms reflecting the luminescence of their realm. With a shared determination, they cast their minds back to the adversities they had triumphed over in the past. They stood prepared to face the looming trials once more, their collective spirit aflame with the unyielding determination to ensure that Keisha's spirit remained unbroken, a testament to the enduring power of light in the face of encroaching darkness.

In the ethereal realm of Kadona, Goddess of Light and Protector of the Eladrin

The chilling echoes of Keisha's capture reverberated through the hallowed, luminescent halls of Kadona's divine realm. There, in the presence of the Goddess of Light and Protector of the Eladrin Elves, a profound sorrow gripped her very being as the dreadful tidings reached her celestial ears. Her resplendent radiance momentarily dimmed, casting a shadow over her ethereal form.

Tears welled in the eyes of Kadona, their glistening trails akin to the stars adorning the midnight sky. In a whisper that carried a symphony of grief and a crescendo of determination, she spoke, "My Guardian," her voice a lament that resonated with the essence of her divine sorrow. "How they have inflicted suffering upon you, how they have twisted the sacred path you tread."

Her gaze remained fixed upon the embodiment of Keisha's anguish, her heart a leaden weight as she took in the desolation that had befallen her cherished Guardian. "This is not the guardian I once knew," Kadona's voice trembled, a tumultuous blend of righteous anger and boundless compassion. "What horrors have they wrought upon your radiant spirit? What darkness have they dared to cast upon your radiant light?" Her divine powers stood poised, a formidable bulwark to defend and protect her sacred realm—a steadfast beacon of hope for the Eladrin Elves and their valiant Guardian.

"My children," Kadona addressed the gathered Eladrin, her voice bearing the weight of her awareness of Keisha's suffering. Her words resounded with unwavering conviction. "Keisha's indomitable strength has ever been a wellspring of inspiration for us. Let this dark transgression serve as a stark reminder of the enduring significance of unity and resilience. We shall not waver. We shall reclaim her."

The Eladrin, bound by their steadfast loyalty to their Goddess, nodded in solemn agreement. In the face of relentless adversity, Kadona's radiant light shone ever more resplendently, an unerring beacon of hope for those who dared to defy the encroaching shadows in their quest to reclaim their Guardian.

As Kadona's voice quivered with the burden of responsibility and the lamentation of being unable to aid her Guardian, her celestial tears fell freely. She whispered, "Why am I confined by such restrictions when my Guardian is in dire need?" Her plea was a haunting echo, a testament to her love and anguish for the one entrusted to her care.

Beneath the depths of the vast ocean, in the domain of Lysander, God of the Sea

The message reached Lysander, the god of the sea, his eyes akin to the ever-shifting tides, flickering with deep concern as the disconcerting news washed over him. By his side, the creatures of the sea congregated, a living testament to the unwavering unity that bound the ocean's residents together.

Lysander's voice resonated like the relentless waves of the deep sea as he addressed the sea creatures and his divine counterparts, who had assembled in the hallowed underwater court. "My brethren," he began, his words carrying the weight of urgency and resolve, "the Dominion's malevolence knows no bounds. Keisha, a cherished friend to both our realms, above and below, has been cruelly seized. We must move with swiftness and unwavering determination to liberate her from their dark clutches."

In response, the sea creatures stirred, their collective resolve palpable as they communicated through mystical channels. Lysander turned his gaze to his fellow gods, a silent accord passing between them. The unity of the realms, their greatest strength, now stood poised to rally together to rescue Keisha and, in doing so, to restore harmony and equilibrium to their intertwined worlds.

A profound melancholy swept over Lysander, the God of the Sea, as he beheld Keisha's torment. The recollection of her visit to his aqueous domain echoed within his consciousness, reminding him of the vibrant spark of life and vitality that had radiated from her. "She was different when she graced our waters," Lysander mused, his voice tinged with heartfelt concern. "There was a luminous spark in her, a profound connection to the rhythm of existence. Her companions, her husband, and the enigmatic creature known as Pumpkin cherished her deeply. I worry for them, for Keisha, and for the bonds that interlace our realms." As the God of the Sea, his dominion extended over vast, unfathomable powers, and his alliance with the Eladrin elves remained steadfast—a source of unwavering aid and support for their time of need.

Lysander could not contain his frustration at the prohibitions imposed upon the gods. "Why are we barred from rendering aid when our assistance is so desperately required?" His booming voice carried his anger like a roaring storm. "This must change!" Like crashing waves upon the shore, his words reverberated through the divine realms, a clarion call for the gods to unite and challenge the oppressive restraints that hindered their intervention in the face of impending darkness.

In Crystal Vale

The chilling message arrived at the throne of King Manard, its ominous weight settling heavily upon his regal shoulders. Once a revered warrior of the resplendent Crystal Vale, Ong had departed to assume the mantle of Guardian of E'vahona, and now his beloved wife lay trapped within the cruel grasp of the Dominion.

The king sank into his majestic throne, his countenance paling as he revisited the haunting words delivered to him. He was intimately aware of the unbreakable bond between Ong and Keisha, and the news bore down upon him with a crushing weight. Crystal Vale, a city seasoned in the crucible of battle, now was embroiled in a different kind of warfare—a war that waged shadows upon the mind and heart alike.

Within the heart of Crystal Vale, a palpable atmosphere of shock and disbelief hung heavy in the air as the harrowing news of Keisha's torment swept through the city's streets. The image of the once-vibrant Eladrin, a Guardian of E'vahona, reduced to a mere specter of her former self, haunted the minds and hearts of all who had known her.

King Manard's eyes, once bright with regal composure, darkened with a fierce fury as he bore witness to the depths of Keisha's suffering. The unparalleled strength and indomitable courage that had once defined her were now overshadowed by the cruel scars etched upon her very being. Whispers of anger, laden with indignation, flowed like an underground river through the veins of Crystal Vale, and even those who had never personally met Keisha were touched by a profound sorrow at the injustice she had endured.

"By the resplendent light of Crystal Vale," King Manard proclaimed, his voice resounding with a steely resolve that sent tremors through the very foundations of his realm, "we shall not remain idle while one of our own languishes in such abhorrent torment. With E'vahona, Goldmoor, and every realm bound by the intricate tapestry of existence, we shall stand together to rescue Keisha and cast aside this encroaching darkness."

A newfound resolve took root in Crystal Vale, nourished by the haunting image of Keisha's suffering. The imperative for unity among the realms had never been more evident, and the memory of Keisha's once-vibrant spirit served as a luminous beacon, igniting the flames of determination against the Dominion's evil grip, ushering in a new era of persistent defiance.

In Goldmoor

A heavy, somber atmosphere settled like a dense mist over Goldmoor, the very city where Ong and Keisha had once been hailed as heroes for liberating it from the clutches of Phoenix's tyranny. The news of Keisha's capture reached the ears of King Alex, and it hung in the air like an unfathomable enigma. He had witnessed firsthand the profound love and unwavering strength that bound Ong and Keisha together, and now, that strength was being subjected to a cruel and relentless test.

King Alex, the embodiment of unyielding fortitude, slouched upon his majestic throne, his visage etched with the deep lines of sorrow. The citizens of Goldmoor, their hearts heavy with the weight of the dire tidings, experienced a poignant blend of shock and unwavering determination. Ong and Keisha had ascended to legendary heroes within the city's annals, and now, they found themselves confronted with a darkness that seemed nigh impossible.

The city of Goldmoor itself quaked with the seismic impact of the message. King Alex, renowned for his indomitable resolve, sank into the grandeur of his throne, his countenance a pallid mask of shock and disbelief. His subjects gathered around him, their expressions mirroring the profound doubt and anguish etched upon his face as the crushing weight of the news descended upon them like an oppressive shroud.

The indelible memory of Ong and Keisha's past heroics for their beloved city hung heavy, an enduring testament to their profound bond with the Guardians of E'vahona. Goldmoor had borne witness to the couple's boundless courage and unwavering determination. Now, beholding Keisha's suffering and the fading ember of vitality in her eyes, they were seized by an all-consuming urgency.

King Alex's voice, although laden with the sorrow of the moment, resounded with an unwavering resolve as he addressed his people, his words serving as a clarion call to unity and defiance. "This travesty shall not stand unchallenged. We shall unite against the Dominion's tyranny and summon the strength to reclaim Keisha."

In Goldmoor, the flames of determination burned brighter than ever, fueled by the collective knowledge of the suffering inflicted upon one of their own and the unshakable resolve to bring her back from the abyss of darkness.

In Coraluna

In the serene realm of the merfolk, the illustrious King Oceanous received heart-wrenching tidings. When the message arrived, he found himself in the company of his beloved daughter, Adrianna, and her devoted mate, Aqilus. Adrianna's azure eyes widened in sheer disbelief as she read the words, her delicate hand instinctively seeking solace over her racing heart.

"Father," she choked out, her voice trembling with a potent mix of shock and anguish. "This cannot be true. Keisha is my friend, my confidante. I have known her for countless tides. This... this cannot be happening to her."

King Oceanous, his stern countenance softened by his profound love for his daughter, placed a consoling hand upon her slender shoulder. His steely gaze bore the weight of his unwavering determination. "Fear not, my dearest Adrianna," he vowed, his voice a steadfast anchor in the storm of their emotions. "Keisha is our cherished friend, and we shall stand united against the encroaching darkness that seeks to engulf her."

Aqilus, Adrianna's steadfast mate, stood beside them, his fists clenched in indignant resolve. His visage bore a complex tapestry of emotions, where anger and determination intermingled like opposing currents. "We shall not remain idle, King Oceanous," he declared, his voice ringing like a turbulent sea. "In this dire hour, we offer our aid without hesitation. This cruelty shall not pass unanswered."

Together, they beheld the harrowing scenes of Keisha's torment. Her tears flowed freely like crystalline droplets, and Adrianna watched as her dear friend endured unimaginable agony. Beside her, Aqilus's voice, heavy with concern, broke the tragic silence. "It's as though they seek to shatter her spirit, to extinguish the very light that has illuminated her soul."

King Oceanous, the embodiment of wisdom and strength, wrapped his sinewy arms around his sobbing daughter. In that moment of profound sorrow, he offered her the warmth of his embrace, a wellspring of comfort and fortitude in the face of such relentless cruelty.

Aqilus, his steely resolve unwavering, reiterated his commitment. "We shall not stand idle, King Oceanous. Our realm shall unite and face this evil darkness with unwavering resolve and determination."

In Hidden Isles

The dragons, stalwart and resolute in their quest to aid the search for Keisha, received the distressing news of her capture and torment. Their reaction was nothing short of draconian fury—an eruption of anger rippled through the foundations of their hidden cliffs and valleys.

Among them, Kimras, a colossal gold dragon, his scales shimmering like molten sunlight, gazed upon his esteemed council members with an air of solemnity that scarcely concealed the seething wrath within him. "This affront," he declared, his voice thunderous and laced with draconian anger, "is not merely an attack on Keisha alone; it is an affront to every realm and an insult to the balance that sustains our existence. Vuarus seeks to parade his power by shattering her spirit, but he has trespassed too far." His eyes bore into his council members with unwavering resolve. "This time, Vuarus must be eradicated, and we shall leave no shadow of doubt in our intent." He turned to Amara, the amethyst dragon, and locked eyes with her, an unspoken pact forming between them. "If my might is required, I shall plunge headlong into the rescue of Keisha, and I trust you shall do the same."

Kimras, his golden form resplendent with fury, unleashed a furious roar that rents the air. Like the thunderous wrath of the heavens, the sound reverberated through their realm—a visceral testament to the depth of the dragon's anger and frustration. Amara, the amethyst dragon, cast a keen and narrowed gaze upon the distressing scene before her, her eyes discerning the unmistakable absence of luster in Keisha's once-vibrant orbs—an undeniable marker of the unspeakable suffering she had endured.

"The Dominion," Amara growled, her voice a melodic yet menacing symphony, "has flagrantly overstepped its boundaries. Keisha has earned our respect and admiration through her courage in the Battle of Goldmoor. We shall not remain passive observers, for the hour has come to take action." Her proclamation resonated with an unwavering commitment to justice and retribution, echoing the dragons' resolve to defend the realms against the Dominion's tyranny.

In E'vahona

The Eladrin and Ong, united in their tireless quest to locate Keisha, came together once more to grapple with the jarring revelation delivered by the Dominion. Their faces bore the weight of the grim tidings, and emotions ran high as they confronted the chilling message that now reverberated across the realms.

"Why now?" Ong's voice quivered with a potent mix of disbelief and frustration as he scrutinized the ominous message. His heart ached with anguish, and Keisha's relentless torment weighed heavily upon him.

Karrenen, known for his unwavering composure and rationality, stepped forward to offer his perspective. His voice, however, carried an undertone of righteous indignation. "They are taunting us, Ong," he declared, his eyes reflecting the storm brewing within his soul. "This revelation is a calculated act to pierce our hearts, to let us know they possess Keisha and have succeeded in breaking her spirit. It is, without a doubt, a psychological tactic."

The air within their assembly grew taut, each group member grappling with a tumultuous mix of emotions. Ong's fists clenched in a silent testament to his frustration and impotent anger as the enormity of Keisha's torment bore down upon him like a crushing weight.

Karrenen's once-calm eyes, now stormy and turbulent, furrowed his brow with seething anger. "The Dominion," he growled, his voice resonating with righteous fury, "seeks not only to imprison her physical form but to subdue her indomitable spirit. Their intent is clear—to showcase their evil power and dominance over her."

Ong's once-resolute jaw tightened, his eyes clouded with a maelstrom of emotions as he struggled to fathom the horrors that Keisha had been enduring. He had heard her pitiful whispers, her voice akin to a fragile thread straining against the unyielding darkness, and it tore at his very soul.

"Four months," he muttered, the words escaping his lips like a venomous hiss, each syllable heavy with a volatile blend of anger and desperation. "Four interminable months she's languished within their vile clutches..."

Turning away, his voice now a furious and solemn vow, he whispered to himself, a promise forged in the crucible of his rage and sorrow, "Phoenix shall pay dearly for the torment he has inflicted upon Keisha. This I swear upon my very essence!"

The Eladrin, their faces etched with concern, exchanged somber glances, realizing that their unity had become an irreplaceable pillar of strength in the wake of this harrowing revelation. As the agonizing tidings of Keisha's torment rippled through the very heart of E'vahona, the realm itself seemed to brace for the impending storm that loomed ominously on the horizon.

Within the tranquil embrace of E'vahona, Ong's troubled gaze locked with Karrenen's concerned eyes, and the raw emotions they shared seemed to ripple through the very fabric of their realm. "Did you see her eyes?" Ong's voice quivered with anguish, his words carrying the weight of unbearable sorrow. "Hear her whisper? 'Ong, help me, please.' She asked me for help, Karrenen. And I'm failing her."

Karrenen, the embodiment of steadfast support, placed a comforting hand upon Ong's trembling shoulder. "Ong," he said softly, his voice carrying the reassurance of a loyal friend, "you're doing everything within your power to save her. We all are. Keisha knows your love and your unwavering determination. She knows we won't rest until we bring her back."

Ong's fists clenched, the muscles in his arms taut with palpable frustration. "Four months," he seethed, his voice a torrent of pent-up fury. "Four long, agonizing months she's endured this torment. It's been too long, and I won't allow her to suffer another day."

Karrenen met Ong's gaze, their shared determination igniting a spark of hope in their troubled hearts. "We will find her, Ong," he declared with a fierce resolve, "and we will wrench her from the clutches of the Dominion. We will show them that they cannot break our indomitable spirit together. We shall stand united, a beacon of light against their oppressive darkness."

Ong inhaled deeply, his resolve resolidifying in the face of his friend's unwavering support. "You're right, Karrenen," he affirmed, his voice now determined and persistent. "We will not falter. We will not yield. We shall bring her home, regardless of the trials."

And so, the two steadfast friends reaffirmed their unwavering commitment to their mission, their bond growing stronger with each passing moment. Instead of sowing fear and surrender, the Abyssal Dominion's malevolence had ignited a blazing resolve within them, a determination to rally the realms and end their darkness as they faced the encroaching shadows that threatened to consume their beloved Keisha. Ong and Karrenen were united by a shared purpose—to rescue her and stand as a formidable barrier against the Dominion's tyranny, proving that love, courage, and unity could triumph over even the most insidious adversaries.

The Abyssal Dominion's Satisfaction

In the hidden recesses of their shadowy enclave, Vuarus and Phoenix wore expressions of dark triumph that glimmered with wicked satisfaction. They reveled in the havoc they had just wrought upon the realms, their nefarious deeds casting a shroud of despair upon the fragile flame of hope.

"Did you witness their reactions?" Phoenix's voice dripped with sadistic glee, his eyes alight with the malicious joy of their scheme's success. "The torment etched upon the faces of the Guardians, the heartache that pierces the hearts of kings and queens—it's an exquisite tapestry of suffering."

Vuarus's sinister grin mirrored the malice in his partner's voice. "Indeed," he purred, his eyes gleaming with cruel satisfaction. "They now grasp the relentless weight of their powerlessness, understanding that even the most formidable among them can be brought low."

Their haunting and malicious chorus of laughter echoed ominously within the shadows—a symphony of malevolence resonating through the realms. It served as a chilling prelude to the depths of their cruelty and the impending storm of darkness that loomed on the horizon.

Amidst their sinister mirth, Vuarus's commanding voice rang out in the dim chamber, calling forth an ominous presence. "Malik, come forth."

Malik materialized before Vuarus, his posture marked by deference. "My lord, you summoned me?" he inquired, his voice tinged with respect.

Vuarus's penetrating gaze bore into Malik's eyes, his expression laden with a palpable malevolence. "In two months," he hissed, his voice dripping with venom, "the altar shall be rebuilt, and I shall tolerate no excuses this time. Every resource shall be gathered, and every preparation made without fail."

Malik maintained a composed exterior, though a fleeting glimpse of unease danced in his eyes. "You have my word, my lord. The necessary measures shall be taken without question."

Vuarus shifted his attention to Phoenix, a sinister smile curling his lips as he spoke. "Two months more, Phoenix," he purred, his voice laced with sadistic delight. "Two months to utterly shatter Keisha's spirit before the sacrifice. See to it that she is rendered beyond recognition."

Phoenix's eyes gleamed with a wicked satisfaction as he responded, "Rest assured, Vuarus. I shall ensure she is broken to the core, a mere shadow of her former self."

With that ominous promise hanging in the air, the Abyssal Dominion's malevolent machinations continued to unfurl, casting a foreboding shadow over
Keisha's fate and the very fabric of the realms.

Chapter 41

Shadows Unveiled: Veil of Desolation

Deep within the heart of a desolation wrought by the sinister influence of the Dominion, there lay the Altar of the Abyss, a haunting monument to an ancient, evil power. The surrounding landscape bore the scars of its malefic touch as once-thriving nature languished in a state of withered despair. Barren trees, like skeletal sentinels, stretched their gnarled branches skyward as if in a futile attempt to claw their way back to life. Their twisted forms, stark against the ashen sky, were a testament to the relentless grip of corruption that clung to every inch of this forsaken land.

Upon the dried and cracked earth, the Altar of the Abyss stood as a forbidding relic of forgotten times. Its foundation, fashioned from blackened stones, bore etchings of sinister symbols, which seemed to pulse with the very essence of the Abyss itself. An eerie aura enveloped the site, where the boundaries between realms blurred and shadows danced like restless spirits. The hostility emanating from the Altar clung to the air, thick as an impenetrable fog, and the ground beneath one's feet felt tainted by the darkness that had taken root here.

The Altar's isolation was absolute, hidden deep within the treacherous heart of Fel Thalor, the city of shadows. To approach it was a journey reserved for only the most persistent and determined souls, for the very landscape seemed to conspire against any intruders. The air hung heavy with foreboding, and every step taken carried travelers deeper into a realm where darkness held sway, where even the bravest souls might find themselves questioning the boundaries of reality.

Nestled in the heart of this desolate wasteland, the Altar of the Abyss loomed like an evil giant. Its obsidian spires reached skyward, casting long, ominous shadows stretching endlessly into the abyss. Within this tower, the Dominion's darkest rituals unfurled, and ancient secrets whispered to those who dared to listen. Its presence exuded an air of foreboding, as if it were a sinister beacon, beckoning the shadows from the depths of the Abyss below, drawing them forth like tendrils of darkness yearning for liberation.

The barren expanse surrounding the Altar seemed to mirror Keisha's anguish; the rocky terrain cracked and lifeless, devoid of even the hardiest vegetation. The air hung heavy with a suffocating aura as though the wind dared not utter a sound in this accursed realm. It was as if the very land itself mourned the presence of the Altar and the evil power it represented.

The Altar, a monstrous structure hewn from ancient stones, stood as a grotesque masterpiece, its form jagged and foreboding. Intricate markings adorned its surface, emitting an eerie crimson glow, symbols of the twisted power that resided within. An abyssal maw yawned at its core, a bottomless chasm leading into the heart of darkness like some evil force had torn the earth, creating a portal to an unholy realm beyond imagination.

As the relentless passage of time dragged on, an unshakable sense of impending doom settled over the area. From the depths of the Abyss, grotesque creatures, born of twisted nightmares, began to slither forth, their sinister forms gliding through the shadowy surroundings. It was as if they sensed the imminent sacrifice, their perverted instincts driving them to converge around the Altar, eager to partake in the evil energy that would soon be unleashed.

The Altar's ominous presence hung like an evil specter, a corporeal manifestation of the darkness that had ensnared Keisha's life. As the Dominion's sinister plans inched closer to fruition, the earth seemed to protest, bearing witness to the impending offering that would forever scar the land with its malevolent mark. It was a place where the boundary between the mortal realm and the Abyss had become tenuous, and the consequences of such a connection were dire.

Amidst the relentless two-month onslaught of desolation, the Altar emerged as the epicenter of the Dominion's evil machinations. Keisha's essence hung in the precarious balance in this forsaken place where darkness reigned supreme and malevolence festered. It became the crucible where her indomitable spirit was subjected to a cruel, systematic dismantling, tearing away the protective veils guarding her inner strength each moment.

The Altar was an ominous relic, a living testament to the Dominion's sinister dominion. Its eerie presence cast an ever-foreboding shadow over the tortured landscape as shadow wraiths, vile emissaries of cruelty, circled relentlessly, weaving a nightmarish tapestry of suffering and torment. Visions of despair, anguish, and gut-wrenching loss danced relentlessly before Keisha's weary eyes, plunging her consciousness into an abyss of unending agony. As the days stretched into weeks and the weeks into agonizing months, the outcome of this relentless ordeal remained uncertain, as the Altar held its grip on both Keisha and the realms, waiting for the moment when shadows would either triumph or be vanquished.

Yet, even as the shadows conspired to consume her, a faint glimmer of resistance clung desperately within the depths of Keisha's soul. Though dimmed by the relentless onslaught, the spark of her spirit stubbornly refused to be extinguished. With unwavering tenacity, she clung to cherished memories of a love once shared with Ong, the bonds forged with loyal friends, and the echoes of happier times. It was a fragile thread of hope, a lifeline to the light in the darkest of hours, and it whispered to her heart that surrender was not an option.

In the heart of E'vahona, Ong and Karrenen found themselves amidst the breathtaking splendor of the Eladrin realm, where the very air pulsed with vibrant energy. But even amidst this natural wonder, the weight of their mission cast a looming shadow. Karrenen's words cut through the beauty like a blade with each step they took.

"The volcanic region surrounding the Altar has been fortified," Karrenen said, his tone heavy with anger that simmered beneath the surface. His gaze bore into Ong, a fiery determination burning in his eyes. "No one can get in. Guards patrol the area, and any attempt to breach the perimeter has been met with swift, merciless retribution."

Ong's brows furrowed deeply, his frustration and concern boiling into a simmering rage. "They're taking no chances," he muttered through gritted teeth, his voice thick with pent-up fury. "Fully aware of what's at stake, they're determined to protect it at any cost."

Karrenen nodded in agreement, his expression mirroring Ong's smoldering anger. "Indeed. The Altar holds a pivotal role in their plans. Whatever dark ritual they intend to perform requires its presence. We must find a way to overcome these defenses."

A tense charged silence enveloped them, the air vibrating with the intensity of their emotions. Ong's fists clenched so tightly that his knuckles turned white, a testament to the storm raging within him. He had relentlessly pursued Keisha's rescue, his determination unwavering. But now, faced with the fortress-like protection surrounding the Altar, the reality of the challenge struck him with renewed, seething force.

"We can't afford to waste any more time," Ong finally declared, his voice cutting through the silence like a battle cry. His eyes blazed with anger and resolve. "Every moment Keisha spends in their clutches is another moment they gain strength. We need a plan—a daring plan—to breach their defenses and rescue her."

Karrenen met Ong's fiery gaze with unwavering determination, his anger fueling his resolve. "Agreed. We will gather our sharpest minds, strategize, and find a way to shatter their fortress. We will fight every ounce for Keisha and what she means to Vacari."

Standing on the precipice of the vibrant realm of E'vahona, the enormity of their mission bore down upon them like an oppressive storm cloud. The destiny of Keisha and the fragile equilibrium of the realms dangled on the precipice of uncertainty, and their resolve to retrieve her burned fiercely in their hearts.

Ong and Karrenen found themselves locked in earnest conversation, their voices lowered but charged with determination, as they delved into the depths of their strategy. The vibrant atmosphere around them quivered, stirred by the weight of their purpose. During their discussion, the air seemed to hold its breath in anticipation.

But then, a sudden interruption shattered their focus. The steady rhythm of their dialogue was pierced by the approaching presence of Lord Thaldir, a figure usually draped in composed grace, now marked by an uncharacteristic gravity that demanded immediate attention. Karrenen's inquisitive gaze met Thaldir's as he drew near, prompting the elder elf to speak without a preamble, his words laced with an urgency that resonated through the very core of their mission. "There's something you both should know," Thaldir began, his voice bearing the weight of

an unsettling discovery that had gnawed at his very core. His words hung in the air, heavy as an impending storm. "I've delved deep into the ancient texts, seeking clues about the Dominion's intentions, sinister rituals, and the chilling purpose behind their actions. What I've uncovered is deeply troubling."

Ong and Karrenen's expressions shifted, anticipation mingled with an undercurrent of gnawing worry that clung to their eyes. "Tell us," Karrenen urged, his voice tinged with a sense of urgency that mirrored the racing of their hearts.

Thaldir paused, inhaling deeply before continuing, his words laden with growing concern. "The Dominion's cruelty, I fear, goes beyond mere sadism. According to my findings, their objective is to shatter Keisha's spirit so thoroughly that it becomes... pliable, moldable to the Dominion's dark magic."

Ong's brow furrowed, a shadow of foreboding descending upon him. "What do you mean?" he asked, his voice trembling with confusion and growing concern.

Thaldir's gaze bore into Ong's, the gravity of the revelation etched in the elder elf 's eyes. "When the time comes for the sacrifice, her very essence will be infused with a hostility that will amplify the potency of their ritual. Her pain, despair, and suffering will converge into a power surge that Vuarus can direct as he sees fit. It is a sinister plan, and it might have been Vuarus's focus from the beginning, not just for revenge but to retain his godhead." Thaldir's voice was sad as he shared this chilling insight.

A heavy, suffocating silence hung in the air as the chilling implications of Thaldir's words seeped into their consciousness. The Dominion's malevolence ran even more profound than they had feared. Karrenen's jaw clenched, his fists tightening in anger.

"So, they're not merely tormenting her for their sadistic pleasure," Karrenen spoke, his voice quivering with a growing fury. "They're using her suffering as a wellspring of dark magic, an unholy power source to fuel their abominable rituals."

Thaldir nodded solemnly, his heart heavy with the realization. "Yes. Her torment is twisted into a weapon—an evil power source they intend to harness for their nefarious designs."

Ong's jaw clenched, the weight of Thaldir's revelation igniting an inferno of resolve within him. "Then there's no alternative—we must rescue her," he declared, his voice unwavering and steely. The depth of his commitment to Keisha and the realms seethed beneath his words. "We shall not permit them to exploit her suffering as a weapon against us."

A flicker of something darker danced in his eyes—a volatile cocktail of anger and disgust. "Phoenix is likely savoring her torment," he seethed, his voice dripping with righteous rage. "Deriving pleasure from her anguish, just as they harvest power from it. This abhorrent game ends before they can see their depraved plans come to fruition."

Karrenen nodded emphatically, his fury barely restrained beneath his calm exterior. "You speak the truth. They tighten their grip on her spirit every moment we delay, edging closer to their sinister objective. Swiftness is our ally."

Thaldir's gaze flitted between the two, his expression a poignant blend of concern and unyielding determination. "We shall need a plan, a strategy to infiltrate their defenses and extract Keisha safely from their clutches."

Ong's eyes bore into Thaldir's, his determination a blazing beacon. "Her spirit shall remain unbroken, and her suffering shall never serve as their vile weapon," he vowed, the fires of determination flickering fiercely in his gaze.

Karrenen's gaze shifted between Ong and Thaldir, his composure momentarily slipping as he swallowed hard. He met Ong's eyes, a silent reminder of the painful truth they all carried—the Dominion had already been breaking Keisha's spirit, piece by agonizing piece.

Ong's jaw tightened in acknowledgment of the painful reality, his eyes reflecting the anguish that gnawed at his soul. "We'll end their torment," he vowed, his voice tinged with sorrow. "And we'll help Keisha rebuild what they've sought to destroy."

As they stood there, a triumvirate bound by an unyielding purpose, the magnitude of their mission stretched out before them like an ominous abyss. The Altar of the Abyss loomed ahead, enshrouded in an unsettling darkness and an aura of malice—a domain firmly under the dominion of Shadow. Yet, forged together by an unwavering resolve, the Guardians of E'vahona were poised to confront the Abyss, to defy the horrors that awaited, and to wrest Keisha from the unforgiving clutches of the encroaching darkness.

Lord Galadon moved with a measured step, approaching Ong, his presence commanding unwavering attention. He laid a hand on Ong's shoulder, his eyes reflecting the weight of their impending ordeal. "Remember," he said, his voice laden with solemnity, "even if we succeed in rescuing Keisha, the battle does not conclude there. The Dominion's machinations run deeper than our comprehension can fathom."

Ong's gaze bore into Galadon's, a fierce determination blazing in his eyes. "I damn well know that" he retorted, his voice carrying a fiery edge. "But we cannot afford to let them exploit her suffering for their twisted goals. We won't allow her pain to catalyze their malice."

Karrenen, sensing Ong's rising temper, stepped forward, his expression grave yet unwavering. He placed a restraining hand on Ong's shoulder and then turned to address Lord Galadon. "Ong is right," he declared firmly. "Our utmost priority is Keisha's safety. We will not imperil her life further by rushing into a confrontation before securing her return."

Ong nodded, his knuckles white as he tightened his grip on his bow. "Keisha will be back with us, safe and sound, in her rightful place—home—before we even entertain the thought of facing the Dominion in battle," he affirmed, his voice unwavering and tinged with a quiet, smoldering determination. "And when that time does come, Phoenix belongs to me," he added, his tone low and unwavering, a promise etched in his words.

Galadon's gaze held a blend of respect and understanding as he offered a solemn nod. "We stand united with you, Ong," he acknowledged. "But let it be known that the Dominion's sinister influence stretches far and wide, seeking to entangle more than Keisha's spirit."

Ong's jaw clenched, his steely resolve undeterred. "We shall not permit them to lay waste to her, nor any facet of our world, without a battle that shall echo through the ages. But for the present, our unwavering focus remains on Keisha and her safe return."

In that profound moment, the weight of their mission hung heavy in the air, binding the Guardians of E'vahona in an unspoken covenant. They comprehended the daunting trials ahead and the looming abyss that awaited them. Yet, they bore within them a resolute determination—to rescue one of their own and to shield their realms from the clutches of the Dominion's malevolence. United, they stood, a bastion against the encroaching darkness, a beacon of hope in a world shadowed by peril.

Ong's steps led him away from the huddled group as the conversation concluded. A tumultuous blend of emotions weighed down his heart. He traversed the verdant woods of E'vahona, the very same woods where he had shared countless moments with Keisha. At last, he arrived at their home, a place of cherished memories and untold dreams. There stood Pumpkin, awaiting him with eyes that mirrored unwavering loyalty and a tail that wagged with unbridled affection. Ong knelt, his arms encircling his faithful companion, and a hint of tears glistened in his eyes. "I won't lose her," he whispered, his voice quivering with both resolve and fear.

Rising to his feet, Ong cast a poignant gaze upon the home he had built with Keisha, his fingers caressing the weathered wood of the doorframe. "I just can't," he confessed, his voice barely more than a breath, his eyes shimmering with determination. The mere notion of losing Keisha, of permitting the Dominion to shatter her spirit and exploit her anguish for their grotesque rituals, tore at his very soul. He understood that they faced a formidable and malevolent adversary. Yet, Ong was prepared to muster every ounce of his strength, to traverse the darkest abyss, to bring Keisha back to safety, and to shield their world from the Dominion's sinister clutches.

Vuarus and Phoenix, enshrouded in inky shadows, moved with purpose through the labyrinthine corridors of their sinister lair. The air bore an evil weight as if it conspired in their wicked designs. Their journey led them to the heart of their venom—Keisha's cell, where her spirit lay in perilous captivity. As they reached their grim destination, Vuarus turned to Phoenix, his eyes gleaming with predatory hunger.

"Let us ascertain the remnants of her spirit," Vuarus purred, his voice thick with anticipation, a sinister cadence lacing his words.

Phoenix's lips twisted into a cruel smile, a chilling echo of his dark delight. "Indeed," he hissed with cold satisfaction. "We have invested so much effort into her torment. It is time to reap the fruits of our malevolent labor."

With a mere flick of Vuarus's hand, the cell's imposing door swung open, revealing the fragile figure of Keisha, huddled on the unforgiving, cold floor. Her once-vibrant eyes, those windows to a fiery soul, had dulled to a lifeless gaze, her spirit crushed beneath the relentless weight of torment. The shadows in the room seemed to conspire, their movements casting an eerie, ethereal glow upon her forlorn form.

As Vuarus and Phoenix drew nearer, Keisha's head lifted, and they were met with a gaze that held no hint of the fierce defiance that had once defined her. Instead, her eyes harbored only a profound, haunting emptiness—an abyss that seemed to stretch to infinity and sent icy shivers coursing down their spines. The essence of her being appeared to have been drained away, leaving behind a mere, fragile shell—a haunting echo of the vibrant soul that had once dwelled within.

Phoenix's nod was filled with a chilling agreement, a triumphant fire dancing in his eyes. "Indeed," he hissed with cruel delight. "She is on the precipice, teetering at the edge of her torment. Just a bit more suffering, and she will be the exquisite vessel, the perfect conduit for our boundless power."

Keisha's gaze flickered hesitantly between them, a faint ember of recognition smoldering within her eyes, though it was tragically eclipsed by the engulfing darkness that had swallowed her essence whole. She existed as nothing more than a hapless pawn in their evil game, a tool carved from the fragments of her suffering wielded to fuel their dread-filled ambitions.

Having indulged their morbid curiosity, Vuarus and Phoenix pivoted to depart the lonely cell. Their departing laughter reverberated in eerie resonance, a haunting echo that hung heavy in the air as they retreated into the comforting embrace of the shadows. Keisha remained trapped where she was, a silent, heart-wrenching testament to her relentless torment and sinister, unfathomable machinations that loomed ominously on her forsaken horizon.

Vuarus's footsteps abruptly stopped, his cruel smile widening as a wicked inspiration took root. Slowly, he pivoted, locking his evil gaze upon Keisha, a sinister excitement lighting up his eyes like malevolent stars. With a flourish of his hand, he conjured forth an ominous image before her, a nightmarish altar poised menacingly over the Abyss itself.

"This, my dear," Vuarus hissed, his voice dripping with unholy malice that seeped into the air, "is a special gift for you." The haunting image hovered, a stark representation of the dread-filled destiny that loomed on the horizon, a cruel promise of what lay ahead in her tortured path. "This is what I had planned for you from the beginning. Your sacrifice will ensure my godhead for centuries."

Keisha's breath seized in her throat, her eyes locked in a harrowing trance upon the ominous tableau that unfolded before her. The Abyss, a yawning void of impenetrable darkness, seemed to beckon to her, its inky depths mirroring the profound despair gnawed at her soul. A tremor, born of mounting panic and abject terror, coursed through her, setting her frail form to quaking.

"N-no...no!" Keisha's voice cracked, a frantic scream clawing its way out of her, the anguished sound reverberating off the frigid walls of her dismal cell. Tears flowed unbidden down her pallid cheeks, mingling with the all-encompassing torment that clung to her like a suffocating shroud. "Ong, you promised," she whimpered, a desperate plea hanging heavy in the lifeless air.

But Vuarus had already turned away, his cruel laughter trailing behind him like a sinister refrain. He strode out of the cell, his malevolent presence receding into the shadows, leaving Keisha alone with her torment. The Altar's eerie image dissolved, yet its symbolism's ominous weight lingered, a cruel specter that taunted her, a relentless reminder of the merciless fate that had been artfully orchestrated for her.

Alone in the oppressive darkness, Keisha curled into a trembling ball, her sobs rending the silence as her fragile form shuddered beneath the weight of relentless fear and despair. She clung desperately to the tattered shreds of her once-indomitable spirit in the suffocating void. The promise of salvation had become a fading specter, a distant memory slipping through her trembling fingers.

As the haunting image of the Abyss loomed relentlessly in her mind, she couldn't escape the chilling sensation that she was being inexorably drawn nearer to the precipice of an abyss from which there might be no return. In her lonely solitude, she cried out again, her voice a heart-wrenching plea, before succumbing to an eerie stillness, a motionless figure imprisoned in the depths of her torment.

Ong's heart convulsed within his chest at the harrowing sound of Keisha's anguished cry, its haunting resonance piercing through the depths of his very soul. "Ong, you promised me," her voice echoed in the recesses of his mind, a ghostly refrain that clawed at his consciousness, searing a vivid reminder of the torment that had trapped her.

His gaze fell upon Pumpkin, the loyal companion who had weathered the storms of their lives together. The feline, too, seemed to sense the anguish that gripped her master, responding with a plaintive whine, a mournful harmony to the agony that hung heavy in the air.

A leaden weight descended upon Ong's shoulders, his knuckles whitening as his fists clenched in the throes of maddening helplessness. The desperation to rescue Keisha, to free her from the abyss of suffering, surged through him, but forces beyond his control bound him, and that gnawing reality tore at his very soul.

Karrenen's voice sliced through the turmoil as he drew near, a palpable worry etching lines of concern across his typically composed features. "Ong, what troubles you?" he inquired, his eyes reflecting genuine apprehension.

Ong's head shook slowly, his voice betraying the storm of emotions within him. "It's Keisha...

I heard her. She... she's in agony, Karrenen. I can scarcely bear it."

A rare, empathetic softening of Karrenen's gaze occurred, and he offered Ong a reassuring touch upon his shoulder. "We shall retrieve her, Ong. We won't permit her suffering to persist."

Ong nodded, his jaw locked in stubborn determination. "Time is of the essence. Every moment she endures there... it tears her apart. I cannot allow that to happen. Not to her, not after all she has endured." His voice wavered, a raw emotion breaking through the typically stoic facade, revealing his love and concern for Keisha.

Karrenen's grip tightened around Ong's shoulder, a wordless testament to the unshakable resolve that bound them together. "We will rescue her, Ong," he affirmed, his voice carrying the weight of their shared determination. "Keisha is strong, and we won't allow the Dominion to break her spirit."

Ong's gaze shifted, a distant and haunted look shadowing his eyes as he recalled the tormenting images he had glimpsed of Keisha's suffering. "Karrenen, they've already torn her apart, piece by piece. The anguish, the despair... It's eroding her from the inside."

Karrenen's expression darkened, a turbulent storm of anger and sorrow swirling within his eyes. "Then we shall rebuild what has been shattered. We shall muster our forces, our allies, and we will uncover a path to reclaim her. Keisha deserves her freedom, Ong, and we shall not rest until she has it."

Ong locked eyes with Karrenen, their shared determination forging an unbreakable bond. "You are right. We owe her that and so much more."

Karrenen regarded Ong with a somber expression, his voice bearing the weight of impending reunion, and he chose his words with great care, seeking to ready Ong for the potential shock that awaited him. "Ong," he began cautiously, his voice breaking ever so slightly, a testament to the depth of his concern, "you must prepare yourself for when Keisha returns. What we glimpsed in her eyes—the void, the extinguished flame—may be deeply unsettling. She might appear utterly drained, for I doubt she has known respite. The cruelties inflicted upon her may have altered her visage, and her sustenance may have been sorely lacking. Please, be ready for these possibilities."

Ong nodded firmly, his unwavering determination shining through his response. "You are correct, Karrenen," he affirmed, his voice a steadfast anchor amidst the turbulent sea of emotions. "I will brace myself for whatever lies ahead, for Keisha's sake. Regardless of our hardships, we shall stand unwaveringly by her side. She has endured far too much and deserves all our love and support. She shall not confront this nightmare alone."

As they stood there, a renewed fire kindled within them, a blazing resolve to confront the encroaching darkness that had ensnared Keisha and reclaim her from its cruel grasp. Their promise to save her remained unbreakable, etched in their hearts, their unwavering loyalty serving as a beacon of hope amidst the shadows that threatened to consume her.

Malrik's entrance into the Dread Spire commanded Vuarus's immediate attention. "The altar is ready, my lord," Malrik reported, his voice conveying reverence and palpable anticipation. With a respectful nod, he pivoted to depart, leaving the chamber.

Vuarus followed Malrik's exit with a calculating gaze, his lips curving into a slow, sinister smile as his attention shifted to Phoenix. "The moment we've awaited draws near," he remarked in hushed tones, his voice a mere murmur that carried a weight of dark significance. "But there remains one final task before the stage is fully set." In his eyes danced a chilling gleam, a precursor of the impending climax of their evil designs.

Chapter 42

Shadows Unveiled: Echoes of Sacrifice

Vuarus and Phoenix enshrouded in the enigmatic embrace of the night, stood resolute at the precipice of the abyss. Below them, profound, unfathomable darkness stretched like an abyssal maw, hungry for the light that dared to venture near. The Altar, a monolithic monument to sinister intentions, cast a long, chilling shadow that seemed to reach into the souls of those who beheld it.

In this desolate realm, where life and hope had long since withered away, the air bore the weight of an unsettling aura. It clung to their skin like a cloak woven from malevolent whispers, whispering secrets of ancient horrors that lay dormant beneath.

Amidst this eerie tableau, dark creatures, born of the Abyss's corrupted heart, skulked and slithered with furious grace. Twisted and malformed, they seemed to have embraced their grotesque existence, their movements like demented waltzes. Their presence hinted at an uncanny awareness as if they were the precursors of a dark ritual soon to be realized.

The door to the Abyss, veiled in inky shadows, pulsing with a rhythm beyond the comprehension of mortal senses. It throbbed like a living entity, as though the very fabric of reality strained to contain the eldritch forces within. The boundaries between worlds seemed to blur, revealing glimpses of the cosmic turmoil held in check.

Phoenix's lips curled with a vicious satisfaction, casting an unsettling gleam in his eyes as he surveyed the grim panorama. "Behold, even the abyssal denizens prepare for the grand spectacle," he mused, his voice dripping with a perverse delight that resonated in the frigid air.

Vuarus nodded, his gaze fixated on the Altar and the churning abyss below, his eyes gleaming like twin stars amidst the stygian gloom. "Indeed," he murmured, his voice a sinister symphony. "The currents of energy swirl, and the threads of fate align. Keisha's torment has become the blood that feeds the roots of our evil tree."

A haunting silence hung in the air, a moment of eerie calm that masked the storm about to be unleashed upon the realms. In that shadowed instant, the duo's presence echoed the explosive forces they had harnessed, a prelude to the impending dark symphony that would resonate through the very fabric of existence.

Vuarus's smirk twisted into a vicious grin. "Keisha's magic has been completely siphoned from her, and the Abyss has taken control of that magic, twisting it for their use. Now, we will use her spirit for my designs."

Vuarus, his gaze withdrawing from the gaping maw of the Abyss, locked eyes with Phoenix, his lips curling into a frigid smile that danced on the precipice of malevolence. His voice slithered forth, a whispered command that carried an icy, bone-chilling edge. "Let us venture forth to oversee our prized sacrifice," he uttered, each word etched in glacial intent. "We must ascertain beyond doubt that Keisha's spirit lies broken and bereft of any lingering resistance."

Phoenix's response mirrored Vuarus's sinister grin, his eyes alight with a wicked, anticipatory gleam. "And," he insinuated with a threatening murmur, "we might consider subjecting her once more to the wraiths' relentless torment. A final crescendo to shatter whatever remnants of her will still cling to the abyss of her soul."

Vuarus nodded as his voice dripped with the darkness of their intent. "A splendid proposition indeed. Let her despair spiral ever deeper, her spirit crumbling like the timeworn ruins of forgotten kingdoms. The more shattered she becomes, the more potent her impending sacrifice shall prove."

As the sinister pair turned away from the abyss, retreating to the heart of their evil domain, their laughter, rich with malice and glee, hung in the air like a haunting overture, foretelling the dire ritual that would soon commence and inexorably rewrite the tapestry of the realms.

Ong's visage contorted, his countenance etched with furrows of dismay as he imbibed Karrenen's dire tidings. Within the depths of his eyes, frustration and urgency churned like turbulent tempests, mirroring the grim news that now coursed through his veins. "No ingress by foot," he muttered, his voice a lament veiled in disenchantment.

Karrenen, standing beside him, nodded solemnly, his manner a canvas painted with a tapestry of concern interwoven with the threads of unwavering resolve. "Indeed," he concurred. "The Dominion's machinations are deliberate, fortifying these environs against intrusion."

Ong's jaw tightened, and the creases on his brow deepened as he grappled with the gravity of their predicament. "We're shackled by the merciless hands of time," he proclaimed with unwavering determination. "Keisha's suffering unfurls with each passing moment, and our hesitation hastens her anguish."

Karrenen's eyes locking with Ong's conveyed a tacit communion of purpose. "I comprehend, Ong," he intoned gravely. "Our movement is undeniable, but we must tread with discernment. Recklessness would only jeopardize her further."

The storm of Ong's emotions swirled within him, his frustration simmering like molten magma. "I refuse to witness her spirit wither to naught," he declared firmly. "We cannot simply await an unexpected deliverance. We must unearth an avenue of access and seize it with urgency." Karrenen's hand found Ong's shoulder, the firm, reassuring grasp, a tether binding them in their shared commitment. "I pledge, Ong, that I shall rest not until we decipher the cryptic gate to her liberation," he vowed. "Each avenue shall be traversed, every stratagem explored, but above all, we shall safeguard Keisha's sanctity."

Ong's gaze, ablaze with the inferno of resolve, met Karrenen's unwavering stare. "You speak truth, Karrenen," he affirmed with steadfast conviction. "Let us assemble our most adept and resourceful confederates. Together, we shall convene and conjure stratagems, for a breach in their defenses must be discovered."

Karrenen acquiesced with a solemn nod. "A group of minds united in purpose we shall organize, and with diligence, we shall commence our deliberations," he agreed resolutely. "No rest shall be taken until we have a viable plan to wrest Keisha from the clutches of her tormentors."

As they exchanged that mutual nod, Ong and Karrenen knew that the road ahead was fraught with peril, its path obscured by the shadows of uncertainty. Yet, the unbreakable bond they shared, their steadfast commitment to Keisha's salvation, fortified their resolve, casting their spirits as unwavering beacons amid the stormy seas ahead.

Within the shadowed confines of the Dread Spire's dimly illuminated chamber, Vuarus, and Phoenix convened in hushed voices, their conspiratorial whispers weaving the threads of an evil design. Like a dark tapestry, the plan unfurled before them, and Vuarus harbored a particularly sinister notion.

"What if," Vuarus contemplated, his eyes agleam with a treacherous blend of anticipation and delight, "we dangle a flicker of hope before their despairing eyes? A ruse, a mere mirage of exchange, if you will."

Phoenix, his curiosity piqued, arched a curious brow. "Pray, explain."

Vuarus's lips stretched into a wicked smile, akin to a serpent unveiling its venomous fangs. "We dispatch a message to Ong and the esteemed Eladrin Council," he elucidated, his tone laden with cruel charm, "extending an invitation for negotiations regarding Keisha's deliverance. We shall grant passage to Ong and a solitary companion, guiding them toward the shadowy corridor leading to the accursed Altar. Yet, as they step into our web, they shall find that genuine discourse remains naught but a beguiling illusion."

Phoenix's laughter reverberated through the chamber, sharp and biting, akin to a chorus of sinister strings. "A delightful ruse indeed," he extolled. "Your mind is a malevolent symphony, Vuarus."

Vuarus's smile deepened as if echoing the treacherous melody of his mind. "It is a plan most poetic," he remarked, his voice dripping with sinister allure. "And, as a touch of irony, it mirrors the tragedy that occurred to her father. I imagine that fool Karrenen would recall that scene all too well."

Vuarus's malevolent smile unfurled like the spreading wings of a vulture, a sinister emblem of his stratagem's dual purpose. "It bears the weight of two burdens," he elucidated, his voice an evil whisper. "First, it shall shatter the frail edifice of hope they clutch in their desperate hands, leaving them bereft of any illusions about rescuing Keisha through the conduits of diplomacy. Second, it shall pave a path, twisted and obscured, leading them to the very epicenter of our dominion, where the Abyss coils like a serpent, and its shadowy progeny weave their malefic dances."

Phoenix, his eyes twin flames of malicious delight, leaned into the macabre symphony of their designs. "As they stand marooned within our unholy sanctum, engulfed by the inky embrace of the Abyss and its grotesque offspring, the gravity of their predicament will unfurl before them like a sinister tapestry."

Vuarus, his satisfaction radiating like an unholy aura, affirmed their evil course. "Precisely. Their vision shall become a mirror, reflecting the sovereignty of our might and the tragic fragility of their endeavors."

Phoenix enshrouded in shadows cast by obsidian pillars, expressed sadistic amusement. "I can already envisage the tumultuous storm brewing within Ong's eyes as the truth gnaws at the edges of his consciousness."

Vuarus's dark laughter resonated like the tolling of a cursed bell. "Oh, the moment shall be a symphony of torment that shall serenade our malevolent desires."

With their plan's sinister wheels set in motion, Vuarus and Phoenix exchanged glances, their eyes like twin omens harboring the foreboding promise of what lay ahead. The forthcoming missive to Ong and the Eladrin Council merely marked the overture of a calculated game, one in which the puppeteers reveled in their malevolent prowess, testing the limits of their adversaries' tenacity while delving ever deeper into the abyss of their maleficence.

Ong stood like a sentinel at the edge of the Emeraldwood Forest, an ancient realm where the trees whispered secrets to the wind, and the earth seemed to pulse with untamed magic. His keen intuition, honed through years of relentless pursuit and unwavering love, guided him to this location. It was where the boundary between the mundane world and the arcane weave of destiny appeared thin, a subtle convergence point he had sensed in his heart.

From the whispered tidings of sympathetic spies and shadowy informants, Ong had gleaned the knowledge of this clandestine meeting with the Dominion's emissary. It was a detail that weighed upon him like a leaden shroud, a choice to stake their hopes on an enigmatic gambit that might secure Keisha's salvation or seal their fate in a darker abyss.

His unwavering vigil continued, each moment etching the lines of anticipation upon his face as the horizon beckoned with the promise of the approaching messenger from the Dread Spire. The air thrummed with premonition, mirroring the storm of thoughts raging within Ong's mind. As the precursor drew nearer, Ong's heart raced with the messenger's deliberate approach. As critical as any in his life's tale, this juncture bore the weight of a future unknown. The messenger's cautious and suspicious demeanor hinted at the gravity of the tidings he carried.

With a solemn nod of gratitude, Ong accepted the sealed parchment, his fingers lingering upon its surface as though hoping to glean its secrets.

With the messenger's departure, Ong's unwavering gaze returned to the message, a parchment harboring the inked prophecies of the Dread Dominion. His breath, measured and deliberate, preceded the shattering of the seal and the unfurling of the enigmatic words penned by Vuarus's hand. The message wove a tale of dangerous machinations—a masquerade of negotiation, a solitary opportunity for Ong and one companion to traverse the enigmatic passage toward the foreboding Altar.

As Ong navigated the labyrinthine verses and deciphered the hidden snares, the Dominion's treacherous motives loomed like ominous storm clouds. Yet, the iridescent lure of glimpsing Keisha, of beholding her torment firsthand, tugged at his soul like an unyielding tempest.

Cradling the parchment in his grasp, Ong determined his course of action. He would bear this heavy burden to the esteemed Eladrin Council, summoning their wisdom and insight. Keisha's life dangled precariously, a fragile ember in the abyss of darkness. Prudence would serve as their guiding light on this treacherous path. With resolute steps, he embarked upon the journey back into the heart of the Emeraldwood Forest, his thoughts awash with uncertainty, his spirit aflame with the unwavering resolve to wrest his beloved from the clutches of malevolence.

The Eladrin Council's chamber exuded an aura of profound silence as Ong entered, his steps echoing like whispers in a sacred temple. The parchment clasped in his hand felt like it carried the weight of the entire world, an oppressive force that permeated the air. He advanced toward the central dais where the council members were seated, their countenances a mosaic of intrigue and trepidation, a congregation of minds poised on the precipice of uncertainty. Ong's throat cleared, and with a respectful gesture, he unfolded the parchment, relinquishing its ominous contents to the council's scrutiny.

As the councilors immersed themselves in words sprawled across the parchment, their brows knit together in pensive contemplation, their thoughts weaving a complex tapestry of deliberation. Karrenen, a sentinel of wisdom amongst them, locked eyes with Ong, a shared understanding coursing through their silent exchange. When the councilors finally raised their gaze, Karrenen, his voice like the resonance of a sacred chant, broke the profound silence.

"As acolytes of our shared wisdom," Karrenen intoned his low and unyielding timbre, "we understand the Dominion's insidious design. Their lust for E'vahona's elusive heartbeats in tandem with their desire to use Keisha as leverage to pry the sanctuary's sacred location from our lips."

Ong's jaw clenched, his heart heavy with the weight of Karrenen's irrefutable revelation. Deep within the recesses of his soul, he had known the Dominion's insatiable hunger for E'vahona's secrets. Yet, betraying the city's location, a haven of light and life, was impossible. It was more than a vow; it was a sacred duty, an oath of preservation that transcended mortal boundaries.

As Ong stood amidst the solemnity of the Eladrin Council chamber, an ancient memory surfaced within him like an ethereal specter. It was a vow made in the distant past, a promise forged in the crucible of trust and bound by the indomitable strength of his love for Keisha. Like a ghostly whisper, the memory unfurled within his consciousness, bringing the chill of regret and the weight of an unyielding oath.

Years ago, when he was first entrusted with the sacred secret of E'vahona's hidden location, Ong had stood with Keisha beneath the stars, their hearts tethered by an unspoken understanding. Then, in the gentle embrace of moonlight, he had made a solemn pledge. With conviction in his eyes and love transcending mortal boundaries, he had vowed to her that he would protect the city's hidden heart at any cost, even if it meant losing her. He had sworn to guard the sanctuary's secret with his life, for E'vahona held within its depths the legacy of their people and the fragile threads of their love.

As the memory resurfaced, Ong shivered, feeling the weight of his past commitment press down upon him like a crushing vice. Back then, the mere thought of parting from Keisha had been a torment, a wound to his soul that he had been willing to bear. But now, as he gazed upon the depths of his love for her, he knew that the prospect of losing her, even to safeguard E'vahona, would be a devastating blow that could shatter the very core of his being.

In the hushed chamber of the council, as deliberations continued around him, Ong's thoughts remained trapped by the memory of his promise. The heartache he had been prepared to endure in the past had transformed into a profound and all-encompassing love. Keisha had become his world, the embodiment of his purpose, and the beacon that illuminated the darkest corners of his existence.

He knew that, as the wheels of destiny turned, he might be faced with a choice—a choice that threatened to tear apart the vow he had once made. The weight of that impending decision hung heavy upon him, a burden he would willingly bear to rescue the woman who had become his everything.

"Keisha's trust in me hinges on my pledge," Ong declared, his voice unwavering, tinged with determination and the bitter taste of regret. "I cannot forsake her, no matter the cost. Disclosing E'vahona's location would not only unleash ruin upon our realm but also imperil Kadona's life, and I shall not allow that shadow to fall upon us."

Karrenen's eyes softened a blend of paternal pride and fraternal concern etched in his gaze. "I understand, my steadfast comrade," he affirmed gently. "And we must also remain vigilant, for the Dominion's treacherous intentions may extend beyond the inked lines of that message."

In unison, Ong and Karrenen nodded, their thoughts a whirlwind of apprehension and resolve, their pact forged in the crucible of adversity. "Agreed," Ong concurred, his voice a steadfast vow. "We shall honor my sacred pledge yet remain wary, for we tread upon the serpent's path and must anticipate its venomous strikes."

Karrenen's grip on Ong's shoulder was a gesture of solidarity and a pledge of unity. "Together we stand, Ong," he intoned with the conviction of a sage, "as guardians of Keisha's well-being. We shall venture forth to the fateful meeting and navigate the labyrinth of deception with a singular purpose—to rescue her from the depths of darkness."

With a heavy exhale, Ong nodded in solemn agreement. The council members, eyes a mosaic of expectation, turned their collective gaze to him, awaiting his decision. Resolutely, he folded the message again, placing it in the outstretched hand of one of the council members. "Return this to the Dread Spire," he instructed, his words resolute. "Inform them that we accept their terms and shall dispatch our representatives to the designated meeting place."

Ong felt a tumultuous fusion of apprehension and unyielding resolve as the parchment was reclaimed. The path ahead was shrouded in shadows, fraught with perils and machinations. Yet, he knew he would brave it all to rescue Keisha from the relentless clutches of darkness, even if it meant confronting the Dominion head-on and navigating their labyrinth of deceit.

Amidst the hallowed confines of the Eladrin Council chamber, Ong's important decision unfolded like a tapestry of fate. As the parchment bearing their assent was handed over, Karrenen, a sentinel of wisdom and an oracle of memories, watched it leave his grasp. The sight triggered a haunting recollection, a sepia-toned vision that beckoned from the annals of time, casting shadows upon the present.

In his mind's eye, Karrenen retraced the steps of a bygone era when Eldric, Keisha's father, had stood on the precipice of peril. The Druchii, relentless in their pursuit, had demanded knowledge hidden within the sacred walls of E'vahona. The stakes had been high, yet Eldric's spirit had remained unbroken, a beacon of unwavering strength.

Karrenen vividly recalled when Eldric, resolute and fearless, had gathered his courage. He had summoned his wife and the council, urging them with a firmness born of determination not to yield E'vahona's secret. The sanctity of their realm had been holy, and he had been willing to protect it at any cost.

But now, as the parchment departed to convey their consent to the Dread Dominion, Karrenen's heart quivered with sorrow and rage. What they had done to Keisha, Eldric's beloved daughter, was an abomination beyond imagination. The stark contrast between the two scenarios, the unbowed spirit of Eldric and Keisha's shattered resolve, gnawed at Karrenen's soul. In the dimly lit chamber, the specter of Eldric's courage lingered—a stark reminder of their duty to protect the realm and a testament to Keisha's unfathomable torment. The chamber itself seemed to resonate with the weight of history and the burdens of the present as the Eladrin Council moved forward into the unknown, their hearts burdened with the promise to rescue Keisha and safeguard E'vahona's hidden heart.

The message's arrival was greeted with a sinister satisfaction within the dimly lit confines of the Dread Spire's clandestine chamber. Vuarus, a maestro of malevolence, regarded the message with a self-assured smirk, his eyes tracing the lines that sealed their adversaries' fate. The words within confirmed their adversaries' compliance with the orchestrated charade, an acceptance tantalizing the Dominion's darkest desires.

A malicious glee danced in Vuarus's eyes as he contemplated the imminent unfolding of their nefarious plan. "Now," he mused, his voice a serpent's whisper, "let us witness whether they will willingly unveil the sanctum of E'vahona to salvage an Eladrin bereft of hope, a soul already consumed by the abyss." His fluid and predatory movements resembled a shadowy waltz as he rose from his seat, the darkness bowing to his evil whims. "Join me, Phoenix," he beckoned, his tone pregnant with anticipation and cruelty. "It is time we administer the final coup de grâce to Keisha's shattered spirit. Once her essence is utterly broken, she shall become the key to unlock the boundless power of the Abyss."

Phoenix, a harbinger of doom with a twisted grin upon his visage, rose in obedient accord. His soul mirrored the wicked fervor that infused their sinister designs.

"Indeed, my lord," he crooned with a hint of sadistic pleasure. "With Keisha's spirit reduced to naught, her very being shall catalyze to unleash the unfathomable might of the Abyss."

In that shadowed chamber, the air pulsed with malice, and both victim and oppressor fates hung in delicate balance, like dark constellations converging upon a cataclysmic event. The Dread Spire's tendrils reached ever deeper into the heart of darkness, where cruelty and cunning were the coin of the realm and where Keisha's torment was poised to reach its zenith.

They traversed the winding, shadow-laden corridors of the Dread Spire, their footfalls resonating like whispers in the oppressive stillness. As they ventured deeper into the fortress of hostility, the atmosphere grew chillier, a bone-deep cold that gnawed at their very souls. Finally, they arrived at the chamber that held Keisha in its cruel embrace.

There, within the heart of the chamber's icy stone confines, Keisha was a pitiful sight. She sat huddled on the frigid ground, her fragile form curled in on itself, a spectral echo of her former self. Her once-fiery eyes now lay vacant, bereft of the spark that had once defined her spirit, now extinguished like a dying star. Her frail body quivered as if beset by an eternal winter, an embodiment of despair's icy grip.

Vuarus, a precursor of malevolence, advanced upon her with a dreadful grace, his eyes aflame with cruel satisfaction. He reveled in the torment that clung to her like a shroud, savoring the exquisite agony of her broken spirit. "Keisha, my dear Guardian," he taunted, his voice dripping with malice, "you are a fallen star, a shattered constellation. Your will has crumbled, and now you stand at the precipice, a vessel yearning to be filled with the unrelenting darkness of the Abyss."

Beside Vuarus, Phoenix, a sinister puppeteer of despair, wore a wicked smile that tugged at the corners of his lips. His words oozed with malefic intent as he gloated over the anguish that had become Keisha's constant companion. "Your pain, your suffering," he proclaimed with a chilling certainty, "shall transcend the boundaries of the mortal realm. You, dear Keisha, shall be the harbinger of a new epoch—a reign of darkness that shall engulf the realms and plunge them into eternal night."

In that wretched chamber, Keisha's misery was the crucible in which their evil designs would be forged, her shattered spirit the key to their darkest ambitions. The Dread Spire's dark embrace held her captive, a vessel poised to unleash a cataclysmic storm upon the realms.

Keisha, a mere wisp of her former self, her spirit tattered and frayed, managed to summon a feeble whisper. "Ong... help me..."

Vuarus, a master of sadistic cruelty, could not resist the urge to twist the knife of despair even further. He laughed as cold and heartless as the abyss, a cruel echo reverberating within the chamber. "Oh," he mocked with a chilling disregard, "like Ong has helped you thus far? Your pleas, my dear, are but a lament sung to the void. Ong's power and love are meaningless now, for you are trapped in a web of darkness from which there is no escape."

With a passive sweep of Vuarus's hand, the obsidian shroud enveloping Keisha thickened, coiling around her like serpentine chains of despair. The chamber seemed to shudder in response to the encroaching darkness, as if nature recoiled from the malevolence at play. Once again, the spectral wraiths materialized, their ethereal forms an eerie dance around the captive Guardian. Keisha's once-resolute gaze now harbored an expression of abject terror as she bore witness to a procession of nightmarish visions, each more grotesque and harrowing than the last.

She whispered, quivering with desperation and heartbreak, "Ong, you promised me... You promised..."

Vuarus and Phoenix, the architects of her torment, beheld the crumbling remnants of her will with a cruel satisfaction that sent shivers down the spine of the very abyss. The unrelenting agony that clawed at Keisha's soul nourished the ever-hungry darkness that yearned to consume her. In her suffering, they discerned the means to harness greater power, realize their sinister designs, and usher in an era of dominance.

Vuarus's malevolent grin expanded. An obscene crescent mirrored the grotesque dance of shadows that held Keisha in thrall. "Indeed," he purred with an unsettling delight, "Keisha, you are the cornerstone of our ascent. Your anguish and desolation shall serve as the lifeblood of the ritual heralding our unassailable Dominion."

As they departed the chamber, leaving behind Keisha's heart-wrenching lamentations that reverberated like the haunting echoes of a lost soul, Vuarus's strides bore an eerie sense of purpose. The inexorable march of destiny drew nearer, the culmination of their sinister plot approaching with each deliberate step. The Abyss seemed to pulsate with anticipation as if the very foundations of reality quivered in response to their impending ritual.

Yet, amidst the resounding cries of a soul bereft of hope, Keisha's form crumpled, her once-indomitable spirit now but a fragile ember. Tears cascaded like liquid crystal down her pallid cheeks, tracing the path of her unrelenting despair. She cried out, her voice but a weak whisper carried away on the winds of agony, a lone word that hung heavy in the air like a requiem, "Ong..."

Chapter 43

Shadows Unveiled: Descent into Darkness: Keisha's Lament

In the Dread Palace, where preparations were underway for Keisha's sacrifice, she languishes in her cell, tormented by the relentless anticipation of her impending fate. Vuarus, impervious to her suffering, advanced relentlessly through the shadowy chamber. The moment had arrived, and the oppressive weight of destiny hung heavily in the air. Before him stood the Altar of the Abyss, beckoning like an evil deity, its obsidian surface shimmering with malevolent intent. Keisha's spirit had been irrevocably shattered, leaving no formidable force poised to thwart their unholy ascendancy."

"Brace yourself, Phoenix," Vuarus intoned, his voice an icy breath that slithered through the marrow of one's bones. The chamber seemed to shiver in response, its cold stone walls bearing witness to the sinister ritual about to unfold. "The next chapter of our malevolent chronicle unfurls before us. The realms shall quiver beneath the shadow of our impending ascendance, and our dominion will transcend the boundaries of imagination."

Drawing closer to the threshold of their nefarious expedition, Phoenix's laughter melded seamlessly with the inky tendrils that clung to them like a loyal specter. Shadows danced and swirled around them as if celebrating their evil intentions. "Indeed, my lord," he chimed, his mirth echoing the sinister resonance of their designs. "Our reign of darkness shall soon cast its oppressive veil over all creation."

And thus, they pressed onward, the weight of their unholy ambitions settling upon them like an indomitable yoke. The ephemeral divide between worlds grew increasingly tenuous, and the Altar of the Abyss beckoned with an insatiable hunger that threatened to consume all in its path. As they crossed the threshold, the very fabric of reality seemed to fray, and the chamber itself seemed to bleed darkness into the void beyond, marking the beginning of an evil saga that would forever scar the tapestry of existence.

Before them, the foreboding city of Fel Thalor loomed, a nightmare-crafted metropolis of dark spires and contorted architecture that mirrored the somber pall that had descended upon Ong and Karrenen. As they ventured through the labyrinthine web of shadowed streets, Karrenen's words lingered in the air like an unshakable specter, casting a leaden pall over their every step.

"Prepare yourself for what may be the most agonizing decision you will ever face," Karrenen intoned his voice, an austere dirge that resonated through the very essence of their being. He strode with unwavering determination, his gaze fixed upon a distant horizon. "You may find yourself in the harrowing position of choosing, Ong, between Keisha's life and the sanctuary of E'vahona."

Ong's heart clenched at the gravity of those words, the stark reality of the choice that loomed ominously before him. He understood all too well the profound implications of such a decision, the heartrending prospect of having to weigh Keisha's existence against the safety of E'vahona. His furrowed brows and con- flicted expression painted a poignant portrait of inner turmoil.

Desperation tugging at the edges of his voice, Ong turned to Karrenen, his eyes searching his friend's countenance for a glimmer of solace. "Karrenen," he con- fessed, his words heavy with the anguish that gnawed at his very core, "I... I cannot fathom how to make such a choice."

Karrenen's gaze softened, his empathy evident as he extended a steadying hand to rest upon Ong's shoulder. "I know, my dear friend," he whispered with a profound understanding that bordered on the divine. "It is a choice forged in the crucible of torment that no soul should ever bear. But we must confront each possibility, however grievous, in our quest to safeguard the realms."

In the ensuing silence, Ong's thoughts surged like a stormy river. He recalled the promise he had once made to Keisha, the solemn vow to protect her and stand firmly at her side. The notion of abandoning her in her darkest hour clawed at his soul like a ravenous beast. Yet, the fate of the realms, the lives of countless beings, hung precipitously in the balance. The choice he was inexorably drawn toward tore at the very fabric of his existence, a decision that threatened to rend his heart asunder.

"Karrenen," Ong's voice quivered with desperation, the weight of his torment evident in every trembling word, "how can I even begin to entertain the notion of turning my back on her? How can I bear to meet her gaze and let her believe that I have forsaken her in her darkest hour?"

Karrenen, ever the wellspring of wisdom and empathy, met Ong's anguished plea with a gaze steeped in profound understanding. His voice, a soothing balm to Ong's troubled soul, bore the weight of a sad truth. "Ong, my cherished friend, I do not envy the harrowing precipice upon which you stand. But you must grasp that even if circumstances compel you to tread the agonizing path of departure, it shall never be deemed abandonment. You are bound by a solemn duty to safeguard E'vahona from the hands that have wrought such anguish upon Keisha's spirit." In the face of such heart-wrenching choices, Karrenen's words offered solace and clarity amidst the tempestuous sea of emotions. Ong understood the relentless nature of his responsibility, the heavy mantle of guardianship he bore, and the unforgiving dichotomy that had become his reality. Yet, the anguish in his heart remained an unyielding storm, a tempest threatening to consume him whole as he treads the path of the impossible.

Ong's fists knotted into unyielding resolve, the fierce conflict within him manifesting in the crushing grip of his clenched hands. "She is my world, Karrenen," he confessed, his voice a raw lamentation, the torment tearing at the very fabric of his being. "After all the trials we've surmounted together, I cannot fathom the prospect of her regarding me with eyes filled with pain and the venom of betrayal."

Karrenen's gaze remained an unwavering beacon, a steadfast bastion of support, as he spoke with a committed and compassionate tone. "Then, Ong, we shall delve into the depths of possibility, seeking out every avenue, exploring every alternative, to avert such a grievous fate. We shall stride into that ominous meeting and unravel the true motives that shroud their intentions." Like the radiant ember within a sea of despair, a glimmer of hope kindled within Ong.

He offered a heartfelt nod, though the weight of his decision bore down upon him, its burden unbowed. "Thank you, Karrenen. In your wisdom and unwavering companionship, I find the strength to navigate these treacherous waters."

Karrenen, his resolve unwavering as the finest steel, smiled with an unwavering determination. "We are bound together in this crucible of tribulation, Ong," he declared, "and no matter the tempests that assail us, we shall uncover the path that leads to our salvation."

In unison, Ong and Karrenen pressed onward through the enigmatic labyrinth of Fel Thalor, their synchronized footfalls echoing their shared pledge to confront the nebulous future ahead. Their hearts remained unwavering in their resolve to shield both Keisha and the sanctuary of E'vahona from the encroaching shadows, no matter the sacrifices their destiny demands.

"In the wretched cell, devoid of light and steeped in a bone-chilling cold that clawed at one's soul, Keisha lay huddled in the corner. The air hung heavy with an evil aura, as if the walls themselves exhaled an icy breath. The darkness seemed to press in from all sides, smothering any trace of hope.

Amidst the frigid gloom, an eerie congregation of wraiths and grotesque creatures, born of Vuarus's twisted machinations, encircled Keisha like spectral sentinels. Their ethereal forms flickered in and out of existence, a dreadful dance that mirrored their evil intent. Their hollow eyes gleamed with a perverse anticipation, for they knew the hour of Keisha's sacrifice was nigh.

The wretched creatures celebrated in their own eerie way, their formless voices joining in a discordant chorus that reverberated through the cell's desolate confines. It was a haunting macabre symphony, heralding the impending doom that hung over Keisha like an inescapable shroud."

"Vuarus's lips curled with sadistic delight as he surveyed the harrowing tableau, his voice a venomous serpent's hiss. 'Behold the remnants of the spirited Eladrin,' he taunted, his words dripping with cruel mockery. 'A mere specter, a whisper of the vibrant soul that once defied us. She's now nothing but a vessel, broken and empty.'

Phoenix's gaze remained unrelenting, his satisfaction palpable. 'Indeed, Vuarus,' he concurred, his tone oozing with wicked glee. 'Her suffering has stripped her bare, erasing every trace of her former self. She's an empty canvas, ready to be painted with the darkest shades, a pawn in our evil game.'

Yet, within her desolation, Keisha existed as a fragile specter, her hollow eyes gazing into the abyss of her torment. Each shallow breath was a gasp of agony. She acknowledged their presence only peripherally, lost in the depths of her despair.

Vuarus's gaze remained unwavering, fixed upon Keisha's tormented figure, his voice soaked in a sinister triumph that reverberated through the confines of the cell. 'But fret not, dearest Keisha. Your suffering has not been in vain. Soon, your agony will transcend mere pain. Your shattered spirit will become a conduit for unparalleled power, and your torment will fuel our Dominion's unholy ascent.

Your buried memories of not belonging and the fear of Ong leaving you have become our instruments of your despair, rendering you defenseless against our evil influence.'"

"Phoenix advanced, his narrowed eyes scrutinizing Keisha's frail form with a calculating intensity. 'Indeed, she may now be an empty vessel, yet even such hollowness may be wielded with great efficacy. Her essence, shattered and fragmented, transmutes into a malleable substance, one receptive to the Dominion's arcane designs. When the hour of sacrifice dawns, her very core shall be steeped in darkness that shall enhance the very essence of our ritual. Her anguish, despair, and agony shall converge into a torrent of power I shall harness as I see fit.'

A macabre grin twisted across Vuarus's visage, embodying wicked satisfaction. 'And thus, my dear Phoenix, the realms shall quiver beneath the weight of our supremacy. The equilibrium shall crumble, and a new epoch of obscurity shall rise, shrouding all in its shadow.'

Phoenix's gaze remained unrelenting as he turned his attention back to Keisha. He leaned closer, his voice dripping with venomous mockery. 'You see, dear Keisha, this is the price you paid for interfering in Goldmoor those years ago,' he taunted, relishing her torment. 'Your misguided heroics have led you to this abyss of despair, a place from which there is no escape. Your sacrifice will serve as a testament to the futility of your resistance.'

For a fleeting moment, Keisha's vacant gaze appeared to waver, a faint glimmer of her former self battling to pierce the encroaching darkness. But like a candle struggling against an unyielding tempest, that glint of light was swiftly extinguished beneath the crushing weight of her agony. In the recesses of her shattered mind, memories of her past actions haunted her, their specters twisting the knife of guilt deeper into her soul."

Vuarus and Phoenix exchanged glances of retribution, their resolve unshaken by the flicker of resistance within Keisha's fading spirit. She was now a vessel devoid of hope, her spirit fractured beyond repair, and they stood upon the precipice of realizing their malevolent aspirations. With one final, appraising look at the hollow vessel that had once been Keisha, they departed the cell, their chilling laughter echoing down the corridor as they advanced toward their next undertaking. The Dominion's nefarious design marched inexorably forward with every passing step.

The aura surrounding the mystical barrier crackled and hummed with ethereal energy, weaving a tangible tension that mirrored the gravity of the decision looming before Ong. Karrenen's gaze, a blend of empathy and profound understanding, shifted toward his friend, his voice an anchor amid uncertainty, laden with deep significance.

"Are you prepared for the trials that await, Ong?" Karrenen inquired his words, a delicate fusion of compassion and unwavering resolve.

Ong's jaw clenched, his attention riveted upon the shimmering veil that barred their path. He drew a slow, steadying breath, his inner turmoil etched upon his forehead increased lines of contemplation. "I am aware of my duty, Karrenen," he replied, resignation palpable in his voice. "Even if it necessitates severing ties with Keisha, I cannot jeopardize the sanctuary of E'vahona and the multitude it shelters."

Karrenen's eyes softened as his hand found its place upon Ong's shoulder, a gesture of solace and unwavering support. "It is a choice wrought with adversity, my dear friend," he murmured tenderly but with unshakable conviction. "Rest assured, you need not shoulder this burden in solitude. We stand united in this ordeal, steadfast and resolute."

Ong's gaze locked onto Karrenen's, a testament to his gratitude and determination. "Your steadfast companionship means more than words can convey, Karrenen. I am indebted to your unwavering loyalty."

Karrenen acknowledged this sentiment with a subtle nod, a faint smile gracing his lips. "Keisha holds a place of profound significance in our hearts, Ong. To relinquish our connection with her shall be an excruciating ordeal. But for the welfare of E'vahona and the glimmer of hope that her salvation remains, I am willing to make this painful sacrifice."

Their resolve solidified in the presence of the barrier, and an unspoken understanding flowed between them. The path they trod was fraught with peril, and the specter of heartache, yet Ong and Karrenen remained resolute in their commitment to confront whatever adversities lay ahead. With a shared nod, they fortified themselves for the formidable journey, their unwavering allegiance steadfast as they marched toward an uncertain destiny, bound by their dedication to their world and those they cherished.

Vuarus and Phoenix, having returned to the cell to retrieve Keisha for the impending sacrifice at the Altar, paused before Malrik. The sinister purpose in their eyes was unmistakable, and the air grew colder in their presence. Keisha's desolation weighed heavily upon the room, casting a pall over their every move.

Turning their attention to Malrik, who stood at the ready, Vuarus's voice pierced the air, a command as chilling as the Abyss itself. "Prepare yourself to rendezvous with us at the Altar. The final act is nigh."

Malrik, his gaze cautiously averted from Keisha's forlorn visage, acknowledged the directive with a brisk nod. The shadow of darkness enveloping her appeared to touch even him, and he hastened to fulfill his assigned duties, his steps resolute and undeterred.

Vuarus and Phoenix moved with a sinister harmony. Their every motion was choreographed in eerie unison as they handled Keisha's frail figure. Her former vibrance had been utterly shattered, leaving behind a haunting echo of the once-potent Eladrin she had been. Once ablaze with determination, her eyes now lay vacant, bereft of the enthusiasm that once defined her existence. In their arms, she seemed ethereal, an almost weightless specter. Her clothing, once a symbol of her strength, now hung from her emaciated frame in tatters, no longer fitting the way it should, a poignant reminder of the suffering she had endured.

With Keisha's frail body in their grasp, Vuarus and Phoenix approached the Altar, its surface gleaming with ominous allure. Her figure, almost spectral against the yawning Abyss that stretched beneath, bore the weight of their sinister intentions.

The air above the abyss was bitterly cold, causing Keisha's body to shiver despite the tense situation. She lay on a cold, hard stone surface, the sinister ropes binding her wrists securely, leaving her with no means of escape.

An eerie chill in the air emanated from the depths below. The stone of the Altar felt like ice against Keisha's skin, while the unforgiving ropes dug into her wrists, as if they had a relentless grip on her, refusing to let go.

The ropes, rough and jagged, dug into her skin with each movement, a cruel reminder of her captivity. They pressed against her as if challenging her to break free, yet she remained powerless, her spirit resigned to her fate.

The relentless rope showed no mercy, its fibers biting into her skin, growing tighter with each passing moment. Her body lay motionless on the ground, any semblance of strength or resistance drained from her, her spirit utterly defeated.

The knots, unyielding, continued to dig into her flesh with every twist and turn. Their cold, unforgiving grasp tightened, sapping her spirit and strength, leaving her with no hope of escape.

With a cruel tug, Vuarus and Phoenix pulled Keisha's limp form up from the cold stone altar. The sinister ropes, once digging into her flesh, now hoisted her above the ominous altar like a grotesque marionette. Her frail body dangled above the unforgiving surface, still bound by the unrelenting cords. Keisha's pale face, etched with fear, stared down at the cold stone below, her body suspended in a deathly display of power, a symbol of her helplessness in the face of her tormentors' evil intentions.

Keisha's body hung in the air, vulnerable and suspended, her pallid face marked by fear and her form trembling. The atmosphere around her was oppressive, heavy with an impending darkness. It felt alive, contracting an imminent sense of doom, sending a cold chill coursing through Keisha's body.

Above the abyss, Keisha's body dangled limply, a picture of helplessness. Fear etched her pale face, and her trembling form bore witness to the oppressive ambiance that filled the space. The air seemed to throb with darkness and foreboding, its thick mist seeping through her skin and into her very being.

Suspended in the air, Keisha's frail figure quivered with fear, her once-majestic presence now contorted in terror. Her pallid skin stood out like a moonbeam in a midnight sky. Below her, the abyss gaped like a hungry maw of darkness while the air surrounding her pulsated with the impending hunger of doom.

Standing next to the Altar, Vuarus and Phoenix loomed over Keisha like ominous shadows, their evil schemes on the brink of realization, sending shivers down her spine. The destiny of Keisha and the world hung by the slenderest of threads, as fragile as a gossamer strand stretched between heaven and earth, poised to snap under the unrelenting hands of fate.

Having completed their preparations, Vuarus and Phoenix exchanged a knowing glance, their malevolence unmistakable. Vuarus's words, dripping with perverse anticipation, found their mark as he turned to Phoenix, their shared purpose etched in his sinister grin.

"Position yourself on that side, Phoenix," Vuarus commanded, his voice laced with chilling resolve. "Should they even contemplate surrendering the sanctum of E'vahona, we shall sever these bindings. By the time their reaction unfolds, it shall be too late."

Phoenix's lips curled into a macabre smile as he assumed his stance. "Agreed," he replied, his voice dripping with sadistic satisfaction. "Their only recourse shall be to witness the horrifying culmination of her sacrifice."

With an evil smirk, Vuarus relished tormenting his helpless victim. "Oh, dear Guardian," he taunted with sadistic pleasure, "how your once-bright light has dimmed. You are utterly at our mercy." Phoenix joined in with an evil laugh, his words dripping with cruelty. "Indeed," he added, "no one shall ever remember the radiant soul you once were."

The formidable gates of Fel Thalor yielded with a mournful groan, granting passage to Ong and Karrenen. As they crossed the threshold, the harrowing tableau of the city unfolded before them. Fel Thalor, stood veiled in darkness. Its streets, veiled in a sinister pall, lay eerily still as though they had succumbed to the shadows that now held dominion over this forsaken place.

Ong's breath hitched in his chest as he beheld the desolation that stretched in every direction. The city, once teeming with vibrant life, now lay prostrate in ruins, its vitality drained away by the insidious forces that had engulfed it. The palpable malevolence hung heavy in the air, an ominous shroud that bore witness to the Dominion's ruthless rule.

Karrenen's touch, a gentle reassurance upon Ong's shoulder, conveyed a wordless pledge of solidarity and unwavering support. "Stand resolute, Ong," he murmured, his voice a hushed vow. "Our purpose remains unwavering—to safeguard Keisha, regardless of the trials that await."

Ong nodded, his gaze fixed on the arduous path that lay ahead. Together, they pressed forward, propelled by a steely determination and an ever-vigilant caution. In these bleak streets, bereft of life's vitality, an unsettling silence reigned, broken only by the distant echoes of their footsteps—a somber cadence marking their relentless pursuit of salvation.

Finally, they reached the very heart of the city, where the Altar of the Abyss sprawled, ominous and foreboding. The tableau that unfolded before them was nothing short of a nightmarish vision. Keisha's ethereal form hung suspended above the yawning Abyss, cruelly ensnared by the Altar's vicious grip. Once radiant and fierce, her spirit lay shattered like shards of a broken star while her body had become naught but a vessel for unrelenting suffering.

For Ong, witnessing his beloved in such a wretched state was an agony. The sight pierced through the armor of his resolve, leaving his heart constricted in its vise-like grip. Keisha, the love of his life, had been irrevocably ensnared by the clutches of darkness, and he, a helpless bystander in her descent into oblivion, teetered on the precipice of a choice that threatened to shatter the very core of his being.

His gaze flitted to Karrenen, their eyes locking in a shared communion of profound sorrow and unwavering determination. In that charged moment, Ong's eyes bore the weight of anguish and resolve, his heart a battlefield where love waged war with the inevitable demands of their mission.

Karrenen's grip on Ong's shoulder tightened, offering silent encouragement. "We're here, Ong. Let's do what needs to be done."

Ong's eyes met Karrenen's, a tumultuous sea of emotions swirling within them. He couldn't contain his distress any longer and found himself whispering, trembling, "Karrenen, what have they done to her?"

Karrenen's response was solemn, his voice a lamentation for the tragedy that had befallen them all. "They've torn her spirit asunder, Ong, and plunged her into despair. But we won't let her sacrifice be in vain. We will find a way to save her, no matter the cost."

With a deep breath, Ong squared his shoulders and turned his attention to the harrowing scene before him. Keisha's suffering was evident, her spirit broken, and the cruel intentions of Vuarus and Phoenix were laid bare for all to see. He clenched his fists, his mind racing as he prepared for the agonizing choice he was about to face.

Vuarus's voice sliced through the tense silence, his eyes locked onto Ong and Karrenen like a predator assessing prey. "You've heard the terms," he declared, his tone a frigid blade of menace. "The fate of this shattered Eladrin rests within your grasp. Surrender E'vahona's sanctuary, and she shall be spared further torment."

Ong's response resounded with unwavering resolve. His steadfast gaze locked onto Vuarus like a stone that could not be moved. "I shall not yield the sanctity of E'vahona to you," his voice carried the weight of love and defiance, a resolute stand in the face of darkness. Then, his eyes turned to Keisha, a tumultuous sea of emotions within them. "Keisha, I love you."

Together with Karrenen, they pivoted to depart, their decision laden with the heavy burden of sacrifice. As they left, Ong couldn't help but make a fierce declaration to Phoenix, his voice filled with righteous anger, "Your day of reckoning is coming, Phoenix!"

Phoenix's maniacal laughter tore through the air, foreshadowing Keisha's grim fate. With a heart as cold as ice, Vuarus severed the bonds that had kept her tethered to safety, and she began her harrowing descent into the yawning abyss below. Vuarus's sadistic words of delight overshadowed the cacophony of her anguished screams. "Welcome, dear Guardian," he taunted with a twisted grin, "to your descent into eternal darkness."

As the cruel bonds were severed, Keisha's anguished cry reverberated through the chamber, a gut-wrenching sound that pierced the very soul. Her body plummeted into the unfathomable abyss below, her paralyzed eyes locking onto Ong, who, with Karrenen by his side, turned away, resolute in his advance. Her voice, filled with desperation and unrelenting longing, escalated to a heart-rending scream that tore through the air, "Help me, please!" Her plea hung in the air like a haunting refrain, an urgent cry for salvation, a poignant plea for redemption amidst the relentless descent into the abyss.

As her gaze fixated on Ong's retreating form, a desperate spark of hope ignited within Keisha, only to be swiftly extinguished. The tattered remnants of her spirit crumbled and faded into the abyss, leaving behind an infinite void of despair. With one last, ear-piercing scream that resonated throughout the abyss, she surrendered to the relentless pull of darkness. Vuarus and Phoenix watched with sadistic glee as her descent into the pit of misery began, a symphony of suffering that heralded the culmination of their evil designs.

As Keisha's agonizing scream reverberated through the area, Ong felt a sharp, searing pain in his chest, like a piece of his soul had been torn away. He turned to Karrenen, his eyes wide with shock and despair, his voice trembling with the moment's weight. "What have I done?" he whispered, words heavy with regret and the realization of the irreversible consequences of his choice.

Karrenen's reassuring hand found its place on Ong's shoulder, a gesture of solace amidst the turmoil. His eyes, filled with sympathy and understanding, locked onto Ong's as if trying to convey the gravity of their choices. "You made the best choice for E'vahona, Ong," he spoke gently but firmly, "I know it's tearing you apart, but we must remember the bigger picture. Keisha wouldn't have wanted her sacrifice to lead to the fall of our world."

Ong's head hung low, his fingers clutching the fabric of his cloak in search of some tangible comfort. In a whisper, to himself, he uttered words heavy with sorrow, "How can I go on without her?"

Karrenen met Ong's gaze with unwavering determination, a flicker of grief in his eyes. "We will honor her sacrifice by fighting for E'vahona's safety," he reassured, gently guiding Ong away from the city's gates. "We'll find a way to free her from Vuarus's grasp and ensure her sacrifice wasn't in vain."

Ong nodded in acknowledgment, his voice barely above a murmur as he spoke, "But I have lost my world." As he hung his head, his eyes fell to the ground, heavy with grief and despair. Then, he noticed another fragment of Keisha's necklace, tarnished and forlorn, lying on the ground.

He bent down to pick it up, his trembling fingers clutching the precious piece of the circlet. Tears welled in his eyes, and he couldn't hold back the flood of emotions any longer. With the necklace fragment in his hand, he knew that he had lost Keisha, and the weight of that realization pressed upon his heart like an impossible burden.

The darkness of the Abyss mirrored the despair in his heart, and for a fleeting moment, hope felt like a distant memory as he accepted the painful truth that he had lost the love of his life.

With each step they took, the weight of their mission pressed upon them, and the resolve to save both Keisha and their world burned brighter within their hearts. The road ahead was fraught with peril, but they were determined to navigate it together, for Keisha and for the realm they held dear.

Vuarus and Phoenix exchanged triumphant smirks, their malevolence mirrored in the cruel curl of their lips as they watched Keisha's limp form descend toward the gaping maw of the Abyss. Time, in this harrowing moment, seemed to stretch its limits, each second echoing like an eternity as if the very fabric of reality conspired to prolong the inevitable.

The chasm of darkness below gradually beckoned her nearer, the void stretching out indefinitely as if yearning to embrace her. As Keisha's body continued its inevitable descent, it was as if the air clung to her, hesitating, almost reluctant to let her go, as if the world paused to witness this heart-wrenching juncture.

It took several agonizing minutes for Keisha's form to reach the very peak of the Abyss, where the boundary between the realm of the living and the abyssal depths blurred and wavered. In that suspended moment, she hung precariously, a fragile soul perched on the precipice of a destiny that was both heartrending and intense. It was a testament to the inevitable turmoil that had brought them all to this fateful crossroads, where the choice between darkness and salvation awaited its final reckoning.

Just as Keisha's fragile form teetered on the precipice of being consumed by the yawning maw of the Abyss, the very atmosphere quivered in anticipation of a seismic shift. A sudden, forceful gust of wind erupted from the abyssal depths, unsettling the delicate balance between light and darkness in this harrowing moment. It was as though the very fabric of reality trembled at the impending turning point.

Emerging from the inky depths of the Abyss, a gnarled and shadowy hand reached forth, its fingers, like tendrils of despair, closing in on Keisha's feeble form. The suffocating grasp of the Abyss threatened to claim her, to shroud her in eternal darkness.

Yet, as the Abyss sought to engulf her, the heavens seemed to respond to this dire plight. With a resounding rupture in the sky, the celestial canvas split open, revealing the awe-inspiring figures of Kimras, the regal Gold Dragon, and Amara, the radiant Amethyst Dragon. They descended upon the scene like divine avatars, their enormous forms casting a glorious glow that banished the oppressive darkness. Their wings unfurled in a magnificent display of power and grace, and their majestic presence filled the void with a newfound hope that sent shockwaves through the very heart of the Abyss.

Kimras, adorned in scales of radiant gold, gleamed like a beacon of hope amidst the encroaching gloom. His very presence heralded the dawn of salvation. Beside him, Amara's amethyst brilliance illuminated the darkness, casting aside the shadows that had dared to lay claim to Keisha's spirit.

In this pivotal moment, the clash between light and darkness, despair and hope, hung in delicate equilibrium as the fate of Keisha and the destiny of worlds swayed in the balance of celestial intervention.

"Hold fast, My Lady," Kimras's resonant voice thundered like a divine proclamation as his colossal claws extended to snatch Keisha from the relentless grasp of the Abyss. He ascended with a powerful beat of his wings in a breathtaking display of strength, bearing Keisha aloft from the precipice of oblivion. Her fragile form rested within his grasp. Kimras held her as gently as the most delicate flower, cradling her with the utmost care as a symbol of an indomitable spirit protected within the mighty embrace of a celestial protector.

Amara, radiant and furious in tandem, directed her unwavering ire towards the accursed Altar, the heart of innumerable torments. A torrent of amethyst energy surged forth from her, a luminous deluge of cosmic might that struck the Altar with the force of a celestial storm. The very earth quaked beneath the weight of her power, and the Altar shattered into fragments, its malevolent dominion rent asunder, scattering its maleficence like seeds on the wind.

Having fulfilled her sacred mission, Amara turned her regal gaze upon the evil duo of Vuarus and Phoenix, her eyes twin vortexes of righteous fury. Her message was unspoken yet undeniable: their dominion of darkness was far from absolute, and the dawn of retribution cast a long shadow upon them.

She spared a deliberate glance toward Vuarus, her words a testament to the impending reckoning. "A message for you, Azeron, from Kimras," she intoned with chilling finality. "You have lost. Your days of reckoning are imminent."

With a single, unwavering roar that reverberated through the air they breathed, Amara, blazing with righteous anger, took to the skies, her form disappearing beyond the horizon.

In the aftermath of the dragons' intervention, a palpable tension lingered in the air, their echoes fading but their impact everlasting. The scales of power had irrevocably shifted, and the battleground of shadows bore the indelible mark of celestial interference.

In the turbulent aftermath of the dragons' unexpected intervention, Vuarus and Phoenix were entangled in an explosive exchange, their words a tumultuous clash of anger and exasperation.

"This was your design! Your execution!" Phoenix's voice erupted like a storm, its thunderous fury mirrored in his blazing eyes. "How did they discern our stratagem? How did the abyssal winds of treachery betray us?"

Vuarus's visage warped with a storm of rage, his retort an equal deluge of ferocity. "Do not dare to besmirch my intelligence with accusations of inadequacy! I held dominion over this enterprise. Keisha's spirit lay shattered, poised for the sacrificial altar!"

"But those dragons... they unraveled the very fabric of our scheme!" Phoenix's fingers balled into fists of impotent wrath. "We held sway, poised for triumph, and they brazenly interceded in our dark affairs."

Vuarus's voice dripped with virulent scorn. "It appears we grievously underestimated the intricate alliances Keisha had woven. She harbored allies in the most unexpected of realms."

"Or, perchance, your hubris clouded our foresight!" Phoenix fired back with bitter fervor. "You believed her spirit utterly broken, yet you failed to fathom the ember of resilience that still burned within her."

Vuarus's eyes seethed with unyielding determination. "We shall reconvene. We will chart an alternate course. And when the ordained moment arrives, E'vahona shall quiver at our dominion."

Phoenix's lips curled into a sinister smile. "And those dragons, those impertinent intruders... they shall render a dear reckoning for their impudence."

The two evil figures, veiled in shadows and unresolved ire, pivoted upon their heels, and commenced their return to the Dread Spire. The echoes of their altercation resonated through the air, a discordant symphony of their partnership's schism. The shadows whispered their discontent, and as the two dark enigmas vanished into the depths of their citadel, it was with an unwavering commitment to reevaluate their designs and to unleash their retribution upon those who dared to disrupt their ambitions.

Amara's amethyst eyes sparkled mischievously as she landed before Ong and Karrenen. Ong's brow furrowed in frustration, his worry for Keisha evident. "Amara, this isn't the best time for your games," he sighed.

The amethyst dragon tilted her head, and her voice tinged with playful teasing. "Oh, Ong, you always take the fun out of my teasing, but this time, I promise it's worth it. I come bearing news about your dear wife."

Karrenen raised an eyebrow, his curiosity piqued. "What news?"

Amara couldn't resist drawing out the suspense. "Well, your wife isn't where you think she is right now."

Ong's patience was wearing thin. "Enough with the riddles, Amara. What are you talking about?"

With a triumphant grin, Amara finally revealed her hand. "She's in the Hidden Isles. Kimras, the regal gold dragon, has whisked her safely away."

Ong's eyes widened in astonishment, a mix of relief and disbelief washing over him. "Hidden Isles? But... how? Why?"

Amara chuckled softly, her wings twitching with suppressed laughter. "You might want to climb onto my back with Karrenen if you want answers. They're waiting for you there."

Amara's playful nature shone through, adding a touch of whimsy to the situation.

Karrenen, ever astute, shared a knowing glance with Amara. "I believe we would be wise to accept your gracious offer, Amara."

With a blend of disbelief and gratitude, Ong addressed Amara. "Lead the way, Amara. And thank you."

Amara stretched her wings wide in regal splendor, a smirk of satisfaction gracing her lips. "Well, Ong, it appears this dragon has played the hero. Now, let us embark."

As Ong and Karrenen ascended onto Amara's back, the dragon rose into the heavens, her laughter trailing behind like a celestial echo, a testament to the whimsical interplay of fate and the grandeur of their world.

As they soared through the skies atop Amara's back, Ong couldn't help but marvel at the majestic dragons and their unwavering loyalty. He spoke in awe, "The dragons of Vacari truly are remarkable beings. I'll forever be indebted to Kimras and you, Amara."

Amara chuckled softly, her voice carrying a playful undertone. "You always had such foolish notions about dragons, Ong. We're not all as terrible as you once believed."

Ong couldn't help but smile at Amara's teasing. "I stand corrected, Amara. You're a shining example of the true nature of dragons – powerful, wise, and, in this case, a savior."

The amethyst dragon's eyes twinkled mischievously. "Perhaps you'll think twice before doubting our kind in the future."

As they continued their journey to the Hidden Isles, Ong couldn't deny that his perspective on dragons had undergone a profound transformation, and he was grateful for the newfound alliance they had forged.

Chapter 44

Shadows Unveiled: Echoes of Renewal

Kimras, the majestic Gold Dragon, descended with the grace of an ethereal deity, his resplendent scales shimmering like molten sunlight as he alighted beside Keisha. They stood amidst the pristine beauty of the Hidden Isles, where the very essence of the world seemed to harmonize. The air carried a melody of serenity, a soothing balm for the scars of torment that Keisha bore.

Fragile as a glass sculpture, Keisha crumpled to the ground, her shivers echoing like the last whispers of a fading storm. Her gaze, a distant constellation adrift in the sea of her thoughts, betrayed the turmoil within. Kimras, his eyes deep pools of infinite empathy, observed her, fully aware of the intricate fragility of her spirit.

In a tender gesture, as if to bridge the chasm between their worlds, Kimras unfurled his majestic wings, their feathers as delicate as gossamer tendrils of hope. These vast and splendid wings spread wide, casting a radiant canopy above them. He folded them gently around Keisha, creating a sanctuary of warmth amidst the world's chill.

Beside them, the waterfall cascaded like liquid crystal, its melodious song a lullaby of forgotten sorrows. As Keisha nestled within the embrace of Kimras' wings, the world beyond seemed to dissolve, leaving only the two souls entwined in a moment of profound solace.

He cleared his throat softly, a deep resonance that sent ripples through the stillness. "My Lady," he began, his words as gentle as the caress of a moonbeam, "you are safe now. Hidden Isles is a sanctuary, a realm untouchable by harm."

Like a shattered mirror, Keisha's gaze slowly found Kimras. Her eyes became a canvas, painted with the hues of her emotions—fear, relief, and the profound weariness of a traveler who had journeyed through the darkest of nights. Her voice emerged as a distant, hollow echo when she finally spoke. "Safe... yet not free from the relentless grip of memories."

Kimras drew closer, his colossal, golden presence casting a protective tapestry around her. "I understand the depths to which the scars reach," he murmured with the empathy of ancient wisdom. "But know this, my Lady, you stand not alone. We, your steadfast companions, are here to cradle you in your ascent from the abyss."

Keisha's fingers, like fragile tendrils, traced intricate patterns in the verdant grass as she contemplated his words. Her response was a whispered breeze, barely there yet laden with vulnerability. "Your kindness is a beacon," she confessed, "but the darkness within me lingers, a stubborn shadow unwilling to dissipate."

Kimras released a soft, resonant sigh, his eyes alight with a profound understanding and unwavering determination. "Time is the elixir for wounds such as these, my Lady. The darkness may have brushed against your soul, but it is not the tapestry of your essence. You stand amidst allies and friends, an unyielding fortress of support. Together, we shall confront the challenges shrouded in tomorrow's mists."

As Keisha's gaze remained locked upon the waterfall, a serene strength descended upon her, like the hush of a forest before a hidden storm. She recognized that the journey to mend her fractured spirit would be a labyrinthine one, a labyrinth of shadows and light interwoven, but her resolve to reclaim her essence blazed like a beacon in her heart.

Kimras, a steadfast sentinel, stood as her guardian, a reminder etched in gold that she walked this path with companions bound by loyalty. The echoes of sacrifice resonated through their shared history, but vibrant and unwavering hope surrounded her like a sanctuary's warm embrace, banishing the chill of despair.

Amara, her wings slicing through the cerulean sky, bore herself alongside Ong and Karrenen, the trio arriving in harmonious flight to the idyllic tableau by the waterfall in Hidden Isles. Kimras, the luminary embodiment of a golden dragon, turned his colossal head to meet their arrival, his eyes twin pools of sagacity, filled with a tacit acknowledgment and an encompassing comprehension. At that moment, he grasped the profound significance of the reunion unfolding. Drawing nearer to the scene, Kimras unfurled one of his magnificent wings, a vast expanse of gilded majesty that provided both shade and an emblematic aegis. Ong's eyes met Kimras's, and within that wordless communion lay a depth of gratitude that transcended mere words. Kimras offered a subtle nod, his countenance a bastion of reassurance, a silent pact to stand as a sentinel over Keisha's well-being.

Amara, ethereal and radiant in her amethyst-hued scales, touched down with a grace that mirrored the fluidity of a lustrous river. She approached Keisha and Kimras, her presence at once a balm of comfort and a testament of reverence. Nestling beside Keisha, Amara met the Eladrin's gaze, her eyes radiant with compassion and an empathetic understanding that transcended the confines of language. "Keisha," she began, her voice a lyrical cadence, a soothing symphony, "you are nestled in safety now, and remember, you are not alone in this odyssey. We are steadfast, here for you, awaiting your call."

Like a leaf carried by a gentle stream, Keisha's gaze traversed from the cascading waterfall to Amara's countenance. In that fleeting instant, a glimmer of recognition danced within her eyes, akin to the rekindling of a long-lost star. A faint smile, as fragile as the first bloom of dawn, graced her lips—an eloquent expression of gratitude for the unwavering friends who stood as guardians by her side.

Proceed with measured steps, Ong. She has borne an ordeal of suffering, and the complicated path to her recovery shall be fraught with tribulations. Steel yourself for what you are about to witness."

Ong inclined his head in solemn acknowledgment, the raw tapestry of his emotions laid bare as he beheld Keisha, a fragile wisp of a soul, perched by the cascading waterfall, her form a mere echo of her former self, trapped within the maze of her ruminations. "I understand," he whispered, his voice an intricate tapestry woven of tender resolve. He bore witness to the truth that while they had rescued her human form from the abyss, the scars of her harrowing ordeal ran far more profound, etched into the very fabric of her being, a testament to the unrelenting passage of time that would be required for her to find solace and mend her fragmented spirit.

Their gazes converged upon Keisha like beams of compassionate light piercing through a shroud of darkness, and their hearts swelled with a poignant ache, tears welling up like glistening jewels in their eyes. What lay before them was an image burdened with profound torment.

Once the possessor of eyes that mirrored the brilliant depths of emerald forests, Keisha had witnessed the vitality and fire within them extinguished. In their place now dwelled shadows of fear and an impenetrable distance, the very essence of her spirit bearing the scars of relentless anguish. Dark crescent moons nestled beneath her delicate features, testimony to the restless nights she had endured, as if sleep had become a fugitive, forever eluding her grasp.

Her glorious mane of fiery red, once a cascading waterfall of lustrous silk, lay in disarray, robbed of its former splendor by the cruel hands of her captivity. She appeared as though she had been drained of life's sustenance, her once-robust frame now reduced to haunting thinness, as if she had not savored a proper meal in an age. Her movements, once graceful and assured, had become hesitant and fragile, her body adjusting to the unfamiliar terrain of freedom after the protracted confines of her prison.

In the wake of their concerned gaze, Keisha, a wounded spirit, stole a furtive glance in their direction before attempting to recede into the protective shroud of shadows. They comprehended the profound depth of her inner turmoil. The radiant bloom of her former self had withered. Her beauty transformed into a haunting testament to the horrors she had faced. Keisha yearned to disappear, to evade the unrelenting gaze that now bore witness to her altered appearance.

Perched in the sad embrace of shadow near the secluded waterfall, her form trembled involuntarily. The echoes of her harrowing ordeal within the freezing chamber still reverberated through her being, sending frigid shivers coursing like ethereal specters along her fragile frame. The ghosts of her past haunted her, their spectral touch a chilling reminder of the scars etched upon her spirit.

Her trembling hand instinctively reached for the space where her necklace had once rested—a symbol of her love with Ong, now lost to the depths of the Abyss. Tears welled up in her eyes, and she couldn't contain the rush of emotions that overwhelmed her. In the solitude of her hiding place, Keisha wept, her heartache echoing through the quiet Hidden Isles, a poignant lament for the love and life she had been torn away from.

As their eyes fell upon Keisha, a storm of sorrow and fury surged within their hearts, emotions as fierce and unyielding as a storm front rolling across the endless expanse of the sea. The weight of what she had endured bore down upon them, a burden too immense for words to convey. The journey to guide Keisha back from the abyss of her suffering loomed before them, a daunting odyssey fraught with trials that reached beyond their understanding.

For Ong, the sight of his cherished Keisha in such fragility tore through his being like a storm. A maelstrom of emotions gripped his heart with a relentless force. He struggled to swallow the lump in his throat, the urge to rush to her side, to wrap her in the warmth of his protective embrace, was almost overwhelming. Yet, he knew the path ahead demanded restraint, a gentleness akin to the soft caress of a whispering breeze. Keisha remained a fragile spirit, a delicate bloom vulnerable to the slightest gust.

For Karrenen, the image of Keisha, once an unyielding beacon of strength, now trapped in the clutches of fear, carved a chasm of profound sorrow within his heart. It was a stark contrast to the woman she had once been, a jarring difference that resonated with the ache of empathy. His heart swelled with a fierce determination, an unwavering resolve to restore her to the luminous being she had once embodied. At that moment, the depths of his commitment mirrored the unyielding force of a tidal wave, surging forth to wash away the remnants of Keisha's torment and unveil the strength that still dwelled within her.

Ong ventured forward, each step measured like a heartbeat echoing through the chamber of his chest. Mixed emotions surged within him, a tumultuous symphony of hope and despair, compassion and fear. As he knelt beside Keisha, the air around them seemed to shimmer with a shared vulnerability. His voice, a soothing cadence like the gentlest of river currents, caressed the broken fragments of her spirit. "Keisha, I acknowledge the deep-rooted shadow that has cloaked your soul, but I'm here to shield you from it. You are not its captive nor its vessel."

Tears, like glistening dewdrops, welled up in the once-haunted emerald pools of Keisha's eyes. She extended a trembling hand, fingers reaching out to graze Ong's, a gesture laden with trepidation yet pulsating with an aching yearning. Her voice, a fragile whisper that resonated like a distant echo, traversed the delicate space between them. "Ong," she breathed, her words a weak plea, "did you hear my cries in the abyss?"

Ong's eyes shimmered with an indefinable blend of sorrow and resolve as he met her gaze, his voice a profound affirmation of his unwavering commitment. "Keisha," he replied, his tone resolute and tender, "I heard the echoes of your pain, even in the deepest abyss, and I came to stand between you and that darkness."

Keisha's tears flowed softly, like the quiet lament of a solitary bird in the night, her voice trembling with the weight of her vulnerability. "I was uncertain if my desperate cries reached your ears," she confessed, her words a fragile thread binding her heart to his. "I feared you, too, had abandoned me, as countless others have in my fractured life. I was enveloped in a shroud of fear." Ong, his heart a storm of emotions that mirrored the turbulent skies before a storm, tightened his grip on her cold hand with a gentle, reassuring squeeze. His unwavering gaze bore into her eyes, a steadfast beacon in the tumultuous sea of her doubts. "Keisha," he breathed, his voice a whispered promise, "I will never abandon you. Even in the darkest abyss, I am here to protect you."

As his fingers interlocked with hers, a shiver coursed through Ong's frame, not from fear but from the stark awareness of the frigid chill that permeated Keisha's touch. His eyes widened, reflecting a blend of concern and realization. He whispered, his breath forming a wisp of warmth against the icy tendrils of her hand, "Keisha, you are as cold as the deepest winter. We must get you warm, bring life back to your frozen spirit."

Keisha's cries echoed through the shadowed chamber, a mournful symphony that bore witness to her harrowing ordeal. "I suffered in a frigid, desolate cell for those interminable months," she sobbed, each word laced with the bitterness of her isolation. "There were times when they sought to strip away even the traces of warmth. I fear that I may never know warmth again."

Ong's heart shattered into a thousand pieces as he listened to her anguished words. The air seemed to resonate with his profound empathy and a burning desire to alleviate her suffering. His gaze darted around the surroundings, searching for something to enfold Keisha in, to wrap her in a cocoon of warmth and solace. A glance at Karrenen revealed the cloak draped upon him, a mantle of protection against the elements.

"Karrenen," Ong implored, his voice heavy with emotion, "may I borrow your cape for Keisha? She is trembling with cold." His plea hung in the air, a testament to his desperate need to shield her from the relentless chill that clung to her fragile form.

Karrenen, without hesitation, stepped forward, his actions embodying the very essence of compassion. He carefully removed his cloak and extended it to Ong, their hands briefly touching like two stars brushing against each other in the midnight sky. "Of course," Karrenen responded, his voice a quiet affirmation. "Anything for Keisha." He withdrew, granting them the space they needed.

With utmost tenderness, Ong wrapped the cloak around Keisha's shivering frame. His brows furrowed with concern as the cloak draped over her, revealing the stark truth of her gaunt state. Her fragility, laid bare by the cape's embrace, was a heart-wrenching sight that tugged at the very fabric of his soul.

Like a tempest-tossed sea, Keisha shifted to Ong, her eyes a mosaic of emotions, each a shard of her fractured spirit. In that fleeting moment, the memories of the visions that had haunted her during her torment resurfaced like ethereal phantoms. These images were a tumultuous tapestry, a haunting blend of past, present, and distorted reality, each thread a fragment of her deepest fears and vulnerabilities.

Tears, glistening like fallen stars in the obsidian abyss of her eyes, welled up, threatening to overflow like a cascading waterfall. Her breath caught in her throat, a fragile dam on the verge of collapse, as the total weight of her agonizing experiences surged over her like a relentless tide. Her voice, a delicate thread stretched to its limit, trembled as she spoke, each word a testament to the raw and exposed pain etched into her soul. "Ong," she began, her voice a mere whisper, as though the utterance of her fears might shatter her, "in those visions... I beheld you with another, as though you had moved on, found another love, another life... It felt as though you had abandoned me."

Like a tightly coiled spring, Ong's heart clenched with the understanding of her anguish. He approached her with deliberate slowness, his presence a steadfast lighthouse in her tumultuous storm. Seating beside her, he offered her both space and solace, a silent promise that he was there, unwavering, and resolute.

"Keisha," he spoke gently, his voice an elixir of compassion, "those visions were naught but twisted illusions, dark sorceries meant to shatter your spirit. Know this, I could never forsake you, not in a thousand lifetimes."

Tenderly, he wiped away her tears, his touch a soothing balm, reassuring her in the language of empathy. "I am here, Keisha," he whispered, the words like a sacred vow, "and my love for you has never wavered. Regardless of the apparitions that sought to sow discord, my heart has always been yours."

Keisha's gaze, a fusion of agony and longing, met Ong's, her voice a fragile reed in the storm of her uncertainty. "I no longer know what is real," she confessed, lamenting her fractured reality. Ong's grip upon her hand tightened, an unbreakable bond forged at that moment, his gaze unwavering, like a sentinel guarding her from the encroaching shadows. "What is real," he affirmed with steadfast conviction, "is the unbreakable connection between us, Keisha. We have faced innumerable trials, emerging stronger after each storm. Those visions were intended to shatter you, yet they failed to sunder the unyielding bond that binds us."

Understanding the depth of her turmoil, he continued, his voice gentle and filled with empathy, "But I also understand that you need time, my love, to discern what is real amidst the echoes of those illusions. I will be here, patiently, as you find your way back to the truth."

Drawing a deep breath, his voice resonated with unwavering certainty. "I shall spend every heartbeat, every breath, proving to you that I am here, love you without measure, and never depart from your side. We shall defeat this darkness that tried to take you from me and everyone else."

Keisha's tears flowed like a river of grief, yet within her eyes shone a fragile glimmer of hope—a spark rekindling the fire that had once blazed with the fierce intensity of her spirit. She held Ong's gaze, a mesmerizing blend of vulnerability and unwavering determination, like a lone ship navigating through the treacherous waters of uncertainty. Her voice, a whisper that hung like a fragile thread suspended in the air, bore the faintest trace of trust as though she dared to believe in the possibility of solace.

Ong's smile was a radiant dawn breaking through the darkest night, his heart soaring at the sight of her resilience. He leaned closer, pressing a tender kiss upon her forehead, a gesture akin to a benediction, a promise forged in the crucible of their shared trials. "Together," he murmured, his words an oath etched in the language of devotion, "we shall tread this path, one step at a time. We shall rebuild the strength the darkness sought to rob from you."

As Keisha surrendered to his touch, a silent pact unfurled between them, a testament to their unwavering commitment to defeating the encroaching shadows that threatened to engulf her. The journey ahead loomed as a formidable challenge, yet in the unity of their spirits, they found the unspoken promise that they would discover their way back to the radiant embrace of the light together.

Keisha's voice quivered, like a fragile leaf trembling in the face of a raging storm, as she turned her gaze toward Ong. Like twin pools of longing and uncertainty, her eyes searched his countenance for answers, seeking a portal into the depths of his concealed emotions. Her words, uttered with a raw intensity that laid bare the core of her soul, carried the weight of her vulnerability and the searing pain etched into her being.

"Why," she implored, her voice a fragile thread stretched to its limit, "did you not cast a backward glance, Ong? When you walked away from me at that sacred altar... it felt as though my world was crumbling, like the sky was collapsing around me. And when the realization struck that you hadn't spared even a fleeting look in my direction, I... I found myself indifferent to the stark contrast of life and death. I was uncertain whether you even heard my voice in that anguish." Tears, like precious gemstones gleaming with sorrow, welled up and cascaded down her cheeks as she spoke, each word a painful echo of the memories that continued to haunt her. In that agonizing juncture, she had been left behind, a fractured soul abandoned amid the ruins, left to grapple with the anguish of being naught but a pawn in an evil game of fate. The hurt had cut through her like a jagged blade, leaving scars that ran deep, wounds that took time to heal, and a vulnerability that lingered like the fading echoes of a lament.

Ong's heart was a symphony of agony, its mournful chords resonating perfectly with Keisha's words. The pain in her voice echoed the storm of emotions he had battled within himself for far too long. With deliberate steps, he closed the distance between them, his eyes locked onto hers, his intent clear—he sought to convey the profound depth of his emotions, to bridge the gulf that had kept them apart.

"Keisha," he began, his voice a soft but unwavering cadence, "I implore you to understand that not a single heartbeat had passed when I did not bear the crushing weight of that moment with me. When I walked away, it was not borne of desire but a dire necessity."

Drawing a deep breath, he held her gaze with an unyielding intensity. "I heard your voice calling out to me, and I heard your anguish as it echoed through the sanctum of our shared memories. In that fleeting moment, doubt clawed at the edges of my resolve. Had I turned back and allowed my eyes to meet yours one final time, I knew I would have been incapable of departure. The mere thought of witnessing the pain in your eyes, the torment I inflicted upon you, was unbearable."

His voice quivered with regret as he recalled that fateful day, the echoes of which had haunted his every step. "Keisha, I made a painful choice and inflicted untold hurt upon you. But I implore you to believe that not a single moment has elapsed when I did not regret it. I believed I could protect you, shield you from the shadows that sought to consume us."

Trembling with remorse, his hand reached out to tenderly brush a tear from her cheek, like a gentle breeze wiping away the anguish etched upon her soul. "Please understand that I never ceased to love you. Even in the darkest hours, you remained the beacon that lit my way, the compass that guided my path." His voice cracked, an undertone of anguish betraying the depths of his torment. "Now, seeing you here, broken and shattered because of me, I... I cannot forgive myself for the pain I have inflicted upon you."

Ong's voice trembled, carrying an undertone of sorrow and determination as he met Keisha's gaze, his eyes a reflection of remorse and unwavering love. He longed to turn back the hands of time, to have found her months ago and spared her the torment inflicted by Vuarus and Phoenix. The weight of responsibility for her suffering bore down upon his heart like a heavy chain that bound him to the past. He clenched his fists, his resolve cementing like iron, and declared, "I promise you, Keisha, Phoenix will face the consequences of his atrocities by my hand. No matter the price, justice shall be served."

His eyes pleaded with her, seeking absolution, understanding, and a chance to mend the tattered fabric of their love. He knew that his words could never fully heal the wounds he had inflicted, but he hoped that, somehow, they could begin to bind the shattered pieces of their souls back together.

Ong's words lingered in the air like an unspoken oath, his emotions a tangible presence that enveloped them both. Without uttering another syllable, he drew nearer to Keisha, his movements graceful and deliberate. His touch, likc a gcntle breeze caressing the petals of a fragile flower, extended toward her. His fingers, like the skilled hand of a master musician, wove their way through her disheveled hair, a tender and empathetic gesture. As he worked to untangle the chaotic strands, he was fully present in the moment, driven by an ardent desire to offer her respite from the nightmarish ordeal she had endured.

Her gaze haunted and distant, Keisha lifted her eyes to meet his. In that instant, a glimmer of recognition flickered within her irises like a faint star piercing through the shroud of an overcast night. It was as if his touch had stirred something dormant within her, a fleeting echo of the vibrant spirit she had once embodied. Ong's heart ached for her, but his touch remained unwavering, a silent vow that he was steadfastly by her side, an unyielding bulwark against the encroaching darkness.

As he continued to comb her hair, Ong's thoughts were a storm of emotions and determination. He was resolute in his commitment to aid her in her healing, to stand as her unwavering support as she confronted the indelible scars of her captivity. Simultaneously, he harbored an unshakable resolve to exact retribution upon Phoenix and Vuarus to ensure they paid a grievous price for their horrendous crimes against her and the realm. Amidst the serene symphony of the waterfall's cascading waters and the burden of their shared trials, Ong's touch transcended the physical realm—it became a symbol of hope and unwavering solidarity, a solemn promise that they would confront every challenge that lay ahead together, united in their quest for justice and healing.

Karrenen quietly approached Keisha, "Keisha," he began, his voice a steady and flowing melody imbued with a tenderness that transcended mere words, "my dear daughter, I understand that my addressing you thus may come as a surprise. Yet, I implore you to grasp the truth that has long remained unspoken. You are my daughter, a cherished soul I have cared for and watched over since you lost your father. I should have revealed this long ago rather than waiting until..."

As the weight of his words settled upon her, Keisha's eyes widened in sudden realization, a storm of emotions surging like a tidal wave. Once buried beneath the sands of time, the reservoirs of her memories flooded to the surface. She recalled when she was but a child, vulnerable and bereft of paternal guidance, and how Karrenen's presence had been a soothing balm to her wounded heart. The loss of her father had torn a chasm in her life, and Karrenen had stepped forth to help bridge that void.

Tears, like dewdrops glistening upon the petals of a forgotten bloom, welled up in her eyes as she regarded Karrenen. A deluge of emotions cascaded within her, rendering her momentarily speechless. The enormity of all that had transpired—the relentless torment she had endured, the bewildering unfamiliarity of her current circumstances—had left her feeling adrift, like a rudderless vessel on a storm-tossed sea. Yet, within Karrenen's words lay an undeniable resonance, a reminder of the enduring bonds that had silently woven between them, uniting their souls in a profound tapestry of shared experiences and unwavering support.

Tears, like glistening pearls, welled up in the reservoir of Keisha's eyes, her voice a quivering testament to the complex tapestry of emotions that engulfed her—a symphony of gratitude harmonizing with a refrain of trepidation. As her words flowed forth, they were like fragile notes of a delicate melody, each a nuanced brushstroke on the canvas of her soul. She could feel the formidable walls she had erected around herself starting to crack, their stony facade yielding to the persistent warmth of a longing she had kept hidden—a yearning to reconnect with the profound bond she had once shared with Karrenen, a connection that time and tribulation had tested but never severed.

Karrenen," she managed to utter, her voice trembling with vulnerability and a profound sense of gratitude. "They siphoned my elemental magic, sending it into the abyss," she confessed, each word carrying the weight of the scars etched onto her very being during her captivity. It was a fragile admission, revealing the depth of her trials and yet the enduring ember of hope within her heart."

Karrenen, his presence a steadfast beacon of support, extended a hand toward her, a silent offer of solace and guidance. Like a soothing balm to her wounded spirit, his words reassured her that she was not alone in her journey. They were here for her, ready to aid in healing, just as she had always stood guard over E'vahona. His voice, gentle as a murmuring brook, spoke of a truth that the shadows had obscured—her magic, though stolen and distant, still held a trace within her, a distant echo. It was like the memory of a pristine stream after a protracted drought, a faint whisper of what once flowed freely. She couldn't wield it or sense its presence anymore, but it lingered in the recesses of her being, awaiting the moment when it might be restored.

Karrenen turned his gaze to Keisha. "We know that the Dominion siphoned your magic, but for now, my daughter, let's set that aside. It would be best to focus on healing after your ordeal. We will address these matters promptly, so please do not burden yourself with them now."

Keisha's tears flowed freely at Karrenen's compassionate words, her emotional turmoil an unrelenting tempest within her. Her voice, trembling like the fragile branches of a winter-blighted tree, quivered as she uttered her lament, 'I want to believe that, but look at what Vuarus has wrought.'

In fleeting desperation, Keisha sought to summon even the faintest glimmer of her once-potent magic—a connection to the ethereal forces that had once coursed through her like a mighty river. Yet, as her words wove the old spells, nothing happened. Tears welled up in her eyes like crystalline dewdrops, blurring the world around her. A heart-wrenching sob escaped her lips, a visceral expression of the profound realization that her once-mighty magic was gone.

The frustration and heartache of this newfound vulnerability consumed her, wrapping around her like the tendrils of a shadowy specter. In this moment of bitter isolation, Keisha grappled with the stark reality of her impotence—a sorceress bereft of her sorcery, a phoenix whose flames had been extinguished, left to navigate a world that had grown infinitely more formidable.

As Keisha's voice faltered and her tears flowed like the mournful rain of a storm, Karrenen couldn't help but feel a rising tempest within himself—an anger, fierce and unyielding, directed squarely at Vuarus, the architect of Keisha's torment. He could feel the embers of his protective instincts stoked by the sight of her suffering, his heart a smoldering furnace of determination.

But when he turned his gaze back to Keisha, that anger transformed into an unwavering resolve. His voice, a soothing balm to the wounds of her soul, carried the promise of a mentor who had stood by her side through the darkest hours. "We will start again, my daughter," he declared, gently affirming their unbreakable bond. "It will take time, but I will help you as I did before."

He saw the fragility that had become Keisha's state—the cracks in the once-unshakable foundation of her spirit. And with a heart full of compassion, he offered her the sanctuary of time and understanding.

As Keisha hesitated, her emotions swirling like turbulent waters, Karrenen maintained a steady and warm gaze, giving her the space she needed to navigate the labyrinth of her feelings. He knew that the path to healing was fraught with uncertainty, but he was there to walk it with her, step by tentative step.

With a soft sigh that carried the weight of both their burdens, Keisha's trembling hand finally reached out, bridging the gap that had grown between her past and present. Like a fragile thread weaving the fabric of their shared history, the simple touch connected her to the familiar support that had been steadfast throughout her journey.

"Thank you," she whispered, her voice a gentle melody filled with the sweet notes of gratitude and the haunting refrain of longing—for the solace she had once found in Karrenen's guidance and for the restoration of the self she had been before the storm had shattered her.

Kimras, the majestic Gold Dragon, orchestrated their gathering with a silent yet compelling urgency in his gaze. His colossal frame descended gracefully, wings folding with an innate regality at his sides. The solemnity that cloaked him lent an air of gravity to the occasion, and Ong and Karrenen exchanged knowing glances, sensing the impending weight of their discussion.

With resolute steps, they closed the distance to where Kimras awaited, the ground beneath them bowing to his immense presence. As they drew near, he began, his voice resonating with solemnity mirrored by the magnitude of the matters at hand.

"Ong, Karrenen," he intoned, each syllable bearing the weight of a world in turmoil, "I understand the relief of Keisha's return, but two pressing matters demand our attention."

Ong's brow furrowed in concentration, his thoughts aligning with the growing foreboding in the air. The unspoken understanding between them was that their journey was far from over, and they would face challenges yet unimagined.

Kimras maintained his commanding presence, his towering figure etched in stubborn determination. His golden eyes, mirrors of ageless wisdom and boundless concern, glistened with a radiant intensity that outshone the sun. He understood the fragility that enveloped Keisha like a fragile blossom caught in an unrelenting storm.

"In her present vulnerability," Kimras continued, his words measured and profound as the echoes of his wisdom resonated, "Keisha may find herself ill-equipped to withstand another relentless onslaught of torment. We must steel ourselves for the grim possibility that Vuarus will continue his relentless pursuit of her."

The gravity of the situation hung over them like a shroud, and each word from Kimras was a chisel shaping the stone of their resolve. The quest for Keisha's safety was a perilous odyssey, one they would embark upon with the unwavering determination of warriors sworn to protect their own.

Kimras's tone held an air of solemnity as he regarded Ong and Karrenen with piercing golden eyes. Each word he uttered struck a chord in the symphony of their shared responsibility.

"The first issue we face," Kimras began, his voice a resonant call to arms, "is Vuarus himself. He is a maestro of shadows, a conductor of malevolence. If he intends to persist in tormenting Keisha, he will undoubtedly exploit her moments of vulnerability."

Ong's brows furrowed, his heart quickening with anxiety and determination. "But she's vulnerable most of the time now. Is there a particular time when she's even more so?" he inquired, his voice quivering with concern.

"Darkness often seeks to ensnare us when we are most defenseless," Kimras elucidated. "For Keisha, that vulnerability manifests when she succumbs to sleep. During those precious moments, her defenses wane, and if Vuarus decides to assail her, it will be then. Our vigilance must extend to her dreams, for it was through these nightmares that her spirit was initially fractured, leaving her in a perpetual state of unrest."

Karrenen's countenance darkened as he absorbed the gravity of their discussion. "So, you suggest that her most vulnerable moments are during sleep, and we must stand watch."

Kimras nodded with unwavering resolve. "Precisely. Whether it is you, Ong, or someone near and dear to her, having a watchful guardian during her slumber is the best defense against the evil forces that Vuarus may send. Given the potency of the visions they've subjected her to, having you, Ong, by her side while she sleeps would likely provide the most comfort and protection."

Ong clenched his jaw, his visage a portrait of frustration and determination. He bore the weight of his commitment with fierce intensity. "I will never leave her alone," he declared, his voice trembling with a potent blend of resolve and anger. "I will ensure her safety, even in her moments of reprieve. I may not have shielded her from their torments in captivity, but I swear, they will not subject her to those nightmarish visions again."

As he spoke, vivid memories of Keisha's harrowing nights in captivity surged to the forefront of his mind. The haunted look in her eyes, her relentless tossing and turning in the clutches of night terrors—these recollections fueled his unwavering dedication to safeguarding her. His love for her blazed as fiercely as a forge's inferno, an unyielding pledge to be her protector, even in the abyss of darkness threatening to engulf them.

They stood united, a trio of guardians, facing the stark reality of their battle against Vuarus. It was not confined solely to physical combat; it encompassed the defense of Keisha's spirit and well-being against the insidious reach of shadows. With steadfast resolve, they acknowledged that their duty transcended the realm of weapons and magic—it extended to safeguarding Keisha's essence from the darkness, seeking to devour it.

Kimras's proclamation reverberated through the air, his voice like the tolling of a solemn bell, carrying the weight of destiny.

"The second dilemma," Kimras declared, his voice unwavering and relentless, "rests upon this truth: Vuarus and Phoenix harbor relentless determination. They shall not know reprieve until their sinister machinations find fruition. We must seize the initiative to mount an offensive that confronts their malevolence at its heart. The path before us is fraught with peril, but it is a path we must traverse to shield E'vahona and its residents from impending darkness."

Ong's jaw tightened, his mettle rekindled by Kimras's words. "You speak the truth," he responded, his voice an alloy of unwavering resolve. "Delay is a luxury we can no longer afford. Keisha has endured most of their cruelty for far too long. It is time we confront Vuarus and Phoenix, extinguishing the darkness they seek to propagate."

Karrenen's gaze became a blade of determination as he locked eyes with Ong. "A strategy is imperative," he interjected, his mind already a cauldron of tactical contemplation.

Kimras nodded with a regal nod of approval. "Indeed. Let us summon the council and those who have previously waged war against Vuarus and Phoenix. We shall confront this looming threat with our combined fortitude and unity of purpose."

Ong's gaze remained unwavering, reflecting the deep concern etched into his eyes. "Kimras," he ventured, his voice bearing the weight of uncertainty, "Vuarus has ascended to godhood, a realm where our efforts have found formidable opposition. The divine order restrains the gods' interference, and we seem to confront impossible odds."

Kimras, the embodiment of regal wisdom, met Ong's gaze with a steady and re-assuring demeanor. "Your assessment is astute, Ong," he acknowledged. "Indeed, Vuarus's newfound divine status complicates the path before us. But within this challenging landscape, a flicker of hope persists, and with it, a conceivable means to thwart him."

Ong's curiosity heightened, his entire being intent upon Kimras's forthcoming words. "A method to overcome him? Pray, share it with me," he implored, his voice intermingled with hope and eager anticipation.

Kimras's countenance momentarily seemed to drift into the annals of history, his words laden with the echoes of ages past. "In the pages of ancient lore, an elusive figure exists—a dragon of grand power and sagacity known as Talleoss. He vanished into antiquity's mists, leaving only cryptic whispers and tales behind. Yet, whispers have resurfaced, insinuating the possibility of his continued existence."

Ong's brow furrowed as he processed this revelation. "Talleoss... the name does ring familiar, a fragment of childhood stories. But if he disappeared, how can he aid us now?"

Kimras's countenance grew solemn as if he were the bearer of age-old truths. "Talleoss possessed knowledge and talents that could rival even the newfound prowess of Vuarus. He delved deep into the intricate tapestry of light and shadow, unraveling arcane secrets few dared to glimpse."

A spark of realization lit up Ong's eyes. "Are you suggesting that he might provide us with a means to counter Vuarus's darkness?"

Kimras's nod was unwavering, akin to the majestic sweep of a golden dragon's wing cutting through the cerulean sky. "Precisely so. If Talleoss yet draws breath, he could possess the key to unraveling the evil magic that cloaks Vuarus. He may offer us insights into how to weaken him, even restore balance to our strife-ridden realm. However, the path that stretches before us is difficult; discovering him and securing his cooperation will not come without confronting treacherous trials and enigmatic riddles."

Karrenen's voice, carrying the weight of cautious determination, interjected like a seasoned navigator guiding a ship through treacherous waters. "Should Talleoss prove to be our most promising recourse, then we must embark on a quest to unearth his elusive presence—a venture fraught with peril, undertaken to safeguard Keisha and the destiny of our realm."

Kimras's regal eyes shimmered with unwavering resolve, like twin orbs of liquid gold reflecting the ancient wisdom of countless ages. "In due course, we shall convene the council assembly. Talleoss's lineage is irrevocably interwoven with the fabric of E'vahona's history; if anyone can fathom the means to combat the enigmatic shroud of Vuarus's malice, it is he."

In the contemplative silence that ensued, the mere mention of Talleoss cast a radiant thread of hope into the labyrinthine tapestry of their ominous circumstances. The impending council gathering bore the gravity of destiny—a moment to unite kindred spirits and choreograph their future dances with fate. As their collective thoughts converged upon Keisha's recovery and the potential key concealed within the enigmatic dragon of yore, Ong, Karrenen, and Kimras readied themselves for the impending odyssey. They were determined to confront whatever trials lay ahead, even if it meant embarking on a quest to seek a dragon lost to the annals of time itself.

Ong and Karrenen, their brows furrowed inquisitively, dared to voice the questions that fluttered through their minds like elusive butterflies. How had Kimras and Amara, their steadfast allies, come to possess knowledge of their dire predicament when Kadona, the deity they faithfully served, was bound by constraints that should have rendered such awareness unattainable?

Kimras, the majestic Gold Dragon, whose ancient wisdom radiated like the golden rays of a setting sun, could not suppress a hearty laugh that echoed through the sacred grove where they had gathered. Beside him, Amara, her presence an ethereal embodiment of celestial grace, joined in the harmonious laughter that seemed to resonate with the very pulse of the land.

"You see," Kimras began, his voice a melodious cadence akin to a forgotten hymn, "our divine alliances extend beyond the singular dominion of Kadona. Within the intricate tapestry of the divine exists another deity, one whose realm lies beneath the boundless depths of the sea—the enigmatic Lysander, the God of the Sea."

Ong, who had once stood in the ethereal presence of Lysander, nodded in profound understanding. "Lysander," he acknowledged with a reverence that mirrored the deep depths of the ocean, "a vital and unwavering pillar of our divine alliances."

Amara, her eyes sparkling with a hint of mischievous wisdom, bestowed upon Ong a knowing smile. "Indeed, dear Ong," she chimed, "Lysander is not one to be bound by the constrictions of divine regulations. If a path exists beyond the boundaries, he shall find it. He uncovered the deceit behind the so-called 'exchange,' a treacherous snare meant to ensnare Keisha forever. When this revelation became known, Lysander, in his boundless wisdom, alerted us to the deception. In response, Kimras and I, taking on the mantle of divine intervention, embarked on a mission to thwart their nefarious designs and liberate Keisha from her harrowing captivity."

Kimras, his majestic form nodding with regal grace, interjected with a resonant tone that resonated like the echoes of ancient wisdom. "As sincere as my desire for vengeance against Vuarus may have been, the paramount concern was the rescue of Keisha from her torment. I must confess that even I, with all my might, may not have been able to halt him. Lysander and Amara, in their formidable union, obliterated the very altar that bound her. If I were to surmise, nothing remains of that loathsome construct but ruin and rubble."

Ong, his gratitude swelling like a mighty tide, stepped forward. His voice, infused with profound emotion, flowed like a river of thankfulness. "Kimras and Amara, words alone cannot convey the depth of our gratitude for your intervention. You have saved Keisha's life and the hope that sustains our world. E'vahona owes you a debt beyond measure."

With a heart ablaze with determination, Ong turned away from the council and those who had gathered. Still shimmering with gratitude, his eyes found Keisha sitting in her fragile vulnerability. Her presence drew him in like a beckoning light in the darkest of nights. He couldn't bear to leave her alone any longer, to let her suffer in solitude. He approached and gently sat beside her with a relentless stride, their shoulders nearly touching. In that quiet moment, amidst the whispers of gratitude and the weight of their shared burdens, Ong realized that he could no longer let her face the shadows alone.

In the dimly lit recesses of the Dread Spire's labyrinthine halls, Vuarus and Phoenix prowled like caged predators, their visages etched with an explosive fusion of frustration and ire. The intrusion of noble dragons, their unexpected intervention, had rudely disrupted the meticulous tapestry of their evil designs. Vuarus, a portrait of maleficence, clenched his formidable fists with an iron grip, his abyssal eyes narrowing into slivers of darkness as a litany of curses danced upon his lips.

"It was as if they possessed an uncanny prescience," Phoenix growled, his voice vibrating with simmering vexation. "How did they discern our very timing?"

A malignant snarl contorted Vuarus's lips as he seethed in response. "An unseen informant, lurking in the shadows, must have betrayed our machinations, revealing our every move to those accursed dragons."

Phoenix's keen intellect sparked with an epiphany in the hollow chambers of their relentless contemplation. "The Eladrin, perhaps? They have always been resourceful in frustrating our diabolical stratagems."

Vuarus's jaw constricted, mirroring his wrath. "Indeed, it is a possibility. Keisha's tether to E'vahona is an unbreakable bond, a thread of connection that may have sensed the discord we sowed and roused them to her defense."

Phoenix, the mastermind of devious schemes, turned his thoughts inward, casting a net of deliberation over the unfolding circumstances. "This setback is far from trivial. Our plans require a recalibration and a strategic reassessment. We cannot persist as though this unforeseen interjection never transpired."

Vuarus's fingers, alabaster and sinewy, drummed restlessly against the obsidian armrest of his malevolent throne. "No, we cannot. Prudence and guile must become our allies. We cannot permit the fierce winds of surprise to buffet us any further."

Silence, an oppressive shroud, descended upon the chamber, casting its weight upon the once-assured rulers of the Dominion, the architects of malevolence. Once brimming with unwavering self-assuredness, their demeanor had now metamorphosed into a disquieting amalgamation of uncertainty.

"In light of these adversities," Vuarus spoke with measured composure, his voice a calculated cadence, "our stratagems necessitate a profound transformation—a stratagem reborn from the crucible of adaptability, one that accommodates the unanticipated intervention of the noble dragons."

Within the chamber of sinister design, the molten intensity of Phoenix's eyes burned with stubborn determination, casting an ominous glow in the dimness. His words, dripping with evil resolve, slithered through the stagnant air like serpents poised to strike.

"This temporary setback," he hissed, "shall not quell our ambitions. Keisha may have eluded our grasp for now, but her spirit is a fractured mosaic, her suffering a canvas yet to be fully painted. We shall weave her anguish into a tapestry of despair, forging her into the willing sacrifice we require."

Vuarus, the architect of malice, consented with a slow, measured nod, the gears of his nefarious machinations grinding relentlessly. "Indeed," he conceded, the tendrils of his contemplation already reaching into the abyss of their subsequent cruel actions. "We must persist in shattering her, pushing her fragile soul to despair. And when the hour is propitious, we shall descend upon her like a storm."

As these two dark specters conspired, the shadows of the Dread Spire seemed to coalesce around them, an eerie embodiment of their unyielding determination. Despite the unforeseen intrusion that had disrupted their designs, Vuarus and Phoenix remained steadfast in their crusade to unleash darkness anew upon the realm. With Keisha ensnared within their malevolent web, the battle for E'va-hona's future continued to smolder, a sinister ember threatening to ignite the world in chaos.

Amidst the conspiratorial air, Lyra, a spectral presence shrouded in shadow, materialized before Vuarus and Phoenix, her very existence a troubling enigma. Her dark, bottomless eyes shimmered with an unsettling curiosity as her melodic voice, as soft as a nocturnal whisper, pierced the heavy silence.

"You have ever been the architects of cunning," she purred, her words laced with a subtle, sardonic amusement. "But with your plaything having slipped your grasp and your visions rendered impotent, how do you intend to weave the threads of her despair and fracture her fragile spirit?"

Vuarus's lips curled upward into a sinister, sardonic smile, a vicious portrait of guile and sinister forethought. "Ah, Lyra," he replied with wicked assurance, "you have always possessed a knack for the penetrating query. Yet, you underestimate the power of psychological manipulation, my dear. Though the visions may have waned, Keisha's psyche remains a fertile ground for our malevolence. We shall cultivate her suffering through alternate means, plucking at the strands of her deepest fears and vulnerabilities until she dances to our macabre symphony of despair."

Phoenix's obsidian eyes gleamed with the malevolent luster of smoldering embers, an unsettling fire ablaze with dark resolve. His voice, an evil serpent coiled and ready to strike, slithered through the air, carrying a promise of relentless cruelty.

"The abyss of her despair," he intoned, his words a sibilant incantation, "is a yawning chasm, Lyra. And within its depths, we hold the very keys to unlock her tormented soul. Through the crucible of pain, through the relentless onslaught of hopelessness, we shall continue to chip away at her spirit until it crumbles like fragile porcelain, ready for the sacrificial altar."

Enigmatic and ethereal, Lyra seemed to sway in the dim-lit chamber, her shadowy form like an apparition of contemplation. Her voice, a mere murmur of intrigue, slipped through the air like a silken thread of doubt.

"What if," she whispered, "she discovers a wellspring of strength within her? What if her resilience proves to be a formidable adversary?"

Vuarus's grin deepened, a predatory expression that bared the fangs of his unwavering conviction. His words hung in the air like the incantations of an unholy ritual.

"Then," he purred, "we shall simply redouble our efforts. Time is our ally, and Keisha's fortitude can only endure so much. Hidden within her, there are abysses of darkness yet uncharted. We shall plumb those depths and exploit them to their fullest."

The cadence of Phoenix's laughter, an eerie reverberation in the chamber, sent shivers through the air. His tone, laced with a sinister delight, carried the weight of impending malevolence.

"Lyra, dear," he laughed, "you underestimate the potency of despair. Even the mightiest spirits can be sundered when thrust to the precipice. Keisha shall be no exception."

Lyra's shadow danced a play of intrigue and skepticism in her ephemeral gaze. Her insubstantial whisper voice hung in the air like a dark prophecy.

"Very well," she conceded, her words a portentous murmur. "But remember, the shadows can be inconsistent. Even the most meticulously woven schemes may unravel in ways unforeseen."

Vuarus and Phoenix exchanged a knowing look, their resolution unwavering. Vuarus's retort, a declaration of unyielding determination, resonated with steadfast certainty.

"We are acutely aware of the risks," he proclaimed, his voice a sinister symphony. "And we shall adapt as exigencies dictate. Keisha's suffering shall become our deadliest weapon, and we shall not permit her to slip through our grasp once more."

With that, Lyra appeared to meld back into the shadowy shroud from whence she had emerged, leaving Vuarus and Phoenix to their nefarious plotting and dark stratagems. As the lingering echoes of her words filled the air, the Dominion's leaders remained steadfast in their evil pursuit of power, unmoved by the shadows of doubt that danced at the periphery of their ambitions.

Chapter 45

Shadows Unveiled: Quest for the Heart of Twilight

In a veil of shifting shadows, Lyra materialized in the chamber where Vuarus and Phoenix, enigmatic figures steeped in arcane secrets, conducted their clandestine conference. Her arrival ushered in a subtle change in the ambiance, as the dim light played host to her presence, casting cryptic glyphs etched into the chamber's walls into dance, their faint luminescence akin to ethereal fireflies. Vuarus's demeanor, tinged with eager anticipation, tore his gaze away from ancient scrolls that held forgotten knowledge, his eyes capturing the essence of mysteries long buried. Phoenix, his eyes like molten embers smoldering with curiosity, fixed his attention on the spectral visitor, his curiosity akin to a blazing inferno that sought to devour every hidden truth.

"Lyra, what tidings do you bear?" Vuarus inquired, his voice a velvet veil concealing secrets veiled in intrigue, a lyrical undercurrent that drew one deeper into the labyrinth of enigma.

Lyra's visage remained a mysterious enigma, veiled by a mask of impenetrable mystery, as she began to weave her tale. "I have ventured into the abyss, delving deeper into the unfathomable quest for the Heart of Twilight. The myth is no mere whisper; the artifact exists, entrusted to the merfolk for the most sacred of safekeeping."

Vuarus leaned forward, an insatiable thirst for knowledge kindling in his eyes, like a torch illuminating the dark recesses of forbidden lore. "And where does this elusive relic reside now?"

A half-smile, as cryptic as the runes that adorned the chamber's walls, graced Lyra's lips—a precursor to secrets yet unveiled. "Ah, therein lies the problem. The Heart of Twilight eludes our grasp, veiled by the cunning and secrecy of the merfolk. Like threads in the grand tapestry of fate, our network of sources remains tangled in their pursuit of the exact merkingdom where it hides."

Phoenix, the embodiment of fiery inquisitiveness, leaned closer, his obsidian pupils narrowing like the winding corridors of a labyrinth as he probed deeper into the significant part. "But what, dear Lyra," he inquired, his voice a molten flow of curiosity, "makes this enigmatic artifact of such paramount interest to our cause?"

Lyra's resolute gaze locked onto Phoenix's, unwavering in its intensity, like a moonbeam piercing the darkest night. "Because, my dear Phoenix, if the ancient legends hold truth, the Heart of Twilight cradles within it a reservoir of unfathomable power—power that could metamorphose the very landscape of E'vahona into our dominion."

Vuarus, the mastermind, steepled his fingers in profound contemplation, his visage a canvas painted with ponderous thoughts, a portrait of scheming intellect. "So, you propose that this enigmatic artifact might be the celestial key capable of tipping the cosmic scales in our favor?"

Lyra affirmed with a subtle yet assured nod, her countenance reflecting unwavering conviction. "Indeed, Vuarus. The Heart of Twilight weaves the essence of radiant light and cloaking shadow into its very being, rendering it a celestial blade of formidable might. If we can grasp its power, we might gain an upper hand over the Guardians and their steadfast allies."

Phoenix, a figure of intrigue and cunning, let a sardonic smirk curl upon his lips like the whispered promise of impending intrigue in a world shrouded in shadows. "A tantalizing proposition, to be sure, but the merfolk, Lyra, are not known to part with their treasured secrets willingly." His words dripped with a wicked undertone as if plotting the intricacies of a grand heist within the confines of their conspiracy.

A fire of determination ignited in Lyra's eyes, casting a shimmering, otherworldly glow that defied the boundaries of their dim chamber. "Indeed, Phoenix," she declared firmly, "but therein lies the essence of our grand strategy. We must embark upon a labyrinthine journey to unveil the veiled, to decipher the cryptic, and to orchestrate a symphony of cunning plots, all in our quest to unearth and secure the elusive location of the Heart of Twilight."

Vuarus, the sage of their clandestine circle, nodded in solemn agreement. "Indeed, Lyra, this revelation could be the elusive break in the storm we've yearned for. Continue your relentless quest within the archives of time, and when you unearth even a glimmer of substantial leads, do not hesitate to beckon us."

With a graceful bow, Lyra receded into the enigmatic embrace of the shadows, her presence dispersing like a whisper in the wind. Left in solitude, Vuarus and Phoenix grappled with the weight of the newfound knowledge. The prospect of harnessing the Heart of Twilight's arcane power stirred their minds, igniting a celestial fire of contemplation.

In their secret chamber, where shadows danced like spectral courtiers, they realized that pursuing this elusive relic would demand a dance of wits and cunning. It was a game played upon a treacherous chessboard, where each move must be calculated, each strategy shrouded in a tapestry of secrecy. In their quest to redefine the course of their ceaseless conflict with E'vahona, they were acutely aware that victory would be born not of sheer might but of outmaneuvering their foes, of capturing the essence of twilight's enigma that lay hidden within the Heart of Twilight itself.

"Vuarus," Phoenix's voice, soft as a serpent's hiss, resonated with a cunning edge, "let your mind dance with the possibilities—the unimaginable power we would wield if the Heart of Twilight were within our grasp. Its ancient energies, woven into the very fabric of existence, mingling with the essence of Keisha's sacrifice, amplifying its formidable might. With such a relic, we would ascend to the realm of the unassailable."

Vuarus pivoted, his gaze locking onto Phoenix with a calculating glint that mirrored the depths of a mysterious abyss. "Indeed, Phoenix. The Heart of Twilight, a jewel coveted even by the heavens, possesses abilities that transcend mortal comprehension. Keisha's torment, her spirit rent asunder by suffering and despair, stands as an offering—a conduit through which we may channel the essence of twilight to elevate our dominion."

Phoenix's smile, a sinister crescent of delight, deepened like the shadowy recesses of their clandestine chamber. "The Abyssal Dominion would cast its shadow upon the realms, forcing them to quiver and fracture beneath our implacable might, while E'vahona would succumb to an eternal eclipse."

Vuarus, the mastermind, mused like the rustling of ancient scrolls. "Yet, Phoenix, while the Heart of Twilight beckons as an alluring prize, let us not forget that our influence remains a potent force, a storm that rages even without it. Keisha's shattered spirit, a fragmented masterpiece of torment, is an advantage we must skillfully exploit in the grand tapestry of our ambitions."

Phoenix leaned in, his intrigue a flickering flame within his eyes as he probed, "Tell me, Vuarus, how do we continue to exert our influence upon her in her current state? With her spirit fractured, she should be as pliable as clay, don't you think?"

A malicious pleasure gleamed in Vuarus's eyes, an ominous glow like the reflection of sinister constellations. "You, my cunning companion, hit the mark precisely. Keisha's spirit lies in shattered ruins, a mosaic of vulnerability ripe for our machinations. And do you not recall the phantasmal tapestry of her past? The lingering specters of her fears, insecurities, darkest nightmares—all threads we can expertly weave into a relentless torment."

Phoenix's grin, embodying sinister delight, widened like a crescent moon in the darkest of nights. "So, you propose that we venture into the recesses of her dreams to haunt her even in the realm of slumber?"

"Indeed," Vuarus confirmed, his voice dripping with satisfaction, like the elixir of malevolence itself. "Within the realms of her dreams, we shall become architects of her reality, magnifying her suffering and trapping her in an unending labyrinth of distress. She shall find no respite, not even in the sanctuary of sleep."

Phoenix's laughter, echoing through their secret chamber, reverberated like the unholy chorus of dark spirits. "Ah, Vuarus, you possess a mind as wicked as the abyss. I find it utterly captivating."

Vuarus's lips curved into a sinister smile, echoing malevolent triumph. "Phoenix, we are not mere mortals; we are gods of shadows, wielders of an art that manipulates the essence of reality itself. We shall weave the threads of her deepest nightmares with deft fingers, trapping her in a tapestry of dread that shrouds even her moments of reprieve."

Phoenix's eyes gleamed with a fevered anticipation, his thirst for darkness unquenchable. "Then, Vuarus, let the symphony of torment commence. Let us reveal to Keisha that there exists no sanctuary, no refuge from the all-encompassing darkness we have meticulously woven around her."

Vuarus leaned closer, his voice a promise of doom, his gaze an abyss of unfaltering intent fixated upon Phoenix. "Remember, my astute companion, her true vulnerability emerges when the shroud of sleep descends. Her mind is laid bare in those moments, her defenses in disarray. That is precisely when we shall strike."

Phoenix nodded, a macabre pact sealed in agreement. "Her dreams shall become her prison, a realm where we hold unwavering dominion."

In that clandestine chamber, the two conspirators exchanged a knowing glance, the prospect of Keisha's suffering perpetuating even within the realm of slumber, adding an ominous layer to their sinister alliance. Yet, they knew that even after they had subjected her to their visions, her nights would remain sleepless, haunted by the specters of their relentless torment. The dreams were a swifter conduit to her anguish, a means to hasten her descent into the abyss of despair.

Lyra's inquisitive spirit blazed like a star in the night sky as she turned her attention to Qellaun, her flesh and blood, a font of knowledge within their enigmatic fellowship. "Qellaun," she began, her voice tinged with eager anticipation, "have the annals of your scholarly pursuits unearthed any cryptic chronicles or ancient legends that might entwine the merfolk with artifacts of unfathomable power?"

Qellaun, the sage with furrowed brows, delved deep into the recesses of his memory as though seeking answers within the labyrinthine passages of forgotten tomes. "Merfolk, you say?" he pondered aloud. "Hmmm, I cannot summon direct recollections of such aquatic beings in conjunction with potent relics. Nevertheless, the dusty corridors of obscurity may conceal answers."

Lyra's curiosity swelled, a surging tide of intrigue. "Obscure records, Qellaun? Pray, where would one embark upon such a quest?"

Qellaun leaned in, his voice hushed, conspiratorial. "Should we chance upon merfolk-related narratives, our voyage may lead us to Fel Thalor's illustrious library. There, beneath its towering shelves, lies an abyss of knowledge—texts known to delve into the esoteric and the forgotten."

Unwavering in her determination, Lyra nodded with a gratitude that sparkled like a gem unearthed from the depths of a hidden cavern. "Fel Thalor's library it is, my dear Qellaun. Your wisdom rings true. And you, my trusted companion of curiosity since our tenderest days, will accompany me, will you not?"

A fond smile graced Qellaun's lips, an unspoken promise. "Without a doubt, Lyra. I shall stand beside you as we embark upon the labyrinth of secrets hidden within those ancient scrolls."

Their pact sealed, the duo of intrepid seekers prepared to delve into the mysteries lurking within the heart of Fel Thalor's library, where the whispers of forgotten tales awaited discovery.

"Thank you," Lyra expressed with heartfelt sincerity. "Together, we shall tread cautiously and unfurl the mysteries that may ultimately guide us to the elusive Heart of Twilight."

As the words of their conversation settled like leaves in a tranquil forest, the sibling duo grasped the undeniable truth—their quest was far from reaching its zenith. The pursuit of the elusive Twilight Heart lay shrouded in an enigmatic tapestry of shadow and uncertainty, and the path ahead beckoned with a siren's call, demanding both courage and the sagacity to navigate the labyrinthine corridors of history and lore.

The atmosphere within Fel Thalor, the air they breathed, diverged markedly from the familiarity of their past, bearing the indelible imprint of the Druchii stronghold. While they ventured through the labyrinthine alleyways and concealed alcoves of this enigmatic place, Qellaun's shoulders, once laden with the weight of the unknown, gradually eased, allowing a nostalgic sigh to slip from his lips.

Lyra observed her brother with eyes as discerning as a hawk's and offered a knowing smile. "You long for our former home, don't you?"

Qellaun, his laughter as melodic as a woodland stream, surrendered to a moment of reminiscence. "Indeed, I do. There's an inexplicable allure to this place despite its ominous reputation."

Lyra nodded in heartfelt understanding. "I recall those bygone days when we roamed these hidden recesses, unraveling the secrets concealed in the shadows. And now, we stand here once more, poised to uncover the answers to yet another enigma."

Qellaun's eyes, pools of wisdom illuminated by the flickering flames of nostalgia and anticipation, sparkled with a brilliance akin to the gems of an age-old treasure chest. "Indeed, Lyra, and perhaps the shadows, those enigmatic custodians of secrets, shall be persuaded to reveal their mysteries once more. Let us entrust our hopes to the sacred archives of Fel Thalor's library." As they journeyed, footsteps tracing the cobblestone streets, the siblings exchanged tales of yore—recollections of shared adventures, of the boundless curiosity that had eternally woven the tapestry of their connection. Lyra's smile, radiant as the sun's first light, proved infectious, a contagion of joy and nostalgia.

"It was an era of daring exploration, Qellaun," Lyra reflected, her voice awash with sentiment as if she were glimpsing through the mists of time. "Fearless, we were, driven by the insatiable hunger for knowledge and the thrill of uncovering the unknown."

Qellaun's grin mirrored his sister's, a mirror reflecting a thousand shared memories. "Indeed, Lyra. We were brave seekers of the hidden, discoverers of treasures veiled within the embrace of shadows."

The very streets of Fel Thalor, like the pages of an ancient chronicle, resonated with their conversation, reverberating with echoes from the past. Before long, they stood before the formidable entrance to the city's renowned library—a tower that stood as a monolithic testament to the Druchii's unquenchable thirst for knowledge and dominion.

Resting gently on her brother's arm, Lyra met his gaze with unwavering resolve. "Let us press on, Qellaun. Our pursuit of the Twilight Heart has led us to this citadel of shadows and enigmas." Qellaun, his eyes aflame with determination, nodded in silent accord. "Indeed, Lyra.

Together, we shall navigate these hallowed halls of knowledge and, by the quill and scroll, reveal the truths that have remained veiled in secrecy for far too long."

The scent of age-old parchment, the echoes of forgotten whispers, and the aura of boundless wisdom enveloped them as they ventured further into the library's depths. Their shared odyssey had only just begun, and amidst the labyrinthine shelves and ancient scrolls of Fel Thalor's library, they fervently hoped to unearth the elusive threads that would draw them closer to the unavailable Heart of Twilight.

The library of Fel Thalor stood as a hallowed sanctuary of ancient wisdom, where the walls exhaled eons' accumulated knowledge. As Lyra and Qellaun meandered through its labyrinthine corridors, their eyes roamed over the shelves, deciphering the cryptic titles and symbols that whispered tantalizing secrets held within the tomes. In the dimly lit recesses of this chamber of enlightenment, Lyra's fingertips brushed against a scroll that seemed to beckon with a promise of revelation.

"Qellaun, look," Lyra's voice quivered with hushed excitement, the echo of discovery. Qellaun, ever the scholar, swiveled his attention toward his sister, his inquisitiveness kindled.

"What have you stumbled upon?"

With meticulous care, Lyra unfurled the aged parchment, her eyes tracing the ancient script that adorned its surface like the tracks of long-forgotten constellations. "It speaks of an artifact, the Heart of Twilight. This artifact, it claims, once graced the possession of a dragon—an entity of radiant light, a sentinel entrusted with the guardianship of ancient realms."

Qellaun, his countenance a mask of rapt attention, leaned closer, his gaze fixed on the words that seemed to dance upon the parchment's weathered canvas. "A dragon of light? That is a significant revelation."

Lyra nodded, her thoughts entwined with the mysteries unfolding before them. "Indeed, but here lies the enigma, Qellaun. The scroll withholds the dragon's name as if this vital puzzle piece had been shrouded in shadow."

Lyra's expression once ignited with unyielding determination, now bore the weight of a solemn revelation. Her voice, a whisper of contemplation, cut through the hallowed silence of the library. "Qellaun, as I delved deeper into the tomes and scrolls, I came across a peculiar pattern—a recurring motif hidden within these ancient texts."

Qellaun's curiosity surged, his scholarly instincts alert. "A recurring motif, you say? Pray, elaborate."

Lyra's eyes sought her brother's understanding like twin beacons of insight. "Dragons, Qellaun. Dragons of various aspects and attributes. It appears that these beings, these dragons, are interwoven with the legends of the Heart of Twilight in manifold forms, each tied to a different aspect of the artifact's power."

Qellaun absorbed this revelation with measured contemplation. "So, we are faced with not just one dragon, but a multitude of them, each with its connection to the Heart of Twilight."

Lyra nodded solemnly. "Indeed, Qellaun. The dragons, these celestial beings of light and power, seem to be guardians and custodians of the Heart. Their roles, aspects, and allegiances vary, but all are intrinsically tied to the artifact's elusive nature."

The weight of this revelation settled upon them like the relentless march of time. In their quest to unravel the enigma of the Heart of Twilight, they now confronted the intricate tapestry of dragonkind, a mosaic of diverse guardians who held within their stories the key to unlocking the artifact's secrets.

Qellaun's gaze once again focused on the shelves of ancient knowledge that surrounded them, holding a glimmer of determination. "Then, Lyra, we shall delve deeper into these texts, explore the legends and lore of these dragons, and discern the threads that connect them to the Heart of Twilight. Our journey into the annals of history takes on a more complex and intricate hue."

Lyra's resolve remained unshaken, her spirit aflame with an unquenchable thirst for knowledge and discovery. "Agreed, Qellaun. Together, we shall navigate this labyrinth of lore, for it is here, within the tales of dragons, that we may find the missing fragments of our puzzle."

And so, with the weight of their newfound revelation pressing upon them, Lyra and Qellaun continued their relentless pursuit of truth amidst the ancient tomes and scrolls of Fel Thalor's library, their quest now intertwined with the myriad stories of dragons who guarded the secrets of the Heart of Twilight.

As they navigated the sea of knowledge within the library's vast chambers, the weight of Phoenix's hidden vendetta lingered like an unspoken specter. Lyra and Qellaun understood that their quest for the Heart of Twilight was fraught with complexities intertwined with the ambitions and animosities of others. Yet, they remained resolute in their pursuit of understanding, driven by the belief that the artifact held a significance far greater than the vendettas of individuals.

The library's shelves held countless tales of dragons, each thread of lore weaving a tapestry of ancient guardians and their connection to the Heart of Twilight. Lyra's fingers traced the embossed covers of dusty tomes, and Qellaun's eyes danced over parchment and ink as they sought to piece together the intricate mosaic of the artifact's history.

As the hours passed, and the library's candlelight cast elongated shadows upon the floor, the siblings exchanged whispered insights and revelations. They uncovered accounts of benevolent dragons who had watched over the Heart of Twilight with celestial grace, their motivations a testament to a higher purpose. They also encountered tales of dragons whom the artifact's power had ensnared, their stories a cautionary parable of the consequences of seeking dominion over twilight's essence.

Lyra's voice, filled with reverence for the knowledge they unearthed, broke the silence of the library's depths. "Qellaun, it is becoming clear that the Heart of Twilight is not just an artifact—it is a nexus of cosmic forces, an embodiment of celestial balance. The dragons, each bearing a unique aspect, are guardians of that balance."

Qellaun nodded, his scholarly spirit resonating with the profundity of their discoveries. "Indeed, Lyra. It is as if the Heart of Twilight represents the convergence of light and shadow, and the dragons are the celestial stewards tasked with maintaining that equilibrium."

Their quest, once a pursuit of the unknown, had evolved into exploring the very fabric of existence. As they delved deeper into the lore of the dragons and the Heart of Twilight, Lyra and Qellaun were acutely aware that their journey was far from over. The complexities of their mission had grown, and they were now tasked with understanding the artifact's power and the intricate web of cosmic forces that bound it to the dragons.

The siblings forged onward in the heart of Fel Thalor's library, where the echoes of countless stories and the weight of boundless wisdom surrounded them. They knew that the secrets they sought were concealed within the pages of time, waiting to be revealed by the diligent hands of seekers of truth. And so, side by side, Lyra and Qellaun continued their quest, driven by an unyielding thirst for knowledge and a shared determination to unravel the enigma of the Heart of Twilight.

Their laughter, a brief interlude of camaraderie amidst the profound quest, echoed through the library's dimly lit chambers, a testament to their journey's unpredictable twists and turns. Amid their scholarly pursuit, Lyra and Qellaun had rediscovered a moment of fun, a reminder that even in the most serious of endeavors, there could be room for joy.

Lyra's eyes sparkled with renewed purpose as their laughter subsided. "Qellaun, let us make haste. The Heart of Twilight and the Dragon of Light await our discovery. We may have stumbled upon the first threads of truth, but there is much more to unravel."

Qellaun, his scholarly spirit rekindled, nodded with fervor. "Indeed, Lyra. We have only scratched the surface of this cosmic enigma. Let us press on and delve deeper into the labyrinth of knowledge."

With newfound determination, the siblings returned to their research, the echoes of their laughter lingering in the air like a fleeting memory. The library's hallowed halls bore witness to their unwavering commitment to uncovering the secrets that had eluded countless seekers before them. In Fel Thalor's repository of wisdom, they would continue their quest, driven by the belief that the Heart of Twilight held the power to reshape the destiny of E'vahona, and that their pursuit of knowledge would lead them ever closer to that elusive truth.

Within the dimly lit sanctum, the play of shadows painted intricate patterns on the walls, mirroring the complexities of the knowledge they pursued. Lyra and

Qellaun, like diligent scribes, immersed themselves in the scrolls and manuscripts that held the essence of bygone eras. The gravity of history and the allure of forgotten wisdom beckoned them onward, propelling them to unearth the dormant enigmas woven within the pages of time. As they ventured deeper into their quest, their dedication to the mission remained unwavering, their hearts steadfast in their pursuit to unlock the truth behind the Heart of Twilight and its cryptic bond with the dragon of light.

Lyra's fingers danced like a sorcerer's magic over the time-worn page within the cocoon of aged parchment's musky aroma and lamplight's gentle, golden embrace. Her heart, aflutter like a caged bird yearning for flight, quickened its pace as her rapt gaze swept across the ancient text. The words before her were like ancient runes, pulsing with the secrets of an age long past. With a barely contained excitement, she leaned in closer, her breath hitching with anticipation like a long-dormant ember springing to life. Ever the vigilant guardian of knowledge, Qellaun noticed his sister's transformative demeanor and leaned in to share the revelation she had unearthed.

"Listen closely," Lyra breathed, her voice barely above a reverent whisper, her words woven with palpable anticipation. "'In the annals of forgotten kingdoms, there lies a tale of a realm beneath the waves, where the merfolk of old sought refuge and protection. Legends speak of a merkingdom nestled in the embrace of the ocean currents. Its shimmering heart said to hold the essence of twilight itself.'"

Qellaun's brows furrowed in tandem with his efforts to fathom the significance of these words, his mind an alchemist's crucible mixing possibilities. "Merkingdom... the essence of twilight..." he murmured, his thoughts racing like galloping steeds. "Could this be an allusion to the Heart of Twilight?"

Lyra nodded vigorously, her enthusiasm spiraling. "It's plausible. Yet, what captures my intrigue is the reference to proximity with Old Flameford."

Qellaun's eyes widened, a luminous orb of comprehension ascending above the horizon of his consciousness. "Indeed, Old Flameford within Vacari. That's the crucial connection. The merkingdom might very well be situated in the waters that stretch between Old Flameford and New Flameford."

The two siblings exchanged a look, a silent pact sealed by shared revelation, the electrifying thrill of discovery coursing through their veins. "So, the Heart of Twilight, perchance, lies hidden in the watery abyss that separates Old Flameford from New Flameford," Lyra contemplated, her voice filled with wonder and possibility.

Qellaun's agreement manifested in the slow nod of his head, a gesture of concurrence and determination. "Indeed, we must delve deeper into this mystery. If the merkingdom holds the elusive Heart of Twilight, our task lies in ascertaining its whereabouts and evaluating the situation."

With measured deliberation, Lyra gently closed the ancient tome, her gaze unyielding, her eyes aflame with resolve. "Then let us set our course for New Flameford. If even a sliver of truth clings to this age-old legend, we must seek knowledge from those who may possess it."

Their research materials packed with meticulous precision, they made ready to depart the hallowed halls of Fel Thalor's library. They felt a burgeoning sense of purpose and anticipation as they ventured forth. The riddles concealed within the mer kingdom, and the Heart of Twilight beckoned, and with every footstep they took, they drew nearer to the revelation that could shape the destiny of E'vahona.

The sun, an ember sinking beneath the tapestry of the horizon, cast elongated shadows upon the bustling thoroughfares of New Flameford. Through the city's labyrinthine lanes, Lyra and Qellaun navigated with a singular destination in their hearts—the towering Dread Tower, a colossal edifice that harbored the enigmatic figures of Vuarus and Phoenix. With resolute strides, Lyra ascended the steps to the tower's entrance, her heartbeat a frantic rhythm of anticipation and trepidation.

The formidable doors, ancient and laden with history, yielded to Lyra's insistent push, unveiling the shadowed recesses of the tower's interior. Within the dimly illuminated chamber stood Vuarus and Phoenix, their presence a palpable force that commandeered the air. Lyra, her throat cleared and voice resolute, prepared to unveil their uncovered secrets.

"Vuarus, Phoenix," she began, her voice akin to the musical cadence of a lute, "we have unearthed a trove of knowledge that may guide us to the elusive Heart of Twilight."

Vuarus, his eyes alight with the enthusiasm of a seasoned explorer, focused intently on Lyra. "Do go on," he urged, his tone a tapestry woven with threads of intrigue.

Lyra, a symphony of emotions coursing beneath her poised exterior, nodded with a measured blend of exhilaration and unease. "Indeed. Within the hallowed tomes of Fel Thalor's ancient library, we chanced upon a passage that reveals the existence of a merkingdom between Old Flameford and New Flameford."

Phoenix, the precursor of inquisitiveness, arched a solitary eyebrow, his intense gaze locked upon Lyra. "A merkingdom?" he echoed, his voice laced with intrigue. "What, pray tell, elevates this merkingdom to such significance?"

Lyra's voice, a river flowing with calculated precision, disclosed the revelation. "It is believed to cradle the Heart of Twilight within its depths. The legends speak of this merkingdom as the sacred vessel, cradling a heart aglow with the essence of twilight itself."

Vuarus's lips curled into a reflective smile, a mastermind contemplating the threads of destiny. "Fascinating. But the crux of our quest lies in the location of this mer kingdom."

Lyra's unwavering gaze met Vuarus's. "It is whispered to lie between Old Flame-ford and New Flameford."

Phoenix's eyes, honed calculation instruments, narrowed with a hint of recognition. "Remarkably close to our current domain," he mused, a sardonic twist tugging at the corners of his mouth. "How fortunate."

Vuarus's smile, akin to the unfolding petals of a rare and exotic bloom, broadened, his interest kindled like a dormant ember now ablaze. "Indeed, Lyra, Qellaun, your diligence in uncovering this revelation has not gone unnoticed. We shall embark upon a search in the waters encompassing this enigmatic realm without delay."

Lyra, a mosaic of emotions etched upon her countenance, grappled with a sensation akin to triumph tinged with disquiet. Vuarus and Phoenix were hastening toward action, and beneath her gratitude lay a shroud of uncertainty. Nevertheless, she met their decision with a dignified nod, her resolve unwavering.

"Your appreciation is duly noted," she conveyed, her voice steady. "We entrust our hopes to the path this revelation may unveil."

Vuarus's gaze, an enigma veiled in obscurity, locked onto Lyra's, his eyes betraying the presence of an unspoken undercurrent. "Rest assured, Lyra. In the fullness of time, the elusive truth shall be uncovered."

As the meeting drew close, Lyra and Qellaun departed from the tower, leaving an atmosphere pregnant with the weight of their newfound knowledge. The waters encircling the territory between Old Flameford and New Flameford held the promise of untold secrets destined to carve the contours of E'vahona's destiny.

"The somber echo of the tower's massive doors resounded as they closed behind Lyra and Qellaun, returning them to the vibrant tapestry of life in New Flameford's bustling streets. An unspoken, burdensome silence enveloped the siblings, a silence laced with the gravity of their recent actions and the ramifications of their choices.

Walking in tandem, their strides echoing the rhythm of their shared apprehension, Lyra could not dispel the lingering disquiet woven into the tapestry of her thoughts. The city of New Flameford, with its ominous crimson and obsidian architecture, loomed above them like the specter of a forgotten prophecy. Dark alleys wound through the heart of the city, their secrets hidden within shadows that clung to every corner.

Eventually, she turned to her steadfast brother, her voice a barely audible whisper that mirrored the depths of her uncertainty. 'Qellaun, do you ever question whether we made the right choice? Sharing that information with Vuarus and Phoenix?'

Qellaun, the thinker and ponderer, met her inquiry with a contemplative expression. 'Our intentions may not mirror theirs entirely,' he began, his voice a reflection of the reflective nature of his thoughts. 'Yet, at this moment, our goals intersected – the defeat of the Eladrin elves. In that sense, it was a necessary step.'

Lyra's understanding nod conveyed her acceptance of his rationale. 'A union of necessity, then. The enemy of our enemy.'

'Indeed,' Qellaun concurred, a note of resignation in his tone. 'It is a precarious alliance, to be sure. However, when confronted by a greater peril, we must set aside our disparities.'

At that juncture, they reached both a figurative and literal crossroads. Qellaun's path diverged from Lyra's as he prepared to resume his duties on patrol. Before their parting, Lyra regarded her brother with determination and anxiety radiating from her gaze.

'May you remain shielded from harm, Qellaun,' she murmured, her voice a soft, heartfelt benediction.

He returned her sentiment with a reassuring smile. 'And you as well, Lyra.'

With each step, an unspoken awareness enveloped them as they embarked on their diverging paths. They comprehended that the forthcoming journey would not be easy but a treacherous passage, fraught with trials and the weight of irksome choices. In the pursuit of victory, the once-distinct boundaries between comrade and adversary, morality, and practicality, had become indistinct, akin to ink dissolving in water.

In a world where the shadows served as both the shroud and the revealer of secrets, their voyage through the labyrinthine convolutions ahead demanded an unwavering tenacity, a resilience that not even the keenest of seers could foresee with absolute certainty."

Chapter 46

Shadows Unveiled: Secrets of the Heart and Allies Assemble

Ong stood there, his gaze a watchful sentinel, vigilant over his comrades who had gathered in a clandestine chamber within the heart of Vacari. His eyes shifted from Kimras, the golden dragon of revered stature, to Keisha, his beloved wife, who had endured unspeakable torture at the hands of the Abyssal Dominion. She sat amidst their assembly, her countenance etched with unwavering resolve, though it bore the telltale weariness of her recent ordeal. The flickering torchlight played upon her face, casting dancing shadows that mirrored the inner turmoil she had endured. Ong's heart ached for her, but duty called him to the grim task.

With a brief, loving acknoweldgment of Keisha's well-being, Ong turned his attention back to Kimras, the majestic dragon who loomed above them all. Like the resonant hum of ancient magic, his voice carried unwavering determination as he began to unfurl a tale that weighed destiny.

"There exists among us," Ong proclaimed, his voice a river of composure, "a mermaid named Nerissa, who stands as a sentinel over an artifact of unparalleled potency known as the Heart of Twilight. With its profound significance, this relic was originally safeguarded by Talleoss, the Silver Dragon who once served Kadona. Yet, when the enigma known as Phoenix entered the stage, the artifact found its sanctuary in the care of the merfolk."

Kimras, the golden dragon, listened with rapt attention, his countenance gravitating towards solemnity. The chamber held its breath, the air tinged with reverence. "The Heart of Twilight," he murmured, his voice carrying the weight of ancient knowledge. "Its existence has graced my ears in whispers of lore. A delicate and unyielding relic poised at the precipice between the realms of light and shadow. The presence of Nerissa, a trusted ally, as its guardian in our midst speaks to its importance."

Ong's nod mirrored the gravity of their shared knowledge. "Indeed," he agreed, his voice a low rumble like distant thunder, "but the path ahead is fraught with peril. With their ever-watchful eyes, the Abyssal Dominion could be privy to the artifact's existence and boundless potential. Should they seize it, the power scales could tip irreversibly in their favor."

The chamber closed around them, a shroud of tension and urgency settling like a heavy cloak. At this moment, they knew that their fate and the fate of Vacari hung in the balance, and the Heart of Twilight held the key to either salvation or destruction.

Karrenen, his voice a clarion call of unwavering resolve, added his voice to the discourse, his words cutting through the chamber's tension like a sword through the darkness. "Now that we stand enlightened about the Heart of Twilight's significance and guardianship within our united alliance, swiftness becomes our imperative. We dare not permit the Abyssal Dominion to lay claim to a relic that could shape the very course of our world."

Ong's gaze briefly shifted to Keisha, a silent acknowledgment of her presence and indomitable fortitude in the face of recent tribulations. Then, he turned back to Kimras, his eyes reflecting the urgency of their situation. "Agreed. Let's send word to our allies immediately. We'll convene the meeting in Hidden Isles later today or early tomorrow. Once everyone is assembled, we can discuss the plan to safeguard the artifact and ensure it remains out of the Abyssal Dominion's reach."

Kimras inclined his noble head with regal grace, his golden scales shimmering in the torchlight. "Very well, Ong. I shall undertake the solemn task of ensuring the message's reach spans the farthest reaches of our realm. The time has come to rally our forces and confront the looming specter of peril."

With unwavering determination coursing through their collective spirit, Ong, Karrenen, and Kimras recognized the daunting challenges ahead. The fate of Vacari now rested precariously in the balance, tethered to the choices they were poised to make in the impending days. The chamber seemed to pulse with a sense of purpose as they prepared to face the darkness that threatened to engulf their world.

As they were poised to strategize, their minds focused on the impending mission. A sudden and blood-curdling scream cleaved the tranquil air, shattering the stillness like a lightning bolt. Ong's heart quickened, and he exchanged wide-eyed glances of alarm with Kimras and Karrenen. Without hesitation, they launched themselves into a sprint, their determined strides aimed toward Keisha's side.

Ong's gentle touch roused her from the depths of her nightmare, his fingers like a lifeline pulling her back to reality. He whispered her name with a tenderness that seemed to weave through the very fabric of her nightmare. "Keisha, awaken, for it is but a nightmare."

Fear gripped her heart as her eyes snapped open, and it took her a fleeting moment to discern the familiar contours of reality. She found herself cradled in the protective embrace of Ong, his sturdy arms a bastion of security. Nearby, the vigilant presences of Kimras and Karrenen offered a silent testament to their concern.

"What transpired within your nightmare, Keisha?" Like a gentle river's flow, Ong's voice encouraged her to unravel the harrowing threads of her ordeal and share the haunting vision that had tormented her rest.

Keisha's voice quivered like a fragile flame in a gusty night as she unraveled the tapestry of her torment, her words a fragile bridge to the terrifying realm of her dreams. "It was as if I was submerged in an abyss of shadows," she began, her words bearing the weight of her ordeal. "They pressed in on me, a suffocating shroud, while whispers, like malicious specters, taunted and jeered, insisting that you, Ong, had forsaken me."

In the wake of her traumatic nightmare, Keisha drew in a trembling breath, her voice still bearing the echoes of her distress as she continued her account. "In that nightmarish abyss, there came a moment when the shadows relented, parting like a sinister curtain, and I glimpsed it—the Heart of Twilight. Enshrouded in a foreboding aura, it seemed like the Dominion's sinister grip was closing in."

Ong's hold tightened, his arms a steadfast anchor in the storm of Keisha's fears. His unwavering gaze locked with hers, a profound blend of reassurance and resolve emanating from his very being. "Keisha," he murmured, his voice a soothing balm, "I am here and shall never abandon you. Those were mere phantoms born of the evil shadows that Vuarus and Phoenix have cast upon your spirit."

Karrenen's voice reverberated with a fusion of righteous fury and heartfelt concern as he addressed Keisha, his words a shield against the darkness that had assailed her. "Their sinister purpose is clear, Keisha, an insidious design to fracture your spirit further. But we shall not permit them to succeed. Our purpose is to safeguard you, to ensure the Dominion's malevolence does not triumph."

Kimras, the embodiment of compassion and unwavering loyalty, added his voice to the chorus of support, his majestic presence a testament to their unbreakable bond. "Remember, Keisha, you stand not alone in this struggle. We are a united front against the tyranny of the Abyssal Dominion, just as we stand united in safeguarding the Heart of Twilight and our cherished Vacari."

As the moments passed, Keisha's frenetic heartbeat found solace, her breaths steadying. Like an unyielding fortress, their collective strength enfolded her, a poignant reminder that she need not face her trials in solitude.

Ong's gaze blazed with an intense resolve as he turned his attention to Kimras and Karrenen, the three of them forming a resolute triumvirate against the encroaching darkness. His jaw tightened, his eyes aflame with determination. "Vuarus and Phoenix shall be made to answer for the anguish they have inflicted upon her. Their reign of darkness ends now."

As the appointed hour neared, the Hidden Isles brimmed with eager anticipation, as the sun descended beneath the horizon, setting the sky with breathtaking hues of oranges and pinks. Meticulous preparations by the dragons had transformed a portion of the Hidden Isles into a communal gathering space tailored to accommodate the diverse attendees. Here, merfolk conversed with the nymphs, their tails gracefully shimmering beneath the water's surface. In proximity to the aquatic denizens, the nymphs exuded an aura of ethereal elegance that left onlookers enchanted.

Representatives from Crystal Vale and envoys from Goldmoor intermingled, their attire reflecting the distinct beauty of their realms, exchanging meaningful glances laden with an unspoken understanding of the impending deliberations' profound significance. Intricately arranged patterns of glowing gems delineated the boundaries of each faction's designated area, enabling them to convene in mutual comfort while preserving a measure of segregation.

As the time of the gathering approached, Ong and Karrenen, standing alongside Kimras, bore expressions that conveyed a potent mixture of determination and concern. Keisha remained protected in Ong's embrace, her presence a poignant reminder of the purpose that fueled their resolve. The destiny of their world hung precariously in the balance, resting heavily upon the deliberations to come. Towering beside them, the ancient and sagacious dragons bore witness, their solemn presence bearing testament to the profound gravity of the impending decisions.

The assembled allies, many of whom had not laid eyes on Keisha since her recent rescue earlier in the day, could scarcely conceal their shock upon seeing her. A collective gasp, followed by hushed murmurs, coursed through the room. Their countenances mirrored various emotions—disbelief, sympathy, and heartfelt concern. The harrowing ordeal had etched its indelible marks upon Keisha's visage, manifesting in her pallor, the fatigue etched into her gaze, and the faint tremor that coursed through her hands.

Some exchanged worried glances, while others instinctively gravitated closer to her, their actions akin to an unspoken offering of solace and support. It was an unambiguous reminder of this battle's toll on their cherished comrade. As the weighty gravity of their situation lingered in the air, a collective awareness permeated the room, crystallizing the understanding that their fight encompassed not only the pursuit of the Heart of Twilight but also the safeguarding of Keisha's well-being and the very future of their realm.

The ambiance brimmed with an electric sense of unity, an understanding that, regardless of their origins, a common purpose bound them—to safeguard Vacari. The gentle cadence of waves caressing the shore reverberated like the very heartbeat of their world, serving as a constant reminder of the life they held steadfast to protect.

Kimras's voice, resonating with solemnity, addressed the assembled allies under the canvas of the twilight sky, its hues a breathtaking tapestry of oranges and pinks as the sun descended beneath the horizon. "Friends and guardians of Vacari, we gather here today, confronted by a threat of unparalleled magnitude. Vuarus, once a trusted companion, has fallen prey to the forces of darkness, emerging as an evil deity—the God of Shadows. His dominion over our world is vast, making his designs grim."

He momentarily paused, his gaze traversing the countenances of those gathered, his golden scales shimmering with an ancient wisdom. "Nevertheless, our hope remains unbroken. A path exists to challenge his dominion, to restore the disrupted equilibrium. That path leads to the return of a dragon long shrouded in myth—Talleoss, the Silver Dragon."

A ripple of astonishment and intrigue cascaded through the assembly, prompting Kimras to continue. "Talleoss, a dragon of profound wisdom and unparalleled might, served Kadona with unwavering loyalty for countless years before vanishing from our realm, leaving behind only tales. These legends speak of his extraordinary capacity to harness the very power of Twilight—a force capable of standing resolute against the encroaching shadows."

Kimras locked eyes with the assembled audience, his gaze an unyielding beacon of determination. "The legends also whisper of Talleoss's sanctuary among the merfolk, concealed within the profound depths of their realm. If we are to harbor any hope of thwarting Vuarus and his evil schemes, we must embark on a quest to find Talleoss and implore his aid. This path will be difficult, but it is the course we must follow."

Kimras's words lingered in the atmosphere, their gravity palpable. The destiny of E'vahona now rested squarely upon their shoulders, and the journey to seek out Talleoss and rekindle his allegiance would be rife with adversities. However, the mere glimmer of hope in his prospective return had ignited a vibrant resurgence of determination amongst the assembly. This hunger would propel them forward in their unyielding struggle against the impending darkness.

Nerissa, the mermaid guardian of Twilight, gracefully stepped into the forefront, her graceful presence a living embodiment of the mystique of the underwater realm. Like the gentle cadence of ocean waves, her voice carried the wisdom of eons past. "Dragons harbor profound memories, as do we merfolk. Talleoss remained imprinted in the depths of our realm's collective consciousness. He entrusted me with a relic—a fragment of his essence, infused with the glorious power of Twilight."

Her utterance carried a profound significance, reverberating through the assembly like a sacred hymn. "He tasked me with the solemn duty of safeguarding this relic, preserving it in secrecy until the hour of its utmost necessity. It was intended for the one capable of wielding its potent force against the advancing shadows. That time has come."

Nerissa's gaze first met Kimras's, her eyes shimmering with a profound understanding that transcended mere words. She then turned her gaze to encompass the diverse assembly of allies, her voice resonating with solemnity and hope. "I have safeguarded this relic through countless centuries, patiently awaiting the destined hour when its power would be summoned into service. If it holds the potential to aid us in our arduous battle against Vuarus, I stand ready to entrust it to those who will wield it in the name of the greater good."

Her words wove an atmosphere of breathless anticipation and deep reverence. The relic, entrusted to Nerissa by Talleoss, could shift the balance in their relentless struggle, countering the encroaching shadows with the iridescent radiance of Twilight. With each passing moment, the pathway forward seemed to crystallize, and the once-disparate fragments of their strategy converged, guided by the ancient wisdom of those who had gone before them.

As the assembly of allies continued their deliberations, a profound hush descended upon the gathering, and an ethereal presence subtly enshrouded the space. It manifested Kadona's spirit—a beacon of divine luminosity amidst the brooding veil of darkness.

Kadona's voice, an ethereal symphony of wisdom and grace, resonated through the assembly, enveloping them in a palpable aura of reverence. Her presence embodied divine guidance sought at this crucial juncture. "Greetings, esteemed allies," she began, her words a soothing balm to the hearts of those who listened. "I have been granted the privilege to partake in your gathering, offering insights into this pivotal moment. The threads of destiny are woven with intricacy, and the choices that unfurl here will inevitably shape the tapestry of E'vahona and Vacari."

She paused, her luminous eyes scanning the faces of those assembled. Her gaze then alighted upon Keisha, her trusted guardian, who had endured countless trials. At first, her presence stirred a bittersweet emotion within Kadona, causing her to falter in her divine address momentarily. Yet, the deity's inherent grace prevailed as she continued. "It warms my heart to witness the unity among you. Guardians of light and defenders of realms, you stand united by a singular purpose, driven by unwavering resolve to thwart Vuarus's nefarious designs."

A sense of collective awe washed over the assembly, their hearts and minds drawn into the ethereal presence of Kadona. They hung on to her every word, absorbing her wisdom as she unveiled the intricacies of their impending quest.

"Yet, let it be known," Kadona continued, her voice a soothing river of knowledge, "that the tale is far more intricate than it first appears. Talleoss, the Silver Dragon of light, is kept within a crystal sanctuary of my creation—a measure taken to safeguard him from the clutches of darkness. This crystal remains under the vigilant watch of Phoenix Shadowwalker, who remains unaware of Talleoss's allegiance to the light. It is a protective shield, securing his safety while monitoring the unfolding events."

Her words weighed heavily upon the gathering, a reminder of the complexities they faced. "But do not despair, for a solution exists to awaken Talleoss from his protective slumber. The crystal's enchantment can be dissolved, but only amid the fierce clash of battle. Within the heart of the impending confrontation, where the forces of light and shadow shall collide, lies the opportunity to free him and rekindle his strength in service of the light."

Kadona's presence seemed to shimmer, infused with the very essence of hope. "As you continue strategizing and uniting, remember that this battle transcends mere victory or defeat. It is a battle for preserving balance and the redemption of even the darkest souls. Stay steadfast, for the dawn of a new era rests within your grasp."

With her final words, Kadona's luminous form began to wane, her presence a fleeting yet unforgettable touch upon the assembly's hearts. The path forward was now illuminated with newfound insights, and the group bore the weight of the future upon their shoulders, united in purpose and fortified by unwavering determination.

As Kadona's ethereal presence gradually dissipated, a hushed anticipation enveloped the assembly. Keisha's voice, trembling with uncertainty, pierced through the quiet, bearing the weight of an unsettling revelation. Ong's reassuring nod encouraged her to continue, and with newfound determination, she spoke.

While I was a prisoner of the Dominion, I had a vision about Talleoss, but I cannot say if the vision was true," Keisha began, her eyes locked on the ground as if seeking refuge from haunting memories. "I beheld the crystal wand imprisoning Talleoss. It resides within a darkened tower in Afor, guarded by evil shadows and forces beyond reckoning. I glimpsed it only fleetingly, an image etched into the very core of my being."

Her voice quivered, and a palpable shiver coursed through her. Drawing a trembling breath, she summoned the strength to reveal the extent of her harrowing ordeal. "The tower exudes an aura of despair, a place steeped in darkness. Yet, amid that darkness, I could sense the presence of Talleoss within the crystal—a loyal heart ensnared by sinister shadows."

A heavy silence descended, Keisha's words lingering in the air, carrying the profound weight of the sacrifice she had endured. Her revelation crystallized the clarity of their mission and served as a chilling reminder of the perils ahead. The path to liberate Talleoss led through a realm shrouded in hostility, demanding the unwavering courage and determination of all present.

As Keisha's voice trailed into silence, Ong's gentle touch and the steadfast support of their allies enveloped her in a comforting embrace amidst the turmoil surrounding them. The unity forged among the guardians and their partners shone as a beacon of hope, even amid the formidable challenges looming.

Karrenen's voice shattered the contemplative silence that enveloped the gathering following Keisha's revelation. His gaze shifted toward Aeliana, the Guardian of Ardinia among the nymphs, a glint of determination in his eyes. His deliberate and resolute words bore a request rooted in strategic foresight.

"As we stand united against a formidable adversary," Karrenen began, his measured tone carrying the weight of their shared mission, "we recognize the diversity of our strengths, each of us bringing unique talents to the impending battle. Aeliana, Guardian of Ardinia, your profound connection to the natural world and its mysteries holds boundless potential."

Aeliana met Karrenen's gaze, her eyes reflecting both the wisdom of ages past and the gravity of their responsibilities. As the nymph entrusted with safeguarding the knowledge of Ardinia's flora and fauna, her abilities were an intricate part of nature's tapestry. She listened intently, poised to receive Karrenen's request.

"During the battle," Karrenen continued, "we humbly seek your assistance in confounding our adversaries, disrupting their comprehension of the terrain and the environment. With your mastery of nature's intricacies, you can craft illusions, altering the perceptions of the shadows that threaten our realm."

Aeliana's demeanor remained contemplative, her gaze briefly encompassing her fellow nymphs as if silently gauging their collective assent. When she spoke, her voice resonated with the essence of nature's grace and unwavering determination.

"While the forces of darkness may wield manipulation and shadow," Aeliana replied, her words carrying the conviction of one intertwined with the natural world, "the resilience and beauty of nature hold their formidable power. I shall lend my abilities to our shared cause, invoking the spirits of the forests, the rivers, and the skies to weave illusions that shall bewilder our adversaries."

The unspoken gratitude in Karrenen's eyes conveyed his deep appreciation for the harmonious alliance they had forged. In unity and determination, they erected a barrier against the encroaching hostility that threatened to plunge their world into darkness. As the discussion progressed and strategies took shape, the forces of light and their steadfast allies fortified their resolve, everyone contributing their unique strengths to the pivotal battle ahead.

Aqilus, a commanding presence imbued with an aura of authority, first focused on Keisha. His smile, warm and genuine, graced his regal countenance. Although his voice carried the weight of nobility, beneath it lay an undertone of sincere relief.

"Welcome back to the embrace of the waters, Keisha," he spoke, his eyes mirroring the profound depths of the oceans from whence he hailed. "Adrianna and her kin have dearly missed you, and their concerns have reverberated through the currents of our realm. Your return shines as a beacon of hope for us all—a testament to your strength and resilience in adversity."

His words resonated with heartfelt warmth, a testament to the friendships that transcended the diverse realms of Vacari. As he shifted his attention to address King Alex, Aqilus's expression transformed into focused determination.

"King Alex," he began, his tone measured and resolute, "our strategic position within the vast expanse of the oceans bestows us a unique advantage. Goldmoor's location places you on the opposite shore of the ocean from Afor, separated by the currents that flow between us. This proximity, while advantageous, calls for prudent measures."

Aqilus's gaze bore the weight of his responsibility as he continued. "The merfolk shall harness the power of the seas, making the very waters our allies. As we traverse the waters through Fel Thalor and Old Flameford, we shall manipulate the currents and tides, shrouding your passage and ensuring the waters conceal your arrival in New Flameford within Afor."

The concept of nature aiding their cause underscored the unity among the citizens of Vacari. In a world where shadows threatened to engulf their realm, the forces of light and their steadfast allies derived strength from their shared purpose and the harmonious collaboration of their diverse talents.

The atmosphere within the chamber bore the weight of impending conflict. Ong, standing firmly at the forefront of the assembly, cast his discerning gaze across the assembled leaders. King Manard of Crystal Vale stood out among them—a ruler renowned for his sagacity and formidable leadership, a guardian of ancient wisdom.

As Ong's gaze found its mark in King Manard, he advanced purposefully. "Your Majesty," he began, his voice resounding throughout the chamber, "we confront a dire juncture that demands the amalgamation of our forces as never before."

King Manard, his countenance etched with solemnity, met Ong's unwavering stare, fully comprehending the gravity of the situation. "Indeed, Ong. We must not underestimate the menace posed by Vuarus and Phoenix."

Ong nodded, his determination unswerving. "This is why I implore you to stand with us, to take your place beside the Eladrin in the impending struggle. We require your strength and the strategic insight that Crystal Vale can bestow."

King Manard's gaze shifted toward the meticulously laid-out maps that adorned the table before them, each representing a piece of the intricate puzzle. Ong pressed on with clarity in his purpose. "Our initial objective," he explained, "is to breach the formidable gates of the Dread Spire. Within those dark walls, the crystal wand, the instrument of Talleoss's imprisonment, lies hidden. We shall liberate him by destroying it, enlisting his formidable might to bolster our ranks for the forthcoming battle."

King Manard's eyes shimmered with understanding. "And upon Talleoss's liberation," Ong continued, "it is only fitting that the Heart of Twilight is entrusted to him, for its power rightly belongs in his grasp. His strength will be invaluable in our confrontation with Vuarus and Phoenix."

A solemn nod from King Manard underscored his concurrence. "You have my commitment, Ong. Crystal Vale shall stand unwaveringly alongside the Eladrin in this impending battle, sparing no effort to secure the triumph."

Gratitude filled Ong's eyes, his demeanor reflecting heartfelt appreciation. "Thank you, Your Majesty. Your unwavering support resonates deeply."

King Manard's countenance softened with a hint of amusement, a chilling glint dancing in his eyes. 'One more thing, Ong,' he added, his voice carrying a foreboding edge, 'you mentioned Phoenix. I doubt you will allow him to escape your path without leaving behind a trail of regrets.'" With their accord sealed, Ong and King Manard exchanged a resolute nod, solidifying their alliance as they prepared to face a common adversary. The impending battle loomed ominously, but they could defeat the encroaching darkness with the united might of Crystal Vale and the Eladrin.

Nerissa's words floated in the air, heavy with the wisdom of ages past. Her serene and confident voice resonated deeply with those gathered in the chamber.

"As Talleoss emerges from his crystalline captivity," Nerissa began, her eyes gleaming with a hint of enigmatic knowledge, "the Heart of Twilight shall naturally gravitate toward its rightful owner. This artifact wields a singular power, one that acknowledges its original possessor. It shall seek out Talleoss, merging with him as it was always meant to."

A ripple of realization and wonder passed through the assembly. The idea that the Heart of Twilight would find its true bearer carried an air of profound magic and destiny.

Nerissa continued, her gaze traversing the faces before her, gauging their determination. "Until Talleoss's liberation, we must safeguard the Heart from the Dominion's relentless pursuit. Its power acts as a beacon, one they can sense, and we cannot afford to let it fall into their clutches."

Ong affirmed with a resolute nod. "We understand, Nerissa. We shall protect the Heart with unwavering devotion until Talleoss reclaims it."

King Manard, his countenance marked by unwavering resolve, voiced his agreement. "Then it is settled. We shall ensure Talleoss's release from his crystalline imprisonment, and in the interim, the Heart of Twilight shall remain concealed and shielded."

Nerissa's gaze pierced the depths of their souls, bearing the weight of countless ages. "Bear in mind that the threads of destiny have woven us together for a purpose," she intoned, her words lingering like an unspoken oath.

With those solemn words, the leaders of their respective realms stood united, bound by a shared purpose and an unwavering determination to confront the looming darkness, and end the reign of Vuarus and Phoenix.

Kimras, his resolute golden gaze, took command of the moment. "The dragons of light shall confront the forces of the Abyssal Dominion's dragons. We will engage them to divert their attention and keep them occupied. Their interference shall not hinder our plans."

Silvara, a majestic silver dragon exuding an aura of wisdom and might, stepped forth. Her eyes locked onto Ong and Keisha, determination gleaming within their depths. "Talleoss is my beloved mate," she proclaimed, her voice resonating with a commanding presence. "I shall be the one to liberate him from that accursed crystal."

A ripple of anticipation surged through the chamber at her resolute declaration. Keisha's heart swelled, moved by the profound connection shared even among the mighty dragons. Silvara then turned her gaze toward the entire assembly, addressing them with authority. "While imprisoned, Phoenix has been siphoning power from Talleoss. When the crystal is shattered, that stolen power shall return to him, weakening Phoenix significantly."

The gathering's collective resolve solidified their determination as a beacon of hope in a world threatened by darkness. The path forward was set, and the roles of each ally were clearly defined as they prepared to face the encroaching malevolence with unity and strength.

Karrenen's countenance shifted from cautious contemplation to genuine intrigue as he considered the profound strategic implications. "If we can weaken Phoenix before the ultimate confrontation, it may tip the power scales decisively in our favor."

Ever the analytical thinker, Alaric quirked an eyebrow as he voiced his concerns. "But what of the Crystal Wand itself? Given its intimate connection to Talleoss, will it naturally return to him after liberation?"

Nerissa, the mermaid guardian, offered a nod of agreement. "Indeed, Alaric speaks truly. The Crystal Wand bears a unique bond with its true owner. Upon Talleoss's release, the wand will instinctively recognize him, and its powers will seamlessly reunite, revitalizing his strength and abilities."

Ong exchanged a meaningful glance with Keisha, their fates irrevocably entwined. The unwavering commitment of Silvara and the stubborn determination of the dragons fueled their resolve. The intricate puzzle pieces of their plan were gradually falling into place, guiding them ever closer to the pivotal and long-awaited confrontation with Phoenix and Vuarus.

As the chamber buzzed with an electric sense of anticipation, Kimras addressed the gathering with a resolute declaration. "Our path is clear. Let us prepare for the impending battle that heralds the rebirth of Talleoss and the reclamation of the Crystal Wand. The encroaching darkness of the Abyssal Dominion shall be met with the unyielding light of our unity."

Galadon, his voice tinged with caution, interjected a note of prudence. "We must not disregard that Vuarus wields the very power of the Abyss, and he shall likely unleash its twisted denizens upon us. We should prepare to confront these nightmarish creatures, for they are the malignant extensions of his evil influence."

Karrenen, his gaze sharp and unwavering, concurred with a solemn nod. "The Eladrin's sorcerers shall employ their mystical talents to counteract the presence of the Abyss. We shall endeavor to dispel these nightmarish apparitions through our arcane arts and weaken their grasp upon the battlefield. However, bear in mind that these creatures are both lethal and unpredictable. Maintain vigilance, and never underestimate their relentless ferocity."

The connections among the varied allies deepened within the heart of their deliberations and the forging of plans. They exchanged the wisdom of their realms, sharpened their tactical understanding, and fortified their resolve to confront the Abyssal Dominion's dark forces with unwavering unity. The destiny of their world teetered upon a precipice, and as one united force, they would stand as a bulwark against the encroaching shadows that hungered to engulf their realm.

Keisha's voice quivered as she quietly expressed her unwavering decision to be at the impending battle, her eyes glistening with unshed tears. Ong's gaze, filled with deep concern and affection, shifted towards her, his worry for her safety etched across his features. He couldn't help but voice his concern, a testament to the love that bound them. "Are you certain about this?" he inquired, his voice gentle yet gauged with apprehension, his heart aching with the fear of what might occur in the looming conflict.

Meeting Ong's gaze with a mix of trepidation and unwavering determination, Keisha replied, her voice breaking as she spoke of her captivity, tears welling up in her eyes. "Yes, Ong. Though I do not have my magic, and fear lingers, I must be there to see Vuarus and Phoenix defeated." She paused, her voice trembling with emotion as she continued, "After the six months of torment, I have to see them destroyed if I am to begin the long healing process." Her tears flowed freely now, a testament to the deep scars and trauma she had endured during her captivity and the arduous journey of recovery that lay ahead.

Kimras, the majestic golden dragon, drew closer, his presence radiating a calming reassurance. "You shall not face this battle in solitude, Keisha," he declared with regal authority and a protective tone. "I willingly offer myself as your guardian. You can ride upon my back, and together, we shall stand as vigilant sentinels over the battlefield." His words carried an unwavering determination as if he would not allow her to be captured again while the battle raged on.

Ong's grip on Keisha's hand tightened, his worry palpable. "Promise me, above all else, that you will exercise caution," he implored, the fear of losing her once more clouding his thoughts. His voice conveyed a deep emotion, expressing his love and concern for her.

A faint but genuine smile graced Keisha's lips, a glimmer of determination shining through the shadows of uncertainty. "I promise," she whispered, her voice quivering with emotion. Her heart was fortified by the unwavering support and love enveloping her. The battles that lay ahead would undoubtedly test their resolve, but their unity and unyielding determination would serve as a guiding light through the looming darkness.

With the imminent battle hanging like a storm cloud over them, Ong's voice rang out, a clarion call that pierced the heavy air of anticipation. His words, laden with purpose, served as a rallying cry, a stark reminder of the impending clash with the Abyssal Dominion. "Return to your realms and ready yourselves as best you can. In three days, our assault on the Abyssal Dominion's stronghold in New Flameford, Afor, shall commence. Until then, remain vigilant against their relentless assaults. Guard our strategy with utmost secrecy; let them be caught unaware."

Ong's penetrating gaze traversed the assembly, and each face was a portrait of unwavering determination mingled with anxious anticipation. "We aim to strike with the element of surprise, to disrupt their preparations. This is our moment to shift the balance of this war." His concluding words reverberated with an unyielding resolve that penetrated the hearts of those present. "Na lû e-govaned vîn. (Translation: Until next we meet.)"

With that, the gathering began to disperse, each member carrying the call to arms and a shared purpose to drive them forward into the imminent battle. The forthcoming week would be one of relentless preparation, a time for honing their skills and steeling themselves for the trials ahead. As they departed, the echo of Ong's words lingered, a promise of unity in the face of the encroaching darkness that threatened their world.

Chapter 47

Shadows Unveiled: Rising Tensions

Vuarus and Phoenix were trapped in a maddening web of frustration that deepened with each passing day. Their relentless quest for the elusive Heart of Twilight had led them to the murky depths beyond New Flameford in the realm of Afor. Yet, like elusive phantoms, the coveted artifact remained beyond their grasp, concealed within the enigma of twilight itself.

Their once-boundless patience had dwindled, replaced by a seething fury that simmered below the surface.

Vuarus, his visage twisted with vexation, clenched his hands into fists, his eyes piercing the dark expanse of the watery abyss before him. "Infuriating!" he seethed as if he could compel the Heart of Twilight to reveal itself through sheer force of will. "How can the Heart of Twilight taunt us with its silence?"

Beside him, Phoenix mirrored his frustration, his jaw tightly clenched and his eyes narrowing with urgency as if he could will the artifact into their possession. "Time is a luxury we can no longer afford," he muttered, his voice tinged with impatience. "We must have that artifact, and we must have it now."

In their mounting desperation, their only semblance of satisfaction came from tormenting Keisha in her sleep, weaving nightmares that echoed the sinister game they played with her subconscious. Despite her vulnerability, her steadfast resistance within the labyrinth of her dreams was a source of grudging admiration. Her subconscious defiance stood as a discordant note in their symphony of control. Still, it was a note they begrudgingly tolerated, for their fixation remained firmly on the Heart of Twilight.

As Vuarus and Phoenix exchanged glances, their frustration coalescing into an unspoken pact, they understood that their pursuit was a dark covenant. The Heart of Twilight stood as the linchpin of their dominion, a source of boundless power to fuel their ambitions. Failure was a luxury they could not afford, for the Heart of Twilight remained their ultimate, elusive prize.

Unbeknownst to the sinister duo, their relentless quest for the Heart of Twilight was a blinding mirage, obscuring the approaching tempest gathering on the horizon. The Alliance of Light and its steadfast allies had forged clandestine bonds, the whispers of a formidable storm of opposition growing louder with each passing day. The world trembled as if it sensed the impending clash determining its existence.

Into the foreboding depths of the Dread Spire, Lyra ventured, her demeanor a reflection of the oppressive atmosphere that clung to the air. The towering, ancient halls whispered their secrets as she approached the formidable figures of Vuarus and Phoenix. Lines of worry etched her face, and her voice, taut with gravity, carried the weight of her report. "We face further trials," she declared, her words laden with apprehension. "Our agents, sent on the dangerous dive in search of the Heart of Twilight, are entangled in a web of futility. The artifact eludes their grasp, and despair shadows their every effort."

Vuarus, a storm of irritation brewing in his eyes, absorbed Lyra's words with a patience worn thin. Frustration permeated the air, and a palpable tension simmered in the silent exchange of glances between him and Phoenix. Their collective vexation swirled like an impending storm.

Without uttering a word, Vuarus strode purposefully from the confines of the Dread Spire, his steps resonating with inner turmoil as he headed toward the water's edge. His aura exuded a seething rage, an emotional storm ready to unleash itself. As he reached the water's edge, his voice pierced the air, and an eerie resonance sent shivers rippling through those who bore witness—a chilling reminder of the Dominion's evil power.

"Listen, all who dare to serve our dark cause!" Vuarus's voice, like a spectral melody, danced upon the waves, sending ripples of dread through those who stood before him. "You bear the mark of the Abyssal Dominion, bound by a mission that admits no failure. The Heart of Twilight must be wrested from the veils of obscurity, and it must be claimed here and now."

The waters themselves stirred as if responding to Vuarus's decree, the world quivering in the presence of forces that threatened to plunge into an abyss of eternal twilight. The impending battle for dominion loomed ever nearer, and the destiny of their world teetered on the precipice—a tale poised to unfold in shadows and light.

Vuarus, the formidable figure of the Abyssal Dominion, fixed a searing gaze upon the chosen servants who stood before him, their faces a tumultuous blend of fear and trepidation. His eyes, as cold and unforgiving as the abyss itself, bore into the very depths of their souls, his words dripping with the venom of impending menace. "Should any among you dare to falter, should incompetence mar your endeavors, understand this: the consequences that await you are darker and more twisted than the deepest realms of your imagination. Your loyalty to the Abyssal Dominion is not a mere oath but an unbreakable covenant. Failure will be met with a retribution that shall haunt every fiber of your existence."

A suffocating tension enveloped the assembled group as Vuarus's ominous threat hung in the air, casting a shadow over their resolve. The servants exchanged uneasy glances in the dim light, their fear tangible, like a creeping chill down their spines. With one final withering glare that seared their consciousness, Vuarus pivoted and strode away from the trembling assembly, leaving them to grapple with the weight of his ominous words.

Within the foreboding embrace of the Dread Spire, the lingering tension persisted like a phantom, a haunting reminder of the unrelenting cruelty of the Abyssal Dominion and the ever-escalating stakes of their undercover mission. It clung to the air like a suffocating mist, thick and palpable.

Vuarus's gaze, as keen as the sharpest of blades, bore into Lyra, her presence fragile amidst the encroaching darkness. Suspicion dripped from his narrowed eyes, his voice a razor-edged instrument honed to perfection. "Are you certain that your interpretation of that scroll was accurate?" he demanded, impatience and skepticism dripping from every word.

Bolstered by a gust of determination welling from within, Lyra swallowed hard, the weight of Vuarus's scrutiny pressing upon her like an unyielding burden. She met his unrelenting gaze, her voice a fortress of resolve tinged with a hint of apprehension. "I have the utmost confidence in the accuracy of my interpretation," she replied, her words a steadfast oath in the face of the gathering storm.

"Confidence?" Vuarus's voice, colder than the darkest abyss, oozed with disdain, a stark reminder that confidence was a fragile commodity in their world, liable to shatter beneath the weight of their ambitions. "This is not a matter of confidence. This is a matter of certainty, of unswerving commitment to ensure the flawless execution of our grand designs." His words carried the weight of an unspoken threat, a serpent lurking in the shadows, warning of the dire consequences that awaited any hint of faltering.

Lyra, standing firm beneath the oppressive scrutiny of Vuarus, felt a shiver of apprehension run down her spine. She knew the stakes were perilously high, and the Abyssal Dominion was not known for its leniency in the face of failure. "I will revisit my notes," she affirmed, her voice unwavering, echoing an unspoken pledge. With that, she turned away, her steps a mixture of determination and anxiety, each a testament to the price of failure in their dark enterprise.

Vuarus, his inscrutable countenance betraying no hint of the tumultuous thoughts within, watched Lyra's departure. The quest for the Heart of Twilight, the crucible of their ambitions, lingered far from its conclusion, and the Abyssal Dominion's patience waned like a fading ember. The artifact, a vessel of unimaginable power, held the destiny of their dominion within its enigmatic embrace—a force that brooked no opposition.

The chamber's atmosphere underwent a subtle, charged shift as Qellaun, an unexpected presence, entered the sanctum, drawing the piercing gazes of both Vuarus and Phoenix. Clearing his throat, he embarked upon a declaration of purpose, outlining the fortifications he had implemented along the waters, his gaze unwavering as if bearing the weight of the entire operation.

Vuarus nodded in approval. "Excellent. We cannot afford the slightest whisper of our machinations to reach the unwelcome ears of our adversaries."

Yet, Phoenix, Vuarus's enigmatic counterpart, raised an eyebrow, his scrutiny unwavering as he probed Qellaun's motivations. "Why, may I ask, do you wish to become entangled in this endeavor, Qellaun?"

There was a momentary pause, a hesitation that hung in the air like a gathering storm before Qellaun replied with unwavering conviction. "I believe in the cause of the Abyssal Dominion and wish to contribute in any way possible. My knowledge of these waters may prove to be an invaluable asset."

Vuarus, the master of calculated choices, leaned back, his gaze locked onto Qellaun as if delving into the depths of his intentions. After a lingering pause, he uttered a single word, a decree with the power to shape destinies: "Very well." With that pronouncement, Qellaun's fate was sealed, joining the relentless hunt for the Heart of Twilight, where secrets of power and darkness lay hidden, waiting to be unveiled.

Ever the harbinger of ominous warnings, Phoenix leaned in closer, his voice a whispered blade cutting through the air. "Remember, Qellaun," he hissed, his tone low and sharp, "the same shadows of consequence that haunt our steps shall also shadow yours. Should you falter in your quest to unearth the Heart of Twilight, know that the price to be paid is one that even your darkest nightmares cannot fathom?"

Vuarus, the mastermind of the Abyssal Dominion, chimed in with a sinister smirk, his voice cutting through the air like a haunting melody. "Indeed," he purred, his words laced with a chilling satisfaction, "the Abyss is ever insatiable, a voracious maw that devours the wayward souls who dare defy its will."

Qellaun, his expression a taut mask concealing a turbulent sea of emotions beneath, could only nod in response. The ghostly flicker of a dying candle played upon his lips, its feeble dance casting fleeting shadows on his face. The weight of his chosen path bore down upon him, a burden as heavy as the abyssal depths. "I understand," he affirmed, his voice carrying the resonance of a vow etched in the annals of his destiny.

With those words, Qellaun turned and departed the chamber, his footsteps echoing with a melancholy cadence, each step bearing the weight of the abyssal depths. The looming demands of the Abyssal Dominion, the darkness, and the unknown hung like a shroud over his shoulders, a relentless specter of destiny that would haunt him every step of the way.

Within the confines of their shadowy sanctum, an atmosphere fraught with tension enveloped them like a shroud. The weight of their evil intent hung heavy as they convened, their dark purposes concealed beneath the guise of their clandestine meeting.

"Phoenix, the orchestrator of torment, cut through the palpable stillness with a voice that sliced like a dagger through the silence. 'Have you decided upon the nightmare to haunt Keisha's slumber tonight?' His words were a chilling reminder of their unrelenting cruelty, a dark symphony that echoed through the chamber.

Vuarus, the architect of despair, leaned back in his chair, a cruel smile curling upon his lips like a serpent basking in its treacherous glory. 'Ah, the nightmares,' he mused, his voice echoing twisted experimentation. 'I have been toying with various scenarios, testing the limits of her endurance, searching for the fractures that break her spirit most swiftly.'

Ever the vigilant enigma, Phoenix raised a quizzical eyebrow, his unwavering gaze boring into Vuarus. 'And pray tell, which of these nefarious concoctions have proven most effective?'

In response, Vuarus's eyes gleamed with sinister amusement, a chilling fire that flickered within their depths. 'Oddly enough,' he mused, his tone dripping with dark satisfaction, 'it is the nightmares of Ong that plague her most profoundly. Even though she now resides in the realm she calls home, the spectral memories of her beloved, those that we subjected her to when she was our prisoner, continue to haunt her the most. The fears and buried past we brought back to the surface during her captivity play a crucial role in amplifying the torment she endures.'

Phoenix, a master of cruelty in his own right, emitted a dark chuckle that reverberated through the chamber like a malevolent symphony. 'Ah, the enduring power of love, even amidst the throes of despair. How poetically cruel.'

Vuarus's smirk widened, a grotesque mask of delight. 'Indeed,' he concurred, his voice resonating with twisted fascination. 'It is nothing short of fascinating to witness her relentless struggle against the haunting specters of her past, the torrent of emotions that tear her from within. The visions we subjected her to when she was our prisoner played their part in destroying her confidence, leaving her adrift in uncertainty, unsure of what is real. The very fabric of her reality is woven with threads of our malevolent design.'"

"The evil architects of torment convened in the heart of their shadowed sanctum, their conversation dripping with malice that seemed to stain the air around them, leaving an ominous residue. Phoenix, the embodiment of darkness, leaned forward with an aura of sinister intent, his voice a venomous caress that sent shivers down the spines of all who listened.

"And how long, I wonder," he hissed, his tone thick with malice, "do you intend to employ this method?"

Vuarus, the orchestrator of their cruel designs, assumed a contemplative demeanor, his visage a mask of calculated maleficence, as if pondering the intricacies of their sinister plot. "Until she has served her purpose, and we have squeezed every ounce of utility from her fragile existence," he replied, his words laced with cold finality, "only then shall we permit her spirit to wither away."

A nod of sinister agreement, subtle but unmistakable, passed between them, sealing their dark compact. "Indeed," Phoenix concurred, his dark eyes glinting with morbid satisfaction. "The longer we can keep her under our thrall, the deeper her suffering will run, and that suffering shall become our most potent weapon."

In response, Vuarus's eyes sparkled with a sinister light, his thoughts dancing with wicked anticipation. "And when the time comes," he added, his voice like a whisper from the abyss, "her shattered spirit shall stand as a chilling testament to our power, a grim reminder to all who dare to defy us."

"Yet, as their chilling discourse continued, Phoenix, the precursor of malevolence, steered the conversation toward an intriguing question. 'Have you, by any chance, detected any anomalies within her nightmares? Any signs of resistance?'

Vuarus's brow furrowed, and he mulled over Phoenix's inquiry as though sifting through the dark tapestry of Keisha's torment. 'Now that you mention it,' he conceded, a hint of unease tainting his tone, 'there have been fleeting moments, even within the confines of her nightmares, where a glimmer of defiance manifests. It's as if her willpower possesses a strength we did not initially anticipate, a hidden current flowing beneath the surface of her nightmares like an unseen tide.'

Phoenix's smile, once cruel, twisted into something altogether more predatory—a hint of sadistic delight coloring his features like shadows deepening in the gloom. 'Fascinating,' he mused, his fingers tapping thoughtfully upon the arm of his chair. 'It appears our captive possesses a reservoir of determination far more formidable than we had presumed.'

Vuarus's amusement returned, a dark ripple in the sea of their wicked intentions, his satisfaction echoing through the shadowed chamber. 'Then,' he declared, 'we shall simply have to break her spirit further to ensure she cannot undermine our malevolent endeavors.'

Within the shadowed recesses of their sinister plotting, the revelation of Keisha's hidden strength in the face of their unrelenting torment added an intriguing layer of complexity to their evil designs, a glimmer of resistance that fueled their dark ambitions."

In the mystical realm of E'vahona, where dreams and reality intertwine like threads of an otherworldly tapestry, Keisha lay nestled in the embrace of her bed, lost in slumber's enigmatic depths. In the stillness of her resting form, the boundaries of her conscious world dissolved, giving way to the realm of nightmare.

Within the ethereal landscape of her nightmare, Keisha found herself upon the desolate shores of a vast and foreboding ocean. The sky above hung heavy with storm-laden clouds, their ominous presence casting a pallor upon the world below, as if the very heavens wept in sync with Keisha's subconscious turmoil. The waters churned restlessly as if echoing the turmoil of her very soul. A deep sense of abandonment and despair coursed through her, their tendrils wrapping around her heart like spectral chains.

A vision unfurled before her as her gaze was drawn toward the turbulent sea, the acrid scent of salt and despair mingling in the air. Standing at the water's edge with his back to her, there was Ong, a specter of the past, an embodiment of longing and loss. Her voice, an echo of pain and yearning, pierced the eerie silence as she called out to him, her words carried away by the relentless wind. Yet, he did not respond. It was as if he stood in a world apart, oblivious to her cries, or, as if he had chosen to turn his back on her, a painful silence that rented her soul asunder.

The nightmare's grip tightened around Keisha's slumbering form, her distress deepening like the abyss before her eyes. Ong, unmoved by her anguish, took deliberate steps into the murky waters, his form gradually vanishing into the darkness below like a fading specter swallowed by the abyss. Desperation seized her, and she extended trembling hands toward him, her cheeks wet with the tears of her heart's torment. But it was a futile endeavor, a heart-wrenching journey into the depths of longing and abandonment.

As the nightmare's ethereal tendrils released their hold, Keisha stirred in her sleep, her voice an anguished murmur that echoed through the night. The nightmare had woven its haunting tapestry, leaving her with an enduring sense of abandonment and heartache, a phantom of emotions that would linger long after the dawn had broken in E'vahona."

"As the first light of day began to grace the world, Keisha awoke from the turbulent embrace of her nightmare, yet the lingering sensation of Ong's departure clung to her like a ghostly specter, an ache that refused to relent, an ethereal weight on her soul. Rising from her slumber, she ventured outside, the morning sun casting its golden rays upon her tear-stained cheeks, each crystalline drop, like fragile mirrors, glistening with the reflections of her inner turmoil.

With a heavy heart, Keisha sought solace in the embrace of the world outside her home. She found respite in the tranquil solitude of her surroundings, a quaint haven that had witnessed the tapestry of her life's moments. Sitting in quiet contemplation, her cheeks still glistening with the remnants of her night's tears, a faithful companion accompanied her. Pumpkin, her steadfast confidant, lay beside her, hier presence a silent source of comfort like a warm embrace amid emotional storms. Her head rested gently on her lap, her eyes mirroring the empathy of a loyal friend.

As Keisha gazed into the horizon, the weight of the nightmare from the previous night pressed heavily upon her heart, an unyielding burden she struggled to cast aside. Her emotions surged like a stormy sea, each wave carrying the echoes of her torment, the shadows of her captivity still haunting her despite her newfound freedom."

"Approaching the scene, Ong, a source of solace and concern, traversed the distance with a furrowed brow, his gaze honing in on Keisha's tears. With a gentle grace, he lowered himself to the ground beside her, his presence offering a semblance of comfort. "Hey," he murmured, his voice a soothing whisper, "what troubles your heart, my dear?"

Keisha, trembling, sniffled as she attempted to wipe away the stubborn traces of her tears with the back of her hand. "Oh, it's nothing," she whispered, her words laced with a vulnerability she could not entirely conceal. "Just a nightmare, nothing more."

Warm and understanding, Ong's eyes held her gaze like gentle beacons amid emotional turbulence as he gently reached out, his fingers lifting her chin, ensuring their eyes met. "You know," he said, his voice filled with the quiet assurance of a kindred spirit, a soothing melody amid emotional discord, "you can always talk to me. Whatever burdens your heart, you need not face it alone. I am here for you, now and always."

The world held its breath as Keisha's gaze met Ong's, a swirling storm of emotions churning within the depths of her eyes. In the tender stillness of the moment, she found the courage to admit the haunting truth that had shadowed her heart like a ghost in the recesses of her emotions.

"It was about you," she confessed, her voice barely above a whisper, as if afraid to give voice to the pain clawed at her soul. "In the nightmare, you walked away from me, just as you did at the altar. And there I stood, alone and shattered."

"Ong's expression softened, a profound understanding dawning in his eyes like the first rays of dawn breaking through the darkness. Without hesitation, he enveloped her in his warm embrace, his arms a sanctuary, a shield against the storm of her anguish, like a steadfast fortress during chaos. "Oh, Keisha," he whispered, his voice a soothing balm laced with empathy, "I'm so sorry that you had to endure such torment."

With her head resting against his shoulder, Keisha surrendered to the solace of his comforting presence, the steady rhythm of his heartbeat echoing like a comforting melody. In the cocoon of Ong's embrace, she found respite from the nightmares that had haunted her. "It felt so real," she confessed, her voice a tremor of vulnerability. "The pain, the heartache... I thought I was reliving that moment all over again."

In that shared moment of vulnerability and understanding, the bonds of their connection deepened—a testament to the enduring strength of their love, even in the face of the darkest of dreams.

In the tranquil embrace of Ong's arms, Keisha felt a profound sense of security, as if the storms of her dreams were held at bay by the strength of his unwavering presence. His hand moved with a soothing rhythm, his touch a tender caress upon her back as if to erase the lingering traces of her torment, like a gentle breeze that dissipates the storm.

"I promise you," Ong vowed, his voice resolute and filled with unwavering determination, "I will never leave you like that again. I should have turned back that day and regret not doing so every moment since. You, Keisha, are the heartbeat of my existence, and I will always fight for you."

"Keisha, her fragile breath steadying in the cocoon of Ong's embrace, allowed herself to release the weight of her sorrow. Tears stained Ong's shirt, a testament to her vulnerability. "I know you will," she whispered, her voice a tremulous admission. "It's just... the fear of losing you again, even in my dreams, it's overwhelming."

Ong, his resolve as unyielding as the mountains surrounding them, pulled back slightly to gaze into her eyes, their depths reflecting the unwavering certainty of his words. "You won't lose me," he declared, the strength in his voice an unbreakable bond. "Whatever challenges may come, we shall face them together."

A tender smile graced the corners of Keisha's lips, a beacon of hope in her emotional upheaval, like the first light breaking through the storm clouds. "I love you," she murmured an earnest declaration, brimming with genuine affection.

Ong's smile matched hers, a reflection of pure, unadulterated love that transcended words, their smiles radiating like a shared warmth that enveloped them. His fingers, like a gentle breeze, brushed away her lingering tears. "And I love you more than words can ever express."

As they held each other in that tranquil moment, the weight of the haunting dream began to fade, replaced by the reassuring certainty of their boundless love, like a dissipating mist yielding to the clarity of a serene morning. They found solace in each other's arms, their hearts committed and determined to face whatever obstacles the future might bring, knowing that their love was an unbreakable shield against the shadows of uncertainty."

Under the gentle caress of the dappled forest canopy, Keisha's gaze sought refuge in the depths of Ong's eyes. Like twin pools of uncertainty, her eyes held a silent plea for reassurance in their shimmering depths. With a hesitant tone, she broached the unsettling question that had gnawed at her soul.

"Do you think," she began, her voice a delicate melody tinged with worry, "that Vuarus is... controlling my nightmares?"

Amid the spotty play of sunlight and shadows within the ancient forest, Ong's features took on a contemplative cast. The memory of Kimras' warning, a dark prophecy about Vuarus seeking to influence Keisha through the realm of her nightmares insidiously, resurfaced in his mind like a specter. With a heavy sigh, he allowed his fingers to trace a gentle path along the curve of Keisha's cheek, the touch a tender reassurance amidst the gathering storm of doubt.

"Yes and no," he replied, his voice a measured reflection of the complexities surrounding them. "Vuarus, it seems, still hungers to fracture your spirit, and in his quest, he may well be manipulating your nightmares. But also," he continued, his gaze locked with hers, "there were nightmares and visions that you were subjected to during those months of captivity, and these memories have the power to weave themselves into your nightmares."

Keisha's shoulders sagged beneath the weight of the revelation, a realization that cast a long shadow over her spirit. "Even after Vuarus is gone," she lamented, her voice trembling with a poignant vulnerability, "these nightmares, especially when I sleep, may persist." Her voice wavered, and tears welled up in her eyes. "When will this all end?"

In the forest's heart, their love was a fragile beacon amidst the encroaching darkness, a poignant reminder of their struggles. And as Keisha wept, Ong held her close, his arms a sanctuary against the relentless tide of nightmares, a silent promise that together, they would find a way to navigate the labyrinthine corridors of her dreams and free her from the clutches of darkness.

Ong's grasp around Keisha tightened, his touch a soothing caress against her delicate skin. With a firm and comforting voice, he offered a glimmer of hope in the depths of their shared uncertainty. "But listen," he began, his tone carrying a quiet resolve, "I have an idea for tonight."

Keisha turned her gaze upon him, her eyes shimmering with a blend of curiosity and hope, her heart yearning for a reprieve from the relentless torment of her nightmares. "What is it?" she inquired, her voice a delicate melody that danced upon the breeze.

A small, tender smile graced Ong's lips as his thumb traced the elegant curve of her jawline. "Tonight," he murmured, his words imbued with a promise, "I shall hold you close as you slumber. Perhaps, just perhaps, if you feel safe and cherished in my embrace, the nightmares will lose some of their power."

Keisha's heart, nestled in the sanctuary of Ong's steadfast love, swelled with warmth, a sense of security enfolding her like the protective arms of the forest itself. "And if the nightmares return?" she inquired, her voice a whisper of vulnerability.

Ong met her gaze with unwavering determination, his eyes like twin beacons of steadfast resolve. "If I hear your cries or sense your distress," he vowed, "I shall wake you, my love. I shall not allow those nightmares to continue their haunting reign over you. You need rest, and I shall be your guardian against the tides of darkness."

In the heart of the forest, as the sunlight waned and the world surrendered to the embrace of night, their love became a beacon of hope, a testament to the enduring strength of their bond. And as Keisha nestled against Ong's chest, the promise of a night free from the clutches of nightmares held the promise of a new dawn, a reprieve from the relentless torment that had plagued her for too long.

Tears welled up in Keisha's eyes, but these tears were not born of fear this time but instead of the overwhelming love that surged within her, a love that transcended the confines of their world. In a moment of profound tenderness, she leaned in, her lips meeting Ong's in a gentle kiss that spoke of promises and shared journeys.

"Thank you," she whispered, her words a soft caress against his mouth, carrying with them the weight of her gratitude and the depth of her emotions.

Ong's arms, strong and unwavering, encircled her, drawing her close into a tender embrace that seemed to defy the encroaching darkness. "Always," he murmured his words a solemn vow, spoken against the canvas of her forehead. "I'll always be here for you."

As the day gradually surrendered to the velvety embrace of night, Ong and Keisha prepared to seek solace in the realm of dreams. The sun's warm, golden glow gave way to the silvery luminescence of the moon, casting an otherworldly radiance over their surroundings. Together, they retreated to the sanctuary of their chamber, where the boundaries between their world and the mystical realms of dreams blurred. Like veils drawn over the mysteries of the night, the curtains swayed gently in the evening breeze, and the scent of the forest's enchantment permeated the air. With each step, they drew closer to the intimate refuge of their shared slumber, where their love would stand as a guardian against the encroaching darkness.

In the heart of their shared chamber, where the boundaries between reality and dreams were as thin as gossamer threads, Ong's protective embrace proved an unyielding fortress against the encroaching nightmares. As Keisha's distress called out in the night, her voice a tremor of vulnerability, Ong responded with a tenderness that transcended the boundaries of the waking world.

His arms around her were a sanctuary, a haven where the storms of her nightmares could find no purchase. Like a gentle breeze through the ancient trees of their mystical realm, Ong's soothing whispers brushed against the edges of her consciousness, offering solace amidst the turmoil.

Slowly but surely, the disruption of Keisha's nightmare began to subside, its tumultuous waves giving way to the tranquil waters of peace. In Ong's loving embrace, she found herself cradled, the remnants of her torment fading like the dissipating shadows of night. The ethereal connection between them, a testament to the strength of their love, had once again thwarted the nightmares that sought to trap her.

As the night resumed its silent vigil, Keisha's slumber found respite, her dreams shifting away from the abyss of torment, and she remained nestled in the protective embrace of her beloved Ong. The night held its secrets, but for now, they had carved out their sanctuary amidst the enigma of dreams.

Their chamber took on a warm and ethereal glow in the soft embrace of the morning's first light. It appears the sun itself painted the room with hues of gold and amber, its gentle fingers caressing every surface. Roused from her slumber, Keisha wore a tender smile that blossomed like a fragile bloom under the sun's tender touch. Her gaze, filled with gratitude, fell upon Ong, whose presence had been her unwavering shield through the night.

She leaned in, her lips a whisper upon Ong's cheek, a wordless declaration of the profound love that had cradled her during the dark hours. "Thank you for being here, Ong," her voice, a delicate murmur, carried the weight of her appreciation, akin to the first rays of dawn piercing through the shroud of night.

Ong, his eyes like warm pools of affection, stirred and slowly opened them, locking his gaze with hers. "I'm glad you got some rest," he replied, touching her cheek as tenderly as the caress of a morning breeze. "It seems like the dream didn't trouble you as much this time."

Keisha's smile, like the sun's rays growing brighter, widened, and her fingers began to trace intricate patterns upon the canvas of Ong's chest. "I don't know how," she admitted, her words as soft as a cherished secret, "but at first, it was like all the other times. Yet, it all vanished when you pulled me closer and whispered. You being there made all the difference."

With a gentle grace, Ong leaned in, his lips brushing against her forehead in a kiss that radiated tenderness, like the sun's kiss upon the earth. "I'll always be here for you," he murmured, his words resonating through the chamber like an unbreakable promise forged in the crucible of their enduring love.

Amidst the quiet sanctuary of their chamber, where shadows danced with the whispers of forgotten enchantments, Keisha sought refuge in Ong's embrace, drawing close to him as if he were her anchor in a world awash with uncertainty. The room held its breath, the air thick with the echoes of their shared moments, a haven where time stood still.

Yet, despite the tranquil surroundings, the weight of Keisha's pain pressed upon her heart, casting a shadow that threatened to engulf her. It loomed like gathering storm clouds heavy with rain, promising a deluge of tears and sorrow. Her usually steady and resolute voice now trembled with the raw emotion that spilled from her heart.

"Ong," she began, her words cracking with the weight of the emotions that surged within her, "I'm not sure if all of this will ever fade. I'm uncertain if I'll ever be the person I once was." She nestled her head against his chest, her voice swallowed by the anguish that gripped her. "I used to think I couldn't be broken, but Vuarus shattered my spirit so completely that I wonder if I'll ever heal fully. There are times I don't even know who I am anymore."

With a shaky sigh, Keisha leaned back slightly, her gaze locking with Ong's, their eyes becoming mirrors of shared vulnerability. "Ong," she whispered, her voice trembling with the weight of her fears, "I'm scared."

Ong's warm and understanding smile touched his eyes as his thumb brushed away her tears as if wiping away the storm clouds that threatened to consume her. "Keisha," he said softly, his voice like a gentle breeze amid the turmoil, "that's perfectly understandable, and it's okay."

Nodding, Keisha allowed herself to be enveloped again in the reassuring embrace of Ong's arms. She knew the road to healing would be long and fraught with challenges, but it felt less daunting and more bearable with Ong by her side. Together, they would navigate the labyrinth of her healing, with the promise of a brighter dawn lighting their way through the darkest of nights. In the heart of E'vahano, a land touched by the delicate hand of magic and steeped in the lore of ages, a small chamber concealed its secrets beneath layers of ancient stone. Here, the leaders of the light gathered their presence, a beacon of hope in a world besieged by shadows. Ong, Karrenen, Keisha, and other brave souls, each bearing the weight of their roles as defenders of the realm, took their seats around a circular table. Before them, maps and plans unfurled like a canvas awaiting the brushstrokes of destiny. Though tense, the air within the chamber brimmed with an unwavering determination.

Karrenen, a figure of regal bearing and strength, leaned forward, his voice a steady clarion call amidst the palpable anticipation. "We stand but two days away from the battle for Vacari," he intoned, his words resonating solemnly. "How are our preparations advancing?"

Ong, a steadfast pillar of resolve, nodded in agreement, his eyes reflecting the spirit of a leader unyielding in the face of adversity. "We've dedicated ourselves to rigorous training," he replied, his voice carrying the resonance of authority, "strengthening our defenses and forging alliances with those who share our cause. The elven warriors, in particular, have displayed remarkable dedication, and I am confident they will be ready when the time comes."

In this chamber, where the threads of fate were woven, and the destinies of many converged, the leaders of the light steeled their hearts for the impending battle. They knew their unity and determination were their greatest weapons against the encroaching darkness. The world's weight rested upon their shoulders, and the land of E'vahano awaited the heroes who would champion its cause.

In the ancient tongue of the Eladrin, known for its lyrical cadence and ethereal beauty, Karrenen turned his gaze to Keisha, the words dripping like honey from his lips. "Keisha, melme nín," he spoke, his voice carrying the weight of a thousand years and the tenderness of a parent's love. "Manke lle ilqua?" ("Keisha, my beloved daughter, how are you holding up?")

As the words "beloved daughter" flowed from Karrenen's lips like a soothing melody, Keisha's gaze remained locked on his, her eyes glistening with the shimmering tears of a soul laid bare. In that tender moment, the weight of her emotions hung heavy in the air, like the fragility of a butterfly's wings against a storm.

Hesitation cast a brief shadow over her countenance, her heart wrestling with the tumultuous currents of her past. Yet, in that fleeting pause, she found the strength to be unflinchingly honest. Her voice, soft and trembling like a fragile leaf quivering in the breeze, broke the silence that enveloped them.

"It's been tough," she confessed her words like whispered secrets carried on the wind. "The nightmares and memories... haunt me, especially when I sleep."

In her vulnerability, Keisha bared her soul, revealing the wounds that still festered within her. The haunting specters of her past clung to her like relentless shadows, and in the sanctuary of this moment, she allowed herself to seek solace and understanding from those who had become her family.

Kimras, a dragon known for his calm composure, could no longer contain the surge of anger and frustration at the mere mention of Keisha's torment. His usual stoic demeanor gave way to a simmering intensity as he spoke, his voice a sword forged in the fires of righteous indignation.

"Vuarus went too far," Kimras declared, his words slicing through the air like a blade seeking justice. "Vuarus' motives were not born of vengeance; he required a sacrifice to fuel his evil transformation. Enough is enough."

Keisha glanced at Kimras, her brow furrowing with confusion and concern. "What do you mean? I thought it was all for Phoenix's revenge, and the sacrifice was part of that."

Karrenen met her gaze, his expression somber. "No, not all of it. When you were captured, we believed it was for revenge, but the more we learned, the more questions we had, so we investigated what was happening. Vuarus needed a sacrifice to retain his godhead, and you had a special connection to nature. Your heritage and elemental magic were too much for Vuarus to ignore. He gave Phoenix what he wanted, but it was his plan all along to sacrifice you."

A shiver ran down Keisha's spine as the weight of Karrenen's words settled upon her. She turned her head toward the floor, her voice trembling as she processed the grim truth. "So, all that happened was for him to continue to be a god, even giving my magic to the abyss?"

Keisha's heart trembled within her chest as she absorbed the revelation. She had believed for so long that her suffering was merely a pawn in Phoenix's quest for revenge. To learn that it was all part of Vuarus's dark plan, that her very essence had been sought after for its power and connection to nature, sent a shiver down her spine. The magnitude of the deception was staggering, leaving her with a profound sense of betrayal.

Karrenen nodded solemnly, understanding the turmoil that gripped Keisha's heart. He motioned to Ong, who approached and gently pulled her into his arms, holding her close. Ong's presence was a source of comfort amid the revelation.

Karrenen turned back to Kimras, his tone resolute. "We won't allow him to perpetuate this darkness," he affirmed, his voice a pledge of unwavering resolve. "We are committed to ending his reign of terror."

With the weight of their collective purpose hanging in the balance, Karrenen, the venerable leader, concluded the meeting. Like a rallying cry, his words echoed through the chamber, carrying the strength and determination of those who had chosen to stand against the encroaching shadows.

"Let us press onward," Karrenen declared, his voice a beacon of unwavering faith. "We shall demonstrate to the Abyssal Dominion that they cannot shatter our spirit. The battle for Vacari will mark a turning point in our struggle."

Chapter 48

Shadows Unveiled: Eldrion's Gambit

Vuarus surveyed the city from his vantage point, a web of intrigue and control spun with malevolent threads binding the city to his dark will. Despite his outward demeanor of confidence, an invisible undercurrent of unease marred the perfection of his countenance. The ominous silhouette of the Dread Spire echoed the turbulence within his mind.

In the heart of this twisted citadel, Vuarus confronted the unsettling truth that fueled his unease. Keisha, the intended sacrifice, had eluded his grasp during a daring rescue. Her unique connection to nature and elemental magic made her essential to retaining his godhead, and the nightmares crafted to break her spirit were a crucial element of his sinister plan. As the sun dipped below the horizon, casting the city in a crimson embrace, Vuarus's gaze remained riveted to the panorama below. Like twin orbs of obsidian, his eyes betrayed no emotion, but within his calculating mind, a storm of thoughts and feelings churned.

With a decisive turn, he departed from his contemplative perch, striding with purposeful steps toward the uppermost level of the Dread Spire. His footfalls echoed through the labyrinthine corridors, resonating with the weight of his vexation and the turbulent sea of thoughts that roiled within him. The path ahead was uncertain, and Vuarus, the master of shadows, faced a future filled with ominous warnings and looming challenges.

"How could she resist that dream?" he seethed, his voice a low, evil hiss that resonated with the acrid taste of thwarted power. "It has grown stronger, more vivid, and yet she defies it. This is not how it's meant to be. She should be broken, a vessel for the Abyss. The rescue thwarted the sacrifice, and her defiance threatens everything."

Within the confines of the foreboding chamber, adorned with obsidian motifs that seemed to writhe with an otherworldly energy, Vuarus sought solace in contemplating his predicament. The very walls seemed to absorb the weight of his dissatisfaction, whispering echoes of ancient secrets that reverberated through the corridors of the Spire.

In the depths of his musings, Vuarus acknowledged that Keisha's resilience posed a formidable challenge. Her indomitable will, a beacon of light within the shadowy realm he sought to control, fueled the flames of his obsession. The battle of wills between them had become a clandestine war, waged in the unseen recesses of the Dread Spire, and Vuarus felt the relentless pull of an adversary who refused to succumb to the abyss.

A sinister glint flickered in Vuarus's obsidian eyes as he paced the darkened chamber. Plans of manipulation and coercion churned within his evil mind, each scheme more insidious than the last. The elusive shadows that slipped through his grasp would not elude him for long. He plotted his next move with renewed determination, bringing Keisha to the precipice of despair, where the shadows converged to consume even the strongest spirits.

The air in the Dread Spire crackled with dark energy, a precursor of the evil designs that brewed within its walls. The battle of wills between Vuarus and Keisha reached a fevered pitch, setting the stage for a confrontation that would shape the destiny of Vacari itself.

His mind was a cauldron of evil intent, concocted schemes that unfolded like dark tapestries. Each thread is intricately woven into the narrative of his sinister machinations. The Heart of Twilight, an elusive artifact with the power to unravel the very essence of E'vahona, remained the linchpin of his grand design.

As the shadows clung to him like loyal servants, Vuarus extended his influence across the mystical realms. Whispers of impending doom echoed through the unseen corridors of E'vahona, a prelude to the vicious storm that threatened to engulf all in its path.

"I shall draw her closer to the precipice," Vuarus murmured, his voice a serpent's hiss in the silent chamber. "The Heart of Twilight will be unveiled, and with it, my ascendancy to a plane of power beyond imagination."

With arcane symbols etched in the air, Vuarus enacted rituals that transcended the boundaries of morality. The very foundations of Vacari quivered as his dark sorcery unfolded, setting in motion events reverberating across the realms.

Within the dimly lit recesses of the Dread Spire, Vuarus paced with restless energy, a figure adrift in the turbulent sea of his thoughts. The weight of his onerous responsibilities bore down upon him like an impossible burden, and the imminent battle loomed like a colossal storm on the horizon. As he muttered to himself, the approaching footsteps of Phoenix, his unwavering partner in their evil pursuits, heralded the intrusion into his solitude.

"Vuarus," Phoenix inquired, his voice a low rumble that resonated with the darkness surrounding them. "Have you unraveled the mystery of breaking her yet? Last night's nightmare... she appeared... different."

Vuarus stopped pacing and turned to regard Phoenix, his eyes betraying a palpable frustration that simmered beneath the surface. "No," he retorted curtly, his voice tinged with impatience. "I haven't. And do not concern yourself with her nightmares; they serve to bring an end. Focus on your assigned tasks, for our time is running out."

In the suffocating gloom of the chamber, their shared determination to achieve their evil ambitions remained unwavering, even as uncertainty and trepidation shadowed their every move.

Phoenix's eyes bore into Vuarus, a defiant glint sparking in his gaze like a smoldering ember in the depths of a raging fire. "We are bound in this endeavor, Vuarus," he declared, his voice resonating with a sense of stubborn defiance. "I won't allow myself to be dismissed as a mere lackey."

Vuarus's strained patience finally snapped, and his words dripped with seething frustration. "Enough of this insubordination!" he thundered, his voice echoing through the chamber. "Time is a luxury we can no longer afford, and we must not yield to distractions. Focus on your designated role and trust that the rest will fall into place."

With a final, contemptuous glance, Phoenix turned sharply on his heel and stalked away, leaving Vuarus alone with his thoughts. As he watched Phoenix's retreating form, Vuarus's lips curled into a sardonic smile, a shadow of amusement flickering in his eyes. "You believe us equals, Phoenix?" he mused softly, his voice tinged with scorn. "You, who were once consumed by a thirst for revenge so potent that you became nothing more than a pawn in my grand design."

In the oppressive ambiance of the chamber, Vuarus grappled with the complexities of their partnership, the tensions simmering beneath the surface, and the knowledge that their dark plans rested on the precipice of culmination.

The chamber, adorned with sinister symbols and bathed in a dim, otherworldly light, seemed to constrict around Vuarus as he paced. Shadows danced with the uncertainty that permeated the air, amplifying the sense of urgency and desperation.

As Qellaun, a loyal operative of the Abyssal Dominion, entered the room, the atmosphere tensed further. His face bore the weight of frustration as he delivered the disheartening report. "Lord Vuarus," Qellaun began, his voice laced with palpable frustration, "we have scoured the perimeters of New Flameford tirelessly, yet we have found no trace of the elusive Heart of Twilight."

Vuarus's jaw clenched in response to the news, his temper simmering beneath the surface like molten lava awaiting release. The notion that the artifact had vanished challenged his belief in his mastery of uncovering hidden treasures. Phoenix, standing nearby, echoed the frustration. "Are you telling me, the one heralded as the Abyssal Dominion's foremost expert in locating concealed artifacts, that you have returned empty-handed?" His voice bore the weight of both anger and disappointment. "Return to your task, Qellaun, and do not return until you have something of substance to report."

Qellaun's face paled in response to the unforgiving command, and he hurriedly exited the chamber. Vuarus's grip on his emotions tightened as he watched the operative's swift departure. The mounting pressure weighed heavily on his shoulders, and with every setback, a sense of desperation and urgency swelled within him.

As Vuarus resumed his restless pacing within the dimly lit chamber, the atmosphere seemed to constrict around him, suffused with an ever-darkening storm of uncertainty, determination, and unrelenting desperation that threatened to consume all in its path.

In a chamber illuminated only by the flickering glow of candles, its walls lined with ancient tomes and scrolls, Lyra was engrossed in her relentless pursuit of knowledge. The elusive location of the Heart of Twilight had eluded them for far too long, and she had become resolute in her mission to decipher the cryptic clues that the scroll she held contained.

Her fingers moved precisely, tracing the intricate lines of text etched onto the aged parchment. Each twist and curve of the script carried a weight of significance, and as she delved deeper into her task, her eyes widened in sudden realization. It was as if the disparate pieces of a jigsaw puzzle were finally falling into place. Once scattered and elusive, the evidence now converged upon a singular conclusion – the Heart of Twilight lay concealed within the waters surrounding New Flameford. A complex mix of emotions enveloped her, a blend of relief and trepidation, as she unraveled the intricate threads of the mystery.

Yet, her solitude was abruptly shattered as swift footsteps approached. The arrival of two formidable figures, Vuarus and Phoenix, their presence filling the room with an intense purpose, disrupted the chamber's tranquility.

The chamber, bathed in the flickering glow of candles, emitted an ancient scent of parchment. Shadows danced across the walls, adorned with mystical symbols, creating an atmosphere steeped in arcane knowledge.

"Lyra, any progress?" Vuarus inquired, his voice betraying a sense of urgency that mirrored the gravity of their situation.

Lyra's gaze lifted from her detailed work, her expression a manifestation of her unwavering determination tinged with the weariness of her efforts. "The location of the Heart of Twilight lies within the waters surrounding New Flameford."

Phoenix's sharp eyes narrowed, suspicion etched across his features. "Are you certain? We've combed those waters exhaustively in search of it. You must be sure."

Lyra's sigh carried both a burden of responsibility and the weight of her honesty. "I've cross-referenced the information from multiple sources. The evidence aligns with this conclusion. But I cannot guarantee its absolute accuracy."

Vuarus's patience wore thin, his frustration manifesting as palpable tension in the chamber. "We cannot afford to be wrong, Lyra. This mission hinges on your interpretation."

"I understand," Lyra replied, her voice unwavering. "I've done all within my power to decipher these enigmatic clues. The rest now lies in your hands."

Phoenix's anger simmered beneath the surface, but he nodded curtly, the severity of the situation leaving no room for further debate. "Very well. If your interpretation proves incorrect, you will bear the consequences."

As the two enigmatic figures left the candlelit chamber, Lyra returned her unwavering focus to her daunting task. The weight of their mission bore heavily upon her, and the knowledge that the fate of their endeavors hinged upon her ability to decipher ancient texts weighed upon her shoulders. Her fervent hope was that her tireless efforts would bear fruit and lead them to the long-sought Heart of Twilight, concealed within the depths of the waters near New Flameford.

Beneath the undulating waves of Coraluna, the mermen of this mystical realm glided with mesmerizing grace, their sleek forms merging harmoniously with the ever-shifting currents. Coral formations of every hue adorned the underwater landscape, casting a vibrant kaleidoscope of colors that danced with the play of light filtering through the water.

Among them swam Aqilus, Oceanus's most trusted confidant and a revered authority figure in Merfolk society. His keen eyes scoured the vicinity surrounding New Flameford, where the relentless Druchii forces tirelessly explored the watery depths.

Concealed amidst the vivid coral formations, Aqilus and his fellow merfolk observed their adversaries with vigilance. The sight of the Druchii invaders filled them with a potent mixture of anxiety and steely determination. Maintaining absolute silence, they communicated through a language of subtle gestures and fluid motions, a dance of understanding that only the keenest of observers could decipher.

As the Druchii continued their methodical search, Aqilus narrowed his eyes, his gaze locked on their every move. The invaders sought something of profound significance beneath the waves, and the thoroughness of their pursuit suggested an object of immense value and desire.

With a series of intricate signals, Aqilus silently communicated with his fellow merfolk, and together, they retreated stealthily, putting a safe distance between themselves and the prying eyes of the Druchii. Once they had distanced themselves adequately, Aqilus signaled for a peaceful gathering.

"We have gathered enough intelligence," Aqilus whispered urgently, his voice tinged with purpose. "The Druchii are searching for something here, something they hold in great esteem. They leave no stone unturned in their quest."

Thalorin, a merman warrior of renowned courage, spoke up. "Should we not engage them, divert their attention?"

Aqilus shook his head thoughtfully. "Not yet. Our priority is to amass more information and decipher their true intentions. This discovery may be intertwined with their grander designs, and we must proceed cautiously."

Another merman, his eyes reflecting the collective resolve of his kin, spoke up inquiringly. "What steps should we take, then?"

Aqilus held their collective attention, his tone unwavering and purposeful. "We shall return to Coraluna immediately and convey everything we have witnessed to King Oceanus and the leaders of our alliance. They must know these developments and prepare for any conceivable outcome."

With synchronized movements and unspoken understanding, the merfolk dispersed soundlessly, their lithe forms melding into the aquatic environment. Aqilus propelled himself toward the water's surface, his thoughts consumed by the impending battle and the enigmatic motives of the Druchii. His unwavering commitment ensured that their allies would be armed with crucial knowledge and poised to confront any challenges on the horizon.

Aqilus, King Oceanus's right hand and a cornerstone of the alliance, reached out to deliver the urgent message concerning the Druchii's activities in the waters near New Flameford. King Oceanus's heartfelt gratitude resonated through their conversation as he expressed his appreciation for Aqilus's invaluable insights. Following their exchange, Aqilus returned to Coraluna, resuming his preparations alongside his fellow merfolk, ready to face the impending storm with unwavering determination.

As Ong received the message from King Oceanus, his thoughts surged forward like a relentless tide. With unwavering determination, he navigated the regal corridors of the kingdom, each step echoing with a sense of purpose. The weight of the impending battle for Vacari pressed upon his mind, an ever-present presence that refused to be ignored. In the intricate dance of warfare, Ong understood that every shard of knowledge, regardless of its perceived insignificance, could shift the balance in their favor.

In the solemn grandeur of the Council Chambers, Ong's presence was a harbinger of important tidings. His gaze was unwavering, finding its mark in Karrenen, who was deeply engrossed in the intricate details sprawled across scrolls and maps. Without hesitation, Ong shared the valuable information Aqilus had conveyed, the words falling from his lips like water from a pristine spring.

Yet, as he delivered the intelligence, he detected an unexpected glint in Karrenen's eyes, a mischievous spark that hinted at something more. Then, as if erupting from a hidden wellspring of humor, Karrenen burst into laughter, his joy catching Ong off guard. Confusion danced across Ong's features, his brows furrowing for understanding. He couldn't help but voice his words heavy with curiosity, "What's so amusing?"

Karrenen's laughter lingered, his eyes glistening with merriment as he finally regained his composure. With a gentle swipe, he brushed away a tear from the corner of his eye and began to explain. "Lord Eldrion played a little trick on the Druchii. He crafted a false scroll filled with misleading information about the Heart of Twilight and cunningly placed it within their library." Ong's surprise deepened as he absorbed the revelation. "So, they're chasing after a phantom?

Eldrion knew they might set their sights on the Heart, and he baited them with a trail of falsehoods?"

Karrenen nodded, his amusement still evident but gradually subsiding. "Precisely, my dear friend. It's a clever stratagem to keep them entangled in a web of deception while we fortify our preparations."

A faint smile tugged at the corners of Ong's lips. "Well, I suppose a touch of artful trickery in our favor is a welcome twist."

Karrenen's grin widened, his eyes twinkling with shared amusement. "At times, a well-timed jest can be as potent a weapon as any blade."

The specter of the impending battle briefly lightened in their camaraderie and the unexpected fun. The alliance, united by purpose, had woven bonds that transcended the heaviness of war, and even in grave peril, the spark of shared humor and resolve remained undiminished.

Chapter 49

Shadows Unveiled: Gathering Storms

The fading light of day bathed the ancient city of E'vahona in a warm, ethereal glow as Ong made his way through the winding streets. The air was thick with anticipation, and the whispers of a thousand secrets seemed to linger in every corner, like ancient echoes of forgotten lore.

Ong's footsteps echoed softly against the cobblestone pathways as he journeyed home. Each step resonated with a sense of purpose and weighed heavily with the gravity of his responsibilities. The looming battle for Vacari, the enigma of the Heart of Twilight, and the fate of the realm itself hung in the balance, casting a shadow over his thoughts.

Upon reaching their dwelling, Ong pushed open the ornate doors that led into the tranquil haven he and Keisha had crafted together. The interior was adorned with vibrant tapestries that came alive with the play of fading daylight, delicate sculptures that whispered of forgotten tales, and the soft glow of enchanting crystals that cast intricate light patterns across the room, painting the walls with dancing colors.

The distant melody of wind chimes played a gentle harmony with the rustling leaves outside, and the subtle fragrance of exotic flowers wafted through the air. Ong took a moment to breathe in the familiar scents of home, a mixture of comforting warmth and the subtle traces of magic that permeated their sanctuary.

With a sigh, Ong shed the armor of duty, each piece clinking softly as it settled, and he found solace in the familiar embrace of their bed. The cool and inviting sheets cradled him, and the plush pillows offered a momentary respite from the burdens of leadership that weighed upon his shoulders. In this moment of reprieve, he longed for the warmth of Keisha's presence, her soothing touch, and the comfort of her unwavering love that had carried them through countless trials.

As the moon began its ascent, casting a silvery sheen over the room, Ong closed his eyes. His thoughts turned toward the promise of rest, a precious commodity in turbulent times, and the hope that the coming day would bring clarity and strength to face the challenges ahead. Beside him, the space Keisha occupied remained empty, awaiting her return, their dreams intertwined with a shared determination to stand firm against the encroaching shadows.

Time slipped by in restless silence until, at last, she returned, her steps hesitant as she slipped beneath the covers. Exhaustion quickly claimed her, pulling her into a fitful sleep.

The tension hung thick in the dimly lit chamber, mingling with the remnants of Keisha's unsettling nightmare. Shadows danced upon the walls, casting eerie silhouettes that mirrored the unease within her, their twisting forms like specters of her fears.

Keisha's breaths gradually steadied as the reassuring touch of Ong's hand on her cheek brought her back from the brink of her nightmarish reverie. His eyes, pools of unwavering concern, met hers in the semi-darkness, a beacon of solace amidst the tumultuous sea of her thoughts.

For a moment, silence enveloped them, broken only by the soft rustling of sheets as they shifted closer, seeking the warmth of each other's presence. The room retained a faint scent of lavender, calming the residual tension that lingered in the air. Keisha could feel the gentle rise and fall of Ong's chest, a comforting rhythm that anchored her in the here and now, like the steady heartbeat of their shared love.

"I... I'm okay," Keisha finally whispered, her voice trembling but filled with gratitude for Ong's unwavering support. The chill of the nightmare still clung to her skin, but Ong's presence acted like a soothing balm. "It was just a nightmare, a bad one."

Ong's thumb caressed her cheek soothingly, a balm to her frazzled nerves. "I'm here, Keisha," he murmured, his words a promise, a gentle affirmation that she wasn't alone in facing these haunting nightmares.

With the weight of her distress shared between them, Keisha nestled into Ong's embrace, finding solace in the warmth of his love. As they lay together in the quiet of the night, the haunting remnants of her dream slowly dissipated. Replaced by the reassurance of Ong's presence by her side, it was like a protective shield against the darkness that sought to intrude.

In the calm stillness of their shared moment, Keisha's tears flowed freely, dampening the fabric of Ong's comforting embrace. Each tear, a testament to the lingering torment of her dream, found solace in the warmth of his chest, like raindrops seeking refuge in the shelter of a gentle tree.

Ong, the steadfast guardian of her heart, cradled her gently, his arms offering a sanctuary from the haunting specters that had invaded her slumber. His touch, a soothing balm, whispered promises of protection and love, reassuring her that she was not adrift in the abyss of her nightmares.

Amidst the soft cries that escaped her trembling lips, Keisha's vulnerability found refuge in Ong's unwavering devotion. His embrace held her close, a lifeline to reality amidst the disorienting dreamscapes that had threatened to pull her under.

"I just wish these would stop," she confessed, her voice laden with heartache. "This one was different; everything was gone, and I was given to the Abyss this time with no one to help me."

Ong's eyes, deep pools of empathy and strength, glistened with a profound understanding. He leaned closer, bridging the emotional chasm that had opened within her, and whispered soothing words that flowed like a gentle river of comfort. "I'm here, Keisha," he promised, his voice a lifeline. "It was just a nightmare. I won't let anything happen to you."

She leaned into his protective embrace, the contours of his body fitting seamlessly against hers as if they were two pieces of a puzzle meant to be joined together. Ong's steady heartbeat became the rhythm of her reassurance, each pulsation a testament to his unwavering presence.

"I know," Keisha breathed, quivering but resolute, "You're here. I just... it felt so real."

Ong gently kissed her furrowed brow with tenderness, a silent vow that spoke louder than words. "I'm not going anywhere, Keisha. You're safe with me." As a soft smile graced Keisha's lips, the room embraced the serenity of their shared moment, a sanctuary against the lingering shadows.

Their embrace persisted as a sanctuary against the residual tremors of the dream that had gripped her so fiercely. Gradually, Keisha's heartbeat returned to its natural cadence, and she clung to Ong like a shipwrecked sailor finding refuge on solid ground. In the cocoon of his love, she began to navigate her way back from the abyss of her fear, the darkness receding in the face of their shared light.

As moments passed, the nightmare's remnants dissipated like morning mists, gradually surrendering to the radiant warmth of Ong's unwavering presence. Keisha's breathing steadied, the quiver in her limbs receding. She looked up at him, her eyes reflecting a kaleidoscope of gratitude and love.

"Thank you," she whispered, her words laden with the profound emotion that swelled within her.

Ong's smile was a beacon of light in the night, his fingers tenderly brushing away the strands of her hair that clung to her cheeks. "Always, Keisha," he vowed, "I'll always be here for you."

In that tender embrace, they found solace in each other's arms, like two warriors ready to face the challenges of their shared path. The nightmare had shaken her, but Ong's presence was a reminder that together, they could brave any storm that sought to test the depths of their love, their bond unbreakable in the face of adversity.

In the shadows of the dimly lit chamber, Vuarus reveled in satisfaction curling his lips into a sinister smirk. The culmination of his recent machinations had yielded the results he craved, a fleeting sense of gratification coursing through his veins. Each delicate thread of his elaborate design wove together seamlessly, an intricate tapestry of malevolence.

His plans, etched with meticulous calculation, remained shrouded in obscurity, a labyrinthine puzzle of deceit and manipulation. With measured steps, he ventured closer to the towering window, gazing upon the sprawling city of New Flameford below.

The city, a living, breathing entity, buzzed with activity, unaware of the sinister forces coiled within its heart. Vuarus surveyed his dominion, eyes gleaming with a veneer of confidence masking the turbulent maelstrom of emotions beneath.

As Twilight's crimson fingers brushed across the cityscape in this pivotal moment, he felt an undeniable surge of self-assuredness. The shadows he had masterfully harnessed responded to his will, coalescing around him like a loyal legion of darkness ready to execute his every command.

Everything, he mused silently, was aligning perfectly, like stars in the night sky forming a constellation of malefic intent. The city below was but a pawn in the grand tapestry of his ambitions, and the threads of fate drew tighter, trapping all who dared to stand in his path.

In the heart of the Hidden Isles, the alliance's leaders convened in secrecy, an air of steadfast determination enveloping the clandestine gathering. The final preparations for the imminent battle surged ahead, the very atmosphere pulsating with the gravity of their impending task. At the forefront stood Kimras, the magnificent Golden Dragon, whose presence alone commanded the respect of all.

As the murmurs of anticipation yielded to a palpable silence, Kimras raised his voice, its resonant tones cutting through the chamber. His words, laden with the weight of destiny, swept over the diverse assembly of races united against the Dominion.

"We've poured over our plans tirelessly," Kimras began, his voice unwavering. "Our objective remains crystal clear: to shatter the Dominion's iron grip on our lands and end their nefarious reign of shadows." His gaze, a reflection of a thousand battles, surveyed the gathered leaders.

Adding sagacious insight, Karrenen, the venerable Eladrin elder, spoke, "Success hinges upon our unity and synchrony. We must strike at the heart of the Dominion's power, securing the release of Talleoss from his captivity. With the aid of the captured archon, our forces will find new strength."

King Alex of Goldmoor, joined the discourse, his eyes ablaze with determination. "The merfolks will veil our approach, concealing us from prying eyes. We shall employ every tactical advantage to infiltrate the stronghold of New Flameford."

Queen Aeliana, the ethereal ruler of the nymphs, her voice as melodic as a forest's sigh, chimed in. "Our magic shall sow confusion amidst the enemy ranks, sowing discord and thwarting their efforts to beckon the denizens of the Abyss."

As deliberations continued, the unspoken understanding among the leaders became tangible – this battle was a last stand, a desperate gambit against impossible odds. The Dominion's forces loomed dark and formidable, the odds uncertain.

Nevertheless, each leader bore the weight of their world's destiny, resolved to give every ounce of their being to ensure its salvation.

Beneath the tapestry of tactical discussions and shared resolve, the unspoken truth lingered like a haunting melody: the outcome of this battle was the linchpin upon which their world's fate was delicately balanced. As the sun descended over the Hidden Isles, casting long, looming shadows upon the gathered council, the alliance's leaders stood united, their hearts steeled for the storm of darkness that awaited them.

As the weighty meeting concluded, Ong and Keisha strolled side by side, their footsteps echoing in the quiet aftermath of deliberations. The Hidden Isles embraced the twilight with an amber aura, a canvas of anticipation for the trials ahead. The air carried the scent of salt from the nearby sea, and a gentle breeze whispered through the leaves, stirring a symphony of rustling leaves.

Approaching the towering figure of Kimras, the radiant golden dragon, Ong and Keisha felt the weight of the impending struggle settle upon their shoulders. The dragon's scales gleamed like molten gold in the fading sunlight, and his eyes, deep pools of ancient wisdom, met theirs with a mixture of assurance and gravity.

In that quiet moment beneath the fading daylight, Ong's hand found Keisha's fingers intertwining in a silent affirmation of shared strength. Their gaze met Kimras's, and an unspoken understanding passed between them, a recognition that the threads of this imminent conflict now bound their destinies together.

Now, a mere sliver on the horizon, the sun painted the sky in fiery orange and dusky purple hues. The Hidden Isles, with its secrets woven into the fabric of its land, stood witness to the unity forged in the crucible of impending adversity. The alliance, each member carrying the weight of their realm's hopes, stood poised on the brink of destiny, ready to face the encroaching darkness with hearts ablaze.

Approaching the colossal dragon, Ong cleared his throat. His voice, threaded with apprehension, reverently addressed the regal creature. "Kimras, during the battle, when Keisha rides upon your back, I implore you to exercise utmost vigilance in her protection. Vuarus and Phoenix will make her a target once they discern her presence. Vuarus would spare no expense to fulfill his sinister designs."

Kimras lowered his gaze, ancient eyes reflecting wisdom forged in the crucible of time. "I share your concerns, Ong," he responded, a sonorous rumble carrying the weight of ages. "Keisha's role in this battle is pivotal, and the Abyssal Dominion will not hesitate to exploit any vulnerabilities they perceive."

Keisha nodded, determination unyielding despite trepidation in her eyes. "Ong, I understand I won't be fighting this time, but I must be there to witness the culmination, especially..."

Ong drew her close, enfolding her in a comforting embrace. "We shall stand with you every step of the way," he affirmed, gaze unwavering. Turning back to Kimras, sincerity edged his voice. "I have faith in your strength and capabilities, Kimras. Understand that she means the world to me."

Kimras inclined his massive head in solemn acknowledgment, a glint of affection gleaming in his ageless eyes. "Rest assured, Ong. I shall exert every ounce of my power to ensure her safety. She is protected as long as she rides upon my back."

"The path that lay ahead twisted through treacherous terrain, each step a challenge mirrored by the daunting odds they faced. Despite the harsh reality of their mission, the leaders and warriors of the alliance moved forward with hearts beating as one—a resounding declaration that they would not yield to the encroaching darkness. The destiny of Vacari hung in the balance, teetering between salvation and annihilation, and they stood undaunted against the storm that awaited.

When venturing deeper into the desolate heart of Afor, where desolation reigned supreme, the terrain would grow harsher, reflecting the grim nature of their mission. Yet, their unbreakable bond remained a beacon of hope amidst the encroaching shadows. Each step forward testified to their unwavering commitment, carving a path through the heart of adversity."

Darkness embraced the land as the sun's final rays dipped below the horizon. However, within the hearts of these warriors, a fierce light burned—a light that would pierce the abyss and usher in a new dawn for Vacari. The battle for the realm had begun, and they were prepared to face whatever horrors awaited, united and unwavering in their quest for victory.

The hours leading up to the fateful clash were tense, a palpable sense of destiny hanging heavy in the air. The alliance's leaders, warriors, and beings of all races converged on the edge of the Abyssal Dominion's stronghold, their eyes fixed on the looming darkness concealing their adversaries.

The flames of determination burned brighter than ever in their hearts, a fierce commitment to justice and retribution. They had come not only to reclaim Vacari but to deliver a resounding message to the Abyssal Dominion: that they would pay dearly for the suffering inflicted upon Keisha, and that their tyranny would be ended.

Ong, bearing the weight of his own vendetta, knew that he was not alone in his quest for vengeance. The support and unity of the alliance were a testament to their shared resolve, a formidable force ready to confront the hostility lurking within the Abyss.

As the ultimate moments before the battle drew near, their collective determination grew stronger, a mighty storm of purpose ready to be unleashed upon the forces of darkness. The destiny of Vacari hung in the balance, and the alliance stood prepared to rewrite the narrative, to emerge victorious and cast aside the shadow of the Abyssal Dominion finally.

Chapter 50

Shadows Unveiled: Battle for Vacari

Keisha's breaths came in shallow gasps, each a fragile whisper of life amidst the somber aftermath ravaging her spirit. The heart of E'vahona, once a sanctuary of serenity, now throbbed with the muted cadence of war—a rhythm harmonizing with the haunting echoes of her captivity. She was standing beside Ong, her once-majestic form now trembling, the remnants of her former strength flickering like a candle battling a storm. His grasp on her hand transcended mere assurance; it was a lifeline, anchoring her to a world that had nearly slipped into the abyss.

Though freedom had been wrested from the clutches of her tormentors, the invisible shackles of her suffering continued to weigh upon her—oppressive as the impending conflict that cast its ominous shadow over Vacari. Ong, her unwavering protector, recognized that the battlefield was no place for Keisha in her current state. Her magic drained, her essence siphoned by unspeakable cruelty, yet her determination to stand shoulder-to-shoulder with her allies remained unbroken. As the majestic Kimras cut through the turbulent skies, a gilded symbol of their last hope, Ong acted with the utmost care, guiding Keisha gently to the margins of safety. The golden dragon's descent stirred the air, a display of powerful grace contrasting starkly with the fragility of their circumstances. Kimras landed with an air of sovereignty that whispered of ancient legacies, standing as a symbol of hope amidst Keisha's newfound fragility."

The decision needed no words. With tender reverence, Ong lifted Keisha, her body feeling weightless in the aftermath of her torment, and placed her upon the warm, scaled sanctuary of Kimras' back. Her voice, a fragile murmur scarred by her imprisonment's shadows, carried her fear and her apology. "I'm sorry, Ong. They left me less than I was."

The kiss that Ong placed upon her brow was a quiet act of defiance against her captors' malevolent intent to shatter her spirit. "There's nothing to forgive, Keisha," he whispered against her skin, his words serving as a balm to heal her fractured soul. "Your strength is not measured by might alone, but by the enduring flame of your heart, which still beats, unyielding." He turned to the dragon, his gaze filled with unwavering trust. "She is my heart's unquenched flame, Kimras. In your guardianship, she remains the beacon of our lives."

In that poignant moment, as E'vahona braced itself for the impending storm, Keisha, cradled by the dragon and cherished by her beloved, became the living embodiment of Vacari's resilience—wounded, yet indomitable.

Kimras's response carried the solemn weight of an oath, and his nod wove an unbreakable vow into the very fabric of the world. "She shall be my charge, as precious to me as the very jewels that adorn my hoard," he rumbled, his voice a resonant thrum that echoed with the certainty of mountains themselves. "Now, we must cast ourselves into the fray, for the threads of fate are taut with the tension of the coming storm."

With a regal grace that defied the urgency of their departure, Kimras stretched his wings, each one a magnificent tapestry woven with the ethereal light of a thousand dawns. The very air yielded to him, parting with a whispered reverence as, with a mighty downbeat, he and Keisha ascended into the vast sky. Below them, Ong stood alone, a solitary figure gazing skyward, his silhouette etched in unyielding determination.

As they climbed higher, the world below transformed, evolving from a mosaic of fear and hope, of impending chaos and the silent prayers of warriors, into a rich tapestry of emerald greens and gleaming golds. Keisha, her grasp firm yet gentle on the reins, became more than a mere passenger; she embodied Vacari's heart ascending to meet its destiny. And Kimras, with the majestic rhythm of his wings, composed a wordless hymn to the courage that awaited their arrival.

The fragile threads of destiny that held Vacari in precarious balance now quivered under the imminent clash, a symphony of powers rising like the prelude to an epic saga. The air held its breath, charged with potent magic and the raw emotions of warriors teetering on the precipice.

A harmonious tapestry of arcane energies pulsed through the atmosphere as the Nymphs of Ardinia, guided by the venerable Queen Aeliana, cast their luminous gaze across the battlefield. Their presence emanated serene authority, a stark counterpoint to the turbulent aggression unfurling around them. With whispers that melded seamlessly with the world's life force, they embarked on their ancient and intricate incantations, invoking the very power of the earth beneath their feet.

The once-quiet land responded with an intimate rumble, the soil, and roots echoing in harmony with the Nymphs' will. Indigo brilliance surged through the foliage, a silent battle cry of nature itself. Above, the heavens draped themselves in obscurity, the moon's glow smothered by the sudden gathering of clouds, as if night sought to claim dominion over the impending conflict. In response to the Nymphs' call, the sea between Old Flameford and New Flameford churned with newfound ferocity. The Nymphs' chants intermingled with the gale, weaving a symphony of sound that danced with the escalating winds, summoning a deluge that descended like crystalline shards upon the earth.

This mystical shroud, spun by the Nymphs' deft hands, became an enigmatic puzzle concealed within the storm. This riddle sowed confusion and doubt among the ranks of the encroaching Abyssal Dominion. The darkened sky and the intensifying tempest were the Nymphs' masterpieces, their spells casting shadows of uncertainty and discord among the enemy's lines.

In the heart of the vortex, the Abyssal forces converging on New Flameford found themselves challenged by the untamed fury of nature. Some, fleet and fortunate, managed to navigate the aquatic chaos, but many were not so fortunate. The whirlpool, a formidable guardian conjured by the Nymphs, served as both shield and spear, disrupting the enemy's advance, and consuming them within its voracious maw.

Amidst the storm's furious onslaught, King Alex and his resolute Goldmoor legions waited patiently, their vessels concealed within the storm's tumultuous embrace. This natural tempest, an ephemeral cloak, shielded them from the watchful eyes of the Abyssal Dominion's sentries stationed in New Flameford. The merfolk's artful ruse played a pivotal role, expertly diverting the enemy's attention and paving the clandestine path for the Goldmoor fleet's advance.

As the storm raged with unrestrained ferocity, King Alex's armada commenced their stealthy approach, capitalizing on the chaotic sea to shroud their movements. His eyes, ablaze with unwavering determination, remained fixed on the distant coastline, fully aware that the impending engagement marked a potential turning point in the battle for their besieged world.

Yet the capricious sea, indifferent to their noble cause, churned with hostility, its towering waves a constant menace to their mission. In this moment of peril, Adrianna and Aqilus, connected intimately to the sea's denizens, sensed the dire straits of their comrades. With a breathtaking display of marine communication, they summoned the aid of the dolphins.

The dolphins sliced through the turbulent waters, their intelligent eyes alighted with shared determination. Guided by Adrianna and Aqilus, these swift denizens of the deep graciously accepted the entrusted ropes, towing the vessels with astonishing strength and precision through the unpredictable swells. Safely escorted to the embattled shoreline, King Alex and his warriors disembarked, poised to breach the formidable fortifications of the Abyssal Dominion.

On the far bank, amidst the pandemonium of thrashing waves and the deluge of torrential rain, Qellaun stood as the embodiment of serene might, a calm center amidst the storm of his inner turmoil and unwavering purpose. His gaze, sharp as the howl of the gale, remained fixed on the ethereal silhouettes of Kaelen and Thalorin, the valiant Coraluna warriors whose magic had given rise to these tumultuous waters, stirring within him a whirlpool of conflicting emotions.

Just as the confrontation between Qellaun and the merfolk warriors climaxes, a deafening roar reverberates through the storm. The rain-drenched sky splits with a blinding flash of lightning, revealing a colossal figure rising from the depths of the sea. King Oceanous, the ancient ruler of the oceans, manifests his wrath and power in a display of dominance over the raging storm.

With swift and resolute strides, Qellaun bridged the distance to the merfolk, his sword an extension of his turbulent spirit. Their confrontation was brief, yet it blazed with the intensity of the surrounding storm. Qellaun's blade, guided by an unrelenting resolve, found its mark with somber finality. The merfolk warriors, entangled in this deadly dance, succumbed to the abyss, their bravery melding with the turmoil of the waters.

Adrianna, her heart heavy witnessing the fall of her kin, shed tears that mingled imperceptibly with the rain. Yet within her, an unwavering determination surged, connecting her with her marine brethren. With the destinies of many intertwined in the chaotic fray, Adrianna fortified her spirit, her resolve solidifying with a silent vow: to ensure that the sacrifices made on this fateful day would carve a path of hope for Keisha and all Vacari, ensuring that none would suffer as those now lost to the depths.

At the front gates of the Abyssal Dominion's formidable stronghold in New Flameford, Ong stood shoulder-to-shoulder with Karrenen and the assembled Eladrin forces. The air hung heavy with tension, and the looming specter of the impending battle cast a palpable weight upon them. The warriors were meticulously positioned, poised for the signal that would unleash their thunderous charge, their weapons gleaming ominously in the dim light, thanks to the Nymphs' enchantment.

Pumpkin, Ong's steadfast companion and trusted confidant, remained loyal. The creature's vigilant presence was a constant reminder of their unbreakable bond, infusing Ong with a deep well of courage. His grip on his weapon tightened, a silent pledge of his unwavering resolve. As he glanced at the Eladrin warriors flanking him, their resolute expressions mirrored his own commitment to the cause, an alliance solidified in the crucible of adversity.

Ong's unwavering focus remained fixated on the imposing gates looming before him. The passage of time seemed to stretch infinitely, each passing moment heavier than the last. A shared glance with Karrenen conveyed their mutual resolve and the profound responsibility they bore for the lives entrusted to their leadership.

Then, as if summoned by destiny itself, a thunderous roar pierced the air, heralding the majestic descent of the dragons from the heavens. This awe-inspiring arrival served as the signal for the Eladrin forces to surge forward. With a battle cry that resonated through the very core of their beings, Ong and his comrades charged headlong into the fray, their weapons flashing brilliantly in the shroud of darkness.

At one of the concealed side gates, a group of Eladrin warriors and fighters from Crystal Vale had assembled in the cloak of darkness, their unwavering determination mirrored in the relentless gaze of King Manard, the ruler of Crystal Vale. This coalition of Eladrin and Crystal Vale forces was poised to embark on a daring mission that demanded the utmost stealth and precision.

With a solemn nod from King Manard, his warriors moved forward with the grace of shadows. Their footsteps were invisible against the darkened earth, their figures seamlessly merging with the obscurity surrounding them. Each warrior was a master of their craft, equally skilled in combat and the mystic arts.

Their resolve was unwavering, and the Eladrin and Crystal Vale forces pressed onward, bearing the immense weight of the alliance's audacious assault. Their mission was to infiltrate the enemy's formidable defenses, carving a clandestine path for others to follow.

The shroud of darkness enveloped them, concealing their advance as they moved stealthily toward the imposing stronghold of the Abyssal Dominion in New Flameford. The raging storm above masked the sound of their movements, and the tumultuous chaos that enveloped them diverted the attention of the Abyssal Dominion's forces. King Manard's heart beat in time with the anticipation of the impending battle. He understood that the success of their mission held the power to tip the scales in their favor, and with each measured step they took, they drew closer to liberating their world.

As the combined forces of the Eladrin and Crystal Vale pressed onward, Queen Aeliana and her Nymphs watched from the shadows, their eyes aglow with hope and determination. Amidst the echoing battle cries, the clashing of weapons, and the crackling of magic, the Battle for Vacari raged on, an epic struggle that would determine the fate of their cherished realm.

King Alex of Goldmoor led a contingent of his most elite warriors through one of the concealed side gates, their gleaming armor casting a muted radiance as they unleashed their resounding battle cries, their determination unwavering.

The mere presence of King Alex on the battlefield served as a beacon of hope for the Alliance, and his warriors fought with renewed vigor. They clashed fiercely with the formidable forces of the Abyssal Dominion, every strike of sword against blade a testament to their unyielding resolve. King Alex and his warriors engaged their foes valiantly, cutting down enemy after enemy in their relentless pursuit.

However, within the chaotic maelstrom of the battlefield, a sudden and deadly threat materialized. A Druchii sorceress, keen-eyed and malevolent, spotted King Alex's entrance through the side gate and directed her dark magic toward him, intent on his destruction.

In a heart-stopping moment, one of King Alex's most loyal and courageous warriors leaped forward, interposing himself between the King and the approaching blast of evil magic. The arcane energy struck the valiant warrior, causing his body to convulse in agonizing torment before collapsing to the ground. It was a selfless and heroic sacrifice, evident in the anguished expression etched on his face.

King Alex's eyes widened in shock and horror as he witnessed the noble act of his fallen comrade. Grief and fury surged within him, intensifying his determination to avenge the fallen warrior's sacrifice. With a thunderous roar reverberating across the battlefield, King Alex redoubled his efforts, rallying his warriors and driving back the forces of the Abyssal Dominion with unwavering resolve.

The fallen warrior's heroic sacrifice became a rallying point for King Alex's men, kindling a blazing determination in their hearts as they fought in his memory. Amidst the ongoing chaos of battle, with the resounding clash of swords and the pulsing roar of magic filling the air, the fallen warrior's sacrifice served as a poignant and unforgettable reminder of the price paid to defend their homeland and defeat the encroaching darkness.

As the minutes ebbed away, the Abyssal Dominion's forces within the stronghold began to stir. The unusual weather and the enshrouding darkness had not gone unnoticed by the keen eyes of the enemy. Whispers of conccrn and confusion rippled through their ranks as they grappled with the unnatural phenomena enveloping them.

The atmosphere hummed with palpable tension within the heart of the foreboding Dread Spire. The hushed sounds of focused preparations were shattered when Qellaun burst through the chamber doors, his breath ragged and urgency blazing in his eyes. "We are under attack!" he bellowed, igniting a surge of urgency among those present.

Phoenix's eyes widened, and without a moment's hesitation, he seized the crystal wand from its resting place. Clenching it tightly, he muttered, "They will pay for this..." His voice resonated with a potent blend of determination and trepidation as he hastily departed the chamber, leaving behind an aura of uncertainty.

Vuarus and Lyra exchanged a fleeting yet resolute glance, understanding the moment's gravity. The time for waiting had passed; the battle had arrived at their very doorstep. Without exchanging a word, they turned and approached the impending chaos. Vuarus moved with measured precision, his eyes ablaze with the fervor that had been building within him for far too long.

Amidst the chaos and urgency gripping the Abyssal Dominion's stronghold, Vuarus couldn't restrain a low, self-assured chuckle that escaped his lips. "They dare to attack us here?" he mused inwardly, his voiceless laughter tinged with a hint of overconfidence. "They have no idea what they've walked into."

His unspoken words lingered in the air for a fleeting moment, a silent testament to his unwavering belief in their own indomitable strength. With that, he joined the fray, ready to demonstrate the true power of the Abyssal Dominion and the formidable challenge their audacious attackers had recklessly chosen to confront.

High above, the Abyssal Dominion's dragons, stationed within the ominous Dread Spire, took to the skies. Their wings beat with powerful strokes as they joined the ranks of their allies, the prevailing darkness imbuing them with an even more foreboding aura. The presence of these dragons served as a stark reminder of the high stakes involved in this dire conflict.

The Abyssal Dominion's stronghold had now transformed into a relentless battleground. The resounding clash of steel against steel, the crackling of potent magic, and the thunderous roars of the formidable dragons melded into a cacophonous symphony of war. The forces of light and darkness collided with fervor, each side fiercely fighting for their vision of the future.

Hidden amidst the turbulent stormy skies, Kimras soared gracefully with Keisha astride his back. Though Keisha's hands twitched with the memory of her lost magic, the once-familiar connection severed by her captivity, she persisted with unwavering determination to find another way to contribute to the battle. Frustration etched lines on her brow as she grappled with her newfound vulnerability.

Sensing her hesitation, Kimras turned his regal head back toward Keisha, his voice as gentle as the breeze, yet reassuring. "Don't worry about contributing; just having you safe is enough for everyone," he said kindly. "I'll take care of this. Stay back and keep yourself safe."

A profound sense of relief washed over Keisha as Kimras stepped forward, his shining golden scales shimmering with unwavering determination. With a potent surge of his own magic, he deftly wove protective barriers and shields for the alliance forces below, shielding them from the evil forces of the Abyssal Dominion.

Keisha watched in awe as Kimras handled the situation with grace and formidable power, ensuring the safety of their allies. She remained concealed in the background, aware that Kimras held the reins of control. Amidst the chaos and uncertainty enveloping them, Kimras' valiant efforts served as a luminous beacon of hope amidst the ferocious battle, a testament to the enduring strength of their alliance.

An intense and climactic confrontation unfolded as Thundria, the majestic topaz dragon, carved a path through the tumultuous battlefield. Her towering presence was a beacon of unwavering determination, his resplendent scales gleaming in the pale light piercing the storm. Across the war-torn field, Aurelia, a formidable crystal dragon, caught sight of her.

With a primal roar reverberating through the air, Aurelia launched herself towards Thundria, her crystalline wings propelling her with deadly speed. The collision of their colossal forms was a remarkable sight, an explosive clash of elemental forces that resonated through the battlefield. They locked jaws and talons, each vying for dominance over the other.

Aurelia's breath weapon surged to life, and a cone of radiant, luminous shards erupted from her gaping maw. These shards streaked through the sky like brilliant meteors, homing in on their target. Thundria, caught amidst the onslaught, struggled to evade the relentless barrage. Each shard that struck her seemed to siphon away her vitality, leaving her once-vibrant scales dull and faded.

Despite the overwhelming assault, Thundria fought on with an enthusiasm that refused to be extinguished. Her roars of defiance echoed across the battlefield, and his massive claws left deep furrows in the earth as he pushed against Aurelia's relentless advance. Her strength and determination surged forth, defying the odds stacked against her.

Yet, Aurelia seized an opportunity at a critical moment in the battle. With a sudden, unexpected movement, she unleashed another shard attack, catching Thundria off guard. The shards struck her with a devastating impact, and for a brief, heart-stopping moment, the battle hung in a precarious balance. Then, with a resounding crash that shook the ground, Thundria fell to the earth, her once-mighty form now still and lifeless.

Thundria's massive body crashed into one of the towering stone pillars as she collapsed, shattering it into a myriad of fragments. The ground quaked beneath the impact force, and the ongoing battle momentarily faltered as warriors from both sides turned their attention to the fallen dragon. A heavy silence descended upon the battlefield, the weight of Thundria's defeat casting a somber shadow over the conflict.

Aurelia hovered majestically above the fallen topaz dragon, her crystalline form radiating an undeniable aura of triumph. The battle continued to rage on around them, but in this fleeting moment, the epic clash between two mighty forces had reached a chilling conclusion. The winds of fate had shifted, leaving behind a fallen champion and a shattered pillar, stark symbols of the unyielding cost of war.

A monumental clash of titans unfolded as Zylron, the fiery red dragon, and Caelum, the formidable copper dragon, locked in a ferocious battle. The air crackled with the raw energy of their elemental power as they circled one another, eyes ablaze with determination and an age-old rivalry that burned hotter than the flames and acid they wielded.

Zylron's scales shimmered like molten lava as he unleashed his scorching breath—a searing torrent that blazed through the sky. Swift and agile, Caelum skillfully evaded the blistering flames, retaliating with a blast of corrosive acid that hissed and sizzled upon meeting Zylron's inferno. The clash of fire and acid sent seismic shockwaves rippling through the battlefield, causing the ground to tremble beneath the colossal magnitude of their struggle.

As these two mighty dragons clashed, their colossal forms hurl debris through the air. Stones and rocks tumbled from the walls and spires of the battleground, crashing down upon the combatants below, adding to the chaotic fury of their confrontation.

The battle between Zylron and Caelum raged on, their thunderous roars echoing across the battlefield as they grappled and exchanged devastating blows. Zylron's fiery breath collided with Caelum's corrosive acid attacks, creating dazzling explosions of steam and smoke that momentarily obscured the battlefield. Their elemental powers clashed in a brilliant spectacle, a breathtaking testament to the ancient might of these formidable creatures.

In the end, after a fierce and grueling struggle, it was Zylron who emerged as the victor. With a final, triumphant roar reverberating through the battlefield, he unleashed a torrent of flames that engulfed Caelum, the searing heat consuming the copper dragon's form. As the dissipating smoke revealed the aftermath, only Zylron remained, his scales scorched and his hard-fought victory a resounding testament to his indomitable strength.

In a distant corner of the battlefield, the clash of two colossal forms resonated across the tumultuous chaos. Drakthor, with scales as black as the Abyss, unleashed torrents of searing acid that sizzled through the air. His mighty wings created gusts that carried the noxious fumes even further. Facing him was Hespherus, a majestic brass dragon, who billowed forth a cloud of fear-inducing gas, causing even the bravest of warriors to falter in their advance.

Their battle was a ferocious spectacle, and the sky above them was tainted with swirling clouds of acid and dread. Drakthor's acid spewed like a deadly rain, corrupting the earth, and hissing against Hespherus' gleaming brass scales. In response, the brass dragon countered with bursts of searing flame, attempting to disperse the corrosive mist that clung to the air. However, as the gas enveloped him, Hespherus' noble demeanor faltered under the weight of his fears.

Amidst the relentless chaos, Drakthor's assault appeared to gain the upper hand. His corrosive acid found its mark, eating away at Hespherus' defenses and weakening the once-proud dragon. But in a final surge of courage and determination, Hespherus summoned the very last of his strength. With a resounding roar that echoed through the battlefield, he unleashed a blast of fire infused with a golden, radiant light. The searing flames cut through the acid-laden air, engulfing Drakthor in a blaze of irrevocable destruction.

As the echoes of their battle gradually faded, only the charred remnants of Drakthor's form remained, a grim testament to their fiery struggle. Hespherus, victorious yet battered, stood amidst the scars of the confrontation. With a triumphant roar that resonated through the battlefield, he spread his mighty wings and soared into the sky, his courage shining as brightly as the sun breaking through the dissipating clouds of war.

Zylron, the red dragon with eyes ablaze with anger, ascended into the heavens with a haunting purpose. He had borne witness to the fall of his black dragon comrade, Drakthor, at the talons of Hespherus, the brass dragon. Now, fueled by a vengeance that devoured his soul, Zylron fixated his wrathful gaze upon the brass dragon who had taken his ally's life.

In the heavens, the air seemed to crackle with tension as Zylron's fiery wings bore him closer to Hespherus. His scales glimmered with infernal intensity, reflecting his burning fury. With a thunderous roar that reverberated like a volcanic eruption, he unleashed torrents of flames that surged forth with the wrath of a smoldering volcano, the very atmosphere shimmering with the intensity of his ire. The very earth quaked beneath the weight of his anger as he drew nearer to Hespherus.

The brass dragon, already wearied from his prior battle and trapped in the aftermath of his fear-inducing gas, had little time to react. As Zylron's flames engulfed him, the once-proud dragon writhed in agonizing torment, his radiant scales dimmed by the relentless assault. Yet, even confronted by such overwhelming power, Hespherus refused to surrender, his defiant roar serving as a testament to the indomitable spirit that defined him.

In one last, desperate act, Hespherus mustered the remnants of his waning strength and unleashed a blinding burst of light that cleaved through the searing flames. Alas, it was too late – Zylron's fury was relentless. With a final, explosive attack, Zylron's flames devoured Hespherus completely, leaving naught but scorched remnants as a somber testament to the fallen dragon's unwavering determination to avenge his comrade's demise.

Amidst the tumult of the battlefield, the skies transformed into their arena, where two colossal dragons clashed with elemental might. Verdantia, the emerald dragon, soared through the sky, her wings outstretched and her scales shimmering with a brilliant, vibrant green. Her eyes blazed with unwavering resolve as she unleashed a loud roar, unleashing sonic shockwaves that rippled through the enemy ranks, sowing chaos, and confusion among their adversaries.

But Venfyr, the vicious green dragon, proved undaunted by her display of power. His scales glinted malevolently with a toxic sheen as he exhaled a noxious cloud of chlorine gas, a lethal weapon that billowed outward, its poisonous tendrils seeking to asphyxiate and incapacitate. The battlefield air grew dense with the acrid stench of the poisonous gas, and the defenders of the Light confronted the Abyssal forces and the choking fumes that threatened to engulf them.

Verdantia's resonating wail persisted amidst the tumult, her sonic vibrations a testament to her unyielding determination. However, as the enveloping gas cloud expanded and obscured her presence, her advantage began to wane. Her cries grew strained, and her once-majestic flight faltered under the relentless assault of the toxic air. Yet, even as her vision blurred and her strength wavered, she continued to battle, refusing to succumb to the corrosive assault.

Then, in a moment of unexpected salvation, the heavens above were torn asunder by the arrival of Dirona, the bronze dragon. Her form gleamed like burnished bronze against the stormy backdrop, her wings slicing through the air as she descended upon the embattled scene below. With a resounding roar that resonated through the heavens, she unleashed a torrent of bronzed energy, manifesting her newfound power as a breath weapon.

The unleashed power struck Venfyr with relentless force, her lightning crackling through him. The evil green dragon's massive form convulsed and writhed, his anguished cries piercing the air as the bronze dragon's energy seared through his scales, penetrating deep into his very core.

Amidst the swirling chaos of the battlefield, where the clash of swords and the roar of magic resounded, a confrontation steeped in the shadows of vengeance came to life. Lyra, a formidable wielder of dark magic, locked her gaze with Lady Mirabelle, an Eladrin sorceress who had long been a thorn in the side of the Dark.

Their magic met with explosive force, tendrils of darkness and radiant energy intertwining as they battled for supremacy. Lyra's malevolent spells lashed like venomous serpents while Lady Mirabelle countered with brilliant bursts of ethereal light. Each attack was met with equal ferocity, their powers colliding in a dazzling display of opposing energies.

As the battle raged on, it became evident that Lyra had the upper hand. Her relentless onslaught began to erode Lady Mirabelle's defenses, her dark magic wearing down the shimmering barriers that shielded the sorceress. Lady Mirabelle fought back with unyielding determination, but the ceaseless assault took its toll.

In a final surge of dark energy, Lyra unleashed a devastating spell that shattered Lady Mirabelle's defenses. The sorceress staggered under the force of the impact, her strength waning. Lyra seized the opportunity, enveloping Lady Mirabelle in an inky maelstrom of dark magic. The sorceress struggled to break free, but her efforts proved futile.

As the dark energy subsided, Lady Mirabelle lay motionless on the ground, her once-bright eyes dulled and lifeless. For a fleeting moment, the battlefield held its breath, the cacophony of combat momentarily muted in the wake of this singular confrontation.

In the hush that followed, a chilling whisper escaped Lyra's lips, carried on the wind like a harbinger of doom. "Only good Eladrin is a dead one," she muttered, her words dripping with malice and triumph. Her victory over Lady Mirabelle was undeniable, a testament to the power of her dark gifts.

With her adversary defeated, Lyra turned away from the fallen sorceress, her dark aura pulsating with a mixture of satisfaction and malevolence. The battle raged on around her, but in this moment, she stood alone in the aftermath of her triumph—a figure cloaked in shadows, consumed by her unrelenting vendetta.

Amidst the chaotic maelstrom of battle, the clash of blades, and the cries of warriors, a fateful confrontation emerged. Lord Eldrion, an Eladrin of noble bearing, and Qellaun, a Druchii warrior with a sinister aura, locked eyes across the battlefield. They had both been drawn into this relentless conflict, their destinies entwined in the dance of war.

Their swords gleamed like ethereal moonlight and shadowy obsidian, symbols of their respective races' grace and brutality. As they closed the distance between them, the air was still, and a circle formed around the impending duel, for the warriors on both sides recognized the significance of this clash.

Lord Eldrion's blade, an exquisite work of Eladrin craftsmanship, sang through the air with the fluid grace of a swan in flight. His movements were a testament to years of training and discipline, each strike and parry executed with a flawless precision that spoke of his noble lineage. Qellaun, on the other hand, wielded his Druchii sword with a predatory finesse, his strikes carrying the evil intent of a cobra poised to strike. He moved with a deadly elegance, his dark eyes locked onto Lord Eldrion's every move, anticipating and countering with lethal accuracy.

The clash of their swords was a mesmerizing spectacle—a dance of light and shadow, grace, and brutality. Lord Eldrion fought with honor, his blade a beacon of the Light's hope, while Qellaun embraced the shadows, his strikes fueled by a desire to conquer and dominate.

Despite Lord Eldrion's noble spirit and exceptional skill, it became apparent that Qellaun possessed a relentless determination that knew no bounds. Slowly but with unwavering purpose, he began to press Lord Eldrion back, driving him further into the heart of the battle.

With a final, devastating blow, Qellaun disarmed Lord Eldrion, clattering his sword to the ground. Lord Eldrion stumbled backward, his noble visage marred by the harsh reality of defeat. Qellaun stood victorious, a dark, triumphant glint in his eyes as he surveyed the fallen Eladrin.

The warriors who had witnessed this duel stepped back in solemn acknowledgment of the outcome. Qellaun's victory over Lord Eldrion would be etched into the annals of history, a testament to the relentless spirit of the Druchii and the inevitable tide of war that swept through the realms.

Amidst the tumultuous chaos of the battlefield, a sinister Druchii warrior, cloaked in shadows, saw an opportunity to deliver a fatal strike to Ong, the stalwart defender. With stealth and lethal intent, he inched closer to his target, his blade poised to deliver a deadly blow from the shadows.

Yet, in a twist of fate that defied expectation, Ong's faithful companion, Pumpkin, leaped into action with unbridled ferocity. A snarl that bared her formidable fangs tore through the air as she lunged at the Druchii assailant. Pumpkin's jaws clamped down on the Druchii's arm with a vice-like grip, causing the warrior to scream in agony and surprise. In the chaos, the Druchii's weapon slipped from his grasp, a fallen instrument of death.

Ong, quick to react and emboldened by Pumpkin's timely intervention, turned to confront his would-be assassin. His sword cleaved through the air in a fluid and precise motion, finding its mark with deadly accuracy. The Druchii's menacing presence was defeated in an instant, extinguished by the unwavering determination of Ong.

Turning to his loyal companion, Ong offered a grateful nod, acknowledging Pumpkin's crucial role in preserving his life. With renewed resolve, they stood together, ready to face the relentless tide of battle, their shared determination a testament to the unbreakable bond between a warrior and his faithful companion.

Phoenix, a precursor of malevolence, loomed at the epicenter of the tumultuous battlefield. His maleficent intent manifested through the crystal wand, a wickedly humming conduit of sinister energies. Dark power crackled and swirled around him like an evil storm, turning the once-innocent artifact into a weapon of destruction.

His gaze, as evil as the abyss, fixated on a group of brave warriors drawn from the Alliance. Among them were Eladrin, Crystal Vale denizens, and Goldmoor champions who had united in their noble quest.

The air quivered with an eerie anticipation, a prelude to the impending calamity. Phoenix, a maestro of malevolence, unleashed a deluge of dark energy from the sinister wand. The unfortunate warriors, trapped in the merciless clutches of this malevolent maelstrom, endured most of its malefic force. Pain and despair contorted their expressions as they frantically sought refuge from the relentless storm.

The once-pristine earth bore the scars of the wand's wrath, its surface marred and scorched by the searing torrent of power. A cataclysmic clash of elemental forces between Phoenix and the resolute alliance fighters unfolded before the horrified onlookers, painting a nightmarish tableau of destruction and anguish. Once a symbol of courage and hope, the battlefield lay in ruins, shattered by the unrelenting battle of wills that rent the very fabric of existence.

Amidst the tumultuous storm of battle, a burst of sinister and bone-chilling laughter echoed, its dark cadence sending shivers down the spines of all who bore witness. Vuarus, an evil master of shadows, fixated his gaze upon the Alliance forces with an unsettling amusement that danced upon the precipice of madness. Like abyssal voids, his eyes gleamed with a twisted delight as his outstretched hands moved with an eerie grace, fingers weaving intricate and eldritch patterns into the very fabric of reality.

An evil grin, a grotesque mockery of goodness itself, twisted Vuarus's lips as he enacted his dark magic. With each arcane gesture, he summoned forth the denizens of the Abyss, creatures born from the most bottomless and most malignant chasms of existence. The atmosphere grew dense with an unsettling anticipation, the very earth trembling under the oppressive weight of their impending arrival.

From the ominous abyssal rifts, nightmarish and contorted forms slithered forth, their visages twisted and marred by the malefic forces that had brought them into being. Their presence sent waves of dread cascading through the hearts of all who saw their monstrous forms. These abominable entities bore the unmistakable mark of their sinister origins, their eyes aglow with an unholy radiance piercing through the fabric of shadows.

In a nightmarish unison, they surged forth as a relentless tide of darkness, their evil intent writ large—to overwhelm and consume the forces of light that dared to defy them. The battlefield, already steeped in despair, was plunged into an even more bottomless abyss of terror as these unholy beings advanced, the living embodiment of the unspeakable horrors that lurked within the darkest recesses of the cosmos.

.Karrenen, a master of formidable magic, harnessed his mystical prowess to dispel the encroaching denizens from the Abyss, a dire threat looming over the alliance. With unwavering focus and intense concentration, he directed his arcane energies toward a specific group of evil entities, his resolve unwavering as he sought to banish them from the battlefield.

Yet, within the depths of his concentrated efforts, a handful of cunning denizens managed to slink unnoticed from the rear, their sinister intentions veiled in the shadows, poised to deliver a treacherous blow against the alliance's defenses. Their malevolent presence was akin to a looming specter, concealed by the din of battle.

However, destiny had a fresh design, as Pumpkin, the vigilant panther and unwavering protector, sprang into action with lightning-fast determination. In a swift and ferocious attack, Pumpkin intercepted the stealthy denizens, thwarting their wicked designs and shielding Karrenen from imminent harm. In that pivotal moment, the unbreakable bond between Ong and his loyal companion emerged as an invaluable bulwark against the encroaching forces of darkness.

Karrenen, his heart brimming with silent gratitude, couldn't help but acknowledge the panther's courage and unwavering loyalty. His thoughts resonated within him, an unspoken testament to his trust in Pumpkin: "Glad Pumpkin came with Ong. That panther is a formidable protector."

Karrenen's vigilance and quick thinking remained steadfast, even amidst such peril. Without hesitation, he shifted his attention to the assembly of magic wielders within the alliance's ranks. His voice, clear and commanding, pierced through the clamor of battle, issuing a resolute directive that brooked no delay. His words carried the weight of authority as he urged, "Dispel their presence, now! Spare no effort!"

With the fluid grace of seasoned magic users, the Eladrin spellcasters synchronized their powers, weaving a mesmerizing tapestry of radiant light. Their incantations flowed in harmonious unison, and with determined gestures, they directed beams of potent energy toward the encroaching denizens from the Abyss. The brilliance of their collective magic struck the evil creatures with devastating force. Some entities disintegrated into ethereal tendrils, their forms unraveling like fragile threads dispersed upon the wind.

The battlefield transformed into a chaotic tableau, a vortex of clashing forces locked in a relentless struggle for supremacy. Gleaming blades, honed to a lethal edge, clashed against elusive, ghostly figures spawned from the darkest abyss. The air crackled with the raw surge of arcane power as both sides fought ferociously. It was a symphony of war, a tumultuous blend of battle cries and the eerie roars of the abyssal entities, creating a haunting cacophony that reverberated across the battlefield like a dire omen.

Amidst the swirling chaos, the unwavering figures of Lord Galadon and Lady Isadora stood back-to-back, embodying the essence of unity and steadfast determination. Together, they confronted the unrelenting onslaught of the abyssal denizens with unwavering courage. Their blades moved with a deadly precision, cutting down several evil creatures in their path. Yet, the odds were a heavy burden to bear, and despite their indomitable spirit, the ceaseless tide of denizens proved overwhelming. With heavy hearts and unyielding resolve, Galadon and Isadora succumbed to the relentless assault, their final stand a poignant testament to their unwavering commitment to the cause.

Karrenen's countenance darkened as the chilling realization struck him – some denizens had breached their defenses. Witnessing these malevolent beings sow chaos and destruction among the Alliance forces filled him with a profound sense of urgency. The battle was far from its conclusion, and the encroaching shadows of the Abyss threatened to engulf them all, a stark reminder of the arduous path that lay ahead.

Keisha's resolute gesture directed Kimras, and with a solemn nod, the majestic dragon advanced toward the encroaching abyssal creatures.

In a breathtaking display of draconic might, Kimras opened his maw wide, and a torrent of scorching flames erupted from its fiery depths. The inferno roared through the air like a vengeful storm, a purifying blaze intent on engulfing the abyssal creatures within its searing embrace. The denizens' eerie screeches and desperate flails filled the battlefield as they withered and disintegrated under the relentless onslaught of the dragon's fiery breath.

The shadows recoiled, their ethereal forms contorting and writhing as Kimras's potent magic tore through their essence. Some creatures emitted anguished cries before fading into oblivion, leaving only a trace of their evil presence.

Despite Kimras's valiant efforts, a few abyssal denizens exhibited a tenacity that allowed them to evade the cleansing flames. These relentless entities surged forward with an unnatural determination, their sinister gazes fixed upon the defenders of the Light. With eerie swiftness, they eluded attacks and unleashed shadowy tendrils that clawed and grasped at their adversaries. The battle continued its relentless cadence, an intricate dance of luminous magic clashing against encroaching darkness. The battlefield transformed into a tumultuous tapestry of swirling enchantments and clashing weapons. At the same time, the air itself became laden with the tang of sorcery and the acrid scent of scorched shadows. Each strike and spell cast held the weight of destiny as the world's fate teetered on the precipice of uncertainty.

Amidst the tumultuous battle, Vuarus wielded his dark powers with a chilling precision that sent shivers down the spines of all who bore witness. His eyes gleamed with malice, a sinister glint that revealed his evil intent as he honed his magical focus on a singular target.

High above the chaotic battlefield, Sylvana, the emerald dragon, soared through the skies with a graceful and mesmerizing elegance. Her scales sparkled like the most precious gems, an awe-inspiring remarkable sight. However, Vuarus's dark sorcery proved relentless as inky shadows began to coil and entwine around her majestic form. The once-graceful movements of the emerald dragon now became sluggish and unsteady.

With a triumphant grin that mirrored the shadows encroaching upon his target, Vuarus intensified his magical assault. His dark powers greedily drained the vitality from the emerald dragon, sapping her once-boundless strength and leaving her helpless against the inexorable pull of gravity. Sylvana's formidable form descended earthward, her descent marked by a sorrowful cascade, until she collided with the unforgiving ground—a poignant testament to the relentless might of Vuarus's dark mastery.

"Within the chaotic maelstrom of battle, Phoenix's eyes narrowed into slits of seething rage as they fell upon Keisha, who rode Kimras, an ever-present irritant in his path. A malicious grin twisted his lips as he shifted his attention to Vuarus, his voice dripping with venom as he taunted, 'Vuarus, look who's joined the festivities! Your cherished little pet has chosen to grace us with her presence.'

Vuarus's sinister gaze obediently followed the accusatory path of Phoenix's outstretched finger, and an evil sneer twisted his lips in response to the taunting words. Vuarus chuckled darkly, his voice laced with a cruel edge as he replied, 'Let us remember to thank them after we win the battle, for returning Keisha to us for the grand finale.'

While Phoenix's words held an evil edge, it was Vuarus's response that sent a chill down Keisha's spine. Kimras, Ong, Karrenen, and the entirety of the Alliance noticed the stark difference in her reaction. A collective sigh of relief escaped their lips as Kimras swiftly acted, pulling back to shield Keisha from the looming threat of Vuarus, momentarily sparing her from Phoenix's malice."

Silvara, the majestic silver dragon, descended from the heavens like a celestial comet, her luminous scales aglint with the ethereal radiance of the moonlight. With elegant yet deadly precision, she unfurled her wings. She unleashed a frigid breath—a sweeping cone of ice and frost directed toward the malevolent artifact held aloft by Phoenix's outstretched hand.

The crystal wand, a conduit for Phoenix's corrupt magic, was ensnared by the icy tendrils of Silvara's assault. Frost crept over the wand's malevolent surface, spreading like a web of crystalline tendrils. This arctic spell disrupted the dark energies within the wand, causing the once-menacing crystal to shatter and splinter into countless shards. With a resounding and final cacophony of splintering, the wand disintegrated entirely, and its nefarious power dissipated into the ether.

Silvara, triumphant in her aerial stance, hovered with a regal bearing, her silvery eyes locked onto Phoenix with an unwavering gaze. Her actions transcended mere victory; they conveyed a profound message—a testament to the enduring power of love and unity, capable of dispelling even the darkest shadows.

Phoenix's eyes, once filled with malevolent confidence, now widened in shock as he beheld the catastrophic disintegration of his formidable weapon. His fingers twitched in futile desperation, the remnants of his grip on the fractured crystal wand slipping away like the sands of time. The once-potent source of his dark power crumbled before his very eyes, its jagged shards cascading to the ground, rendering it naught but a pile of shattered crystals.

Within Phoenix's breast, the blazing flames of his rage were abruptly doused, replaced by a guttural cry of anguish that pierced the air—a lamentation echoing across the battlefield. His desperate fists clenched in agony, the aura of dominance he had once radiated now diminished, a dark ember in the wake of extinguished power.

Disbelief rippled through the battleground, a collective gasp of astonishment and hope, as the once-imposing crystal wand shattered into irreparable fragments. Even Vuarus and Phoenix, their countenances etched with doubt, could only watch in disbelief as the evil power they had so arrogantly harnessed was cruelly wrenched from their grasp. Their eyes, once filled with malice, now widened in tandem as a radiant figure emerged from the dissipating shroud of dark energy.

Talleoss, once imprisoned within the malevolent crystal, emerged reborn and transformed into a glorious silver dragon. His scales, bathed in an ethereal radiance, shimmered like the moon's glow, and his wings unfurled with newfound freedom. As he ascended into the boundless skies, a palpable surge of energy rippled around him, a manifestation of Phoenix's stolen power returning to its rightful source.

Talleoss's silver eyes, gleaming with wisdom and authority, surveyed the battlefield with a commanding presence that could not be ignored. He exuded an aura of unparalleled might and purpose, a living symbol of hope for all who fought on the side of light. Amidst the tumultuous chaos of battle, the silver dragon's very presence became a luminous beacon of unwavering determination, a source of inspiration for the brave souls battling against the suffocating shadow of the Abyssal Dominion.

Nerissa, the guardian of the merfolk, emerged from the depths of the ocean with a graceful flourish. Her outstretched hand beckoned forth the Heart of Twilight, a legendary artifact that had rested in the ocean's embrace for eons. The iridescent relic floated above the waves, casting a gentle, soothing radiance contrasting the turmoil. Guided by an invisible hand, it soared through the air, its trajectory aimed directly at Talleoss. However, an evil force intervened before reaching its destined recipient, shattering the moment's tranquility.

Vuarus, his eyes brimming with hostility, unleashed a devastating surge of destructive energy that tore the serenity asunder. In a cruel act, he struck down Nerissa, the mermaid guardian, whose life was extinguished instantly.

Nerissa's lifeless form tumbled towards the sea, and the Heart of Twilight momentarily faltered in its course. Talleoss, the majestic silver dragon who had broken free from his crystal prison, gazed upon the unfolding tragedy with mounting horror.

Vuarus, consumed by fury and thwarted ambition, roared in a storm of rage. The artifact's rejection of his darkness was a profound blow to his nefarious designs, a symbol of renewed hope amidst the chaos. Talleoss, a majestic silver dragon now reborn and empowered, gazed upon the unfolding tragedy with mounting horror. However, he was not one to succumb to despair. He summoned his magic with unwavering determination, entwining it with the artifact's innate power.

Against Vuarus's evil influence, the Heart of Twilight resisted, its trajectory shifting again. It veered away from the fallen mermaid and resumed its path towards Talleoss. The silver dragon extended his colossal wings, his eyes locked onto the approaching relic, and his heart filled with anticipation and trepidation. The artifact drew nearer, inexorably pulled towards its rightful possessor until it merged seamlessly with Talleoss, enveloping him in a radiant luminance.

As the Heart of Twilight melded seamlessly with Talleoss's essence, the artifact's light was interwoven with the brilliance of his silver scales, magnifying his might and presence. An echoing harmony enveloped the battleground, signifying Talleoss's rightful ascension. His eyes, a complex fusion of understanding and challenge, turned to Vuarus. The air seemed to quiver with the weight of their shared history, fraught with secrets, betrayals, and a long-anticipated reckoning.

Talleoss, now infused with the Heart of Twilight's potent energies, radiated a luminous aura across the battlefield, pushing back the encroaching darkness of the Abyssal Dominion. The earth seemed to respond to his presence, the ground beneath their feet trembling as if acknowledging his newfound power.

Vuarus, consumed by fury and thwarted ambition, roared in a storm of rage. The artifact's rejection of his darkness was a profound blow to his nefarious designs, a symbol of renewed hope amidst the chaos. Talleoss, now fused with the Heart of Twilight's potent energies, turned his unwavering gaze upon Vuarus. Their eyes locked, two forces irrevocably linked by destiny. The battlefield raged around them, but a spark of light had been rekindled amidst the maelstrom.

During the chaotic fray of battle, Vuarus's voice cut through the clamor like a dagger of anger and desperation. His fiery gaze fixated upon Lyra, his words dripping with accusation and spite. "Lyra, you've been played for a fool! The Heart of Twilight was in their possession all along!" His utterance hung heavily, a curse that shattered any lingering illusions.

Vuarus summoned additional denizens from the Abyss with a surge of dark energy. These grotesque creatures swarmed around him, an unrelenting tide of hostility. The warriors of the Alliance met their advance with fierce resistance, the clash of weapons resounding amidst the nightmarish entities. Magic crackled through the air, and blades sang as they fought valiantly to stem the tide of darkness.

As Talleoss, the silver dragon, ascended into the boundless skies with the Heart of Twilight's power coursing through him, a palpable surge of energy rippled around him — interwoven with the essence of the Heart of Twilight. This surge had a profound effect on Vuarus's godly form. The very fabric of existence rejected his twisted power.

Within Vuarus, a profound transformation unfolded, a spectacle defying reality's law. The essence of his godly form wavered and flickered, as though the very fabric of existence rejected his twisted power. His once-majestic visage twisted and contorted in a grotesque display of corruption.

A guttural cry of denial erupted from Vuarus as his godly form unraveled. The shadows that had once danced to his command now rebelled, writhing, and swirling like sentient entities seeking liberation from their master's malevolence. The shroud of his divine might tore asunder, revealing the fractured and tainted soul beneath.

"No!" Vuarus's voice rent the air — a tortured scream merging agony and defiance. He fought vehemently against the inevitable unraveling of his once-potent power, remnants of darkness clawing desperately at the fabric of reality. But the forces he had manipulated and perverted now turned against him, unbound by his will.

Vuarus's anguished screams echoed across the battlefield as his form disintegrated — a mournful dirge for a dominion built upon deceit and malice. The battle raged on, the symphony of clashing wills and weapons harmonized with the elemental chaos. Amidst this turmoil, the fall of a self-proclaimed god sent shockwaves through the very foundations of Vacari.

In the heavens above, a fierce spectacle unfolded as Talleoss, the magnificent silver dragon, locked eyes with the transformed Vuarus — now a grotesque and mighty black dragon. The two dragons engaged in a deadly aerial dance, their movements graceful yet lethal, a convergence of power and destiny."

The air crackled with raw energy as Talleoss and Vuarus clashed, their roars resonating through the battlefield like thunder. Shockwaves radiated through the earth with each strike, the ground trembling beneath the titanic conflict. With each beat of their massive wings, they stirred up winds that swirled with debris, adding to the battle's chaos.

The silver and black dragons proved evenly matched, each employing their unique abilities to counter the other's onslaughts. Talleoss's frosty breath met the searing flames of Vuarus, generating plumes of steam that dispersed in the vortex. Their claws clashed, tails lashed, and roars reverberated through the skies, a testament to their colossal power and unwavering resolve. As they circled each other amidst the turbulent heavens, Talleoss's eyes blazed with relentless determination, reflecting his unwavering commitment to protecting his realm. Vuarus exuded a sinister aura in stark contrast, his dark scales gleaming with malice. The fate of Vacari hung in the balance, and the outcome of their world's destiny depended on the clash of these titanic forces.

The battle between Talleoss and Vuarus raged on, transcending the boundaries of mere dragons. It was a battle for the very heart and soul of Vacari, a conflict that would determine the fate of their world for generations to come. The land below bore witness to their titanic duel, the very essence of Vacari quivering under the impact of their monumental blows.

The ground beneath them began to tremble as the battle continued, manifesting the tumultuous struggle waged above. With a final surge of strength, Talleoss gained the upper hand, delivering a devastating blow that sent Vuarus hurtling to the ground below. The impact was thunderous, and the very earth quaked as the stronghold of the Abyssal Dominion crumbled, mirroring the dark power that had once held sway here.

Talleoss, the majestic silver dragon, gazed down at the fallen form of the black dragon that had once been Vuarus. The once-mighty God of Shadows now lay defeated, his once-imposing form twisted and shattered, a grotesque reflection of his former glory. The dark scales that had once gleamed with malice now crumbled and charred, a testament to the overwhelming might of Talleoss and the forces of light.

Amidst the turmoil of the battlefield, Ong's every step resonated with unwavering resolve, even as the very ground trembled beneath his feet. By his side, Pumpkin, the loyal panther, moved with a graceful determination as they carved a path through the chaotic battleground, their singular goal clear: to confront Phoenix. A palpable tension hung in the air as their eyes locked onto each other, culminating in years of festering hostility and unresolved conflict.

Phoenix couldn't resist the urge to taunt, his laughter a venomous undercurrent to the din of battle. "I see you still need that panther for help," he sneered, his gaze shifting to Pumpkin. However, Ong had different plans. With a whispered command, Pumpkin gracefully parted ways, joining Karrenen nearby, while Ong redirected his unwavering focus back to Phoenix. "Not this time," Ong retorted, his determination etched into every word.

This battle transcended mere martial glory or territorial conquest. It was a reckoning, a deep-seated resolve to ensure that Phoenix would never again inflict harm upon Keisha or anyone else. Ong vividly recalled their last encounter when they had allowed Phoenix to escape. This time, however, was different. It was a battle to settle scores, an unyielding determination to put an end to the tormentor who had caused so much pain and suffering.

Keisha watched from a distance, her heart pounding in her chest, as Ong confronted the once-dreaded Phoenix. She could sense the fiery determination in Ong's eyes, a genuine resolve to bring an end to the tormentor who had caused her so much anguish. Amidst the chaos of the battlefield, a fellow warrior rushed toward Ong, but he waved them off with a determined shake of his head. This battle was his to face alone, a long-overdue reckoning that had finally arrived.

As Ong and Phoenix clashed, their battle became a mesmerizing symphony of steel against dark magic. Each strike bore witness to their unmatched skill and unwavering determination. Ong wielded his sword with precision, deflecting Phoenix's malevolent spells and meeting his dark strikes with swift parries. The air around them crackled with energy, their conflicting forces generating dazzling bursts of light and resonating sound clashes illuminating the entire battlefield.

Phoenix's cruel laughter cut through the chaos as he confronted Ong, his eyes gleaming with malice. "Oh, Ong, how delightful it is to see you again," he sneered, his words dripping with sadistic glee. "And look, you've brought Keisha with you.

How precious. Tell me, Ong, does witnessing her weakness and powerlessness pain you? We've done quite a number on her spirit, haven't we? It's almost a shame she's still breathing." Each word he uttered carried the weight of the torment he had inflicted upon Keisha.

Ong's eyes blazed with an inferno of fury as he faced Phoenix. His voice, like a thunderclap, reverberated with anger and unyielding determination. "Phoenix, you vile creature," he growled, the very scales on his being shimmering with an intense, fiery light. "I won't allow you to escape from this battle as you did before. You may have tried to break Keisha's spirit, but you underestimate her strength and mine. You'll pay for your cruelty, and I won't rest until you're stopped, once and for all."

The battle between Ong and Phoenix intensified with each passing moment. The ground trembled beneath their feet as Phoenix hurled dark incantations and conjured ethereal fire, while Ong deftly parried with his sword, sparks flying with each clash. This battle was deeply personal for Ong, who fought not just for victory but for Keisha's safety, determined to fulfill a promise that Phoenix would never again harm her.

As they circled each other amidst the tumultuous battlefield, their combat skills and magical prowess pushed them to the limits of their abilities. Ong's determination blazed even brighter, his resolve unyielding as he faced the warlock who had tormented Keisha and threatened their world.

Phoenix's sinister grin remained undiminished, and he continued to taunt Ong with cruel words, his aim to break his spirit. Yet Ong's fiery determination only intensified, and he fought back with unparalleled ferocity. The clash between these two adversaries reached a crescendo, the very earth quaking beneath the weight of their battle.

In a desperate moment, Phoenix's attacks became more erratic, the ground trembling beneath him. He stumbled, losing focus instantly, and Ong seized the opportunity. With a fierce yell, Ong pressed forward, his sword gleaming brilliantly in the battlefield's light. Phoenix attempted to counter, but Ong's determination was unwavering.

Their swords clashed once more; this time, Ong's strike found its mark. The blade pierced through Phoenix's defenses, sinking deep into his heart. An expression of shock and disbelief contorted Phoenix's face as pain seared through him. Ong's voice rose above the chaos, filled with unyielding resolve and simmering fury.

"No!" Phoenix screamed, his voice echoing with a mix of rage and disbelief. "How could you defeat me?"

"That was for Keisha," Ong declared, his words echoing with the weight of justice.

With a final, shuddering breath, Phoenix's form began to dissolve, fading away like a wisp of smoke carried by the wind. As his presence vanished from the battlefield, Ong felt a profound sense of closure. He had fulfilled a promise, avenging the torment inflicted upon Keisha and ending a chapter of darkness that had plagued their lives.

Keisha leaned down, her voice a soft, reassuring whisper to Kimras. With a graceful descent, the majestic dragon landed beside Ong, his eyes filled with warmth and understanding. "I kept her safe," Kimras conveyed to Ong, his voice a soothing balm. "But now, I think she needs to be with you. The battle has ended, and Vacari is safe."

Ong nodded in gratitude, his heart swelling with a profound sense of relief and love. With gentle care, he lifted Keisha from her perch, setting her feet on the ground, and then pulled her into a tender embrace, their hearts entwined in that moment of shared victory and newfound peace.

Kimras, understanding the bond between them, gave a dignified nod before taking to the skies again. With each majestic beat of his wings, he left Keisha and Ong to cherish the embrace of newfound tranquility and the promise of a brighter future.

As the dust settled and the divine energies receded, a collective sigh seemed to ripple through the battle-scarred landscape. The forces of light and darkness had waged their cataclysmic clash, and though the price had been steep, the light had emerged victorious. Above, the heavens began to clear, revealing the stars silently witnessing the epic confrontation. Now, their distant light symbolized hope and the triumph of good over evil.

The leaders of the alliance gathered, their expressions bearing the marks of exhaustion and relief. Ong, Keisha, and Pumpkin stood united, surveying the aftermath of the battle that had brought them to the precipice of despair and back. Fallen warriors, Eladrin, dragon, merfolk, or human, lay at rest, their sacrifices etched into the earth they fiercely defended.

Lord Karrenen approached Ong, wordlessly handing him the reins of Thunder, Ong's loyal black horse. Without a spoken exchange, Ong lifted Keisha onto the horse, and they shared a silent understanding, ready to leave the battlefield behind as they began their journey towards healing and a brighter future.

In the distance, the luminous lights of E'vahona began to twinkle, a beacon of safety and hope that remained steadfast even in the darkest of hours. The battle for Vacari had been hard-fought, and the cost would forever be etched into their memories. As the alliance began their journey homeward, a prevailing sense of unity and purpose enveloped them, a reminder that even in the bleakest of times, there was always a guiding light to lead them forward.

"Thank you for reading Shadows Unveiled. If you enjoyed the book, we would be immensely grateful if you could take a moment to leave a review at the location where you purchased the book. Your feedback is invaluable to us and helps other readers discover our work. Thank you for being so supportive!"

Epilogue

T he night hung over New Flameford like a thick, inky shroud, enshrouding the city in an oppressive darkness. A clandestine gathering was taking place in the heart of this city of shadows. Lyra and Qellaun, two of the most cunning and powerful Druchii sorcerers, stood at its edge, within the ruins of the once-mighty Abyssal Dominion.

Lyra summoned a shadowy portal with a whispered incantation, its edges shimmering with malevolent energy. It served as a gateway to Fel Thalor, their ancestral home—a city steeped in dark magic and hidden away from prying eyes. As the portal rippled into existence, its dark magic spread like ripples on a still pond, masking their presence and intentions from any who might sense their passage.

Qellaun, his dark hair gleaming like moonlight, cast a cautious glance at Lyra. "Are you certain about this, Lyra? Returning to Fel Thalor is a risky gambit, especially with Phoenix and Vuarus vanquished, New Flameford, and the Abyssal Dominion stronghold in ruins. Our people are scattered, their strength fractured."

Lyra's crimson eyes burned with determination. "It is our only recourse, Qellaun. New Flameford's defenses have weakened, and we can no longer rely on its feeble protection. We must fortify our city with the potent magic of our ancestral home. Yet, we shall not reveal our return until we are fully prepared for revenge—to make the Eladrin elves and their allies pay for thwarting our plans time and time again."

As one, they stepped through the portal, emerging in the heart of Fel Thalor. This city was a nightmarish labyrinth of winding streets and towering spires, all hewn from obsidian and adorned with grotesque, yet strangely alluring, statues. The air thrummed with arcane energy, and the ground pulsed with malevolence.

Their destination was the ancient library of Fel Thalor, a vast repository of forbidden knowledge. Within its shadow-draped confines, Lyra and Qellaun commenced their dark work. Ancient tomes and scrolls, pages filled with incantations and rituals long forgotten by the outside world, were summoned.

Hours blurred into days as they wove their dark magic, crafting potent wards and enchantments to safeguard Fel Thalor. Their spells were insidious, capable of trapping even the most skilled high elf mages who might dare approach. As they worked, they could feel Fel Thalor, their true home, calling out to them, its essence woven into their being.

Beyond the library's walls, the sun began the ascent, casting long, eerie shadows across Fel Thalor. Their task was complete, and Fel Thalor now lay concealed beneath a veil of clouds so impenetrable that even the most vigilant high elf sentinels would remain oblivious.

Lyra and Qellaun, their faces etched with weariness, emerged from their labor. But fatigue was a small price to pay for the safety of their people. The dark magic they had summoned would shield their city, and none would suspect the Druchii's silent return to Fel Thalor.

Leaving the library behind, they stepped again through the portal to New Flameford. As they did, Lyra couldn't help but feel a sense of satisfaction. Their covert journey back to Fel Thalor had been fraught with danger, but it had secured the survival of their people and the continued dominance of the Druchii. In this world, darkness and shadows were their most significant allies. It was time to gather the rest of their scattered brethren and return to Fel Thalor, their true sanctuary.

AS THE SUN SETS ON the shadowy revelations of 'Shadows Unveiled,' Book 2 of the Elves of Vacari series, a new chapter awaits. Join us in 'Vacari's Resurgence,' Book 3 of the Elves of Vacari series, where the scars of the past will heal, forgiveness will bloom, and the resilient spirit of Vacari will rise stronger than ever b efore."

Teaser

Vacari Resurgence

Amidst the renewed hope of Vacari's healing, a quiet struggle unfolds in the heart of Ong. The shattered necklace, a symbol of his love for Keisha, remains broken, hidden away from her eyes. Once intertwined with precious gems, its delicate silver chain is in fragmented disarray.

He had vowed to mend it, to restore its beauty and significance, a promise of unwavering devotion. Yet, as days turn into weeks, frustration gnaws at him. Each failed attempt to repair the intricate circlet necklace feels like another failure, a reminder of his perceived inadequacy. The pieces, once so familiar in his hands, have become elusive puzzles that defy his skill.

He can't bring himself to tell Keisha, for he yearns to surprise her with the gift of their love made whole once more. The weight of his unspoken promise presses upon him, mingling with the fear that the unrepaired necklace will symbolize his doubts and fears.

As Vacari embarks on a healing journey, Ong must find the strength and skill to mend what is broken within himself and in the face of external threats. The unrepaired necklace is a silent testament to his determination, a reflection of his love, and a challenge he cannot ignore. In the intricate threads of their personal stories, the characters weave the broader narrative of Vacari's resurgence, where healing takes many forms, and challenges are faced with unwavering resolve.

Acknowledgements

Jean McEvoy

To my wonderful mother—your red pen and unwavering belief in me will never be forgotten. Thank you for always standing by me.

Caroline Otto

To my best friend from high school, Caroline, thank you for taking the time to read the rough drafts. Thank you for also being there for me during high school and believing in me now. Her friendship has meant a lot to me. She is more of like a sister.

Steven Thomas

To my dear friend, Steven, who took the time to read early drafts of the chapters. Your friendship and feedback mean the world to me.

Special Acknowledgements to the Fur Babies (whose names are used in the book

Pumpkin

I rescued my little black panther over five years ago, and her playful spirit became the inspiration for Pumpkin in this book.

About the author

T. McEvoy, a native of Corpus Christi, Texas, has made Anderson, South Carolina, her home for over a decade. With a lifelong passion for writing that ignited during her high school years, she has now ventured into the realm of self-publishing fantasy fiction novels. 'The Wicked Phoenix,' her inaugural creation, introduces readers to the enchanting world of 'The Elves of Vacari' series. Shadows Unveiled is the second book in the Elves of Vacari. T. McEvoy has another book plan for this series so her journey as an author promises a captivating continuation of fantastical adventures

In addition to her writing pursuits, Theresa holds an associate degree in paralegal studies and has gained over five years of experience working in a law firm in Texas. Since relocating to South Carolina, she has dedicated her time to being a caregiver for her mother.

Beyond the world of words, Theresa finds creative expression through painting and enjoys immersing herself in the world of video games."

"Thank you for reading Shadows Unveiled. If you enjoyed the book, we would be immensely grateful if you could take a moment to leave a review at the location where you purchased the book. Your feedback is invaluable to us and helps other readers discover our work. Thank you for your support!"